SAINT GEORGE

and

THE DRAGON

* * *

A Martyr's Faith

Brent Colton

Saint George and The Dragon: A Martyr's Faith is a work of historical fiction. Many of the characters and events are based on the historical record, but the work as a whole is a product of the author's creation.

This work incorporates some material that is copyrighted by others, and has been used with permission of the copyright owners. However, this in no way implies their agreement with or support of the application of their materials in this story.

"This material is neither made, provided, approved, nor endorsed by Intellectual Reserve, Inc. or The Church of Jesus Christ of Latter-day Saints. Any content or opinions expressed, implied or included in or with the material are solely those of the owner and not those of Intellectual Reserve, Inc. or The Church of Jesus Christ of Latter-day Saints."

"I Feel My Savior's Love" *Words Verses 1-3:* Ralph Rodgers, Jr.; K. Newell Dayley; and Laurie Huffman; (Ref. John 15:10-12); *Music:* K. Newell Dayley; © 1979 K. Newell Dayley. Used with permission. Jackman Music Corporation is the publisher of commercial arrangements for this song.

****

Although many sacred sources are cited extensively in this work, no pretense is asserted that any of this work is scripture aside from the verbatim scriptural references cited. Any changes to or modifications of the sacred texts represent an expression of the author's frame of mind, understanding, and attempts to apply the references more seamlessly into this story. In all instances the author defers to the sacred word of God, which stands on its own and should always be considered in its original context. Some citations are direct quotes, but many others simply identify sources for ideas used in the book and starting points for further research by readers.

****

Copyright © 2019 by Brent Colton
All Rights Reserved
ISBN: 978-1-0746-2460-6
saintgeorgemartyr@gmail.com

ACKNOWLEDGMENTS

    First and last, praise be to God for all that is good. Next, I am grateful to George for his life which has inspired me to greater courage in righteousness, mercy, and freedom. I am also grateful for the editing assistance of Crystal Hunt who rose gently to the task of telling me hard things. I am grateful for the encouragement and creative inspiration of my son, Bruce, who is a far better story teller than I could ever hope to be. I appreciate the support and assistance of my parents, Larry and Jean, my brother Jim and his wife Cindy, my wife, Cheryl, and many others who picked me up at critical times and urged me onward. I give thanks also to Cara Jernigan for her help in designing and formatting the book cover.

    I acknowledge that most of my learning in life has been vicarious, receiving the counsel or observing the experiences and actions of others, to whom credit is due for many of the principles and lessons I have learned. I've lost track of most of the sources to whom credit is rightfully due for the knowledge, insights, and blessings I now possess. However, I feel a strong desire to share with others some of the vision I've gained. I've made my best effort to do so in this historical fiction based upon the actual life of one of our Heavenly Father's truly faithful and magnificent sons, Saint George, the martyr and witness for Jesus Christ.

CONTENTS

Introduction   1

PART I.   The Boy

1. The Young Maiden   3
2. George's Covenant   7
3. A Good Report   12
4. George Defeats the Beast   15
5. Witness Faith in Christ   19
6. Imperial Politics   24
7. The Theban Legion   31
8. Engineering Skills   40
9. David and Goliath   47
10. The Honor of Ascalon   50
11. Heaven and Earth   60
12. Father Prepares for Death   66
13. Caring for Mother   72
14. Uniting the People   79
15. A Market for All   87
16. Mother Prepares for Death   93

PART II: The Man

17. About My Father's Business   97
18. Joining Diocletian's Army   103
19. Centurion in Battle   112
20. Battle Reputation Grows   126
21. The Word in Vision   135
22. The Spoils of Battle   145
23. Pure Religion   152
24. Mercy and Justice   161

25. The Covenants of Peace	170
26. Conquer and Stabilize	183
27. Insulted by a Messenger	196
28. Trust in the Lord	205
29. Peace and Prosperity	214
30. Others Surrender	223
31. Prosperity Celebrations	235
32. The Glorious Report	245
33. A Few Good Men	249
34. Final Promotion	257
35. Back to the Palace	265
36. Faithful Tribune	272
37. A Burning Conspiracy	281
38. Evil Hearts Aflame	293

PART III: The Martyr

39. Persecution Order	303
40. Prisoner for Christ	311
41. Every Man Has His Price	319
42. God and His Witnesses	327
43. Dispensations and Apostasy	335
44. The Plan of Redemption	343
45. The Atonement of Christ	354
46. Priesthood Keys and Covenants	365
47. A House Upon a Rock	376
48. Obedience and Repentance	387
49. The Eve of Trial	399
50. Trial and Testimony	408
51. Conversion of Others	417
52. Sabra Visits	422
53. Preparing to Meet God	432
54. Sabra Prepares	436
55. Truth Stands	440

56. Torture and Dragging	447
57. The Quicklime Casket	453
58. The Wheel of Swords	455
59. Testimony and Execution	458
60. Behold the Glory	463
61. Habeas Corpus	467
62. The Mantle Passes	473
63. Other Martyrs	477
64. Rest in Peace	482
65. The Dragon Wounded	485
Epilogue: The Ripple Effect	491
Author's Witness	499
Discussion Questions	502
Chapter Notes	504

INTRODUCTION

Saint George was born Georgios, son of Gerontius and Polychronia, most likely in Lydda, Palestine, around 275 AD. He died on Good Friday, April 23, 303 AD, in Nicodemia, which was the eastern capital of the Roman Empire, and is near modern day Ismit, Turkey. He was executed at the inception of the final and most severe state-sanctioned persecution of Christians in Roman history.

During the 28 years of his life, George set an example so amazing that memory of him and his goodness have endured. He was a military officer who was loved by the people he conquered. The records of his military successes and powerful witness of faith have largely been destroyed, but what remains recounts a life that inspired many to believe in the living God.

George is somewhat of an exception among great men and saints in that he is known and respected by Christians, Jews and Muslims throughout the Middle East, from Africa to Asia, and in Europe. These honor him as a martyr for bending his will fully to their common deity, the one true and living God of Abraham. He defied the dominant secular authority of the Roman Empire which had declared itself in opposition to the God of Abraham.

George's fame and popularity grew steadily, even after he was condemned by the Emperor and executed for his faith in God and Christ. Many made pilgrimages to his grave and the cathedral constructed in his honor by Constantine's mother in Lydda, Palestine. In 494 AD, George was beatified as a saint by Pope Gelasius I, who described him as among those "whose names are justly reverenced among men, but whose acts are known only to [God]."

Historically, Saint George has been revered for his military conquests, his liberation of the oppressed and his unbounded commitment and uncompromising fidelity to Almighty God. His fame was so enduring in the Middle East that some 800 years after his death, many Christians and non-Christians alike still honored him as a saint who brought peace, prosperity, and religious tolerance to their people. When the Crusaders entered the Holy

Land in the late 11th and early 12th centuries, they collectively adopted the banner and colors of Saint George, a red cross on a white field. Upon their return to Europe, these soldiers romanticized the legend of Saint George with a symbolic account of his mythical battle with a dragon for the life of a princess and access to the water of life. This tale had no prior historical reference.

George is the Patron Saint of the following nations: Aragon, Bulgaria, Catalonia, Egypt, England, Ethiopia, Georgia, Greece, India, Iraq, Israel, Lebanon, Lithuania, Malta, Palestine, Portugal, Serbia, Syria, Russia and Ukraine. He is the proclaimed protector of many cities throughout the ancient Roman Empire. He was also the model character for the Boy Scout movement. He is often depicted in art on a horse with a spear, above a dragon.

George was a true saint and the type of person who would have lived, "by every word that proceedeth out of the mouth of the Lord."[1] Therefore the scriptures have been used extensively to recreate pieces of the puzzle for this historical fiction based on his inspiring life.

It is my intent to honor God's word in all things as I apply it and what little I understand of His mysteries to my life and my work. The truths in this work are God's. The errors are mine.

—Brent Colton

CHAPTER ONE
The Young Maiden

Lydda, Palestine
280 AD

"A Father of the fatherless, and a Judge of widows, is God in His holy habitation."[1]
Psalm 68:5

****

    Callidora put her weight into the coarse cloth as she struggled to remove the dirt and bright grass stains from the two small pairs of pants in her wash bucket. "These boys wrestle like the Emperor's pigs wallowing in a rainstorm," she muttered to herself. The green stains seemed to have mostly transferred to the skin on her fingertips, but she knew these pants would never be pure white again. She sighed lightly and mused, "Well, if master Gerontius really wanted these pants white, he wouldn't have let his boys wear them…or he would've had daughters instead of sons. Perhaps if he had given me milk to wash them in…" She shook her head as she beat the pants against the outside of the wash bucket before hanging them out to dry.
    She looked up to check on her daughter Sabra, who was all of three years old. A stone's throw from where she stood, there was a white "flower" patch where Sabra had been playing. It was really just a weed patch, but to Sabra, anything with a blossom that wasn't grass or trees was "flowers," and Sabra loved playing in flowers. Callidora could see a small circle in the center of the weed patch where much of the flowers and grass had been pulled up by the roots. The rest of the flowers were trampled to the ground. But there was no Sabra.
    Callidora's eyes shifted frantically about the weed patch and she felt her throat tighten with fear. "Sabra?" she called out, but there was no answer. She lifted her skirt slightly and stepped quickly through the weeds towards the trampled flower patch. "Sabra!" she called again. "Heavens! Where have you gone? Come back to mother now!" At the sound of a muffled giggle behind her, she turned around.
    "I'm right here Mama," Sabra called as a gentle breeze carried a lock of her wavy black hair up to the corner of her smiling little mouth. She was standing next to the wash bucket, her head tilted down as she pushed

her hands in under the water.

Holding the hem of her skirt, Callidora turned and paced back through the weeds toward her daughter. "What are you doing, my little angel?" she asked.

"Ba'tizing!" Sabra declared with enthusiastic innocence.

"You're what?" Callidora asked as she leaned over the wash bucket and saw Sabra's two little dirt-stained hands plunge into the water again.

A smile beamed on Sabra's shining face as she looked back up at her mother, her little tongue resting between the rows of her baby teeth. "They're flower babies…from the flower patch. And they need to be ba'tized!" The soapy water darkened with the dirt. Bits of grass rose to the surface.

Gently Callidora took hold of her daughter's small hands and lifted them firmly out of the water. Sabra's tiny fists were holding a dozen bright pink earthworms that were squirming anxiously. Silently, Callidora counted to five before she spoke. "Sabra, that was very…thoughtful of you to baptize the…flower babies. But you must not do that anymore. Only people get baptized…and only men with the priesthood of God can baptize them, okay? Now, please put your flower babies back in the flower patch and let's go home."

Sabra held the worms to her chest. Her smile became a thin line. "Yes, Mama, I'll put them back." She looked down at the worms and softened her grip. "I'll take you back to the flower patch, little babies. You're all clean now," she whispered victoriously. She tiptoed back to the matted weed area and carefully laid down her precious tiny converts. Her little chest expanded out and relaxed back in with a satisfied sigh. She filled her hands with weed blossoms again and hurried after her mother, who was already heading for their cottage with the wash bucket in tow.

Twisting her hands into her thick apron, Callidora paused just outside the door of their one-room quarters to watch Sabra, making sure she came home. Her princess entered the room and began dancing along the walls, decorating the cracks in the mud mortar with her blossoms. Callidora smiled with joy as she thought, *How blessed I am to have my beautiful little daughter.* "Sabra, I have a very important job for you," she said. Sabra spun around and looked expectantly at her mother. "I need you to fetch me some of your favorite vegetables from the wooden bins outside the master's kitchen. You can pick whichever ones you like. Please go fill your apron and bring them back to me quick."

Sabra dropped her remaining handful of weeds onto the dirt floor and ran out the door past her mother chanting, "I get to pick! I get to pick!"

Callidora eased herself into her heavy wooden rocker. It creaked gently beneath her, seeming to conform willingly to her body. Her husband had built it for her in his carpentry shop a few months before she'd given birth to Sabra. Then one night, a few weeks after Sabra's birth, he hadn't come home. His body was found the next morning in a back alley near his shop. He had several knife wounds, and his money pouch and shoes were gone.

"What a blessing Gerontius and his family have been," she reflected to herself. "We had nothing, but they provided a means for me to care for myself and Sabra, with an honorable job as a servant and modest living quarters. I shall always be grateful for their kindness and charity, embracing us as we passed through our desperate tragedy."

Gerontius and his family were well respected in the region. Greek by birth, Gerontius had joined the Roman army and proved himself faithful. He had risen to become one of the Emperor's personal guards. He'd been discharged after he injured his low back when he was thrown from his horse in battle. It took many months for the injury to stabilize and Gerontius was never the same physically powerful man he'd been previously. Upon his discharge, he had received some farm land and money. With hard work, he and his wife had quickly improved their modest estate.

His skills with people also served him well. As his health improved, he was rewarded with an administrative post in Palestine. The local people had given the Romans no end of civil trouble, but since Gerontius had taken charge he'd helped all the factions under his stewardship to work together more peaceably, benefitting everyone.

An excellent teacher and trainer, Gerontius used his abilities to educate his sons and his servants in all of the farm operations. He also instructed his sons in combat skills and political principles. The boys received religious education from both of their parents but Gerontius' wife, Polychronia, or Polly as she was known to her friends, clearly took the lead in this subject.

Gerontius' older son was Gregorios, or Gregor. He was nearly eleven, and was quickly changing from boy to man. His disposition was pleasant and his character was true. He'd been taught well by his parents. He knew the importance of obedience to God and choosing the right, even in the face of adversity.[2] He was already making good decisions as to what manner of man he would be.

The younger son was Georgios, or George. He was only five, but he was growing tall and strong, like his father and older brother. He had keen intelligence for his age, and great talent and coordination. George's name meant "worker of the land" and was an indication of how his father had envisioned that he might use his life for good. His father and older brother were his heroes. He followed them everywhere, imitating them whenever he could.

In the two years since Callidora had joined Gerontius and his family as a free servant, she had grown to love her master's family. She covered her face with her hands and rocked gently in her chair. Peeking through her fingers, she looked out the front door, which Sabra had left open, and watched as Sabra returned with her apron full of vegetables.

In a blink my darling little Sabra will become a young woman, she thought. *Then men of every character will be watching, including men like those who took the life of my husband. But they won't be interested in Sabra's shoes or money pouch. They'll want something else.* Callidora couldn't shake the anxiety she felt for her daughter. Again and again she prayed to God for inspiration, and pondered on what she could do to help keep Sabra safe.[3] She patted her own cheeks with both hands as if to wake herself up. With a sigh she pulled herself from the comforting embrace of her rocking chair and set a pot of water in the fireplace to boil.

****

CHAPTER TWO
George's Covenant

Lydda, Palestine
280 AD

"Heaven and earth shall pass away, but My words shall not pass away."[1]
Matthew 24:35

****

"Hah! You missed me!" George shouted at Gregor in his rowdy, high-pitched voice. He quickly dodged another blow from his older brother's sword, and taunted, "I bet you couldn't hit the broad side of a bear with the butt end of Pa's sword!"

"I'll bet I could hit your butt end with the point end of Pa's sword," Gregor responded, and the two boys burst out laughing.

Callidora stepped out through her cottage door. Following the voices, she turned toward the boys. Sternly she addressed them. "Well, if it isn't the two young wrestling masters. I'll have you know I spent a good bit of my morning beating the dirt and grass stains from your last tussle out of your pants." She paused briefly, and then added gravely, "The next time you stain your pants like that, I'll start the beatings while you're still wearing them!"

The boys stopped cold and turned to look at her. They eyed Callidora cautiously for a moment, until they saw just a hint of a smile at the corners of her mouth. Looking back at each other they cautiously resumed their laughter.

"Come on in, Gregor. George, you come too. If you're hungry I'm making vegetable soup. What have you two been doing today?"

Gregor held up his soiled wooden weapon and answered, "Practicing swords." George noted Gregor's raised sword and raised his own filthy sword to match.

Callidora looked at the boys and their swords. "I see," she said, raising her eyebrows and nodding her head gently as she examined a prominent bruise on the outside of George's left heel that matched the tip of Gregor's sword.

George wasn't big on vegetable soup so he added, "Mother will be expecting us for lunch soon."

"George is gettin' better at swords, but his arms must be too short 'cause he still can't seem to stab me," Gregor chided with an arrogant smirk.

"I wasn't trying to stab you!" George protested. "I was blocking! And my arms are not short." He sent an exaggerated scowl Gregor's direction, but his brother ignored it.

Gregor shifted his smirk into a smile as he looked up at their hostess. Gregor's smug smile made George wonder if now was the time to get his older brother's word on a very important and sensitive matter. "I'll bet you Pa's battle sword Ascalon that I'll best you at swords some day," George challenged intently.

Responding too quickly, Gregor took the bait. "Listen here, Pip, the day you best me at swords is the day I'll be too old to lift Pa's battle sword. You can have it then, if you're man enough to pick it up."[2]

Maintaining his intensity, George asked a bit too politely, "Do I have your word on that?"

Gregor hesitated, sensing he'd just bragged himself into a corner. But it wouldn't do to back down now, not to his little brother in front of witnesses. "Of course you have my word on it," he said, feeling sober and very uneasy about whether his promise would bring him honor.

Callidora loved Gregor and George as if they were her own sons. Still, she worried about how they would treat Sabra when she began to develop sufficiently to attract the attention of boys and men alike. She had been pondering on this for some time, and had prayed mightily for inspiration on what she should do to help keep her daughter safe. Finally, she'd settled on a strategy that she prayed would provide Sabra with some protection as she grew older. "George, would you take some feed to the chickens for me?" she asked. "I have it right here for you," she said as she pulled a fist full of corn meal out of a bin and held it towards George.

Putting his wooden sword in his belt, George responded, "Yes, ma'am." Callidora poured the feed down into his cupped hands. As he went out the door he quickly made his best imitation of a rooster call, "Urha-urha-urrr!"

Callidora turned to the older boy. "Gregor, I would like to talk privately with you for a moment. I've been meaning to ask you something very important."

"If I'll feed the goats?" Gregor guessed.

Callidora stifled a laugh. "No, my boy, not the goats." She set down her wooden spoon and knelt in front of Gregor, taking him by both hands. "Gregor, I am worried about my little Sabra and how she'll be treated in life. You know her father is gone, and she has no family but me to look to her needs. I want to know that she will always be safe, even if I'm not always there to take care of her. I would like your help. Will you help me?"

"I'll try," Gregor replied uncertainly. "What kind of help do you need?"

Callidora knew how important a man's word was to the members of her master's family, so she addressed the issue directly and somewhat formally. "Will you give me your word, your solemn promise, that you will always be kind to Sabra throughout her life?"

Gregor considered the question soberly. He'd been taught never to give his word lightly, and having once given his word, to do everything in his power to keep all his promises. His father had taught him that the true measure of a man was his commitment to righteousness and keeping his word, especially when keeping it became unexpectedly difficult. Gregor knew he needed to be more careful about giving his word lightly, but he could see that Callidora was earnest in her request. He recognized this request as more than a simple task that could easily be completed and then forgotten. He looked squarely into Callidora's face and thought of all the kindness she had shown him since she and Sabra had come to be with their family. She had helped his mother in raising him and George. She'd always been patient and kind in helping others on the farm to complete their work. Gregor looked to heaven for just a moment and, knowing it was the right thing to do, he looked back to Callidora and spoke soberly, "Yes, I give you my word that I'll always be kind to Sabra throughout her life."

Callidora squeezed Gregor's hands together. "God bless you, my boy. You're such a fine young man, and great with your sword, and obedient to your parents. You truly are a valiant hero!" Gregor straightened up as he thought a hero might do. Callidora smiled and continued, "Now, would you go find George and send him to me? I would like to ask him to give me the same promise."

Gregor recognized this request to find George and send him back as a simple task, to be done quickly and forgotten quickly. However, if the task was not done quickly, there was a risk that it might still be forgotten quickly. "You have my word," he pledged, determined to locate George immediately and send him back, as promised. Then he would finish his own chores quickly before lunch, as he remembered he'd given his word on that as well, to his mother. He stepped out the door, wooden sword in hand, and made his best imitation of a rooster call, "Urha-urha-urrr!" After a moment he heard George's answering call and headed towards it.

Callidora paused, closing her eyes, thinking again of faceless evil men bent on stealing her daughter's virtue. After an involuntary shudder, she opened her eyes to the light. Soon George appeared, his right hand holding the hilt of his little wooden practice sword. Callidora took another look at the bruise on George's left foot and asked, "Is your heel okay?"

"Aw, it's just fine," George reassured her. "Gregor isn't as good at swords as he thinks. I wish he'd give me a little more respect at swords. It won't be fun if I have to prove I deserve it."

Callidora smiled at such big talk from such a young man. "I'm sure you'll measure up in Gregor's eyes someday. Just remember, no matter how big and tall your father is you still have to do your own growing."[3]

Callidora had an instinctive feeling that getting this promise from George might be much more important than getting the word of his older brother. Perhaps that was because George and Sabra were close enough in age that he might take more than just a passing interest in her at some point in the future.

"Gregor said you wanted to talk to me," George stated, looking curious as he rocked back and forth on his feet.

"Yes, I do," Callidora answered. "Did your brother tell you why I wanted to speak with you?"

"He just said it was about Sabra, that's all. Is she alright?" George wondered.

"Yes, Sabra's fine. I want to ask you to promise me something. I want you to give me your word," Callidora said.

George's eyes got big. "Give you my word? You're the first grown-up, besides my parents, who has ever asked me to give my word on anything."

"Well I think you're grown up enough to do it. Do you know what it means to give your word?" Callidora asked gently.

George laid his wooden sword on the table, his right hand still clutching the hilt and his eyes resting on the blade. "I do. My mother taught me that to give my word is to bind my soul. To keep my word I must do everything in my power to keep the promise, no matter how difficult that is, even if it leads me to my death. Father told me the true measure of a man is if he keeps his word in righteousness," George said as he looked back up at Callidora.

She looked back, amazed at his sober and sincere response, considering his tender age. Her heart grew warm in her chest as she spoke. "George, will you give me your word that you will always be kind to my daughter Sabra throughout her life?"

George continued to look up at her, not blinking. Not moving. Barely breathing. If the cottage had caught fire, neither of them might have noticed. Finally, he shifted his gaze toward heaven and, holding it there for a moment, he let go of the sword hilt. Looking back to Callidora, he took her two hands in his own, knelt on one knee, and broke the silence. "Callidora, I give you my word that I will always be kind to Sabra." As he stood back up and grasped the hilt of his small wooden sword, George felt enthusiasm in this sacred moment and added boldly, "And with God's help I swear to protect her, with my own sword, and my own life, for as long as I shall live!" Exuberantly he slashed the air with his sword, adding emphasis to his oath.

Warmth flooded Callidora's heart and, taking his hand again, she knelt on both knees before him. "George, you truly are a man of honor," she whispered. As she kissed his forehead, a tear fell from her lashes and ran down her cheek. Though she still feared the shadowy deeds of evil men in her daughter's future, she knew in her heart that George would keep his vow to be kind and protect her cherished Sabra.

George bowed his head slightly before leaving. For a moment, Callidora thought she could see the tousled hair of a grown man with an iron will, the light of God radiating from him. George looked back up at her, sweat glistening on his angelic little cheeks, and then he turned to leave.

****

CHAPTER THREE
A Good Report

Lydda, Palestine
280 AD

"...for them that honor Me I will honor..."[1]
1 Samuel 2:30

****

George knelt on the floor beside the bed where he laid his wooden sword. The sword was covered with scratches and dents from his endless battles with his "dragons" and with Gregor, but he had carefully washed all the mud off the blade. Father had told him that often the difference between life and death in combat was determined by which soldier's weapon was in better condition. "A sword kept sharp and clean gives its master a truer swing, a deeper cut, and a better chance to survive the battle," he had said. George had seen the battle scars on his father's chest and wondered if the enemies' blades had stopped short of piercing his heart because they had been dull or unclean.

While stroking his cherished weapon, George heard three quick knocks on his bedroom door. As he jumped onto his straw mattress and flipped onto his back, Polly entered the room to tuck him in for the night. She picked up the sword from the covers beside him and gave George a careful look. "Did you slay any dragons today?" she asked with playful curiosity.

George wrinkled his brow as he looked from his sword to his mother. "Aw, I only kilt three today, Ma." He meant to look down in mock embarrassment, but he couldn't resist watching his mother's face for a reaction. A slight smile on his own face betrayed him.

"Oh, only three?" Polly echoed questioningly, bemoaning the awful shame of it.

"Ma, I need to start exploring way past the garden and the yard 'cause I've already kilt all the close-in dragons. May I...please, may I go out into the field with you tomorrow so I can hunt for bigger dragons?" George begged.

"We'll see about that," Polly answered with a smile. "What else did you do today?"

"Me an' Gregor practiced swords. And I helped feed the chickens.

Oh, and I and gave Callidora my word."

Mother's eyebrows rose slightly. "Really? You gave your word to Callidora? What did you promise?" Polly asked with intense interest.

"Yes. I gave her my word that I'll always be kind and protect little Sabra. I want to be a great protector, like Pa," George declared.

Polly was amused, seeing her young son acting all grown up. *But then,* she pondered, *acting grown up is certainly the beginning of actually being grown up. Perhaps my beloved Georgios is coming of age before his time.* "How exactly did you decide to give your word to Callidora, my curious little man?" she asked thoughtfully.

"I did like you said," George replied. "I thought about what she was asking and how long it would take. I thought about whether I could do it…and whether I should do it…and whether God would do it."

"And?" Polly prodded.

"I knew God would give His word to always be kind, so I did too. You said God protects us all, so I thought it would be okay for me to promise that too, since I had my sword ready and all."

Polly paused, considering her son's answer carefully. "So you gave your word?"

"I did, Ma. I gave my word," George confirmed. "And now I'm bound, for as long as I live."

Mother tilted her head slightly forward. "For this life, and beyond." It was George's turn to question with his eyes. "Not all promises end when you die, George. Remember what Jesus said to Peter when He gave him the keys to His kingdom: 'Whatsoever thou shalt bind on earth shall be bound in heaven.'"[2]

"What does that mean, Ma?"

"That means our promises to God go on after this life. Jesus said, 'If ye love Me, keep My commandments.'[3] Our promises to obey God's commandments don't end when we die. Our spirits live on after this life. Some day we'll be resurrected. Our spirits will receive new bodies that are perfect, and we will live with God. Our promises to love others and be kind to others don't end either. You think on that. We can talk more about it tomorrow if you want."

George settled in to bed, looking at the two lumps where his feet pushed up his covers. Then he looked back up at his mother.

"Georgios, you made some very good choices today. I'm so proud that you decided to follow God. You're right that He will protect us all as long as we keep His commandments and obey the voice of His Spirit. If we do the work Jesus would do, and if we are His servants, God will fill us with His Spirit and with courage to overcome all our fears. I'm so pleased that you want to be a great protector like your father. He is trying to be a perfect protector like God. Now let's kneel together for prayer before you go to sleep."

George knelt on the cool stone floor, and bowed his head. Polly knelt with him beside the bed as he prayed. "Dear Father in heaven, we praise Thee. We thank Thee for all our blessings. We thank Thee for our Savior, Jesus Christ. We thank Thee for our family. Please help me to be obedient. And please help me to keep my promise to always be kind and protect Sabra. Please help me to be a great protector like Pa, and like Thee. We pray in Jesus' name. Amen."

"Amen," Polly whispered as she smiled at George, rejoicing in his enthusiasm for good. He certainly was catching on to the lessons she had been carefully teaching him about righteousness. He was learning to have faith in Christ and follow His example in love to all, and in obedience to Heavenly Father.

****

CHAPTER FOUR
George Defeats the Beast

Lydda, Palestine
283 AD

"The sword of the LORD, and of Gideon."[1]
Judges 7:20

****

"Father, thank you so much for my new full-sized practice sword," Gregor said. "I've really enjoyed training with a more grown-up weapon. I've been feeling that it's time to set some of the things of my childhood aside.[2] I was wondering if it would be alright for me to pass on my medium-sized wooden sword to George for his eighth birthday? I think it would be a good gift that might encourage him into believing that he isn't falling too far behind me in development of his battle skills and sparring."

"That's a great idea," Gerontius replied. "I think your perpetual shadow would really appreciate such a worthy gift. You'll still have the medium-sized sword of fine steel I gave you as a prize for placing third in Lydda's youth battle skills tournament last year. Your achievement was unprecedented for a 12-year-old."

*****

George was very pleased to advance from his little wooden sword, which he was sure he'd outgrown, to the larger practice sword. Although he was getting older and more mature, George still took his sword to bed with him every night. Each night Polly would move it off his bed while she told him a story, only to find it back beside George on the bed in the morning. *Tonight*, Polly thought, *I'll share a special story about a special sword.*

She ended her story with these words: "On the signal, Gideon's 300 men all blew their trumpets and broke the pitchers off their lamps and held them up high. With lamps in their left hands and trumpets in their right hands, they all cried aloud together, 'The sword of the Lord, and of Gideon.' And the Lord set every man's sword against his fellow in the camp of the Midianites."[3]

15

As Polly finished telling of Gideon's victory over the hundreds of thousands of Midianites, she asked, "Who held the sword of the Lord in this battle?"

"Gideon did," George responded confidently.

"But Gideon and each of his men had a lamp in the left hand and a trumpet in the right, so where was the sword of the Lord?" Polly challenged.

This time George didn't respond quite so quickly. After thinking it over for a moment he said, "The swords that killed all the Midianites were their own, but I don't think those were the swords of the Lord. I guess the sword of the Lord was His power, given to Gideon because of his faith and righteousness and obedience to God. God held His own sword and won this battle Himself."

"That's right, George," Polly agreed. "God won the battle, and Gideon was His faithful servant."

George thought a little longer. Looking at his own sword he said, "I know that faith in God is more important and more powerful than any man's sword, but I sure wish Gideon had a fine steel sword in his hand to do the work of the Lord, like Pa's battle sword, Ascalon."

Polly smiled. "Gideon had a real sword too. He was very good with it and won many victories in the name of the Lord. But he understood, just like you do, that his faith in God and his obedience to all of God's commandments were even more important than his real sword.

"Your father and Gregor will be going to town tomorrow, and I'll be out in the field with the servants. Callidora said you can have lunch with her after your morning chores are done. Now, it's time for your prayers."

"Okay. Good night, Mother. I love you," George said as he slid out of bed and onto his knees.

*****

George completed his daily sword training with Gregor early in the morning and then he helped load the cart for their trip into town. He finished his other chores by midday and went to the barn to wash up for lunch. Before he went in, George struck a pose, his new wooden sword in his right hand held high before him, pointing toward heaven. Dramatically he proclaimed, "Behold, the sword of the Lord and of Georgios!"[4]

Inside the barn he cleaned his sword first and laid it on the bench next to the wash basin before washing himself. Although George's medium-sized sword was used and worn, it was still new to him. He thought

A Martyr's Faith

again about how his sword resembled a wooden cross, which led him to think of Jesus. Carefully he washed his hands and face. As he wiped them dry before going to Callidora's, he heard a startled cry out in the yard.

"Dear God, help us!" the voice pleaded.

Quickly George went out to investigate. He found Callidora in the yard, frozen in her tracks, staring at her daughter.

Callidora spoke quietly but very firmly, "Sabra, stop! Don't move! Stay...very...still!" Sabra was a few feet away, seemingly frozen in place too, staring at the sitting rock by the well.

George approached cautiously, uncertain what was happening but knowing something was terribly wrong. "What's the matter, Callidora?" he asked. "Did you call for help?"

"No, George, I didn't call to you, but I surely need help right now!" she replied.

Just then, George saw the huge snake on the bare ground near the sitting rock by the well. The cobra was coiled and rising up, as if it was preparing to strike.

"That snake surprised us. It must have been warming itself near the large rock," Callidora spoke earnestly. "The beast is close enough to strike Sabra. If it bites her, its venom will kill her. Quickly, go and get your father to help!"

"Father and Gregor went to town, and mother is out in the far field," George replied as he stared at the large serpent that had them frozen with fear. The asp was easily longer than George was tall, and as big around as his upper arm. It was very menacing and frightening. "If mother was here, she would tell us to pray," George said.

Callidora kept her eyes fastened on her daughter as she pleaded in a strained whisper, "Dear God, please protect my little Sabra."

George had never liked snakes, and this one was very frightening, but as he heard Callidora's anguished plea, his mind flooded with memories of the day he had promised to be Sabra's protector. Knowing of his mother's faith in Christ as the source of all courage and power, he looked quickly to heaven and pleaded, "Almighty God, please bless me with courage and help me to protect Sabra."

As he thought about how he could keep his vow to protect Sabra, his mind returned to the day of his promise and to his little wooden sword slicing the air. "I'll go for help," he said. Carefully he withdrew and returned to the bench in the barn where he had just laid his sword as he washed. Taking the weapon firmly in his hands he returned to the yard and approached cautiously.

"Did you find any help?" Callidora pleaded anxiously.

Raising his sword ahead of him, George responded, "This and God are the only help I can find." As he moved slowly toward the snake, the beast took notice of him. George was much larger than Sabra, and obviously a greater threat than the little girl. With deliberate caution he moved toward a position between Sabra and the beast. As he advanced, George waved his sword in front of him, swinging the tip slowly from the foreground on his left, rising waist high in a broad arc, coming down on the foreground to his right and back again. Slowly but intently, he warned the viper of the territory he and his sword were claiming from the beast. The back of George's clothes just barely brushed the front of the little girl as he got into position between Sabra and the snake. George felt the hair rising on the back of his neck as he began to speak. "Sabra, go to your mother now…slowly!" He commanded, but Sabra hadn't waited for the last word. She quickly darted back and away to his right, running to her mother.

Sabra's sudden move startled the beast, and it struck reflexively. So did George. As the viper sprang to his right to attack the moving girl, George's sword came down forcefully on his right, crossing the path of the attacking demon. The tip of the blunted blade struck with such power that it separated the snake's head from its body, crushing it in one swift, decisive blow.

As the realization of what had just happened began to sink in, George began to tremble. He stared at the body and severed head of the snake. Taking a few steps back, he dropped to his knees. Tears of relief edged down his cheeks as he bowed his head and whispered, "Praise God. Praises to Thee and to Thy Holy Son, Jesus Christ."

Callidora caught Sabra up into her arms and burst into tears of joy and relief. Gratefully she surveyed the scene and pondered on this miracle. She also remembered the day she had gotten George's promise to be kind to Sabra, and the feelings she'd had. She remembered distinctly his additional promise to protect Sabra, with God's help. Callidora gushed with emotion, having seen the hand of God. "George, you are a saint!" she declared as she gathered him in a nearly crushing embrace. Then she whispered, "Praise God for keeping my daughter safe, and for giving George such a miraculous victory over this beast."

****

CHAPTER FIVE
Witness Faith in Christ

Lydda, Palestine
283 AD

"Be ye holy; for I am holy."[1]
1 Peter 1:16

****

    Gerontius was passionate about learning. He loved to spend quiet time reading. He had a comfortable chair in his library that eased the pressure and pain in his lower back. His government post and financial means had allowed him to gather one of the most extensive collections of academic, historical, and religious texts in the province. He had carefully acquired copies of the Jewish scriptures and many of the writings of Christ's apostles. Aside from these sacred records, one of his most prized acquisitions was a series of Roman architectural books with diagrams. His architectural collection included books on roads and bridges, walls and fences, buildings, towers, cellars, sewage systems, wells, canals and aqueducts. The volume on buildings included diagrams for markets, libraries and hospitals.
    He used his library for private meetings with important visitors and for regularly interviewing his family and servants regarding their responsibilities and plans for the future. Anyone who had dealings with Gerontius quickly learned that he expected all people to carefully plan to achieve appropriate goals in their assigned work and in their personal lives. Those who didn't know how to plan for the future would be taught this important skill. His sons had been instructed not to interrupt him in this room, except with very important matters.
    Sometimes Gerontius would discover George in the library, staring at his battle sword, Ascalon, which was mounted there on the wall. More commonly he could be found reading, escaping from the afternoon heat. Generally, George would be straining through the sacred texts or looking at the engineering books. Gerontius wasn't sure how much his son was getting from these studies. However, he showed such care and respect for the books that no caution or rebuke was required, except to remind him that the library was no place for wearing a sword.
    Father was beaming with pride as George came into the library.

"Mother said you called for me," George offered as his reason for invading his father's sanctuary.

"Your mother tells me that you finally killed a real dragon. Come tell me about it," Gerontius said in his business voice, a slight smile rising on his face.

"Well, first of all, it wasn't a real dragon. I think I would know a real dragon if I ever saw one. But it was a monster of a snake. I had just finished washing up for lunch after my chores when I heard Callidora out in the yard call out for help. I went to see if I could help her. She said she needed help from you or Mama. Then I saw the snake near the well. It was one of the biggest cobras I've ever seen. I got scared just looking at it. Sabra had gotten too close to the beast and it had coiled up ready to strike her.

"Since you and Mama weren't close enough to help, I thought about who else could protect Sabra. Then I remembered when I was little and I gave my word that I would protect Sabra, with God's help. I knew that God was pleased with my choice when I gave my word to do that. I trusted God to help me keep my word. So I prayed quickly. I'm not exactly sure what I said but I know I begged God to help me protect Sabra and so I wouldn't be afraid. Then I remembered my new sword that Gregor gave me, so I hurried and got it from the barn. I thought if I went slowly towards the snake and didn't startle it, I could show it how far my sword could reach and maybe the beast would go away.

"Just when I got between the beast and Sabra, she ran to her mother. Her sudden move surprised me. It must have startled the cobra too because in a flash, the viper struck at Sabra to my right. My sword was already coming down in that direction, so I put all my strength into the blow. With God's help, the tip of the sword came down hard exactly behind the head of the serpent, separating its head from its body and crushing it. I didn't know I could swing the sword that hard. It felt like when you're helping to train me and you wrap your arms around me and help me swing the sword with power."

The smile on Gerontius' face widened. He was impressed with George's faith, and with the detail and accuracy of his report on this dramatic event. He also appreciated that George spoke the truth without much self-serving embellishment. "The field servants seemed a lot more excited about your victory than you do. They told me about a great demon that you miraculously destroyed. The shepherds said there is plenty of snake meat for you and any who like it, with maybe some left over to help the poor. One shepherd is preparing the hide for you as a prize for your victory. You could keep it or trade it in the market."

"No thanks, Father. I didn't kill it for the flesh. I don't like snakes, especially poison ones. I don't want the snake skin as a trophy, and I don't ever want a snake to be my symbol for victory. The meat and hide can be given away to any folks who might need them or want them."

Gerontius felt the honest charity in his son, and he swelled with honor.[2] "Well, if you get nothing more from this than the experience, tell me what you learned from it," he said.

"I was surprised at how dangerous my wooden sword was, even after all the warnings you've given me about it. But even more amazing was the awesome power of God in answering my sincere prayer of faith, giving me courage to do His work as He would have it done, and helping me to protect Sabra from the beast." George paused for a moment and then added, "Father, I felt God's hand in me, and it was a miracle."

Gerontius felt the spirit and truth of his son's testimony and confirmed, "Yes, George, it was a miracle, and glory be to God."

"Father, Callidora said I was a saint. What exactly does that mean, and what do I have to do to be one?" George asked.

Father thought for a moment and then picked a scripture to share. "The Psalm says: 'For the Lord loves judgment, and forsakes not his saints. They are preserved forever. But the seed of the wicked shall be cut off. The righteous shall inherit the land, and dwell therein forever.'[3] Saints choose righteousness and follow God, making and keeping sacred covenants with Him, being sanctified or made holy through the atoning sacrifice of Jesus Christ."

"Are saints perfect?" George asked anxiously.

"Not quite," Father replied. "Like all of us, saints are sinners, but instead of giving in to Satan, they just keep trying to be righteous. They follow Jesus' example, calling upon God and doing His will in all things. Saints remember and strive earnestly to live by every word that proceeds from the mouth of God.[4] They are servants of Jesus.[5] They love God and have charity, or the pure love of Christ, towards all men.[6] Children of God who strive in patience and faith to act in all holiness before the Lord become saints.[7] Do you know what faith is?"

George thought for a moment and then responded, "I'm sure I don't know everything, but I think faith starts with believing that God is our Father in heaven, and that He loves all his children.[8] Mother says that faith is trusting in God and following the example of Jesus. God will grant all power for His true servants to do what He would do if He faced the same problems. I'm sure mother knows that God lives and that He loves us. I have some other ideas of my own about faith, but I want to learn what you think I should know about faith."

"That was a very good answer, George." Gerontius appreciated that George chose to be guided by what he knew and not by doubts and fears of what he didn't know. He thought carefully for a moment, praying for the best way to add to his son's understanding of faith, uncertain of what George was prepared to learn. "Faith has been described as the substance of things hoped for, the evidence of things not seen.[9] The essence of faith is a belief in the divinity of Jesus Christ, that He is the Son of God, and that He has all power to save God's children from this world of sin if they will turn to Him and obey Him. He has power to do all that is good. He can bestow that power on His servants. Faith works on the principle of pure love.[10] Without faith it is impossible to please God. He that comes to God must believe that He is, and that He will reward those who diligently seek Him."[11]

George considered his father's words. "God filled me with His Spirit and directed my thoughts and actions in overcoming the snake. But I feel my faith began long before this confrontation with evil. Father, I think faith starts with a desire and hope for things which are not seen, but which are true. When we draw close to the Lord, He reveals Himself to us so that, as long as we believe, our faith grows until we come to know what is true. We gain power from our obedience to the truths we know and the truths we believe, and from our faith in Jesus Christ. As we act in faith, God will continue to reveal His truths to us. Faith in God is like a seed within us. If we nourish it, it grows and bears fruit. If we uproot it with unbelief, it dies; not because there is no God, but because we have made no place for Him in our hearts."[12]

Reaching out, Gerontius took George in his arms and said, "That's an excellent description of faith. I didn't expect you to enlighten me on faith, but you have. I know Mother often teaches you principles of faith, but I've never heard her explain it that way." Staring gently at his young son he asked, "But what do we do if our obedience to truth is not perfect and we offend God?"

George enjoyed his father's powerful but gentle embrace. He felt a rush of confidence as he began to explain, "If we do wrong, we must repent. We must learn to see ourselves as God sees us, and fix anything that is not approved of God. We must become what Jesus commanded us to be; perfect, even as our Father in heaven is perfect.[13] When Jesus wanted reassurance from His Father, He prayed, 'Father, if it be possible, let this cup pass from Me: nevertheless not as I will, but as Thou wilt.'[14] He set the example for us to seek God's will and obey Him. If we follow His example in all things, He'll lead us back to our Father in heaven. With charity, we can learn to see all men as God sees them and to love all men as God loves them."[15]

As Gerontius listened, he felt the growing weight of his own example in George's life. Obviously, his son was learning faster than he had been intending to teach. He thought to himself, *I must watch my thoughts, words, and deeds, observing the commandments of God, and continuing in the faith of what I have heard concerning Jesus Christ, even unto the end, lest I corrupt this most precious gift that God has entrusted to me, and I perish.*[16]

*****

Later that evening, Gerontius prayed again, pleading for wisdom to guide his boys properly in developing their characters as servants of the Lord. As he pondered, the Spirit filled him with peace. A strong impression came into his mind that, even as God had given Moses power over water, so George would be blessed with wisdom and power to overcome dragons, beasts, and evil men, to protect God's humble and innocent children, and especially His precious daughters.

In a quiet moment, Gerontius confided in Polly. "I spoke with George today about his victory over the dragon. The Spirit impressed upon me that George has a mission in this life, to slay even greater dragons, and to protect the innocent sons and daughters of God from the assaults of men and beasts alike. I don't know all the details, but I know the Lord has work for him to do."

Polly hugged her husband tightly and whispered, "Yes, I know it too."

****

CHAPTER SIX
Imperial Politics

Lydda, Palestine
284-286 AD

"Render therefore unto Caesar the things which are Caesar's; and unto God the things which are God's."[1]
Matthew 22:21

****

"Will you call the boys to dinner?" Polly asked again patiently.

"Of course I will. I'm sorry," Gerontius replied, straining to turn his mind to the task. "You know, Polly, I have these persistent forebodings that prompt a constant sense of urgency to train our sons early and prepare them in all things."

"Those feelings are probably due to your injury," Polly suggested.

"I'm sure you're right, but I think there are other reasons I can't completely explain," he responded. "I count it a blessing that our boys are growing quickly so that, in addition to their academic lessons, they are able to handle the physical demands of farm work, combat training, and battle strategy. These skills are in constant demand throughout the region. I'm also anxious that they receive a careful education in politics, consistent with their position as sons of a provincial official who once had the honor of serving as a Roman tribune."

"Just remember that the most important training we can give them is in establishing a personal connection with God," Polly smiled.

*****

As the family enjoyed a quiet dinner, Gerontius spoke soberly. "The Roman army in the east has proclaimed Diocles as Emperor. He's taken the name of Gaius Aurelius Valerius Diocletian as his imperial title."

"What a mouthful!" Polly laughed. "That's another strike against a life of imperial politics."

"Most officials are referring to him simply as Diocletian or the Emperor," Gerontius responded.

"How well do you know him?" Polly asked.

"Quite well," Father replied. "We joined the army close to the same time and kept pace with each other for over ten years as we rose quickly through the ranks. Diocles was a commander in Moesia, recognized for his loyalty and capable leadership in battle. He was promoted to tribune as part of the Emperor's personal guard, where we served together. We were friends. We had mutual respect, owing our lives to each other more than once. After my back was injured in battle I was discharged. Diocles stayed with the imperial guard and was appointed its captain."

"In the military, your father built a strong reputation for faithful and effective service," Polly explained to the boys. "Among the soldiers in the army he was known as a peace maker who could get almost any quarreling men to see themselves on the same side of more important issues and set aside their petty differences for the good of all. I think that's partly why he was given this civil administrative post in Lydda after his discharge. His peace making skills have helped him succeed in this position."

"If Father has a job as a government official, then why do we have to do all this farm work?" Gregor asked politely.

"I received land and some money when I was discharged," Gerontius answered. "The official position came later. Being dependent upon the government will never be as secure as farming our own land. Therefore, we've been using our income to add to the estate, hoping to become self-sufficient. We're doing well enough now that we can hire laborers to do most of the heavy work. That's fortunate because my back isn't getting any better and I'm concerned about how our family will manage if I can't do any of the work. If I can teach you boys what to do, we'll be fine. In any case, we'll seek the blessings of God and make the best of our situation."

"What about Diocles?" George asked, anxious to hear the rest of the story.

"As commander of the imperial guard, Diocles was appointed second in command over all the eastern army by Emperor Carus," Gerontius explained. "When Carus was killed in battle, his sons ascended to the throne, with Numerian in the east, and Carinus as co-emperor in the west. However, Numerian was soon killed by a traitor within his own camp.

"Diocles was chosen by Numerian's army to lead them in avenging his death. He charged Numerian's top general, Arrius Aper, with the crime and sentenced him to death. Thereafter, he personally executed Aper in front of the troops. Shortly after that Diocles was acclaimed Emperor by the eastern army."

"Is this change in emperor a good change, or not?" George asked.

"That's an excellent question," Father replied. "Whether this change is good or not will depend upon how Diocletian rules. If he promotes peace and prosperity among the subjects of the Republic, that will be good. If he places the excessive burdens of a gluttonous ruling class upon his people, or if he aggressively promotes class distinction and is continually abusing men just to show off his power that would be bad. In any case, this matter won't be resolved unless Diocletian and Carinus can agree on how they will share power. Nearly all men will stand adversity, but if you truly want to test a man's character, give him power."[2]

"Is our family loyal to Diocletian?" George asked bluntly.

Gerontius wasn't surprised. With George, there was almost always another question. *Well, at least the boy doesn't waste time beating about the bushes*, he thought. However, the question required a careful response and some essential training in politics and loyalty. He began, "Jesus taught that we are to 'render unto Caesar that which is Caesar's, and unto God that which is God's.'[3] As Christians we are bound to support and sustain the Emperor as long as he doesn't fight against God. Our family is loyal to the Emperor, and to the Republic. Diocletian has risen to the throne and become the Emperor of the Republic, mostly because he now has the strongest loyal army. In the history of the Empire, the Emperor has almost always been the man who can raise and maintain the largest or strongest loyal army."

George considered his father's words. Finally, he asked about the logical conclusion of his own deep thinking. "Isn't this way of choosing leaders like letting the biggest bully be the boss?"

Father stifled a nervous chuckle and then responded, "Isn't that the way it works with the boys in town? Don't the other kids all submit to the biggest bully?"

"Of course not!" George declared. "If there's a bully being mean to the kids in town, either me or Gregor would take him down."

Father smiled at this reply and continued, "See there, not all strong men are bullies. Some are protectors who love and serve God and the people. It's very important for good men to be strong too, so evil men won't be so anxious to cross them and abuse others. When men battle for power, the people always suffer, even when the good men win. An evil leader will often cause much sin among his people. But taking down a wicked leader is usually a horrible and bloody task.[4] That's why it's so important for good men to be as strong as they can, to maintain peace through strength, and thus discourage evil men from battling for abusive power."

George thought on his father's counsel, and then asked his next question, "How does the Emperor keep track of all the men who are trying to become emperor?"

Father responded carefully, "The Emperor doesn't have to keep track of all the ambitious dreamers. Most of them talk big but think small. They get into arguments and get weeded out by other ambitious dreamers. The Emperor only needs to deal with men who present an actual threat to his position. First, he needs protection from those who would try to kill him secretly. That's why he has a group of loyal bodyguards called tribunes. Before I was injured, I had the great honor to serve as a tribune, protecting the Emperor for the Republic.

"Next, the Emperor must deal with those who would challenge him openly. Such men are generally easy to identify because they must, of necessity, amass to themselves a sizeable loyal army. Depending on the extent of his success in gathering an army, a challenger may choose to try and conquer the entire empire. With a lesser force, he may choose to try and separate a portion of the empire as a kingdom of his own. Frequently, such actions are taken against the Emperor when he is new or distracted by war with other foes, or when many of his subjects have shown a strong willingness to die rather than continue as his subjects. In any case, the Emperor and his allies regularly assess those who have been delegated power and those who appear to be gathering power. Any who have exceeded the bounds of delegated authority, having excessive support, or holding the loyalty of any formidable host become targets of the Emperor."

"Does that mean a man with a big army is a more likely to be attacked by the Emperor than a man with a small army?" George asked.

"That's partly correct," Father replied. "The other important factor is the loyalty of the army. If a big army is given to a commander by the Emperor, but that army remains loyal to the Emperor, then there shouldn't be much suspicion. However, if the Emperor believes the loyalty of the army is changing from him to the appointed leader, the Emperor will likely take action to separate that leader from his army, resolving the issue by force, if necessary."

"What happens when the leader of the army gets killed in the heat of battle? Who becomes the new leader of the army?" George asked with intense interest.

Father smiled patiently. "Well, if the Emperor is close by, he can either take personal command, or he can appoint a new leader of the army. If he's not close by, then the leadership of the army passes to the next highest ranking officer. If there is more than one man of the next highest rank, they can make an agreement on who will lead. If they don't agree on who should lead, usually they appeal to the whole army for support. Generally, it quickly becomes obvious who the men trust and respect and therefore who they are willing to accept and support as their new leader.

"When the battle is over, the Emperor must decide whether to ratify these battlefield promotions or to replace the leaders with new commanders of his own choosing. It's important for the Emperor to assure that the loyalty of both the leaders and the army remains with him. If the army ever loses confidence in the Emperor, it may try to get another leader to overthrow him and take power. Such rebellions are very bloody. They exact a terrible toll on the peace and prosperity of the entire Republic. Regardless of who wins, the people all suffer."

"You make farming sound better all the time," Gregor sighed. "I think I might stick with that."

George pondered the words of his father. As always, he still had another question. "If I'm in the army and I have to help pick a new leader, how will I know which man to pick?"

Gerontius struggled for an answer that would always be right, considering George's unnerving gift of remembering with exactness nearly all he heard and read. "That will depend on so many factors that it's very hard to give you a single right answer. But I trust in the counsel of Jesus who taught us to 'seek first the kingdom of God, and His righteousness; and all these things shall be added unto us.'[5] That promise means that if we always put God first, He will inspire us with truth and reveal to us the right things to do by the power of His Holy Spirit according to our needs. Because of this promise from God, we have every reason to rejoice and little reason to fear. If we follow the promptings of the Spirit, we will be safe, whatever the future holds. We will be shown what we need to do."[6]

George thought that answer seemed simple and made sense. He didn't know why Father struggled over it. "That sounds a lot like God's plan for how we get rich," George said.

"Get rich?" Father responded dubiously. "And what is God's plan for us to get rich?"

"First we seek the kingdom of God. After we've gained a hope in Christ we'll gain riches, if we seek them with the intent to do good, to clothe the naked, to feed the hungry, to liberate the captive, and to give relief to the sick and the afflicted.[7] But I don't think the riches are money. I think they are the riches of God, like charity and humility."

"How do we clothe the naked with humility, or feed charity to the hungry," Polly asked with great interest.

"We can't," George responded. "But we can let our hearts fill with humility and charity, and that will help us find ways to properly do all of God's work."

Gerontius looked to his wife and raised his eyebrows. Polly shrugged her shoulders. With a slight giggle she said, "Don't look at me. I didn't teach him that…but I wish I had."

*****

When Gerontius received word that the civil war in the east had ended, he was greatly relieved. At dinner that evening he related what had taken place. "Shortly after Diocletian was named Emperor by his army, Carinus marched east with his forces, intent on destroying Diocletian and subjecting the entire empire to himself. In response, Diocletian crossed the Bosporus Strait from Asia into Europe and met the forces of Carinus in the Balkans. Diocletian's army was losing the battle when Carinus was assassinated by one of his officers, leaving his army with no emperor.

"The western army was unable to agree on a new leader from within its own ranks, but the men were united in their respect for Diocletian, believing he was the one most likely to pay them for their military service. Therefore, they surrendered to Diocletian, accepting him as their emperor. As a token of goodwill to their newly sworn allegiance, Diocletian kept in place Aristobolus, the highest ranking officer of the western army, as well as many of the government officials."

"I'm happy that's all resolved," Gregor stated.

"Oh, it's not all resolved," Father responded. "Though the civil war with Carinus is over, the empire is now under attack by foreign invaders in the Danube River region. They are mostly ambitious and opportunistic Germanic tribes from the north and Sarmatians from the northeast. If Diocletian focuses fully on defense of the northeastern frontier, he won't be able to personally attend to the assimilation and management of the west. There is also word that Carausius, the commander of the North Sea fleet, has given in to his own ambitions and declared himself emperor of Britannia. He's probably hoping the civil war and invaders in the northeast will exhaust Diocletian's forces enabling him to consolidate loyal support and maintain his claims.

"War and politics are dangerous businesses. Perhaps the only more dangerous business would be an unhappy marriage." Gerontius paused to glance at Polly, and then continued with a smile, "But then, I wouldn't know anything about that."

"Deep water. Very deep water. Tread carefully," Polly said, returning her husband's smile.

Gregor and George both felt they were missing something from their parents' exchange, but it seemed to be all in fun, so they joined in with a few sympathetic chuckles.

Gerontius continued with his analysis. "Assassination is a tactic commonly used by commanders of inferior forces. It's often easier to arrange the death of the opposing leader than it is to overcome the strength of the opposing army. That's one reason why the Emperor surrounds himself with only the most trusted and proven men as tribunes, who will personally protect his life. When I served as a tribune, I considered it one of the highest honors to bear that trust.

"The assassination tactic applies to supposedly loyal forces as well. If a leader suspects a subordinate is becoming a threat, he may arrange the death of that subordinate, even if the man has remained loyal, with no ambitions for rebellion. The larger the subordinate's army, the greater the shadow of suspicion that naturally falls upon him. This is especially true if the superior commander is insecure in himself or his own army."

George thought carefully and then posed his next questions. "Father, what are they all fighting over? Who would want a job where other people are trying to kill you all the time? Why do they even want to be emperor? It seems like being the head of the Republic is a lot of work, taking care of all your subjects."

"Those are great questions, George," Father responded. "However, many men who seek power don't have the best interests of the people at heart. When the righteous are in authority, the people rejoice. But when the wicked bear rule, the people mourn.[8] Many ambitious men tell themselves that control of the military, or the economy, or the people will allow them to stabilize things so the people can have peace and prosperity. However, all too frequently this control is coupled with excess and waste in government, and greedy politicians who seek to fill their own purses with the taxes and labor of the poor. Frequently, such leaders drag the people into immorality and other sins, bringing a curse upon their entire nation."

"Do money and power make good people become evil?" George pondered aloud.

Father paused to let George think on his own question before he shared his opinion. "I don't believe that either money or power corrupt men's souls, but I do believe that both money and power magnify and reveal any corruption that's been hidden, however carefully, in the deepest recesses of each man's heart."

****

CHAPTER SEVEN
The Theban Legion

Lydda, Palestine
285-286 AD

"For whosoever will save his life shall lose it; but whosoever shall lose his life for My sake and the gospel's, the same shall save it."[1]
Mark 8:35

****

Diocletian looked his most trusted general in the eye. "Maximian, I have a problem. I must secure the empire. I need to lead our army in repelling the attacks of the Alamanni in the north and the Sarmatians in the northeast. I can't do that and oversee the assimilation of the western provinces at the same time."

"What would you have me do?" Maximian responded.

"I need a strong leader I can trust to help me. You are that man. I'm renewing the division of the empire between east and west, and placing the west in your charge. I have no son as a natural heir to share this burden, and in any case, I favor promotions based on merit. As my Caesar, my second in command, I choose you to administer the western provinces while I resolve matters in the northeast. You must quell the rebellions and make an orderly transition of power to ministers loyal to us. I grant you full authority to rule the west, subject only to me."

"As you command!" Maximian barked, an excited twinkle in his eyes.

*****

Winter had been brutal with battle to stabilize the borders against all foes. As spring came, Diocletian concluded the empire would always be too big for one man to rule alone, so he wrote:

Most Noble Emperor Maximian, Augustus of the Western Empire:

I have reviewed your status report. I'm pleased that you have solidified the support of the western army and put down the southern rebellions. I urge you to move quickly and crush the rebellions in Gaul and Britannia.

I have decided to make permanent the division of the empire between east and west. In honor of your loyalty, trustworthiness, and success I promote you to Augustus over the west. I will remain the senior Augustus over the entire empire, possessing veto power over any edicts you issue. I expect you will retain Milan as your capital, but you may decide that matter. Keep me informed of any important developments.
    Always faithful!
– *Emperor Diocletian Augustus*

*****

Most Noble Emperor Diocletian Augustus:
    As you suspected, I will retain Milan as my capital for now. The western army is making progress against the rebellions in Gaul but the task may not be complete by the end of this fighting season. I expect we will subdue Gaul next year and then begin preparations to retake Britannia. I note with concern the growing Christian influence among both the Romans and the rebels. Reports indicate that Christianity has become particularly prominent among the rebel leadership, especially in Gaul and Burgundy. Although the Christian soldiers in the western army have generally been loyal to us, it is apparent they are even more loyal to their God and their families. I have taken steps to reform their priorities, placing the Emperor and empire first, Roman gods next, and finally family. My plan to accomplish this reformation of priorities has been simple. I have instructed my commanders to keep the Christians dispersed in the various battle groups with the intent of undermining their ability to sustain each other in their faith. I have also ordered these men to posts far from home to weaken their family ties. Prior to each major battle I require every soldier to make sacrifices to the Roman gods, and to swear absolute allegiance to me. Finally, as a direct assault on their Christian values, I have encouraged these men in looting conquered villages and brutally ravishing local women after battle victories. These measures appear to have been effective in muting the Christian influence in the western army. Perhaps such measures may be helpful to you going forward.
    Always faithful!
– *Emperor Maximian Augustus*

*****

Most Noble Emperor Maximian Augustus:
    Our warfare has gone well. We have repelled many of the invaders.

A Martyr's Faith

I make particular praise of our Theban Legion and their faithfulness and valiance in restoring peace and stability in the Danube River region. Christianity has also been expanding in the east, taking hold more rapidly among the subjects of the empire than among the foreigners. We've had some trouble with Christians placing God and family ahead of the empire, but that has been inconsistent among the professed believers. I've heard that many Christians have banded together in the Theban Legion, which complicates efforts to reset their priorities, placing Emperor and empire first. Keep me informed of your progress, and let me know if I can assist you.
  Always faithful!
– Emperor Diocletian Augustus

*****

Most Noble Emperor Diocletian Augustus:
  Distancing the Theban Legion from their families may be the key to your Christian problem. Perhaps you should send that legion to assist me in the conquest of Gaul and Burgundy, and leave the discipline to me.
  Always faithful!
– Emperor Maximian Augustus

*****

It was a cool September morning, but a strange northeast wind was whispering through the trees of Gaul, carrying an ominous shroud of fog with it. The morning fog had been the same for several days, burning off by the early afternoon. Maximian mounted his horse and stood up in his stirrups, thinking. *This is not the weather I want. The rebels have better knowledge of these woods and the lay of the land. Foggy conditions will be a great advantage to them in the impending battle. I want a clear morning to improve the odds for my army. We should start our attack early, reducing the chances of our enemies escaping later under cover of darkness. Though I'm uncertain of the strength of the rebel forces, we must crush them decisively before bad weather comes bringing an end to the fighting season. It's likely we can succeed with the legions we have, but to strengthen our hand we will use the Theban Legion to make a surprise attack on the rebels, firmly tipping the scales in favor of the empire.*

Normally, a legion had 3,000 to 5,000 men in it, and was divided into several millenniums, each comprised of 700 to 1,000 men, commanded by a millenary. Each millennium was further divided into centuries of 70 to 100 men, commanded by a centurion. The Theban Legion was over 6,000 men strong, all proven in battle. But they were late. Maximian waited anxiously for them as a messenger approached.

"My lord, we have word from a scout. The Theban Legion will arrive in camp early this afternoon," the messenger reported.

"It's about time," Maximian responded in frustration. "They should've been here a week ago so we could've won this battle before the bad weather set in."

"It's just bad luck, sir," the messenger consoled.

"I believe a bit in luck, but only that it favors the prepared," Maximian replied. "I don't believe in superstition, but I know many of the men do and that's a problem. I've seen too many battles in which men have given in to superstitions, withdrawing from combat and losing when, if they had pressed the fight, they surely would have won. Because of that, I keep a steady schedule of pre-battle activities. The Theban Legion has upset that. Perhaps I'll reposition them to lead the battle charge when the time comes. Notify me immediately when they arrive."

"As you command, my lord," the messenger confirmed.

Maximian returned to his tent. Still seething a bit, he thought, *How can I overcome the men's superstitions? I must have their complete submission. This day will be no different.* "Rufus!" he called. "Come take my orders!"

"Yes, sir!" the aide responded as he popped in through the tent door.

"All soldiers will assemble two hours before dusk. Each man will make sacrifices to the Roman gods for strength and victory in the coming battle. Once the sacrifices are complete, each man who has not previously sworn an oath of allegiance to me will appear before me personally, to worship me and to swear allegiance to me and no other. Finally, because the rebel leaders are Christian, I will require every soldier to swear an oath to assist in the extermination of Christianity from Gaul and Burgundy. Make sure the Theban Legion is given notice of these orders immediately upon their arrival. That's all for now."

"As you command," Rufus replied, and then he quickly disappeared.

Now we'll see whose faith is real and whose is pretend among the Theban Legion, Maximian thought. "The Roman gods should smile upon us before the night is over," he muttered.

*****

Rufus met the Theban Legion commanders in their tent. Mauritius, Candidus, and Exupernis were all seasoned men of war. There was no nonsense in any of them. Rufus prefaced the orders with his own commentary. "Maximian believes there may be some disciplinary issues among the Christians within your legion. He intends to address that directly, as you can see from the orders." He handed the leaders a written copy for their review. Immediately he saw a shadow of anger cross the men's faces.

"And what of the men who refuse these orders?" Mauritius asked bluntly, restrained anger evident in each word.

"I can't speak for the Emperor," Rufus replied, "but in the past he has ordered such stubborn souls to night watch guard duty before battle, coupled with the command that they lead the attack in the morning. He says with men who are so sure of their God's favor in battle, we will stand behind them from the start."

"There may be a lot of men standing guard tonight," Ex mused. "You see, every man in the Theban Legion is a devout Christian. All 6,666 of us. We'll talk to the men and let you know when we have their voice on the matter. Please return in an hour. Until then, we won't pretend to speak for the men on this issue."

Rufus was surprised by the news that the entire legion was Christian, including the commanders. Concerned, he proceeded on his rounds to meet with and notify the other legion commanders.

*****

Quickly, the Theban Legion commanders called in their millenaries and centurions. As they relayed the Emperor's orders, these men were shocked and angered. Immediately they separated and met with their soldiers and relayed the orders, noting how each man intended to respond. As the last of the centurions returned with his report, Mauritius concluded, "That's it then. To a man, all have chosen to refuse these commands. As all who live a godly life in Christ shall suffer persecution, we shall now see what measure of suffering our faith demands of us."[2]

*****

"My Lord, the Theban Legion has refused to comply with your orders," Rufus reported, fearing Maximian's response and regretting his role as the messenger.

Maximian raised his eyebrows and looked directly into Rufus' face. "How many refused?" he asked.

"All of them," Rufus replied. "All 6,666. Including their

commanders."

The rage within Maximian was inconsistent with his sober and calculating demeanor. He stifled his reaction and tried to think for a moment. *This is not how I intend to start this critical battle. I can't trust these Theban men.* He thought a moment longer and decided how he would handle their refusal. Turning to Rufus he ordered, "Call all the men to assembly at the appointed hour!"

*****

"Most noble Emperor Maximian," Mauritius addressed his commander uncomfortably. "The Theban Legion are all devout Christians. Therefore, we affirm our loyalty to Rome and to you as her emperor. We will faithfully sustain you in battle against the rebels. However, we respectfully decline the proscribed sacrifices and oaths."

Scanning the assembly of soldiers, the Emperor could see that the Theban men were predictably anxious, but so were the men of the other three legions as they observed the defiance. "Disarm the Theban Legion while I consider their refusal of my commands!" Maximian charged. Cautiously, the other legions approached to fulfill the order.

"We willingly surrender our weapons," Mauritius called out to his men. "We shall wait to see if Maximian will make exception for us, or take exception to us, imposing a punishment."

When the Thebans were disarmed, Maximian commanded, "Separate out every tenth man from this legion!" With 666 men set apart for the initial punishment, Maximian roared, "Put these men to the sword!" In just moments all 666 men were killed, decimating the Christian legion.

Maximian's other three legions braced for a melee as the Emperor loudly proclaimed, "These men have died for their faith. I now renew my commands, that others may choose a different course. Each of you men of the Theban Legion must make the required sacrifices to the Roman gods, swear allegiance to me, and swear to assist in the extermination of Christianity from Gaul and Burgundy. Those who will comply should move slowly to my left on the assembly field. Those refusing to comply with my commands should move slowly to my right on the field. You have two minutes to show where you stand."

It only took a minute for the Theban centurions to assess the minds of their remaining soldiers. The entire group faced Maximian and, in measured cadence, moved to signify they would not comply.
Maximian's rage increased at their united defiance. Again he ordered, "Separate out every tenth man from the defiant legion!" These 600 stood courageously, fully anticipating the worst. "Put these men to the sword!"

Maximian bellowed. Immediately, these 600 were killed, decimating the legion a second time.

Maximian renewed his commands a third time.

Gathering his leaders for consultation, Mauritius counseled them to make a counter-offer to Maximian, and the men readily agreed. Stepping boldly ahead of his men he said, "Most noble Emperor Maximian, our legion swears allegiance to you, and we volunteer to lead the attack in the coming battle, but we refuse to worship any but our God and we refuse the oath to exterminate the Christians."

Further infuriated at the Christians' persistent refusal of his commands, and rather than consider any compromise, Maximian raged, "Kill them all, to the last man!"

Spurred by the injustice of Maximian's order, Mauritius declared to his men with determination, "Let us hold fast to our faith and not waver, for He that promised us His eternal blessings is faithful.[3] Great and terrible shall be the day of judgment for the wicked because they cast out the saints, and slay them. The blood of the saints shall cry out from the earth and ascend up to God for justice against the wicked at that day, and all the proud and they that do wickedly shall burn as stubble at the coming of the Lord."[4]

*****

It was early October when an official came and met with George's father. Gerontius stayed in his library after the meeting. When George came to study in the early afternoon, he heard his father talking. Thinking he may have another meeting, George slipped in very quietly to find a book and read. Soon he realized the anguish in his father's voice as he prayed to God for understanding.

"O Lord, how long wilt Thou suffer that Thy servants shall dwell here below in the flesh, to behold such gross wickedness among the children of men? O Lord God, how long wilt Thou suffer that such wickedness and infidelity shall be among this people? O Lord, wilt Thou give me strength that I may bear my infirmities, for I am weak, and such wickedness among the leaders of this people pains my soul, and my heart is exceedingly sorrowful. Wilt Thou comfort my soul in Christ. O Lord, wilt Thou grant unto me that I may have strength, that I may suffer with patience these afflictions which have come upon me because of this great iniquity."[5]

When Gerontius had finished his prayer, George quietly approached and asked, "Father, why is your heart so heavy with grief?"

In a strained voice, and with tears flowing, he responded, "Maximian, the Emperor in the west, has killed all 6,666 soldiers of the Theban Legion because they were Christians. They utterly refused to worship the Roman gods and would not take an oath to exterminate the Christians from Gaul. Therefore they were executed, martyred for their faith in Jesus Christ.[6] The Theban Legion offered no other resistance as the surrounding legions swept over them with their swords, fulfilling Maximian's order. I can hardly bear this atrocity. I have been pleading with God for understanding."

George felt tears begin to run down his own cheeks as he asked, "Why are Christians hated and persecuted so? Why would God allow it?"

"Those are my questions too, George," Father replied. "I don't know all the reasons God has for allowing wickedness among His children. The apostle Paul taught that all who live godly lives shall suffer persecution.[7] He also taught that persecutions should be borne with patience and faith, counting it an honor to be worthy to suffer for the kingdom of God.[8] I feel in my heart that God allows the righteous to be persecuted and slain by evil men, who act according to the hardness of their hearts, that the wrath of His final judgments upon the wicked may be just. The blood of the innocent shall stand as a witness against the wicked and cry mightily against them at the last day. I have faith in Jesus that the righteous are not lost because they are slain. Surely they enter into the rest and glory of the Lord their God.[9]

"One of the Psalms says, 'I humbled my soul with fasting; and my prayer returned into my own bosom.'[10] Whenever I've felt my spirit this low before, I've found it helps me to fast and pray, seeking humility and greater faith in Christ, trusting in His will and not trying to change it. I fast and pray until God fills my soul with joy and consolation.[11] Fasting and prayer will help you too, George."

"Father, did the Christian soldiers do the right thing? I mean, couldn't they have just pretended to agree in order to get their weapons back, and then fought their way out?"

"When Jesus was crucified, should He have fought for His life?" Gerontius questioned.

"If that would have been right, Jesus would have done it," George replied.

Gerontius continued, "Sometimes a witness must seal his testimony with his own blood.[12] Sometimes it's best if we sacrifice ourselves rather than send others through the veil of death, unprepared to meet their God. Which were more prepared to meet God, the Theban Legion of Christian soldiers, or Maximian's soldiers, who hadn't yet found faith in Christ?"

"The Theban Legion was better prepared to meet God," George

answered.

"That's right," Father confirmed. "The Theban Legion did what was right by God. They had taken upon them the name of Christ, taking His burden upon themselves. They may have been justified in fighting for their own lives. They would have been more justified in fighting for the lives of their brethren, but the men they would have killed in protecting each other were Maximian's soldiers, who were just following orders. The innocent blood of the Theban Legion will mainly stain Maximian's hands, not the hands of his soldiers."

Gerontius breathed deeply, trying to bleed off the grief. After a few quiet moments he spoke reassuringly to his son, "Follow the Spirit, George, and you will always do right."

"Yes, Father." George wiped a tear from his own cheek as he pondered for the first time what he would do if evil men demanded that he deny his faith in Christ or be put to death.

*****

Alone again, Gerontius searched the scriptures until he found these passages: *Precious in the sight of the Lord is the death of His saints. O Lord, truly I am Thy servant. I am Thy servant, and the son of Thine handmaid. Thou hast loosed my bonds, for Thou hast delivered my soul from death, mine eyes from tears, and my feet from falling. I will walk before the Lord in the land of the living. Return unto thy rest, O my soul, for the Lord hath dealt bountifully with thee.*[13]

****

CHAPTER EIGHT
Engineering Skills

Lydda, Palestine
286 AD

"But to be learned is good if they hearken unto the counsels of God."[1]
2 Nephi 9:29

****

It was early afternoon and Gerontius had gone to his library to escape the heat of the day. This was his usual time to study the Holy Scriptures. As he entered the room, he saw his son in one corner, carefully shifting a rather large book that he was studying intently. "George, what are you working on there?" he asked.

"I'm just reading this book about building things. It's very interesting. The diagrams really help me understand what it's all about. I'm reading about wells again. I might want to dig one someday. It's really amazing that land can be dry on top, but there's plenty of water not far underground."

Gerontius nodded in agreement. "You know, I have been thinking about hiring some men from town to dig a well for us down by the servants' quarters so they won't have to carry their fresh water so far to their homes. Maybe when we do that you can watch and learn something. Have you looked at any of the other engineering books?"

"Sure," George replied. "I've read each of them several times. I like the simple way they show how we can build things with wood and stone that make our lives much better, like roads, bridges, walls, towers, and wells."

"Have you read the other books on sewage, irrigation, hospitals, libraries, and markets too?" Father wondered out loud.

"Yes, I've read all those books," George responded. "The instructions seem simple to follow. Once you think about them, they make a lot of sense."

"Can you build any of those things?" Father asked, trying to gauge George's level of ambition.

"I don't have much experience building things yet, but I think I could if I had a little training working with wood and stone. Speaking of training, I've been meaning to ask you, would you permit me to work

A Martyr's Faith

with Lucius, the stone cutter in Lydda, helping him haul stone to his work projects in exchange for him training me how to work with stone? It would just be in the evenings, and I promise it won't interfere with my chores or training at home. May I do that, Father, please?"

Gerontius thought he could see where this was going. "Boys at your age are almost always looking for any excuse to get some distance from their parents so they can do a little growing up of their own. At least your proposal is calculated to accomplish something worthwhile. I'll speak to your mother about it and let you know," he replied.

"Oh, she said she's fine with it, if it's okay with you," George responded, as if he'd ridden this horse before.

"Oh, she did, huh?" Gerontius chuckled. "Then you have my blessing, as long as your work for Lucius doesn't interfere with your duties or training at home."

"It won't, I promise. Thanks, Father," George said. "My training with Lucius starts this evening. I'll run to his place just after dinner, work for about an hour, and then run back home. I won't keep you or mother up late. Lucius said the first thing he'll teach me, after we haul stone to his job, is how to care for the tools. Then he'll teach me to cut and shape stones. As we deliver stone each evening to his jobs, I'll get to see how the work progresses."

Father noted that George had set things up with Lucius before getting his permission. He smiled to himself as he thought, *There's no lack of confidence with George. But, I wonder how good Lucius will be at getting work done while answering an endless chain of complex questions from one very curious and ambitious young man.*

*****

"Where's George?" Gerontius asked Polly as he sat down to lunch.

"Oh, he's out digging his well. The time must have gotten away from him."

"Digging his well? What kind of a well is he digging and where is it?" Gerontius asked.

"It's just a common water well," Polly replied. "He's digging it down by the servants' quarters. He's been at it since just before sunrise. Maybe you should go down there and give him a little…supervision. I know your back won't let you do this kind of labor, but George has young muscles to spare. He'll do his own digging. I think he would appreciate your encouragement."

"Wells are dangerous projects!" Gerontius declared. "Many men have tried to improve their land by digging wells, only to get buried alive when the walls have collapsed on them. If you'll excuse me, I'll go down right away and encourage him not to kill himself."

*****

When Gerontius rounded the corner of the main house, he could see a new pile of dirt in the distance by the servants' quarters. It took him over a minute to walk the hundred yards to the project site. As he got past the mounds of earth he couldn't see George, but he could hear him down in the hole. Sabra was sitting on a rock a few feet from the hole. A broad cloth had been rigged above her head for shade. She was quietly drawing letters with a stick in the fresh soil. The mouth of the well was small, only twice the width of George's shoulders. A notched wooden pole inserted in the hole served the same function as a ladder, but was much easier to move out of the way of the work down the hole.

"George, would you come up and talk with me for a minute?" Gerontius called down the well.

"Sure, Father. I'll be right up," was the slightly hollow reply.

"Sabra, are you spying on George again?" Gerontius teased.

"No sir, master Gerontius. I'm working," Sabra responded with pride.

"Really? And just exactly what work are you doing?"

"I'm watching George…and he's paying me to do it. He gave me a copper coin."

Father stifled a chuckle as he thought how many times George had made careful arrangements to avoid having Sabra tag along on his adventures. "Why would George pay you to watch him dig dirt?" he asked.

"To be safe," Sabra answered smartly. "George came last evening and asked mama if he could hire me to watch him today. He said he was going to dig a well and it would be dangerous. He said he would need someone to watch him once the hole got over his head, and to get help in case the dirt fell in on him. He said he would start digging a little before sunrise, but he wouldn't need me to watch until about the third hour, once the hole was over his head. When I heard the shovel this morning, I came out to watch, but he said he wouldn't pay me for watching until the third hour, like we agreed. I didn't mind. Besides, he digs faster than he thought he would. The hole was over his head by the second hour, so then he said he would start paying me. But I told him the third hour was our agreement, and I would do the second hour for free. He set up this sun shade for me and said I could work on my letters while I watch."

Soon, a very sweaty, dirty George popped his head up from the hole, a big smile on his face.

"Here's your water," Sabra said as she handed George a jug from under her shade.

"How's your well coming along?" Father asked.

"I'm happy with the progress so far," George said between gulps from the jug. "I didn't think it would go this fast. The soil at the bottom of the hole is already starting to get moist. It looks like it will be a good water well, so I've started lining the upper walls with stone as I work my way down. That reduces the risk of earth falling down on me. I've used nearly all the stone I brought to line the inside of the well down to where I have dug so far. That's okay because I need to quit for the day so I can get my training and chores done. Tonight I'll go get another load of stone to line the well further down when I dig tomorrow morning."

"The size of your dirt pile is surprisingly big, but it looks like you've done a good job of spreading it out evenly as you've worked," Father said, inspecting the project more closely. "I'm impressed that you planned ahead and took precautions to increase your safety on this job. You've got a lot of great ideas and you've proven you'll work hard to accomplish any goals you set. However, I'd still appreciate it if you'd run your big ideas by me before you get started so I can at least pretend to help you think them through."

"Okay, Father," George agreed. "I'll work harder at that from now on. I just remembered you talking about what a blessing it would be to have a second well down by the servants' quarters. I remembered our discussion about the best location for the well based on the lay of the land. I thought the only question left was who would do the work."

"It was on my wish list," father admitted. "But I hadn't planned to do it until next year, or the year after. Since you're nearly done, tell me about your plan and what it'll cost me."

"Oh, it won't cost you anything," George assured. "Like we discussed last month, I started working with Lucius, helping him haul rock to his different projects in Lydda. I've been working with him in the evenings, every day but Sundays. In exchange for my help hauling stone, he's been teaching me to quarry and shape stone. He said I could have as much stone as I can quarry myself, as long as I keep up in my work for him. I made a plan for how much stone I would need to finish this well, and what sizes and shapes of stones I would need. I've been hauling loads of stones home this week, so I'd have them ready for my well.

"So far, I've set the ring of large stones at the mouth of the well, so the edges of the hole won't cave in. As I've deepened the well, every three feet I've carved a deep ring into the well wall and put a ring of larger stones actually set into the wall, like the ring of stone at the top of the well. I've been using smaller stones to line the wall between each deep set ring of stones. If I set the lining stones correctly, they will be tight all the way to the top, except for maybe the last one or two stones, but those can be tightened with rock chips. As long as I don't dig more than a few feet below the rock lining the inside of the well, I stay better protected from the walls caving in on me. It's a slow but safe process, working alone."

"Hey, you're not workin' alone! I'm workin' here too, remember?" Sabra protested at the unpardonable oversight.

Gerontius laughed as George smiled apologetically and replied, "Sure, Sabra. How could I forget that you're working here too? Would you be kind enough to help by bringing me the next bucket of stones to line the well wall?"

"That's too heavy for me!" Sabra objected. "Besides, that's not the work we agreed for me to do. My job is to watch over your life, and to get help if the earth comes down on you," she said with an air of importance and a sweet little smile. As an afterthought she offered, "I guess I could bring the stones from the bucket one at a time and drop them down to you in the well."

Gerontius laughed again as he imagined Sabra dropping stones down the well onto George while he was digging. However, he was in no hurry to find out how thick George's skull was by having stones dropped onto his head. Turning to George he said, "Agree with thy adversary quickly, while thou art in the way with her, lest at any time she cast thee into a pit and stone thee, and none can deliver."[2]

George chuckled uneasily as he withdrew his request. "You're right, Sabra. The stones aren't part of your work. I'll have Gregor help me with them and the dirt tomorrow."

"Okay," Sabra chirped. Then, turning to pierce Gerontius with her eyes she exclaimed, "Besides, I'm NOT his adversary! And I didn't cast him into this pit! He dug it himself. And I wouldn't stone him! I would think you of all people could see that I'm his guardian angel!" Sabra looked truly pained by the fun at her expense.

Gerontius looked at Sabra and thought, *This one is very intense and quick-witted for only being nine years old. I'll have to be much more careful of my words around her from now on.* Apologetically he responded "You're right. You are his guardian angel. I'm sorry I didn't see that completely before. Will you please forgive me?"

"Sure I forgive you," Sabra said with a quick smile.

"I wish I hadn't been injured and could help you more with projects like this," Gerontius said to George. "I'm grateful that you and Gregor have both grown big and strong, but I'm also grateful for my own adversity. My injury has taught me that the help people need is not always the kind that relieves their burdens of labor. I've helped many with wisdom and encouragement that I couldn't help with physical strength. Even so, I'm truly impressed with your work here. You've thought of things I wouldn't have on my own. Did Lucius teach you to dig wells?"

"No," George replied. "He's been working on building a shop at the market square. The plans for digging and finishing wells are in the architectural books in your library. I love those books. Most of the projects can be done if a person just learns how to work with wood and stone."

Oh, it's that simple, is it, thought Gerontius, as if George believed these skills would come naturally to everyone. "George, I'm pleased with the progress you've been making in your studies. I don't think much of men who are no wiser today than they were yesterday.[3] But you do understand you have many gifts and talents from God that other people don't have, right?"

"I know God has blessed me with many gifts that other people don't have," George agreed. "But many people do have gifts just waiting to be discovered and developed."

Father smiled. "Not everyone understands what they read in books. Few can quickly develop the skills to shape and fit stones or wood. Just be mindful of the Source of your gifts. Don't neglect them.[4] Use them for good. Never despise others because they are weak. Just give thanks that God has made you strong, and bless others with the talents He has given you."

"I will, Father," George promised. "When I started working for Lucius, two of the older servants here, Jason and Erastus, took an interest. I've been teaching them the things I've been learning and they've been helping me shape the stones for the well. They have real talent working with stone. I told Lucius about them. He might want to apprentice them, if you would agree to that."

Gerontius considered for a moment. "We'd lose their labor on the farm, but the apprenticeships would greatly improve their prospects in life." Turning to George he continued, "Digging a well for the servants and field workers is an excellent example of using your gifts for good, but guiding others in developing their talents is even more valuable. I think you're doing a great job with this well, but an even better job in working with Jason and Erastus. I'm sure we'll be able to support them in apprenticeships, if that's what they want. I love you, Son."

"I love you too, Father," George replied. "I know I can't do everything alone. That's why I have Gregor, Jason, and Erastus to help me when I get down to digging in the water. And that's why I have Sabra here working for me," he said with a smile and a sideways glance at his vigilant helper. "I think it's going to be a great well."

"Do you love me too?" Sabra asked, staring intently at George. "Or am I just your little guardian angel?"

Gerontius measured Sabra's intense stare at George. George looked confused, and then he began rapidly turning red. Gerontius wasn't confused. Sensing his son really did need his help, he gently confirmed in a reverent tone, "Sabra, we all love you too."

*****

Gerontius washed his hands and returned to lunch with his wife. Polly took note of her husband's distant stare and asked, "So, were you able to cheat death with your amazing supervisory skills?"

Thoughtfully he replied, "Perhaps. It's hard to believe that George is just going on twelve years old. He's certainly sharp for his age, and very big and strong too. I tell you Polly, every time I try to teach that boy something new, I learn something from him. But it's a good thing I went down there to supervise because George was obviously in over his head on at least one count," he added with a chuckle.

Polly stood up from the table and cleared the dishes away. She returned to where Gerontius was sitting, lost again in his thoughts. Gently she moved behind her husband and, wrapping her arms around him in a bear hug, whispered into his ear, "I'm glad you're not afraid to learn new things. Maybe I can still teach you a thing or two myself."

"I'd like that," he said as he turned to face her embrace. "I think George got big and strong from his father, but handsome and intelligent definitely came from his mother."

"Being full of faith is a gift from his loving Heavenly Father," Polly added.

"The more I think on George's amazing gifts, the more determined I am to seek the guidance of the Lord in training both our sons and helping them to become true men of righteousness," Gerontius shared.

****

CHAPTER NINE
David and Goliath

Lydda, Palestine
286 AD

"...that all the earth may know that there is a God in Israel."[1]
1 Samuel 17:46

****

Gregor was in the yard practicing attacks and defenses with his sword. George approached and sat on the rock by the well to watch. After a few passes through his exercises, Gregor stopped and faced George. "Did you want something, Pip? Or are you just here in awe of the master?"

"I came to thank you for helping me with the well project down by the servants' quarters," George responded, not taking the bait. "Without help from you and Jason and Erastus, I'd probably still be digging. I think the well will be a really good one."

"Don't forget thanks for all the help from your little guardian angel, Sabra," Gregor teased.

"Well, I'm still not sure if there's more danger with her around or not, but it worked out this time and I am grateful for her too," George said honestly.

"You're welcome for the help. That was a good project," Gregor replied. "Just remember, you owe me. I'll expect you to step up the next time I come to you for help, okay?"

"Now that you mention it, I've been watching your sword practice and it looks like you could use a little help with your right overhand attack," George offered.

Feeling a bit indignant at his younger brother's offer of counsel, Gregor responded curtly, "Listen, Pip. It's better to keep your mouth shut and have others think you're a fool, than to open your mouth and remove all doubt.[2] I'm sure I know what I'm doing here. I'll let you know if and when I ever need your help."

"Okay," George replied, but he stayed on the rock, quietly watching Gregor practice.

After a few minutes, Gregor stopped again and asked, "Is there something else you want, Pip?"

"I was just reading about King David, before he became the king. He had great faith that allowed God to help him be victorious in battle," George said.

Despite his sense of superiority over his little brother, Gregor loved to hear George retell stories of battle heroes from the scriptures. George had a way of really bringing the stories to life, even if Gregor questioned some of the details. "Tell me about it," Gregor invited.

"When David was still too young to be in the army of Israel, he went to take food to his brothers who were soldiers. When he got there, Goliath the Philistine was cursing the hosts of Israel by the Philistine gods, and cursing and reviling the God of Israel. Even though Goliath was nine feet tall and had massive weapons, David was astonished that none in the camp of Israel would go fight him. With faith in God, David volunteered to fight Goliath.

"King Saul told David he was too young and inexperienced to fight Goliath, who was a seasoned man of war. Then David told the king about when he had rescued sheep from a lion and from a bear, and that he had killed both the lion and the bear. David gave the glory to God, saying, 'Moreover, the Lord that delivered me out of the paw of the lion, and out of the paw of the bear, He will deliver me out of the hand of the Philistine.' He told the king he would kill the giant because Goliath had defied the living God and His armies. Impressed by David's faith, King Saul agreed to let him fight. He offered to let David use his own armor. Trusting in God, David refused Saul's armor. In faith, he took only his staff, five stones, and a sling to the battle.

"Goliath despised him because of his youth saying, 'Am I a dog that thou comest to me with sticks. Come to me and I will feed thy flesh to the fowls of the air and the beasts of the field.'

"David answered, 'Thou comest to me with a sword, and with a spear, and with a shield: but I come to thee in the name of the Lord of hosts, the God of the armies of Israel, whom thou hast defied. This day will the Lord deliver thee into my hand, and I will smite thee, and take thine head from thee...that all the earth may know that there is a God in Israel. And all this assembly shall know that the Lord saveth not with sword and spear: for the battle is the Lord's, and He will give you into our hands.' David used his sling to smite Goliath in the forehead with a stone. Since he had no sword, David used Goliath's own sword to cut off the giant's head."[3]

Gregor enjoyed the story, but he couldn't help challenging George's admiration of David. "If you aspire to be as David, then you must see me as Goliath. You should remember, in the battle skills tournament no slings are allowed. Perhaps if David had been forced to face Goliath with a sword, you would be singing the praises of Goliath instead."

George considered for a moment and then responded, "I don't think so. David's greatest weapons were his faith in God and his pure heart. He knew he was on the Lord's errand, and would be sustained by Him. I don't think it would have mattered which weapon he used, because the Lord was fighting the battle."

"Then I guess the trick is finding a way to make sure that, in every battle you join, you're on the Lord's errand," Gregor said. "Otherwise, you have no promise of God's help."

After considering Gregor's counsel George agreed, "I'm sure you're right. I think that's the point of the cautions Father often gives us to be careful picking our battles," he added.

****

CHAPTER TEN
The Honor of Ascalon

Lydda, Palestine
287 AD

"...he also shall be great: but truly his younger brother shall be greater than he..."[1]
Genesis 48:19

****

"Time for supper," Polly called to Gerontius, who was in his library thinking.

"Polly, please come here for a minute. I want to talk with you," Gerontius responded.

"Sure, my love. What's the topic of torture for today?" she teased as she entered the room.

Gerontius gazed up at his battle sword which was mounted on the wall. "I've been thinking about Ascalon. You know it's my most prized weapon. I had it custom made especially for me by a master craftsman, gifted in working fine steel. He knew how to balance the blade and match the shaft and hilt to the stature and strength of a man. Ascalon was indispensible in my career as a soldier. There are few people who could use it effectively because it's simply too big and heavy for most men to wield properly. But, for those who can use it properly, it offers a supreme advantage in personal combat."

"I'm not as excited about swords as you and the boys," Polly replied quietly. "But this sword I love. It has preserved your life for me too many times not to deserve my honor."

"That's just it!" Gerontius exclaimed. "Ascalon is a sword of honor, proven many times in battle. As my heir, Gregor will inherit it. But I keep thinking there's a more honorable way to pass this battle sword on to my son. I want to give him the privilege of winning it in combat!"

Polly looked dubious. "Will Gregor have to kill you in combat in order to rightfully claim your weapon? Because 'honor' would then require that I kill my son in order to avenge your death, wouldn't it?" Polly pondered aloud with a smile.

Gerontius grinned. Polly's sense of humor was definitely one of the many reasons he loved her so. "No," he replied. "I've thought this through carefully to find a solution in which Ascalon is honorably conferred, and I continue to live. I would like to donate Ascalon as a prize, to be awarded to the champion of Lydda's youth battle skills tournament this year. That way our son can legitimately win the sword in open combat."

"What would you do if Gregor didn't win the tournament?" Polly asked mildly.

"I think we both know he'll win," Gerontius responded confidently. "He's easily the strongest competitor."

"Yes," Polly agreed. "But what would you do if Gregor didn't win the tournament and Ascalon was claimed by a challenger?"

"Well, first I think I'd be in shock! Next, I'd fall into a deep depression. Finally, my heart would break and I would die. Oh…I see your point." Gerontius smiled slyly. "But the risk of loss is what makes the victory honorable! Gregor has won this tournament three years in a row. The competition was stronger when he first won. Since then, his skills have increased while the more skilled competitors have aged out of the tournament. Unfortunately, his dominance has stifled enthusiasm for the tournament. The big question now is who will win second place. It might even be George though he's just now old enough to participate. He's been the most skilled opponent for at least the past two years, but even he has never beaten Gregor. I was hoping that having Ascalon as a prize might bring more excitement to the tournament this year."

Polly loved her husband's sincere motivation to guide their boys to honorable manhood. "If you think this is the best way to strengthen the honor of your son, I support you completely. I suppose if we lose Ascalon, we can try to buy it back, or we can simply have another battle sword custom made for Gregor once he stops growing."

Acknowledging Polly's cautious support, Gerontius responded enthusiastically, "I'll inform the tournament officials of the prize donation. Hopefully this will spur interest in the tournament, and, God willing, Ascalon will pass on to its rightful heir through the honor of open combat, and will be returned peaceably to our home."

*****

"Tomorrow is the big day!" Gerontius exclaimed when Polly entered their bedroom for the night.

"The boys are feeling it too," Polly replied. "Gregor speaks confidently of winning another solid victory and bringing Ascalon back home as his final prize."

"I'm proud of Gregor," Gerontius said. "It will be nice to have another championship this year."

"George could barely contain his excitement," Polly continued. "He's been dreaming of this day for years. He was stunned when you donated Ascalon as the victor's prize in the tournament. He has always understood that Ascalon would be passed down to Gregor, as your first born heir. His prayer tonight was interesting. He told God he knew that coveting what he could not rightfully possess was a sin,[2] and that there was no honor in whining, so he has never asked to have the honor of Ascalon as his own. But with the sword as the prize, he proposed that seeking God's help to obtain what he could rightfully possess would not be a sin. He prayed earnestly for God's help, if it be His will, that he might do his best and be honorable in combat. Afterwards, he told me the more he prays to be in line with God's will, the more his faith in God increases, and at the same time, the more uncertain he becomes of success in the tournament. Still, he has high hopes of doing well tomorrow."

*****

George lay awake, barely able to contain his excitement. He thought, *Nearly everyone expects Gregor to win and claim Ascalon as his prize. But this will likely be my only chance to claim the sword with honor. Though I've never won a match against Gregor, I haven't really tried to win in several years.*

Their matches now followed a predictable pattern. Gregor was always the aggressor. George preferred to focus on defensive techniques. The duels were grueling in length and intensity. By and by, Gregor would score several hits on George. George didn't want to embarrass or anger his brother, but by the time Gregor had scored three or four hits, George would be sure to sting him with one good whack. Gregor always responded with a furious attack which George would hold off as long as he could before taking the fifth and final whack.

Amused by Gregor's pride in the effectiveness of his furious attacks, George thought, *During his attacks there are many defensive lapses that leave him exposed and vulnerable to counter-attacks. I'm not sure I can beat Gregor, but I am sure I can do better than I've ever done before. I'm a little concerned that Gregor is the only opponent I've ever faced. I'm not sure how I'll do against the other young men who have different training and fighting styles. In any case, I'm determined to trust in God and do my best.*

*****

With Gregor and George taking part in the tournament and Gerontius helping to coordinate the events, Polly invited Callidora and Sabra to attend the celebration as her companions. As Sabra dragged her and Callidora along, hurrying from booth to booth, inspecting every display, Polly wondered if she'd chosen her companions wisely. She laughed at Sabra's infectious enthusiasm.

When they reached the dueling arenas, Polly explained to her companions, "The battle skills tournament was created to encourage young men to prepare for service as soldiers. Most boys without trade skills will either become farmers or join the army. Soldiers get paid better than farm workers, but the military is definitely more dangerous. We hope those who join the army will return home safely with the means to support a family.

"The major competition in the tournament is young men on foot with swords and shields. Each contestant brings his own wooden sword, with tip and edges blunted to reduce the danger of severe injury. The young men are also required to use arm shields and breast shields, and to wear leather leggings, and leather covers for the upper and lower areas of their arms. Each participant chooses how thick his protective clothing will be, but the thicker the clothing, the less agile he will be in combat. Leather head protection is also allowed, but head hits are strictly forbidden and will disqualify an offender. The first contestant to score five solid hits against his opponent in the upper body, upper arms, or upper legs is declared the victor in each match."

"Does anybody get killed?" Sabra asked anxiously.

"I worry about that too," Polly replied. "So far, no one has been killed in Lydda's tournament. Bones sometimes get broken, but not often. If a participant feels he's been injured, he can withdraw at any time."

"I'm excited for George," Sabra said. "He doesn't talk much about his ambitions, but I saw the way he looked at Ascalon. I think he really wants to win the prize."

"It's fun to watch the people admiring Ascalon, the battle sword that saved the Emperor's life," Callidora observed. "It's clearly a prize that any hearty young man with an inclination for combat would treasure and cherish, even if he doesn't grow into it. However, I think everyone is expecting that Gregor will win the tournament again this year and claim Ascalon as his prize."

Sabra scanned the competitors in their various stages of preparation and her eyes fixed on George. He appeared to be meditating, filtering out all the distractions. Determination was evident in his countenance.

"I don't think everyone is expecting that," Sabra observed.

*****

"Gregor has dominated his matches, occasionally taking a hit here or there, but quickly dispatching his opponents and advancing," Callidora observed.

"George's matches take much longer," Sabra noted. "Some might think he is struggling, but I don't think I've seen him take any hits in his lengthy duels. The tournament lists only show the victors, not the match scores, so I'm not sure about that."

*****

As George finished his semi-final match with victory, Polly beamed at Gerontius, "At least now we know the honor of Ascalon will remain in the family, at no additional cost to us."

Gerontius was more sober than Polly expected as he answered, "Yes, but I'm not certain this will work out as I intended. I've been watching the matches closely. Both boys have done well. Gregor is doing just as I'd expected. However, George has added several attack moves that are unfamiliar to me. His primary focus on defensive techniques has allowed him time to learn each new opponent's fighting style, tendencies, and weaknesses. As his confidence rises during each match, he adds offensive moves to his approach. With each attack, he seems to note his opponent's defensive response, and also where his opponent has left himself unguarded. Next, he strikes quickly, combining his attack with a counter to his opponent's defense that scores a point in the unprotected area. He repeats this approach until his opponent successfully defends the attack combination, and then he begins to probe with other attacks."

"Are you saying that George is studying his opponents' weaknesses and then planning his attacks to take advantage of them?" Sabra asked. "That doesn't seem very charitable."

"Perhaps there are still a few things you have yet to learn about the art of war, young lady," Gerontius replied to with a smile. Turning back to Polly he continued, "He's using different attacks for each new opponent. I'd be more certain of the outcome of this final match, except I've never seen George approach his sparring with Gregor in this manner. I just don't know how it will end if he does."

"Have faith, Gerontius," Polly charmed with a smile. "God is over all. It will all be okay."

*****

George's excitement peaked as he entered the championship match against Gregor. His success in the earlier matches had boosted his confidence. *Stay focused on the prize,* he thought. *This match alone will decide the honor of Ascalon. All I can do is pray for success and do my very best, accepting God's judgment of what will be best for me. I know that to win, I cannot simply defend, getting in one good whack at the end. I will have to attack the most skilled opponent I've ever faced.* "Good luck," he said to Gregor.

"Luck is the dream of the unprepared, my little Pip," Gregor chided. "I expect to teach you that lesson yet again today." In the back of his mind, he knew he wouldn't be calling George his 'little Pip' much longer, as they would likely be the same size within a year or two, and it appeared certain George would eventually be the bigger man.

As the match began, it followed the pattern familiar to the dueling brothers. Gregor was the aggressor, rotating through various attack moves. George was cautious and defensive at first, but on his brother's first right overhand attack, George brought his blade up and across his body to his left, blocking the attack. As he deflected Gregor's blow, George simply continued his body rotation to the left, immediately crossing his right foot in front of his left, pivoting and spinning counter-clockwise with his sword extended low. He continued turning to his left until his sword slapped the outside of Gregor's left thigh. George had scored the first point.

Gregor was a little surprised at George's attack, but not as surprised as Gerontius was. He could already see how this was going to end. Gregor began another series of attack moves, expecting to wear George down. The trouble was that just after he started his attack George made an unfamiliar counter-attack and whacked Gregor again, scoring a second time.

Gregor had thought George's first point was simply a lucky strike, but the second point sobered him up thoroughly. He defaulted to what had always worked in the past. He made a furious attack on George. George was a little surprised as he had expected this type of attack to come later and he hadn't thought through which counter-attack he would use in order to score. Just that quickly, George felt the sword whack his left shoulder as Gregor scored his first point.

Gregor initiated a second furious attack, only to be surprised by George's quick counter-attack that scored another point, striking Gregor's left thigh again.

Still confident in his own skills, Gregor made a third furious attack with the same result. George scored again on the outside of Gregor's left thigh.

At the call to engage, the brothers faced each other hesitantly. "What are they waiting for?" Sabra asked.

"With the score at four hits to one in George's favor and barely a few moments of sparring complete, Gregor must adjust his approach to be much more defensive and cautious. He can't afford even one more hit," Gerontius responded. He watched his younger son carefully. "George is more intense than I've ever seen him, looking for any tell Gregor might give that would guide him to the opening he needs to score the final point."

Suddenly, the intensity on George's face triggered a distant memory in Gregor. He could hear himself saying, *Listen here, Pip, the day you best me at swords is the day I'll be too old to pick up Pa's battle sword. You can have it then, if you're man enough to pick it up.* Sober and concerned, he began to think through each of his attacks and where they would leave him open if he didn't cover quickly. Carefully following each attack with the proper counter-defense, he successfully avoided several of George's attacking blows. Considering George's moves carefully, Gregor feigned an attack and went directly to the opening created by George's counter-attack, scoring his point and shifting just barely in time to avoid George's strike.

With the score now at four hits to two in George's favor, Gregor decided to gamble on how quickly George was learning. Gregor tried the same feigned attack he had just used to score. As he shifted and went immediately to the opening that would be created by George's anticipated counter-attack, George was not where he expected. Immediately, Gregor felt the sickening thud of George's sword blade as it struck his right lower ribs.

The crowd roared in amazed approval for the young man who had just beaten their reigning champion. Sabra yelled her support with great satisfaction. Quietly she vowed, "I shall never doubt my hero again, he who has rightly gained the honor of Ascalon."

Nearby an excited boy commented to his group of friends, "You see that kid, the new champion that won the sword? I think that's the same one who killed the viper snake and saved that little girl's life a few years back."

Another of the boys confirmed, "I'm sure it is. My mother has told me that story many times."

*****

A Martyr's Faith

Gerontius watched, still in stunned amazement, as Gregor and George approached the victor's stand together. Gregor, as reigning champion, crowned George as the new champion. Having won the victory, George was presented with Ascalon by the tournament officials. Pausing before the prize he had long admired, George knelt humbly on one knee. Bowing his head reverently, he asked, "Father, and Gregor, I beg leave of you to claim the honor of Ascalon as my own."

Gregor was first to respond. "Brother, you've won this honor in open combat. No man could deny you what is now rightfully yours and still retain his own honor. I honor you now. By God, Ascalon is yours."

Father was choking with emotion as he saw Gregor set aside his own wounded pride and properly honor his younger brother. As he looked steadily on Gregor, his mind was filled with the words of the Lord to the prophet Samuel: *Look not on his countenance, or on the height of his stature; because I have refused him: for the Lord seeth not as a man seeth; for man looketh on the outward appearance, but the Lord looketh on the heart.*[3] Also into his mind came the prophetic words spoken by Israel when blessing his grandsons Manasseh and Ephraim: *He also shall become a people, and he also shall become great: but truly his younger brother shall be greater than he.*[4]

Gerontius shifted his focus from Gregor to George, who waited patiently at the stand for his consent to claim Ascalon as his prize. "Yes, George. The sword is yours. Claim it and bring it home. Let it stand as a symbol of your honor and the honor of our family." As Father spoke these words, a further impression came to his mind and heart revealing, *It will thus be so for George, for truly the younger son shall be made greater than the elder.*

*****

At home that evening Gerontius went directly into his library for some quiet reflection. Inspired by the personal revelations of the day regarding his sons, he pled with God for wisdom to guide them properly in the development of their faith in Christ, and their characters in service to God and to all men.

Presently, George came into the library with his prize in hand. "Father, I'd like to return Ascalon to its wall mount, until such time as I might need it for true battle. May I do that?"

"Of course you can, George. It's a symbol of honor for our whole family, but it's yours to use and care for as God wills."

After watching George replace Ascalon on the wall mount in the library, Gerontius spoke with joy as he counseled his rapidly maturing young son. "George, you did extremely well today in the tournament. I've never seen you show as much skill and ability as I saw today. You did things I couldn't have taught you because they exceed my own level of skill, and yet you're only twelve years old. I'm certain God was with you this day. You should consider carefully the gifts and talents God has given you, and plan your life to use all that you have and all that you are for His glory. Wisdom whispers that when we are in the service of others, we are only in the service of God.[5] The Lord taught that as He loved us, we should love one another and care for one another. This is how we show true discipleship of our Savior, Jesus Christ."[6]

"I will, Father," George promised. "I know God blessed me today. I'm nothing without Him."

*****

The morning after the Sabbath, Gerontius, Gregor, and George all gathered for sword practice as usual. Gregor was seriously perplexed as he asked, "George, where did you learn the attacking techniques you used in our match in the tournament? I've never seen you use them before."

Suddenly embarrassed, George answered honestly, "I've used those attacking techniques before during our sword practices here, but I've only used each technique once, and that was only at the very end of our sparring. Otherwise, I was mostly just studying your moves and attacks and looking for openings in your defenses."

"If that's true, little Brother, why didn't you use your skills more in our sparring and push me harder to learn?" Gregor challenged.

"Well, I thought if I beat you, it might make you feel bad," George replied. "I really didn't have any reason to try to win until Ascalon was made a prize for the tournament."

"Ascalon, eh?" Gregor responded without any accusing glance at his father. Continuing earnestly he stated, "Well what makes me 'feel bad' is finding out that you've been holding back on me, failing to expose my weaknesses, and not helping me to develop and improve my skills for the mutual safety of us all."

George looked Gregor respectfully in the eye and asked, "Do you remember that I once offered you a suggestion on how to fight better, and you told me it would be better for me to remain silent and be thought a fool than to open my mouth and remove all doubt?"[7]

"Oh, yeah," Gregor groaned. "I thought my jab was fairly clever at the time. I would've done better to heed my own advice rather than pushing it arrogantly on another. I'm sorry. I take back my mistaken counsel."

"Then I shall henceforth consider myself at liberty to offer you honest counsel. Apology accepted," George affirmed.

"George, what have you learned that might help Gregor to improve his skills?" Father asked.

"First of all, Gregor has always brought his shield too high on the left when attacking with an overhand right, leaving himself exposed on his lower left side."

"Yeah, I learned that one yesterday," Gregor winced. "I've got three overlapping bruises on my left thigh to prove it."

As the sword practice and sparring continued, it was obvious to each of them that George had taken to heart the challenge to teach his older brother something new with each engagement. Although Gregor did improve with his sword, so did George. Gregor still got in his whacks, but try as he might he was never again able to win any sparring contests with George.

****

CHAPTER ELEVEN
Heaven and Earth Meet

Lydda, Palestine
287 AD

*"...and the Lord whom ye seek, shall suddenly come to His temple,
even the Messenger of the covenant, whom ye delight in:
behold, He shall come, saith the Lord of hosts."*[1]
Malachi 3:1

****

"When Gregor was twelve, he finished third in the battle skills tournament," Gerontius said quietly to Polly in their room that evening. "I rewarded him with a new medium-sized steel sword. Now, George has won the tournament in his first year and gained the honor of Ascalon. A new steel sword would pale in comparison to the prize he has already won. So I asked him if he had any ideas for how I could honor his tournament victory. Would you care to guess what he said?"

Polly smiled. "Would you care to just tell me, or is this the topic of torture for this evening?"

"He said there's really only one thing he wants and that's for me to take him to the temple in Jerusalem, if my back can bear the journey," Gerontius replied. "He knows the temple was destroyed and there isn't much more than a wall left, but he would still like to see where heaven once touched earth in the house of God, and where Jesus ministered and made His atoning sacrifice. It was such a great idea that I just couldn't refuse."

"When will you go?" Polly asked.

"George said he'll be sleeping outside in a tent, with the door facing the temple,[2] until we've completed the trip. I'm planning to go early next week. We'll take the cart so I can lie on some blankets in the bed if I need to ease my back pain. We should only be away for three days. One day traveling there, a day in Jerusalem, and one day traveling back."

*****

As they approached the city, George recalled part of a psalm he had memorized, which he recited for his father. "Great is the Lord, and greatly to be praised in the city of our God, in the mountain of His holiness. Beautiful for situation, the joy of the whole earth is mount Zion, on the sides of the north, the city of the great King. We have thought of Thy loving kindness, O God, in the midst of Thy temple. According to Thy name, O God, so is Thy praise unto the ends of the earth. Thy right hand is full of righteousness. Let mount Zion rejoice, let the daughters of Judah be glad, because of Thy judgments. For this God is our God forever and ever: He will be our Guide even unto death."[3]

"That was wonderful," Father said. "Thank you for sharing that."

*****

"The vibrant activity here is amazing," George observed as they entered the city.

"With all its troubles throughout history, God's covenant people are always returning to renew their faith and to rebuild the holy city," Gerontius responded.

"Why is Jerusalem always getting destroyed?" George asked soberly.

Gerontius thought it over and replied, "I guess it's because the Lord has given the inhabitants of Jerusalem the Law and the Gospel, but the people have repeatedly turned away from God. If they would just return, repent, and obey Him, He would bless them and preserve them from destruction. Jesus lamented, 'Jerusalem, how oft I would have gathered you as a hen gathereth her chicks, and ye would not.'"[4]

*****

Quietly they climbed the hill to the garden of Gethsemane where they sat and rested. "I wish I'd brought the holy books that tell of Christ's suffering and atonement," Father said wistfully.

"I love the scriptures," George replied. "I always feel the Spirit of the Lord when I focus on the word of God. I've memorized a few other passages that I could share with you," he offered.

"That would please me," Father encouraged.

Carefully, George began to quote from memory, "And He came out, and went…to the mount of Olives…and kneeled down and prayed…[5] And He…began to be sore amazed, and to be very heavy; and said…My soul is exceeding sorrowful unto death…[6] And He…prayed, saying, Father, if Thou be willing, remove this cup from Me, nevertheless not My will, but Thine be done. And there appeared an angel unto Him from heaven, strengthening Him. And being in an agony He prayed more earnestly...[7] O My Father, if this cup may not pass away from Me, except I drink it, Thy will be done.[8] And His sweat was as it were great drops of blood falling down to the ground.[9] And Jesus...lifted up His eyes to heaven, and said, Father, the hour is come; glorify Thy Son, that Thy Son also may glorify Thee. And now, O Father, glorify Thou Me with Thine own Self with the glory which I had with Thee before the world was."[10]

Impressed with his son, Gerontius said, "You've been reading up for this trip, haven't you?"

"Not really," George replied. "I learned those passages some time ago. Ever since you taught me that a saint lives by every word that proceeds forth from the mouth of God,[11] I've been studying the sacred records more intently. Each week, usually on Sunday evening, I pick a new passage of scripture and copy it down. I recite it several times that day, and each morning and night during the week when I say my prayers. By the end of the week I have it memorized."

"That's a great way to learn the scriptures," Father marveled.

"It is," George agreed. "One of the greatest blessing for me in doing this is that, whenever I don't have anything specific to think about, my mind almost automatically goes to the passage of scripture I'm learning, and I can feel the Spirit of the Lord with me."[12]

O, my son, Gerontius thought, *God has truly blessed your mind and your heart.*

*****

Next, Gerontius took his son to Golgotha, the place where Christ was hung on the cross. Again George began to quote from memory, "And when they were come to a place called Golgotha...they crucified Him...And set up over His head His accusation written, THIS IS JESUS THE KING OF THE JEWS.[13] And about the ninth hour Jesus cried with a loud voice, saying...My God, My God, why hast Thou forsaken Me?[14] And the sun was darkened, and the veil of the temple was rent in the midst.[15] And...Jesus...said, It is finished. Father, into Thy hands I commend My spirit:[16] and He bowed His head and gave up the ghost.[17] And when the centurion...saw that He so cried out, and gave up the ghost, he said, Truly this Man was the Son of God."[18]

Gerontius couldn't remember all the verses George quoted, but he had no doubt the words were inspired. Again he was amazed at the retention and comprehension of his young son.

"Father, what did Jesus mean when He asked why God had forsaken Him?"

Gerontius thought for a few moments before answering. "I'm not exactly certain about that, but I think in Jesus' final hours of agony, the Father withdrew His presence from the Son, so Jesus could make the required sacrifice on His own. Sometimes there are things in our lives that we just have to do alone, like exercising faith and submitting our wills completely to the will of the God. Isaiah speaks of the year of redemption in which the Lord will answer, 'I have trodden the winepress alone.'[19] Perhaps this was a requirement to fulfill that prophecy. Do you have any other ideas about that?"

"I'm still just thinking about it. It's a hard one for me," George replied mildly.

Together they left Golgotha and went to the garden tomb of Joseph of Arimathaea. As they peered inside the empty tomb, George recited from memory, "And when Joseph had taken the body, he wrapped it in a clean linen cloth and laid it in his own new tomb, which he had hewn out in the rock: and he rolled a great stone to the door of the sepulcher..."[20]

"Actually," Father said, "I think it was the Roman soldiers who rolled the great stone to block the door of the tomb, so no one could disturb the body."

George thought for a moment and then responded. "Matthew says Joseph had the stone rolled to block the tomb door the evening of the crucifixion. The next day was the Sabbath. That's when the Pilate sent the Roman watch to secure and seal the tomb.[21] The third day, the day of Christ's resurrection, was the first day of the week.[22] Matthew said, 'And...the angel of the Lord descended from heaven, and came and rolled back the stone from the door, and sat upon it. His countenance was like lightning, and his raiment white as snow...and the angel answered...fear not...for I know that ye seek Jesus, which was crucified. He is not here, for He is risen....'"[23]

"Thank you so much for sharing those scriptures," Gerontius praised thankfully. "I'm grateful you chose to memorize those passages. Your memory and willingness to share are such wonderful gifts from God." Both sat silently, working through the flood of emotions that overwhelmed them as they were filled with the Spirit of peace, humility, and gratitude at the Savior's willing sacrifice and at the promise of redemption and the power of His resurrection. Finally Gerontius looked at his son and reverently testified, "He is not here, for He is risen!"[24]

*****

As they approached the temple wall, many people were there praying. George thought about Jesus' experience in the temple when He was only twelve years old: *And it came to pass that after three days they found Him in the temple, sitting in the midst of the doctors, and they were hearing Him and asking Him questions. And all that heard Him were astonished at His understanding and answers.*[25]

George was impressed with the massive foundation stones that were a remnant of the temple wall, which had obviously been intended to endure to the end of the world. Imagining the past majesty of the temple, George thought of the words of King David: *Lord, I have loved the habitation of Thy house, and the place where Thine honor dwells.*[26]

After some quiet reflection of his own, Father spoke. "The prophecies of old foretell that the temple of our God will yet be rebuilt by the Jews. Their long-awaited Messiah will come to them here, and they will be surprised to learn from the marks in His hands and feet and side that He is Jesus, Whom they rejected and crucified.[27] He will redeem them and bless them. These stones stand as a testament to the history and to the glorious future of the House of Israel, and particularly of the Jews."

Close by a young man suddenly perked up from his prayer. Turning to George he said, "Excuse me. My name is Nicholas. I don't mean to intrude on your private conversation, but I feel I must stand as a second witness to the truths that were just shared. I testify of those truths too. God seeks our glory as we seek His. May the Lord's gifts and blessings abide with you both."

"I'm George and this is my father, Gerontius," George replied as he extended a hand in greeting. "Thank you for your witness. It's most welcome. We pray that the Lord's gifts and blessings may abide with you as well and that you may ever be able to share them with others."

As Nicholas returned to his solitude, George removed a small bundle of stone working tools from the cart. Reverently, he selected a stone from the ground that matched the temple stones, and he began to shape it. After a few minutes he compared his small stone with a gap between two of the wall stones and then continued shaping it. When he was done, he took a large wooden mallet from the cart and, placing the narrow end of his carved stone into the gap between two large temple stones, he gave his stone two firm strikes, driving it into the temple wall. The final match was precise, appearing as if the smaller stone had been in its position of honor for centuries. With tears in his eyes he spoke to his father. "This little stone may not mean much to anybody else, but to me it is a symbol of my covenant to do God's will and to support His works. Here I accept my accountability to Him."

George stepped back, eyeing the temple wall, memorizing the location of his stone. Resolving to always remember his commitment to

God, he quoted, "Who shall ascend into the hill of the Lord? Or who shall stand in His holy place? He that hath clean hands, and a pure heart; who hath not lifted up his soul unto vanity, nor sworn deceitfully. He shall receive the blessing from the Lord, and righteousness from the God of his salvation.[28] One thing have I desired of the Lord, that will I seek after; that I may dwell in the house of the Lord all the days of my life, to behold the beauty of the Lord, and to enquire in His temple…When Thou said, Seek ye My face; my heart said unto Thee, Thy face, Lord, will I seek."[29]

"Father, thank you for bringing me here. We can go home now."

****

CHAPTER TWELVE
Father Prepares for Death

Lydda, Palestine
289 AD

*"Counsel with the Lord in all thy doings,
and He will direct thee for good..."*[1]
Alma 37:37

****

Gerontius lay upon his bed in obvious distress, unable to move his legs. "Don't worry, my love," Polly reassured. "It's only been a few days since your back gave out. You were down like this once before when you were first injured."

"That was almost ten years ago. This time is different," he responded quietly, straining to control the pain. "Though I've managed mostly on my own until now, I never healed completely from the original injury. For a couple of years my back pain seemed to gradually improve, and then leveled off. These last few years the pain has been increasing. Riding horses or heavy lifting has caused a sharp tingling in my lower back, the body's reminder of its abiding promise that the price for my physical pride will someday be required in full. Lately it's been difficult simply riding in carts and the pain has been persistent whenever I've been up and about."

"Initially, you were completely unable to move your legs for a couple of weeks," Polly recalled. "Few dared to hope that you would ever walk again. But you surprised everyone when you began to recover. Even though it took months, you still regained the ability to walk," she said encouragingly.

"This time, instead of fighting to overcome the paralysis and regain function, I can feel my body submitting and shutting down," he frowned. "I just have a feeling that this old battle wound, my constant but unwelcome companion, will soon overcome me."

"Just rest and be patient," Polly urged. "We'll get through this together."

"Yes, dear," was Gerontius' subdued response.

"I'll fix you some soup. That should help you feel better," Polly said as she left the room.

Alone he observed to himself, "My time to die is quickly drawing near. I have covenanted with God for His blessings. My death will not impair those blessings in eternity. There are no more bargains to be made. With precious little time to prepare for my passing, I can't afford to linger in depression, nor will I waste myself in anger against God or men, or in a fight against my body that I can't win. I need to prepare myself, and more importantly, I need to prepare my family."

He thought of the words of Jesus: "...*all they that take the sword shall perish with the sword.*"[2] He also reflected on the words of John the Revelator who wrote: "...*he that killeth with the sword must be killed with the sword. Here is the patience and the faith of the saints.*"[3] He found something comforting in the final sentence of the scripture, for just as surely as pain had become his constant companion, patience and faith had come to abide with him. These brought him peace even as this ominous illness struggled to grip his body with finality.

Quietly he prayed, "Dear God, forgive me. I've given faithful service in battle, but I am far from perfect. My mistakes have cost men their lives. I pray that the price of my shortened life might in some way offset my imperfections in the use of the sword. I've done my best to fight for peace and to protect the innocent. Thou that knowest all, know my heart and have compassion on me. Redeem me as a follower of Thy Holy Son. Watch over and keep my family."

*****

Polly spoke gently to her boys, "Gregor, George, Father is calling for us. Come. Let's answer his call with courage."

As the boys came into their father's bedroom, George was surprised that his father's body was noticeably swollen. He didn't understand exactly what was happening, but the intensity of his father's pain and the labor of his breathing were obvious. Gerontius struggled to reposition himself so he could speak more easily from his bed. The provincial administrator who had recently been appointed to replace him was already in the room, as was his official scribe.

"Thank you for coming," Gerontius began. "I don't want to scare anyone, but I feel it's time to put my affairs in order and to make a record of my last will and testament, in the presence of my family and witnesses."

"Of course," the administrator replied. "Scribe, make record of Gerontius' will as he dictates."

"Thank you," Gerontius sighed. After briefly reviewing some notes he continued, "Over the past year I have spent the vast majority of my personal wealth in completely resolving all of my debts for lands purchased. At my passing, the accumulated land will all pass to my first born son and heir, Gregorios. With this bestowal of land, I charge my son with the care of his mother, Polychronia, and his brother, Georgios.

"Recently, I've also purchased or accepted as payment for debts owed to me, some slaves and the contracts of several indentured servants who have proven to be honest, talented, and humble in their service to others. To these faithful souls, and to all who have served me and my family, I express my deepest appreciation and gratitude.

"Further, I hereby make my legal declaration that, at my passing, the few remaining debts that are owed to me are forgiven, and all slaves and indentured servants in my care are released and freed from their bonds. Further, I charge Gregorios to read aloud the following declaration to all in our service, upon my passing: *Just as master Gerontius has been released by God from the bonds of this life, so with his passing you are all released from your bonds of servitude to Gerontius and to our family. We pray that each of you will consider joining yourselves with us voluntarily, by just and mutually agreeable covenants with me, as Gerontius' heir, and with our family, as long as you may desire into the future. We are all strengthened by our unity. We thank you all for your service, and commend you to a just and merciful God.*

Father continued, "Regarding my personal wealth other than the land holdings, it shall be divided into three equal portions, with the double portion going to Gregorios, for himself and the care of his mother and the household, and the third portion going to Georgios. My treasured library will pass to Gregorios and will become a part of his stewardship from Almighty God. The battle sword Ascalon is no longer mine to give. Georgios has claimed it in honorable combat and it will remain with him as a part of his stewardship from Almighty God. This is my will, as all here witness this day.

"That should be sufficient for the record," Father confirmed to the administrator with a sigh of relief. "Please send me two copies of the will. I will sign both of them and return one for the provincial records. Thank you for your help."

"As you will," the official responded respectfully.

Polly escorted their guests to the door and, after seeing them off, returned to her husband's side. "Lay back and relax, Papa. Let me help you take a little water."

"Not yet, Polly. We're done with the legal administration, but I still have some private counsel for my family." Carefully raising himself a bit more on the pillows, Gerontius continued, "I now seek a covenant from each of my sons that you will do my will in each and all of these

A Martyr's Faith

matters. Gregorios, do you give me your word, your solemn promise that you will abide by my will in all these matters, and especially in the care of your mother?"

"Yes, Father. I give you my word that I shall do according to your will in all these matters, and especially in the care of my mother, as God is my witness."

"Georgios, do you give me your word that you will abide by my will in all these matters?"

"Father, I give you my word I shall abide by your will and honor you in all these matters. Also, I freely bind myself to our mother's care, till we are separated by death, as God is my witness."

"Thank you," father smiled weakly. "I am so grateful for the men you have become. As I humbly prepare to return to that God who gave me life, I cannot pass peacefully out of this world without reaffirming my witness to you that God lives. He is our Eternal Father. He loves us and is ever anxious for our success and blessing. He sent His Son, our Lord and Savior Jesus Christ, who has atoned for our sins with His holy blood, that He might establish a sure path, on conditions of repentance, for our redemption and return to our Heavenly Father, pure and clean and worthy of His richest blessings, as joint-heirs with Christ.[4]

"Remember, man does not live by bread alone, but by every word that proceeds forth out of the mouth of God.[5] Jesus quoted this passage of Moses when the adversary came tempting Him to turn stones into bread to satisfy His bodily hunger after fasting. The bread we eat sustains physical life, but our individual obedience to God's word and His law sustains spiritual life, and prepares us for glory in the hereafter. Blessed is the man that honors the Lord and delights greatly in His commandments.[6]

"I counsel you to be wise in the days of your probation on earth. Come unto Christ. Strip yourselves of all uncleanness, and deny yourselves of all ungodliness. Ask the true and living God, with a firmness unshaken, that you will yield to no temptation, but lay hold upon every good gift, that you might obey and serve Him, and have His Spirit to ever abide in you.[7]

"Polly, I promise that you shall always have my eternal love, which shall endure beyond this life, as God is my witness. You shall also retain mortal stewardship over our two sons, who have been raised up unto the Lord, until you pass on and relinquish their mortal care solely to that God who is their Father. I give you my assurance that you are an heir to the love of God. Through your faithfulness, you will remain an heir to His mercy also. I am your witness. Do you accept these gifts and will you honor them?"

"Yes, my love. I accept these gifts of love. I swear that you have my eternal love. I will honor you in all you have entrusted to me, as God is my witness. I love you, my dear."

"May you all be blessed of the Lord Jesus Christ, and may He prosper you in this land," Gerontius concluded as he eased himself down to rest.[8]

*****

Several days later, Gerontius lay in bed alone with his thoughts, a signed copy of his will beside him. He could hardly breathe. He felt terrible pain and nausea. But more than this, he felt the urgent need to call down the blessings of a merciful and loving God upon his family. Straining slightly, he raised himself back to a sitting position and meekly bowed his head. Tears flowed freely down his cheeks as he quietly pleaded, "Beloved Father, please fill Polly with peace and comfort at my passing. Sustain her with a measure of joy until it is her time to pass through the veil and we are reunited in eternal glory.

"I pray that Thou wouldst bless Gregor that he may prosper in his care of all those who look to him and our family for stability in a complex and challenging world. Surely, where much is required, much will be given of Thee to those who serve the Lord faithfully.[9]

"Please remember George in mercy. While worldly possessions may not be significant in his life, I pray that Thou wouldst bless him with Thy Spirit continually."

As he prayed, he felt the strong impression confirming, *George has been chosen for a greater work, and his name will be known for good or evil among many nations in this world, but will only be known for good in God's kingdom.*[10] *As a servant of the Lord Jesus Christ, George will have power over dragons and beasts, and over the oppressors of this world, to relieve suffering, especially among the humble and virtuous daughters of God.*

As he finished his prayer, there was a soft knock at his door. "Come in," he responded.

George entered quietly, carrying a bowl of warm chicken broth. "Mother sent this for you. She'll be coming soon."

"Close the door please," Gerontius directed his son. "I have some things I want to tell you." Quickly father shared the impressions he had received during his prayer. "George, I need you to hear my words and heed my counsel.[11] Be faithful to the Lord in all things. Don't seek to counsel the Lord, but seek to take counsel from Him.[12] Don't despise the chastening of the Lord, nor be weary of His correction, for whom the Lord loves, He corrects, even as a Father corrects the son whom He loves.[13] Counsel with the Lord in all your doings, and He will direct you for good.[14] Plead with Him to teach you His statutes and commandments.[15]

"You will have much tribulation, but be faithful unto death and God will give you a crown of life.[16] Never doubt the Lord, but believe in Him,[17] for God shall give His angels charge over you, and they shall bear you up in their hands, and you shall trample the dragon under your feet.[18] You should use your gifts from God to resist the oppressors of this world and to relieve suffering, especially among the humble and virtuous daughters of God. Promise me you will receive my words and treasure them, having reverence for sacred things. Share them only in wisdom with those who share your faith or when moved upon by the Holy Spirit."[19]

Though George didn't fully understand his father's counsel, he paused to commit it to memory and then solemnly replied, "I promise, Father, as God is my witness."

Just then, Polly entered the room. "Papa, you should eat the soup I sent you," she urged.

"I needed to talk with George more than I needed the soup. But we've finished our talking." With that signal, George excused himself and left to finish his chores.

Gerontius strained to shift himself in bed. He winced involuntarily at the pain he felt, which wouldn't quit. He gasped for breath, and spoke to Polly, "What I need now is for you to sit by me on the bed so I can put my head on your lap. And I need you to hold my hand."

Polly adjusted herself on the bed as her husband had asked. Gently she took his right hand in her right hand, and then began to massage his scalp and fuss at his hair with her left hand. As Gerontius began to relax, she spoke softly, "I will always love you with my whole soul."

In a moment, Gerontius let out his last breath, relaxed his grip on Polly's hand, and passed on peacefully through the darkness toward the ever growing Light.

****

CHAPTER THIRTEEN
Caring for Mother

Lydda, Palestine
290 AD

"And the child...grew on, and was in favor both with the LORD, and also with men."[1]
1 Samuel 2:26

****

George poked his head in through the kitchen door. Softly he called, "Mother, the cart's ready. If you're ready, we can go to Lydda now."

Polly quit rummaging through the chest beside her and closed it. She scooped up a handful of clothes she planned to give away to the poor and inspected them more carefully. Satisfied, she took the clothes and passed through the kitchen, picked up a basket of fresh bread rolls she had made, stepped out the door and headed toward the cart. "Thanks for helping me, George. I love helping the poor in Lydda, but I feel much safer when you or Gregor go with me."

"Mother, you are much safer when Gregor or I go with you!" George exclaimed pleasantly as he gave his mother a hand up to the seat.

Polly checked the cart's contents to make sure they were secure and then looked forward down the road toward the low hills that rose between their land and Lydda. "I used to enjoy taking your father with me on my errands, even though his back could barely stand the ride. I miss him deeply. I'm sorry the burden of my personal safety has fallen mainly on you lately. Gregor has been so busy at home this season doing the farm work father used to do."

"That's okay," George replied. "When I think about father, I get an ache in my chest. I wish he was still here with us. I always felt we were all safe when he was here."

"I feel that ache too," Polly agreed. "I feel sad without him. I don't know how I would bear it if I didn't know that I would see him again someday. But I do know we'll be reunited with your father again in the eternities. We have every reason to rejoice. If we follow the promptings of the Spirit, we'll be safe, whatever the future holds.[2] Our secret yearnings are known to God and surely will touch His heart."[3]

The cart gave a slight lurch as George gently urged the horse forward.

"So, how exactly does it work for you to see father again?" he asked.

"Oh, not just me, George, but you and Gregor will be reunited with father too. In fact, your grandparents and all the generations before, along with all those that come after us, will be reunited with us too. If we are faithful to God and live worthy to return to His presence, we'll all be in the same place, associating together, filled with the love of God for all men, and raised up to incorruption with perfect bodies in a glorious resurrection. I truly look forward to the day when I shall pass through the veil of death and be reunited with my husband."

George thought about his mother's words. He wasn't sure how to ask his next question, but since they were alone on the road, he thought it might be okay even if it was a bit awkward. "So, are you saying you're looking forward to dying?"

"Oh, gracious no, I'm not looking forward to dying," Polly replied in surprise. "I expect that experience will be miserable. It's what comes after the release of death. That's what I look forward to. Do you remember when your father finally passed away, after all that straining pain and anguish? Remember how peaceful his face became? I want that peace too."

"I thought father looked more lifeless than peaceful," George replied. "Although, I guess he did look relieved from all the pain before his passing, so he must have been a lot happier."

Mother continued, "The peace of the body is small compared to the peace and joy of the Spirit for those who have true hope in Christ. What I hope and believe with all my heart is that through the atonement of Christ and the power of His resurrection, we can be raised to eternal life, and this because of our faith in Him according to His promise.[4] I have hope for a joyful reunion with all my loved ones and for a glorious resurrection from the dead."

George pondered his own faith. He knew that God lives and that He loves His children. He knew Jesus Christ is the Son of God and that He fulfilled the will of His Father in giving His life as an atoning sacrifice for all men. He was a little unclear on exactly what it would be like in heaven after this life, but he believed he could be with God and with all of God's righteous sons and daughters through faith in the atoning blood of Jesus Christ, repentance from all sin, and strict obedience to God's laws.[5] George put his arm around his mother and said, "I don't know all the things you know about God and His ways, but when you tell me what you know, I'm certain you know it…if that makes any sense. Hearing you speak of the glories prepared for the righteous after this life gives me courage and casts out all my fears, even the fear of death."[6]

Polly smiled. "If you don't doubt, God will deliver you from all adversity and fear. Just think upon the liberty with which God has made us free to choose righteousness and eternal life. Dedicate your life to securing that liberty for all of God's children."

"I will, Mother. I will," George reassured. After a quiet moment he continued, "I really don't mind going to town with you. I like working with other people and helping them through tough times. I really like helping people figure out how they can earn money and manage their own situations better so they feel better about themselves and have more choices in life. It's great when people learn to set their own worthy goals and then make plans to achieve them."

*****

As they reached the edge of Lydda, Polly directed George toward the town's trash pit. The people they were seeking were often down in this area scrounging for food or anything of value. Mother observed, "This isn't the most luxurious place to give service, but I know the people here really need our help, and they appreciate it. I often think about how Jesus was willing to descend below all things in order to prepare a path for us back to our Heavenly Father."[7]

George quoted from memory: "Pure religion and undefiled before God and the Father is this, to visit the fatherless and widows in their affliction, and to keep ourselves unspotted from the world.[8] Though I bestow all my goods to feed the poor, and though I give my body to be burned, and have not charity, it profits me nothing. Though I speak with the tongues of men and of angels, and have not charity, I am become as sounding brass, or a tinkling cymbal. And though I have the gift of prophecy, and understand all mysteries, and all knowledge, and though I have all faith, so that I could remove mountains, and have not charity, I am nothing."[9]

Polly thought for a moment, and then asked, "So what is this charity that is so essential?"

George considered, and then responded, "I think charity is the pure love Christ has for all men. It is so important because it endures forever."[10]

"Amen," Mother agreed. Speaking further from her heart she added, "It's important to know that when we give service to others we are in the service of God. He is our King, and through His divine mercy He answers our sincere prayers, helping each of us through life. As He is our Example in all things, we know He desires that we help and bless each other, just as He blesses us.[11] Jesus taught, 'Inasmuch as ye have done it unto the least of these My brethren, ye have done it unto Me.'"[12]

Polly climbed down from the cart and grabbed her basket of bread to distribute. "I'll give out the clothes later, when I can take more time to talk with the people. For now, hunger is their first concern. George, would you run through the neighborhood and let people know we will be working on reading and math skills today? Tell them we'll start at the third hour."

"Sure, Mother." George replied. He was familiar with the assistance plan his mother had put together. Monday was instruction on raising chickens and selling eggs. Tuesday was instruction on gardening. Wednesday was training in reading and math skills. Thursday was healthcare, cooking, and sewing. Friday was another reading day, spent mostly in the scriptures. George stayed close until there were at least a few familiar people around so Mother wasn't alone.

"If I need more help, I'll let you know. Otherwise, you're free to run your own errands for a couple of hours until it's time for our trip home. If there are any changes in our plans, we'll need to meet and agree upon them in advance," Polly instructed.

"Yes, Mother," George confirmed. "I don't have too many errands of my own. Do you have a list of things that need doing while you do group instruction?"

"I have just a few items," Polly replied. "One family needs a leak in their roof patched. Another needs waste water runoff diverted around their home, instead of through it. I'm sure there will be more needs revealed as I talk to people while I'm distributing bread and clothing."

"I'm happy to help," George replied.

"At least being the youth battle skills champion is good for something," Polly noted. "People recognized you quickly, and they're willing to listen to your ideas. Most don't believe you're only fifteen years old. I sometimes wonder about that myself."

"It makes me chuckle when people see me coming and light up exclaiming, 'Our champion is here to help us!' I usually reply, 'I'm here to help you help yourselves.' I find that more gets done if I explain my ideas to people and then show them how to begin working to solve their own problems. Once they understand what to do, I get out of their way so they can succeed. If they get stuck and need more guidance, I'll provide it until their confidence is restored. Then again, I'll encourage them to finish the projects on their own. A lot more gets done that way than when I try doing everything myself."

"I'm so grateful that you are willing to be my hands as I try to be the hands of the Lord in service to others," Polly responded thankfully.

*****

"I'm really impressed with your skill in teaching others and the success you're having with your students during these months we've been traveling to Lydda," George said with true admiration. "When I was younger, I hadn't noticed how you had cultivated ideas in my mind. But watching you work with the poor, it's easy to see your guiding methods and their obvious effectiveness."

"Thank you," Mother replied. "I've noticed that you have natural skill in training others too."

"I think I've been blessed with many friends who are very bright," George responded. "In any case, we have a surprise for you today. We've been working on a project for several weeks now. It's for the people of Lydda. Would you like to go see it?"

"Of course I would," Mother answered with enthusiasm.

Quickly, George turned the cart toward a low hill not far from their usual destination. "The owner of this land is a charitable man who has also been looking for ways to help the poor. He has provided enthusiastic support for our plan."

Polly strained her eyes toward the hill and noticed a doorway set at a slant leading into the hill. "Is it a root cellar? Oh, it is. This is wonderful!" she beamed. "This will protect and preserve the precious food donations for the poor. Excess crops and bulk produce purchases can be stored safely much longer, so there won't be so much hunger and fear during the winter season. This is marvelous! How did you do it?" she asked.

"Working with a few young men in town, we dug a deep rectangular pit into the hill," George replied. "We lined the floor and walls with rough cut stone. We extended the walls a few feet up with lumber and built a supportive ceiling above the pit. Then we covered the structure with a two foot layer of dirt and capped it with the original sod. We made fitted stone walls to hold back the dirt on either side of the stairway and set the door at a slant above the steps."

After admiring the structure a bit longer, Polly asked, "What did you do with all the extra dirt?"

"About a third of it went on top of the cellar," George explained. "We used the rest of it for another project, the housing area you showed me on the lowlands with lots of standing water and mosquitoes. We raised the ground level in a few places so storm water runoff would go directly into the creek. The area dries quickly now in good weather. I'm hoping this will improve the health of the residents. Lots of people helped after I explained what I thought we could do."

Mother stepped close to George and gave him a quick but firm hug

A Martyr's Faith

that caught him a little off guard. "Thank you so much!" was all she could say.

*****

"I'm surprised at how many people gave me credit for our project ideas," George told the inn keeper. "I've shared with many of them how the ideas have come from books in our family's library, but a collection of books is something most of them have never seen. I'm determined to change that. My mother has often told me that literacy is the doorway out of poverty, and I've seen the truth of it."

"So how does this involve me?" the man questioned skeptically.

"If you will allow me to build shelves along a wall in the common room, we'll stock them with books for anyone to read," George urged. We'll cover the cost of the shelves and books, and you can promote your inn as a community resource, hopefully increasing your business."

"Since it costs me nothing, I'll give it a try," the merchant agreed.

*****

At George's request, Gregor contacted many of the wealthier families, proposing that they support the new public library by donating one book each, which he would match, book for book from Gerontius' family library. If they didn't have any books they were willing to give away, Gregor invited them to loan their books so he could have copies made. "The loaned book proposal has been accepted by many, so I offered Sabra a modest fee to make copies of the books that were loaned to us," Gregor explained to George. "Sabra agreed to make the copies, but refused any fees saying the project was a community service so she would donate her work."

*****

Shortly after it was established, George enlisted Sabra to look after the public library. A few weeks later she reported back to him. "With books on the innkeeper's shelves, community interest has increased, and so has his business. Some of the books I copied have disappeared, but they were replaced on the shelves by the exact aging originals from which I made the copies," she explained. "After some inquiries, I learned that an enterprising young man in Lydda has been taking the copies I made to the families who possessed the originals. In exchange for their worn originals, plus a handsome fee of course, he's trading them for my copies."

"What should we do about that?" George asked.

"I've taken care of it," Sabra replied with a smile. "Now, when I borrow books to copy, I make the same offer directly to the owners. If they want the new copies of their books, instead of the worn originals, they pay me the fee. I still donate the original to the public library."

"Work as a scribe can be a good source of income," George said. "You're making the right contacts to establish a reputation for high quality work among civil officials and the wealthy."

"It's been a blessing to me and my mother," Sabra responded. "I had another idea, too. Because the library was intended especially for the poor, I've been inviting the poor to share their own family stories and add them to the library. I've been helping those who want to participate, collecting their stories and family histories and writing them down. Many of the wealthy families have offered to pay me to help them do their own family story projects.

"These family stories are amazing. Many families in the province trace their Christian conversions back to miracles done by Christ's apostles. Peter healed Aeneas of the palsy in Lydda.[13] My mother told me that in the nearby town of Joppa, Peter had raised Tabitha from the dead. Tabitha was my great grandmother many generations back."[14]

*****

Polly's cough struck hard. After three months it seemed to be getting worse. "I refuse to cut back on my care for the poor," she said. "However, I will try to spend more time on indoor activities where I can continue to promote literacy."

****

CHAPTER FOURTEEN
Uniting the People

Lydda, Palestine
290 AD

*"For unto whomsoever much is given,
of him shall be much required:..."*[1]
Luke 12:48

****

As they finished sword practice one morning, Gregor sat down next to George, resting for a moment while they drank cool water drawn from the well. "You know, George, I've been thinking," Gregor began. "After your dramatic victory in your first tournament, there were many more challengers the following year. However, you provided ample evidence that your initial championship was born of more than luck, as you again won every battle without ever taking a hit. There were fewer competitors in your third tournament. Again, you took no hits on your way to victory in the championship."

"What's your point?" George asked.

"Your dominance in the tournaments is discouraging participation, frustrating the purpose that motivated Father to help establish this event. He wanted as many young men as possible to take an interest in combat skills, with the intent of improving their chances of coming home safely from military service. Though I'm very proud of your success, I think I should do something to honor father's vision of young men preparing to survive and return with honor. Besides, you need better competition to improve your skills."

"What have you got in mind?" George probed.

Gregor thought for a moment longer and then responded, laying out his plan, "I think I'll contact each of the wealthy families, with sons of the right age, and offer to train them in combat skills, for a modest fee. I'll emphasize the point that, although I lost the championship to you, I'm the only competitor who has ever gotten a hit on you. If the boys will learn all I can teach, and bring even a few of their own natural skills and aptitudes to bear in competition, they'll greatly improve their chances of success. In any case, if their skills improve, their chances of surviving actual combat in war will increase, and that was always

Father's goal."

"I think that's a great idea," George said as his mind began to flood with ideas of his own.

*****

"With the spring planting complete, I contacted the wealthy families with my training proposal," Gregor remarked. "Many of the parents recognized the fundamental benefits of such skills and quickly accepted my offer to train their sons in the art of combat. Nearly all of these noble sons believe that their own unique skills will allow them to win, if they can just learn what we learned from our father. Teaching these boys without destroying their self-confidence in the process will be the true challenge," he observed wistfully.

"Perhaps I can help, indirectly," George offered, trying to be supportive without interfering.

"How would you do that?" Gregor probed.

"I'll watch from a distance as your boys practice in the cool of the mornings," George answered. "Each evening, after I've returned from Lydda with Mother, I'll offer you my best counsel for each young man's development."

"That's a great idea," Gregor replied. "Just be sure not to discuss the training with my boys. After all, you are the enemy and it might unnerve them."

*****

"Your counsel has been excellent," Gregor complimented George. "My students are making rapid progress. The more they learn, the more they realize how much they have yet to master. Their pride is beginning to melt away, yet their self-confidence is increasing because they know their skills are increasing. It's taken a while to firm up my training routine, but I'm feeling good about the group's development."

*****

As the summer came to a close, George decided to implement an idea of his own. "Listen, Gregor," George began. "I have a plan to provide a little competition for your students."

"I'm not so sure about that," Gregor responded. "They're not ready yet and I won't have you destroying their confidence now."

"Oh, I wasn't planning to spar with them myself, at least not yet. I've been thinking about the other young men in Lydda who need battle skills training too, but can't afford to pay for private lessons. I'm thinking of training a group of them for free," George explained. "I want to start by focusing on those young men who are the most likely to enter the military, based on their limited prospects in other careers. I'll begin training the oldest first, and then work down from there."

"If you're going to give free training, I hope the young men I'm training don't come whining for a return of the fees I'm charging," Gregor said lightly.

"Oh, I don't think you have to worry about that," George responded. "You know how the wealthy often despise anything within the grasp of the poor. They'll keep paying you just to keep their club exclusive." Both brothers smiled knowingly.

*****

As he and Polly arrived in Lydda, George explained, "Mother, I've got a few important errands of my own to run today. Will you be alright without me for a while?"

"I've been feeling a little poorly and short of breath," Polly admitted, "but it's the same irritating cough that's plagued me for months. I may have caught something from one of the people I've been caring for here. No matter. Those are the risks. I'm sure I'll be fine, George. Meet me back here in two hours," she said just as a coughing fit struck. After it subsided, she reassured, "I may be a little weak, but I'll be alright. You go on."

Quickly George headed for Joshua's carpentry shop, a place he'd visited many times before with his father and sometimes on his own. He'd come here to select and purchase a full-sized practice sword when he turned eleven, so he would be ready for the tournament the following year. He loved to look at the things Joshua could make from wood. Joshua had a gift for explaining things and he was patient with young men and their questions, as long as they were truly interested in learning. He taught George about the different types of wood and which worked best for making things like swords, and in construction. He'd also provided the wood used in constructing the community root cellar. It was still early in the day when George approached the carpenter's shop. "Joshua, how are you today?" he asked.

"I'm doing well, thank you. What can this old carpenter do for you today?" Joshua responded.

"Well, I have another idea to run past you. Have you got a few minutes?" George inquired.

"Anything for our young champion," Joshua replied easily. "What's on your mind?"

"I want to start a combat skills training group for the young men in town who can't afford Gregor's training."

"That sounds great," Joshua responded. "But I don't have the time to train boys and I can't afford to work for free, though I'm flattered that you'd think of me." There was a teasing smile on his face as he tried to back George into an awkward corner with his wit.

"Well, that's the beauty of my plan," George countered. "You don't have to do the combat training, and you might even get some help with your work around the shop."

"I'm listening," Joshua sighed. "Give me enough of the plan so I can judge for myself whether it's God's hand or the devil's in the details. Then I'll let you know if I'm in."

"Well, we need a central place for training. I was hoping my group could use the back corner of your lumber yard. We would need to reorganize the yard a little, but our boys will provide all the muscle for that, under your direction of course. I'm hoping to clear an area large enough that several groups of sparring partners can be active at the same time. I expect there will be other kids watching, and maybe they could sit on some raw lumber, stacked into benches."

"So, how does this help me?" the merchant probed.

George was encouraged that Joshua's initial response hadn't been negative. He continued, "The young men I plan to train can't afford the things they need. If you'll allow me to assign them in rotation as carpenter's helpers, they could give you a hand around the shop and at your work sites. In exchange, you would teach each boy some basics about working with wood, and help him make his own high quality wooden sword. When the sword is done, the young man is discharged from your service, but he keeps his sword. Then I'll assign a new helper. If you like the work of any young man, you're free to try and apprentice him on your own terms."

"What about wooden shields?" Joshua asked.

"Shields would be great if you want to work a deal on that, but I'm not asking for shields yet. I need each young man to have a sword first. Initially, I'm planning to train in combat skills using the sword for both attack and defense. If the young men learn quickly, we'll move on to combat training coordinating the use of sword and shield later."

What a blessing it would've been if someone had given me some training before I served in the army, Joshua thought. "I like your plan, but discipline must be the first rule of order. I can't have kids playing around the lumber yard instead of training. I need your word that you'll send away any young man who won't stay focused on the training. What do you say?"

"It's a deal! You have my word!" George agreed enthusiastically.

*****

Many young men appeared for the free training. From this assembly, George organized his first group of students, explaining the opportunity to everyone. "Any young man twelve years or older may participate. The first lesson for all is discipline. Following instructions with exactness, especially Joshua's lumber yard rules, is essential to learning and success. Discipline is strengthened when it is practiced consistently. I'll be training the oldest young men first. If you stay focused, you younger boys can watch and learn as you wait your turns. Anyone who fails to maintain discipline and focus will be dismissed from the training group for the week and will go to the end of the line for active battle skills training. Understand?"

All agreed, though many still seemed unclear on how this training would work beyond having to do everything George said or be dismissed. Still, George was pleased with the enthusiasm that these young men displayed.

Reviewing his notes on his trainees, George remarked, "I see six of you are within a year of the minimum age for military enlistment. In addition to you six, I've selected six others to be in the first group to receive combat skills training. These second six have claimed a willingness and ability to teach others."

As George was organizing the group, Joshua appeared from his shop with a rack of new wooden practice swords. "I know we've got our deal on making swords," the carpenter said, "but I thought it would be best if you started with twelve swords that can be used only in the lumber yard, for supervised training. The boys can take their own swords home, once they've made them. I took the liberty of making six full sized swords and six medium swords, which should work well since you're training the oldest young men first."

"Thank you so much," George responded sincerely. "This will really help speed up the training. How can we pay you for this help?"

"Aw, forget about it," Joshua said briskly. "I made those quick from scrap wood. They probably won't last through a single sparring match."

George had never known Joshua to produce anything but the best. As he and the other boys examined the rack of new swords, he could easily see they were high quality. He knew Joshua was just being modest. "Well, if these are your shoddy scraps, I can't wait to see the masterpieces these young men will make with your help," George said gratefully.

Turning to his first group of trainees, George said, "Each of you will trade labor to Joshua and he will help you make your own practice swords. Who wants to go first?" Several hands shot up. "Persis and Quartus, you are the oldest. Introduce yourselves to Joshua and make your arrangements." As the carpenter assigned work schedules to them, George assigned two more volunteers to rotate into Joshua's service as each of the first two completed their own swords.

The practice area in the lumber yard was wide enough for four trainees, two pairs of sparring partners, in each row. It was deep enough to permit three rows of trainees. All the other young men who wanted to learn were allowed to sit down on the lumber stacks and observe the instruction George was giving. "The most important skill each of us must develop is discipline. Discipline can be practiced by anyone doing anything, even just sitting on a stack of lumber watching other people in training. Those who work hard and stay focused will do best."

George was pleased with the intensity and focus of the initial group receiving active training. *These older boys will serve as great examples for the younger ones*, he thought.

At the close of the first training session, George spoke to all the boys. "Thank you for your careful attention during today's training. I suspect that may be more a result of the swordplay than my brilliant instruction. I encourage all of you to practice these skills on your own and with each other. Through my own experience I've found that one of the best tools for learning is teaching newly acquired skills and truths to others. Therefore, every young man who receives direct instruction will be required to teach their newly acquired skills to others. At the end of the first day of training each week, I will divide up all the others boys who have been watching. They will be assigned to the various sparring partnerships in the active training group. The active trainees will give the training they received from me to their own assigned trainees for the remainder of the week. I'll attend the final training session on the last day of each week to observe so I can plan more effectively what to teach and how to teach it in the following week. The lumber yard will be closed and there will not be any group training on the Sabbath."

*****

"I'm curious about what you boys are doing," Polly announced at dinner. "Gregor, have any of your students or their families complained about being charged for training when George is giving free training in town?"

"Not many," Gregor responded. "There were a couple of families who raised the issue lightly. When I countered that my training was a good deal at the price they are paying, and they shouldn't think me evil just because my brother is doing something good with his own time and talents, they let it go.[2] I even suggested that if they thought George's offer was better, they could withdraw and join his training. Only one family was sharp enough to do that. The others seemed satisfied that George is only training one day a week, while I train five days a week. Also, I think some of the parents like their sons participating in a group that is exclusive and not available to the common young men in town.

"Sometimes I go with George at the end of the week to watch his students teach others. I'm really impressed with how well they're doing and how much better they learn by teaching. I've decided I need to split my training sessions so at the beginning of practice my students teach each other what they learned the day before, and then later in practice I teach them something new. This is one of the best ways to train them to be leaders."

"Gregor and I have set up monthly sparring competitions to provide greater motivation," George added with modest excitement. "We hand pick the match-ups and then instruct the competitors on the strengths and weaknesses of their opponents. Young men who pay attention are able to prepare and improve. Those who give poor attention to instruction suffer in the sparring contests. However, they do learn the hard way to work at improving their skills."

Gregor agreed, adding, "I'd rather have these young men learn from the rod of a friend, than be obliged to learn from the cold steel kiss of an enemy.[3] All the boys involved are learning quickly. They're recognizing the growth of their own skills and their confidence is increasing. They're also learning the equality of classes in combat. Because we teach discipline and respect like we learned from Father, the young men are learning to respect each other. This has been breaking down barriers and uniting many of the youth in the community."

*****

"This training has worked out well for me," Joshua assured George. "I've found several young men who have proven very skillful with wood. I've engaged some of them in apprenticeships, greatly easing the growth of my business."

"That's wonderful," George replied. "Based on the success of my deal with you, I've been able to work out similar deals with the tanner and the blacksmith. The tanner agreed to let the young men work to acquire leather protective gear for arms, legs and chest. The blacksmith agreed to let the oldest young men work for steel swords, shields, and helmets. The thing I've found most encouraging in all of this is that several of the young men have been able to develop trade skills, opening opportunities for them in careers other than agriculture and the military."

****

CHAPTER FIFTEEN
A Market for All

Lydda, Palestine
291 AD

"Say not, I will do so to him as he hath done to me..."[1]
Proverbs 24:29

****

Quietly Gregor entered the library where he found George reading one of the holy records, an open engineering book pushed to one side. "I don't know how you find time to study books with all you do. Caring for Mother, helping her give service to the poor in Lydda, and keeping up with battle skills training for the other young men doesn't leave you much time for yourself."

"It's like juggling," George responded. "If I train well and delegate properly, I never feel too much weight in my own hands at any one time. It's a fun challenge. Did you need some help with the crops or livestock?"

"No," Gregor replied. "Although you're still getting bigger, stronger, faster, and wiser,[2] I thought you might want to have a sparring session with me to prepare for tomorrow's tournament. The level of competition has improved significantly, due in large measure to the training we've provided. A few of our young men have even won similar tournaments in neighboring communities such as Joppa. Some that we've trained have already joined Diocletian's army. The recruits from Lydda are getting noticed for their fighting skills. The training they've received is being recognized as superior preparation for true battle, raising hopes that more sons of Lydda will eventually return safely home."

"You offered a sparring session?" George asked with a smile.

"Yes," Gregor replied. Noting the sparkle in George's eye, he quickly added, "This time you get to be Goliath."

*****

In accepting the return of the champion's crown after his fourth tournament victory, George proclaimed to the assembly, "I'm honored and greatly blessed by your encouragement and by the hand of Almighty

God. Henceforth I shall strive to be a more effective servant of Christ, working more diligently for the welfare of all men, helping others in any way I can. I see myself as equal to those who stand in need. I will enjoy prosperity only as those around me are released from the curse and bondage of poverty. I have no promise of success, but I'm bound in gratitude to God to live up to the light I have and to bless others with the talents God has given me."[3]

*****

The cart creaked gently as George and his family made their way down the road through the low hills from Lydda to home. Exhausted by the day's activities, Mother was trying to relax when another coughing fit began. These attacks were getting more frequent now, but Polly refused to reduce her service to others. As the attack subsided, she put on the best appearance she could and struck up a conversation to get her boys' minds off her health. "That was the best harvest celebration Lydda has had since I can remember," she said.

"Absolutely," Gregor responded. "More people attended than ever before. The amount and variety of trade goods were the best outside of Jerusalem."

"It was fun," George agreed, as he rode a horse alongside the cart. "I'm really happy for all the merchants and their families. I never thought this holiday would rival the tournament for excitement and activity."

"Some credit is due to you on that account, George," Polly praised.

"I really think the merchants made their own success," George said with a smile.

Gregor was uncertain of what his mother meant. Turning slightly toward her, he asked, "What credit would you have me give George for the success of the harvest celebration?"

Mother perked up a bit to tell her proud tale. "You've been busy spending nearly all your time at home tending to the fields and cattle or training young men with sword and shield so you may be unaware. However, early last spring, George told me he had an idea that might help some of the less fortunate young men in Lydda and their families. He really has a soft spot in his heart for the ones he's been training at the carpenter's yard."

"I see greatness in those young men," George commented. "As I've gotten to know them and their families better, I've been impressed that some, though blessed with great hearts, lack the aptitude, intelligence, or social skills to pull themselves out of poverty. I wonder if these were the ones Christ was speaking of when He said, 'For ye have the poor always with you....'"[4]

"Even so," Polly continued, "he mentioned how many of these boys have real talent and the ability to escape poverty but simply lack the skills or training in a trade. Some of the boys have made opportunities for themselves as they've apprenticed with the carpenter, blacksmith, and tanner to earn and make their own equipment. Others have done well working with the stone mason when they built the community root cellar. But some young men, often coming from merchant families, seemed best suited to work in the markets, buying and selling. However, many merchant families have only been marginally successful because their shops were in the back alleys instead of being on the main road through town."

"I really thought I could help them too," George added.

"When he looked into it," Polly continued, "George saw that the shops on the main road were nearly all taken. Also, competitors were scattered around town, avoiding each other."

"It wasn't very efficient and it didn't attract much trade from people outside of Lydda," George noted.

"So what did George do?" Gregor asked his mother with interest.

"Well," mother beamed, "George had an idea about building a market. He got it from one of those engineering books. He prepared a master plan for construction of the market, having high quality merchant booths made of stone, with good drainage and sewer systems. Somehow, he was able to persuade many of the back alley merchants into pooling enough money to buy land for the new market on the main road, at the eastern edge of town."

"The key to the project was persuading the back alley merchants to work together and trust my assurances that putting all their shops in a central location on the main road would make them a more attractive destination for more customers and other merchants," George commented. "They finally agreed to the plan once I committed to dig a well for the new market. I guess that's when they knew I really believed in my own proposal. Funny how good merchants have a sense for true commitment."

Polly stifled a cough and continued, "These merchants bought the land on both sides of the road in order to have the greatest display area and to control the growth of the market. As part of their mutual covenant to lift the oppressed, the back alley merchants agreed they would work together, donating their time to build the market, one stone shop at a time. As each shop was completed, they drew lots to decide who would get the new shop."[5]

"I got that idea from the way the tribes of Israel cooperated under Joshua when they came out of Egypt and conquered the land of Canaan, dividing it by lot," George offered, wanting to make sure proper credit was given where it was truly due.

Mother continued her story. "The merchants all agreed to give one full day of labor each week towards the project until all the merchants involved were relocated together in the new market. Once the well and the first few shops were complete, it didn't take long for business to pick up. Then the merchants and their families got very excited about the project, volunteering much more time than their original commitments in order to finish the market and make it great."

"Once all the back alley merchants were relocated, we reorganized the new market by trades, allowing customers to see the broadest variety of wares in the shortest amount of time," George explained. "The new market has quickly become the focus of trade in the community, lifting the previously marginal shopkeepers to more comfortable levels of success.

"Seeing their success, many of the main street merchants wanted to participate in the new market. The prospering shop keepers had to decide whether they would now include those who had previously excluded them. At first, the merchants in the new market were reluctant, feeling they had been despised by the other merchants. They were planning to deny the other merchants' requests. When I questioned them, they cited the Savior's injunction, 'Therefore all things whatsoever ye would that men should do to you, do ye even so to them: for this is the law and the prophets.'[6] They reasoned that what had been done to them, being shut out of the main road market, is what they should do in return.

"I shared my belief that the Savior's words were looking forward, not backward, meaning they should treat others as they would want to be treated in the future. I reminded them of their covenant to lift the oppressed. I asked if they would now stubbornly delay until those with diminishing means became destitute before they embraced them. If so, what lesson would they teach the community regarding how they wished to be treated in the future, should any of them suffer financial or personal adversity? I suggested that responding in like manner was the lesser law, not the higher law of forgiveness given by Christ. I shared with them a verse from Proverbs regarding the backward looking view and refusing to forgive. It says, 'Say not, I will do so to him as he hath done to me....'[7] Then I shared the words of Paul: 'Rejoice with them that do rejoice, and weep with them that weep...Be not overcome of evil, but overcome evil with good.'[8] Finally, I pointed out to them how beneficial it had already been for them to cooperate and work together, suggesting that unity and cooperation are the keys to prosperity for the whole community. After much consideration on the matter, the new market merchants decided to set aside past wrongs and work together with the other merchants toward a brighter future."

"So, you started quoting scriptures and they all backed down, huh?" Gregor summarized with a chuckle. "You have the power of a preacher amongst an unlearned flock."

"I think they did the right thing because they respect George so much," Mother observed. "He's a natural engineer, planning and envisioning things as they should be or could be. Amazingly, he seems to do as well envisioning events and relationships as he does with physical structures. As an added benefit, many of the young men in his training group have earned enough money by working at the new market place to purchase their own practice equipment."

Gregor chuckled at his mother's gushing. With sincere admiration he turned to his younger brother and nodded, "Very impressive…for a Pip!" The brothers laughed together.

"The new market merchants began making additional shops and renting them out to other merchants, at a fair but handsome profit," George added. "They have improved their business district by including more merchants, and strengthened the incomes for their families. With the additional merchants, general trade has increased substantially for everyone. Now, the merchants communicate more freely about suppliers and business opportunities, and their market is becoming more efficient, driven by competition. They are working together to each specialize in a few unique items, enhancing the market's reputation as the best place in the region, aside from Jerusalem and the coastal ports, to find a wide variety and low prices."

"The Lord truly blesses those who are united," Polly declared just before being overcome by a coughing fit so severe they had to stop the cart.

After dismounting, George held his mother gently. "I'm starting to feel like my next great cause should be organizing a community hospital," he said. And so the planning began.

*****

"Honestly Mother, your condition has only gotten worse as the weeks have gone by. You should stay home and rest. We will deliver the bread and clothes to the poor for you," Gregor pleaded, with George nodding agreement.

"Thank you boys, but I need to do it," she said. "The greater the distance between the giver and the receiver, the more the receiver develops a sense of entitlement, which undermines the motivation to self-reliance intended by the giver.[9] Let us never distance ourselves from the Ultimate Giver, nor take Him for granted or fail to do our part."[10]

****

CHAPTER SIXTEEN
Mother Prepares for Death

Lydda, Palestine
292 AD

"...rejoice in hope of the glory of God...And hope maketh not ashamed; because the love of God is shed abroad in our hearts by the Holy Ghost which is given unto us."[1]
Romans 5:2, 5

****

"Mother's looking very thin and frail there in bed," Gregor whispered to George. "This illness just won't ease its grip on her. Lately her coughing fits have become so violent that she's spitting up small clots of blood with each episode."

"She likely caught this illness from some of the poor she's been caring for in Lydda," George responded. "But as far as she's concerned, God can heal her or take her as He sees fit. I just wish she would fight this. I still feel the loss of Father. I can't bear losing mother too, so soon."

*****

With strained courage, George entered his mother's room. As he sat by and peacefully held her hand, Polly tried to guide his perspective. "Don't be angry at life's twists and turns. God is over all. He'll decide when each of us has been tried sufficiently to be fit for His kingdom. On the good side, I'm no longer worried about how long it will be until the Lord sees fit to reunite me with your father. I'm looking forward to being with him again. I'm also looking forward to a glorious resurrection in God's kingdom where I'll have a perfected body that's no longer subject to sickness, disease, or death."

"It would be a great favor to me if you would fight this thing," George begged. "I still need you to guide me."

Polly sighed lightly and was immediately besieged by another involuntary coughing fit. Recovering a bit, she added, "These attacks sure give emphasis to the value of my hope. George, you have your own work to do for the Lord. You don't need anything more from me to succeed. You need God's help."

"I know," George responded quietly, "but I can still desire that which I don't need. I can still pray for a miracle, can't I?"

"Of course you can, George," Polly replied. "Ours is a heritage of faith. Have you read the account in the Acts of the Apostles when Peter came to Lydda and healed Aeneas who had been sick in bed with the palsy for eight years? Soon thereafter, Peter went to nearby Joppa, and raised Tabitha from the dead."[2]

"I've read those stories," George replied. "They strengthen my belief in healing."

"Did you know that Tabitha was Callidora's seventh great grandmother, and Sabra's eighth?" Polly asked.

"Sabra mentioned that once, but I've never heard Callidora speak of it," George answered.

"You should ask her sometime to share her witness of Christ and how important that family history is to her as she faces life's adversities as a widow with a young daughter," Mother encouraged. "All the families in this area know of these miracles in our community history. No man can do such miracles, except God be with him.[3]

"I know God lives and loves us. Surely He would not have created such beings as men and women to exist only for a day! We were made for immortality.[4] God has designed eternal glory for the obedient. My son, hear and give heed to the law of the Lord, for it has become the law of your mother, which I pray you will never forsake."[5]

Mother's witness and counsel were uplifting, and George's faith grew as he heard her testify. He didn't doubt that she knew God and that she knew she would soon see her beloved husband again.[6] "I will always honor your law. You have my word," he replied solemnly.

"You can pray for a healing miracle if you want," Polly added. "But if you truly know God, you'll know that He loves us completely. It's His intent to give us His richest blessings, now and in eternity. Whenever we undertake to negotiate with God for what we want, instead of what He desires for us, we are doubtless negotiating for a lesser blessing. It's best if you make sure the miracle you seek is the one God has selected for you so you don't end up with a lesser blessing than God intended."

"I'll try," George promised.

"I'm a little hesitant to bring up the next topic for fear it might upset you, but I'm not sure a better time to share will come, so please hear me out," he asked. "I've been considering joining Diocletian's army soon, when your illness has resolved. I want you and Father to be proud of me and how I'm using my life and the talents God has given me for good. I was wondering what counsel you might give me about that."

Polly took a cautious breath and asked, "Is this the topic of torture for the evening? Well, at least it's nice to know you will be joining your father and me on the other side of the veil soon after I'm gone," she teased. Noticing her humor wasn't having the desired effect on her son, she put aside her teasing and spoke plainly. "George, you need to know that your father and I are already very proud of you. We respect your faithfulness to God and your exercise of good judgment. Why don't you share with me why you plan to join the Emperor's army?"

"Well, it's not because I'm the most capable in personal combat, although that's clearly a talent I've been given. It's more a feeling of concern I have for the young men who are going into the army unprepared to handle themselves and even less prepared to lead others to safety and security. The more I fast and pray about this decision, the more I remember Daniel's interpretation of King Nebuchadnezzar's dream.[7] I believe the two iron legs of the image clearly represent the Roman Empire, split between east and west. If it's God's will that this Republic lead the world at this time, then I want to help establish peace among all nations and tribes by bringing about Roman control and administration, through strength, in order to secure the peace. But I would be happy if my efforts were simply helpful in bringing some of my friends safely home when otherwise they might not make it."

"If the Holy Spirit leads you down this path, go with God," Polly assured. "I have no greater joy than to know that my children walk in light and truth.[8] Call on the Lord privately in humility.[9] Always follow what you are taught by inspiration from the Lord.[10] If you value your reputation and you sincerely desire to help your true friends, limit your associations to men of good quality, for it is far better to be alone, than to be in bad company.[11]

"Regardless of your chosen occupation, the two greatest decisions you will make in life are whether you will put God first in all things, and whether you will select a woman of faith to marry. Focus on pure relationships. I promise you the best opportunities in life, and in eternity, arise out of the best relationships. The church is the bride of Christ. You should base your choice of a spouse on who you love enough to live for, and die for, and who you trust to raise your children up unto the Lord.

"As for the army, your father used to tell me that a faithful soldier must always be ready to sacrifice his life for a cause he supports. Therefore, he must always be ready to meet God. This preparation is done by receiving and retaining the Holy Spirit as your constant companion. When we are filled with the Spirit of God, we can be sure we are prepared to meet Him. If there is anything amiss in our lives we must quickly repent. Be reconciled to God, void of offense toward Him and all men, that you may merit the companionship of His Holy Spirit always."[12]

"Oh, Mother," George replied, giving Polly's hand a firm but gentle squeeze. "How will I ever remember all you've taught me after you've gone to be with father?"

After a muffled cough, Polly replied, "It's more important for you to seek and follow the Lord than it is for you to remember what I've tried to teach you about His ways. Jesus said, 'If a man love Me, he will keep My words: and My Father will love him, and We will come unto him, and make Our abode with him. But the Comforter, which is the Holy Ghost, whom the Father will send in My name, He shall teach you all things, and bring all things to your remembrance, whatsoever I have said unto you.'[13] If you seek the Lord in humility, He will tell you all truth, in your mind and your heart, by the Holy Ghost, which shall come and dwell in your heart."[14]

Mother paused, a distant look in her eyes. When she refocused on George she counseled in a weakening whisper, "Go forth among the armies of the Emperor. The Lord will make you an instrument in His hands in bringing about the salvation of many souls.[15] Your father also used to say, 'The soldier, above all other people, prays for peace, for he must suffer and bear the deepest wounds and scars of war.'[16] Pray always, George.[17] When the world around you melts into confusion, be still and let the Holy Spirit guide you home."

****

CHAPTER SEVENTEEN
About My Father's Business

Lydda, Palestine
292 AD

"...wist ye not that I must be about my Father's business?"[1]
Luke 2:49

****

Respectfully George approached his older brother. "Gregor, I come seeking your counsel, and your blessing."

"What about, Brother?" Gregor replied, concerned by George's serious expression.

"For some time I've felt in my mind and in my heart that I should follow in our father's footsteps and pursue a military career. With mother's passing this winter and the month of mourning over, I feel a strong impression to be about my mission in life. I clearly recall father's final inspired charge to use the gifts God has given me to resist the oppressors of this world and to relieve the suffering of the weak and innocent. Each time I consider joining the army, I feel the calm assurance of the Spirit confirming father's charge and urging me to take action. I'm planning to join Diocletian's army."

"Mother warned me this might be coming," Gregor replied. "Still, I've dreaded the day I would lose the direct support of the man I most admire in the world." He eyed his younger brother, who now stood six feet four inches tall and weighed a lean 240 pounds. With encouragement in his voice he continued, "George, I'm sometimes amazed that you still look to me for approval. Aside from our parents, there is no one who has helped me more in my life than you. But if the Holy Spirit bids you to another path, I'm confident the Lord will still continue to bless and prosper me on this land so I can bless the lives of those who depend on us for support.

"Your life is your stewardship from God. At seventeen, you're old enough to join the military without my consent. Beyond your age, your size and skills make you the kind of physically intimidating man that inspires courage in all but your foes. There is little doubt the army will take you. The only question is whether they can handle you.

"You have my blessing and my prayer of faith for your success. As for counsel, keep the commandments of God. Be established in righteousness. By these means shall you be free from fear, neither shall terror abide in you.[2] When you search for peace and cannot find it in the world there will always be a place of peace and rest for you here. If you are on the Lord's errand, I trust God will sustain us both until you return."

"Thank you Brother. I also trust that God will sustain us," George replied. "I feel strength whenever I reflect on the happy reunion between our parents at Mother's passing. Perhaps you feel it too. The words which they often spoke concerning eternal life and the joy of the saints has sunk deep into my heart.[3] Their faith has guided my perspective on eternity. I feel my own mighty change of heart through the Spirit, independent of the faith of our parents. Still, their lives and testimonies are a constant comfort to me."[4]

*****

"I can't find George. He hasn't left already, has he?" Sabra asked anxiously.

"Not to Nicodemia," Gregor replied passively, teasing with silence.

"Well, where did he go and when will he be back?" she spouted.

"He said he was going to make a quick visit to the temple mount in Jerusalem, seeking God's blessings in the sacred place where heaven once touched earth," Gregor responded, noting the relief in the young girl's eyes. "He'll be back tomorrow."

*****

As George neared the temple wall, he thought, *I remember when Father brought me to Jerusalem as a reward for my first tournament victory. He shared the prophecies that God will yet establish a new temple in this place, gathering in His scattered people, and restoring that which has been lost.*[5] *The stones of the temple wall remain as an enduring testament to God's covenants with His ancient and future people.*

Pondering on his plan to join the Roman army, he felt strongly it was the right thing to do, but he wanted reassurance from God. With his eyes fixed upon the wall, he silently prayed, *Forsake me not, O Lord: O my God, be not far from me. Make haste to help me, O Lord my salvation.*[6]

Carefully George looked for the small stone he had added to the temple wall as a token of his faith in the mighty hand of God and of his own commitment to serve Him. It didn't take long to find the object of his search. "There you are, just where I set you five years ago," he greeted, testing the stone with his hand. "Still set solidly in the wall, with all its promise of glories to come, eh?" With a brief glance toward heaven and renewed determination, he pled, "Eternal Father, be with me and bless my efforts in helping to establish peace among Thy children."[7] He enjoyed the warm flush of calming reassurance he felt immediately.

During his travel home, George reflected again and again on his covenant to help God in His work. *I love to ponder on the promises of the Lord, for I know that God is bound by His own word to those who keep their covenants with Him.*[8] *I know I can't dictate terms of service to the Lord. If any terms of service are to be set, let them be set by the Lord, and rejoice in His tender mercies. At baptism, I covenanted to take upon myself the name of Christ, to serve Him and keep all His commandments. God's promise to me was that if I would do those things, the Holy Spirit would abide with me.*[9]

*****

As he packed for his travel to Nicodemia, George went into the library to look at Ascalon. Although he had won his father's battle sword in the tournament, he revered it as a family heirloom. As he stared at his treasure, Gregor entered the library behind him.

Measuring George's gaze, Gregor asked, "Will you take it with you?"

"I had just decided to leave it mounted on the wall when you came in," George replied.

"Take Ascalon with you," Gregor urged. "It will likely save you in battle, just as it saved Father. I recall Mother saying how she honored that sword for bringing Father safely home. I want your safe return so much more than I want Ascalon hanging on the wall. Please take it, for me."

"Trusting your counsel, Brother, I will," George replied, feeling a pleasant strain of emotion.

"And you," Gregor spoke with intensity to the battle sword, "I charge you to be valiant in defense of George and of all that's just and true."

Removing the weapon from its wall mounts, George added, "There, Ascalon. You have your charge. Heed it well!"

*****

On the morning of George's departure, Gregor, Sabra, and Callidora gathered to see him off. Gregor surprised him with a pair of three-year-old stallion chargers born of a common sire. One was obsidian black and the other was brilliant white.

"I've always known you to be generous," George said to his brother, true pleasure ringing in his voice, "but I never dreamed you'd buy such beauties and give them up to the battlefield."

"Why not?" Gregor replied. "They were born for it. They both have powerful hindquarters and short backs with strong bones. They're well trained and easily capable of coiling and springing, stopping quickly, turning or even spinning, and sprinting forward on command. They're superior in combat, inspiring assurances of successful journeys into the perilous lands held by their enemies. Besides, I'm giving up my little Pip to the battlefield and you're worth more to me than any old horses."

"Careful there," George cautioned playfully. "You'll hurt their feelings before we even start on our journey."

"I knew you had worked with the prior owner before and he said that you favored these two horses," Gregor noted. "I suspect you've already given them names that suit you."

George smiled. "I call the black one Joshua, because he inclines to service in battle. The white charger is Caleb, because he inclines toward peace, seeming pleased to bear burdens without the rush of battle."

"Then Joshua and Caleb they are!" Gregor declared. "Now, since it's apparently your intent to make yourself a prodigal son, and your return is uncertain, I'm giving you all the trappings of the son welcomed home, to assure you of your abiding place at our table.[10] The fatted calf was served at dinner here last night with all your friends."

"Thank you, Brother. You're too generous. But I give you my word I shall not be prodigal," George promised.

"Nonsense!" Gregor replied. "It's not enough. Here we have a new pair of shoes in your size. I think you'll find these are better suited to travel and battle, once they're broken in. Here's the ring I had made for you. It has the monogram "G" flanked by tiny chargers, with a cross at the top and a battle sword on the right side."

George accepted it and tried to put it on his smallest finger, but the ring was too small. He smiled anyway, liking the design of the jewel.

Gregor frowned, seeing the predicament and without time to get it fixed. "Well, it was only a signet ring anyway," he said, regaining his smile. "Now, this new riding cloak should work well for travel in bad weather. That about does it."

George looked carefully into his brother's eyes. "I believe there is still one more gift the father had for his prodigal son, isn't there?"

Gregor's eyes filled with tears as he stepped forward, embracing his beloved brother. Kissing him lightly on the cheek he whispered, "No, Brother, I didn't forget. I love you."

As they parted, each quickly wiped at his cheeks and struggled to swallow the lump in his throat. After a moment, Gregor coughed slightly and said, "There is still one final gift for your journey which I'd thought to give you, but my patronage was denied. Sabra, it's your turn."

Sabra had tears streaming down her face as she handed George a thick packet of bound papers. George accepted the packet and opened it carefully to examine the contents. "The sacred records!" he declared in amazement. "Oh, thank you!"

Sabra looked George in the eyes and mustered a smile. "The packet includes many of the Jewish scriptures, Psalms, Proverbs, the Gospels and many letters of the Apostle's. It was Gregor's idea. He said he would pay me to do this copy work for him, but I refused him, saying I would do it as my gift to you."

"And it's a good thing too," Gregor laughed. "I'm not sure I could've afforded her work. Sabra took a long time copying, probably making a matching copy for herself."

"If you don't study and understand what you're copying you make more mistakes," Sabra spoke politely to Gregor. "Is there a problem if I made a matching copy for myself?"

"No problem at all," Gregor replied. "There's a reason why I appointed you as keeper of the library on our estate. We all know you excel at reading and writing, and that your mind is sharp and quick. You've done well copying the books we've borrowed and adding the copies to our library. Your initiative in making and selling copies of the books most frequently borrowed from us has opened the door to work for you outside the estate. Your growing reputation for excellence has brought in many other requests for personal and even official copy work, which have provided you a secure and independent income. You've also helped expand the cause of literacy in the region. I'm sure my mother is proud. But, the reason I appointed you as keeper of our library is because you have always treated the sacred texts with such reverence."

Sabra blushed at the sincere praise.

Offering a final bit of brotherly advice, Gregor said, "George, be sure to feast upon the words of Christ, for they will tell you all things that you should do.[11] Follow the path of King David in his youth, and beware of pride that by and by leads to sin."

"I will," George reassured his brother.

As he turned the packet of pages back to the front, George detected a personal note that Sabra had included with the scriptures. The note read, *My soul delights in the scriptures and the things of the Lord. My heart ponders continually upon the things of God which I have both seen and heard. I write the things of God that they may be of benefit to future generations, and I rejoice in the goodness of the Lord.*[12] *Thank you for saving my life. Perhaps someday I can return the favor. I will pray for you every day. I love you.*

George looked up from the packet into Sabra's eyes. She saw that he had read her note and she wasn't embarrassed. Casually he stepped toward her. "I also delight in the scriptures and the things of the Lord. Thank you so much for your gift. I will hold it sacred." His words were coupled with a firm but gentle hug.

Maintaining her composure, Sabra begged, "Let me have your ring." Obediently, George handed her the signet ring. Pulling a small cord from her pocket, she made a quick loop through the ring and tied the ends together. "Here is your ring," she said as she handed it back to him. "Now you can wear it around your neck as a symbol of home that remains near your heart."

George was thrilled with each gift. Quickly he began to discard some of his extra food supplies to make room for these cherished items. "There's no need to unpack those things," Callidora said, stepping forward with some gifts of her own. "I made a leather horse pack for you. It has several pockets large enough to hold your packet of sacred scriptures. I also made a leather breastplate for you with many hidden pockets on the body side. They can hold protective metal scales over the vital organs, or they can be used to carry secret documents."

"Thank you. May God bless you always," George said as he embraced Callidora.

*****

Loaded for the journey, George urged his horses forward. As the road cut behind a low hill where he knew those at home had lost sight of him, he heard Gregor's familiar call, "Urha-urha-urrr!"

With a warm smile George thought, *I hear you Brother and I'll answer the call!* Turning to face home he loudly replied, "Urha-urha-urrr!"

****

CHAPTER EIGHTEEN
Joining Diocletian's Army

On to Nicodemia, Eastern Roman Capital
292 AD

"Wherefore take unto you the whole armor of God, that ye may be able to withstand in the evil day, and having done all, to stand."[1]
Ephesians 6:13

****

At George's urging, the black charger led the white one carefully along the dusty road towards the city of Nicodemia, the capital of the eastern empire. George enjoyed the travel because it gave him time to think. *I believe the Roman Empire is the fourth kingdom of Nebuchadnezzar's dream, as revealed by the prophet Daniel.*[2] *Diocletian's renewed division of the empire between east and west, like the iron legs of the image in the dream, strengthens my belief. If God has established this Republic, I want to support it, promoting peace and religious freedom for all. I'm not certain how my life will play out, but I know I want to make a difference for the good. I can still hear Mother's words encouraging me to prepare myself so that each day I will be ready to meet God.*

Just off the road ahead a few trees promised a bit of shade for rest and relief from the midday heat, so George turned the horses toward them. Feeling the pace of the horses increase, he suspected a likely water source which would add to this welcome relief.

Near the cluster of trees, George located a small spring leading to a little pool of water. After directing the horses downstream and staking them in a patch of grass, he checked on Ascalon. Then he went to Caleb's pack and retrieved his scriptures. There was a specific passage he found helpful and inspiring, especially considering the path he'd chosen, and he'd been working to memorize it. Carefully he read it: *Finally, my brethren, be strong in the Lord, and in the power of His might. Put on the whole armor of God, that ye may be able to stand against the wiles of the devil. For we wrestle not against flesh and blood, but against principalities, against powers, against the rulers of the darkness of this world, against spiritual wickedness in high places. Wherefore take unto you the whole armor of God, that ye may be able to withstand in the evil day, and having done all, to stand. Stand therefore, having your loins girt about with truth, and having on the breastplate of righteousness, and your feet shod with the preparation of the gospel of peace, above all, taking the shield of faith, wherewith ye shall be able to quench all the fiery darts of the wicked. And take the helmet of salvation, and the sword of the Spirit, which is the word of God. Praying always with all prayer and supplication in the Spirit, and watching thereunto with all perseverance and supplication for all saints....*[3]

I love to ponder on the scriptures and apply them to my life, for my benefit and learning,[4] George thought. *Most passages of scripture have some beneficial application, if a person will just look for it in humility before God. I know there is no protection comparable to the armor of God and His blessings. This passage makes clear how we qualify for that divine protection. The shield of faith is the best preparation, but the breastplate of righteousness is the best raiment, righteousness being among the clearest signs of humility before God in all men who seek His guidance.*[5]

George's mind turned to another passage of scripture: *My son, despise not thou the chastening of the Lord, nor faint when thou art rebuked of Him, for whom the Lord loveth He chasteneth, and scourgeth every son whom He receiveth. If ye endure chastening, God dealeth with you as with sons; for what son is he whom the father chasteneth not? But if ye be without chastisement, whereof all are partakers, then are ye bastards, and not sons. Furthermore we have had fathers of our flesh which corrected us, and we gave them reverence. Shall we not much rather be in subjection unto the Father of spirits, and live? For they verily for a few days chastened us after their own pleasure; but He for our profit, that we might be partakers of His holiness.*[6]

What a blessing is the chastening hand of the Lord! he marveled. *How much we learn through adversity that would be difficult to understand in the absence of experience. It's difficult to explain to others why a loving Heavenly Father allows us to be tested with adversity and calls it a blessing, but I know it's true.*[7] *Father taught that saints live by every word that proceeds out of the mouth of God.*[8] *This was taught by the Lord who spoke these words in the face of hunger and adversity. Father also made it clear that bread sustains physical life, but obedience to God sustains spiritual life and glory hereafter.*

George rested in the shade with his thoughts and his horses until the heat of the day had passed. A slight cooling breeze was his signal to move on. Carefully he placed the scriptures back in his saddle pack, secured his gear, and headed north again. He wondered, *What adversity might the Lord allow me to experience on the path I've chosen?* Deep in thought, he traveled with the Mediterranean Sea to his left until the shoreline turned west. Then he turned northwest to Nicodemia.

*****

Just before sunset George guided the horses away from the road again to camp for the night. It was a dry camp, but George wasn't worried as he considered, *The horses watered well earlier and the road is well worn, suggesting water shouldn't be too far away. Besides, water sources are often dangerous at night, attracting all manner of wild creatures.* After prayer, George ate a small meal from his supplies and drank sparingly from his water pouch. He checked the horses' tethers carefully and then bedded down. Somewhere in his pondering, he drifted off to sleep.

*****

"George...George...George," Gerontius called out.
"I'm here, Father," George answered.
"George, be ever mindful of all your covenants with God," Gerontius spoke gently but firmly. "Be faithful and God will give you power to slay dragons, extending mercy to His innocent children, and especially to His virtuous daughters, in whom He delights."
"I will be faithful," George whispered. "I trust that God will prepare a way for me to accomplish all He commands."[9]

*****

George's dream had been brief, but was still vivid in his mind when he awoke. *That was an amazing experience,* he thought. *But what specifically must I do about it?* He thought about his covenants with God. These reflections still left his course unclear, so George began to review the counsel his father had often given him. He could almost hear his father's words: *Pursue righteousness. Follow God's will in all things. Live by every word of God.*[10] *Love God and have charity towards all men.*[11] *Act in all holiness before the Lord, in patience and faith.*[12] *Seek not to counsel the Lord, but seek to take counsel from Him.*[13] *Despise not the chastening of the Lord, nor be weary of His correction, for whom the Lord loves, He corrects, even as a Father corrects the son whom He loves.*[14] *Plead with God to teach you His statutes and commandments.*[15] *Use your gifts from God to resist the oppressors of this world and to relieve suffering, especially among the humble and virtuous daughters of God. Have reverence for sacred things.*[16] *Share them only in wisdom, when moved upon by the Holy Spirit. You will have much tribulation, but be faithful unto death and God will give you a crown of life.*[17]

Determined to keep all these counsels, George was still uncertain what specific things he needed to do. Praying for guidance, he felt an impression. Just then, his horse snorted, anxious to go forward. With a whisper he urged the horse on, "That's right, boy. We already know the next few steps of our path. We'll join the army and seek to secure peace for all men. If we show faith and take a few steps into the darkness, the Lord will surely light our way."

*****

Having arrived at Nicodemia, George proceeded directly to the barracks and armory. There he found himself among hundreds of men, young and old, seeking the honor of appointment to Diocletian's army, with its promise of a reliable income. It was rumored that the Emperor was raising 10,000 additional soldiers to be trained and deployed for the coming fighting season.

George secured his gear and reported to the registrar's table. The grizzly old registrar tilted back on his stool, looking up to see who had cast such a big shadow. He was visibly impressed with George's size, but his eyes fixed on Ascalon. "Brought your own weapon, eh?" he croaked, raising one eyebrow a bit. Cocking his head to the side he continued, "Sign in here and head straight over to that sparring group near the armory well. They'll test your fighting skills."

"Yes, sir," George replied respectfully.

As he approached the sparring area, the group gradually fell silent, each hopeful recruit quietly comparing himself to the mountain moving in among them. Constantine, the legion commander, had been overseeing the work of several sparring groups, but he also stopped and turned his full attention to the new recruit. With an air of confidence he spoke to George. "Now you're the size of man we need. I can see why they sent you directly here. Let's see if you're a force to be reckoned with, or if you're just a bigger target." Selecting one of his most capable combat veterans who had proven the superiority of his fighting skills the previous year, Constantine called out, "Quartus, take this man through his paces so we can measure his skills!"

Quartus stepped forward, meeting George's eyes with a solid stare. Both men began to smile. Without changing his gaze, Quartus called loudly to Constantine, "Sir, perhaps you would like to select a more…expendable soldier to draw out this man's skills to your view."

Constantine was surprised and confused. "What's the problem, man? Do your duty," he urged.

Again, Quartus held his position while speaking his piece. "My lord, if my duty is to prove this recruit's battle skills, let me witness to you that I have sparred with this man many times before I joined the army, for we are from the same town in Palestine. I've been tested many times by his battle skills and know them to be far superior to my own, for he trained me."

Constantine looked at George again, considering him carefully. Finally overcome with curiosity he spoke. "Fair enough, Quartus. I accept your word that this man's skills are superior to your own. Still, I must see his abilities for myself. Being just as expendable as any man in this army, I pledge myself to the task," he said, strapping on a leather breastplate and picking up a sword.

Bowing slightly, Quartus stepped aside. His smile grew with high expectations as he watched.

"Are you ready?" Constantine asked, raising his wooden sword.

George selected an appropriate wooden sword and announced, "Ready, sir!"

The assembled group stepped back, forming a ring of sorts, as Constantine and George began to circle each other. Constantine was a favorite among all the men, providing an excellent example personally, inspiring confidence, and training effectively for success. He took the initiative with several attacks. George deftly countered each attack with his wooden blade. As the intensity of the match grew, the other sparring pairs broke down, gathering to witness this heated duel. After several intense engagements neither man had taken a hit. Constantine called out, "Quartus, I see your man here has mastered his defenses, but his attacks appear weak."

With a knowing smile Quartus loudly replied, "My man hasn't attacked yet, not that he couldn't have scored. He's still evaluating your habits and skills before revealing his own."

Annoyed by this comment, Constantine stared at George and challenged, "Is this true? Do you stand in judgment of my skills?"

"Life stands in judgment of all men's skills," George responded calmly.

"Ah, so you're a judge and a philosopher!" Constantine ribbed. "Show me what you've learned. Strike me if you can!"

At the command, George nodded slightly and closed the gap a half step before initiating his attack. Constantine defended well, deflecting George's blows. "Again!" he demanded.

Anxiously the men in the crowd placed their bets on the outcome of this epic duel, heavily favoring their commander. It took George three attacks before he scored a hit. Still, the blow surprised the crowd and his opponent. "Again!" Constantine shouted as he initiated a furious attack of his own. George defended every blow, passing on several openings for counter-strikes. Suddenly, the image of Gregor's furious attacks flooded his mind. Carefully, he guided Constantine to an opening, allowing the commander to strike his thigh to even the score, so none of the men would lose money betting on their leader.

"Hah! You are mortal!" Constantine exclaimed as he withdrew a pace to regroup.

"Well done!" George laughed, a wide grin covering his face.

"What's so funny?" the commander challenged.

"Oh, I thought I might feel out of place here," George responded. "But now I see you've taken the place of my older brother. I welcome that, knowing I'll feel right at home with you."

"Shall we call it a draw for now, Brother?" Constantine offered, extending a hand and a smile to George. "It's been a long time since I've taken a whack, but I'm pleased that my sparring time promises to be more competitive and educational in the future."

*****

By the end of the day, the camp was abuzz with word of the contest between George and Constantine. "The new recruit bested the legion commander," some said.

"I saw it the opposite," others replied. "In the end, we should agree that in such close matches, we can't know for sure who wins unless the swords are real." Many who hadn't seen the match resolved with determination that they wouldn't miss the next one.

Rumors began to spread regarding this challenger who had dueled the commander to a draw. One popular story was told by a soldier from Joppa, who had been with the army for three years now. Claiming personal knowledge of the new recruit's unnatural powers, he shared his tale in hushed tones:

In Cappadocia there was a spring that provided sweet water for all the people of the village. One day, as they went to fetch water, a crocodile appeared at the spring. It caught one of the children and ate her. With the beast distracted by its prey, the other people were able to quickly fill their water pots and return home. Every day the beast continued to threaten all who approached the spring, becoming more angry and aggressive with each encounter.

A few hearty souls battled the crocodile, trying to rid the village of the scourge. But the beast with its fierce teeth and jaws was too powerful and quick. None were able to kill it or drive it away, and more than a few lost their lives in these battles. In desperation the people agreed to feed one sheep a week to the monster to appease it so they could draw water.

By and by the lot fell upon a poor family to give its only sheep to the crocodile. However, their brave daughter, Sabra, swore that instead of sacrificing the lamb, she would distract the beast with a long wooden pole, so others could fill their water jugs.

By chance, at that very moment, George happened past the village in his travels. Upon seeing the innocent young maiden courageously engaged with the crocodile, he vowed to rid the village of the beastly scourge. After calling upon God to bless his efforts, George fortified himself with the sign of the cross and approached. As the people watched intently, he took his battle sword and confronted the monster.

The crocodile made a sudden lunge for the maiden. Instantly, George brought his sword down on the head of the beast. Enraged, the monster twisted viciously to face his foe. The duel was fierce but finally George stabbed the crocodile to the heart, bringing great relief to all. He presented the crocodile's hide to Sabra for her courage.

To thank him the villagers offered George his choice of any young maiden in marriage, and pled with him to make their village his home. He refused, but gave thanks to God in Christ's name. Before taking leave of the village, he charged the people to learn of Christ and worship Him. Many of the people, including Sabra, converted to Christianity and are faithful to this day.

*****

Diocletian stood upon the rampart overlooking the armory and barracks, assessing the new recruits. Stepping closer to Galerius, his second in command, who was also inspecting the new recruits, Diocletian observed with satisfaction, "I've been a soldier from my youth, but I still enjoy watching the training of strong fighting men. These recruits look very promising to me."

"Fresh meat," Galerius grunted. "Should be enough to reinforce our northern legions."

"We can't afford any miscalculations there," the Emperor replied. "It takes more men to reconquer territory than it does to hold it. I refuse to squander our hard fought victories of the last several years in the Danube River valley. If we can keep the Germanic tribes and the Sarmatians at bay in the northeast, then we can properly address the Saracens from Sinai and their invasions of Syria. We need decisive victories and secure reinforcements if we're going to expand the empire and achieve any lasting peace."

"Perhaps the gods will favor us this year," Galerius mused sarcastically.

"We worship all the Roman gods and accept worship from common men out of respect for the power of their superstitions," Diocletian replied soberly. "However, the only divine law I recognize is that might makes right!"

As he continued to observe, Diocletian noted, "Constantine has done excellent work selecting and training these men. Lately, he seems more enthusiastic about his work, and perhaps a bit more ambitious. We'll need to keep a close eye on him."

Cringing slightly at the Emperor's praise for the legion commander, Galerius replied, "He's got himself a prodigy too. See the big guy sparring with him now? He's the one. His name is George, from Palestine. He's already built a strong reputation for skill at arms. His mastery of advanced fighting skills is obvious. He rivals Constantine with the sword."

Focusing on George, the Emperor added absently, "He appears to have the stature, physical strength, and military bearing of a natural leader."

"He's the only one who consistently wins the three-against-one drills," Galerius remarked begrudgingly. "Constantine says he has a quick clear mind, skill with weapons, combat experience, and training in strategy which has conditioned him to focus immediately on the key elements in any battle scenario. He excels with any weapon, but his favorite is a battle sword he brought with him that makes him nearly invincible. You can see it there by the well."

"I know that sword," Diocletian smiled with wonder. "My life has been preserved by it more than once. It's called Ascalon and it belonged to Gerontius. He was my best tribune when we served in the imperial guard together. If he hadn't been injured in battle, he might have been in the palace instead of me. He was a man I could have followed. This George must be his son," Diocletian concluded curiously. After watching a little longer he observed happily, "He does stand out among the other soldiers. I expect we'll see he excels in courage and valor, just as his father did."

"Best keep a wary eye on him, too," Galerius murmured to himself.

*****

A Martyr's Faith

"Congratulations, men!" Constantine spoke firmly to the assembly of new recruits. "Each of you has been selected for appointment to the Roman army. As a part of your induction, you will be required to take the oath of enlistment, administered by the highest ranking officer present. It will be your honor to make your oath as a group directly to our most noble Emperor Diocletian. Each man will stand at attention. On a signal, each will draw his sword in his right hand and, raising it to heaven, repeat the oath of your commanding officer."

George repeated the oath as follows:

"I do solemnly swear that I freely accept the honor of my appointment in the Roman legion and the trust and brotherhood that attend it. I further accept the duties and responsibilities, inseparable from my appointment to this honor, to the senate and people of the Roman Republic, the Emperor, my legion commander, and my brothers in arms. I swear that I will bear true faith, allegiance, and loyalty to each of them, supporting and defending them against all enemies, understanding that my duty may require the sacrifice of all things, including my own life. I will faithfully discharge my duties as given by the orders of the Emperor and the orders of my legion commander until I be duly released from this oath by the Emperor or by my legion commander, or by *God* through my death. If I fail in my oath, my life is forfeit, as *God* is my witness."

George had no reservations about modifying his oath from the proscribed references of 'the gods through my death,' and 'as the gods do witness.' As he suspected, in the sea of voices swearing allegiance, none seemed to notice his changes, but George knew One had noticed.

*****

Taking charge of the newly sworn soldiers, Constantine explained the next rite of passage. "Each soldier will now receive the legion emblem, an eagle surrounded by a laurel wreath, tattooed on his right arm near the shoulder. Below the wreath are the letters *SPQR*, an acronym for the Latin 'Senatus Populusque Romanus,' which means 'The Senate and People of Rome.' The tattoo is an emblem of fitness for service, signifying sufficient strength, aptitude, and courage. It also signifies that you understand that bravery, not numbers, will carry the day."

****

CHAPTER NINETEEN
Centurion in Battle

Northeastern Frontier, Eastern Roman Empire
293 AD

"What mean these stones?"[1]
Joshua 4:21

****

Most Noble Emperor Maximian, Augustus of the Western Empire:
Our warfare in the northeast has been successful. However, effective government and peaceful change of leadership have weighed heavily upon my mind of late. It is apparent that the Roman Empire is simply too extensive to be ruled efficiently by only two men. Therefore, I am dividing north from south in each half of the empire, creating quarters and establishing a tetrarchy, or rule of four. Each quarter will have its own emperor and its own capital city, but, as Augustus in the east and the senior of all emperors, the entire empire will remain under my command. You will remain Augustus in the west, answering only to me. Continuing strength of leadership will be achieved as each of us selects a man of proven ability to serve as Caesar, or junior emperor and heir to our thrones. We will legally adopt our Caesars as sons, confirming their positions as heirs to our thrones. If possible, these adoptions should be further strengthened by marriage, with each Caesar becoming a son-in-law to his Augustus. Each heir should be ruling as Caesar long before he becomes the Augustus, when that position is vacated. By merit the new Augusti will appoint their own Caesars, adopting them as their respective heirs. This succession plan should ensure that only the most qualified men rule, minimizing the scourge of civil war that has been pervasive in the course of past leadership changes.

To achieve success, all tetrarchs must fully cooperate in maintaining order throughout the Republic, but each will act with primary authority within the domain of his quarter of the empire, subject to our approval. I'm considering Galerius as my Caesar in the east. I would adopt him as my son and give him my daughter, Valeria, to wife. Notify me promptly of your proposal for Caesar in the west. Keep me informed of your progress and let me know if I can assist you.

Always faithful!

– Emperor Diocletian Augustus

*****

Most Noble Emperor Diocletian Augustus:
  I sense great wisdom in your organization of the empire. I was initially surprised by your consideration of Galerius as Caesar in the east, though the herdsman has come a long way. He has served with distinction under your command, yet it seems difficult for him to connect with the people and build trusting relationships. I'm suspicious that he cannot maintain loyalty without buying it. He despises those born to privilege. He only respects those who've taken wealth and power at the point of a sword, as we have. He is a godless man, brutal and barbaric in his manners and demeanor. However, these past two years in Egypt he has demonstrated his ability to command an army and to subject a rebellious people. Perhaps he is the perfect choice to serve as the point of the spear in future conflicts.
  I have stabilized the southern half of the western empire. However, the northern half is rife with rebellion on many sides. My gut tells me the man for the task is Constantius. He has the loyalty of a formidable army, inspiring confidence and success among his men. He divorced Helena a few years ago and married my daughter, Flavia, anticipating the terms for advancement. He is cunning and charismatic. However, I'm wary of his ambitions. If you would hold his son, Constantine, in the east as leverage, I would be confident in appointing Constantius as my Caesar and charging him to quell the rebellions in the northwest. I expect the campaign will be brutal and will likely thin his army considerably. In any case, with all four emperors from Moesia, we give ourselves the best chance of coordinating and controlling the empire effectively.
  Always faithful!
– Emperor Maximian, Augustus of the Western Empire

*****

Most Noble Emperor Maximian, Augustus of the Western Empire:
  I sanction Constantius as Caesar in the west subject to the terms previously agreed upon. As you have requested, I will keep Constantine in the east. This should be a simple arrangement given his popularity among the legions and his skill on the battlefield. He has proven to be a superb strategist. We will likely be quite active this fighting season in the northeast along the Danube River securing our positions against the continuing threats of the Alamanni and other Germanic tribes to the

north and the Sarmatians to the northeast. Fortunately, our southeastern frontier with Persia has been relatively peaceful. Their young ruler, Bahram II, may be facing an internal power struggle, but he paid the annual treaty tribute. He doesn't appear to present any immediate threat. Therefore, I plan to deploy nearly all of my new recruits in the Danube River region, pursuing an offensive strategy. Constantine and his legion will be with me continually.

Finally, I have ordered Galerius to take command of our legions in the provinces west of Nicodemia but east of the Adriatic Sea. From there he can monitor the movements of Constantius and his army to the northwest. Fare well my brother.

Always faithful!
– Emperor Diocletian Augustus

*****

Most Noble Emperor Constantius, Caesar of the Western Empire:

Emperor Diocletian has charged me with establishing an heir to the throne in the western empire. Therefore, as my son-in-law, I am naming you as my Caesar, or junior emperor. You will have primary administration of the northern half of the western empire, subject to me, and we will both continue to serve Diocletian, the senior emperor. In order to confirm you as the clear heir to my throne, I will legally adopt you as my son.

Your initial charge is to take your army northwest to Gaul and put down the usurper Carausius and his Frankish allies, thus securing your domain in the empire. I will look for your coming by the next full moon so we can attend to all the legal necessities.

It may interest you to know that Diocletian has chosen Galerius as his Caesar in the east.

Fare well my son.

Always faithful!
– Emperor Maximian, Augustus of the Western Empire

*****

Although George was a subordinate, he counseled frankly with Constantine. "You know, Brother, I once received the rebuke of my older brother for holding back and thereby failing to help him improve his skills and raise his chances for success in battle. His reasoning was persuasive and applies to us, so with each match I'll strive to teach you something new about yourself. Therefore, I won't hold back in our future sparring."

"Fair enough, Brother!" Constantine boomed, the corners of his mouth turning slightly higher. "Persuaded by your brother's reasoning, I too vow that I shall no longer hold back in our future sparring." There was just enough mischief in the commander's voice to keep George cautious.

*****

As he prepared to cross the Danube River and deploy his men for the fighting season, Diocletian approached Constantine. "I see you've appointed George as a centurion in your legion even though this is his first campaign and he is unproven in battle. Do you think that's wise?"

Constantine turned slightly on his horse, giving the Emperor his full attention. "I do," he replied firmly. "He is a Roman citizen by birth. His experience in training others in combat and in managing laborers in agricultural and construction projects has proven a great advantage in leading and preparing his men for battle. He demands strict personal discipline from each man, forbidding excessive levity on duty and gluttony at any time. He requires obedience with exactness and trust in the command structure. He has his men practice marching and running, which keeps them lean. He encourages them to volunteer their labor on stonework projects, which appears to build their strength. He requires his men to train each other in combat, which greatly improves their skills as they teach. Though he's young, his stature and skill inspire the men. Also, he has a keen sense of diplomacy and political skill with his superiors and his men."

"Talents probably gained by observing his father deal with such issues," Diocletian chuckled.

Constantine continued, "George has a knack for explaining things at whatever level his men need to increase their understanding and motivate them. His men are gaining confidence and humility at the same time. It's truly unique. They are convinced that by following his counsel and training, their skills and abilities will improve, increasing their chances for success and survival."

"His father used to teach soldiers to study the weaknesses of their enemies, including weaknesses in their defensive implements such as shields and armor," the Emperor offered. "He also taught them to understand the vital points of attack on the body that would enable them to kill or incapacitate their enemies efficiently."

"George does the same," Constantine confirmed. "It doesn't surprise me that he's learning about battle strategy and military resource management. But the rate at which he internalizes and then applies the lessons and principles is simply amazing. He often identifies weaknesses and advantages gleaned from the training he's been given that leave his trainers in awe as they learn from his observations. He views the battlefield strategically, considering the impact of variables that others ignore to their peril. He continually thinks several moves ahead of his opponents. He really enjoys working with the men to raise their skills and confidence. He teaches the strategies and dynamics of combat, preparing them to think and act more effectively as a group in the heat of battle, thus increasing the odds that they'll survive once we've engaged the enemy. I'm confident that George is a man to lead other men to victory."

"I take you at your word," the Emperor affirmed with a smile.

*****

Constantine stood close, observing as George addressed his men. "Today we train for the battle to save lives that inevitably accompanies every battle to take them. Each man will learn to stop bleeding with direct pressure and heated blades, and to properly clean and dress wounds. We will also learn to set fractures and to relocate dislocated joints. Learning to recognize mortal wounds is an unfortunate necessity that will enable us to quickly move on to others we can help. These skills will serve us well in battle, and in managing our own affairs and those of our families." As the instructors began the training, George thought to himself, *So little time, so much to do. Literacy, mathematics, trade skills. These men need education and opportunities.*

"The Emperor has his eye on you," Constantine remarked lightly. "He's heard rumors circulating among the men of your immense wisdom."

"The fear of God is the beginning of wisdom," George replied confidently. "I teach truths that apply to battle and to life. I'm pleased to hear these principles have been well received, especially if my men are always prepared to make the ultimate sacrifice, being ever ready to meet their God. Understanding comes to all who keep God's laws."[2]

Constantine continued more cautiously, "Your godly talk is starting to attract zealots and philosophers from every quarter seeking assignment under your command. They want liberty and enlightenment. Such men are often ineffective in battle. You should be careful."

"No fear, Brother," George smiled. "I'll train them well for combat, and for life. Fasting and prayer will bring them self-discipline and an understanding of the Spirit and power of God."[3]

*****

Most Noble Emperor Maximian, Augustus of the Western Empire:
We located the forces of Carausius in Gaul. We destroyed his main army and captured his treasury. Our spies report that after the rout, Carausius was assassinated by Allectus, who took command of the remaining enemy forces in northern Gaul and Britannia. Allectus then fled to Britannia to rule. We'll see about that. It will take some time to organize and train new civil authorities in Gaul who will be loyal to us. However, in light of our decisive victory and the recovery of substantial spoils, we are receiving broad cooperation. We have yet to crush the remaining Frankish allies of Allectus. Once I've stabilized the tax base in Gaul, I will push eastward to the Rhine River, attacking the western flank of the Alamanni, creating a second front to assist Diocletian in his war against them. With all the volunteers joining our army, which is now over 100,000 strong, I don't foresee the need to call upon your forces for assistance.
Finally, I've dispatched Asclepiodotus and his men to the mouth of the Seine to begin construction of the invasion fleet that will be required for Britannia.
Always faithful!
– Emperor Constantius, Caesar of the Western Empire

*****

Most Noble Emperor Diocletian Augustus:
I'm concerned that we may have unleashed the bear before we tamed him. Constantius achieved more immediate success in Gaul than I had anticipated. His popularity is growing rapidly, swelling the ranks of his legions. His army is larger now than when he began his campaign against the army of Carausius. Given the constant and disgustingly overwhelming display of adulation by the people toward him, it's more crucial than ever before that you keep Constantine tethered as leverage against his father. I'm uncertain of any other method for controlling him. Enclosed is a copy of his most recent report. He'll push eastward till he engages the Alamanni, possibly threatening your western flank. I'm more wary of his ambitions now than ever.
Always faithful!
– Emperor Maximian, Augustus of the Western Empire

*****

Most Noble Emperor Galerius Caesar:

Enclosed for your review is a copy of Maximian's recent report. It appears that no matter how carefully I design the tetrarchy to operate based on merit there is an ever-present shadow of hereditary privilege. Maximian has a son, Maxentius, who carries enough of the qualities of his father to be an obvious candidate to become a future Caesar. The problem is the perception of a familial dynasty such a choice would create, benefitting the empire for a generation or two, but then dooming it to suffer unfit leaders for generations as in the past. Constantine also presents just such a concern. He is much like his father. He has made the most of his palace education, mastering agriculture, architecture, medicine, Greek and Latin literature, and the arts. He is even well versed in philosophy and religion. His military bearing, proven leadership skill in battle, and unconquerable spirit have made him a popular heir apparent for future appointment as Caesar. We must maintain close supervision over him constantly as a precaution against him joining forces with his father against the other tetrarchs. But I warn you against giving any offense to the son lest we unleash a popular backlash in support of the fury of the father.

Always faithful!
– Emperor Diocletian Augustus

*****

Beloved mother Helena:

As the day of battle approaches my thoughts turn frequently to you. I can bear the thought of dying with honor and glory, but I anguish over the prospect of leaving you alone. I know you would say you have your God and that is sufficient, but I feel an intense desire to live that I may protect and honor you. I've become good friends with one of my centurions. His name is George. You would like him. He prays regularly and doesn't seem to mind much who sees him. He earnestly seeks wisdom from the Fountain of all Truth. His devotions have spawned a bit of playful banter among the men, though none dare take serious issue with his worship. In fact, as battle draws near, the ranks of worshipping soldiers have blossomed and many men have been drawn to him. Because the Romans worship so many gods, his actions don't seem that peculiar though I'm not sure how many have bothered to ask which God he worships. In any case, the men are inspired by his sincere faith. As for me, I pray for you and for victory!

With love and devotion,

– *Constantine*

*****

"Meeting the Sarmatian army on an open field was a good initial test for you and the new recruits," Constantine observed when George approached with his post-battle report.

"It was challenging," George replied, "but our army had the numerical advantage and the high ground on the battle field. Even more important, our men supported each other and followed orders with exactness."

"We had better commanders as well," Constantine praised. "You were more dominant in the heat of battle than you've been in sparring sessions with our own men. You rendered your opponents efficiently and moved quickly to shore up weak spots among your century. I was very impressed that your men were particularly unified in their actions, achieving their objectives rapidly with a minimum of casualties. I saw no fear in you during the battle today. Well done."

"My mother taught me to fear God, not man," George responded. "She taught that the soldier, of all men, must be constantly ready to make the ultimate sacrifice and meet his Maker. Shall I take for my protector any other than God, the Creator of the heavens and the earth?[4]

"So, you're a man of faith after the battle as well as before." the commander observed. "It would appear that your God has been on your side today."

"It is I who seek to be on the side of God in my battles with other men," George assured. "My ambition is to relieve oppression and dispense mercy if possible, believing that freedom and lasting peace through strength are among the foundations of prosperity. If I have faithfully sided with God, I'm just as safe leading my men in the heat of battle as I would be at home in my bed.[5] Even if others had remained in their homes, those for whom death was decreed would certainly have gone forth to the places of their deaths, for God is over all."[6] Contemplating further he added, "Even in the struggles within myself, I find it wiser to seek God's position and stand with Him than venturing to plead with God to stand with me."

*****

"Constantine," the Emperor called out, "I have a task for you and your men at our northern outpost. There's a village there of moderate size that submitted to Roman rule last year. Though it's on the borders of the frontier, the outpost is important to our control and defense of the region, being well positioned on high ground overlooking a narrow valley split by a river. Our garrison there is three days late on its post dispatch, without explanation. Send George's century with an early resupply to the outpost to investigate the delay."

"As you command," Constantine replied.

*****

After nearly four days of travel, George's century approached the northern outpost. A scout returned with his report. "There's naught but a few stray dogs and an unwelcome stench to meet us before we reach the wood picket walls of the village," he said.

Entering the gate, George wrinkled his nose and scanned the scene. Several men and boys bawled out their mournful cries. A few were sifting through the ashes of burned out huts. The bloated bodies of nearly a hundred soldiers and several hundred peasants, mostly women and children, littered the ground in all directions. The scene was physically sickening to the men observing it. Even those who had seen battle and death had not seen it like this. "You sir, give me your name and tell me what happened here," George called out to a solemn old man.

The old man looked up at the centurion astride his white horse. Narrowing his eyes against the sun, which was high and bright behind George's back, he explained, "I'm Sipatros, my lord. It was the Visigoths from the north. They surprised the guard and slaughtered the village."

"And how did you survive?" George asked.

"Many of the men and older boys went up the mountain before dawn to fish in the lake. We do this every spring. While we fish, the men tell tales of their youth, fishing in the Aegean Sea. We were nearly at the lake when we heard the screams and cries from below. We gathered the boys and made our way through the trees back down the mountain." The old man's voice broke with emotion and tears rolled down his cheeks as he cried, "The villagers had no weapons. There were rumors that we preferred Germanic rule to the rod of Rome so we were disarmed. With weapons, they could've made a difference. Now we have young ones with no fathers or mothers." Staring numbly at the carnage, Sipatros continued, "There weren't that many attackers. The villagers outnumbered them maybe five or six to one, but with only rocks and sticks they had no chance against the swords of death coming down on them."

As George surveyed the scene again, it wasn't difficult to understand what had happened. He could envision the events in his mind's eye. *On a signal,* he thought, *the watch was cut down by archers a moment before the raiding party rushed the open gate. The enemy entered the village quickly, heading straight for the barracks, separating the defenders from their weapons. The bodies of Roman soldiers were spread randomly throughout the village, each engaged in his own idle pursuits. They were attacked and killed without ever forming into a unit. The raiders were an efficient group, sent to destroy the village, but not to maintain it. Their strategy was to eliminate the village tax base and wait to see if the Romans would abandon it.*

With equal measures of pain and defiance the old man continued, "The defenseless villagers were executed for their cooperation with the Romans. The attackers took all the weapons, money, and property they could carry and departed quickly. Rome could have protected us, or she could have armed us so we could protect ourselves. Because she did neither, she is left without loyal subjects here."

Ignoring the pained inference of disloyalty, George replied respectfully, "Father, we share your loss. Rome wasn't properly prepared and thus has lost many of her sons and daughters. Still, we can work together to save what has not yet been lost and, as far as possible, to restore what can be reclaimed." Climbing down from his horse, George drew his sword. Extending the hilt to the old man he said, "Will you join me in protecting our survivors while we give an honorable burial to all our dead?"

The old man turned to scan the faces of the surviving men and boys. He knew the only way was forward, but he couldn't go there in anger. Turning back, he stared into George's eyes and began to feel the beginnings of trust and healing. With a deep sigh, he let go of his pain and set aside his pride. Taking hold of the sword, he affirmed, "Yes, sir. Together we will honor our dead and move forward in life."

*****

Under the protection of a perimeter guard, they began the gruesome task of gathering and burying the dead. "Such a slaughter of women and little ones challenges the belief in a benevolent God," Sipatros observed soberly.

George strained at the lump in his throat as he acknowledged, "It is hard to understand how or why a loving God would allow such evil among His children."

In the depths of his soul George felt the need to reconnect with God to receive understanding as to why such things happen, and to gain reassurance that His love endures. Mentally, George began to review the evidence of God's love in his life. He pondered on the love of our Eternal Father, and thought of the love of his own parents. *They were great examples with the caring help they always provided. I know they loved me and that knowledge is the foundation of my relationship with them which endures beyond death. I count this heritage as a marvelous gift.*

Beyond the persuasive blessing of my family, there is the love and kindness I felt from Callidora. Also, there is the unity, peace, and prosperity of the people in Lydda. And when I protected Sabra from the serpent, I knew of God's love and help. This reassures me now of God's constant love for all His children. I'm certain that faith in God's love for His children is part of a sure foundation for personal revelation.[7] *I trust in God's mercy to those who either have no such loving examples or, worse yet, have been subjected to terrible family relationships.* As the light within him brightened and he felt the Spirit flood his soul he concluded, *Surely, faith can be restored by truly remembering the blessings of the Lord.*

"Devastation such as this is not God's doing," George reassured Sipatros. "This is the iniquity of evil men who have rejected the God of heaven. In the mortal test of adversity, God suffers the righteous to be slain that His eternal judgments upon the wicked may be just. The righteous are not lost because they are slain, but they enter into the rest of the Lord their God."[8]

As he spoke these words, George received a clear witness of their truth. He pondered on the blessing of God's love, remembering the words of Jesus, *Come unto Me, all ye that labor and are heavy laden, and I will give you rest. Take My yoke upon you, and learn of Me; for I am meek and lowly in heart: and ye shall find rest unto your souls. For My yoke is easy, and My burden is light.*[9] He was certain that in the end God will not be judged by the injustices of men in the world, but by His healing power in the eternities.

*****

Once the dead were all buried, George scouted the perimeter of the village looking for ways to improve the defenses against future raids. He carefully examined the small stream that provided fresh water to the village and followed it upward to its source. Alone, he thought about Joshua and the camp of Israel crossing the Jordan River. *At God's command, the waters were parted for the people, showing them that, even though Moses was gone, He was still with them. There they built a monument of stones as a token of their renewed faith in Him.*[10]

Thoughtfully, George collected twelve large stones from the stream and placed them in a tight ring around the spring of water, as a token of his renewed faith in God and in memory of the tribes of Israel and the Apostles who surrounded the Fount of Living Water. Reverently, he prayed, "O God, Eternal Father, these stones shall stand as a symbol of my faith in Thy judgment, mercy, and might, for which I give thanks.[11] I renew my covenant to submit to Thy will. Thou knowest all things and it is Thy right to call home each of Thy children in Thine own wisdom and time, to accomplish Thy purposes. I pledge myself to Thee, as a servant of Thy Son, in Jesus' name. Amen."

*****

When George returned to the village, Sipatros and his people were discussing whether they would rebuild, relying upon agriculture and trade, or abandon the village to settle in a new place. Cautiously, George approached the group and spoke. "Your village has been devastated. Anyone would understand if you chose to leave. But, if you want prosperity, I ask you to consider staying and rebuilding. This place has great value to Rome. It is the key to control of the region. It will be maintained by Rome, but this time with a much stronger force. The memory of the losses suffered in this raid will keep future soldiers more vigilant."

"We've been cursed in this place," Sipatros replied quietly. "We've lost everything. We have no women and no future. We have no harvest and no money. What will Rome do for us now?"

"Rome lost many men too," George responded. "However, this place has not been cursed of God, but only of our enemies. We must fight that curse. If your people choose to stay, I promise that those among you who are able will get work with the legion, either as soldiers, craftsmen, or laborers. With the supplies we brought for the garrison we'll meet your needs until harvest time. Then, we'll buy your grain and produce at fair prices. We'll organize a militia for your village, supplying your people with weapons and training for battle.

"Beyond what Rome will do, there are many things you can do for yourselves. There are nearby villages to the southeast that have lost men to the wars. Their women need faithful husbands, and their children need fathers. If you answer their needs, you can all escape the curse of an enduring destruction of the family. I'll lead in rebuilding the village and improving its defensive structures. Because of its strategic position, this place should develop into a prime market for future trade. I invite you to stay and work with us to restore your home and your prosperity."

Sipatros was surprised by the centurion's humble yet passionate proposal. He couldn't remember such a man of authority ever approaching him as an equal. "I'll consult with my people and let you know their will in the matter," he replied.

After much discussion, Sipatros reported to George. "My people have chosen to hold to the promise this place offered when they first settled here. They have chosen me to be their leader."

*****

Constantine, Legion Commander in the Northeast:
Our forces arrived at the northern outpost only to witness that the entire garrison has been destroyed by the Visigoths. Many of the villagers were also killed but many remain faithful to Rome and ready to rebuild. It is my opinion that the outpost can and should be restored and strengthened. Because of its strategic position, I believe it would be wise to post a century in the village for at least the remainder of the fighting season. I volunteer my command for the assignment. It is also my opinion that the outpost provides a serviceable base of operations if you are inclined to send additional forces for the purpose of claiming and stabilizing more territory in the north. In humility I await further orders.
Always faithful!
– George, Centurion under the command of Constantine

*****

"Sipatros," George called. "While we await a reply, we should prepare the people to meet the coming challenges. We will begin by arming them and providing combat training. My men will take up defensive positions within the village as others complete repairs on the wood picket wall. We will restore the buildings within the village after the wall and gates are secure. We will convert the entry into a dual gate structure. Only the outer or the inner gate may be opened, but never both at the same time. We will dig a trench around the outside of the wall and pile the dirt up against the wall. Also, I have ordered my men to cut down several trees outside the wall that gave the enemy cover too close to the watch towers. Thus we can prepare to support our liberty, our lands, and our peace, that we might choose righteousness and prosper."[12]

*****

"You've done a great job explaining the work so all the people know what to do," Sipatros praised. "They're feeling confident in the integrity of the village. They understand how a superior enemy force can be held off with these defensive structures and by using the features of the land to their greatest advantage. They are inspired by your confidence and energy. Though young, you are a man of strength, might, and understanding, taking joy in the liberty and the freedom of all men."[13]

"Thank you for your kind words," George responded graciously. "My heart rejoices in thanksgiving to God for the many privileges and blessings which He bestows upon His people. I'm anxious for their safety and welfare. I will defend them and my country, my rights and my faith with my life, raising my sword against our enemies to preserve the lives of the people. I trust that God will prosper the faithful, and that He will sustain us, inspiring us as to how we should defend ourselves against our enemies."[14]

****

CHAPTER TWENTY
Battle Reputation Grows

Northeast Frontier, Eastern Roman Empire
293 AD

"He keepeth the paths of judgment, and preserveth the way of His saints."[1]
Proverbs 2:8

****

The legion reached the outpost a week after George had sent the messenger with his report. "Ho, Brother," Constantine greeted his friend. "The Emperor was impressed with your report and your strategic analysis and proposals for the region in response to the loss of the garrison. He sent me to confirm the situation, along with resources to implement the strategy you proposed. Shall we scout the territory now, or later?"

"I'll be ready in a couple of hours," George replied. "I'm set to receive status reports from the work crews before we go. Perhaps you could use a short break after your hard ride."

Constantine stood in his stirrups and surveyed the various work projects. "It looks like you've been working much harder than me lately," he replied.

George didn't argue. "Did you share my full report with the Emperor?" he asked.

"Yes, we reviewed it together," Constantine answered.

"This was the most senseless loss of life I've ever seen," George seethed. "I swear I will never let this happen again, as God is my witness."

"That sounds like an oath to never lose another battle," Constantine observed skeptically.

"Oh, I may lose a battle, and even my life if it be God's will, but I will never have innocent people under my charge slaughtered because I've denied them the means to defend themselves and their God-given liberty," George responded. "My hope and my faith are in my God."

Constantine smiled. "Pray tell, which God is that in whom you have such hope and faith?"

George looked back at his friend. "My God is The Holy One of

Israel, the Lord Jesus Christ."

Constantine smiled again and spoke. "The voice of Thy thunder was in the heavens[2]...yet Thy mercy endureth forever."[3]

"So, you know your Psalms," George observed.

"Was that scripture?" Constantine replied coyly. "I thought it was just something my blessed mother used to say. She is a woman of faith. She raised me to believe, though I confess, I'm still uncertain about the role of religion in my life. I'm certain the gods of wood and stone have no power, but I'm still pondering on the living God of love." After a brief pause he asked, "Brother, is it possible to reconcile a God of peace and love with a life of war?"

"There are some righteous justifications for war," George assured. "I wouldn't fear the wrath of God in defending land, homes, wives, and children from the hands of our enemies and in preserving our rights of liberty and freedom to worship God according to our desires.[4] Just wars are generally defensive, to protect the innocent or to recover that which has been taken. There may be just cause to bring down oppressive rulers and to establish and preserve peace and liberty.[5] Anger and vengeance are not just causes. The holy word commands, 'Let not anger rule thy mind, for the wrath of man worketh not the righteousness of God.'[6] Anger clouds judgment in these matters, leading to bad decisions, for the spirit of contention is not of God but is of the devil, who is the father of contention. He stirs up the hearts of men to contend with anger, one with another.[7] We must seek to do the will of the Lord, acting in mercy to relieve oppression and expand peace and freedom, for God is faithful to those who serve Him."

*****

"The tour of the region was enlightening," Constantine remarked to George. "I'll back your proposal to drive out the Visigoth raiders, expanding and stabilizing the borders of the empire and securing peace for the people. I'm appointing you administrator of the outpost. We'll work together to secure the region. Your century will join in the battle duty rotation."

*****

Prior to one battle, a young soldier named Andronicus approached George. He was a village survivor who demonstrated skill in weapons training and was added as a recruit to George's century. "Will God be on our side in this battle?" he asked in simple humility.

Putting a gentle hand on the anxious young man's shoulder, George responded, "My concern is not whether God is on our side. My greatest concern is to be on God's side.[8] You would do well to seek the will of God and battle for His purposes. Battle for peace, not for dominance. If we are serving God's purposes, He will be for us, and if God be for us, who can be against us?"[9]

"How can I seek God that I might know His will?" Andronicus asked earnestly.

George smiled encouragingly, "Pray with all your heart for wisdom and understanding. When you understand reverence for the Lord, you will find the knowledge of God. For the Lord gives wisdom, and out of His mouth comes knowledge and understanding. He lays up sound wisdom for the righteous. He is a shield to them that walk uprightly before Him. He keeps the paths of judgment and preserves the way of His saints. Persevere in this course and you will understand God's righteousness, judgment, equity, and every good path."[10]

"But will God preserve me in the battle?" Andronicus persisted anxiously.

"I don't know everything, but I know enough to continue in faith on the path God has prepared for me," George replied. "Would you rather be preserved in battle or resurrected in glory, never to die again?" George asked, pausing briefly before he continued. "For whether we live, we live unto the Lord. Whether we die, we die unto the Lord. Therefore, whether we live or die, we are the Lord's.[11] Knowing the Lord is my Helper, I will not fear what man shall do to me."[12]

After the young man had left, George sought solitude. Finding a quiet spot to be alone, he knelt and bowed his head. Reverently he pleaded, "O my God, I trust in Thee. Let me not be ashamed. Let not mine enemies triumph over me. Let none that wait on Thee be ashamed."[13]

*****

Most Royal and Honorable Narseh,

Our nation has been on the precipice of ruin with weak leadership since the death of your brother, Bahram, nearly 20 years ago. These charges are not directed against any in your honorable family, but they are directed at the ministers who have manipulated Bahram II from his ascension to the throne as an infant to his passing last year. These ministers are traitors to the people and to heaven. After these infidels lost Armenia to the Romans seven years ago, we had hoped that Bahram II would awaken to their treachery and throw off their yoke, reigning in his own right. Now these same cowardly puppet-masters conspire to hold power by acting in the name of the infant, Bahram III. We honor your family, but we are unwilling to bear the rule of traitors over another manipulated child. We demand a mighty leader who will throw off this yoke of weakness and restore dignity to our nation. As the son of our great monarch and the brother of two other monarchs, you have a rightful claim to the throne. If you accept it, we swear allegiance to you as our new ruler. We swear to support you in removing the cowards who have dishonored your family and this people. We defer to your wisdom in the disposition of your great-nephew, Bahram III. We look to you for salvation from the shame of Persia.

Narseh read the letter carefully again. Though it was unsigned, he was confident of the identities of the main conspirators. *I feel much of what they describe,* he thought. *With their help, I can reclaim my honor and the dignity of his nation...and I will!*

*****

Late in the fall, George spoke with Sipatros. "Rome will purchase all the excess of your harvest. If you have any extra livestock, we will purchase that as well. If there is another market where you can get a better price, let me know and we will match that price."

Sipatros breathed deeply and easily as he reflected on the choice the surviving villagers had made to stay and rebuild. "Our people relied heavily on your word and you have been true to it. As you promised, the Roman army has come in force, clearly establishing a permanent presence in this outpost. Defenses have been restored and greatly improved with stone walls replacing the wooden pickets and with additional watch towers added to provide better warnings of enemy attacks. Paying work had been available for those in need. Many of our men have taken wives from the widows of nearby villages, restoring family structures and taking in orphans. We've been blessed with a bountiful harvest. We've had peace in the village since the day you arrived. You have labored diligently for the safety and welfare of our people, inspiring them to maintain their liberty, strengthening the villagers and your armies in preparation for battle. We have hope for the future and it's easy to see how our lives have been blessed. We're grateful to you."

"I feel the weight of my responsibility for this people," George replied. "I'm determined to prepare them to support their liberty, lands, and people. By continually seeking righteousness and peace, God will bless us for our obedience, preserving us from our enemies and prospering us in the land. I trust God to reveal how we should defend ourselves that we might be delivered. My heart glories in doing good and resisting iniquity, not in the shedding of blood. Because this people have humbled themselves and dealt righteously with all men, God has preserved us and we have been highly favored of the Lord, enjoying peace and prosperity.[14] All thanks should be given to Him."

"I have questions about your God," the old man ventured. "I've heard of your faith, and I've seen your character shown forth in deeds. When we met I was so far from faith in a just God that I had no desire to believe, but now I see something in you that urges me to learn more. At the risk of disunity, may I ask more about your faith?"

"Honest inquiry is no threat to unity," George assured. "Sincere inquiry makes men stronger. Hypocrites bear terror in their hearts sent by God, because they are void of understanding. Some might think they are united, but their hearts are divided, because they are devoid of wisdom.[15] The insincere and unbelieving man cannot unite with other men. Only in a world of sincere men is unity possible, and there, in the long run, it is as good as certain.[16] Ask what you will."

"How can I learn more of your God and know what is true?" Sipatros asked.

"Believe, obey in faith, and then know," George responded encouragingly. "Believe in God. Believe that He is and that He has created all things, both in heaven and in earth. Believe that He has all wisdom and power. Believe that men do not understand all the things which the Lord can understand. Believe that you must repent of your sins and forsake them. Humble yourself before God, and ask in sincerity of heart that He would forgive you. Believe all these things and do them. If you have come to know the goodness of God and have tasted of His love, being filled with His joy, humble yourself in the depths of your soul, call on the Lord daily and stand firm in the faith of Jesus Christ who has come. If you do this, you shall always rejoice and be filled with the love of God, always retaining a remission of your sins. You will grow in the knowledge of the glory of Him that created you and in the knowledge of that which is just and true."[17]

"Was the destruction of our village the punishment of God?" the old man asked earnestly.

"I don't think so," George replied. "But I can't see as God sees, to judge righteously the hearts of men. However, I know that those who pass from mortality to the eternal world will surely reap the rewards of their works, whether they were good or evil.[18] God's punishments endure for the wicked. But for the repentant righteous, the punishments of God are overcome through the atoning sacrifice of His Son, which brings mercy and healing to His people. Thus, the righteous are received into peace and rest. The judgments of God come upon many because they reject the laws of righteousness and neglect their brethren. However, those who go forth in the strength of unity and righteousness before the Lord shall overcome their enemies.[19] We mourn the loss of our kindred, yet we rejoice in the hope that they are raised to dwell at the right hand of God in a state of endless happiness because of the light and mercy of Christ."[20]

*****

Near the conclusion of the fighting season, Constantine called George to his quarters. "I'll be reporting to the Emperor soon," he said. "I trust he'll be pleased with the great successes we've had in battle. You've led your century well. They've performed every word of command with exactness. They are firm and undaunted before the enemy, administering death to all who oppose them. They've fought valiantly for you. Their reputation for overcoming opposing forces is powerful, curbing the ambitions of many enemies. They shall fare well in my report."

"They are faithful, trusting that God will preserve and deliver them,"[21] George observed.

"It's no surprise that you've found favor with your men," Constantine added. "Your might and success inspire them. It seems as if your words and counsel are consistently honored by God.[22] Your men believe that God is with you as everything committed to your hand has prospered. Others of like character and faith still seek assignment under your command. You've also found favor in the eyes of the villagers. They support you in all your works."[23]

*****

Diocletian and Galerius listened carefully to Constantine's report outlining the success of his legion in stabilizing the northern borders of the Danube River region. "Your conquests come as a pleasant surprise," the Emperor praised. "I had expected you to simply restore the outpost, but you've given us a great advantage for the coming year. We will position our forces for the winter and you will accompany me to Sirmium to pass the winter and prepare the new recruits for the spring. Galerius, you will retain command of the northwest provinces. You will also take command of the legions in the northeast that have been reporting to me and to Constantine."

"As you command, my Lord," Galerius agreed. "Is that all?"

"Just one more thing," Constantine replied to Galerius. "I recommend that you promote George to millenary. If you would like any other recommendations, just let me know."

"George, eh?" Galerius sighed. "Your report of his dominance in battle was very impressive. You think he's capable of managing ten centurions and a thousand men under his command? I'll think about it."

"Thank you," Constantine said as he left to prepare for his journey with the Emperor.

When they were alone, Galerius waited for comment. "George is dominant in battle," Diocletian offered, "but I'm even more impressed with his strategic planning. His first assessment of the northern outpost and his proposal for gaining control of the region proved completely accurate."

"So he's a leader," Galerius admitted. "But I'm wary of his alliance with Constantine. We don't need the whelp establishing his own base of loyal subordinate officers. I support the promotion with the stipulation that George be assigned to a legion commander other than Constantine."

"Fair enough!" Diocletian smiled. "Although, they have had incredible and inspiring success together. If I only had a son like one of them," he added wistfully, chafing his Caesar.

*****

Upon receiving his new contingent of soldiers in the northeast, George began a review of the men under his command. As he personally interviewed each of his centurions he explained, "It's important for each man to know the leaders who commanded him, to minimize any hesitation in following orders in the heat of battle. It's just as important for leaders to learn each man's motivations, and who they respect enough to follow with courage and faith into battle." He monitored the men in their sparring sessions, gauging their combat skills and counseling with his centurions on how to help their men improve.

He also met personally with each of the soldiers in his millennium, making careful notes of each man's religious convictions, if any, and what leave he sought for worship each week, offering reasonable support to believers of all faiths. Gradually, he reorganized his centuries based on religious faith and combat skill, encouraging all groups to worship faithfully as prescribed by their own beliefs. To his centurions he gave strict orders, "Let there be no compulsion in religion. Truth will stand for itself against error. Whoever rejects evil and believes in God has grasped the most trustworthy hand hold that never breaks."[24]

*****

"My lord," Tertius began, "Nereus has assigned me as your aid and scribe. Here are my orders for your review."

Thus far, George had been keeping his own records of military activity and writing his own reports. With his expanded responsibilities, he could see how a capable assistant could improve the efficiency of his work. "What are your skills and abilities?" he asked.

Tertius swallowed hard. "I'm not much with weapons, unless you count the quill pen as one."

"Oh, I do!" George responded emphatically. "I can defend myself against the sword. It's the poisoned pen that has me in mortal fear. Can you write as fast as I normally speak?"

Relaxing a little, Tertius replied, "Yes, sir, I most certainly can. And it's readable. More important, I can keep confidences. I'm very capable as an accountant and quartermaster. And I'll keep your records and letters perfectly organized and accessible."

"You sound too good to be true," George smiled. "We'll see about that. Is there some reason your prior commander agreed to let you go?"

"Perhaps," Tertius hesitated. "No one has charged me to keep this in confidence so I'll tell you. I'm a Christian. Nereus was annoyed with that. In fact, he and some of the millenaries have heard about your support for religious faith among the men. Some appreciate the support for religious convictions, but most just scoff at religious practices. Many of the other leaders are looking for chances to rid themselves of the prudish believers, as they refer to them."

George raised his eyebrows and looked at Tertius. "Welcome to the new millennium," he said. "It sounds like bargaining time is upon us. Prepare to take notes. Here is a list of men I don't want under my command. Add to it any in our millennium with recent disciplinary issues, the angry and sullen, those lusting for battle, and those prone to liquor. Take this list and trade these men out for men of faith, any faith. Listen carefully and keep notes of other men of faith for future reference. We'll consider our next move after the first exchange is complete."

"Yes, sir!" Tertius replied. "There is one soldier I know of who professes to believe in both the Roman gods and the Christian God. Shall we take him?" he asked.

George paused, glancing briefly toward heaven. Returning his gaze to Tertius he said, "No. Not him. The man who worships all gods has no true faith in any God, for God is not the author of confusion. We want men who believe God is good, and who act in righteousness to please Him. We don't want men who believe their god has power and simply seek his favor so they can control and abuse others. A false man merely struggles to believe that he believes, but he does not. False beliefs lead to rationalization and to immorality. There is no point in men praying to a God they do not know, who is a stranger to their hearts. Therefore, we must begin to teach men of faith of the true and living God they worship. Line upon line they can learn to be obedient to all truth. Just as physical preparation for battle saves lives in combat, so does spiritual preparation. While the will to win in battle is important, the will to prepare is more important. I have no doubt that those who are faithful believers in truth and righteousness shall know the truth of God by the Spirit, for He persuades men to do good."[25]

*****

Beloved Gregor:

With the blessings of the Lord, I have survived my first year of battle. I've been promoted to millenary which I appreciate. However, I am sad that my assignment has taken me away from Sipatros and his people, and Constantine. Yet I know the Lord is mindful of me. He will light my path forward. I now report to Nereus, commander of the Second Italica legion. He reports directly to Galerius Caesar. Our base of operation is at Lauriacum, in the northeast province of Noricum. We are located where the Enns River enters the Danube. I'm grateful my promotion came at the end of the fighting season, giving me all winter to prepare my men to serve effectively together. I wish I could have come home and passed the winter with you but duty calls. Perhaps next year. Give my love to all, especially Callidora.

   Always faithful, Brother!
– George

*****

"The task is complete, my Lord," the messenger reported to Narseh. "The treasonous ministers have all been captured and executed, and the child is no more. Your words have inspired the dignity of the Persian nation. Support for you and your cause have become dominant."

"Excellent," Narseh replied. "Now we begin preparations to deal with the Romans!"

****

CHAPTER TWENTY-ONE
The Word in Vision

Northeast Frontier, Eastern Roman Empire
294 AD

"In a dream, in a vision of the night, when deep sleep falleth upon men... then He openeth the ears of men, and sealeth their instructions..."[1]
Job 33:15-16

****

"We aren't ready yet!" Narseh declared, silencing the clamor of the hawks. "We will not begin that which we cannot finish, lest our end becomes worse than our beginning. It requires more to wage an offensive campaign than a defensive one so we must gather resources and make careful plans to maintain that which we conquer."

Sensing wisdom and strength, his ministers asked, "What would you have us do?"

"We must prepare for the confrontation with Rome by gathering the men, materials, and wealth that will be required to restore pride to this nation," Narseh replied. "Further, we must prepare the minds and hearts of our people for great sacrifice and great glory. We will suppress the memory of weak leadership, erasing 'Bahram' from all public monuments. We will reclaim the heritage of my father, Shapur I, who sacked the Roman stronghold of Antioch in Syria, capturing, torturing, and executing their Emperor, Valerian. These images will inspire our people." After a brief pause, he added, "Send the Romans our treaty tribute for the year. That should mute their concerns and enhance the element of surprise for us when we attack."

*****

Most Noble Emperor Galerius, Caesar of the Eastern Empire:
I have word from Maximian that Constantius continues to add to his army, which is already the largest in the empire. It seems his rapid success against Carausius and his Frankish allies in Gaul has yielded tens of thousands of volunteers to his banner. There is no question of his commanding presence, but his celebrated reputation even among the soldiers in our armies is a serious concern. My determination to keep a

tether on Constantine grows. We must retain him as leverage to dampen any unsanctioned ambitions from Constantius. Constantine will remain with me this season fighting the Sarmatians. You must return to the eastern provinces west of Nicodemia to monitor Constantius and his army. Fare well my brother.
    Always faithful!
– Emperor Diocletian Augustus

*****

"We have orders to capture a walled town north of the Danube," Nereus announced to his millenaries. "An Alamanni tribe held this town till near the end of the last fighting season when they were overrun by a semi-nomadic band of Carpiani. I don't think they've planned on us."

*****

    Vlad, the Carpiani leader, called his top four officers to counsel together. "When we conquered this town, we knew the Romans had posted a garrison just south of the Danube River. We thought this would deter the Alamanni and they would abandon the town with the Romans so close. As enemies to the Alamanni and located north of the Danube, we expected the Romans to ignore us. We were right about the Alamanni, but wrong about the Romans. Our scouts report they have deployed a legion north of the Danube. With 3,000 to 5,000 men approaching our gates, we anticipate an attack. Now we must decide our own course.
    "I say we should stay. I've had my eye on this town for a long time now. It's a good location inside thick stone walls and with a deep cool well. With these stone walls, ample fresh water, and our current provisions, we could outlast a Roman siege for an entire fighting season. We're at the very edge of the frontier. If we hold this town, and make the Romans pay a high price for their attempts to conquer it, they may decide it's not worth taking. It could become a stronghold for us and a secure base for our raiding parties in the future. It'll cost us less lives to maintain this town than to retake it if we abandon it now. With our superior fighting skills, and a fortified stone wall, we can win this battle."
    Zelimir considered the matter and then spoke, "We can defend this town at the cost of many lives, or we can abandon it and avoid the coming legion, plundering villages in our path as we've always done. If we choose to defend the town, our men will be outnumbered, and any

path for retreat will be cut off once the battle is joined."

Kostya spoke cautiously, "We have sacked many villages lately, amassing much wealth and capturing many women for our pleasure. It will be easier to assimilate these women if we keep them in the walled town until they are pregnant and feeling dependent on us. I'm proud of our fighting skills, but I'm concerned that this time our pride might cost us our lives. Being outnumbered is one thing, but if instead of just laying siege the Romans attack and breach the gate as we did, this legion appears too strong for us to survive. The town's walls are a great advantage, but they are insufficient to assure our victory. We must have a plan we all believe can succeed, or we need to abandon the town before we get slaughtered."

"I have a plan," Vlad assured. "Though we'll be outnumbered, we won't be outmanned. Our fighters have all been bred for battle. Our code, which requires that we put to death our female babies, has been a great benefit to our people, motivating our young men to prepare for battle, so they can gain wives through warfare and conquest as they must. Many of these Roman soldiers are mere peasant boys who don't know how to use the swords they hold."

"Although they'll have many untried soldiers at the beginning of the fighting season, they'll have many others, including their leaders, who won't be so green," Kostya stated. "Once the Romans get a small group through the gate, we can be sure they'll press to keep it open."

"The walls will provide much more security than they did for the Alamanni," Vlad reassured. "We were only able to take the town by seizing the gate with a surprise attack against a people who were too casual about their security. They thought they were safe and would never be attacked within their thick stone walls. The main gate to the east of the town is the only major point of vulnerability. If the Romans breach it, we could work that to our advantage."

"How can we do that?" Kostya countered.

"Because the square opens up just inside the gate, spreading out in all directions, we can maintain superior numbers in combat over any invading force within the gate," Vlad said. "The square provides very little cover for attacking forces and close combat is our greatest strength."

"To succeed we would have to control the flow of enemies through the gate?" Kostya mused.

"We can do that if we prepare," Vlad responded. "We can reinforce the gates with massive stone blocks set back a few feet behind them toward the hinges. These will prevent the gates from fully opening, restricting the flow of men in and out. With archers on the walls keeping the Roman cavalry back, we can allow small groups of soldiers to enter the gate. We can beat them one group at a time. And then what will happen?" Vlad probed.

"If we can't close the gate, we will kill many of the Romans as they come into the square, but eventually they will take control of it," Zelimir concluded.

"If the gate stays open, the Romans will overwhelm our fighters and slaughter us!" Lel responded in anxious agreement.

"Then what will happen?" Vlad pressed.

Lel sighed in distress and responded, "At that point, what would it matter? We'd all be dead."

"But then what will happen?" Vlad persisted.

"The Romans will loot the town, stealing our treasures and ravishing our women," Lel replied.

"While the Roman soldiers are ravishing our women, what will happen to their weapons and armor?" Vlad asked with growing excitement.

"The Romans will lay aside their weapons and armor as they ravish our women," Lel responded.

"Exactly!" Vlad exclaimed with great satisfaction, surprising the other men. Finally, Vlad posed his real question. "Once the Romans have discarded their weapons and armor to satisfy their lusts, what will happen if we suddenly come back to life?"

"What do you mean, come back to life?" Lel asked, thoroughly confused.

"We stand up alive again, fully armed, with swords and shields in hand, and rejoin the battle," Vlad responded, his excitement barely contained.

"We would…destroy the Roman soldiers before they could rearm?" Lel guessed tentatively.

"Exactly!" Vlad crowed. "With our young men as a deception and our women as bait, we can win. We'll have our young men massed just inside the gate to defend the town. Our most seasoned fighting men will be hidden in the barns at the west end of the town for a surprise counter-attack. Our young men will be expecting the counter-attack once the gate is breached, while they are still fighting, but that would be too soon. We'll let the young men take the loss, allowing enough time for the Romans to disarm before we make our counter-attack. At that point, we'll slaughter the Roman soldiers and recover any spoils they have seized. We can eliminate any women who've been violated by the Romans, so we don't subject ourselves to the soldiers' diseases. Then we will loot their treasury and armory, and take their provisions!" Vlad waited cautiously for the reactions of his most trusted men.

"This plan…could work," Lel admitted cautiously. "I like this town and its fortified walls. It's a good location for us, with a good water supply. I don't want to run. I say we stay and fight."

After a long pause, with no other counsel offered, Vlad concluded, "Then it's settled. Our best fighting men will hide themselves for the counter-attack. With promises of glory and honor, the young men will be ordered to defend the square and hold the gate to protect our town and the women and children.

"Once our sons have been defeated, the Romans will loot the town, laying aside their weapons and armor to ravish our women. When our enemies have blown their victory horn, we'll wait ten minutes before our hidden fighters begin the counter-attack. We should catch the legionnaires disarmed and possibly disrobed. We'll slaughter them and any women they have violated. With this town as our base of operations, we can easily replenish our people by stealing new wives from the other villages on the frontier."

Zelimir spoke cautiously, "I expect some of our best fighting men will refuse to follow this plan, preferring to stay and defend their wives and children rather than to survive themselves."

Vlad had thought of this as well. "All who reject our plan and refuse to join the counter-attack will be ordered to lead our young men, with assurances that the counter-attack won't be delayed. This should make our initial defenses as effective and convincing as possible. But we don't change the plan. When it's all over, the men of questionable loyalty and discipline will likely be eliminated, strengthening the core of our band."

The die is cast, Zelimir concluded. *Nothing I say now will change Vlad's mind so I'll hold my peace and do my best to conceal my emotions from my countenance. I disagree with this plan, but I won't desert my people in this conflict. Though I'm not ready to challenge Vlad for leadership of our people, it makes me boil to hear him claim that such a plan will make our people stronger. It makes no more sense than killing our own baby daughters.*

*****

"The late spring rains made crossing the Danube very treacherous and the muddy roads complicated our march to the town," Nereus admitted. "But I still need to know if your men are ready for battle."

Each of the millenaries responded the same. "My men are exhausted. They could use some rest, but we stand ready to obey our legion commander."

"Some may have hoped the enemy would run rather than fight it out, but even with an entire legion prepared to attack, the Carpiani have dug in behind the fortified walls of the town," Nereus noted. "These raiders are a strong, well-disciplined lot, but their numbers are not enough to win the day. I want this battle won promptly. Therefore, if the victory horn is sounded before the sixth hour, I authorize a full hour of looting thereafter. Otherwise there will only be a half hour of looting. With the rumors of Carpiani wealth, our men should have ample motivation."

*****

George had worked diligently to prepare his men for the coming battle, but most of that training had been physical. Now he focused on mental, emotional, and spiritual preparation. "Swords, shields, supper, sleep!" George shouted his command for the eve of attack. "A sword kept sharp and clean gives its master a faster swing, a cleaner cut, and a better chance of victory and life. Make sure your shield straps are sturdy and in good repair. Eat only lightly and get some rest. You'll need all your strength tomorrow. You won't know what the battle will require of you until it's over. If you are men of faith, you should draw near to your God, that your minds may be clear as you risk harm and death in the cause of your country."

George entered his tent alone and presented his own petition to God for strength and victory, and for the lives of his men and his enemies. After checking with his night watch one last time, he laid down to sleep.

*****

"George…George…George."

George heard the familiar voice call and responded, "I'm here."

As he focused on the figure drawing near to him and the voice calling his name, he recognized his father. George was amazed at his countenance. His father's whole being shone like lightning, with brilliant luminescence emanating from his whole body and also from his white linen robe. He was mature and lean, without the familiar limp in his stride.

"George, wilt thou serve the Lord with all thy heart?" Gerontius asked with reverent power.

"Yes, Father, I will," George replied. "But, how have you come to me?"

"My son, the miracles of God have not ceased, neither have angels ceased to minister unto the children of men. We are subject unto Him, to minister according to the word of His command, showing ourselves unto them of strong faith and a firm mind in every form of godliness."[2]

"How shall I serve the Lord, Father?" George inquired.

"Heed this warning! Fulfill thy military duties, but do not participate in the looting. Do not consent to sinners who entice thee to conspire with promises of precious riches for spoils. My son, walk not in the way with them. Refrain from their path, for their feet run to evil, and they make haste to shed blood. By their evil, they spill their own blood. So are the ways of every one that is greedy of gain.[3] Thou shalt not ravish any whom thou hast conquered, and thou shalt command thy men to refrain from this evil. In the coming battle, those who loot the town and ravage the precious daughters of God shall be destroyed. Command thy men to pursue only righteous conduct in battle.

"George, thou hast been chosen to assist the Lord in His work of relieving men and women from lives of oppression. Obey the Lord in all His commands. Protect the virtue of the innocent daughters of God. Rescue and shield them from abuse. If thou art obedient, thy name will be spoken of, for good among many nations.[4] If thou wilt abide in the Lord, thou shalt receive power over evil men, beasts, and dragons, to relieve and protect the oppressed, especially God's humble and virtuous daughters. Abide in Him, that when He shall appear, thou mayest have confidence, and not be ashamed before Him at His coming.[5] Trifle not with sacred things. Share thy visions only with men of faith among the believers."[6]

*****

When George awoke, his father was gone, but the clarity of the vision remained. Filled with an intensity he had rarely felt before, he ordered his men awake a half hour early so he could give them additional final commands prior to battle.

With his men assembled, George began his solemn charge. "My valiant soldiers of the Roman Republic, I give you your final charge in preparation for battle. Put aside your wine, for it clouds the mind. Don't allow anger, greed, or lust to guide your actions, for surely these lead to captivity and destruction. Keep your minds and your senses clear and be your brothers' keepers. Together we shall conquer, and save each other from destruction. Above all, I command you not to engage in the looting of this people or the ravishing of its women. At the signal of the victory horn, I command every man to return immediately to the town square, inside the main gate, and form ranks. I'll meet you there with further orders. I assure you that each man who obeys will receive his share of the spoils of our victory, but you must follow my commands with exactness or you shall be destroyed. Now, deploy to your assigned attack positions."

Surprised by the order, Florian[7] and a few other centurions cautiously sought more understanding of George's commands. "Never before have the men been denied the privilege of looting a town that has refused the legion's command to surrender," he noted.

Looking over the few men who had approached, George noted they were all men of faith so he quickly shared the truth of the matter. "I was visited by my father in a dream last night. He told me to protect the innocent women of this town or we would all be destroyed. As Christ died to make men and women holy, it is our sacred duty to live to make them free to worship God and work out their own salvation.[8]

"The Spirit of God bids me to heed my father's counsel. If we are obedient and God be for us, who can be against us?[9] My brethren, let us cheerfully do all things that lie in our power, and then may we stand still, with the utmost assurance, to see the salvation of God, and for His arm to be revealed.[10] With the Lord as our helper, we shall fear no man.[11] Those who strive in God's cause, He will certainly guide to safe paths, for truly God is with those who do right.[12] See that you and your men strictly obey my commands." With that, the centurions returned to their men and led them to their battle positions.

*****

"It didn't take long for word of your heavenly dream to spread among the men," Florian noted. "Some men believe your father appeared, giving you direction in your management of this battle. These are humble and submissive to God, feeling the still small voice of the Spirit confirming your counsel. They don't know what manner of protection will come from their obedience to your orders, but they are confident God is with their leader. Therefore, they appear inclined to heed your commands with exactness.

"A few others are superstitious and fear your vision. Still others scoff at the suggestion of inspired direction. They weigh in their minds their desires to loot against the probable penalties for violating the direct command you've given to reassemble at the main gate and await further orders immediately after the sound of the victory horn."

Concerned over the dissatisfaction among his men, George quickly gathered all his centurions and reiterated his prior commands so there could be no misunderstanding. "Let us put our trust in God and He will extend the arm of mercy to us, for thus does He work with His power in all cases among the children of men."[13]

"What about this vision we've heard about?" one of the centurions asked.

"There's no time to debate the issue now. Obey my commands with exactness and all will be made clear after our victory," George responded urgently, closing further discussion. Briefly he pondered how he would explain the matter later. He knew he'd seen a vision, and though he might be questioned, challenged, and reviled for speaking of it, this did not destroy the reality of the vision. He'd seen a vision. He knew it, and he knew that God knew it, and he could not deny it, lest by so doing he should offend God and come under condemnation, subjecting himself and all his men to destruction.[14] "Put your trust in God, my brothers. Be faithful in all my commands," he whispered to himself.

*****

As the centurions returned to their posts, one veteran soldier asked Florian, "Do you think George is wrong? Has he gone too far in denying the men their right of looting the town?"

"First, I don't think against my orders; I obey," Florian responded sternly. "Second, looting is not a right, but a privilege among the spoils of war. Besides, if George has had a vision from God, what could he do more wrong than rejecting the sign and turning away from it?"[15]

*****

George dropped to his knees as the moment for attack approached. He wished to be alone, but that was not an option and, at this point, he didn't care who saw him praying for deliverance. With several of his centurions looking on, he pled with the Lord vocally in prayer. "Almighty God, I put my trust in Thee. Let me never be ashamed. Deliver me in Thy righteousness.[16] Have mercy and spare my life that I may be an instrument in Thy hands to save and preserve Thy people.[17] I plead with Thee to strengthen me and my men with the arm of Thy power and deliver us out of the hands of our enemies this day. Give us strength that we might retain our lives and better serve Thee and Thy people, according to our faith in Thy Son, Jesus Christ.[18] Amen."

"Does God answer, my lord?" Tertius asked quietly.

"God speaks peace to my soul, strengthening my faith, leading to hope for deliverance," George replied. "The Spirit provides assurance that God will deliver me and my obedient men."[19]

*****

At the legion commander's signal, the attack began. As anticipated, the town walls presented a formidable challenge to the Roman army. However, with determination they repeatedly attacked the main gate until they were able to splash it with oil and set fire to it. In response, the Carpiani opened one side of the gate in a feigned attempt to douse the flames. Their real intent was to tempt the Romans into sending foot soldiers through the gate, knowing the mounted soldiers would have difficulty following as their horses would shy away from the flaming gate.

Though many small groups of Roman soldiers went through the partially opened gate, none were able to secure it until George's millennium made its attack. As they beat back the Carpiani and held the gate, a flood of other soldiers flowed through the narrow passage. By the time the square was cleared, many of the soldiers from the initial attacks had been killed or wounded.

Inside the town walls, George's men worked aggressively to secure the square and reinforce the ranks of soldiers battling the enemy for control of the buildings. However, the Carpiani truly were a host of warriors. They fought like dragons, inflicting heavy losses on the legion before finally being overcome. When the victory horn sounded, the majority of the remaining Roman soldiers immediately began looting and ravaging. There was a lot of treasure for the taking, and many frightened women and children terrified by the panic and chaos.

Most of George's command remembered his orders and quickly reassembled near the main gate inside the town. "Florian!" George called out. "Take your century and tend to the wounded, but don't leave the square. After you've seen to the soldiers, see what you can do for the Carpiani. Many of them seem too young to die like this."

"Yes, sir!" Florian acknowledged.

As they watched their comrades discard their humanity in lustful aggression, there was an uncertainty among George's men. But true to his promise, he had assembled with his millennium, so none dared violate his commands. Still the muffled whispers were heard, "He promised us our share of the spoils. He'd better deliver."

****

CHAPTER TWENTY-TWO
The Spoils of Battle

Northeast Frontier, Eastern Roman Empire
294 AD

"Better it is to be of an humble spirit with the lowly, than to divide the spoil with the proud."[1]
Proverbs 16:19

****

Thus far the battle had played out just as Vlad had foreseen. In the barns at the west end of town the hidden Carpiani fighters had heard the Roman legion's victory horn. Within minutes, the deep-toned yells of anguished men in battle had been drowned out by higher pitched cries of frightened women and children. Mixed in among their screams were the abusive commands and occasional cruel laughter of the pillaging soldiers.

The hidden Carpiani warriors waited, silent and still. Sweat emerged on a few anxious brows. After what seemed an eternity, the hushed command was given, "Begin the counter-attack!" Quickly and quietly, Vlad and his men spread out, moving from the back end of town forward. Their plan had been laid carefully and it was executed with swift precision. They moved rapidly from building to building, favoring the alleys and back entrances, hiding their own numbers and avoiding open confrontations. As they had anticipated, most of the Roman soldiers they encountered were now disarmed and distracted, looting the town and ravishing the women. Vlad and his men caught most of the Roman soldiers off guard and unprepared, sometimes literally bare. Methodically they isolated and eliminated the enemy soldiers as they cleared each building, moving quickly and efficiently east toward the town square.

As Vlad entered his own quarters, he found Nereus, commander of the Roman legion, disarmed and attempting to force himself upon one of his young wives. With his rage for blood unleashed, Vlad picked up the commander's own sword and thrust it down, driving it through Nereus and the terrified woman pinned beneath him.

*****

George's men remained in their ranks near the main gate, standing at attention, awaiting orders, just as he had commanded. After nearly fifteen minutes of tense waiting, amid the screams of women and children alike, George noted from the back of the town a rising tide of screaming men yelling, "Help!" and "It's a trap!"

"The screams of our men betray the enemy!" George declared. "The battle rages on! Sound the battle horn to arms! Stay close together in patrols of five men or more. Move out through the town and clear it from the east gate to the west wall. We must locate the enemy and destroy their forces! Follow me now!"

With the main force of his soldiers following closely, George hurried towards the sounds of the screaming men. At each intersection he issued orders to his centurions, dividing his forces to address all threats, carefully clearing the buildings and alleys as they advanced in order to avoid being ambushed themselves. Soon they met the Carpiani fighters.

Vlad's men were surprised at the sudden approach of hundreds of fully armed and well disciplined Roman soldiers. The Carpiani men hadn't anticipated this, but they knew what to do. Immediately they formed ranks to take this battle head-on. Believing that victory was their only chance for survival, the Carpiani fighters exerted themselves with a fury of desperation, fighting like dragons for their prey.[2]

Through the few minutes of intense fighting, George's well trained soldiers, with their superior weapons and defensive armor, were able to prevail, where many of their disarmed comrades had been killed. George's men killed or subdued most of the Carpiani leaders in less time than it had taken the remaining disarmed Roman soldiers to stop their abuses, dress and re-arm.

Zelimir could clearly see the Carpiani had lost the battle. Instinctively he ordered, "Retreat! Retreat! Retreat!" But there was nowhere to go. The Carpiani were surrounded by Roman soldiers. Still, the order had prompted men on both sides to step back momentarily to regroup.

Observing their predicament and noting the loss of many of their leaders, even the seasoned Carpiani fighters were struck with fear. Seeing this, George commanded his men, "Legionnaires! Stop the bloodshed![3] Withdraw five paces! Weapons ready for battle!"

Next, he stepped ahead of his line of soldiers to address the remaining Carpiani men. "Enemies of Rome, I am George, a commander in the Roman army. You see that God has given you into our hands. We have power to destroy you or to save you as we choose. Yet we don't want to shed your blood.[4] Enough precious blood has been spilt this day, on both sides. Now, you have a choice between peace and life, or battle and death. Wisdom and understanding support the path of peace and life.[5] If you want to live, you must come forward and surrender your weapons as a sign that you choose peace and life, rather than battle and death. If you surrender your weapons now, you will become our prisoners, but you will be treated fairly. I give you my word, as God is my witness. However, if you refuse to surrender, we will rejoin the battle and spill your blood to the end. Now the choice is yours. Submit or die!"

The Carpiani warriors were conflicted. The older ones warned against Roman treachery and torture, which were common. However, many of the younger men were certain if they didn't surrender they would be killed in this battle. Some spoke in favor of laying their weapons down on the ground at George's feet. Others appeared intent on rejecting the promise of life and taking their chances, holding fast to the weapons of their rebellion.

As if on a signal, two of the most powerful Carpiani warriors rushed at George with their swords drawn. Moving easily, George brought up Ascalon and deflected their attacks, inflicting mortal wounds to each man with his own counter-attacks. George's men rushed to assist, but the skirmish was already done. With a steady voice George commanded, "Hold your ranks men! So far only two Carpiani have chosen death. Let's wait and see what the others will choose."

The Carpiani, also surprised by the attacks, had immediately withdrawn several more steps from the Romans, raising their weapons in anticipation of the coming press of battle. Seeing George's reaction to the abrupt attack, and the result, Zelimir, the senior Carpiani commander in this battle, knew he must act now to protect his people. He stared intently at the young Roman commander, as if weighing his honor and integrity on some imaginary scale. Finally he stepped forward and turned to face his own men. Raising his voice, he spoke boldly. "My brothers, it's plain to see we are in the hands of the Romans. Our battle plan has failed, but there is no need for any more to die this day. The gods have given us into the hands of strangers. We should submit and obey, that we might live to die another day. Each of you must choose for himself, but I counsel you to accept the honor of this man's oath. Let us surrender our weapons now and live for our people, instead of dying for nothing."

Slowly Zelimir turned to face George. Deliberately he took two more steps forward. Calmly, he set his weapons down midway between his army and the imposing commander. Taking two steps back, he knelt down. Looking George steadily in the eyes he put his hands behind his head and called out, "I choose life. I submit myself to your honor and will."

Zelimir's actions were quickly followed by a disjointed chorus of voices echoing, "Life! Life! I choose life." Man by man the Carpiani came cautiously forward, weapons clanking as they struck the ground. Kneeling, they surrendered to George and the Roman army. The battle was over. The victory horn sounded again, but this time the Roman soldiers held to their ranks. There was no more chaotic looting or ravishing.

*****

At his command, George's men returned to gather near the east gate. "All your men who are still living have been brought to the square," Tertius reported. "Nearly all your men suffered wounds in this battle," he observed.

"But only those who disregarded my commands lost their lives," George noted. "Those who obeyed my commands stand fast in that liberty wherewith God has made them free, retaining their lives and their agency."

"The men marvel at their miraculous preservation!" Tertius declared. "Many are convinced of God's power. They want to learn of His statutes, judgments, and commandments. They hope that by obeying Him they might receive His favor and blessings continually."[6]

*****

"Tertius," George called out. "I need a report on the status of the other millenniums."

"The casualties are very high," Tertius replied. "The other four millenniums all fared poorly under the devastating Carpiani counter-attack. Their remnants are gathering into the square. They're anxious to be with friendly comrades after the terrors of the ambush. We've confirmed that Nereus and two of the five millenaries are among the dead. Their bodies, and the bodies of any centurions killed in the battle, are being brought to the square as confirmation of their deaths. Only your millennium has been substantially preserved."

Taking charge, George called his centurions together. "Blessed be the name of our God, for it is He that has done this great thing in delivering us from the hands of our enemies and preserving us this day that we might not perish.[7] Rejoice in His word, for in it we find life, our greatest spoil.[8] Now, we have work to do."

Quickly he divided the essential tasks among his men. "The first, third, and fourth centuries will secure the prisoners, tying their hands behind them and taking them to the square near the gate. First will lead out. The second, fifth, and sixth centuries will scour the town for any remaining enemy fighters still in hiding, and secure all discarded weapons. Fifth will lead out. The seventh and eighth centuries will gather any surviving Roman soldiers. See to their wounds and bring them to the town square to receive further care for their injuries. Eighth will lead out. The ninth and tenth centuries will bring all the Carpiani women and children to the square for care and protection. Florian, you and the ninth century will lead out. Go now, and be faithful!"

"Tertius, invite the other two millenaries to meet with me to coordinate our response to this tragedy," George instructed. "As the wounded soldiers are brought in for treatment, and the death toll is tabulated, keep me advised."

*****

Roman soldiers surrounded the perimeter of the entire square. Standing on the walkway of the wall, above the gate, George directed his men. "The square will be divided into four quarters. The enemy fighters will be restrained in the northeast quarter, against the town wall. The southeast quarter of the square will serve as an assembly area for the Roman soldiers awaiting dispatch. The southwest quarter will be for the care of wounded Roman soldiers. The Carpiani women and children will be organized in the northwest quarter." Next, George gave instructions for the care of the wounded soldiers and made allowances for the Carpiani women to care for the wounded of their people.

As he came down from the wall, George met with Florian and ordered, "See that food rations from the Roman army are provided to all in the square. I know the Carpiani have their own food, but with the devastation of the battle, I'm concerned about their ability to secure more food on their own. I want to make sure the surviving women won't have Rome to blame if they are going to see their children starve in the coming months. I'm determined to help these people survive and succeed, but their success will depend primarily upon their obedience and willingness to work. Besides, the Roman army lost so many men in the battle that our food supplies are now excessive and would just be a burden to store or haul."

"As you command," Florian replied.

*****

With immediate needs addressed, George met with the other two millenaries to reorganize their legion. In gratitude and humility the officers confessed, "We know your leadership has saved our lives and the lives of our surviving men. We join the men in respect for you and your vision. Therefore, although you are the junior millenary, we offer you promotion to the rank of legion commander. We swear to submit to your commands in all our military duties and privileges."

George thought back on the words of his father and how some decisions were simply a function of which leader happened to have the largest loyal army at the time. George had the largest loyal army. However, he didn't doubt the sincerity of his fellow millenaries. More importantly, he felt the hand of the Lord in this responsibility. "I accept this command and honor on condition that in unity you present me to the full assembly of legionnaires and they affirm my appointment by acclamation."

*****

There was little surprise as this battlefield promotion was presented. Without hesitation the legionnaires acclaimed George as their new legion commander. They all knew they owed their lives to his wise leadership. Also, they were genuinely inspired with confidence by his stature, ability, and bearing. They trusted that he valued each of them individually, and that he was committed to protecting every life within his stewardship.

"Thank you for your support and confidence," George said to the assembly. "I name Florian as millenary in my stead. Florian, I charge you with reorganizing the men in your millennium under the remaining nine centurions. I hereby order the men of the first millennium to join the command of the second millenary. The men of the fourth millennium are ordered to join the command of the third millenary. These millenaries are directed to reorganize their commands, absorbing all the surviving men. As the legion is rebuilt, other promotions will be announced as the millenaries identify needs and as men prove themselves worthy of command."

*****

George was sober as he met with his millenaries. "I'm gravely concerned about the tragic toll this battle had taken on both sides. War is a terrible thing, but sometimes it is the only path to peace. Still, war remains an uncertain path. Unless we bind the wounded hearts, and especially the hearts of the innocent, we cannot achieve peace. However, I feel the greater urgency is to prepare everyone for a possible attack by the Alamanni or Sarmatians. This walled town is still a coveted prize on the frontier, and our defenses are possibly the weakest they will ever be.

"For the security of all, administration of the town will be organized into four work groups. The first group will guard the town square and the prisoners. The second group will handle all assignments outside the square but still within the town walls. The third group will handle all assignments outside the town walls including coordination of defenses and burial of the dead. The fourth group will be stationed in the town square, preparing and distributing food, and assisting any of the first three groups as needed. To support this administration, each millenary will divide his command into two main patrols. At any given time, four of the six patrols will cover the assignments, while the other two patrols are assigned to quarters for rest."

*****

Tertius appeared at George's side. "Your orders regarding the spoils of victory, Sir?"

"The spoils?" George responded numbly. "Pride goeth before destruction, and a haughty spirit before a fall. It is better to be of a humble spirit with the lowly, than to divide the spoil with the proud."[9]

"Excuse me?" Tertius asked, a little confused by George's response.

"Oh, nothing," George replied thoughtfully. "God has blessed the survivors with life and with the hope of peace and prosperity. These are the true spoils of victory and they will suffice. The division of treasure will have to wait. We have more important concerns to address now."

****

CHAPTER TWENTY-THREE
Pure Religion

Northeast Frontier, Eastern Roman Empire
294 AD

"Pure religion and undefiled before God and the Father is this, to visit the fatherless and widows in their affliction, and to keep himself unspotted from the world."[1]
James 1:27

****

The cost of the Roman victory had been enormous, but something else pressed more urgently upon George's mind. Calling all his millenaries and centurions together, he issued careful orders for the care of the women, children, and enemy combatant prisoners. "Our battle to win their confidence and loyalty has already begun, and our duty to care for the innocent is before the eyes of God. To remain undefiled before Him, we must minister to the fatherless and widows in their affliction and keep ourselves unspotted from the abuses of the world.[2] We must have charity for all those who are subject to us through the grace of God. Without charity, which is the pure love of Christ, we are nothing. With charity, we and this people can bear all things and endure all things, rejoicing in the truth, for charity never fails.[3] Unless we act according to the principles of righteousness, we can't free this people from oppression, and we jeopardize our ability to preserve ourselves and to strengthen our Republic."

*****

"We've got to bury the dead soon to curb the spread of diseases and to prevent the stench of death from covering the town," Florian urged. "The problem is that we don't have enough men to do that and all the other urgent tasks."

George considered the issue and replied, "You know, it's much easier to guard prisoners while they work. I suggest that we require the captured Carpiani combatants to labor for their food, first by burying all the dead, and then second, by helping to restore the town's defenses."[4]

"Excellent idea," Florian agreed. Turning to the combatant prisoners he ordered, "All able-bodied Carpiani men are now required to work for your food. The work will be hard but not abusive. To begin, we will organize you into work patrols to bury the dead. You will gather the bodies of those who have died in battle and lay them just outside the wall of the town in preparation for burial. Separate areas will be designated for the bodies of Roman soldiers and those of the Carpiani dead."

*****

George pondered on where the bodies should be buried, sensing it would be important. "The people will hold sacred the ground where we place their honored dead as long as the memory of those who have hallowed it remains," he told his millenaries. Turning to the soldiers and prisoners charged with the burials, he declared, "All our dead will be buried with respect, returning them to their mother earth, for God loves all His children. However, those who died without honor will not share the hallowed ground of our honored dead.

"The field of honor for burial will be just outside the town walls, to the sides of the main gate, on ground that must be crossed by any attackers. Such an attack across the graves of these honored dead should remind this people of the high price already paid for their liberty and security. Evil men and abusers shall not be buried in these fields of honor, but must be buried elsewhere. There's an alkali field a half mile southeast of town where all who are denied an honorable burial will be laid to rest, away from the fertile ground surrounding the town.

"The Roman soldiers who died with their armor on will be honored," George ordered. "But those who discarded their armor before they died, who spent the last ounce of their strength abusing the innocent, will be taken to the alkali field where they can be buried with dignity but without honor. May the memory of their dishonor pass quickly from our minds.

"After all the Roman dead are buried, the Carpiani may designate who among their own dead shall be honored by them in death and who should be forgotten for their evil."

*****

"My lord, they've found the Carpiani leader among the dead," Tertius reported excitedly. "His name is Vlad. He's wounded but will most likely survive.[5] He wore the scabbard of Nereus around his waist and the bloody sword lay nearby."

"Dress his wounds and see that he is restrained with the other prisoners," George ordered. "Then bring the legion commander's sword to me."

*****

Outside the wall, the bodies of the Roman soldiers were reviewed first, their names recorded and their personal effects secured for the next of kin. The Carpiani prisoners, in rotating four-man crews escorted by six soldiers, took turns burying the honored Roman dead immediately next to the wall by the gate. "Look lively men!" the centurion called to the burial patrols. "The Carpiani dead will only be honored in burial after all Roman dead have been buried."

After all the Roman dead had been buried, the Carpiani prisoners, a few at a time, were allowed to identify their dead and indicate who should be honored in burial and who should not. Anxious to establish a reminder for the people to inspire their future defense of the town, George chose an area a few paces further from the Roman burials for burial of the honored Carpiani dead. Noting that several Carpiani dead hadn't been claimed, he asked, "Are there none to claim these men?"

Zelimir responded, "These men were evil. They are despised by the people, who would drag them far away and leave their bodies to rot. If they are to be buried, you must order us to do it, but we ask that it be in a field of shame."

"They'll be buried with the respect and dignity given to all men, but away from the town in the alkali field where the abusive Roman soldiers were buried," George replied firmly.

*****

George watched carefully as the Carpiani began to bury their honored dead. "Each grave is started by the oldest next of kin," Zelimir explained. "Others who wish to honor the deceased are then allowed to help with the digging. When the grave depth is approved by the Roman guards those honoring the deceased help to place the body in the grave."

Silently, the families stood around the open graves, waiting. "What are the Carpiani waiting for?" George asked.

The centurion in charge of the burial detail responded quietly, "They've requested knives, and we've refused them."

"Why do they want knives?" George probed.

"I don't know," the centurion answered. "I didn't think we'd give the prisoners weapons, so I didn't ask."

Turning to Zelimir, George asked, "Why do the families want

knives?"

"Tradition," Zelimir replied. "The Carpiani have a custom among family and friends. They spill blood into the graves of the honored dead before the burial is complete. They'll use the knife to make a slight cut in their own hands so they can add a drop of blood to the blood of their dead, as a token of honor to their commitment, fulfilling a covenant to bleed for each other until death, further hallowing already sacred ground for the memory of those who live on."

"Thank you," George said. Calmly he walked toward the group surrounding the first Carpiani grave. The prisoners gave way at his approach. Peering into the grave he saw the lifeless body of a boy, perhaps fourteen or fifteen years old, who hadn't fully filled out in the shoulders. He looked at the faces of the family members and identified the mother. Silently, with tears rolling down her cheeks, her eyes met his and he felt his heart break. Drawing the dagger from his belt, George carefully pricked his thumb and let a drop of his own blood fall into the grave. Holding the blade, he extended the handle toward the grieving mother, who took the dagger, cut her thumb, and let a drop of her own blood fall.

"Centurion!" George called out, "I've given the Carpiani my dagger that they may honor their dead as they see fit. See that it's returned to me when the burials are complete."

"Yes, my lord!" was the stout reply.

Seeing his dagger had been used by all the mourners at the first grave and then passed to the family at the second, George picked up a shovel to help bury the boy he had honored.

*****

When all the dead were buried, George called all to assemble at the burial site of the honored dead. The Carpiani prisoners were heavily guarded, but it was important to George that they be witnesses and participants in all that would take place in turning their conquered people from death to life. In solemnity George began, "I speak first to my soldiers who have dishonored themselves by disarming in battle that they might abuse others. You who have survived have been delivered from your enemies; nevertheless, you are not excused in your disgraces. Return now to honor and tarnish yourselves no more lest the evil one lay claim upon you.[6]

"To all assembled I declare: our honored dead are buried in unity at the base of this wall, beside this gate. These stand as symbols of security and defense for this town and our people. But the walls and the gate cannot compare to the protection of God for those who honor Him. Any attacking enemies must cross this field in their advance, and in so doing they will call to our minds and hearts the sacred sacrifices of our fallen dead. We gather in a single assembly to dedicate this field of honor as the final resting place for those who have given their lives in honor for the causes of their people. As our futures are now bound together, it is fitting and proper that we do this together.[7]

"Though we dedicate this sacred place to those who have fallen, we have no power to consecrate this ground beyond the hallowing blood of the righteous on both sides, slain in this conflict. These honored dead have consecrated this ground far above our poor power to add or detract, for it truly is the innocent blood of the Righteous, unjustly spilt, which sanctifies the earth.[8]

"Though few may long remember our words, none should ever forget the deeds of these honored dead. Now it is for us, the living, to dedicate ourselves to the righteousness and honor for which these fallen dead have given their full devotion.[9]

"We also bid farewell to other fallen men who have been denied burial in this field of honor. These other men failed themselves and those who had claim upon them in this life, yet they are still received by their mother earth, and they are still loved by their Father God, who grieves that He cannot honor and glorify them because they have rejected His principles of righteousness.

"We are now bound together in a great war against sin and death, testing whether those who were once enemies can unite in peace and righteousness, that all may endure and prosper. This is the great task that remains before us.[10] We can and must become a new people, dedicated to the ideals of righteousness, liberty, peace, and prosperity for all. To the Carpiani, I give my word, if you will now embrace the cause of the Roman Republic, you shall have a path to citizenship, just as Romulus promised his war captives centuries ago upon the founding of Rome.

"Now we must draw upon the memories of those who have passed on, resolving to press forward on the path of life secured for us by our honored dead, that they shall not have died in vain. Let us claim this new birth of freedom together, that under this Republic our families may endure in prosperity and not perish from the earth."[11]

Zelimir was greatly impressed with the dignity of the ceremony and the clear message of hope George had offered. He thought, *I've long wished for such a commander to lead me on my path. Still, I will reserve judgment until I've seen if George will honor his word to treat his captives fairly and help us rebuild as a people.*

*****

"All the spoils of our victory have been gathered in as you ordered," Tertius reported. "The confiscated treasure is substantial, which is exciting to the soldiers. Our supplies greatly exceed the requirements for our depleted forces. The Carpiani food supplies have also been inventoried. Their provisions appear to be more than ample to get the remainder of their people through until harvest when they can replenish their stores, so neither captives nor captors shall be a burden on the sustenance of the other."

"Return the Carpiani food to the captive women to secure and distribute among their people. Then call all the people to assemble in the town square," George ordered.

*****

"Legionnaires, we gather to account for and divide the rightfully gained spoils of this victory," George announced to an enthusiastic cheer from the soldiers. "First in our accounting, we must account to God for sparing our lives and for giving us clear signs that He lives and blesses those who are obedient to His word. God has blessed each of us with life and with the hope of peace and prosperity. These are the true spoils of victory.

"As to the treasure, one half will be sent to the treasury of the Republic to cover the cost of supporting peace and public works throughout the empire. Much of this will find its way to our brothers in arms on other battlefields, that together we might remain strong. The other half will be divided equally to every man, woman, and child who remain to secure peace and to rebuild this broken people." George paused a moment for reaction and heard what he expected.

"We've already returned all the prisoners' food. Why should we share the spoils of treasure with them?" one of the centurions asked while many others mumbled similar challenges.

George scanned the crowd of soldiers as he waited for silence. Firmly he declared, "We cannot hope to succeed in our mission to secure peace in this region for ourselves and those we conquer if we leave our new subjects without the means to lift themselves! Let us claim our reward, but not be greedy. Greed and covetousness are tools of the adversary, forbidden by God, turning brother against brother in sin from the beginning.[12] By the grace of God we live, and we are the keepers of our brethren, whom we must lift and not trample upon."[13] Some grumbling continued amongst the soldiers, but there were no further vocal challenges.

There were mixed emotions among the Carpiani. Most were surprised and disbelieving. Zelimir remained cautious. "Perhaps we won't be left destitute or be subjected to humiliating abuses just to secure what little money we need," he whispered to those around him. "Still, I see this issue may become an enduring wedge between captors and captives that might tempt the undisciplined to try and further enrich themselves by force, one captive at a time."

George continued with his instructions. "The weapons gathered will be taken to the blacksmith's shop, which will serve as our temporary armory. Soldiers may go there to exchange weapons and armor for the best that's available. The surplus will be retained for the day when we re-arm our captives under covenants of mutual support and security.

"Finally, I invite all within the sound of my voice to awaken to righteousness.[14] Your lives have been preserved as evidence there is a God, if you will just open your eyes to His glory. May we all abide in the liberty wherewith He has made us free from death. Let us separate from sin and let our hands remain clean until we meet Him."[15]

*****

Most Noble Emperor Diocletian Augustus:

As you commanded, the walled town occupied by the Carpiani has been captured, but our victory has come at great cost in Roman lives. Enclosed are lists of the casualties. We have also sent along a chest containing the personal effects of those killed, to be sent on to their families. A second chest containing the battle spoils for the Republic's treasury is sent with an escort of ten guards to you for disposition. These guards are prepared to accompany the treasure back to the capital if that is your will. If you have other men for the task, please command these guards to return to us as we are short of soldiers and need all the help we can secure.

Enclosed you will also find a report of all the battlefield promotions that have been awarded, listed by rank. As Nereus, the legion commander, was killed, I have referenced my promotion to legion commander which has been signed by each of the millenaries. We request that you respond by return messenger with orders ratifying these promotions or with orders changing the leadership to conform to your will.

There is an urgent need for the town's defenses to be rebuilt and improved as this region is still unsafe and insecure due to the diminished strength of our legion and the ever present ambitions of our enemies.

Therefore, we request authorization to restore our legion strength back to the previously authorized 5,000 men. We await your orders.
   Always faithful!
– George, Commander of the Second Italica legion, Noricum province

*****

"I'm concerned about the great number of Carpiani women," George confided to his millenaries. "They far exceed the number of Carpiani men who survived the battle. Many of these women are pregnant. Fatherless children are another grave matter. Because of the number of their men killed in battle, their children nearly double the number of their surviving adults."[16]

"How shall we minister to their needs?" one millenary asked.

"I charge every legionnaire to look to the needs and impart to the support of all the women and children," George replied. "I order that no Romans partake of or disturb the Carpiani food supply. In time, they should be able to secure their own fruits, vegetables, grain and animals.[17] If additional support is needed, we will assist them from the supplies of the Roman army."

"I think the men's hearts will soften towards the women and children and they will comply with your orders," Florian replied. "Though there were reservations about your decisions on sharing the spoils of victory, the treasure was substantial and most of the men seem satisfied with their portions. Aside from the division of the spoils, there are a great many men who are still struck by how the battle played out, wondering at the heavenly vision that preserved them. Whether through faith or simple superstition, these men speak strongly in support of you, inspiring cooperation among the soldiers as your commands are given."

*****

George, Commander of the Second Italica legion, Noricum province:
   Reviewing your battle report, I give thanks for the success of the legion. I anguish at the surprising loss of so many noble brothers. Receipt of this treasure was most timely as we are hard pressed in our battles with the Sarmatians and we need these resources here.
Therefore, I am returning your guard patrol directly. I've reviewed the promotions arising from the battle casualties and I ratify them all. You may assure these men that they all have my support in their charges. I authorize you to restore the legion strength to 5,000 men. I command you to maintain a defensive posture, securing the town you've taken.

Constantine and I have battle plans for the Sarmatians that will hopefully draw them away from your position.
　Always faithful!
– Emperor Diocletian Augustus

*****

As George entered the forge area of the blacksmith's shop, his millenaries all fell silent, staring intently at their new legion commander. "Should my ears be burning?" he asked lightly.

After an awkward moment of silence, Florian spoke up. "There's been continued talk and rumors about your vision that saved us in the battle. Some of the men are saying that God speaks to you. They want to know the truth. What should we tell them?"

"Tell them the truth," George replied. "God is always speaking to everyone. It is we who must learn to listen."

"Apparently," Florian responded, "you know how to listen better than the rest of us. Will you teach us more of God and His ways?"

George considered for a moment and then spoke. "If you would learn of God, you must be prepared to embrace all truth. God will reveal truth to those who exercise faith in Him and obey His word, acting with honor according to every truth they know. Faith in God requires each man to act, trusting in the word of God. God revealed His will to me in a warning dream. I obeyed the divine warning and we were spared in the battle. Do you consider that a miracle?"

Florian hesitated only slightly before responding. "It was a miracle. I know it."

George continued. "God is a God of miracles and an unchangeable Being.[18] He has revealed Himself to you in this miracle. Now, how does that change your heart and mind and your path forward through life?"

"I'll have to think on that," Florian replied cautiously. "Will there be any other miracles?"

"Because God is a God of miracles and an unchangeable Being, if He ceased to do miracles, He would cease to be God. But He hasn't ceased to be God, and He is a God of miracles. The reason miracles cease among some men is because they dwindle in unbelief and depart from the right way and know not the God in whom they should trust.[19] The unbelieving are unable to perceive the miracles of God though miracles are everywhere."

****

CHAPTER TWENTY-FOUR
Mercy and Justice

Northeast Frontier, Eastern Roman Empire
294 AD

"If it be possible, as much as lieth in you, live peaceably with all men."[1]
Romans 12:18

****

"We've completed our list of the Carpiani leaders for execution," the millenaries offered.

"What law compels this action?" George asked curiously.

"I'm not sure any law compels it," one millenary responded. "But it's longstanding tradition that when a town refuses to submit and has to be taken by force, especially when the cost in Roman lives is significant, we take the leaders of the conquered people and crucify them on the main road just outside the town for all to see. This is done as a punishment for their refusal to submit and as a deterrent to all people, discouraging rebellion and civil unrest."

"Have we so quickly forgotten God's mercy in delivering us from our enemies that we should obtain peace?[2] Are abuse and intimidation sure foundations upon which we can establish this people as confident allies?" George asked. "There's been too much thoughtless death here. Let us not aid the cause of the evil one any further. We must show our subjects the honor of Rome and persuade them to believe in the peace of the Republic. We can't remain their enemies, relying on fear and intimidation, and hope to restore their honor. We must gain their support if we are to survive the Alamanni and the Sarmatians."

"What would you have us do?" the millenaries asked.

"We must repel evil with good," George replied. "Then those who hate us will become our friends and confidants.[3] Crucifying the leaders of our opponents is simply an act of intimidation, borne out of frustration. We can't be ruled by these forces and hope to win the approval of God in ruling over His children. The men you've identified openly declared themselves in opposition to Rome, and they've been conquered in battle. They shall be presented to all for public trial. We must show these new Roman subjects that they are governed by law and due process, not by whim or emotion. Thus may we balance justice and mercy for all."

*****

The trial was promptly organized before the full assembly of soldiers and captives. Vlad and Zelimir, along with a handful of other leaders, were presented bound before the assembly. At the conclusion of the evidence, George, acting as judge in the matter, addressed the Carpiani leaders. "Enemies of Rome, you stand accused of refusal to submit to Roman authority and unlawfully taking the lives of Roman citizens. The millenaries have testified that each of you led enemy fighters in battle against the Roman legion. For your part, you have not denied this.

"As to your refusal to submit to Roman authority, the undisputed testimony is that, prior to the battle, none of you ever made any oath to submit to Rome or to any of her commanders. Therefore, none of you has broken any such oath.

"As to the charge of having taken the lives of Roman citizens, you admit this was done, but you claim it was done lawfully under a banner of open warfare and in defense of your people. The town you possessed was not taken from Rome, and you did not initiate the battle with Rome."

George paused for a moment, gathering his thoughts. "Good judgment would have prompted you to retreat or submit, but you had no duty to submit. Instead, you chose a defensive strategy, which was your right. Your acts in this combat, including killing the Roman legion commander, were part of your strategy of open warfare in defense of your people. There can be no lawful punishments for these defensive actions. If there could, I hereby pardon you for these actions, including your refusal to surrender, and even for killing the legion commander in mortal combat.

"However, because you lost the battle, you are now prisoners of Rome. You will submit to the Republic, by covenant, or you will be put to death. The covenant of peace and loyalty required of you is that you swear allegiance to the Roman Republic and further covenant that you will never again take up arms against her, agreeing to abide by all Roman laws and to participate faithfully in rebuilding this town and this conquered people for the Republic."

The acquitted Carpiani prisoners stood in confusion, uncertain if they should be relieved, or simply wait for the axe to fall.

Having given his verdict regarding the leading Carpiani men, George turned to the remainder of the assembled Carpiani men, women, and children, and spoke. "Though you are captives in our hands, if God finds any good in your hearts, He will give you something better than what has been taken from you.[4] Submit by covenant and be faithful that your hands may be clean, and that you also may abide in the liberty wherewith you are made free.[5] Be not afraid. Only believe in the power, justice and mercy of God.[6] Believers, men and women, are protectors of one another. Believers enjoin what is just and forbid what is evil. Believers pray regularly, dispensing charity and obeying God in all things.[7] If you are faithful in making and keeping the required covenants with Rome, you have my word you will be treated fairly and eventually, you will have a path to become Roman citizens."

Turning to the assembled Roman soldiers George charged, "Soldiers of the Roman Republic, we are now bound to the Carpiani, as God has given them into our hands. We will answer to Him for our conduct towards these, our brothers and sisters. No nation can be strong except in the strength of God or safe except in His defense. Our trust in God should be declared in our actions.[8] Therefore, see that you are merciful to these people. Deal justly, judge righteously, and do good continually. If you do all these things then shall you receive mercy, righteous judgment, and good rewarded to you again."[9]

As George was about to dismiss Vlad and the other acquitted Carpiani leaders, one of Vlad's wives stood to protest saying, "Great and honored commander of the Roman legion, I am Beyla. I beg leave of you to speak for the residue of the Carpiani, that we may be heard."

George was intrigued by the boldness and intensity of this woman. "With my leave, woman, you may speak your piece," he replied.

Beyla addressed George respectfully, yet spoke with conviction. "Although Vlad and his men have been mercifully acquitted and pardoned by Rome for their acts of war, Vlad is accused by the residue of his own people, the Carpiani, of betrayal and murder. There can be no pardon for his terrible abuses of his people, stealing girls for wives, forcing us against our wills, putting our infant daughters to death, and using women and children as dross bait in battle."

Beyla looked earnestly at the faces of the Carpiani women and children. Finally she looked back at Vlad and proclaimed emphatically, "You've stolen me from my family. You've used me to satisfy your carnal lusts. You've killed my daughters who were your own flesh. You've ordered my son into a battle trap that has cost him his life. Through your persistent evil you've betrayed the trust of all our people in this same manner, making you worthy of death, which we now demand under our law." A shout of acclamation arose from the conquered people.

George felt a burning certainty of the righteousness of this woman's cause against the vile evil she was fighting to stop. Still he called out,

"Are there any here who would speak as witnesses for Vlad against these accusations?"

Vlad looked to Zelimir, who returned his stare but made no move to act. Realizing that all who might have been inclined to speak in support of his actions had likely been killed, Vlad spoke. "My lord, it appears you have already dispatched all my witnesses in battle. Therefore, I ask leave to speak for myself."

"You may speak," George consented.

Vlad had been surprised by Beyla's boldness, but he was determined to be even bolder in his own defense. "I've lived a hard life and I've given hard laws, but they were all for the benefit of my people. Our young men have grown up strong, knowing they'd have to fight for everything they would possess in life. Women don't know the true burdens of this life, having been sheltered by their men. Women are weak and can't fight for their own needs. They're kept at a price. They're not much good for anything but pleasure and breeding. If they can't meet our needs in these ways, they're good for nothing. I despise their weakness. Women are to be herded, not followed!" he proclaimed emphatically, staring down at his men.

As Vlad spoke, tears flowed down the faces of many of the Carpiani women. Though they didn't believe his words, it still hurt to be spoken of in this way. The humiliation was coupled with an anger few of them had felt before. It required great effort to restrain their rage, even against the peril of their captors' swords.

George also felt anger and contempt for Vlad. But he'd long since determined he wouldn't be ruled by these demons. Calmly he addressed the gathered crowd. "Will any others speak for Vlad against these accusations?" None responded to his query, so he proceeded, addressing himself to Vlad. "Those who deny dignity, honor, freedom, and life to their own people do not deserve it for themselves.[10] You stand accused of having continually shed the blood of the innocent among your own people. You've confirmed these charges by your own witness. Were we to spare your life, the blood of your innocent victims would also come upon us for vengeance.[11] As with every man that is cursed, you've brought upon yourself your own condemnation.[12] For your iniquities you shall be cut off from among the people."[13]

Determined to preserve confidence in his promise that prisoners would be treated fairly, George turned to the assembled masses and loudly proclaimed, "This man, Vlad, has been convicted under Carpiani law of crimes against his own people. The penalty is death. By the authority of the Roman Republic, I consent to the sentence of death in this matter. The execution of this punishment will be at the hands of the

Carpiani. What man among you will stand to serve justice?"

Though several men stepped forward, Beyla moved ahead with determination. "I am man enough for the task. How shall I proceed?" she asked earnestly.

As he looked at Beyla, George felt a strong desire to spare her the violence and see to the task himself, but he couldn't deny her the justice she had demanded. Responding to her anguished plea he said, "I entrust the sword of Rome to you for this brutal task." Then, he handed her the sword of Nereus, the deceased Legion commander, and stepped aside for her to approach her restrained husband.

Beyla grasped the hilt of the sword in both hands. The weapon was much heavier than she had expected. Still, she raised it and turned to face her people again. "No longer will our swords be stained with the blood of the innocent, nor will we stand as idle witnesses of such evil as this man has done.[14] From this day forth we shall stand as a shield for the innocent against all abuse, sacrificing our own lives rather than violating the trust and confidence of our little ones."

With the sword of justice in her newly liberated hands, she drew near, looking Vlad squarely in the eye. He quickly spat upon her with disdain. Unmoved, she declared, "You can never give back what you've taken from us, but you shall take no more than this!" With righteous determination, she brought the sword up and thrust it with all her might into Vlad's heart. As he crumpled in shock, she released the hilt and turned to face her people and proclaimed, "Now, we will seek God that He may forgive us our sins and change our hearts forever."

Calmly, George stepped forward. Looking upon the limp body of the fallen man he whispered, "All the kings of the nations lie in glory, every one in his own house. But you are cast out of your house, thrust through with the sword. You shall not be joined with the honorable in burial because you've destroyed your inheritance and slain your people."[15] Firmly grasping the hilt, he withdrew the sword from the lifeless body and wiped the blade clean on the dead man's shirt. Returning the sword to its sheath, George commanded, "The body of this man will be removed from the town and taken to the alkali field for burial without honor, along with all the dead who were abusers of women and children."

*****

"I feel the eyes of spies upon my back," George confided in Florian as they inspected their defenses. "I count it a great blessing that we've not been attacked since our victory over the Carpiani. We are so weak and exposed here at the edge of the frontier."

"I'm worried about the Germanic tribes and the Sarmatians, too," Florian responded. "We have many wounded here, but daily burials have nearly stopped, freeing up some soldiers for defense, but increasing the restlessness of the idle prisoners. Though the main gate has nearly been repaired, there is still much to do to secure the town against future enemy attacks."

"I want the town so thoroughly reinforced with new defenses that enemy spies will counsel their commanders to keep moving in search of easier targets!" George proclaimed. "Every time I think of the changing situation, weighing the outside enemy threats, I keep feeling that the key to fortifying the town and to our defense is to gain the cooperation and loyalty of the Carpiani. We must find a way to safely re-arm them as soon as possible."

"Thus ended the career of the youngest legion commander, who armed his prisoners only to be slaughtered by them," Florian jabbed sarcastically.

"I keep thinking of how Zelimir called on his men to trust the honor of the Roman commander," George continued. "Zelimir seems to be a man of honor who can be trusted at his word. I'm also impressed with the determination of the Carpiani to spill their blood in their burial ceremonies in order to fulfill covenants they've made to bleed together to the end. The more I think about it, the more my mind is clear on how we might quickly gain their cooperation. We must administer covenants to these people and call upon their honor for the security of all."

*****

With the trial complete, George met with the Carpiani men to reorganize the leadership of their people. Beyla was also present as his guest. 'The Sarmatians are pressing battle in our direction," he announced. "The survival of your people now depends on your ability to put aside past contentions and work together with each other, and with your captors. I require, insofar as is possible, that you organize the leadership of your own people and work out your own disputes among yourselves, maintaining peace and working diligently for the prosperity of all. Rome will tax you and help protect you, but she has no intention of settling all your internal grievances. You must choose one from among you who has the respect of all to serve as your new chief leader and as a liaison with the Roman army. Your chief must have my support and the support of Beyla who will continue to speak for the women and children among you. You can also choose other lower leaders to judge and settle smaller disagreements among your people. However, any lower leaders must be approved by your new chief leader."

After a few moments considering George's words, the men began to scan the room, where eventually all eyes rested upon one man. "Zelimir has always given us wise counsel. We'll follow his lead," one voice said. Many heads nodded their assent and none spoke against him.

George was encouraged, having seen Zelimir lead his men wisely out of battle and on to peace. "Are there any others to consider?" he asked the group. None spoke, so George turned his attention to the woman. "Beyla, will you and the other Carpiani women accept Zelimir as the new leader among the men of your people?"

With tears streaming down her face, Beyla replied, "Zelimir has already earned the trust of the women. He's a good man who didn't agree with the order to kill our daughters. He's helped many of our women to give away their baby daughters to other villages so they might live. His plan was carried out in the course of the raids, taking young women from other villages as wives, and leaving our baby daughters in their stead. The Carpiani women have been heartbroken at these losses. Yet they are grateful that at least a few men were willing to risk punishment to give their daughters a chance to live rather than being slaughtered by their own fathers, as was the law imposed by Vlad. The women will support Zelimir."

"Zelimir, will you freely accept the duty and honor of faithfully serving as the leader of this people?" George asked.

Zelimir looked at the faces of the men surrounding him. Those who had been with him in the surrender were still with him. Most who had been against the surrender had already changed their minds, in light of the trial results. Glancing briefly at Beyla, he looked to George and replied, "If the people will follow, I will help lead them to peace and prosperity."

"Very well," George concluded, looking intently on Beyla and Zelimir. "I accept both of you and will rely on you to speak for the Carpiani people. I promise you that God will give wisdom and understanding to you and to all leaders who sincerely put the interests of their people ahead of their own and who seek diligently after righteousness." Looking back to the Roman guards, George ordered, "Return these men to their quarters."

*****

"Millenaries and centurions," George announced, "Zelimir and Beyla have been chosen and confirmed as the new leaders of the Carpiani.

They will act as their liaisons with our army."

One anxious young centurion asked, "In honor of your vision and your God who has given the Carpiani into our hands, should we restrict the Carpiani in their religious worship?"

The question appeared to be common in the faces of many leaders. Raising his voice firmly, George instructed, "We shall make no law against a man's beliefs. It is strictly contrary to the commands of God that there should be any law to constrain men because of their beliefs. Our laws will be clear and strictly enforced against violators, but our people will only be punished for crimes they have committed and not for their beliefs. This life is given to men to choose what they will believe, and who they will trust and serve. Therefore, choose this day who you will serve. For those who desire to serve God, it will be their privilege to serve Him. But there will be no punishment under our law for those who choose not to serve God. These cut themselves off from the blessings of obedience to the Lord and thereby punish themselves. In this, we trust in God, for He loves all His children and will continue to feel after them with His Spirit, that He might bless them.[16] As for me and my house, we will serve the Lord."[17]

"But what of those who worship gods we know to be false? Shall we endure the wrath of God for allowing such blasphemy?" the young centurion asked.

George thought on the laws of agency and redemption for the righteous. "Don't revile against those who worship any besides the Almighty, lest out of spite, they revile the one true and living God in their ignorance. If they are sincere in their search for truth, in the end they'll return to the Lord.[18] If they're not sincere, it doesn't matter what they worship.

"Tertius!" George called out, "Record these orders and distribute copies to the millenaries, centurions, and to the Carpiani leaders:

I, George, commander of the Second Italica Roman legion, order that there shall be no more sharp contentions, especially those that come to blows, among my legion and all the people subject to my authority. We no longer settle disputes among us in that manner, for such evil causes the hearts of a people to harden one against another and the Spirit and blessings of the Lord are withdrawn. We must be steadfast and immoveable in keeping our laws, bearing with patience the minor offenses, and appealing to our chosen leaders to resolve major offenses.[19] *As abuses are discovered by our leaders and legion administrators, they will be put down.*
Further, among my legion and the people subject to my authority, there

shall be no persecutions of any people for their faith in God, nor for their worship or failure to worship any gods. In religious matters, all men are ordered to view themselves as equals, esteeming their neighbors as themselves, not allowing pride or haughtiness to disturb our peace. Each man shall do his best to labor for his own support, except in case of sickness or much want, in which case those with substance shall administer to those in need, binding our people together in unity and grace."[20]

After concluding his dictation to Tertius, George turned to his assembled leaders. "My brothers, I promise you that if we will trust in God and do good, we shall dwell safely in this land, enjoying peace, prosperity, and mercy such that all the hungry shall be fed."[21]

****

CHAPTER TWENTY-FIVE
The Covenants of Peace

Northeast Frontier, Eastern Roman Empire
294 AD

"...My kindness shall not depart from thee, neither shall the covenant of My peace be removed, saith the Lord that hath mercy on thee."[1]
Isaiah 54:10

****

    The assembly in the town square came to order as George stood to speak. "Let all within the sound of my voice know that all men here are bound together by the hand of God. We, the Romans and the Carpiani, must be united in our defense or we will surely bleed together to destruction at the hands of our common enemies. Like wolves of the forest they test the air for the smell of fear and the sounds of contention among us. We must not give place to the weakness of such strife. We cannot remain foes and survive. Though we were enemies, we must now be one. We must embrace unity in our common defense. Therefore, I've called this council that all may witness and none dispute the reorganization of the legion and the establishment of the Carpiani people as our allies by solemn covenant. As you've once chosen life and laid down your weapons, I now invite you to choose life again by taking up your weapons as our allies.

    "We must all make changes in order to survive. With integrity we must move forward, being true to each other at all times and in all places and conditions.[2] We begin with the legion officers, who will be bound by covenant to be faithful to the Roman Republic and to their legion commander or be immediately discharged from the army and banished from this post." Calling forth his millenaries one by one, George administered the oath to each man who knelt before his legion commander and readily accepted and covenanted as follows:

I solemnly swear that I freely accept the honor, trust, and brotherhood of my appointment as an officer in the Roman legion. I accept my duties to establish and maintain peace throughout the empire and to remain always faithful to the Republic and to my brothers in arms. I will judge righteously, bringing offenders to justice, esteeming all men as equals in the causes of peace, prosperity, and freedom of worship, keeping myself free of vices that impair righteous judgment.[3] *I acknowledge my duties and obligations to my legion commander, to the people of the Roman Republic, to the senate that represents the people, and to our sovereign Emperor. I swear I will bear true faith, allegiance, and loyalty to each of them, supporting and defending them against all enemies. My duties will require sacrifice and may require the sacrifice of my life, which I now pledge. I will faithfully discharge my duties and the orders of the Emperor and my legion commander until I be duly released from this oath by the Emperor, the legion commander, or by God through my death. If I fail in my oath, my life is forfeit. All here this day are witnesses.*

After putting each of the millenaries under covenant individually, George administered slightly different oaths by group to the centurions and legionnaires. These men were also required to swear their allegiance or be immediately discharged and banished. None of the soldiers withdrew or refused the invitation to covenant.

With the order of the legion established for all to see, George surveyed the assembly. Facing his men, he spoke forcefully. "As you have covenanted with me, I now covenant with you…and with all men, before God," he continued, turning to face the Carpiani:

I solemnly swear that I freely accept the honor, trust, and brotherhood of my appointment as commander of the Roman legion. I also accept my duties to establish and maintain peace among the people throughout the empire. Remaining always faithful to my brothers in arms, I will administer righteous judgment, bringing offenders to justice, esteeming all men as equals in the causes of peace, prosperity, and freedom of worship. I will keep myself free from all vices that impair righteous judgment.[4] *These duties are inseparable from the great honor given to me. I acknowledge my duties and obligations to God, to the people of the Roman Republic, to the senate that represents the people, and to our sovereign Emperor. I swear I will bear true faith, allegiance, and loyalty to each of them, supporting and defending them against all enemies. My duties will require sacrifice and may require that I sacrifice my own life, which I now solemnly pledge. I will faithfully discharge my duties to God, the Republic, the Emperor, and to all men until I be duly released from this oath by the Emperor or by God through my death. If I fail in my oath, my life is forfeit. All here this day stand as my witnesses.*

Having given his oath to his legion and to the Carpiani, George now focused his attention on the prisoners. Speaking clearly for all to hear, he said, "As I would not be a slave, so I would not be a master.[5] For those who lead into captivity will surely find themselves there one day.[6] But those who lead to peace and liberty shall be made free. Prisoners of Rome, I renew my promise: those who receive and honor covenants of peace, mutual support, and security with Rome will have the support of Rome and a pathway to citizenship within the Republic. Further, I promise the blessings of the God of heaven to those who receive and keep the covenants of peace."

"What God is this, and must we believe in Him to obtain the promised blessings?" Beyla asked.

"The God of whom I speak is the true and living God who gave us victory over your people in battle," George responded. "Every blessing received by man is based upon obedience to God's laws.[7] You aren't required to believe in Him to be blessed, but choosing righteousness and peace will assure that you receive His greater blessings. Because we are all God's children, He will teach every one of us, line upon line, precept upon precept until we all come to a unity of faith, every man having a knowledge of the truth and perfection of God for himself.[8]

"However, the covenant I invite you to make at this time is a covenant with Rome. No religious obligations are attached, but truth and honor are essential, for Rome and its officers under my command will not abide infidelity or deceit. I invite all who did not take up arms against Rome to submit yourselves as faithful subjects of Rome with the following oath:

In submission to the authority of the Roman Republic, I covenant to faithfully obey her laws and to support and defend the Republic and her people against all who oppose us. I pledge my life as a Roman subject until I be duly released from this oath by the Emperor, the legion commander, or by God through my death. If I fail in my oath, my life is forfeit. All here this day stand as my witnesses.

"Will you submit with this oath or be cast out?" George asked.

Beyla weighed the options while scanning the faces of the women and children. Her decision was not hard, nor long in coming. "I will accept this oath and submit," she stated with assurance. The women who now looked to Beyla for leadership quickly followed her lead, uncertain how their world was changing but certain they wanted to deal with the changes as a unified group.

With this covenant in place, George immediately dismissed their guards and began instructing the Carpiani women. "As faithful subjects of Rome, I now place the west half of the town, furthest from the main gate, under your control, separate from the Romans and the Carpiani men. I will look to Beyla as your leader, accountable to you and to me, unless as a group you designate another to bear that duty and honor. The entire Carpiani food supply will remain in your control. I also order that each woman be paid the share of the spoils due to her and to her children. In light of past abuses, I declare all marriages under Carpiani law to be null and void. However, I promise that any who desire to renew their marriages may do so, having them recorded under Roman law as long as both parties are freely consenting. All Carpiani children remain bound to their mothers. Further, I order that each of these women be issued a weapon for self defense. A centurion will be appointed to train those lacking in combat skills."

Concluding his work with the women and children, George charged them, "Organize yourselves, select leaders and assign properties equitably among all in your group. Provide the Romans with a record of the leaders chosen and the property assigned." Solemnly, George offered the women another bit of advice. "For the covenants of security and the safeguards to be enjoyed by this people, let them adore the Lord who provides them with food against hunger and with security against fear of danger."[9]

The Carpiani men, still under guard, waited anxiously. Some of them had worried that they might share the fate suffered by Vlad once the burial work was complete. Now they were stunned by what had been done for the women and children. Zelimir, however, felt confident that his faith in the honor of the young legion commander had not been misplaced.

George scanned the faces of his prisoners. He needed their support to preserve the Carpiani and Romans from their common enemies. Speaking slowly and clearly he began, "In reverence before God I take my sword to defend the cause of my country and those who have claim upon me for protection. The time is now at hand, that except we all rouse ourselves in defense of our country and our little ones, the sword of destruction hangs over us all. Unless we unite firmly, it shall fall upon us, even to our utter extinction. Now I'm constrained, according to the covenants which I've made, to keep the commandments of my God and protect the innocent among us. Therefore, I would that you Carpiani men should stand forth in this cause of righteousness and join me in the covenants of peace and the protection and defense of our people. I seek not for power but to set all men equal before God. I seek not the honor of the world but for the glory of my God and the freedom and welfare of my country."[10]

Zelimir understood George's words in favor of unity, for the safety and defense of all. He had heard George's statement rejecting slavery and inclining toward freedom and his promise that the women would be able to choose to have marriages recorded under Roman law. Patiently he waited for his men to be invited to covenant for peace and prosperity.

George looked on the restrained Carpiani men and spoke. "Prisoners of Rome, you who have borne arms against your captors, thus far you have remained in bonds, working under guard for your daily bread, conscripted in the cause of Rome. Because you've not broken any covenants with Rome or its representatives, I offer you a covenant of peace and loyalty at this time. I invite you to swear allegiance to Rome and to covenant that you will never again take up arms against the Republic or its subjects. However I caution you, the covenants of peace are not bitter. They cannot be administered to the angry or vengeful, who should remain in bonds until all their seething rage is gone and they are ready to join the cause of peace. It would be better for each of you to reject this covenant than to accept it lightly and then violate it. Truth and honor are required from each recipient of the covenant.

"Because you've borne arms against Rome, those entering into this covenant will also receive a small branded mark, the size of a signet ring, behind the right ear. The mark is a dagger crossed by a sword and is a reminder of how you've been blessed in your choice of life this day. The mark will be hidden so as not to be unsightly, but it will be easily verifiable. Any of you who attempt to usurp power or dominion over others or abandon support for the widows and orphans will be in violation of this covenant of mutual support, freedom, and peace. As prior enemies of Rome, any breach of your covenants, any infidelity, will result in your banishment or execution.

"Now, I repeat my promise: those who receive and honor these covenants of mutual support, freedom, and peace with Rome will have the support of Rome and a pathway to citizenship. Again, I promise God's blessings to all who receive and keep the covenants of peace. I now invite each of you to voluntarily submit, by covenant, to the authority of Rome, as her faithful subjects, with the following oath:

In submission to the authority of the Roman Republic, I covenant to faithfully obey her laws and to support and defend the Republic, her people, and land against all who oppose us. Further, having once crossed Rome in battle, I accept the brand of a dagger crossed by a sword behind my right ear as a mark in evidence of my covenant that I will never again take up arms against Rome or her subjects. I pledge my life as a Roman subject until I be duly released from this oath by the Emperor, the legion commander, or by God through my death. If I fail in my oath, my life is forfeit. All here this day stand as my witnesses.

"Those who receive this covenant will be granted reasonable liberty and may seek, through gentle persuasion, to renew any desired marriage covenants under Roman law. Those who refuse this covenant of peace will remain in bondage, toiling for daily bread, until Rome determines it is safe to banish you or until you are put to death for violation of the terms of your bondage. Will you submit to Rome with this covenant or remain imprisoned, to be banished?"

Zelimir was impressed with the wisdom of the covenants offered, relying upon the honor of each man to establish and maintain order and prosperity, rejecting fear as the motivator among those who must become allies to survive. Stepping forward, careful not to cast an intimidating eye upon his own men, he stated, "I accept this covenant, and again, I choose life. I greatly desire that my people will also be ruled by honor and not by fear."

Most of the Carpiani men entered into the covenant to fight for the liberty of the Republic and her subjects, vowing to protect the people and the land with their lives. After the small brands were administered behind the right ear of each man receiving the covenant, George ordered, "Release these men and give each a week's rations from the Roman army. Return to each man an equal share of the spoils, along with the weapons needed to defend himself, his people, and his country. Under these covenants, the Carpiani will be a great support to our army."[11]

"The freed Carpiani men shall have the northeast portion of the town for their quarters. But I strictly charge all men, both Carpiani and Roman, not to enter the western half of the town where the women and children are living. Any meetings with women or children must take place in the town square, unless marriages have been renewed as proscribed under Roman law. Living quarters for those who marry will be assigned by the women along the borders between their area and those occupied by the men they have married, be they Roman or Carpiani."

"What of the few Carpiani men who rejected the covenant you offered them?" Tertius asked.

"They will remain in bondage, obliged to continue in daily menial labor under the supervision of the other Carpiani men," George replied. Turning to Zelimir he continued, "I charge you to persuade these men to submit, or to recommend their banishment."

"I will meet with them frequently, urging them to humble themselves, set aside their anger, and choose the best path forward given their circumstances," Zelimir assured. "Some just need more time. Most will come around as they learn to believe in your covenants."

*****

"Tertius, come here," George called out. "I require each person subject to my authority to appear before me, one by one, to affirm to his or her required covenants. Set a schedule each day, between the first and the third hours, until the task is complete. Start with the centurions and the legionnaires, and then include the Carpiani men and women."

"Yes, my lord, as you command," Tertius replied.

*****

"I've been watching your militia drills," George commented to Zelimir. "The Carpiani are more skilled fighters than most of the Roman soldiers."

"Yes," Zelimir agreed. "But numbers were against us and our strategy failed."

"Together, we must coordinate our efforts so they won't fail," George responded.

"It appears most of the soldiers are more comfortable in formations," Zelimir observed. "They don't have the natural stealth and woodcraft skills that have long been cultivated among the Carpiani. Because of this, we would do well to have a few Carpiani assigned as scouts to each Roman century. The Carpiani scouts should receive soldiers' wages for their services, whereas our militia men will only be paid for their labor for the legion."

"I see wisdom in your proposal. We'll implement it for the protection of our patrols," George replied. "Beyond just the scouts, I offer regular enlistment in the army for those Carpiani who prefer it to farming. Any who decline the invitation to military service will still have militia duties, but we should be happy to have such men as these for our farmers, raising grain and flocks, and stabilizing families."

*****

For weeks the men had been anxiously engaged in strengthening and improving the defensive structures of the town and coordinating the militia and army. "Our arrangement with the Carpiani scouts has proven very effective," George informed Zelimir. "The scouting reports have been excellent in identifying positions, movements, battle strength, and weapons among the Alamanni, the Sarmatians, and a few smaller tribes nearby. Not only have the Carpiani proven their skill and stealth as spies, but they've also shown excellence in disrupting enemies without getting caught, and often without even being detected. In our few skirmishes with the Alamanni raiders, our scouts have been a key to our victories, discouraging further attacks."

"Are you referring to the burning of the Sarmatian supply carts?" Zelimir smiled.

"That's just one of many reported successes," George confirmed. "They've kept the battle from us which has been a great blessing. Their proven value has persuaded me to order the centurions to pair a Roman soldier with each Carpiani scout to learn their skills. Building further on our cooperative success, I invite you to identify some of your men to learn the trades of the Roman soldiers such as blacksmithing, carpentry, masonry and general construction."

"That's a generous offer," Zelimir replied. "I'll make sure we take full advantage of it. Our men learn quickly when given the chance. They have gained much respect for the Carpiani women who, though they have been busy raising children, have shown abundant knowledge and great skill in agriculture based on their upbringing among peoples who relied heavily on farming. The women have been eager to share their skills and training with the men in exchange for labor in working the land. Being excellent woodsmen, the men have hunted in their spare time, providing the town with meat and pelts which they have traded to the women for grain and baked goods. Our culture is changing for the good."

"We should also have our people who are most skilled in medicine work together, sharing knowledge and labor," George urged. "Finally, I invite all the Carpiani to join in our literacy training which strengthens the ability to learn, plan, keep records, and prosper."

*****

It was evening when the Carpiani women gathered in the barns near the western wall of the town. "We meet to discuss what we have learned and to make plans to improve our futures," Beyla began. "It's helpful for us to discuss our new liberty and the covenants by which we are bound. We may also talk of issues as they arise, so we can deal with them before they become big problems. Who has issues or concerns to present for our consideration?"

Timidly a young woman began to speak. "I feel lost. I know our lot has improved greatly with our covenants of protection, mutual support, and liberty. Many of us feel more secure with greater control over our own happiness than we've ever dreamed possible. However, what I want most is to be released from my covenants with Rome and to return to my own people."

"Well spoken," Beyla encouraged, knowing many felt this way. "Still, I've seen enough to know that although I have been abused by the Carpiani, I would've been abused by my own people as well. I urge all of you to carefully consider all you've seen, heard, and felt since the awful battle with the Romans that has put us in their hands. Since we've been subjected to the mercy of the legion commander, I've seen a leader who truly honors his God, caring for the innocent and those who have acted honorably, treating all subjects and prisoners justly and mercifully. This George is a man of honor. He has provided protection and care for the Carpiani women and children, treating the Carpiani men honorably as well. He is the first man I've ever seen who has shown determination to persuade his enemies to become his friends and allies.

"I've heard many reports of the miraculous vision by which he preserved his men in battle. These men soberly attribute their victory to George and to his God. I've heard and seen how the Roman soldiers now trust his leadership and fear his God. We've all heard his invitations to covenant and his promises to those who faithfully keep their covenants. I've felt true guidance toward righteous living, free from oppression, bringing justice, peace, prosperity, and life to all. For me, I feel it's best to trust in the one who divided the spoils of the battle with us, leaving our children, food, and shelter undisturbed and protected."

"Should we not go back to our own people?" another young woman asked tearfully.

"I can't tell you that," Beyla replied. "Each of you must decide for herself. I believe your cause is just. I think it's likely that George will act favorably toward any who seek his leave to return to their families, but I'm choosing to stay."

*****

George carefully considered Beyla's request on behalf of some of the Carpiani women. "When I think what I would want if I had a sister who had been stolen, I know what we must do. These women will need an armed patrol to ensure a safe return to their people, but I can't spare the men until winter, after the fighting season has ended and our defenses are fully set. Once that's done and we're secure, I'll release these women from their covenants as Roman subjects and return them with an escort to their own people if they can be found."

"Thank you," Beyla replied. "They'll wait with courage knowing they have your word."

"Is there something more?" George asked, as Beyla had made no move to leave the room.

"Yes, my lord," Beyla replied. "Many of the women have heard accounts of your vision. They're struck by the faith in God shown by your soldiers. Can someone teach us of this God of justice, mercy, and love, in whose name you promise prosperity for righteousness?"

George was surprised. He hadn't expected this, but again he knew what he must do. Cautiously he gave Beyla the names of three of his officers. "These men can teach you the truth of our God and how you can know all truth for yourselves. The instruction will be provided in the women's part of the town, but the instructors must be in pairs, with each other or with me."

"Thank you, my lord. It will give us something interesting to discuss while many of the women wait to be returned to their people," Beyla noted gratefully.

"It'll give you much more than that if you sincerely seek the God of truth," George replied. "Simply put, if you would know more of God, plant the seed of faith in your hearts and approach Him in prayer. Prophets of old have taught that He hears all who plead to Him in the wilderness of their affliction. He hears us in our closets when we pray to be heard of Him and not of men. He fills our souls with joy and peace. He hears us in our homes and blesses our families. He hears us in our fields and blesses our crops. He even softens the hearts of our enemies towards us. By His Son, He has turned away His judgments from us."[12]

*****

"He is a God of love," Beyla said.

"Yes, but He also expects works from His people," Milica responded. "We were taught the first fruit of repentance is baptism. Baptism comes by faith in Jesus, which brings obedience to His commandments. Obedience to God and His covenants invites the visitation of the Holy Ghost and a remission of sins. In this way, God purges our hearts of all that is wrong and we begin again on the path to all that is right. The Holy Ghost, or Comforter, fills us with hope and perfect love, which love endures by diligence in prayer until the end shall come, when all the saints shall dwell with God.[13] I feel the truth of this. This is what I want for my children."

"It may be the path to all that is right," Velika conceded, "but it's only the beginning of the work this God requires. The faithful must honor the Lord with their substance beginning with a tithe on the first fruits of all their increase. For obedience to this, the Lord has promised, 'So shall your barns be filled with plenty, and your presses shall burst out with new wine.'[14] That's a great promise, but those so blessed are also bound to impart of their substance, every man according to that which he has, to the poor and the needy, the sick and the afflicted, taking no pride in wearing costly apparel, yet keeping themselves neat and clean."[15]

"Aren't these things we already expect of ourselves and hope for in others?" Beyla asked.

"They are," Velika agreed. "I'm just not sure why a covenant is required."

"You only need to consider the covenant if there truly is a living God," Milica observed. "For me it's easy to see how such diligent labor and harmony would bring about great prosperity in flocks, herds, grain, gold, silver, fine linen, and cloth. With such blessings we could clothe the naked, feed the hungry, and care for the sick and the afflicted, being liberal to all.[16]

"George said that for those who keep their covenants with God, He will ease their burdens that they can't even feel them upon their backs. Thus they may stand as witnesses for Him hereafter, knowing of a surety that God visits His people and succors them in their afflictions. God will strengthen us so we can bear our burdens with ease, that we might submit cheerfully and with patience to all the will of the Lord. With such great faith and patience in the Lord, He will surely deliver us from bondage and oppression.[17] We will join the people of God, the Lord will fill us with His Spirit, and we'll be blessed and prospered in the land."[18]

*****

"I hope you're not here because of any abuses by the men," George sighed as Beyla led a group of women in to meet with him. "In any case, how may I serve you?"

"We want to make a covenant with God," Beyla responded simply.

George was surprised. "What type of covenant were you thinking of?" he asked cautiously.

Beyla furrowed her brow uncertainly for a moment, and then, with a look of determination she said, "We have vowed to worship the one true and living God and no others. We'll obey His laws. We won't steal. We won't commit adultery or fornication. We'll never be part of killing our children. We'll never intentionally utter falsehoods and we'll obey Roman laws in every just matter."[19] She paused, waiting for some response.

"Why do you seek this covenant with God?" George probed.

"You told us that who we are is not who we can become," Beyla replied. "Through repentance we can change and be purified, gaining integrity, becoming true at all times, in all places, and with all people. We've fasted and prayed that we might turn away from all evil ways, that our hands might be clean and pure.[20] We've felt God's Spirit. We believe if we follow Him we can become holy. For God has called upon us, in the name of His Son, to repent and soften our hearts to Him that He may have mercy on us through His Only Begotten Son unto a remission of our sins that we may enter into His rest, this being His plan of redemption."[21]

George was moved by the sincerity of Beyla's plea. "The vow you've made is a righteous covenant. Because of this covenant which you've made you shall be called the daughters of Christ, for your hearts have been changed through faith in Him. This day has He spiritually begotten you, therefore you are born of Him.[22] The Spirit bears witness that you are true believers in the living God and we shall associate with you as such. We won't send you back to the unbelievers, but shall covenant with you, as your brethren in faith, to guard and protect you, keeping you safe and secure with us, setting aside all that is in the past, praying to God that He will forgive your sins, and asking that you pray that He will forgive our sins."[23]

Beyla was grateful for George's kind words, but they weren't what she and the other women had come for. Patiently she pleaded, "We want to be baptized in the name of the Lord as a token of our covenant with Him."

George smiled softly as he explained, "I'm a follower of Jesus Christ. I worship the true and living God. I do my best to live by every word that proceeds from His mouth. However, I don't have the priesthood of God required to administer these sacred ordinances in His name. I have not been called of God by one having proper authority from Him. I have not been ordained to His priesthood by one authorized of Him to confer His power.[24] We are on the war-ravaged frontier. Christ's church is not well organized here. I'm not aware of any here who have authority to administer these ordinances. We must await the coming of a servant of the Lord with proper priesthood authority."

George could see the disappointment in the women's faces. Considering the choice they had made, hope and joy would've been more appropriate. Trying to inspire them, George added, "I'll send for Bishop Nicholas of Myra.[25] He may have proper authority to perform these ordinances. It's said that he and his wife are just the kind of people who would travel the world to provide such gifts and blessings as these to all of God's children.

"For now, keep your vows to God. Be steadfast and immovable, always abounding in good works, that Christ the Lord Omnipotent may seal you His, that you may inherit heaven and have everlasting salvation and eternal life, through the wisdom, power, justice, and mercy of Him who created all things in heaven and in earth, who is God above all.[26] Continue in prayer and faith and I promise our Father will bless and prosper you. The Lord is merciful to all who believe in Him and in the sincerity of their hearts call upon His holy name."[27]

****

CHAPTER TWENTY-SIX
Conquer and Stabilize

Northeast Frontier, Eastern Roman Empire
294 AD

"...by small and simple things are great things brought to pass;..."[1]
Alma 37:6

****

George, Commander of the Second Italica legion, Noricum province:
Your report that the Germanic tribes have curbed their ambitions and withdrawn their scouts for the winter is a great relief. After battling the Sarmatians through the summer, Constantine and I finally achieved a decisive victory over them in the fall. To secure our conquests I am ordering all legion commanders in the northeast to build new fortresses north of the Danube during the winter. The seven new fortresses will serve as a defensive line securing complete control of the Danube River valley for the Roman Empire. Your legion is ordered to establish a fortress between Lauriacum and Carnuntum. Keep me posted on your progress in construction, and notify me of the man you appoint as garrison commander for the fortress.
    Always faithful!
– Emperor Diocletian Augustus

*****

"I'm encouraged by the restoration of our town and the improvement of our defenses," George said to Zelimir and Beyla. "I'm also pleased that many of the women have remarried their Carpiani husbands under Roman law. These women have given their children a great blessing, that they might have good fathers in their homes. I hope that the women who lost their husbands in battle or have refused their prior husbands' proposals might yet find appropriate husbands and happiness, strengthening our people in this place. The work continues, but it's time for me to fulfill my promise to the women who desire to return to their own people."

"There are more women in that group than I had hoped, but it's right that you should honor your word," Zelimir replied. "The task will be perilous, but the solution is simple. The safest and fastest way to return these women is for the Carpiani men to do it. Roman soldiers wouldn't know how to find the raided villages. They would slow the group's travel. With your permission, I'll lead the return party. I suggest we pick twelve Carpiani scouts to protect us."

"I support Zelimir's plan," Beyla responded.

"Then you pick eight scouts and I'll pick four," George told Zelimir confidently. "Upon your return, each man will receive four weeks' Roman army wages for his services. When your group is ready to leave, I'll release the departing women from their oaths as Roman subjects, but they must swear an oath of peace with Rome. Subject to these terms, they'll be allowed to take their children and their share of the spoils in treasure, weapons, and food and depart in peace."

*****

Twenty-five days after their departure, Zelimir returned with the remains of his party and reported to George. "The mission went better than I had expected," he said. "Two of the scouts broke with Rome to seek other Carpiani, I think because their wives wouldn't remarry them. I thought we might lose more, but the men have come to trust you. Some of the villages we returned to had been destroyed, probably by the Sarmatians. Therefore, some of the women chose to come back, desiring to renew their covenants as subjects of Rome. I think they'll likely choose husbands from among the Carpiani or even the Romans given the situation. Also, we brought back three young girls from one of the villages."

George cocked his head in surprise. "Did I authorize that?" he asked directly.

Zelimir smiled at George and continued, "No, you didn't. These girls were babies I had placed with a village when we raided it two years ago. I knew who their mothers were so when they were offered, I accepted them graciously. The women returning with us cared for the girls as we traveled. One little girl is Beyla's daughter and she looks the part. The mothers of the other two girls are sisters. I can't tell the difference between their little ones. The daughters have the same father so I'm sure the mothers will manage raising them together."

George put his hand on Zelimir's shoulder. "What a blessing. I hadn't thought of recovering any of the abandoned daughters. I fully support your decision to restore them to their mothers. Thank you for helping me keep my word in returning these women to their people."

"I expect other mothers will want to see if they can recover their

A Martyr's Faith

daughters," Zelimir speculated.

"I'm likely to approve such efforts to reunite children to mothers, but you must get approval from me before each mission," George responded. "There must not be any breach of the peace between Rome and those who now possess these precious daughters. Gentle persuasion will be the limit of your authorization."

"What of the men who broke their covenants with Rome?" Zelimir asked in dismay. "I feel I've failed you with them."

"Don't be concerned over those who have abandoned their covenants and left," George replied. "There's a reason I sent unsettled men with you. Those who have returned to us now know they are here by choice. They should be more settled. Those who left shouldn't have much problem as long as they don't cross the Romans again. I'm certain we'll be stronger without them."

*****

Most Noble Emperor Diocletian Augustus:
We have completed the restoration of defenses that were damaged in our battle with the Carpiani. Though we are adequately secure at present, we continue to work at improving our position. We've restored our legion strength to 5,000 men with recruits from this region. Most of them have been proven in battle. Many of the new recruits are trained horsemen who brought their own mounts to the legion. A list of the officers' promotions is enclosed for your records. With our restored forces, we have uncontested control of the surrounding area.
The fortress between Lauriacum and Carnuntum has been established, enclosed, and secured with a picket wall. Our engineering corps and a couple of millenniums will be working through the winter to raise stone walls to improve the security of that structure. Once that is complete we will assign a permanent garrison to the fortress.
　Always faithful!
– George, Commander of the Second Italica legion, Noricum province

*****

George, Commander of the Second Italica legion, Noricum province, and the Tenth Gemina legion, Pannonia province:
I have reviewed your status report for the Second Italica legion. I am pleasantly surprised that you were able to restore your legion forces so promptly, and with men proven in battle. In honor of your success, I promote you to commander of the Tenth Gemina legion at Vindobona,

near Carnuntum. You are authorized to raise the Tenth Gemina legion strength to 7,000 men, and you are appointed as senior commander over the man you appoint as commander to replace you in leading the Second Italica legion. With these resources I charge you to lay siege to the last remaining walled town held by the Sarmatians in the Pannonia province north of the Danube. If this final outpost can be taken before spring, that would be optimal. It is imperative that we deny the enemy the only viable staging location for their anticipated campaign to reclaim territory we have taken in battle this year. Take the town if possible, but in any case, see that no supplies or reinforcements get through to our foes. Keep me informed of any significant developments.
    Always faithful!
– Emperor Diocletian Augustus

*****

"Take a look at our orders from Diocletian," George urged Florian. "Initially, I was surprised, but I can see how the conquest of this last walled town held by the Sarmatians will preserve many lives in the coming fighting season. I'm determined to take the town quickly in order to save both sides from another year of war. You're going to help me do it. I'm promoting you to commander of the Second Italica legion. I charge you with administration of the base at Lauriacum and the Carpiani outpost, and reinforcement of the northern fortress."

"And you?" Florian asked.

"I'm taking Tertius and a few hundred men to Vindobona. After reorganizing the Tenth Gemina legion, seeding it with strong leaders and Carpiani scouts, I'll leave two millenniums to protect Carnuntum and Pannonia while I take three millenniums and march against the Sarmatians."

*****

"Per your orders, we've recruited additional men throughout our march," Tertius reported. "Many have been persuaded that their security is dependent upon a decisive victory, believing there is far more danger for their families if we don't remove the Sarmatians promptly and forcefully. We've added nearly 1,500 recruits on our march. Some have agreed to join the military. Many others are farmers who have joined for this battle only. They're simply looking to earn a bit of hard money before planting season. I'm not sure they'll be much use to us."

"We'll train them and arm them," George replied. "Though a capable man with a sword may be more valuable in a fight, a less skilled laborer is no less serviceable if he frees up a capable man with a sword to join the battle. The men who don't show much aptitude for combat will move supplies, marching with us as a key part of our battle support, freeing up other soldiers for battle. Besides, an armed population is the proper foundation of a more secure nation."

*****

The millenaries entered George's tent quietly, waiting for instructions. "The Sarmatians have refused to receive our representative," George reported. "They wouldn't even hear our terms for their surrender. The leaders on both sides know our legion is sufficient to take the town in battle, but victory will have a terrible cost due to the walls and defensive structures. Seeing our forces deployed in siege positions, they suspect that's a price we don't want to pay. Gambling that we won't attack, they've assured us they have sufficient provisions to outlast our siege until they're resupplied with a much stronger force in the spring. They have two strong warriors on their side: time and patience.[2] Any suggestions on how we should proceed against them?" George asked.

"I take the Sarmatians at their word," one man responded. "Assuming they can outlast our siege, we need to attack sooner, not later. Though we're not complaining, there are reasons why we don't normally battle through the winter. Delays favor our enemies who are warm and dry. The weather on our march here was miserable. Now the misty rain has turned to a light snow. The wet and cold will rapidly dampen the spirits of our men. We should strike forcefully at dawn."

"We'll not attack on the Sabbath," George responded thoughtfully, intending to train rather than rebuke. "We'll keep the Sabbath holy unto our God. However, if we are attacked on the Sabbath, we'll defend ourselves even to the shedding of blood."

"Shall we join the battle today then and pray for God's favor in victory before His holy day?" another man asked hopefully.

"This battle is likely to extend well beyond the remains of the day," George observed. "Though God allows for a man to pull his ox from the mire on the Sabbath, surely He isn't pleased with that man who spends the Sabbath eve pushing his ox into the mire. Patience and time can be our great warriors as well if we wait upon the Lord and act in His time. Have your men make all things ready today and then rest, staying warm and dry. They shall rest tomorrow too. I want all men well rested for the labor that shall come after the Sabbath."

*****

Dawn rose brightly, ushering in a Sabbath that was unusually warm for the winter. "We shall get no better weather for battle," one of the millenaries spoke tentatively. "Is this not a sign from God? Has He not given us this day to fight?"

"It is a sign from God," George responded. "He has given us this day to worship. Worship as you will, but keep this day holy. Let us not be among those who continually pray for God to be on their side. Instead, let us be among the steady who, with determination, put themselves on the side of God. Only thus can we win the greatest of life's battles which are fought out daily within the quiet chambers of our own souls.[3] I shall cry unto my God in faith, for I know He will hear my cry.[4] 'Be not afraid. Only believe.'"[5] As George uttered these words of the Savior, he felt the Spirit and sensed the desire within his millenaries to know the truth of this admonition. "Let us wait upon the Lord a bit longer so that when He appears we will be prepared."

*****

The Sabbath passed and the next day dawned even brighter, yet George ordered his men not to initiate any attacks. Though his millenaries protested vigorously, George wouldn't relent. He explained, "I've prayed for wisdom, that lives on both sides might be spared. I stand upon the principles of righteousness. I cannot show I truly love God if I take no thought of how to spare the lives of as many of His children as possible. We will wait upon the living God."

*****

Reviewing the siege positions in the afternoon, George saw a rabbit grazing near the highest section of wall surrounding the town. Quickly he called a group of his best archers to the location. "It's not time for our attack," he began, "but it is time for us to have a bit of fun. See that rabbit grazing by the wall? I was thinking how discouraging it would be to the Sarmatian tower guards if one of our archers was to hit that rabbit with an arrow from this distance."

The men chuckled. "They would surely be discouraged, but they might also be scared enough to need a change of clothes," one man said, garnering more laughter from the group.

"So, who's up for the shot?" George asked. Getting no quick

response, he made it a challenge. "I'll put my penny against any man's who says he can make the shot."

"I'll take that bet!" a cocky young archer responded, stepping forward with his bow and coin.

"Money and pride are in the balance!" the centurion declared as he took the coins to hold for the victor. A respectful hush came over the group as the archer set his arrow and drew back his bow. With a slow exhale he let the arrow fly. It struck the ground just an inch short of the rabbit. Startled by the arrow, the rabbit quickly disappeared down a hole at the base of the wall.

"Hah! You missed by a hair!" the centurion mocked the archer as he tossed the coins to George.

Almost immediately a chorus of voices from the other side of the wall began yelling, "Rabbit! Rabbit! Get him!" followed quickly by the distressed exclamation, "Aw, he got away!" Promptly, the rabbit reappeared outside the wall and sped away.

George stared intently at the place where the rabbit had performed its disappearing act. Scanning the wall from the base to the top, it suddenly came to him. "Your miss was better than a hit," he said with a sly smile to the young archer as he tossed him both coins. "You and the rabbit have given me God's answer. By small and simple things are great things brought to pass, and by very small means the Lord confounds the wise and brings about the salvation of many souls."[6]

*****

George gathered his millenaries and engineers to the spot where he'd challenged the archers. After relating the story of the rabbit, he concluded, "Based on the rabbit's quick passage under, I suspect that's a 'Jericho wall.'"[7]

The engineers studied the wall carefully and all began to smile. The millenaries looked gravely at the high wall, uncertain about what they were studying. "What's a Jericho wall?" one asked.

George's smile grew. "See how the high wall is set between two towers? It appears to be an expansion that was built upside down, as if the construction was completed by taking down old walls from the top and immediately placing the blocks in the bottom line for the new wall. It also appears that their engineer failed to sink the wall's foundation sufficiently deep."

"So how does that help us?" the millenary inquired.

"We will attack at dawn!" George declared. Turning to his chief engineer he asked, "How shall the battle go?"

The chief engineer responded confidently, "The cavalry, archers, and half the infantry will mass toward the main gate at the east of town so the sun will be in the enemies' eyes. Make a lot of noise, but stay out of archer's range. The engineers will take a few archers, the other half of the infantry, and heavily loaded carts and attack the high wall with long ropes and grappling hooks."

Due to the persistent confusion on his millenaries' faces, George urged the engineer, "Please explain why."

"The high wall was built with a shallow and inadequate foundation. It's higher than the adjoining walls, but it lacks stability. Further, it was built upside down making it top heavy. See how the smaller blocks are at the bottom of the wall and the larger blocks are at the top? We'll have to work out the calculations, but with a few sturdy ropes hooked at the top near the center of the wall, and pulled by weighted carts with a little momentum, we should be able to tip the high wall just enough that it will fall under its own weight. That's why we call it a Jericho wall." Now the millenaries were smiling too.

"Once the wall comes down, the battle will end quickly," George predicted. "But, after you enter, hold your attack for my signal. I prefer to gain the victory with the least casualties."

*****

"What's all the noise?" Rorik demanded as he approached the officer on watch.

"It's the Roman army, sir," the officer replied. "They've been repositioning all night and now they're massed out to the east of the gate. They began their screams the moment sunlight struck the city wall."

"Ah, the yell of mass hysteria intended to mute the fear of death when the risk is high," the Sarmatian commander stated. "Most likely it's a mere ruse intended to unsettle us. This stiff wind from the east makes them seem louder than they really are. We have nothing to fear. The town walls are thick and our archers are capable and fully deployed to repel any attack. See how their commanders ride back and forth in front of them to rouse their passions. They just keep yelling, but they are careful to stay out of archer range."

Suddenly Rorik felt an unexpectedly forceful gust of wind from the east which was followed by a tremendous clap of rolling thunder from the west. Immediately a horn blew the attack signal from west of the town. It was echoed by several horns in succession passing the signal to the Romans who were east of the gate. In response, the Roman cavalry rode quickly from the east around the town toward the first horn.

"It's a trick! Stay with the east gate!" Rorik yelled. Turning to his aid he demanded, "Get me a report from the west watch explaining that loud boom!"

A few moments later the aid returned accompanied by a trembling soldier. "My lord," the pale watchman said, "they've tilted the high wall on the west side of the town. It went down nearly flat before breaking up. The back quarter of the town is already flooded with heavily armed Roman soldiers who are holding their positions. They've sent an embassy inviting you to meet with the Roman commander to discuss terms for our surrender. I'm sorry my lord."

In shock Rorik numbly concluded, "If the wall is down, we must surrender or be slaughtered."

*****

Standing tall in George's tent, Rorik tried to project courage and dignity "I am Rorik, commander of this Sarmatian army. I give myself as ransom for my people. Execute me if you must, but I beg you, let my people go, otherwise, they shall fight until they are all dead."

"We don't kill those whose only offense is defending the lives of their people," George replied. "The objectives of the Roman Republic are to neutralize threats and generate cooperative tax bases and trading partners, establishing a secure territory for peaceful living, and a thriving market for all. Frontier towns are like cows. If you slaughter your cows, they don't give you any milk. If you slaughter a conquered people, no tax revenues are generated."

"But you still control the land," Rorik countered uncertainly.

George smiled. "Land is a fine thing to possess, but it's awfully hard to farm with a sword in one hand. Better to retain alive as many cooperating people as possible. A wise leader will work to persuade his subjects to prefer his rule over any others. If this is the case, the people will readily join in their own defense, making them a much less enticing target for opposing forces."

Though these words made sense to the Sarmatian, he returned to his main objective. "If you don't intend to kill anyone, then what are your terms for peace?" he asked directly.

"Our terms for peace are simple," George said. "Rome will take control of the town. All your weapons will be surrendered to us. Your people may depart peacefully by sundown today, taking only what they can carry on their backs. We'll return one weapon to every fifth man, so your people can travel with some safety. We'll provide a cart for every ten women and children in the departing group, but you may not load it with any goods before it departs. Those wishing to stay and swear allegiance to Rome may do so and they'll be treated fairly."

"What does 'fairly' mean?" Rorik probed uneasily.

"Those who align with Rome by covenant, including any of your men, will be put in charge of their own security," George replied. "Their weapons will be returned, along with a share in the spoils of our victory. Finally, they will be given a path to Roman citizenship if they prove faithful. However, those who stay but refuse the covenants of peace will eventually be banished or executed.[8] Our Carpiani scouts can explain it best. You should talk to them."

*****

"I've accepted the terms for our surrender," Rorik reported frankly to his officers. Quickly he outlined the agreement and began organizing the evacuation. "Be ready to leave by mid-day. We have three long days of marching ahead to make our retreat."

*****

George called his leaders to assemble. After informing them of the terms of surrender which had been accepted by the Sarmatian commander, he said, "Again I praise God, for it is He who has done this great thing in delivering us from battle. I rejoice for the goodness of God in preserving us this day, that none have perished.[9] I urge each man to worship God, rejoicing in His blessings and praying for forgiveness and guidance at the break of each day."[10]

*****

"Because none of our men lost their lives in the conquest of the town, there isn't much lust for revenge," Tertius observed. "It should be much easier to instruct your new millenaries and centurions in the covenants of peace and their duty to treat all subjects fairly. With the help of the Carpiani, you should be able to convince your new legionnaires to work diligently in lifting these people to mutual prosperity, rather than oppressing them into desperate poverty."

Calling his men together, George warned, "We will answer to God for how we treat His children. Therefore, we must show patience, firmness, and self-control. We must be true in word and deed. Bear in mind that opposing fighters who obeyed orders are not the enemies who gave the orders. There shall be no torture of the people in our care. As our laws require, no Roman subjects will be executed without my approval as legion commander, and no Roman citizen may be executed without personal approval of the Emperor. We must use gentle persuasion and give fair treatment to all. If we are to destroy our enemies, let it be by making them our friends."[11]

*****

"Our people are inexperienced in leadership, as we had no such privilege under the Sarmatians," the blacksmith said. "However, we've chosen as leaders those among us who can be trusted. These men are humble enough to embrace the training you provide."

"The lessons are simple and quick," George replied. "First, we must put the interests of our people ahead of our own. The people need liberty and security. Individually, property rights must be simple and secure, rewarding those who work and build. Also, we'll rebuild the wall, and this time we'll do it right. Next, we must lead in service by example.[12] Therefore, with swords in hand, the leaders will personally join in the great work of rebuilding the wall."[13]

*****

"These are all who will be leaving with us," the officer reported to Rorik. "Most of the local people have chosen to stay, as have some of our own men who've become attached to the locals. They've heard reports of this Roman commander and his honor."

"Those who spoke with the Carpiani scouts are convinced that life under this new administration will be much more favorable than it has been under the Sarmatians," Rorik admitted. "This word of reassurance has spread rapidly. The people were fearful of the coming Romans. Now they feel secure, believing we are unlikely to return, so they can remain in peace."

Making his final pass through town, calling for those who would leave freely with his army, Rorik saw the Roman engineers and laborers had already made great progress in digging a deep foundation trench to reset the fallen wall. "They'll likely have the wall complete before we could possibly return with more men for a counter-attack," he muttered lightly.

As Rorik prepared for the retreat, George assessed the provisions of the departing army. "They have insufficient for their needs. Get two more carts of food for their journey," he ordered.

"Thank you for the supplies," Rorik responded. *I regret that I can't stay and become part of something better according to the covenant which you have offered*, he thought.

*****

By mid afternoon those working on the wall were exhausted. The engineers were greatly relieved when George and the town leaders arrived with many men from the town to keep the work advancing. "I'm pleased with the willing effort these people are making to support each other," he told the chief engineer. "They will develop talents and resources, individually and as a group. Those who spend their energy and substance in service to each other magnify the prosperity of all."[14]

As George worked alongside these new leaders, he prayed silently but earnestly, *Holy Father, please bless this people that they may ever remember Thee as they enjoy the blessings of liberty and peace with their wives and their children. May the blessings of liberty rest upon this people so long as the righteous possess the land. May the cause of Christ and freedom spread. May those who have taken upon them the name of Christ not be trodden down nor destroyed, unless we forfeit our blessings by our own transgressions.*[15] *Almighty God, please strengthen us and deliver us out of the hands of our enemies. Give us strength that we might retain this city, and these lands and possessions, for the support of our people.*

George continued pondering upon the will and ways of the Lord, and the Holy Spirit was with him, speaking peace to his soul and strengthening his faith with assurances that God would deliver them. Thus he thought, *I take courage that our forces will be sufficient to resist our enemies and maintain our lands and possessions, sustaining our families and the cause of liberty, peace, and prosperity, having our hope for deliverance continually rooted in Christ.*[16]

*****

"The cold and snow has returned with a vengeance, but it is a welcome blanket of added protection against any Sarmatian attacks before spring," Florian observed.

"And then the rains will favor those defending walled towns," George agreed. "Shall we finalize our plans for deployment of soldiers for the winter?"

"Perhaps we should redeploy our mobile patrols to the positions that were our weakest at the end of the last fighting season," Florian proposed. "Hopefully that will leave our enemies uncertain if still more men are coming."

"I agree," George confirmed. "I'm also ordering that each soldier be given a month leave, in three equal rotations, with every man to be back in place before mid-spring. I'll take the first month off, assuring that I'll be back to direct the strategic deployment of troops in the spring. I'm giving you charge over the tenth Gemina legion during my absence, with power to conduct war in defense of the region, according to the Spirit of God and the spirit of liberty."[17]

*****

Packing lightly, George took his horses, Joshua and Caleb, and traveled quickly to Antioch, in Syria. There he reported to Diocletian. "I'm very impressed with your success this past year. You've done your father proud," the Emperor praised. "I can hardly believe you've already conquered the final Sarmatian post in the Danube River valley, and without suffering any casualties. Won't you join me in Nicodemia for the winter?" Diocletian invited.

Politely George responded, "My lord, I must decline your generous offer. I've been away from home for nearly three years. I must see my brother and pay my respects at my parents' graves."

"Very well," the Emperor responded, appreciating men of power who didn't forget their heritage. "Remember me to your father when you are there," he concluded.

****

CHAPTER TWENTY-SEVEN
Insulted by a Messenger

Northeast Frontier, Eastern Roman Empire
295 AD

"...whosoever shall smite thee on thy right cheek, turn to him the other also."[1]
Matthew 5:39

****

"I'm going to be a god!" Diocletian declared to the Empress with sarcastic enthusiasm.

"How's that?" Alexandria questioned.

"It's a move the imperial priest proposed for the purpose of undermining the influence of the imperial council," the Emperor replied. "Embracing the concept of deified emperors and openly encouraging the people to worship me can only draw power away from the senators. I've been the Emperor for over ten years yet still they vex me. They can't be easily discarded. These men were born to wealth and power. They know how to manage it. However, along with this, I've got a few other reforms I plan to implement to hopefully promote a more general prosperity among my subjects, further diluting the power of the council."

*****

"It's good to have you back, sir," Tertius stated after he had completed his report to George. "Though we don't know much about your home in Palestine, many of the men have commented that they can easily see that your time there has done you much good."

"Really?" George smiled.

"Yes," Tertius replied. "Your entire countenance is lifted. You've shown greater patience and determination to protect all men. Your fortification of every defensive position has made the people feel more secure. Your plan to establish new tower fortresses in areas where there have previously been none has had the same effect. New wells within walled towns have enhanced the security of several locations. With these added protections, the people have greatly expanded their cultivation in the fertile Danube River valley. They have also planted vineyards and

A Martyr's Faith

olive groves in the low hills by the valley. Their flocks and herds have multiplied greatly and they have prospered."

"It is the blessings of heaven for those who love peace," George replied. "But there is still much to do. We must forge ahead in developing local militias to further strengthen the security of the people. After providing the locals with swords, shields, armor and other weapons, we will train them in all the skills of war so they will be resourceful in all circumstances."[2]

"The people are already much more comfortable bearing arms," Tertius observed. "I see evidence of this in the ease with which we were able to restore the legion ranks to their authorized levels. Though I'm sure our success is also due to our miraculous victory over Rorik's army. Your wisdom and fame have spread abroad. It is well known that you prevail through faith, skill, planning, and diplomacy, lifting all men in righteousness."

*****

Most Noble Emperor Galerius Caesar:
With the return of the fighting season, I have deployed my legion commanders and the thousands of new recruits according to the enclosed list. Maximian reports that Constantius put down much of the Frankish rebel alliance in Gaul this past year. Now he is campaigning eastward across northern Europe at the head of the largest army in the empire, intent on finishing the job. My concern over his ambitions remains. Therefore, you must return to the provinces west of Nicodemia but northeast of the Adriatic Sea to monitor him and his army in case they should prevail and turn southeast. Constantine will remain with me to battle our enemies in the Danube River valley, from Pannonia in the west to the Black Sea in the east. If you need help, look to George first. He will remain at Vindobona, near Carnuntum, guarding the northern frontier.
Fare well my brother.
Always faithful!
– Emperor Diocletian Augustus

*****

Florian, Commander of the Second Italica legion, Noricum province:
I repeat my earlier counsel to you. Trust, covenants, and accountability will be your greatest tools in lifting and strengthening the people within your stewardship. As you diligently seek the will of the

Lord and greater wisdom by study of the holy records and by faith, God will prosper all things committed to your hand. Now that we have positioned the majority of our forces in heavily strengthened defensive positions, we will proceed with the organization of our "Mighty Men of Valor."[3] This will be an elite mobile force of our strongest and most skilled fighting men, positioned to rapidly deploy and stabilize any developing trouble spots. Our Carpiani recruits may be strong candidates for these critical positions. Send me your list of men for these positions. I will likely be familiar with most of them so it shouldn't take long to make our selections.

Always faithful Brother!
– George, Commander of the Tenth Gemina legion, Pannonia province

*****

Most Noble Emperor Galerius Caesar:
Narseh has taken advantage of our preoccupation with the Sarmatians and broken the treaty between Persia and Rome. His forces came north from Persia, invading eastern Armenia. The Persian cavalry then advanced quickly to the western border of Armenia, seizing all the land Rome conquered eight years ago. Narseh has now turned his forces south and is threatening to conquer all of Mesopotamia. Rome's vassal king in Armenia, Tiridates III, has fled into exile. He is seeking our assistance in recovering his throne.

I am locked in battle with the Sarmatians and I must press our advantage. You must go to Syria immediately. Take personal command of all the legions opposing Narseh's forces. Tiridates should be helpful in getting support from the local people. I am sending Constantine to assist you. He will meet you in Antioch to help plan the counter-attack. Hear me in this. Do not have him killed. We still need him as leverage with his father. In any case, he has been most useful in developing battle strategies on the northeast frontier and he can help you. We will just have to trust our foes and the gods to check Constantius' ambitions for now. Keep me informed as matters progress. Fare well, brother.

Always faithful!
– Emperor Diocletian Augustus

Galerius smiled as he read Diocletian's letter. "Blood and treasure!" he declared.

*****

When Galerius and his legions arrived in Antioch, Constantine went out to meet him. "I've reviewed the scouting reports on the Sassanian army's positions," Constantine reported. "I recommend that Tiridates and I take one legion to block the western border of Armenia, leaving you to stage an attack on Narseh from the south with the remaining legions."

As Galerius considered for a brief moment, he was certain Constantine's request of a single legion was foolishly inadequate for the task. "I accept your proposal," he confirmed.

*****

Vallen spoke earnestly to his aged messenger. "Andrik, I have a difficult but important task for you. The Alamanni and the Sarmatians in this region are fighting each other. With the Romans to the south, we're getting caught in the middle. We aren't strong enough to resist any forceful attack on our own, so I'm considering a treaty of submission to the Alamanni, the Sarmatians, or the Romans, for the sake of our people."

"But they're all brutal. They would abuse our people. Better for us to fight and die than to submit!" Andrik argued.

"Words easily spoken by an old man who is nearly dead already," Vallen ribbed. "It's the young people who need a chance for a better life. Anyway, I've formed my opinions of the Alamanni and Sarmatian leaders, but the Romans have a new commander named George. He's very young and untested. I need you to seek him out and evaluate his integrity and benevolence to his subjects and his skill at administration. Do this and report back to me."

"Very well, my lord. How shall I make this evaluation?" Andrik questioned.

"That's the difficult part," Vallen responded soberly. "You must find a way to give offense to this George, testing his reaction. If he has you killed, then I'll have my answer."

"So it's really just one and done," Andrik laughed. "That doesn't sound so difficult."

Soberly Vallen continued, "Fulfilling this mission might be the best thing you can do to help our children and grandchildren secure the brightest future possible."

"I'll do it!" Andrik declared.

*****

"My lord," Tertius began, "an old man named Andrik has come as a messenger from one of the minor tribes to the north. He seeks an audience with you for diplomacy."

"Invite him in," George directed.

"Yes, my lord," Tertius replied.

George stood to receive the diplomatic messenger. The aged man shook visibly as he shuffled in. They each took a quick measure of the other. Before George could even welcome his guest, the old man demanded indignantly, "Where is your commander, boy! I was promised an audience with the legion commander!"

"I am the legion commander," George responded firmly. "How may I help you?"

"You...the legion commander? Don't be ridiculous!" Andrik hooted. "You're a big boy alright, but you've none of the battle scars of an experienced and sage leader, nor any silver hair of wisdom upon your head. I see no slaves in your service. You can't possibly be the commander. You're just a pretender sent to make sport of a sincere old man. You insult me!"

Outside Tertius couldn't help overhearing Andrik's intensely disrespectful rants. Abruptly he entered the tent, his sword drawn. "Shall I dispatch this doddling fool?" he shouted angrily.

Ah, that's it, thought Andrik. *One and done!* Silently he dropped to his knees, slowly raising his hands defensively.

"No, Tertius!" George commanded. "Don't kill him! Curb yourself! He must not die at our hands, for though his wisdom is in doubt, he is an innocent man and his blood would cry from the ground to the Lord God for vengeance upon us and perhaps we would lose our souls,[4] for the wrath of man does not work the righteousness of God."[5]

Turning to the cowering old man George said simply, "As I would not be a slave, so I would not be a master.[6] Surely you've come for a more noble purpose than to hurl insults. I beg of you, please state your business and let's look for common ground."

Slowly Andrik raised his head and, for a long moment, he stared intently at George. Certain now that he was speaking with the legion commander, he revealed the second part of his mission. "My lord and master, Vallen, desires to know what terms you would impose in a treaty of submission to the Romans."

"Can you show me on a map where Vallen and his people are located?" George asked.

Andrik still felt cautious, but knowing this to be a reasonable request, he complied.

George carefully reviewed the position and his scouting reports on enemy fighters in the area. "If we make a treaty with Vallen and his people, we will require each man and woman to enter into a covenant of peace with Rome, swearing they will bear arms in defense of the Republic and her people and the liberty with which they are made free. Each must covenant to obey Roman authorities in the administration of Roman laws, including tax assessments and military conscriptions. Each must also covenant to the mutual support of those who stand in need. Those who are faithful to their covenants will be given a path to citizenship. Those who are not faithful will be punished or expelled."

"Don't you need to know how many we are?" Andrik asked.

"Not to decide on the terms for peace and unity," George responded confidently. "Those terms remain constant. If you are many and we can safely defend your position, your people may stay. If you are few and need to gather with us for protection, that's what we'll do. If we make a treaty, you will submit to the wisdom of Rome on the best defense of your people."

"Vallen will weigh your proposal against those of the Alamanni and the Sarmatians," Andrik assured respectfully. "Before I return to my master, I beg leave of you to question your men, as witnesses to your integrity and benevolence and your skill in administration."

"He mocks you again, my lord!" Tertius protested, his hand firmly grasping the hilt of his sword.

"Calm yourself, Tertius!" George ordered. "His plea is made in good faith. Andrik, you may interrogate five people before you leave. You pick three and I'll pick two for you. After you're done, you let me know if you have all you need. Agreed?"

"Agreed," Andrik replied quickly. Casting a scathing glance toward Tertius, he walked out.

"Tertius!" George barked. "Come answer for yourself."

"Yes, my lord?" Tertius responded somewhat submissively.

"What's gotten into you, man?" George asked intently. "You treated our guest rather rudely."

"But my lord," Tertius replied earnestly, "he had no right to disparage you that way. He seemed intent on giving offense to you and to all of us by association. I guess I just got angry."

"I felt Andrik was intentionally trying to give offense, too," George admitted. "But I've seen this many times before. Men would discuss things with my father and try to distract him from the real issues, with flattery or with insults, hoping to gain some advantage. Father always said, 'The man who takes offense when none is intended is a fool. But the man who takes offense when it is intended is a greater fool.'[7] The Apostle Paul warned, 'Therefore, neither avenge yourself, nor dispense wrath, for it is written, *Vengeance is Mine; I will repay, saith the Lord.* Therefore, if thine enemy hunger, feed him; if he thirst, give him drink: for in so doing thou shalt heap coals of fire on his head. Be not overcome of evil, but overcome evil with good.'"[8]

"I guess it's just a weakness I have," Tertius confessed. "I just don't like being insulted."

"Remember, we were given this life to overcome our weaknesses, not to defend them," George counseled. "It takes humility to suffer through insults and remain focused on the real issues. A wise man will hear, and thereby learn and understand.[9] The holy records speak of righteous men who, out of weakness, were made strong by faith such that they escaped the edge of the sword, waxed valiant in fight, and turned to flight the armies of their enemies.[10] If we take our weaknesses to God in humility and faith, He'll help us turn them into strengths."[11]

*****

"Those are the Roman commander's terms," Andrik stated. "He calls them the 'covenants of peace,' and they aren't negotiable."

"Who would need to negotiate?" Vallen responded. "They're not very punitive. Still, what concerns me most is whether this George is a man of his word or whether he's a deceiver. I need to know if he truly is a good man and if I can trust the future of my people to him."

"I met with him myself, as you commanded, and I was liberal with the insults," Andrik assured. "I saw him restrain himself and his men, showing no inclination to wrath, pride, or arrogance. Those in his care walked with self-assurance rather than fear. He selected a Carpiani scout for me to interview, but he also let me choose some of his people for questioning. I heard the scout describe how he had fought against Rome as part of a people who were later conquered. Now, by covenant, he serves in the Roman army. The scout testified to George's faithfulness in word and deed. I could feel that they all trust him to protect them and extend to them as many of the blessings of liberty as possible. With my own eyes I've seen that he's patient in affliction, not reviling against those who revile. He governs his people in mighty meekness. He governs himself by faith, not by wrath. He is steadfast and his will is unbending."

"Tell me all you heard from those you interviewed." Vallen ordered.

Andrik took a deep breath and continued. "I spoke with several of his people. They had no chance to conspire in their answers. They were consistent and, I believe, truthful in their speech. Each assured me that George is not a power monger, motivated by conquest or violence. His primary desire is to save his people from destruction.[12] He's a strong and mighty man of sound understanding who seeks earnestly to avoid bloodshed. He labors diligently with his own hands for the welfare and safety of his people. He rejoices in the liberty and the freedom of his country and his people from bondage and slavery. He's a gracious man who praises God for the many privileges and blessings which He has bestowed upon His people. He's firm in the faith of Christ, and he's sworn with an oath to defend his people and his country, their rights and their liberties to worship freely, even to the loss of his blood.[13]

"George is diligent in preparing the minds of the people to act righteously and to be faithful to God. He strengthens his armies, improving their skills, building and improving their places of resort. He has great skill in battle strategy and in engineering which he uses to encircle and protect his people that they might be preserved.[14] He arms the subjects in his care, just as he has promised to do with our people if we make our treaty with Rome. He has no fear of the people rising up against his armies because of the benevolence with which the soldiers are required to treat the people. Thus he has prepared all his subjects to support their liberty, their lands, their wives and their children, and their peace, and to prefer their covenants with Rome to subjection by any other power.[15]

"Though a Christian himself, he strictly enforces religious tolerance for all men that they might live unto righteousness in unity. It is his faith that if all people truly seek and sustain the will of God as they know it, the Almighty will prosper them in the land, warning them to flee or to prepare for war according to their danger, and making known to them how they should defend themselves against their enemies. By doing this, George believes the Lord will deliver them. His heart glories in keeping the commandments of God, resisting iniquity, doing good, and preserving his people.[16]

"One centurion said if all men were like George, evil and war would be done away forever, and all men would live in peace continually. Although he doesn't claim it for himself, those I spoke with say he's a man of God.[17] This Roman commander, George, is a good man," Andrik concluded. "He valued my life though I gave spiteful offense. I would trust my grandchildren to his care."

Vallen sat silent for a moment, carefully pondering the choice he needed to make for his people. Gradually his face lightened as he looked to the distance and spoke. "Unbelieving people want their lives to be God's cause. But true believers, whether they live or die, seek diligently to be in the cause of God, that they might do His will, acting in mercy to relieve oppression and to expand peace and freedom. They honor liberty as a cause greater than death." Vallen paused another moment and then continued. "If all you say is true, though all his acts are known only to God, George is rightly among those whose names are justly reverenced among men.[18] May God, who sees his secret acts of obedience, reward him openly.[19] I judge that the hearts of the people will be open to him and they will receive him.[20] I'll place my trust, and the hope of our people, in this man of God."

*****

Shortly after meeting George, Vallen saw clearly for himself that Andrik had been both accurate and perceptive in his appraisal of the young legion commander. Though tested, George wouldn't recall the words he'd spoken defining the covenants of peace and liberty.[21] Vallen spoke candidly to George. "I agree to the terms you require and I accept the treaty by which my domain will be annexed into the Roman Empire. By these covenants, I've chosen to save my people, but I'll never compromise my faith by worshipping the Emperor of Rome. Therefore I must abdicate my leadership of this people under Roman occupation."

George smiled as he responded, "Then pray with me that the Emperor never comes demanding such worship, for that would cross both of us. If you refuse to help your people, that is a matter between you and them. I won't appoint your replacement. If your people can't agree on new civil leaders, or if they choose unwisely, they'll heap suffering upon themselves as they are forced to seek judgment at the hands of the Roman soldiers. They must still pay their taxes, but it will be best if they still bear the burden of resolving most of their own problems. I think your continued leadership would be very helpful in keeping them unified and easing the transition. It's up to you and them."

Vallen thought carefully about how difficult this transition would be for his people. After a sober moment considering George's faith, he relented. "I'll continue to serve my people, and I'll pray with you that the Emperor never comes demanding that we worship him."

****

CHAPTER TWENTY-EIGHT
Trust in the Lord

Northeast Frontier, Eastern Roman Empire
295 AD

"Trust in the Lord with all thine heart...."[1]
Proverbs 3:5

****

The Carpiani scout reported to George in careful detail. "My lord, our century traveled to Vallen's town, as you commanded. The town and its defenses appear reasonable, but they can easily be improved. The wall is solid with a broad rampart shielded by a sturdy parapet providing excellent protection. The centurion put the town through a defensive drill to assess their readiness for an outside attack, assuming no help from Rome. Soon after the people had taken up their defensive positions, a patrol of Alamanni soldiers attacked the town from the valley road on the northwest. The attack was sudden, and it might have been successful for them had they maintained the element of surprise and not had the misfortune of meeting the century of Roman soldiers you had sent to protect Vallen's people. The locals handled themselves valiantly in the skirmish, allowing the Roman soldiers to quickly surround and capture all of the surviving Alamanni. We took twenty-one prisoners. None escaped. The Alamanni lost fifteen men. Unfortunately, two of our men were also killed. The prisoners have buried all the dead."

"Did you look for other Alamanni in the area?" George asked.

"Yes," the scout replied. "It took a day to locate their camp northwest of the town. I estimate their forces to be about eight hundred men who are three days' march away from Vallen's town. They weren't making any preparations for imminent battle, which suggests those who attacked us were simply ambitious rouges, but they'll soon be missed.

"The prisoners have seen the defenses inside our town and know the strength of our army there, so we can't release them or they'll bring the main body of the Alamanni to overwhelm us. If they attack us with their full army, we would need a full millennium of soldiers to defend the town, and even then we might lose a number of our men. Either way, the Alamanni will pose a continuing threat to our people until we evacuate them unless we drive the enemy from the region. The centurion awaits your orders regarding defense or evacuation of the town."

"Thank you for your excellent report," George praised. He paused to ponder all he'd heard and what he knew of the status of his legion. Turning to a table of maps, George carefully examined the terrain surrounding Vallen's town. Turning back to the scout he asked, "Are the roads, hills, and valleys on this map accurate?"

After his own careful review, the scout replied confidently, "Yes, sir."

"Then I have a plan…and orders for your centurion," George smiled.

*****

The centurion raised his eyebrows as he read over George's orders. "Vallen's people are to pack up for evacuation in two days. Carts with treasure will be stationed in view of the prisoners. There is to be much talk of how the streets, alleys, and buildings are also full of treasure, with a common fear that the people won't be able to carry it all to safety when they evacuate. Citing a recall to legion headquarters, our century will withdraw from the town. The people will let word slip to the prisoners that they are desperate to evacuate but it'll be a week or more before the Romans are prepared to relocate them southward, and they are on their own defending themselves and the town until the Romans send an escort for them." Looking up from the paper to the scout, the centurion said, "I don't understand these orders."

"Keep reading," the scout urged. "We're going to ambush the Alamanni!"

*****

As ordered, two days later, in the early afternoon, the scout met with George at the Roman army camp two miles southeast of the town. The soldiers were busy but quiet, in obedience to his commands. "I brought three millenniums with me," George stated. "That should be sufficient. Still, let's go to town so I can see it for myself."

Silently, George and the scout rode into town where they found all things prepared as he had ordered. After methodically making his own review of the town and its defenses, he met with the engineering centurion. "I agree with your assessment," George said. "The town is very defensible with a few strategic improvements. It's easy to see how best to position our troops to repel an attacking army."

After satisfying himself that a single millennium could easily hold their position within the solid stone walls, George took a position where he could observe their captured enemies. It didn't take him long to identify the three men he needed to serve his purposes. These prisoners were troublemakers, angry and arrogant, bitterly despising their captors and continually breathing out threats. George's thoughts were clear: *We are for peace, but when we speak, they are for war.*[2] *But the judgments of God will overtake them, for it is the wicked that stir up the hearts of the children of men unto bloodshed, and it is by the wicked that the wicked are punished.*[3] *For the wisdom of this world is foolishness with God. For it is written, He taketh the wise in their own craftiness.*[4] These were the men who needed to escape, and he would arrange it.

*****

When the heat of the day had broken, the centurion led his men away from the town to join the Roman army camp. Vallen's people kept watch over the prisoners for the night. Late in the second watch, a disturbance outside woke the prisoners and drew the prison guard away, allowing the three troublemaking prisoners to escape through an unsecured door. As expected, the escapees stopped by the treasure wagons on their way out of town, taking handfuls of treasure before they were spooked by the night watch which prompted their hasty departure.

*****

"My lord, it's done!" the scout reported. "All went just as you planned."

"Wonderful!" George replied. "Get word to the millenaries and centurions. At the second hour of the morning we will meet in their camp for a council of war."

"As you command, my lord," the scout replied and then departed.

*****

"Men of Rome," George began, "we must be ready for battle by the end of the third day. The escaped prisoners should reach the Alamanni camp before nightfall. With the treasures they carry, it shouldn't take them long to convince the Alamanni commander to make an immediate attack on this town. They may take another day to plan their attack. Finally, they may take two or three days to reach their attack positions. If they waste no time, pack lightly and move quickly, they could be here for the attack in less than four days. We must be ready.

"The town will be presented as a poorly defended prize. We'll conceal one millennium of soldiers within the town. The other two millenniums will be positioned behind low forested hills, one on either side of the road which enters the valley and approaches the town from the northwest. A small train of loaded carts will be outside the main gate, by the wall, attended by a few soldiers dressed as farmers. When the Alamanni appear, the farmers will abandon the loaded carts in a panic and disappear inside the wall, failing to close the gate.

"The carts and open gate should be an irresistible temptation for the Alamanni, who will likely rush their attack. The gates will be backed by large granite blocks braced with stakes so they won't open wide. The Roman infantry will overwhelm the few Alamanni who enter, while the archers will rise up on the wall and decimate the rushing forces. The flanking legions, with the help of the cavalry from the town legion, will cut off the Alamanni retreat, which should be chaotic. The infantry from the town will follow the retreating Alamanni, surrounding them, which should result in their surrender or annihilation. Are there any questions?"

*****

Most Noble Emperor Diocletian Augustus:
I write to report the success of the Roman legions in the Noricum and Pannonia provinces. With the great help of the local subjects of Rome, we have destroyed or captured all of the Alamanni soldiers in the territories bordering our provinces. The patrol delivering this report will also render to you the Republic's share of the spoils. In exchange for their freedom, the Alamanni leaders have surrendered their weapons and sworn to a treaty of peace, recognizing by covenant all our territorial claims in the north. Thus we have successfully headed the Alamanni, pushing them west toward the heart of Constantius' army. Without the Alamanni to counter them in the northeast, I fear the Sarmatians will come against you with intensity unless we immediately attack their western flank and rear guard with my legions. We are currently at full strength. I believe we can commit seven millenniums to your campaign without compromising the security or control of our own provinces. I await your orders and will proceed accordingly.
Always faithful!
– George, Commander of the Second Italica legion and the Tenth Gemina legion

*****

Vallen's men had gathered to celebrate their victory over the

Alamanni. They were anxious to learn more about their new commander. While most of them had remained within the walls of the town, George had led one of the flanking millenniums and Florian had led the other. Having only seen George from a distance, they listened intently as one Roman soldier shared his story.

"He stands out among the men in camp with his military bearing, but he's really impressive in battle," the soldier explained to a huddled group of men. "He inspires those around him to believe in victory. I've heard him praise the faith of his mother who taught him that if he placed himself on God's side and didn't doubt, God would deliver him. Trusting in God, he has no fear of death. Rather, he thinks more upon the lives of his men and the liberty of the people than he does upon his own life.[5]

"I've been in the same legion with George since he joined Diocletian's army, but even before then his greatness was told. This much I know:

In the town of Lasia in the east where I was raised, there was a large pond the people went to daily for water. One day a menacing dragon came and nested near the spring of sweet water at the edge of the pond. The beast was as big as the largest horse. Its teeth and claws were sharp as swords. It's thick skin was covered with hard scales. The vile demon tore and killed all who came near to get water from the pond.

Selinus, the ruler of Lasia, commanded his people to feed the dragon a sheep each morning to appease and distract it, so water could be gathered. Daily the people would tether a sheep near the pond. While the dragon was away devouring the sheep, the people would quickly get fresh water near the spring and return without harm.

When they had no more sheep, the idolatrous ruler commanded his people to feed the dragon one child each day to appease it. The child to be sacrificed would be chosen by lottery, with no child exempt. Once a child was chosen, the father could battle the dragon instead of sacrificing his child. Many strong men chose to battle the dragon, but none had been able to kill it or drive it away. Most of these courageous men had lost their lives. Grief mounted daily as the awful beast took its toll on the people.

Now the ruler's daughter Sabra was a comely young maiden, well beloved by the people. But by and by, the lot fell on her to be sacrificed to the dragon. In desperation the ruler, unwilling to offer himself, offered gold and silver for the life of his daughter. But the people refused. Then the ruler offered half his estate to any man who would slay the dragon. Again, the people refused. Honoring his word, the ruler presented his daughter for the sacrifice. Sabra came willingly, adorned in a beautiful white dress of purity and innocence.

Just then in his travels, George arrived at the town. He approached on his sturdy white horse and inquired into the commotion. A kindly woman in the crowd quickly explained about the terrible dragon. In response, George boldly declared that he would fight the dragon for the life of the maiden. Sabra sought to send him away so he would not perish too. But George swore to the people that he would stay and conquer or die.

As the demon came out to devour its prey, George faced it and fortified himself with the sign of the cross. The duel began with a thunderous clap as he spurred his horse forward and into the beast. In the violent collision, George's lance broke and he was knocked off his mount. Regrouping on foot with just sword and shield, he met the dragon in a furious clash of claws and steel, yet neither prevailed. With the beast so close, George could see that the powerful strike of his lance, though failing to pierce the beast, had dislodged a scale near the dragon's heart.

As the rage-filled demon reared back with a thunderous roar, George lunged in to stab at the missing scale. But the dragon was quick and caught him with a furious strike, slashing across him with three vicious talons, breaking his sword, crushing his shield, splitting his armor, and knocking him to the ground. Having suffered a blow to his head, the dragon retreated to the pond and left George for dead.

Slowly George roused. Unsure how to defeat this beast, but trusting in God, he knelt up and bowed his head, pleading with the Almighty for strength to overcome. Recovering a bit he rose to his feet. Setting down his sword with its jagged split blade, he took off the broken armor of men, trusting only in the full armor of God.

In his tattered white tunic, George again fortified himself with the sign of the cross and, keeping his word, prepared to return to the battle. Feeling his strength restored, he reached for his broken sword, keeping his eyes fixed on the menacing beast. As he brought up his weapon, the sword shined with light. Silently he prayed that God would guide his every stroke.

Bent on revenge, ruled by anger and rage, the serpent returned to the battle. Boldly George faced the vile beast, standing between the dragon and the maiden. The demon made a vicious strike, but George withstood the violent attack, delivering another crushing blow with his sword to the dragon's head. Stunned by the hit, the serpent recoiled. As the beast rose up rampant, George thrust the shining blade with his might at the missing scale, piercing the dragon's heart.

George gently freed the maiden and returned her to her father. With gratitude, the ruler pledged half his estate and gold and silver as the reward. George humbly declined the generous gifts, assuring the ruler that the triumph of good over evil was sufficient reward for him. He then asked the ruler to divide the gold and silver among the people. That way, he said, the wealth of the town will remain for the good of all. Finally, he asked that the Princess Sabra be free to choose her own destiny.

George told the people not to eat the dragon's flesh, but to bury it deep in the ground. Again giving honor to Christ for the miraculous victory, George invited all to worship with him. The ruler and many of his people, who until then had been pagans, swore they would serve the Lord forever. Over 15,000 men, along with women and children, submitted to God and were baptized as a token of their covenant. The ruler and the people built a church in honor of the Lord and they remain faithful to this day. With gratitude for her life and her freedom, the fair Sabra devoted her life to Christ and to serving others.

Though Vallen's men had much to learn about George, the laws of Rome, and their covenants of peace and mutual support, they were pleased to have a new story to tell, and they shared it freely.

*****

"I rejoice in our victory for Vallen's people," George told Florian and the millenaries. "However, I feel an urgency to train our officers in the righteous exercise of dominion, uplifting all people and securing for them the blessings of liberty as far as possible. Persuasion, not compulsion, is the enduring tool of peace, prosperity, and happiness. Those we govern will be blessed if they embrace as much self-rule as possible with swift justice for offenders. For our mutual security, all Roman subjects should receive combat training and be part of our self-defense strategy. They should also support consistent public works. Required taxes will be imposed and must be paid. Religious freedom and tolerance shall be enjoined."

Continuing his training, George counseled, "As military leaders, you would do well to watch the men in their games. Men who cheat in small things will eventually abuse authority because they despise the honor of others. Men who are true in small things can be trusted with responsibility and authority.[6] Be wary of the earnest gambler who seeks to cheat life of his labor and is happily willing to heap his burdens on other men.[7] In a society governed by mutual trust, there can be no tolerance of corruption. Cursed are those who take bribes, turning aside the poor and choosing blindness to evil, for such are incapable of righteous judgment.[8] Give no honor to those who invite conspiracy with promises of precious riches for spoils. Refuse them, for their feet run to evil, and they are quick to shed innocent blood. By their evil, they spill their own blood. So are the ways of every one that is greedy of gain.[9]

"The tests of adversity and integrity are sharpest when we are assured of men's punishments for acting in righteousness, or when we are assured of men's rewards for our complicity in their evil. I plead with you to turn to the Lord with full purpose of heart. Put your trust in Him and serve Him with all diligence of mind. If we do this, He will, according to His own will and pleasure, deliver us from our foes."[10]

*****

As time and opportunity permitted, George reached out to the ranks of his legionnaires, seeking to cultivate more leadership qualities among the common soldiers. He taught, "The greatest quality of leadership is knowing who to follow and following with exactness. Success is the process of change from what we are to something better physically, mentally, socially, and spiritually. You men would do well to gain and improve upon skills in reading, writing, calculating, design and construction, general problem solving, and the exercise of faith. Wisdom calls for covenants of mutual support. We must bind ourselves together in service to each other. Wisdom also seeks soberness in battle, controlling our passions, thinking clearly and not giving place for the rage which leads to self-destruction. Men who learn wisdom are prepared to serve God in leading others to peace."[11]

George's men soon began to recognize the inseparable nature of the leadership principles he taught and the principles of righteousness and righteous dominion encompassed in his faith. As their confidence increased, men would often approach to inquire, as did Archeantus, "Who is this King of glory in whom you place your trust?"

"He is the Lord, strong and mighty in all things and surely mighty in battle,"[12] George replied. "If you seek His blessings you must trust in the Lord with all your heart, setting aside your own defiant wisdom. Seek not to counsel the Lord, but seek to take counsel from Him.[13] Acknowledge the Lord of all. Keep His commandments. Counsel with the Lord in all you do and He will direct your paths for good.[14] Humble yourself before Him so He will have no need to humble you with His might.[15] Set aside your pride and be ruled by faith. Fear the Lord and depart from evil. So shall all men find wisdom and favor in the sight of

A Martyr's Faith

God and man."[16]

"How shall I know when I'm sufficiently humble that I might be favored of God?" Archeantus probed further.

"Are you stripped of pride, envy, mockery, and persecution against your brethren?" George asked. "If not, then you're not prepared to meet God.[17] Seek no contention against your brethren, for he that has the spirit of contention is not of God, but is of the devil, who is the father of contention. He stirs up the hearts of men to contend with anger, one with another. This is not the doctrine of God, to stir up the hearts of men with anger, one against another. His doctrine is that such things should be done away.[18] The Lord said, 'He that loveth not his brother abideth in death.'"[19]

"And who is my brother?"[20] Archeantus inquired.

"When you see all men as God sees them," George testified, "you will know that we are all His children, and therefore all are brothers and sisters in the family of God."

****

CHAPTER TWENTY-NINE
Peace and Prosperity

Northeast Frontier, Eastern Roman Empire
295-296 AD

"...thousands did flock unto his standard, and did take up arms in the defense of their freedom..."[1]
Alma 62:5

****

Diocletian reviewed his map of the empire with his legion commanders in the northeast. "We've had great success against the Sarmatians this fighting season. Still, our enemies won't go quietly. Full control of the Danube River valley will require yet another year."

"We may not have another year, my lord," one legion commander observed cautiously. "There are rumors that Constantius has routed the Alamanni at the mouth of the Rhine. This winter he's reorganizing his legions for further conquests in the spring."

"The rumors of Constantius' victory over the Alamanni are true," the Emperor replied. "However, Maximian has ordered him to prepare for the invasion to reclaim Britannia in the spring. His forces, from Gaul to the Rhine along the North Sea, have been replaced by a large contingent of Maximian's men."

"Where do we stand in our war with the Persians?" another legion commander asked.

Diocletian retrieved a letter from the table and quickly reviewed it. "Constantine and Tiridates have blocked Narseh's advances west of Armenia. Galerius has the Persian army blocked to the south. He assures me he will destroy the Persians with the forces under his command, but that campaign will likely require all of the coming year. We can't count on him to help us in the northeast. On the other hand, the legions under George's command, between us and Maximian, may be able to help. Those provinces have been remarkably quiet, no doubt due to the Alamanni preoccupation with Constantius and the Sarmatian engagement with our forces."

"George has benefitted greatly from those factors," another legion commander agreed. "Yet to his credit, he's been especially effective in using his engineers to improve defensive structures, making his positions less attractive for enemy attacks, otherwise our enemies would have pressed the battle through George's provinces in order to outflank our forces. The security he has provided for us with the limited forces allotted to him has been impressive, as has his willingness to share those forces with us."

Yet another admiring legion commander added, "George teaches his people that liberty and peace always come at a high price. He persuades them that it's better to voluntarily pay the price early in sweat, rather than being compelled to pay it later in blood. With great effort, his people have prospered."

"Let that be a lesson to us all!" the Emperor declared. "Peace begets prosperity, and prosperity begets peace! Are there any other reports or questions?" No one responded so Diocletian concluded his year end war council, "We must always be wary, but I feel with Constantius heading west, we can now safely focus on securing our northeast frontier. Even so, I sense it would be wise for us to quickly put an end to our conflict with the Sarmatians in the spring. Always faithful, brothers! Back to your posts!"

*****

Most Noble Emperor Maximian Augustus:

I am convinced that a strong Republic requires an enhanced social fabric. Therefore, I am initiating a series of social reforms that will place renewed emphasis on the just rule of law founded upon a high regard for truth. Penalties for deception and falsehood must be swift, severe, and consistent. I am also seeking to restore the virtues of proper family relationships. Please see to it that these reforms are implemented in the west.

With the new territory added to the empire, I am reorganizing the provinces, doubling their number to 100. This should further reduce the influence of each provincial governor, making it more difficult for them to launch rebellions. I have created thirteen dioceses to serve as regional authorities over the provinces. In turn, the dioceses administrators will act under the direction of four prefects, one for each tetrarch and his quarter of the empire. See the enclosed maps. The prefects will not be part of the regular military, but they can be former military commanders with proven skills in civil administration. These prefects will manage the affairs of the Republic, subject to the Emperors and our formidable armies. Select your leaders and report back.

Always faithful!
– Emperor Diocletian Augustus

*****

George, Commander of the Diocese of Pannonia:

I have reorganized the provinces, doubling their number to 100. I have also created thirteen dioceses to serve as regional authorities over the provinces. I hereby promote you to serve as commander of the Diocese of Pannonia and its eight provinces. This command would normally report to Galerius, but as he is engaged in the Persian war, you will report directly to me until further notice. There is no change in the authorized level of men for each of the legions at your command. Send me your proposals for provincial administrators and legion commanders for approval before awarding any promotions to these positions. Officers subordinate to these positions may be appointed at your discretion. Keep me informed as matters develop.

Always faithful!
– Emperor Diocletian Augustus

*****

George handed the Emperor's orders to Tertius for review. "We have work to do to get things organized. I'm familiar with the security needs of the four border provinces from Carnuntum to the west edge of the eastern empire. But the four provinces to the south on the interior of the empire appear to need much more economic guidance than military defense."

"How will you select administrators for the new provinces?" Tertius asked.

"I'll probably consult with the local beggars," George replied. "Back home the beggars always knew which leaders in the community were charitable and committed to lifting all people and which were miserly, selfishly hoarding the wealth they received. For a minor incentive they will likely give me all the information I need to start my review of qualified men. We're seeking competent men of faith—Jews, Christians, and even pagan Romans—but all righteous men, devout in their beliefs, committed to serving and strengthening others."

*****

Having learned from his experiences with the Carpiani, George traveled throughout his region, setting both the Roman army and the subjects under his administration in order. He instructed his direct reports, "We must be consistent. First, we will organize our people to rule themselves locally as much as possible under covenants of peace and mutual support. We cannot help men permanently by doing for them what they can and should do for themselves.[2] We must look forward in wisdom and do that which will make for the peace of this people. We will appoint wise men by the voice of the people to judge them according to our laws. Working together we'll establish peace throughout the land, putting an end to wars and contentions, stealing, plundering, murdering, whoredoms, and all manner of iniquity, for these destroy prosperity and they are especially repugnant to God. Oh, that all men might be equal, that each man might enjoy his rights and privileges alike, each bearing his portion of the burdens of his people.[3]

"Each province must produce a plan for improved defensive structures and weapons training for the local people. Being prepared for war is one of the most effective ways to preserve peace.[4] It restores self-confidence and a true sense of liberty in the people."

*****

"The plan I like best for improving the people's security and prosperity is through the organization of local militias," George announced to his legion commanders and provincial governors. "Each militia will be led by a three man administrative council. Initially this council will be comprised of Roman soldiers, but as the locals show sufficient skill and ability, the councils will transition to a commander from the local militia, with first and second assistants from adjoining communities to strengthen cooperation among the militias.

"As men excel in battle skills they can be considered for positions in the Roman army, helping us maintain authorized levels of soldiers. Half of these recruits will receive only two year enlistments in the army, providing the militias a stream of men trained in military strategy and civil administration, who have proven their skills and loyalty. Keeping these army recruits as local as possible will enable the return of taxes as wages, helping to strengthen local economies.

"All male subjects between the ages of sixteen and twenty will serve in either the militias or the Roman army so that all will be trained. Militia service will generally be unpaid, but weapons will be provided. Each local militia will have authority to retain up to a tenth of its strength in career militia men through twenty years of service. Payment for these career militia men will be provided by local officials.

"Finally, we must emphasize literacy and public works, further liberating the people from reliance on the central government. Each militia unit will be required to engage in public works when not in training or battle. Those not in the militia will be organized to tithe their time into public works, some serving every tenth day as labor in support of such public projects and others serving every tenth week as supervisors and trainers. Men with skills requiring their full time commitment to public projects will be paid wages by local authorities. Thus all will help shore up defensive structures, secure water supplies, repair roads, complete sanitation projects, build public markets, and minister to the needs of the widows and orphans."

The governors of the four provinces that were newly assigned to George had seen many mighty men with swords come and go, leaving little record of their passing. They suspected George would be the same…until they met him. "He inspires the masses, yet he appears easily capable of leading the wisest among us," one observed. "We should not challenge him on his economic reforms. However, we may venture to inquire further regarding his faith."

Together they approached George. "Honored commander, we respect and support your orders of religious tolerance, for surely religious friction undermines the prosperity of all. But you can't really believe in the imagined gods of the masses, can you?" one probed cautiously.

In his mind, George recalled the words of his father: *Defend your beliefs, my son. Do it with courtesy and compassion, but defend them!*[5] *And then invite all men to come unto Christ.* George smiled easily as he responded. "I don't believe in the imagined gods of the masses, with their idols of wood and stone. However, I do have faith in the true and living God and in His Son, Jesus Christ."

"Not to be disrespectful," the governor replied, "but how can one believe in a God who is unable to avoid death at the hands of mere mortals?"

"Do you truly desire to learn the doctrine of Christ?" George asked. "Or does your challenge adequately satisfy your need to declare your unbelief?"

The governor had not anticipated being pressed on the sincerity of his inquiry. Good manners obliged him to invite the instruction George was offering. "I'm interested in this doctrine of Christ," he replied. "Teach us of this God that we may consider His existence and nature." The other governors all smiled uneasily, uncertain if they were in for torture or a treat.

"First," George began, "Christ was fully able to avoid the death He suffered, but He chose to endure it to fulfill the will of His Father."

"What father would require the death of a righteous son?" the governor asked.

"A Father who loves all His children," George responded. "To overcome the effects of our sins, God sent Jesus Christ, His Only Begotten Son in the flesh, to come and live a perfect life, preserving Himself as a sinless and unblemished offering in sacrifice for the sins of all those who believe on His name and exercise faith unto repentance, renewing their obedience to God in all things. Thus, our redemption is brought about through the sacrificial shedding of the holy blood of Christ, who has taken upon Himself the transgressions of all, on conditions of repentance. Christ paid the price for all of us that He might draw all men unto Him and restore us to life through the resurrection.[6] The Father required this of the Son, because the Father loved us."

"What do you mean by 'redemption…on conditions of repentance?'" the governor inquired.

Carefully George clarified, "In His mercy, God has made His plan of redemption known to us that we might not perish. By the voice of His holy angels He has revealed these truths, because He loves our souls, as we are His children.[7] Now we must choose the way of righteousness and life. Christ suffered for the sins of all men. However, to qualify for His redemption, we must repent. If we repent and turn back to God and His ways, we shall be saved. But if we don't repent, we will be cast off at the last day.[8]

"God invites all men to have hope in Christ, that we may enter into the rest of the Lord, both in this life and in the next. But we must set aside our rebellion and become peaceable followers of Christ, having a peaceable walk with the children of men. It is by the light of Christ that we may judge with a perfect knowledge righteousness and truth, that by faith we may lay hold on every good thing. Through faith in Christ we can do all things that are expedient in Him."[9]

"That's all good for you," the governor responded. "But I'm not sure I believe in angels and ghosts and such, since I haven't seen any." The other governors chuckled lightly.

"The truth stands independent," George replied. "To love and honor the Lord is the beginning of knowledge, but fools despise wisdom and instruction.[10] Wo unto them that spurn at the doings of the Lord. Wo unto them that shall deny the Christ and His works. Wo unto them that shall deny the revelations of the Lord and the power of the Holy Ghost."[11]

Seeing that George remained sober, firm and unshaken, the governors tried to turn the discussion back to business. Before he moved on, George extended an invitation to these influential men. "My brothers, if it is prosperity you seek, I encourage you to nourish your people in truth and righteousness, which yields prosperity and peace. Teach your people to be saints, living by every word that proceeds from the mouth of God, making and keeping His holy covenants, that they may be sanctified by His Holy Spirit. Then shall you reap the rewards of faith, diligence, patience, and longsuffering. The knowledge of the Lord will increase and faith in God will take root, bringing forth a fruit which is most precious and sweet above all that is sweet and pure above all that is pure. Then shall you feast on peace and prosperity with this people until you are filled.[12] Therefore, deal justly, judge righteously, do good continually, and see that you are merciful, and you shall have mercy restored unto you again. For that which you send out shall return and be restored unto you again forever.[13]

"Finally, I invite you to come unto Christ, who is the Holy One of Israel, and partake of His salvation and the power of His redemption. Come unto Him, and offer your whole souls as an offering unto Him and endure to the end. If you do, as the Lord lives, you shall be saved."[14]

*****

George was pleased to see Florian, who had travelled to the diocese headquarters to personally report the status of his legion. "Increased prosperity has made it easier for our people to pay the required taxes and still retain sufficient resources to invest in their futures," Florian said with a smile. "The people have become more confident that you aren't a tyrant seeking for riches, nor a man who delights in the shedding of blood. They rejoice that you have established peace in the land, granting liberty to all who enter into and abide by the covenants of peace. They have become anxious that every man should live in equality, each man exercising his own rights and privileges, and answering for his own actions. They have become more serious in selecting those among them who will be their judges, subject to your administration. Thus has order been established within the diocese and the people have become convinced of the correctness of the principles you teach. They rejoice in the reality of their liberty."[15]

"I'm impressed with the success of you and your people," George responded. "Let's truly be grateful for the continued peace we have enjoyed."

"Isn't it curious how we enjoy peace while all around us continue under the scourge of war?" Florian observed. "Our determined efforts to strengthen our defenses have clearly promoted peace and prosperity, which have inspired hope within our people. Clearly, peace achieved through strength is preferable to peace through submission to one's enemies."

"Amen, Brother. However, there remains a delicate balance between life in the military and the abiding desire for peace as a disciple of the Prince of Peace," George responded. "I see many parallels between our day and the time of Christ, with the Republic establishing peace and a measure of liberty embodied in the freedom of religion. Still, though we've enforced religious freedom and tolerance, I greatly desire to bless the people by sharing the true principles of the gospel of Jesus Christ. For the word of God has a more powerful effect upon the minds of the people than the sword or anything else they've experienced. Therefore, it is important to share the virtue of the word of God."[16]

With delight in his voice, Florian replied, "Hope in this life has made it easier to guide them to a hope in Christ, that through His atoning sacrifice and the power of His resurrection we may be raised unto life eternal because of our faith in Him according to His promise.[17] The eye of the Lord is upon them that fear Him and have hope in His mercy to deliver their souls from death. Our hearts shall rejoice in Him, because we have trusted in His holy name."

"May the mercy of the Lord be upon us according to our hope in Him,"[18] George pleaded.

"Because of your tolerance of others' beliefs and teachings, many have become tolerant of your beliefs," Florian assured. "Though not all are receptive to the gospel of Jesus Christ, none can credibly argue against the virtues of truth, righteousness, kindness, and charity. A few still grasp for power, advocating war and the spoils as a means of subjugating and enslaving others, but as peace spreads more firmly and prosperity begins to abound among the people, the opponents of peace melt away like the dews before the sun."[19]

"I hope, through gentle persuasion, to inspire faith, repentance, obedience, and tolerance by choice," George replied. "Then might the people experience the mighty change of heart and be filled with the Holy Spirit and the joy that surpasses all understanding."[20]

"You preach plenty through your actions, sir," Tertius chimed in. "Many in the army have heard the story of your vision in the night, before the battle with the Carpiani. Because of your great success in preserving the men under your command, they view you as a holy man. Many seek to learn more of your God and are converted or have their faith restored, choosing to give away all their sins to learn God's ways and know of His mercy and righteousness.[21]

"These men of faith are distinguished for their zeal towards God and men. They are honest and upright in all things, firm in the faith of Christ unto the end. They no longer look upon death with fear or terror, for their hope and views of Christ and the resurrection sustain them. Yet they are zealous in taking up the sword for the cause of peace and in defense of the innocent. They don't lust for blood but administer solemn covenants of peace to their subdued enemies. Thus they have become a beloved people, highly favored of the Lord.[22] They have taken as their motto: *Through God we shall do valiantly, for it is He that shall tread down our enemies.*"[23]

*****

When the fighting season was over and the Roman army had settled in for the winter, George received a letter from Diocletian calling for a report on his diocese. The news was very positive for his area, so he hastily dictated a reply to Tertius.

Most Noble Emperor Diocletian Augustus:
I write to report the success of the provinces in the Diocese of Pannonia. We have enjoyed the blessings of peace this year. That suggests a poor return of war spoils to the Republic, and such is the case. However, as you can see from the accompanying chest of tax receipts, we have had a very prosperous year. The tax revenues of peace greatly exceed the war spoils in any recent year. We trust this will meet with your satisfaction.
My legions are currently at full strength with a total of 29,000 men in the regular army, positioned as shown on the enclosed map. I don't anticipate needing any additional recruits from Nicodemia in the coming year. Based on our scouting reports on enemy troop movements, I believe we can commit six millenniums to assist against the Sarmatians without compromising the security or control of our provinces. Perhaps this would allow you to commit an additional legion or two to the Persian war. I await your orders and will proceed accordingly.
Always faithful!
– George, Commander of the Diocese of Pannonia

*****

"Thank God for His mercy and grace in granting my people peace, liberty, and prosperity," George told Florian. "Now, keep the peace till I return!" With anticipation he mounted his white charger and headed to Lydda, to home and family for his favorite month of the year.

****

CHAPTER THIRTY
Others Surrender

Frontier, Eastern Roman Empire
296 AD

"And why should ye not fight in the cause of God and of those who, being weak, are ill-treated and oppressed?"[1]
Qur'an 4:75

****

Diocletian and Galerius held their winter meeting in Antioch to plan their campaigns for the coming year. "I take great comfort that Constantius obeyed Maximian's order to take his army and reclaim Britannia," Diocletian confided. "What's your report on the Persian war?"

"That conflict is well in hand," Galerius replied. "Narseh's advances have been halted in Armenia. Tiridates III has command of Constantine's legion, securing Syria at the western border of Armenia. The other legions already deployed in the southeast will surely be sufficient for me to attack from the south and drive Narseh and his Sassanian army back to Persia."

"Then I'll take Constantine back to the Danube River valley to campaign against the barbarians to the northeast, leaving the glory of victory over Narseh all to you!" Diocletian replied.

*****

Constantius knew Maximian was right in ordering him to Britannia. "We need to crush the rebellion of Allectus and restore our primary tax base," he explained to a legion commander. "Regardless of what other plans we may have had with our army, circumstances require us to change course to the isles and immediately put down the usurper. One thought keeps churning in my mind. If a man cannot rule his own house, how shall he succeed in ruling others?"[2]

*****

Most Noble Emperor Diocletian Augustus:

According to our plans, I took the main force of our army to the northern part of Roman Mesopotamia, south of Armenia. There I staged for a decisive attack on the Persians, to push them north and then east, to drive them from Armenia. To our great surprise, Narseh's forces were prepared for us. There were three major battles, with the first two being inconclusive. The final battle was joined in the region between Carrhae and Callinicum. Our forces were greatly outnumbered and though we fought valiantly, we were overwhelmed and defeated with a great number of our army being slaughtered.

Narseh's army has swept south across the valley west of the Euphrates to occupy all of Roman Mesopotamia. I have led the decimated legions in flight to Syria where we await your orders.

Always faithful!
– Emperor Galerius Caesar

*****

"Unbelievable!" Diocletian exclaimed. "What do you make of this?" he asked as he handed Galerius' letter to Constantine. "How could this have happened? How do we respond? We're fully engaged in our own campaign. We must stay and press our advantage."

"Galerius was the commander in this battle," Constantine noted. "I feel unqualified to judge his efforts as I wasn't there. However, I can share Tiridates' concerns in the letter he sent me that also just arrived. He wrote, *I am uncertain how we could have lost the Persian campaign with all the forces that were committed to it. We might have been successful had we waited for the scouting reports before joining the battle. The scouts reported that tales of the Persian victories in Armenia and the spoils that were taken prompted a flood of volunteers into Narseh's army. Had we known of their superior numbers, perhaps we would have taken a more defensive posture in the battle. Had we taken a more defensive approach and respected the advantage of the high ground held by the enemy, perhaps we wouldn't have been surprised by their vast cavalry attack coming south out of the Armenian mountains. Perhaps if the Christians hadn't been sent away from our forces before the battle we wouldn't have been overwhelmed by the enemy. Perhaps the Christians wouldn't have withdrawn if they hadn't been declared unfit for duty and therefore ineligible for a share of the spoils. Perhaps they would have been fit for duty had they not been subjected to a beating for refusing to worship the Roman gods prior to the battle. Perhaps our soldiers who fought in the battle would have fared better if they hadn't been exhausted from beating their unarmed brothers in arms.*

Again, I'm quite uncertain as to how we could have possibly lost to Narseh's army."

"For a man who is 'quite uncertain,' he paints a fairly detailed picture of the scene!" Diocletian declared. "I'm sending orders to Galerius to regroup at Antioch, where we'll meet him once matters are settled here in the northeast."

*****

Narseh spoke soberly to his chief officers. "Having seized complete control of Mesopotamia, we face a dilemma. We don't have sufficient forces to occupy all the newly conquered territory and also pursue further conquests into Syria. We'll hold our positions."

"The men have been invigorated by our victory," an officer responded dispassionately. "If we strike Syria now, they will be with us. However, if we hold our positions, withdrawing the promise of further victory and spoils, many will abandon their posts and return home."

"It's better for us to solidify our gains than to expose ourselves to a counter-attack. We'll hold our positions!" Narseh commanded.

*****

Most Noble Emperor Maximian Augustus:
As you commanded, we completed our fleets by late spring and sailed for Britannia. The fleet, commanded by Asclepiodotus, sailed from the mouth of the Seine River in Gaul. Arriving first, they fought and destroyed the main army of Allectus, killing the usurper in the battle.
My fleet sailed from Bononia to London where the Frankish mercenaries, having lost their paymaster Allectus, were terrorizing the people. We slaughtered the Franks to the great relief of the people. I stayed in Britannia only long enough to restore civil order with loyal ministers. I have since returned to northern Gaul to crush the remnants of Allectus' allies.
Always faithful!
– Emperor Constantius Caesar

*****

Most Noble Emperor Galerius Caesar:
Summer is nearly gone, but we have finally driven the last of the Sarmatians from the Danube River valley. We also won a great victory over the main body of the Carpiani in the east. With these decisive

conflicts favorably resolved, I am charging Constantine with command of our legions controlling the northeast borders from Carnuntum to the Black Sea. I am marching to Antioch with two legions to unite with the forces under your command against the Persians. You and Tiridates must hold your positions until I arrive.

Always faithful!
– Emperor Diocletian Augustus

*****

As the summer was coming to a close, Constantine traveled to Carnuntum and met with George. "We beat the Sarmatians into a full retreat, but the stubborn Carpiani have been almost completely wiped out because they got caught between us and the Sarmatians and wouldn't surrender," Constantine noted with some regret. "There are still many other minor tribes to deal with in order to secure the peace. I'm confident in my ability to control the territory subject to my command, but I think we'll both benefit by coordinating our efforts. Besides, I enjoy learning from you. In light of your success, I'm hoping you will teach me better ways to gain the support of the people in securing the peace initially imposed by military conquest."

"I'm not sure I can improve upon your natural skills, but I'm willing to teach what I know," George replied. "If you would persuade your people to peace, you must first protect them from abuse. If you allow your soldiers to torture those they have conquered, the people will never have confidence in the liberty you promise. You cannot gain the trust of those who see you punish others unjustly. However, the people will bear just punishment with confidence, and mercy will inspire hope."

"Do you really believe that?" Constantine asked soberly.

"I've seen it," George replied. "I spoke with the leader of a group of Alamanni who had surrendered. He told me that his men would not fight in the face of doubtful victory because they knew they could safely surrender to our legion. This convinced me that, in the long run, refraining from torture and intimidation can save lives on both sides because the enemy knows he can safely surrender and therefore lacks the motivation to fight to the death. One of the greatest weapons against the enemy is inspiring all men to believe in liberty."

"How shall I teach men to believe in liberty?" Constantine asked.

"Prepare them to defend themselves," George replied. "As their confidence in defending themselves against abuse from others grows, freedom and liberty will instill within their souls. Then organize them as much as possible to solve their own problems and quarrels. As they do,

A Martyr's Faith

they will see the blessings of unity, and they'll accept their duty to establish peace among themselves. Moses was weighed down with the burden of judging the house of Israel until he set up a system of judges for them to govern themselves on all small matters."[3]

"Moses, eh?" Constantine sighed. "'Thou hast delivered me from the strivings of the people; and Thou hast made me the head of the heathen: a people whom I have not known shall serve me. As soon as they hear of me, they shall obey me: the strangers shall submit themselves unto me. The Lord liveth; and blessed be my Rock; and let the God of my salvation be exalted.'"[4]

"I see you still favor the Psalms," George laughed.

"My mother favors the Psalms," Constantine rebutted. "So, set them up to judge themselves. Then what?"

"Train them in perpetual service to each other," George said. "This will liberate them in great measure from excessive dependence on an inefficient central government. Such liberated people firmly establish themselves as part of the solution to most social problems."

"What of those who don't serve the living God?" Constantine inquired.

George raised his eyebrows as he considered the question carefully before answering. "There are really only two kinds of men in this world: those who seek a god who pleases them, to justify their own misconduct, and those who seek the one true and living God, to know Him, that they might worship Him and please Him and thereby become partakers of the heavenly gifts of peace, true freedom, and His glory. Some argue there are those that seek no god at all, but all such men I've known eventually declare themselves to the right or left when they come to an anguishing crossroad in life, which prompts a need for answers beyond themselves.

"You'd be surprised how many men serve the living God, though they don't fully know Him yet. If they are men devoted to learning the ways of truth, who've renounced the world and laid aside their pride, they're nearest among men to the believers in charity.[5] Praise all men who seek to follow a greater power in righteousness. Have faith that right makes might, and in that faith let us, to the end, dare to do our duty as we understand it.[6] Eventually God will lead all men back home to Him if they truly seek truth and righteousness. As for us, we must observe good faith and justice toward all nations, cultivating peace and harmony with all.[7] If our enemies incline toward peace, we should also incline toward peace and trust in God."[8]

"So, free oppressed people and provide security, economic freedom, and religious liberty," Constantine summarized. "Is this how you've gotten nations to place themselves at your mercy, seeking treaties for the

227

protection of Rome to avoid the oppression of the Germanic tribes and the Sarmatians?"

"That's it," George confirmed. "But with each treaty, you must carefully outline the covenants of peace required. In this manner, we have received many foreigners into the protection of Rome upon their submission to Roman administration and taxation."

*****

"George is in a treaty meeting," Tertius told the legion commander. "I could send for you when he is through."

"Which pitiful souls are surrendering this time?" the legion commander asked with a smile.

"It's a minor tribe from the northeast," Tertius replied. "They want to surrender to George rather than to the Sarmatians. I asked their leader why he and his people chose to submit to the Romans. He related how some of their daughters had been stolen by the Carpiani and were later returned. The daughters told of their experiences and spoke convincingly of George's actions as a fair and trustworthy leader. They even taught stories of a hero named George to the children. This leader soberly admitted the hand that rocks the cradle rules the world.[9] To their people, these women stand as faithful witnesses of George's goodness and honor, and of his God."

"This is the third time I've heard nearly the same report," the legion commander responded.

*****

Galerius had his orders and he stuck with them. He and his men spent the summer in Antioch tending to wounds, reorganizing legions, and preparing to defend against any attacks on Syria.

*****

Diocletian arrived at Antioch in the fall where he met with Galerius and joined his legions to those that had escaped being slaughtered by Narseh's army. Diocletian hadn't required Maximian to answer for the slaughter of the Theban legion, but then Maximian had won the succeeding battle. Galerius would have to answer for his actions leading to this devastating loss. "Losing this battle was a mistake," Diocletian observed. "But it would be an even greater mistake if we failed to learn from the experience for which we paid so high a price. You assured me you would win. No one interfered with your strategy. Is there anyone to blame but you?"

"No, my lord," Galerius replied, acknowledging what they both already knew.

"What went wrong?" the Emperor challenged, his steel-eyed stare prompting a confession.

Knowing Diocletian was no fool, Galerius frankly acknowledged, "I'm to blame for the loss. I underestimated the number of volunteers who would join the Persian army. In anger I declared many of my soldiers unfit for battle, upsetting the coordination of several legions. It won't happen again."

"What issues spurred your anger?" the Emperor questioned.

"Prior to the final battle, I ordered sacrifices to the Roman gods, to inspire the men. The cursed Christians in the ranks refused to bow to the pagan gods, creating a backlash of superstition among the men. In my anger I ordered the beating of all non-compliant Christians. I then declared them unfit for battle and ineligible to share in the spoils of victory. At my command, the Christian soldiers withdrew toward Syria to await the results of the battle. Fortunately, the remnants of my retreating army found refuge behind a solid line of able Christian soldiers.

Upset, Diocletian responded, "If you allow anger to rule your thinking, I can only conclude that someone else must be better suited to rule after me. I'll mark a path for your redemption this time, but don't fail me again."

*****

"What's going on?" Tiridates asked one of the legion commanders.

"Diocletian wants his soldiers to know he blames his son-in-law for these battle losses and that such failures won't be tolerated," the officer replied. "He also wants to restore the men's confidence in the man who will remain their commander. As symbolic punishment in token humiliation for his failure, Diocletian has ordered Galerius to take a turn at the scout position, marching at the front of the army as they advance toward their new positions to counter the Persian army advances. During the humiliating mile march, Galerius is required to wear the purple robes of an emperor. This exposes him as a prime target for any enemy scouts, and reinforces to his men that he still has sufficient courage to lead."

*****

Because George had established peace in the land, granting the people true liberation from bondage, the people held him in the highest regard,[10] and many inquired after his God. One old woman demanded, "Tell us about your vision before the Carpiani battle! I've heard the story a few times, but I want to hear the truth of it from you."

Such inquiries were generally respectful, still George tended to confirm the event and then bypass the details in favor of discussion on the nature of God. "Who wishes to know?" he responded lightly.

"I'm Fanya, and I'm not getting any younger so be quick about it!" she replied abruptly.

George chuckled to himself as he thought how none dare give orders to the Commander of Legions, but this tiny frail woman was unafraid, and she spoke with power. It was apparent that she needed to know. Riding the courage of the ancient woman, people began to gather and listen. "Do you believe there is a God?" George asked.

"If you say there is a God, we will believe," the old woman replied, speaking for all.

"Most assuredly there is a God, the God of Israel, who is our Father,"[11] George replied.

"Who is this God of Israel?" Fanya persisted, pressing for a full explanation.

"Who is this God of Israel?" George responded. "Have you not heard? He is our Lord and Savior Jesus Christ, the Creator of the heavens and the earth, who neither wearies nor faints. His understanding is beyond mortal capacity. To them that wait upon Him He gives power and increase, and renews their strength that they might mount up as with the wings of eagles, and they shall run and not be weary, and they shall walk and not faint."[12]

"Teach us more of this God who gives such visions and victories," the woman urged.

Though the crowd was growing rapidly, George didn't hesitate. "Our Heavenly Father loves us and seeks to bless us as we obey His commandments. Now is the kingdom of heaven at hand, for the Son of God has come upon the face of the earth. He was born of Mary, at Jerusalem, the land of my fathers, she being a virgin, a precious and chosen vessel, who was overshadowed and conceived by the power of the Holy Ghost, and she brought forth a Son, even the Son of God.

"Jesus Christ, the Son of God, went forth suffering pains and afflictions and temptations of every kind that the word of God might be fulfilled. He took upon Him death that He might loose the bands of death which bind His people. And He took upon Him their infirmities that His bowels might be filled with mercy, according to the flesh. Thus

He knows according to the flesh how to succor His people according to their infirmities. Now the Spirit knows all things; nevertheless, the Son of God suffers according to the flesh that He might take upon Him the sins of His people that He might blot out their transgressions according to the power of His deliverance. Now this is the testimony which is in me."[13]

Fanya thought for a moment and then asked, "What does God require of us, for which He will blot out our sins and deliver us?"

"We must have faith in Him and in His redeeming power, and then we must repent and be born again, for the Spirit whispers if we are not born again we cannot inherit the kingdom of heaven,"[14] George explained.

"How can I have faith in that which I only believe?" the little woman pondered aloud.

"Let your belief and your desire to know truth move you to action in faith, and try the word of God. Pray for His Spirit to reveal His truth to you. If you nurture the seed of faith in the word of God, it will swell within you and begin to enlarge your soul and enlighten your understanding, that the word will be delicious to you.[15] If you plant this seed within you and nourish it by your obedience to God, it will become a tree, springing up in you unto eternal life. May God grant unto you that your burdens may be light through the joy of His Son. Each of you can do this, if you will do it in faith.[16] For you shall live by every word that proceeds forth from the mouth of God. For the word of the Lord is truth, and whatsoever is truth is light, and whatsoever is light is Spirit, even the Spirit of Jesus Christ."[17]

"When does God speak, and to whom?" Fanya probed further.

"God is always speaking," George replied. "It is we who must learn to listen. The Spirit gives light to every man that comes into the world. The Spirit further enlightens every man who hearkens to the voice of the Spirit and comes unto God, even the Father, and the Father teaches of the covenant which He has renewed and confirmed through faith on the blood of His Son, Jesus Christ.[18] God sends His invitation unto all men, and the arms of His mercy are extended towards them as He pleads, 'Repent, and I will receive you. Come unto Me and ye shall partake of the fruit of the tree of life; yea, ye shall eat and drink of the bread and the waters of life freely; yea, come unto Me and bring forth works of righteousness.'"[19]

"How can I come unto Christ?" the old woman asked quietly.

George smiled easily. "Come and fear not. Lay aside every sin which easily besets you, which binds you down to destruction. Come and go forth, and show unto God that you are willing to repent of your sins and enter into a covenant with Him to keep His commandments, and witness it unto Him this day by going into the waters of baptism. Come and be baptized unto repentance that you may be washed from your sins, that you may have faith on the Lamb of God who has taken away the sins of the world, who is mighty to save and to cleanse from all unrighteousness. Whosoever does this and keeps the commandments of God from thenceforth, he shall have eternal life, according to the testimony of the Holy Spirit, of which I testify."[20]

George paused for a moment to scan the large crowd that had gathered. Earnestly he urged, "All you that are desirous to follow the voice of the Good Shepherd, come out from among the wicked. Separate yourselves and deny yourselves of all ungodliness, and touch not the unclean things of the unbelievers. For the names of the righteous shall be written in the book of life, and they shall be granted an inheritance at the right hand of God."[21]

Now there were many who manifested a sincere desire to enter into a covenant with God, to serve Him and keep His commandments.[22] As George observed these faithful ones enter the waters of baptism, a scripture came into his mind. *Thou didst divide the sea by Thy strength. Thou brakest the heads of the dragons in the waters.*[23] Pondering on that, he noted to himself, *the natural man, the dragon, is destroyed by covenant in the waters of baptism and by receipt of the Holy Ghost as we become the sons and daughters of God.*

*****

A distressed group of officers entered George's quarters. "My lord," one said, "we're having a bit of trouble with a growing number of enlisted men who've embraced Christianity. They seem confused about how to balance their oaths of military service with their oaths to God to seek peace and extend charity and love to all men. We're hoping you can give some guidance to us or them so we won't be forced to punish them just to maintain discipline in the ranks."

"Gather the distressed men to assembly and I'll speak to them," George quickly agreed.

When the soldiers and their commanders were gathered, George spoke easily. "Brothers, we must do our duty to God, for the Lord God has said, 'Inasmuch as ye are not guilty of the first offense, neither the second, ye shall not suffer yourselves to be slain by the hands of your enemies. Ye shall defend your families even unto bloodshed.' Therefore, we will defend ourselves and our families, our lands and our country, our rights, our freedoms and our religion.[24] Our cause is just in defending land, homes, wives, and children from the hands of our enemies and in preserving our rights of liberty and freedom to worship God according to our desires.[25] Let us press forward for peace, always mindful of our God, our religion and freedom, our wives and our children."[26]

Inviting these faithful men to join him, George led them in a declaration of their commitments. Raising their voices they declared, "We covenant with our God that we shall be destroyed if we shall fall into transgression. He may cast us at the feet of our enemies, to be trodden under foot, if we shall fall into transgression."[27]

George concluded saying, "Now let us remember to keep the commandments of our God, that He may bless us and strengthen us, preserving our lives and our liberty that we may be free from bondage and freely worship Him and His Son, Jesus Christ."[28]

*****

"You have truly had many chances to share your faith in God, yet there are many others who have had similar opportunities," Tertius observed. "Throughout the diocese, many people have converted to the Lord. There are few contentions or disputations among the Roman subjects and men deal justly with each other. They have free exchange between them, ministering generously to those who stand in need. Therefore, they are not rich and poor, bond and free, but they are all made free, becoming partakers of many heavenly gifts."[29]

"We have been blessed greatly by our God," George acknowledged.

"Will you dictate a letter to the Emperor reporting on the diocese?" Tertius inquired.

"No, thanks," George replied. "I'm going to Lydda for a month. I'll stop in Antioch to deliver my report. I've thoroughly reviewed the legion commanders' reports on troop strength and deployment, and I've inspected the harvest and tax records for each province. Such good news is best delivered in person. Besides, this will allow me to assess the Persian campaign so I can make arrangements for the protection of my family if there is a threat to Palestine."

*****

Arriving in Antioch, George met first with Galerius who was abrupt and dismissive. "I'm just awaiting the order to destroy Narseh. You keep your report until Diocletian arrives," he ordered.

Wary of Galerius' insecurity regarding his spring battle plans, George reviewed the legion commanders' reports giving details of the Persian army's strength and deployment. *Clearly, Narseh is in a defensive posture,* he thought. *I feel confident the Roman army can hold the line, but I have no confidence in their ability to regain the territory they lost earlier in the year.*

*****

"I'm very pleased with your report, George," Diocletian praised. "I've been short on good news since I got here!" he announced emphatically, greatly annoying Galerius.

"Thank you, my lord," George replied. Following a strong prompting he continued, "Looking to the future, we are planning a Harvest Celebration in Carnuntum this fall. It would be a great honor to the people if you would attend as our guest and preside over the festivities."

"I would enjoy seeing the bounty that peaceful cultivation has brought to the fertile Danube River valley," Diocletian sighed. "I can't guarantee it, but I'll try to attend this celebration in my honor. Plan to see me there."

Concluding his business, George rode his white charger home to Lydda, family, and peace.

****

CHAPTER THIRTY-ONE
Prosperity Celebrations

Northeast Frontier, Eastern Roman Empire
297 AD

*"...the LORD was with him, and...the LORD made
all that he did to prosper in his hand."*[1]
Genesis 39:3

****

Constantine, Commander of legions:
I feel a compelling urgency to turn the tide against the Persians. Therefore, I order you to select three legions from the northeast and bring them to Syria to join the battle. I have written to George, promoting him to Commander of the northeast legions while we deal with Narseh and his army. I look to your arrival by spring.
Always faithful!
– Emperor Diocletian Augustus

*****

George was surprised by the honor and trust he had been given. He responded affirmatively:

Most Noble Emperor Diocletian Augustus:
I acknowledge receipt of your orders charging me with all the affairs of the army in this quarter of the empire. Reviewing the status reports for the Danube River valley dioceses, I am confident we can maintain stability along the frontier if we enlist new recruits and restore our forces to their levels under Constantine. We can accomplish this locally, supporting your use of all the new recruits from the capital in your campaign. We've had great success with a well trained, highly mobile cavalry unit in our furthest west diocese. I will be developing similar cavalry units in the other dioceses. Our engineers will plan new defensive structures to provide greater protection and security to our soldiers and our people.
With our increasing security, the subjects of Rome have shown more ambition in their spring planting. We anticipate another very

prosperous harvest after so many years of war. We are most pleased that you plan to attend our great Harvest Celebration at Carnuntum in the fall, that we may honor you as our victorious Emperor at the festival, if you are not detained by the campaign in Syria. In any case, I will send regular reports to keep you informed, that you may rest assured of our success and support. We pray for your swift victory against Narseh.
   Always faithful!
– George, Commander of the northeast legions

*****

"I'm giving you the chance to redeem yourself in battle. Don't fail me!" Diocletian admonished Galerius. "I'm taking Constantine and Tiridates and assuming personal command of the legions in western Armenia. You will have the majority of the army to drive Narseh's forces out of Roman Mesopotamia. I'm expecting a prompt victory against the Persians so I won't have to miss the Harvest Celebration in my honor at Carnuntum."

*****

"Should we do more than just maintain our supportive flanking position in western Armenia?" Constantine asked Diocletian. "We've seen how Narseh and his cavalry have outmaneuvered Galerius in Mesopotamia. Though he has superior forces, Galerius isn't making any progress against the Persian army. Their cavalry is simply too quick for the Roman infantry to counter. The Persians quickly load their point of attack until they have the advantage, inflicting heavy casualties on our legions. When they can't gain the advantage, they retreat quickly, greatly minimizing their own losses. The spring enthusiasm among the Roman army has been crushed into a summer fatigue as the campaign has dragged on, with no advantage gained."

"Hold your positions," Diocletian responded. "If Galerius can't conquer, he's finished. However, I am impressed with the power and effectiveness of the mobile cavalry forces under Narseh, George, and your father. I must begin to emphasize the use of cavalry to complement our infantry, especially in battles on the lowland plains."

*****

Diocletian read the letter twice and swore. "Defiance is infectious!"
"More bad news?" Constantine asked.

"The Persian victories in battle, especially Narseh's defeat of Galerius at Carrhae, have inspired revolt in Egypt. Lucius Domitius Domitianus has refused to pay the annual taxes on the harvest and has declared himself Augustus of Egypt. He probably believes our war with the Persians has drained the empire of its ability to maintain control over the outlying provinces. His actions are rash, but I know exactly how to respond. He has underestimated us and it will cost him his life."

*****

Taking two legions from western Armenia, Diocletian marched southeast to meet with Galerius. "You will hold defensive positions for the remainder of the season," he instructed his Caesar. "And again I warn you not to harm Constantine as we still need him for leverage against his father, though Constantius is still busily occupied quelling rebellions in the northwest."

Moving past his frustration, Diocletian wrote to George advising that he would be unable to attend the celebration due to the rebellion in Egypt. Taking two more legions from Galerius, Diocletian departed for Africa. By fall he had reached southern Egypt and overcome the rebels there. He then moved north to the Nile River delta and laid siege to Alexandria.

*****

Galerius was irritated by the nagging feeling that Diocletian had lost confidence in him. Still, he tightened his forces in a defensive posture as commanded. As he pondered his position, he thought, *The way the men worship Constantine is disgusting. Even my officers favor his commands and strategies, thinking they'll win, rather than fighting at my command, thinking they'll lose. Strategy isn't much more than controlling the battlefield with a larger force. No matter. I'll kill him soon enough. But for now, I still need him to hold western Armenia, protecting Syria and the northwestern flank of my army. I can wait until after my victory over Narseh to rid myself of Constantine.*

*****

George met with the prefect near the end of spring planting. "I'm grateful that you've worked so closely with me to establish order throughout the northeast quarter of the empire," he praised.

"My experience with you in the northwestern diocese last year has raised my confidence," the prefect replied. "I'm determined to be cooperative and helpful in the two new dioceses, expecting similar results."

*****

At harvest time, the prefect observed, "The people have been inspired by peace, security, and liberty. Their hard work has greatly improved their herds, crops, and communities."

"I give thanks to God for the many privileges and blessings He has bestowed upon the people,"[2] George replied.

*****

As they met for the Harvest Celebration, George led the people in honoring the nation and the Emperor. "Blessed subjects of Rome, I'm honored to gather with you to celebrate the rich blessings of this year and to honor those who have guided us to this prosperity. First, let us honor our great Emperor, Diocletian Augustus, who has brought us peace through strength."

The assembly answered George with the stout reply, "Hazzah! Hazzah! Hazzah for Diocletian!"

When the crowd had quieted, George continued, "I witness that you have honored your covenants with Rome. The required taxes have been delivered to Nicodemia, to the treasury of the Republic. You shall keep all the remaining wealth in your possession." George paused for another deafening cheer before proceeding.

"As we begin our celebration, I call upon all men to remember the great things the Lord has done in establishing this Republic, bringing peace and prosperity to His children. He has preserved us from destruction at the hands of our enemies and has given us this choice land for our inheritance.[3] This land has been consecrated by the Lord. If we serve Him according to the commandments He has given, we will prosper in the land, for this land shall be blessed unto the righteous forever.[4] Awake and put on the armor of righteousness. Arise and be faithful to God, one in mind and one in heart, united in all things that we may not incur the displeasure of a just God upon us. Oh, that we might shake off the chains of iniquity forever and be a choice and a favored people of the Lord, for His ways are righteous forever, and His will be done.[5] Now let us celebrate our peace, liberty, and prosperity!"

*****

The crowd was festive as George moved about the fairgrounds, congratulating many on their bountiful harvests and carefully examining the various physical and mental contests open to all. "The celebration was initially planned to follow the pattern of the harvest celebration and youth battle skills tournament in Lydda," George told the prefect. "However, the organizing committee kept adding more and more ideas to make the celebration more fun and interesting."

"I like the displays of livestock and produce, along with the baked goods and other food and drink abundantly available for purchase," the prefect replied. "I like the toys and crafts for the kids, but my favorites are the many games set up for diversion, with modified games for the younger children. Sheep riding and pig wrestling appear very popular."

"Yes, but I think we could do without the kissing booth," George said with a little cringe.

"The battle skills competitions for sword combat and targets for spears, arrows, and slings are getting the most attention," the prefect noted. "But I've also seen an obstacle course, foot races, rock lifting, and team tug-of-war."

"The serious games are geared toward the twelve to seventeen-year-old age group for both girls and boys," George explained. "I try hard to attend as many competitions as possible, always looking for the unpolished gems of youth."

"I've noticed a host of statues and images of the various gods that are being displayed, bought, sold, and worshipped," the prefect observed. "Doesn't that irritate you?"

"Though they know not the one true and living God, it's good to see so many giving thanks and honor in their own way," George said. "Let them live by what they believe, and diligently seek to gain more truth. This is the day which the Lord hath made; we will rejoice and be glad in it."[6]

*****

George moved easily through the celebrating crowds until he came upon a small assembly of Christians. Enthusiastically they hailed him, inviting him to speak to their group. With a silent prayer to God for the guidance of His Spirit, George joined the people and declared, "Let us praise the Lord for His goodness and for His wonderful works to the children of men! Let our sacrifices be the sacrifices of thanksgiving, declaring His works with rejoicing.[7] Let us contend no more against the Holy Ghost but receive it and take upon us the name of Christ. Let us humble ourselves to the dust and worship God in spirit and in truth, living in thanksgiving daily for the many mercies and blessings which He has bestowed upon us.[8]

"Let us bear joyful witness of our faith in God by our actions,[9] following the example of His Son, Jesus Christ, in charity and service. There are many ways to serve others. We can share skills in preservation, storage, preparation, and distribution of food. We can teach reading and writing. We can train in cleanliness and sanitation. Those with skills in medicine should seek to learn from others and to teach others, that all may benefit. Organize yourselves to care for the poor and the needy, for to bear another's burden is an invitation for the Lord to bear your burdens. Truly, to ease another's heartache is to forget your own.[10]

"Believers are blessed by and should act according to the Spirit of God,[11] which is also the spirit of freedom which is in us. Those who serve God need not fear, for God will deliver all those who stand fast in that liberty wherewith He has made us free.[12] Think not that God will spare you from all adversity, for all who live godly lives shall suffer persecution.[13] There are many tests of integrity in mortal life. One of the most important is the test of adversity, which reveals whether we will hold to righteousness in the face of persecution and punishment and not only for promised rewards. Another important test of adversity is whether we will refuse evil, even when we are promised great rewards for embracing it.

"Trust in God at all times. Pour out your hearts before Him in prayer. God is a refuge for us in joy and peace.[14] Follow the example of Christ, being obedient to the Father in all things, making and keeping all the covenants extended to us by our God. Notwithstanding Christ being holy, He showed unto men that, according to the flesh, He humbled Himself before the Father and witnessed obedience unto the Father by keeping all His commandments. Wherefore, can we follow Jesus except we shall keep the commandments of the Father?[15] Therefore, repent and be baptized in the name of Jesus Christ that He may redeem you in the great day of judgment. For He is faithful, redeeming those who delight in His laws and keep His covenants. Praise the Lord, for His truth endures forever."[16]

"Amen, Brother. Your words are well spoken," the group leader said graciously. "We feel the depth of your convictions. The Spirit has inspired many to that mighty change of heart that awakens within us a new man in Christ.[17] Your example has brought the knowledge of the truth to many and turned them to God, calling on His name and confessing their sins before Him."[18]

*****

People enjoying the celebration spoke frequently about George and his part in leading them to prosperity. "He's helped us shore up our defenses against invaders," the prefect explained to one group. "Though he imposes the required taxes upon the people, he doesn't steal from them. He deals swiftly and harshly with those taking bribes or attempting to bribe. It's clear that he's not seeking for power, but for peace and liberty for his people."[19]

As the closing ceremonies of the celebration began, one of the local authorities in Carnuntum rose to speak. Standing on the wall above the gate, his message was simple: "Let us sing praises." Then with a rich voice and in a joyful and exultant tempo he sang:

He shall judge the poor of the people, He shall save the children of the needy.
Oppressors shall fear Him as long as the sun and moon endure, throughout all generations.
In His days shall the righteous flourish; and peace abound as long as the sun and moon endure.
They that dwell in the wilderness shall bow before Him; and His enemies shall lick the dust.
He shall deliver the needy when they cry; the poor also, and them that have no helper.
He shall spare the poor and the needy, and shall save the souls of the needy.
He shall redeem their souls from deceit and violence. Precious is their blood in His sight.[20]

The people had anticipated celebrating the Emperor for his victories against the Sarmatians, but realizing how valuable George's leadership had been in maintaining peace through strength, they had little trouble in redirecting the focus of their celebration onto him as the presiding dignitary. And so the chant arose: *"George! George! George!"*

George knew the sacred words of this hymn of praise were meant for Another. Rising to speak he signaled for quiet. "Great people of the Roman Republic, I love you, but I cannot accept the praise you so generously offer. For all praise, glory, and honor belong to God, our Savior and Redeemer."

*****

"Tales of the celebration have spread quickly throughout the northeast quarter of the empire," Tertius reported. "They have inspired many successful smaller celebrations elsewhere."

"When the people are war-weary and starved for a celebration, it's easy to get support and have success," George replied. "However, these people truly have cause for celebration. Peace, liberty, and prosperity. Yet I feel a bit uncomfortable with how frequently and generously I am honored in these festivities. I'm also uncomfortable with the embellished story of my epic battle with a dragon."

"Tolerance, my lord," Tertius said defensively. "The people need good stories to inspire them."

*****

With the harvest celebrations throughout the northeast concluded, George turned his attention back to reviewing his legions and protecting his people. The commands he had given regarding religious tolerance were generally being honored, promoting a mutual respect among many faiths and encouraging many to seek greater truth and an increase in righteousness. The blessings of righteousness and continued peace were undeniable.

As George met with his legion commanders, he encouraged them, "Be examples in might and humility, praising God for His bounties. How great reason we have to rejoice! Could we have supposed God would grant unto us such great blessings? We came into this land, not to destroy the people, but with the intent that we might save them and bring them true peace.[21] Remember how generous God has been in sparing our lives and how many miracles He has wrought in this land as our brethren have been released from the oppression of other nations.[22] This great people have suffered every affliction in the course of their deliverance, but they've been patient, and now they've become heirs of peace and prosperity as subjects of the Roman Republic. Together we shall dwell in safety and shall withstand the fierce thrusts of the enemy.[23]

"These people have accepted us into their homes and we've taught them of the God of peace. Thousands rejoice, having been brought into His fold. They were encircled about with darkness, but God has loosed their chains and brought them into His everlasting light. Because of the power of His word, they feel to sing the song of His redeeming love.[24]

"My heart is full of joy for God's children and I will rejoice in Him. Who can glory too much in the blessings of our God? Have we not great reason to rejoice? We are in the hands of the Lord of the harvest, and He will raise us up.[25] Now we see that God is mindful of every people, whatsoever land they may be in, and His bowels of mercy are over all the earth. Now this is my joy and my great thanksgiving. I will give thanks unto my God forever."[26]

*****

Diocletian was still in Egypt when he received word that, due to a bountiful harvest, the northeast quarter of the empire had remitted much more in taxes than had been expected. "This is welcome news," he told his aid. "It reassures me of the loyalty of George and my new subjects in the northeast. Take down my reply."

George, Commander of the northeast legions:
Your report and the substantial contribution to the treasury are most welcome. The people have truly been blessed by the peace and prosperity I have provided. Pass on my gratitude for their loyal support. The ample tax remittance from the northeast will greatly offset the unpaid Egyptian revenues, though I'm confident they will surely be recovered in full, with interest, once the rebellion is crushed. Though it's already December, I have full control of rural Egypt and I've laid siege to Alexandria. Domitianus has died under questionable circumstances, but Aurelius Achilleus has succeeded him, claiming Egypt as his own. I shall prove otherwise.
Always faithful!
– Emperor Diocletian Augustus

*****

"There's been much fighting with the Persians, but no real progress by either side," Galerius confided to the senator. "I stayed in Syria till the winter troop deployments were complete. I left Constantine in charge and traveled to Antioch, and now I've come here to Nicodemia to gather new recruits for the coming year. I'm anxious to redeem myself by destroying Narseh's army, but Diocletian's delay in Egypt and his order to remain defensive is damaging my reputation."

"Why do you think he's stifling your success?" the senator chided as he poured more wine for Galerius. "Is it possible that Diocletian has his eye on another potential successor?

"Not a chance," Galerius grunted. "He distrusts Constantine as much as I do."

"What about George?" the senator prodded. "He is the talk of the capital with all the territory he's annexed and the people he's subjected to Rome, not to mention the wealth he's remitted to the imperial treasury. In every part of the capital they're singing his praises."

"George, the son of Gerontius? He's just an overgrown boy," Galerius replied without convincing himself. "I need to stay focused on my strategy. I need treasury money for the war and more fighting men. When Narseh is dead, then I can focus on any ambitious competitors and figure out how to eliminate them. Constantine and George should be wary."

*****

Carefully George reviewed the contents of the Emperor's note. It struck him that the Emperor's sole focus in conquest was on the establishment and prosperity of the tax base. George thought, *The primary blessings are peace, liberty, and prosperity through righteousness. The spread of the gospel of Jesus Christ is the greatest bounty of all, with all praise and glory to the Father and His Son.* George reflected on the path his life had taken since joining Diocletian's army and the great goodness of the Lord in revealing His great and marvelous works.[27] He was confident as he thought, *I know in Whom I have trusted. My God has been my support.*[28] *Let them shout for joy and be glad that favor God's righteous cause. Let them say continually, Let the Lord be magnified, which has pleasure in the prosperity of His servant. And my tongue shall speak of Thy righteousness and of Thy praise all the day long.*[29] *I will offer to Thee the sacrifice of thanksgiving and will call upon the name of the Lord.*[30]

*****

"The northeast quarter of the empire continues to expand by degrees," George said to Tertius. "The press of tribes and kingdoms seeking security and prosperity by treaty is a good problem for us. Happily, I'm taking a much needed break, traveling home again to Lydda to pass the new year with family."

****

CHAPTER THIRTY-TWO
The Glorious Report

Northeast Frontier, Eastern Roman Empire
298 AD

"To every thing there is a season, and a time to every purpose under the heaven:...a time to keep silence, and a time to speak;..."[1]
Ecclesiastes 3:1, 7

****

As next in authority in the northeast quarter of the empire, it was Urbane's duty to immediately review all military communications received in George's absence. The request appeared to be fairly routine. "Tertius," he called, "the fighting season is coming and Galerius requires a report on troop strength and positions to guide his planning for deployment of the new recruits. His mighty struggle with the Persians is still unresolved. He has over 120,000 men at his command, but it hasn't been enough. Now he's asking specifically how George has been able to secure the entire northeast quarter with only 80,000 soldiers, as identified in our previous report. I need you to draft a response to Galerius. Once you have it prepared, submit it to me for review before any action is taken."

"Yes, sir!" Tertius responded. He'd seen these types of requests before and felt confident he could draft an appropriate reply in George's absence. *In fact*, he thought, *I might even be able to improve upon George's prior reports.*

After studying the reports from the legion and militia commanders, Tertius compiled his facts and figures and drafted his report:

Most Noble Emperor Galerius Caesar,
The northeast command is in receipt of your recent post. In response, I offer the following updated report on the status of our administration, troop strength, and resources.
We began the year with 80,000 trained soldiers under arms. During the year, we lost approximately 10,000 men whose enlistments expired or who requested and were granted voluntary discharges. We lost a few through skirmishes with our enemies and a few to training injuries. During the course of the year, we enlisted and trained about 15,000 new

recruits, bringing our total enlistment of trained men at arms to roughly 85,000.

Beyond the limited numbers of men in the regular Roman army, the strength of our defensive forces is magnified greatly by the local militias that have been established. The local militias are filled with young men, many of whom have served two years in the Roman army before returning to their villages. Others have been trained by the Roman soldiers and have been armed to protect their villages, which has discouraged the ambitions of our enemies and has brought a great measure of peace to these people. Our militias are extremely effective in their cooperation with the regular Roman army, and they display a heightened sense of commitment, not only for their own villages, but also for all the territory of the empire.

George has altered the management of the army so that each of the three dioceses has 20,000 soldiers posted in the villages and along the borders to protect the people. Mobile troops numbering 25,000 have been stationed so that a minimum of 10,000 are within a day's ride of any point in each diocese. If any attack is made, all the groups shift half their forces one position toward the attack and then await further orders. Response drills are held randomly each month to keep the forces familiar with procedures and to keep ambitious invaders uncertain as to what level of defenses they might encounter in any attack. Physical defenses such as walls and towers have been erected, restored, expanded, and improved through public works projects.

In the event of an outside attack, signal fires can also be lit, allowing an attacked village to call for help from the militias of the adjoining villages who share common economic and familial ties. Each of the three dioceses has between 25,000 and 30,000 trained fighting men, either active in the militia or normally engaged in other trades, who are armed and available in the villages. Considering the nearly 90,000 armed militia men, together with the 85,000 soldiers currently enlisted in the regular army, the overall battle strength under George's command is a minimum of 175,000 men. If the need were to arise and all available hands were pressed into service on short notice, the number of loyal soldiers in George's army would immediately double and possibly triple the regular army census in just a few short weeks.

George has won the confidence of the conquered people who revere him for his leadership, protection, and justice. They sincerely praise him for the peace he has established in their lands after so many years of continuous war. Some are calling him their Prince of Peace. A few groups have designated holiday celebrations specifically to George and Freedom. These events sometimes rival the Celebration of the Emperors

in their pomp and festivity.
I, Tertius, who wrote this epistle, salute you most noble Galerius.[2]

With Urbane's uncertain review, the response was approved and sent.

*****

When George returned from Lydda to his post, he reviewed the work done in his absence. Seeing the order for a report on troop strength from Galerius, he considered how best to respond. As he pondered, he found a copy of the response Tertius had sent and read it.

"Tertius," George called out, "Come to my quarters. We need to discuss the report you sent to Galerius."

"Yes, sir!" Tertius replied, smiling proudly as he entered George's quarters.

Quietly, George closed the door behind Tertius. "Sit down with me. I'm greatly concerned over the report you sent. I wish you hadn't sent it."

Tertius was surprised and devastated. "What did I do wrong?" he asked. "The report was true and accurate. Though it highlights your success and popularity, it's not self-serving."

"It's accurate," George admitted, "...to a fault. I've been organizing our forces to effectively defend the people of this region. To do that, we've needed more men at arms than the size of army I've been authorized to establish and maintain. As you so clearly noted, we've covered the difference with our system of local militias. Since they're not part of the regular army, I've never included them in the troop strength reports. I didn't want anyone to feel threatened by the size of our loyal forces. Galerius has 120,000 soldiers at his command, but many of them are battle-weary and must be kept in place to counter the Persians. If he was confronted by an ambitious usurper, he couldn't bring that many soldiers to bear in a civil conflict. Now our report has informed him that a commander in a comparatively peaceful region has 175,000 or more fiercely loyal soldiers ready at his command, when a troop strength of only 100,000 has been authorized."

"Oh, no! Now I see what I've done," Tertius moaned. "Based on that report, I might view you as a threat to my succession, if I was an insecure commander."

"Precisely," George confirmed. "You and I know we have no ambitions beyond the peace and protection of the people of this Republic. What we shall soon learn is whether Galerius is a man who knows in whom he should place his trust and whether he trusts in us as well."

"I pray he's not one of the people who buy the life of this world at the price of the hereafter," Tertius replied.[3] "George, I'm so sorry I've let you down. I did what I thought was best, and now I feel just terrible. I'll resign my commission immediately, if you wish."

"Don't be ridiculous," George laughed. "You haven't let me down, nor will you. God is over all. I remain confident in your faith and loyalty. If I'm a success today, it's because I had a Friend who believed in me, and I didn't have the heart to let Him down.[4] Besides, I'm just getting you trained. I don't want to start over from nothing with some raw recruit."

As George pondered on the situation a moment, he felt increasing confidence and a determination to exercise faith and trust in God that all would work out to His glory. "Blessed is the man that makes the Lord his trust, and respects not the proud, nor such as turn aside to lies.[5] Have no fear, brother Tertius. I'm sure the Lord's hand will be in anything that comes."

****

CHAPTER THIRTY-THREE
A Few Good Men

Eastern Roman Empire
298 AD

"The people that are with thee are too many for Me..."[1]
Judges 7:2

****

Galerius silently scanned the report from Tertius. He was unsettled by the claim of 175,000 or more trained fighters loyal to George's commands. There was no mistaking the unmasked ambition of George and his legion commanders. They were an undeniable threat to Galerius' plan to seize control of the empire. *Almost as dangerous as an opponent with a larger loyal army is an ambitious man who mistakenly thinks he has a larger loyal army*, Galerius thought.

Anxiously Galerius discussed the matter with his top commanders. "What is the mood of the army, and how will they respond to threats from another quarter of the empire?" he asked.

"We have 120,000 men who are exhausted from battle, but their loyalty for Diocletian remains very strong," one officer replied. "If Constantius turned southeast, we would have to leave a sizeable army in Syria to counter the Persians, but we would gain a sizeable force from George in the northeast. His men have been very effective in battle and there are relatively few issues currently distracting his army."

"And what of George and his ambitions?" Galerius asked, pressing toward his real concern.

"He kilt a beastly dragon with naught but a stick in me own province," one officer joked drawing a light bit of laughter from the group. Galerius' face showed he was not in a joking mood.

Cautiously, another man observed, "Beyond his success leading men into battle, George has many achievements in civil administration. He has shown faithful support of the Republic through remitted tax revenues. He consistently protects those within his care and it's apparent that his people love and reverence him."

Galerius was irritated that his own commanders held George in such obviously high regard. He was also annoyed that any of the Emperor's subjects would be described as George's people. "Does any man here view George as a threat to the Emperor?" He finally asked in a thinly veiled thrust at the crux of the matter.

"My Lord, we all agree that George has been a faithful servant of the Emperor in every particular. However, his demonstrated capacity, his growing reputation, and his personal bearing suggest his potential to be a serious threat to imperial succession as long as he commands his army. Thus far he has truly overcome any man who has opposed him."

"That will be all. You're dismissed," Galerius said, sensing the need to hide his jealousy. *I must avoid causing a rift in the loyalties of my officers as I plan to destroy George,* he thought. *Separating George from his army is obviously the first step in my plan.*

*****

"Galerius has ordered us to transfer 30,000 soldiers to his army immediately to assist in the war against the Persians," George announced to his legion commanders. "I believe he may have some concerns that our armed forces are stronger than necessary. He may also suspect that some of us have ambitions."

"He's a man of war who is neither secure in nor content with the ambition of peace," Florian observed.

"Still, his request is not unreasonable," George concluded. "I believe Diocletian would support it given the peace in the northeastern provinces and the lack of progress in the Persian war."

"But the loss of six entire legions is an open invitation to our enemies!" Urbane declared.

"Not if we manage the transition well and follow the Spirit," George replied.

"Will we draw lots then to select which of our legions must go?" Urbane asked.

"Not this time," George answered. "We'll fare better if we apply wisdom instead of luck." As he spoke, George's mind filled with a proverb: *These six things doth the Lord hate: yea, seven are an abomination unto Him: a proud look, a lying tongue, hands that shed innocent blood, a heart that deviseth wicked imaginations, feet that be swift in running to mischief, a false witness that speaketh lies, and he that soweth discord among his brethren.*[2] This gave him a few ideas about how this transfer of troops should be handled from his end.

"We will answer the call, but we won't be sending any of our standing legions," George replied. "We'll be forming five new legions with 6,000 men each to transfer to Syria. We'll organize them and take a week to train them as units. Then we'll send them on to Galerius. You

A Martyr's Faith

men must identify who will be sent to the battle front. My guidelines for selecting which men to send include the following:

1. Men who are currently subject to disciplinary action within our ranks.
2. Men who are greedy, bragging about expected gains from the spoils of war, for they shall not walk with us.[3]
3. Men who speak lies for entertainment or gain.
4. Men who bear a spirit of anger and contention, lusting for blood and battle, preferring warfare to peace, seeking conquest and power over liberty and prosperity.[4]
5. Men who take gifts and bribes, for they choose blindness to evil and become incapable of righteous judgment, turning aside the poor without cause.[5]
6. Men who frequent the tents of sultry women who follow the legions' camp. These men and the women with them will be sent to Galerius' army, for we must be moral and abide in our covenants if we are to abide in the favor of God.[6]
7. Men who witness falsely against others.
8. Men who are malevolent gossips and backbiters. We will not retain any trouble makers.
9. Men who gamble in earnest, for he who gambles earnestly seeks to cheat life of his labor and seeks to heap his burdens on other men.[7]
10. Men who are gluttonous, wasting excessively, destroying for no purpose but spite.[8]
11. Men who are slothful, lazy, and remiss in their duties, taxing unity and security.[9]
12. Men who take the name of our God in vain. The most beautiful names belong to God, so let us use them to call upon Him with reverence and rid ourselves of such men as use His names profanely.[10]
13. Men who make light of their own faith or the faith of others, for we must not walk with those who trifle with sacred things.[11] We distance ourselves from those who take their religion to be mere play and amusement and are deceived by the life of this world.[12]
14. Men who volunteer for their own personal reasons, such as those who desire to be elsewhere.
15. Men who are chosen by lot, only after all other methods of selection are exhausted.

"I'll distribute written copies of these guidelines to each of you, but you will make the final decisions as to who we send. I urge you to make these decisions a matter of prayer before you report back to me with your lists of men for transfer."

Again Urbane spoke. "These men are accustomed to volunteering and lotteries. I'm just not sure how well they'll respond to these other methods of selection."

"The Roman army is not a democracy!" George declared abruptly. "These men will take orders. They've made their oaths and will now be held to them. As God is over all, these men will be just as safe and blessed if they choose to obey Him in the southeast as in the northeast. Otherwise, they have no promise. I know my guidelines speak harshly against the ungodly, according to the truth. The righteous I've justified. The guilty take the truth to be hard, for it cuts them to the very center.[13] Our charge is to use every means at our disposal to strengthen our army and to secure peace and prosperity for the area under our administration. We'll keep the most faithful soldiers under our command and seek the blessings of God in preserving peace. We'll send those who seek other paths to answer the call of Galerius. Now, return to your posts and do the work that must be done. The sooner we complete this task, the sooner we can reorganize our remaining forces and begin training our own new recruits, lest being unprepared we entice ambition from our neighbors to the north and east."

"Yes, sir!" was the responsive chorus as the legion commanders departed.

*****

"Tertius, I'm anxious about the toll this conscription will take on our forces," George explained. "I want an open call put out to former soldiers in the local militias and villages. Any who have similar desires for battle or relocation will be sworn back into the regular army and assigned to one of the five new legions. Any men who simply want back into the military in the northeast will be considered for replacement positions in our standing legions."

*****

"We've been able to cull the troublemakers and those with a lust for violence and bloodshed out of our ranks," the legion commanders reported. "We've also selected most of the men who have shown discomfort with the rising standard of conduct expected by all in the northeast army. Few of these men have objected to their new assignments, sensing the opportunity is a match to their need for a change. The new legions have been organized with leadership and they have begun drilling for unity."

*****

As George watched these men work hard to mesh and bond, he felt love for them and hope for their futures despite their faults. Earnestly he prayed, "Father, bless these men with success that they might survive the coming battles, that they might yet have further opportunities to repent and come unto Christ and overcome the hardness of their hearts."[14]

*****

Having complied with the order for redeployment of 30,000 soldiers to Galerius' army, George reviewed the remaining troops with his legion commanders. "See how good it is for brethren to dwell together in unity!"[15] he declared with enthusiasm. "However, there is much work to do. We've renewed local recruiting to restore the strength of our regular army back to the previously authorized levels."

"Many men in our provinces are anxious to join up for several reasons," Urbane noted. "Some see you as an inspired protector. Others simply want work that provides a solid income for their struggling families. Still others have heard that, in addition to battle training, we provide opportunities for training in literacy and trade skills."

*****

Most Noble Emperor Galerius Caesar, Commander of the Syrian legions:
Alexandria withstood the siege until March, when I was able to finally put down the revolt and execute Achilleus. I feel a growing weariness in my bones. Perhaps that is brought on by the extended length of the fighting season in the warmer climates. In any case, I've decided to remain in Egypt through the end of the year, restoring civil order with new leaders worthy of my trust. With the legions from the northeast, I expect you and Constantine will soon cry "Victory!"
Always faithful!
– Emperor Diocletian Augustus

*****

When the legions from the northeast arrived at the camp in Syria, Galerius was initially wary of the new soldiers, but with battle imminent he had no time to waste on suspicions. Assigning each new legion to report to a commander of one of his own legions, he called the men to assemble, administered the oaths of allegiance to the Emperor and to himself and then assigned each legion to its post. As he left the assembly field, the new legions stood firm. "What are they waiting for?" Galerius demanded.

"They are expecting a reciprocating oath of allegiance from you to them," an officer responded.

After a few awkward moments Galerius replied, "That's ridiculous! Go to your posts!"

*****

Constantine reviewed the troop positions and the terrain. "Narseh's forces appear ready to defend against an attack on the western Mesopotamian valley," he noted. "Perhaps they can be overcome if we attack from northern Syria, heading east into Armenia. If the main body of our army pushes east across Armenia, turning south into the heart of the eastern Mesopotamian valley, we can outflank the Persians and cut their supply lines. Tiridates could remain in Armenia to restore civil administration there. One of us should stay in Syria, protecting the rear guard of our main army, defending any westward attacks by Narseh from Mesopotamia. Do you want to attack or defend, Galerius?"

Even Galerius could see great wisdom in Constantine's plan, yet it annoyed him that such a strategy had never occurred to him. "I'll be leading the main army," he replied gruffly and then left.

"I'm happy to let Galerius' forces do the heavy lifting and take all the glory, so long as I don't have to spend much time in the presence of the barbarian," Constantine whispered to Tiridates.

*****

As the campaign against the Persians progressed, Galerius was surprised at the respect these new soldiers had for George, who had just sent them to the battle front. One of his own legion commanders observed, "Aside from some normal disciplinary issues, the men George sent are well trained for combat and are generally anxious to be in battle. With their skills and brutal aggression, they're worth 50,000 of the standard fare of soldiers. These are the type of men I would have kept with me to strengthen my position."

*****

Most Noble Emperor Diocletian Augustus:
   Victory! Victory! Victory! That echoing cry you hear is mine. I engaged Narseh's army much more aggressively, rapidly turning the tide in our favor. I personally led the attack against the Persians in Armenia. The rugged mountain terrain was favorable to my infantry over the enemy's cavalry. Working with Tiridates and some local Armenians, my attack was a surprise. I was victorious in two successive battles. It should please you to know that during our second encounter at Satala, I captured Narseh's treasury and his royal harem. The spoils were substantial, containing all the wealth the Persians had taken from Tiridates' people. I've claimed half in the name of the Republic. I gave a fourth to Tiridates and his people. The other fourth I gave to the soldiers to divide. Narseh sent an ambassador to plead for the return of his wives and children, but I refused. I then won a string of victories, advancing by the fall into Media and Adiabene. Having gotten behind Narseh's army, I pushed down the Tigris River, south into Persian Mesopotamia, taking Narseh's capital at Ctesiphon, filling the roads with blood. It was glorious. I could almost see the ruins of Babylon before I turned west and swept the Persians from all of Roman Mesopotamia, from the Tigris to the Euphrates River. I expect you will want to join me for peace negotiations in the spring. It promises to be such a delight.
   Always faithful!
– *Emperor Galerius Caesar, Commander of the Syrian legions*

*****

Most Noble Emperor Diocletian Augustus:
   By slaughtering the rogue Frankish mercenaries, Constantius has endeared himself to the people of Britannia. Returning to Gaul, he quickly put down the allies of Allectus. Now he's taken his army east, gaining great victories over the Alamanni at Lingones and then at Vindonissa, near the Alps mountains. I exhort you to be wary. I don't know where he will stop.
   Always faithful!
– *Emperor Maximian Augustus*

*****

Feeling invincible, Galerius pondered how he might remove Diocletian. "I've got money to fund my plans, but I still need to deal with Constantius, Constantine, and George," he muttered.

****

CHAPTER THIRTY-FOUR
Final Promotion

Eastern Roman Empire
299 AD

*"For promotion cometh neither from the east, nor from the west,
nor from the south. But God is the judge:
He putteth down one, and setteth up another."*[1]
Psalm 75:6-7

****

Most Noble Emperor Maximian Augustus:
 I am also wary of Constantius. For our own protection, I am reintroducing conscription for citizens of the Republic. This will support a substantial increase in our military expansion. As our armies grow to keep pace with Constantius, collectively we will have well over half a million men at arms throughout the empire. The frontiers and borders are currently being defended by garrisons of regular infantry. However, my observations of the Persian cavalry and the mounted forces under Constantius and George prompt me to establish centralized divisions of highly mobile mounted fighters. These will be based well within the borders of the empire, in posts where they can quickly respond to any trouble spots. I have also ordered the expansion of our fleet. This grand military expansion will require a severe tax burden. It may be difficult for the people to bear and they may believe it is strangling their struggling economy. However, I'm confident this change will stabilize peace through strength in the Republic. Our people will prosper greatly in the absence of the scourge of war, enabling them to bear the tax burden.
 Always faithful!
– Emperor Diocletian Augustus

*****

Peace negotiations with Narseh were undertaken in the spring, with both Diocletian and Galerius attending. Diocletian's personal assistant, Sicorius Probus, was sent to relay terms of peace, which were quite severe for the Persians. Upon his return, Sicorius relayed the counter-proposal from Narseh to the Roman Emperor. "In exchange for the return of his wives and children, the Persian monarch offers to give up territory to Rome, making the Tigris the boundary between the two empires. Further, Armenia will be returned to Roman dominion."

"No!" Diocletian boomed. "His offer is nothing beyond what we've already taken by force. Rome must control all the trade routes between Armenia and Persia. This is not negotiable! Relay these terms. Report back when we have an accord."

"I'll reiterate the terms to Narseh," Sicorius replied anxiously. "Is there anything else?"

"No. That should be all," the Emperor responded. With that, the messenger departed.

"Diocletian, you've got the upper hand, and you're playing it well," Constantine said with some admiration. "I think Narseh will agree to your terms this time as long as Sicorius doesn't flinch when he presents them. History teaches that men and nations behave wisely once they've exhausted all other alternatives."[2]

"Yes," agreed the Emperor. "My goal is to exhaust all other alternatives for our enemies as promptly as possible."

Moments later Sicorius returned, breathless, but smiling. "We have an accord!" he spouted.

"With control of these territories, we will have a great advantage in defending against any future Persian advances through the region," Diocletian responded with a sense of relief.

*****

Most Noble Emperor Galerius Caesar, Commander of the Syrian legions:

Congratulations on your victory over the Persians and your favorable treaty. As you have requested, enclosed is a current status report on our regular army census. As you can see, overall we have been able to restore our forces to 80,000 men at arms. That is just 5,000 men short of what we had when you requisitioned men for the Persian war. We are secure in our ability to keep the peace with the forces we have. It will take some time, but we feel confident we can raise forces to the previously ordered level of 100,000 men. The legions we sent can remain deployed in the southeast while the peace cures. We have heard rumors that Diocletian is considering raising troop levels generally. Any information you can provide on that would be appreciated. Finally, with the treaty in place, I encourage you to come and personally inspect the forces at your command in the northeast.

Always faithful!
– George, Commander of the northeast legions

*****

It was late evening as Galerius walked silently through the camp to his tent. *I'm sick of these groups of men always praising George and sharing countless tales of his heroics,* he thought. *What burns me even more is the startled hush that comes over the men whenever I enter their presence and persists until I leave.*

As he entered his tent, he noticed a rather large mongrel dog sitting patiently by his table. The strange dog's eyes begged for some small morsel to eat in exchange for quiet companionship. Desiring the same, Galerius chose to suffer the dog a bit and test its loyalty. Sitting down, he ate a little and tossed a few scraps to the dog. After quickly gulping the offerings, the dog continued to stare patiently at him. Smiling, Galerius reached out and patted the dog's head roughly. "Well then, let's talk about it," he said.

"George had little trouble quickly replenishing his forces. He probably has more men under arms than he reports. Now he challenges me to come inspect his troops. The unseasoned peace with Persia would keep me from taking a sufficient escort to withstand any assassination attempt by George and his men. Further, my soldiers appear even more taken with George, attributing my victory to the skills of his men. Finally, if Diocletian discovers what I've truly taken from Narseh's treasury, he'll be after my head too. You see my problems?"

Maintaining its stare, the mutt begged responsively with an impatient whimper.

Tossing the dog another scrap, Galerius continued. "Besides, the men George sent are problems. Though they're effective in battle, they keep starting fights among the soldiers in camp. I can't quite put my finger on it, but I keep feeling these men are some type of deceptive gift-curse. There's just no evidence of any conspiracy and no discernible pattern of misconduct."

After stretching forth its paws in a respectful bow, the mongrel resumed its begging pose.

"With my victory in hand, no other foes should dare to openly oppose my army. Still, I must find a way to separate George from his army. The trouble is there's no longer any reason to demand more men from him."

Impatiently, the dog edged a bit closer to the table, his eyes now focused on the remaining scraps. Galerius sensed the mutt was looking for opportunity, not approval. Suddenly, he gave the animal a swift, sharp kick which sent it yelping away. The dog stopped at the door to the tent and looked back at his new enemy. "That's right!" the man exclaimed. "Keep your friends close, and your enemies closer.[3] I'll draw George in to take him down. Then the battle will begin in earnest back at the palace in Nicodemia. You'll keep our little secret, won't you?" he begged mockingly. Abruptly the dog left the tent, barking and howling in protest for all to hear.

*****

Most Noble Emperor Diocletian Augustus:
 Having proven himself loyal, capable, and trustworthy in every assignment given, I offer my recommendation that George be promoted to serve as a tribune in your imperial guard, bringing him to Nicodemia. Surely, we can make much better use of his talents there.
 Always faithful!
– Emperor Galerius Caesar, Commander of the Syrian legions

*****

George, Commander of the northeast legions:
 At present I can't spare the men required to make the trip to inspect the legions in the northeast. Instead, I suggest we meet back in Nicodemia before the beginning of the next fighting season. I anticipate the next time we meet battle will soon be upon the empire.
 Always faithful!
– Emperor Galerius Caesar, Commander of the Syrian legions

*****

 After reading the reply to Tertius, George said, "Galerius has thousands of soldiers freely available to him now that the peace accord has been reached. There's no reason he couldn't come inspect our legions, unless he suspects treachery. Perhaps he made a subconscious slip, indicating the next time we meet, he anticipates battle. We must be wary. If he expects treachery, no doubt he'll craft a scheme to overcome what's not there. The righteous are bold as lions, but the wicked flee when no man pursues.[4] He who despises and abhors the statutes and judgments of the Lord, his pride and power shall be broken and his strength spent in vain."[5]

*****

Diocletian raised his voice to address the imperial council. "Galerius has recommended that George be promoted from commander of the Roman legions in the northeast, to tribune and personal bodyguard for the Emperor. I seek your counsel on this proposed honor."

With a slight chuckle one minister asked innocently, "Is this the George who defeated the dragon, saving the maiden princess? As I recall, that happened not far from where I was born." Several other ministers laughed uneasily, uncertain whether the Emperor wanted positive or negative feedback. Those already in league with Galerius in his plan to destroy Diocletian and George hoped to avoid being noticed on this issue.

"My Lord, for some time now we've all been aware of George's success and efficiency in both military and civil assignments," one wary soul offered. "He's ever been a faithful supporter of the Emperor. The provinces under his command are operating smoothly and contributing abundantly to the Republic's treasury. The enemies of Rome are hesitant to challenge him with their ambitions. Peace and prosperity are the fruits of his labors. We've all heard of the success in the Persian war that's been attributed in large measure to the five legions George trained and sent to support Galerius. What a victory! We have no reservations in how you choose to honor such a man, or in how you wish him to serve you. But if you bring him to the palace, who will keep the peace in the northeast?"

Diocletian smiled. "I've met the legion commanders, millenaries, and centurions George appointed, trained, and ordered to the southeast. These men know much more than war. They are formidable in battle, to be sure, but they also know how to lead in peace in order to avoid war. This is common among those under his command in the northeast too. They work well together. They're noticeably devoid of the ordinary vices of crudeness, foul manners, love of strong drink, immorality, arrogance, and pride. Their men, even those who've been disciplined, love and respect their leaders. I'm certain we'll find a suitable commander to replace our mythical hero if we bring him here to the capital to be honored and to serve."

With the Emperor tipping his hand in favor of George's promotion, the favorable recommendations began to flow. "George wisely protects those within his care, and love and reverence for him is shown by all his subjects," another council member reported.

Irritated by this remark, Galerius responded, "Would any man ascribe to another the subjects of our great Emperor? Surely this bodes ill of

George and his ambitions, which remain uncertain."

Diocletian had serious doubt about his selection of Galerius as next in line to be the Emperor, but he wasn't ready to address that issue directly. "Galerius, do I detect a bit of jealousy in you? Weren't you the one who recommended George for this promotion?" he challenged, enjoying the chafing Galerius obviously felt at all the fawning over George.

Galerius was surprised and embarrassed by the Emperor's accusation and by his apparent lack of concern over George's increasing popularity. *The destruction of great men is a process that often requires much patience and great discipline,* he reminded himself. *I shouldn't act rashly now.* "Jealous? Of what? I brought the Emperor victory in the Persian war, capturing their treasury, their royal harem, and sacking their capital. I stand second only to the Emperor in the east. I affirm my recommendation for George's promotion to tribune in the imperial guard."

"Well said!" Diocletian declared. "My primary concern is the ambition of men. There has been no testimony suggesting George has any ambitions against me or the empire. He is clearly capable and will be a valuable addition to the imperial guard." Turning to his scribe, the Emperor continued, "I hereby decree the promotion of George of Lydda in Palestine to tribune in the imperial guard. I command an orderly transition to this new assignment during the coming month. We shall identify his replacement in the northeast in the coming weeks. Send a dispatch to George advising him of this action and seeking his recommendations of three men who he believes are qualified to replace him."

"As you will, my lord," the scribe responded.

*****

George stared at the order effecting his promotion and reassignment. "I sense the real purpose of this change is simply to separate me from my military, political, and popular support which, with this transition, will be anticipated to dissipate over time in the shadow of the Emperor," he said to Tertius. "However, I recognize the undeniable honor of being assigned to the Emperor's personal guard, a position previously held by my father. Theoretically, there could be no greater honor bestowed by the Emperor than to be entrusted with directly protecting his life. Still, it's an honor laced with forebodings."

"This is all my fault," Tertius moaned with remorse. "What will you do?"

"My God has been my support. He has led me through adversity and affliction and has preserved me in battle. He has filled me with His love until I've been overcome with His joy. He has confounded my enemies, causing them to fear and tremble before me. He has heard my cries by day, and He has given me knowledge by visions in the night. By day I've waxed bold in mighty prayer before Him. I have sent my voice up on high, and He has answered, revealing to me His great and marvelous works. O then, if I've seen so great things, if the Lord has visited me in so much mercy, why should my soul linger in the valley of sorrow, that the evil one have place in my heart to destroy my peace and afflict my soul? Awake my soul! Rejoice, O my heart, and give place no more for the enemy of my soul.[6] The steps of a good man are ordered by the Lord, and he delights in His way. Though he falls, he shall not be utterly cast down, for the Lord upholds him with His hand.[7] I shall trust in the Lord and go to Nicodemia, ever an instrument in the hands of my God."

"Shall I summon the legion commanders to council so you can inform them?"

"Not yet. I need some time alone before we address this issue. I need to settle on my recommendations for replacement before there is any speculation about coming changes."

"I'll take my leave then, but I'll be close by. Just call out when you need me," Tertius said as he withdrew from George's quarters.

Alone, George knelt before God. Pondering on his new orders, he felt the Spirit speak peace to his mind and heart. *For promotion cometh neither from the east, nor from the west, nor from the south. But God is the judge: He putteth down one, and setteth up another.*[8] *He shall give his angels charge over thee…They shall bear thee up in their hands…The dragon shalt thou trample under feet.*[9]

"I shall not fear to go to Nicodemia, as the Lord will be with me, going before me and following behind to protect me," George said quietly to himself. "As a servant of Jesus Christ, I will not be confounded."[10]

Reassured by the Spirit, he prayed, "O Lord, I will praise Thee forever. My soul will rejoice in Thee, my God, and the Rock of my salvation."[11]

*****

Each legion commander called his legionnaires to assemble. The men were curious as they rarely met in full assembly. The commanders got right to the point, revealing what George had previously shared with them about the coming changes. Many were surprised, feeling the promotion to be a slight against their commander. Leaving little room for doubt in his response, one legion commander explained, "George has gladly accepted the honor of serving as a tribune in the imperial guard. He describes this as a position made honorable by the men who have previously served faithfully, such as his own father. It's also worth remembering that our Emperor previously served as a member of the imperial guard, and as its captain, before being elevated to Emperor." These words were effective in silencing the debate about any slight.

The men's thoughts soon turned to who would lead them going forward. As Florian explained to his legion, "At the Emperor's order, George has recommended leadership changes in the northeast. The Emperor will make the final decisions. It is your duty to support him in his selections. Beyond fulfilling your duties to the Republic, we beg you to awake to a sense of your duty to God that you may walk blamelessly before Him. We ask that you be humble before God, submissive, gentle, easy to be entreated, full of patience and long-suffering, and temperate in all things. Be diligent in keeping the commandments of God, asking Him for whatsoever you need, spiritually and temporally, always returning thanks to Him for His mercy and blessings upon you. Cleave unto faith, hope and charity, and then you will always abound in good works. May the Lord bless you and keep your garments spotless and white that you may stand without shame before Him at the last day. May the peace of God rest upon you, upon your houses and lands, upon your flocks and herds, and all that you posses, your women and your children, according to your faith and good works, from this time forth and forever."[12]

****

CHAPTER THIRTY-FIVE
Back to the Palace

Nicodemia, Eastern Roman Capital
300 AD

"...the young lion and the dragon shalt thou trample under feet."[1]
Psalm 91:13

****

After settling his affairs in the northeast, George made his way directly to Nicodemia to join the imperial guard. Upon his arrival at the palace, he reported to the Emperor and the imperial council. Though his reputation preceded him, there were many people in the capital with whom he was not personally acquainted, having spent nearly all his time either in the field with his men or at home in Lydda with family. "Brother, it's good to see you among the prominent crowd at this reception," he greeted Constantine.

Diocletian smiled slyly as George was presenting himself for duty. With a bit of drama he announced, "Welcome, great deliverer of captives, defender of the poor, healer of the infirm, champion of kings, victorious in battle.[2] We've heard many legends of a hero named George. The tale of his crushing victory over the beastly dragon has become a favorite in every province in the empire. In fact, it's one of my personal favorites at bedtime," he added with a chuckle.

George flushed with embarrassment, but waited patiently.

Diocletian continued, "Some have whispered that you are the hero of these legends. We shall examine you now and discover the truth. Are you the hero of these legends?"

George couldn't see any benefit in this. Hoping to avoid the issue, he responded casually, "My Lord, there are many great legends circulating in honor of many brave men, including you. I can't be certain of the basis of your inquiry without hearing the legends of which you speak, though I doubt I'm the subject." George hoped the burden of reciting any legend would prove tiresome and deter further questioning.

There was a visible twinkle in the Emperor's eye as he commanded, "Alexandria, tell us again *The Legend of George and the Dragon*. Then we'll prevail upon our heralded new tribune to make plain the truth of this matter, once and for all."

George flushed more deeply, realizing he'd been ambushed. He thought, *Well, let them have their fun. No matter. At least this assignment in Nicodemia is closer to home.*

Galerius seethed in the background of the imperial chamber, chafing at the thought of any further honor or praise being heaped upon this man he meant to destroy.

"As you command, my lord," the young Empress replied with a smile. Stepping to the center of the room, she began to rotate slowly in a circle, speaking clearly to all as she retold her legend. A bit melodramatically she began, "All gather round and I'll tell you a tale of our hero, George, out on the trail, who once on his many travels was seen, approaching the desperate city Silene."

The Legend of George and the Dragon

Now in Silene of Libya, there was a great lake where all the people of the city went daily to fetch their water. One day a venomous dragon came and made its nest at the edge of the lake where a spring of fresh sweet water fed the pool. The dragon was huge and fierce, measuring fifty feet from the point of its beak to the tip of its spiked tail. Its claws and teeth were strong as steel and sharp as razors. Much of the beast's thick skin was covered with diamond hard scales which could not be pierced. This monstrous serpent was a scourge to all in the countryside, tearing and killing those who came near to take fresh water from the lake. The dragon was rife with diseased rotting flesh in its teeth which spread grave sicknesses to the people, increasing the terrible toll of death in the land.

At the direction of the king, the people of Silene agreed upon a strategy to appease the dragon and daily draw it away from the spring. Each morning they would tether a sheep at the far end of the lake, away from the dragon's nest and the fresh sweet water spring. As the vicious creature would go and consume the sacrificial lamb, the people would quickly fetch fresh water from the spring, and return to the city unharmed.

By and by the sheep were all gone, so the king ordered his people to appease the dragon by feeding it one child each day. In anger and despair the people refused, though they knew that without water, they would all die. Soon their water was gone. Again their king commanded them to sacrifice one child to appease the dragon. To gain their support, the king swore that the sacrificed child would be chosen by lottery and that his own daughter, the beautiful Princess Sabra, would not be exempt. The king agreed that once a child was chosen, the father could substitute himself and battle the dragon instead of sacrificing his child.

Reluctantly, the people agreed and did as their king commanded. Many innocent children were sacrificed. Many others were spared when their fathers battled the dragon. Few of these fathers survived their battles and none had been able to kill the dragon or drive it away. Grief in the city grew by the day as their fair sons and daughters were sacrificed to the beast as tribute for their fresh water.

Now, the Princess Sabra was a beautiful maiden of marriageable age, beloved by all the people. But by and by, the lot fell on her to be offered as the sacrifice to the dragon. The king was distraught and the people wondered if he would be true to his word. Desperately he offered his people all the gold and silver he possessed if they would spare his daughter's life. But the people refused. As the king's anguish grew, he offered half his kingdom to anyone who would slay the dragon and save his daughter alive. Again, the people refused.

Though the king fell into a dark depression, he kept his word to his people and sent his precious Sabra to be sacrificed to the dragon. Grieved that his beautiful daughter would never marry, the king dressed the Princess in the most elegant white silk wedding dress, adorned with gold, diamonds, and other precious jewels. Accepting her duty but not her fate, Sabra asked for and was granted a sword to fight for her own life. As Sabra courageously led the procession to the tether post at the lake, the king made one final plea, offering to give the Princess in marriage to any man who would save her by destroying the dragon.

At that very moment, by chance in his travels, our hero George arrived at the city on his gallant white charger and heard the commotion near the lake. A kindly hermit at the edge of the crowd quickly explained the dire circumstances to George who went before those gathered and boldly proclaimed that he would accept the challenge to fight the dragon for the life of the fair maiden Princess. Sabra trembled with fear at the terrible thought of her likely demise. But with great courage she sought to send George away so he wouldn't share her fate for naught. But our hero George vowed that he would remain valiant and conquer or perish.

The crowd scattered back as the beast reared up out of the lake to devour its prey. Fortifying himself with the sign of his God, George spurred his noble steed forward and met the attack of the monstrous dragon. The clash was tremendous, the sound rolled like thunder. George's lance broke and his horse tilted over. The charger was stunned by a blow to the head and lay on the ground as if it were dead. Quickly the dragon clawed, slashing George's body.

Now, dragons will eat a man's flesh, it is true. But men fit in armor are quite tough to chew. So the beast hooked George's breastplate and dragged him around, and then picked him up and threw him back down.

Saint George and The Dragon

  Stunned for a moment, George backed away hoping to recover and rejoin the fray. Some strong men had taken his horse from the field, so George met the dragon with just sword and shield. The demon came close, and George saw at a glance that some good had been done by his now broken lance. The powerful strike, though missing its mark, had dislodged a scale near the vile beast's heart.
  The dragon moved toward the Princess Sabra, but George intervened. With a mighty swing of his sword, he slashed off a few feet of the proud serpent's tail. In anger the dragon turned to counter the blow with a furious attack to the face of its foe. With scales protecting its more vital parts, the beast did not fear a sword to the heart. Quickly the dragon coiled 'round the man, clawing fiercely at his armor. George fought back at the beast's snapping jaws, jabbing his sword toward the serpent's eyes. With its head raised high, just over the man, poisonous venom dripped from the dragon's gaping jaws onto George's body, seeping into his open wounds. Rapidly the poison took effect, numbing the strength of our valiant champion. George fell limp and helpless. The monster batted him roughly, sending him sprawling into the shallow water.
  As it turned again toward the breathless princess, the dragon saw one of its own horns on the ground, broken off from the crown of its proud head by the pounding steel of the man's sword. Caught in its own vanity, the dragon stared for a moment at its own marred reflection in the lake and felt a burning anger surging within.
  The shallow water cooled George from the fury of the battle and diluted the poisonous venom, washing it away until he had regained his strength. With determination he rose from the water and retrieved his sword for the battle. Again he positioned himself between the fierce dragon and the fair Princess Sabra.
  The rage-filled dragon attacked with another thunderous roar. The clash was intense as sword struck at beast and claws flashed at man. With a fierce stroke, George cut off the dragon's ear. When the beast reared back, George could see the missing scale near the demon's heart. He lunged in to stab it but was caught by a furious blow. The dragon slashed him with three vicious talons, breaking his sword, splitting his armor and severely slicing his arms and his legs.
  George was knocked to the ground and left for dead by the dragon, which had withdrawn to the lake to grieve its lost ear. Recovering a bit, George rose to his feet. Staggering back he called to the crowd, "Please, help me! This armor is crushing me. Please help me remove it." He put down his sword with its jagged split blade, and took off man's armor with a small bit of aid.

Soon the dragon took notice that George was preparing to rejoin the duel in a manner most daring. Some inner sense let the beast know that where this man stood no dragon should go. But bent on revenge, ruled by anger and rage, the serpent returned to the violent stage. The dragon closed in on the fair maiden again, but this time help came from the gathering of men. Though none dared get near, they hurled stones with their slings, distracting the dragon and disrupting things.

George was unsure how to conquer the beast. In the filth of his blood-stained tunic he humbly dropped to his knees, bowed his head, and pled to his God for strength to overcome this dragon that had killed so many young innocent ones. Fortifying himself with the sign of his God and, keeping his vow, he returned valiantly to the battle to overcome or perish.

Filled with a warm assurance and feeling his strength was restored, George kept his eyes fixed on his menacing foe as he reached for the hilt of his now broken sword. The people gasped as he brought up his weapon, for the broken sword still lay upon the ground. In his right hand George held a perfect flaming sword of light, a gift from his God.

Boldly George rebuked the evil beast of the pit, again putting himself between the dragon and the pure maiden Princess. At George's command, Sabra threw off her sash, momentarily distracting the dragon. As she ran to the far end of the tether, the dragon made a vicious strike. Courageously, George intervened again, withstanding the dragon's violent attack, delivering a crushing blow to the top of its head with his sword of light. Stunned by the blow, the dragon recoiled. As the beast rose up rampant, George thrust the flaming sword with all his might into the void of the missing scale, striking the dragon, inflicting a mortal wound to the heart.

As the beast collapsed, George cautiously withdrew his sword of light. Drawing near to Sabra, he cut off the tether that held the Princess bound. Gently he guided the beautiful maiden to her father, the king. Flush with emotion and gratitude, the king awarded his precious daughter Sabra to George, the dragon slayer. The king proved again he was good to his word and pledged half his kingdom and all his gold and silver as reward.

George bowed humbly before the king and accepted his daughter and the pledge of his treasury. However, he declined the half of the kingdom, assuring the king that the triumph of good over evil was sufficient reward. Next, he turned to the people and conferred upon them each their equal shares of the king's treasury. Thus, he explained, the wealth of the city would remain for the benefit of all. Finally, George turned to Sabra. He was captivated by her beauty and courage, but true to his *oath to seek naught for himself, he set her free, relieving her from the oppressions of men and beasts.*

George warned the people not to partake of the flesh of the beast, but to bury it deep in an alkali field, to which the dragon's body was carted on four ox-carts. Giving praise to his God for the miraculous victory, George invited all to worship with him. The king and all the people swore to honor the God of George. The burial of the dragon had created a very great hill near the city, which the king chose as the place to build a church in honor of George and his God. From the altar of this church a spring arose whose waters, it is said, cured all manner of diseases.

With the gift of her freedom and the wealth of jewels from her wedding dress, the beautiful Princess Sabra followed after George on his travels, continually offering to serve others with him as a token of gratitude for her life.

As the Empress fell silent a round of enthusiastic applause rang out. Finally the Emperor raised his hand for quiet and spoke. "George, make plain the truth of this matter to us. Are you the hero of this legend?"

Considering the situation, George was now even more certain that he'd been set up. Whoever had suggested to the Emperor that he be challenged on this matter had intended, whether subtly or brazenly, to make a mockery of his faith, his life, and his popularity and to incite an offense between him and the Emperor. George noted with interest that whoever had taught the story to the Empress had been careful not to specify which God had sustained the hero in the story. Perhaps this version offered more universal acceptance by the followers of the pagan gods. George wondered just how much of his popularity had been passed on from those who had been the subjects of his rule in the northeast quarter of the empire. Apparently, it was too much.

After more awkward silence, the Empress spoke, offering her own enthusiastic encouragement, "Please, George, tell us. Are you really the hero of this legend?"

Choosing his words carefully, George replied to the Emperor, "My Lord, no man could possibly be the hero of that legend. If I had been the hero, I would have dug a well for the people within the city walls." A low wave of muffled laughter swept the crowd. George continued, "I'm just an ordinary man and a servant of the Emperor. I have no mystical or magical powers. I strive for honesty, truth, benevolence, virtue, and doing good to all men.[3]

"All men have been blessed by God with various talents, and so have I. These I have tried to magnify by obedience to the training of my parents, my commanders, and many others. I've been blessed with success in the charges given to me thus far. I've been blessed to be guided by others of greater capacity and wisdom than my own, who have shared their visions with me. Together we have accomplished marvelous things for the prosperity of the Republic, its Emperor and its people. As for me, I'm just an ordinary man and a faithful servant of the Emperor. Therefore, whatsoever you desire of me, which is right, that I will do."[4]

"Well spoken, and yet what a pity," the Emperor laughed cordially. "Had the tale been true, we were prepared to have your likeness cast in bronze for all in the capital to pay homage. Perhaps your faithful service will yet provide you opportunities to merit such glory."

****

CHAPTER THIRTY-SIX
Faithful Tribune

Nicodemia, Eastern Roman Capital
301/302 AD

"And the LORD went before them...by night in a pillar of fire, to give them light..."[1]
Exodus 13:21

****

"Inn keeper, another bottle of wine for my friend," the senator ordered.

Galerius lowered his head a bit and tried to whisper, though he had never quite mastered that skill. "I'm tired of waiting for the old man to die and vacate the throne. I have what we need to move forward with our plan. I took it from Narseh at the point of my sword," he said with a sinister smile. "That's how things get done. I want control now, and I'm willing to reward those who help me take it."

"The old man has always been a formidable enemy," the senator responded. "He isn't to be trifled with. We may not be in a position to safely remove him yet, but when he's uncertain about matters or seeks the guidance and support of the council, you have the power to control many decisions through your influential allies. There are many on the council who see his advancing age and declining vigor as liabilities. Soon others will be willing to help. Your goal is too close to become a casualty of carelessness."

"I've been working this problem more cautiously than anything in my life, yet nobody gives me credit for patience as a virtue." Galerius responded. "Perhaps I have been too patient. The longer I wait, the more challenging my contenders become. Constantine is with me on most of my travels, so I can keep an eye on him. I'm confident the old man shares my wariness over the whelp and his father."

"How will you dispose of him?" the senator asked.

"I'm not limiting my options, but whenever the opportunity presents itself, I send him into battle with too few men, hoping he will fall," Galerius replied. "Thus far, my hopes have always been dashed as he returns victorious, against all odds. His stupid popularity feeds on these victories. But I only need him to die once.

"Now I've got our hero George to eliminate, too. I've spent the fall on the northern frontier, assessing things. The legions there continue to show a strong allegiance to their former commander. His destruction weighs heavily on my mind, as I don't trust the old man to restrain him, making George the more crucial foe."

*****

"I hear you've been assigned the personal security of the Emperor when he's in Nicodemia. That's quite an honor," Constantine praised.

"How does that happen?" George asked in mock bewilderment.

"It probably took only a few sparring sessions among the imperial guards for the captain to recognize that you are the new master of combat, with or without arms," Constantine guessed. "Any contrived contests you can't win with superior skill or strength, I'm sure you'll win with your wits. I've also heard that your positive attitude and willingness to teach the other tribunes how to improve their already superior fighting skills, has won friends for you among your peers. Even those who aren't the friendly type have seen and experienced enough to respect you and your abilities."

"It is an honor," George admitted. "It's a duty I enjoy. The captain's tolerance for politics doesn't extend much past the end of his sword, so he prefers the nightly security duty with its peace and quiet. This puts me at the Emperor's side in the imperial chambers, daily observing all the business of the Republic, which I find quite interesting."

*****

One day the keeper of the imperial stables approached the Emperor about required preparations for an outing set for later that afternoon. Diocletian, feeling out of sorts, responded abruptly, "Just make ready for the outing!"

Rather than leaving the court with the urgency implied by the Emperor's command, the stable keeper paused, still unclear as to how exactly things needed to be made ready. Cautiously, he looked to George for guidance. Seeing the man's distress, George motioned him to wait at the door where he met him with a few quickly whispered words of clarification to ensure the proper action and result. As George returned to the Emperor's side, he responded to the ruler's inquiring glance. "Don't worry. He knows what you need. He'll have it ready for you."

"Yes, but your coordination was so blatantly obvious that I couldn't focus on anything else," Diocletian complained. "Now that I think about it, I realize the pinch I caused with my abrupt and incomplete instructions." Continuing with a show of good humor, he laughingly asked, "Why is it that every time I give a command, all men look to you for approval before they act?"

"Is it every time?" George responded with a confident chuckle of his own. "Perhaps those who look to me simply want to be certain of meeting with your approval, which you've told many that I do without fail."

*****

"What's wrong Diocletian?" Alexandria asked.

"Oh, I'm just feeling old in my bones," the Emperor replied with a heavy sigh. "You wouldn't know anything about that yet. But the years and mortal combat have taken their toll on me. Though none dare ask, and I would not admit it yet, I'm growing weary of ruling the empire."

"Well then, what's right?" the Empress urged, unwilling to dwell on the dark path.

"I'm constantly searching for faithful servants to help me carry this burden," Diocletian replied. "I see George's arrival in Nicodemia as a provident answer to my needs."

"What do you mean by that?" Alexandria prodded.

"Sometimes when I'm tired I get short with people when we talk, often giving only partial information coupled with inflexibly urgent commands," the Emperor observed.

"No! Really?" Alexandria replied with a knowing smile.

"Alas, it's true," Diocletian confirmed. "However, noting this habit, George has taken up a supporting role for both ends of each exchange. He patiently seeks additional guidance from me when necessary and confidentially clarifies my commands for my subjects. This has been a great relief to many who have faced me, as it allows them to fulfill my desires with a much higher success rate, thereby gaining praise and avoiding retribution.

"George is faithful to his own counsel, advocating for any who have followed his directions. If I can't remember my own commands or don't understand the value in doing things differently than I thought I had ordered, George is always able to explain things in a way that I understand, without giving offense. I appreciate the fact that things are running much more smoothly in Nicodemia. I'm getting superior results without so much drama and boring detail. Naturally, I'm relying heavily on George to manage more things in the capital."

*****

"Wow! Only a few months in the capital and already you are the captain of the guard. Impressive!" Constantine gloated.

"Who is to say how such things happen?" George responded.

"I'm not certain how this thing happened," Constantine replied. "However, when the captain of the guard falls asleep at his post while guarding the Emperor in his sleep, change is usually quick. I'm impressed with Diocletian's sensitivity. Galerius would have executed the man himself, on the spot. Diocletian gave the captain a graceful exit, allowing him to announce his own retirement, rather than castigating him publicly with shame or punishment."

"So that's how a man falls," George noted. "But how does a man rise?"

"You, my friend, were appointed as the new captain due to your obvious capacity, record of success, and favorable reputation with the guards and with many on the imperial council," Constantine observed. "Beyond that, I suspect Diocletian may be feeling that the son of his old friend Gerontius is becoming more like a son to him."

*****

"I have an announcement," Diocletian said to the assembled imperial council. "I've heard too many complaints about improper sewage systems and poor water quality in Nicodemia. We need to make improvements, so I'm streamlining that process. I'm putting George in charge of public works in the capital." With a sly smile he added, "I've charged him with either slaying the dragon or digging new wells as he proposed." His quip brought the light laughter he desired, so he continued. "George has successfully resolved similar issues before throughout the northeast region. He understands what the engineers are saying, and he has ideas they value. I've also instructed him to look into the increasing crime and vagrancy. I trust his judgment in these matters. I have full confidence in him. Therefore, I'm also making him administrator of all palace operations. While the imperial council will not be subject to his oversight, I will expect your support for him as he addresses these issues and complaints. That's all."

*****

"I'm amazed by all the responsibilities I've been given," George said.

"You don't seem overwhelmed," Constantine replied.

"Oh, I'm confident in exercising the authority I've been given to put the palace and all of Nicodemia in order," George affirmed. "Though as I walk the halls of the palace, I still smile each time I enter the prison area, for without fail the words of the holy records come into my mind. 'But the Lord was with Joseph, and showed him mercy, and gave him favor in the sight of the keeper of the prison. And the keeper of the prison committed to Joseph's hand all the prisoners that were in the prison; and whatsoever they did there, he was the doer of it. The keeper of the prison looked not to anything that was under his hand; because the Lord was with him, and that which he did, the Lord made it to prosper.'"[2]

*****

"I told you, he didn't consult me!" Galerius snapped.

"In either case," the senator replied, "we're concerned that greater authority and responsibility have been given to a man we've targeted for destruction. It's distressing that Diocletian and George are strengthening their positions while you spend so much time away on the frontier. George is winning over many on the council who believe he will address the public works issues more effectively and efficiently than the Emperor."

*****

"George," the Emperor began, "I feel like I've been on holiday these last few months, and it's been wonderful. Things seem to be going much more smoothly now. Still, I feel a bit awkward because more is getting done without my oversight than with it. A little voice inside my head keeps telling me that the monarch who spends too much time on holiday is soon replaced by a more ambitious man. I'm not disappointed at all, but I need a full report on what you've been doing in the palace and in the capital."

George sighed lightly. "Well, as you're already aware, I've changed your personal bodyguard from two twelve-hour shifts to three eight-hour shifts. All who wish to speak with you are still required to appear at the first hour. I filter through them less formally, resolving as many issues as possible before you begin to give audience at the third hour when my shift as guard starts. This way, your days are managed more efficiently and more focus is given to the critical issues."

"Yes, things have been running more efficiently," Diocletian agreed.

"I did some research into the poor water quality and poor sewage management," George explained. "It appears the capital has simply grown too fast and there hasn't been sufficient skilled labor to properly develop the growing areas and keep up the maintenance of established areas. It's also apparent that some people lack common sense about what to put upstream and what to put downstream in a clean water system."

"What do you mean?" the Emperor asked.

"One simple but highly effective solution we implemented was a forced relocation of all the livestock holding pens and all the butcher shops to the downstream areas of the city. Domestic service animals aren't subject to this order. This one change has made a huge difference in water quality throughout the capital. Also, we dug several new public wells, increasing the supply of naturally filtered water to more citizens, greatly improving health.

"In relation to the water and sewage projects, we've required the engineers and masons to split their labor forces in half between critical objectives, such as water source purification, and less critical issues, such as responding to citizen complaints in the housing sections of the city. We have required every laborer in the housing area to be paired up with a local resident, to teach him the trade, so more citizens can simply solve their own problems. Once replacements are trained, the skilled workers are reassigned to more critical objectives. Those workers with the greatest skill have been assigned as inspectors, to give more guidance to others. The process has taken some time, but the acute shortage of trained laborers is resolving. Putting more people to work has also provided some relief from the vagrancy and crime issues."

"How are you selecting your critical objectives?" Diocletian asked.

"We're focusing on water sources and distribution channels first, weighing which projects will help the most people against the level of resources required to get the work done correctly. It's different from prioritizing based on connections or bribes, but it yields better results that are sustainable in the longer term and are broadly evident to citizens and government officials."

"I've heard about your crack down on bribes from a few bruised egos, but overall the mood in the capital has been improving," the Emperor observed. "I credit you, George. You have my gratitude and confidence. What other public works are you planning?"

George thought for a moment. "Right now we have every available engineer and stone mason working to secure clean water sources. As those projects are completed, we'll work on the problems with drainage and sewage. Those will be followed by road repairs and improvements. After that, we're planning to review the security of our food supply and storage. There are few things more dangerous than a starving city."

"I can attest to that," Diocletian replied soberly. "I saw that in Egypt at the siege of Alexandria."

"I think we should consider building at least one more flour mill," George suggested. "I'll let you know when the review is complete. Finally, we're planning to build a hospital. The current system of physicians attending the majority of patients in their homes isn't very efficient and mainly functions only for the wealthy. If we establish a central location for the infirm, the physicians will be able to care more effectively for greater numbers of people. It'll be easier for them to monitor general health concerns and to exchange skilled knowledge in the treatment of many different ailments. It will also provide a central location for our archives on medical care, which will be readily available to our physicians. Along with this, we plan regular exchanges of skilled physicians with the frontier provinces so we can record and preserve their vast knowledge of health issues unique to their areas. We can also share our knowledge with them. Vigilant sanitation will be a key to the success of the hospital."

"How will you find time to get all this done?" the Emperor questioned sincerely.

"Oh, I'm not getting it done. One of the main reasons I adjusted your personal guard to three shifts was to give me more time in the morning and in the evening to meet with the planners and leaders to review and approve their work. I just guide and monitor, but the genius and skill comes from the engineers, masons, and laborers. Our greatest assets are our people."

"And I thought the imperial treasury was our greatest asset," Diocletian quipped.

"Proper treasury management is critical to keeping things moving," George agreed. "But the real sign things are improving is seen when private groups and individuals begin to invest and spend their money, creating demand for goods and services and jobs for all who need them."

"And more tax revenues," the Emperor noted optimistically.

*****

George was honored to receive the Christian Bishop of Nicodemia with his proposal for the construction of a new cathedral in the capital. He was also pleased to see his friend, Bishop Nicholas of Myra, in the delegation. The plans were elaborate, but not extreme. The building would be a jewel, not far from the palace, improving its own location and inviting more refinement and improvement in the properties around it.

One important factor was that the church treasury already had all the funds set aside to assure the completion of the building. Approving the project enthusiastically, George declared, "God speed, Brothers!"

*****

"What's got you smiling?" the Empress asked one evening.

"George," the Emperor replied. "He's doing a great job managing the palace and the public works in the capital. Clean water is readily available and the sewage and trash issues have been resolved. Kitchen sanitation is greatly improved, as are conditions in the stables and the prison. One area George has yet to address is the imperial council chamber. Several members of the council seem to be offended by George's accomplishments. Perhaps he'll make them wait for help until they're sufficiently humble to ask for it.

"His character, integrity, competence and humility inspire trust and a fatherly love. Surely I've never had any man among all my tribunes that's been as capable and faithful as this man. He remembers all my commands and fulfills them.[3] He seems to think of everything before the needs become apparent to others, creating an image unique to him of always being prepared. Further, he inspires fear in his enemies and in my enemies, too."

*****

"Brother, what has you back in the capital in the middle of fighting season?" George asked.

"Galerius sent me for some menial task," Constantine replied. "I think he's sick of me."

"I hear the trust and confidence of the men who follow you continues to increase, fueling further jealousy and suspicion in him," George observed. "I think it's more likely that he's sick of losing the popularity contest among the men."

"He'd better get used to it," Constantine jabbed. "He couldn't win a popularity contest if he was the only man in the race! But he has made an effort at some strategy. He keeps sending me to quell the attacks of rogue Persian commanders along the border without giving me enough men to succeed. I think he's trying to create a Roman battle loss that he can blame on me as a pretext to retaliate against the Persians with a much larger force, hoping to gain more treasure and expand the borders of his future empire. If I am killed in the process, he won't shed any tears."

"How are you holding up?" George prodded.

"As the target of his jealousy I approach these poorly veiled suicide missions very cautiously. In spite of his plotting against me, I've taken my small forces to the assigned battles. Favoring soldiers trained in the northeast, I've gathered additional men along the way, offering a share of any spoils. I carefully plan each engagement to the advantage of my army. With each successive victory against the odds, the local civilians have been more willing to seek alliances with my army, instead of aligning with opposing forces."

"You are a great strategist and teacher, and a very charismatic and inspiring leader," George praised. "These qualities, ever underestimated by your foes, including Galerius, have brought you success where other men surely would have failed. Such a string of good fortune in battle might lead many men to believe they are invincible."

"Not me," Constantine replied. "I understand battle strategy well enough to know that nothing but the provident hand of God can explain my success. My experiences have led me to increased faith and humility before the true and living God. But for now, it's back to the battle."

*****

Most Beloved Alexandria,

I hope this finds you in good health and good spirits. As I planned at the inception of the year, I have spent the spring and summer along the southeastern border, verifying our army deployment and reviewing fortifications and battle strength. I have also been observing the Persian positions across the way to assure compliance with the terms of our treaty. Their men look dejected, which is good. All seems well.

I will stay in Syria at Antioch for the fall to hear appeals. I look forward to this much deserved holiday from Galerius, who will be riding the circuit to the northeast, checking positions with the local commanders before winter. We will meet back in Nicodemia for the winter.

It would please me greatly if you would join me in Antioch, but if the burden of travel is too much, I will see you later back at the palace. I miss you desperately.

Always faithful!
– Diocletian Augustus

****

CHAPTER THIRTY-SEVEN
A Burning Conspiracy

Nicodemia, Eastern Roman Capital
302/303 AD

"The kings of the earth set themselves, and the rulers take counsel together, against the LORD, and against His anointed,..."[1]
Psalm 2:2

****

"Thank you for coming to Antioch," Diocletian said as he hugged Alexandria. "Your presence is such a blessing in my life!"

"This travel has been good for me," the Empress replied. "I needed a break from all the drama in the capital. Will we be here long?"

"Not long," Diocletian responded. "However, you'll find that Nicodemia has not cornered the market on drama. My border review went well, as did the harvest and tax revenues. The tribute from Narseh was an added bonus to the imperial treasury. The more time I spend out here, the more secure I feel about the loyalty of the legion commanders and the people in this region. Unfortunately, there's a perplexing issue I must address before we return to Nicodemia."

"What's that?" Alexandria inquired.

"A religious zealot!" Diocletian declared. "In the military, I was taught to worship all Roman gods. The throne has urged me to worship myself too. However, with the violence, injustice, and bloodshed I've seen in life, I honestly don't believe in any gods. For a long time I've carefully cultivated religious tolerance throughout the empire, mainly for economic reasons. Religious discord undermines the prosperity of nations. I've seen religions and zealots come and go and I'm not easily inflamed by them or against them. So I've listened to the growing complaints against the Christians with muted concern. But this one has me annoyed."

*****

The Emperor sat patiently as the tribunes brought the shackled man before him. The prisoner was gagged and had obviously been severely beaten. "Who is this man and what are the charges against him?" the

Emperor asked, already knowing the answers.

"My lord," one of the tribunes responded, "this man is Romanus. He is from Caesarea. He claims to be a Christian official there. He disrupted the harvest sacrifices to the Roman gods, making a great spectacle of himself, screaming at the assembly and turning over the priests' altars and tables. The priests were so distraught by the disruption that they couldn't read the sacrificial entrails. This has set many people on edge, leading them to believe they'll suffer in battle and in the next harvest because the gods have been offended."

Men like Romanus infuriate me, Diocletian thought. *I can abide tolerant men, allowing them time to regain their sensibilities, but patience is a luxury I don't waste on the intolerant.* "Romanus, citizen of Rome, you are permitted to speak," he said sternly.

Quickly one of the tribunes removed the gag from the prisoner. After spitting at the feet of the Emperor, Romanus unleashed a string of degrading epithets against the ignorant people, the sinister priests, the false Roman gods, the nation, and the Emperor, cursing them in the name of all that is holy.

"Smite him!" Diocletian commanded.

The tribune struck the prisoner's head with the hilt of his sword, knocking the captive down. After recovering from the stunning blow, Romanus continued his ranting, prompting a swift kick to the gut by the tribune.

The Emperor rose from his throne to look down upon the gasping prisoner. "Romanus, citizen of Rome, for your disruption of the harvest sacrifices to the gods, and for your continued insolence, I command that your tongue be cut out and that you be imprisoned for five years at hard labor. Any further defiance shall result in your prompt execution."

Before Romanus could speak in reply, the tribune struck him again with the hilt of his sword, knocking him unconscious so the punishment could be carried out.

*****

"I'm surprised to see Constantine back in Nicodemia and being hailed even more than ever before as a brightly rising star of the Republic," the senator grimaced.

"No one is more surprised than me," Galerius retorted. "I did everything I could to arrange his death, but he just keeps getting lucky. With the fighting season over, he remains an irritating thorn in my side, but now I have my eye on a bigger prize. If I can take the old man's place, it will be easy to deal with the growing ambitions of Constantine and George."

*****

"These are impressive improvements in the public works and palace operations," Constantine observed. "I guess you drew the long straw, enjoying all the comforts of home. Anyway, it beats being sent to hell repeatedly by a commander who can only be seeking your death."

"I confess, being tethered to Galerius, you must have drawn the short straw," George admitted.

Lowering his voice, Constantine confided, "He was a despicable companion in the field but he's gotten worse since our return. Have you got any ideas on how to get him off my aching back?"

George thought carefully for a moment about his friend's perplexing situation. "I know what you mean. He's distressed. He probably fears us as competitors. Perhaps he's too fearful to even consider soliciting us as future allies. I have no idea how to improve things with him."

Still speaking lowly, Constantine said, "You're more religious than I am. Can't you just arrange a meeting between Galerius and God to relieve his distress?"

George laughed lightly at his friend's suggestion. "The only way I know to arrange for someone to meet God is to send them through the veil of death. I'm not sure that's what you meant. Even if I could arrange a meeting between him and God, Galerius would be miserable in the presence of such a just and holy Being, with a consciousness of his own filthiness before Him. He would feel less distress and misery dwelling with the other damned souls in hell."[2] With a shadow of a smile and a twinkle in his eye, George added, "Besides, Brother, you misunderstand my gift. As legend has it, I'm blessed with the unique ability to save *damsels* in distress. Alas, I have no such gift for *damned souls* in distress."

Constantine couldn't restrain a solid laugh. Sobering a bit he said, "Another issue you should consider is the growing antagonism Galerius has shown against the Christians on the frontier. He blames them for his early losses in the Persian war. If he can find an opportune incident, there's little doubt that he'll unleash openly brutal abuses on the Christians generally, especially if he can get the imperial council and Diocletian to back him."

"I don't think Diocletian would do that," George responded optimistically. "Still, we should be ready to answer if challenged on Christianity. I'll likely appeal to Diocletian and trust in God."

Saint George and The Dragon

*****

The next time Diocletian met with Galerius in Nicodemia, he related the incident with Romanus. As he anticipated, Galerius was outraged, calling for more severe retribution. "The purpose of this discussion is not to revisit the punishment of Romanus," Diocletian said. "It is to begin formulation of a consistent policy for the empire regarding the Christians. The Christians have generally not been oppressive to others, but their numbers and influence are growing rapidly. As with any such movement, Christianity has attracted many misguided men, zealots, and power mongers in both the leadership and the membership of the churches. Such people have provided many bad examples of unchecked pride, tarnishing the good name of the faith and its believers. How would you deal with the Christians?" the Emperor asked.

Galerius considered the question carefully, sensing an opportunity. "From all I've seen, the Christians do far more harm than good," he began. "They're forever spouting about their one true and living God, despising and repudiating all other gods and the people who worship them. They upset the sacrifices before battle, casting a pall over the army. And they'll never pay homage to the divinity of our Emperor. Their pride and arrogance in these matters has caused repeated violence between them and many of the non-Christians."

"This wedge of recurring friction has just as often been the fault of the pagans as it has been the fault of the Christians," Diocletian countered.

"It's been the basis for many episodes of vicious persecution by Roman Emperors against the Christians in the past," Galerius responded. "Surely this history is worth consideration." Diocletian had implied a willingness to take measures against the Christians, so Galerius proceeded boldly. "The Christians are becoming a wealthy lot, but we are better off without them. We should make careful plans for their extermination and confiscate their wealth for the imperial treasury."

Diocletian raised his eyebrows a bit as he thought, *Galerius, you truly are a brute, with naught but ambition for money and power.* Calmly he replied, "I'm surprised you feel so strongly about them, especially after the lesson you should have learned in the Persian war. We could destroy the Christians' and take their treasures, or we could allow them to prosper and tax them annually." The Emperor paused a moment to allow Galerius the chance to reconsider his position and speak again before he made his decision. Galerius said nothing, so Diocletian continued, "There's a big difference between abstaining from sacrifices and obstructing them. I've had experience with many Christians who aren't so offensive as this Romanus. They may be uncooperative with pre-battle sacrifices unsettling some, yet they show less fear of battle than others. It's sufficient to forbid Christian participation in government and as military leaders. We shall proceed to identify and remove them from these honored positions."

It was a rare violation of protocol for a subordinate officer to speak after his superior had decided a matter, so it surprised the Emperor a little when Galerius spoke again. "My lord, your wisdom is sure, but I sense the imperial council will chafe at these measures as insufficient. Might I suggest that you consult the oracle of Apollo at Didyma regarding the question of the Christians, not that you lack proper judgment, but simply that the council may be more settled with your plan, with the support of the oracle?"

Diocletian considered his Caesar's request. Though Galerius sometimes showed glimmers of improvement in his manners, the Emperor still wondered if someone else would be better to succeed him on the throne. *Consulting the oracle shouldn't create any great problem,* he thought, *for it is unlikely to favor a policy setting the precedent of exterminating any religion. Its counsel is predictable: Hinder the Christians and tax them, but don't kill them unless they threaten us. In any case, the consultation will buy me some time to come up with a better solution.* "Your reasoning has merit. We'll consult the oracle of Apollo and then decide our course," the Emperor replied as he departed for court and the business of the day.

*****

Less than an hour later, Galerius appeared at court with an inquiry his scribe had prepared for consultation with the oracle of Apollo. Receiving it, the Emperor read: *Are the Christians a threat to the Roman Empire? If so, should every action necessary be taken to assure their true allegiance to the Emperor and the Roman gods?* Although he would have handled the inquiry differently, Diocletian didn't think it mattered since he didn't believe in the oracle anyway. Rather than agitate the council with debate on the matter, and in order to maintain the appearance of strength, he signed the inquiry immediately and returned it to Galerius.

Quickly Galerius passed the order to a waiting messenger for delivery to the oracle of Apollo. Galerius smiled at the senator outside the council chambers. "Things have gone better than we planned," he said. "Now we have other plans and arrangements to make to ensure things will go exactly as we intend when the messenger returns from the oracle."

*****

"Inn keeper, get us another bottle of wine!" the senator ordered.

"I want the Emperor to issue an extermination order against the Christians," Galerius confided. "But how do I get Diocletian to turn fully against them such that he will issue an order for severe persecution, if not complete extermination?"

"We must publicly raise the specter of Christianity as a growing threat to the existing power structure in the Republic," the senator whispered. "I've seen distress on the council for the empire's tolerant approach to religion. Many have noted how the poor are attracted to this gospel that emphasizes charity, love, and the riches of eternity over the material things of this world. The council members have also noted that the poor who embrace and are faithful to the tenets of Christianity seem, as a group, to quickly raise themselves from poverty into positions of learning, wealth, and even influence."

"The council members know Christianity is on the rise throughout the empire," Galerius agreed. "I've even heard that the king of Armenia has adopted Christianity as his state religion."

"Such developments are a threat to the imperial power structure which is founded on imagined gods who have no power to bring forth similar miracles in the lives of the people," the senator observed. "Although most on the council don't believe in any gods, they are determined to retain control over the gods of their people, and to assert a divine right of imperial rule. These should be easily persuaded to join our campaign, as Christianity can't be tolerated by the ruling class in the empire. We must quickly meet with the council members individually about these issues. Those who show distress and concern will be invited to organizing meetings where we'll evaluate which council members are willing to use their power to act against the Christians.

"Those willing to abuse their power in causes they rationalize as just, are soon willing to abuse their power in causes which they know are unjust, especially if they believe they will be shielded from prosecution," the senator added. "Having once entangled themselves in a web of abuse, they fear punishment for past sins more than they fear the path on to greater iniquity.

"Once we've organized our group, we'll coordinate our efforts, making frequent complaints of Christian subversions to the Emperor. Then we'll incite and highlight every disturbance between Christians and non-Christians. Further, we'll persistently emphasize how the Christians defiantly honor their God and repudiate the divine claims of the Emperor. By the time the oracle of Apollo responds, Diocletian should be irritated enough to act."

"Good!" Galerius exclaimed, feeling a rush of pleasure at the long-awaited bloom of his campaign to seize power.

*****

The hour was very late and the palace stables were completely dark inside. However, the men who had gathered there didn't need much light to recognize each other as their voices were familiar. "We've done well, my friends," Galerius tried to whisper. "The Christians will soon be the irritant they must be if we are to accomplish our purposes. Surely, we are better than them and all the citizens and subjects in the empire. We are their leaders. We are entitled to the privileges and wealth of this nation.[3]

"Once the persecution orders are issued we must be prepared to act quickly, putting down the most influential Christians and confiscating their treasures. As you know, a lot of treasure can get lost between confiscation and the imperial treasury. If you act aggressively, I'll defend your actions and you won't have to answer for any acts against the Christians. However, if we are to succeed, we must swear cooperation and secrecy in all we do. Are you with me?"

Though it was dark, Galerius could see each man's head nodding in agreement. Therefore, he continued, "I promise that each of you will be more powerful rulers under me, but all must agree to cooperate in whatever wickedness each man desires, seeking power and plunder by our lies, treachery, and murders. You must swear by your heads to assist as needed and to keep all our works of darkness secret or forfeit your lives."[4] Each man in turn quietly voiced agreement.
Having administered his oath of fidelity in iniquity, Galerius spoke openly. "I'm going to take Diocletian's throne. He's grown old and weak, so this change is necessary," he argued.

A deep voice whispered cautiously, "The Emperor's hand has been greatly strengthened while you've been away. It's true that he's not getting any younger, but his support has stabilized since conditions have improved in Nicodemia. We sent you letters advising when George was appointed captain of the imperial guard and then later when Diocletian gave him authority to oversee the public works and the palace."

"Anybody could have pulled things together like George did and maybe done better if they just had the chance," another faceless voice whined with envy. "The Emperor was losing control of the situation.

Now the palace and all of Nicodemia look up to high and mighty George instead of complaining about Diocletian's incompetence."

"Then we should give more consideration to separating George from the Emperor," Galerius rasped out, not quite mastering the whisper. "How can we make George vulnerable?"

The deep voice spoke again, with hushed soberness. "George is much more than just a figure-head. He involves himself personally in the details of many complex matters. He understands them and, thus far, he's given sound guidance. Conditions here have improved measurably in the short time under his administration. This has strengthened and secured his position with the Emperor and the Emperor's position with the people. With George at his side, Diocletian, though weary with age, still presents a formidable obstacle to any grasp for power."

Galerius was disturbed by this talk, but he needed to hear every detail. He had to know the exact status in the capital to be sure it would not upset his plan for the rapid transfer of power into his own hands. As he continued listening, many of the conspirators candidly admitted their jealousy of George, his talents, popularity, and influence.

"The people are struck with George's personal bearing and his record of success," the deep voice noted. "His conduct has been above reproach and his heroic reputation just keeps growing. Yet, we are wary of his humility and loyalty. He's a dangerous threat to any man who opposes him. He has the potential to be a threat to you and us whether he has ambitions or not."

Galerius listened to a few others babble on about George and how they despised him. *They imagine up in their hearts foolish and vain offenses they've endured at his hands*, he thought. *I'm not impressed with their whining, but I'm pleased that they're clearly much disturbed, spreading rumors and contentions against George, trying to harden the hearts of others. Such conspirators can easily be stirred to all manner of iniquity against that which is good, even to fight against God.*[5]

Hearing these complaints, Galerius was certain that separating George from his army had been insufficient to curb his growing influence. "Though Constantine vexes me daily and my plan to destroy him has yet been unfruitful, I'm sure it will bear fruit soon enough. Eliminating George is clearly my highest priority. He will be the first target of our winter treachery. There must be a way to separate him from the Emperor and ruin him publicly, finally putting an end to him once and for all. He must be eliminated. But how can we do that without alienating the Emperor?"

"We'll need a wedge to bring him down," the deep voice observed. "Undermining his public works projects is a possibility, but we really need the wedge to come between George and the Emperor first, and then between George and the people. Perhaps it would be best if you could get the Emperor to eliminate George," he suggested.

With a flash of insight Galerius explained, "Not all are aware, but as commander of the northeast legions, George's policies of religious tolerance resulted in the rapid spread of Christianity in that region. Now, with the construction of the Christian cathedral which he approved, things have become intolerable in the capital. Brothers, what shall we do? If we let him alone, won't all men follow after him? Must we lose our place and our nation to him?"[6]

The conspirators' responses were immediate and vicious as they contended sharply whether to kill George or just try to ruin him publicly.[7] Galerius smiled as he thought to himself, *There are few people who actually have the nerve to kill someone, but there are many with murder in their hearts, who will assent as long as someone else wields the sword. This group is soaked in the spirit of lust, anger, and contention. I'll have my way with them. But I still need to consolidate more power on the imperial council. I'll spend a bit more time recruiting conspirators, fanning their jealousies of George, and promising more money and power for their support.*

"We must take down Diocletian and all threats to my ascension," he reiterated. "As for the Christians, we must continue our relentless complaints, accusing them of sedition and treason for their violence and their persistent refusal to pay homage to the Emperor as a deity. However, I'm not sure that will be sufficient as Diocletian has less vanity than most Emperors."

"We'll need a spark to ignite the flare of an angry backlash in him," the deep voice replied.

The strain of scheming gave Galerius a burning headache. If there were any gods, he hoped they would reward his efforts, making the pain worthwhile. Peering out through a stable window, he saw a torch light in the bell tower of the new Christian cathedral. "I have an idea!" he declared.

*****

Constantine was in his quarters when George appeared while making his palace rounds. "Hey, follow me to the roof," he whispered. "I want you to see something."

"It's a little cold out here for just romance," Constantine jested as they emerged on the palace roof. "Are we looking at something more than just the moon and stars?" he asked.

Ducking low, George pointed and whispered, "Over there, at the stables. Keep quiet and watch."

As they looked carefully, a few members of the imperial council emerged from the darkened stables, hesitantly scanned the area, and then scattered. These were followed shortly by another small group which included Galerius. "What are you up to, Galerius?" George whispered. "It can't be for good, for God works in light. But the evil one works in darkness, to hide the secrets of iniquity and murder, until he has bound men down to his evil with strong cords."[8]

"But there is nothing hid which shall not be manifested,"[9] Constantine added. "Do you suspect a conspiracy?"

"They're not scouting a new location for their imperial council chambers," George replied.

They continued to watch intently as another small group of men departed from the stables. Constantine spoke his mind quietly, "Wo unto them, for they are like whited sepulchers which indeed appear outwardly beautiful, but within are full of decay and all manner of uncleanness.[10] Who do you suppose is their target?" he finally inquired.

"There's only one real target for Galerius and his minions," George said. "They want more power. The only person who has more power is the Emperor. I think Diocletian is the target, along with any who would support him."

As they continued to watch, one of the tribunes approached the stables. "Look there," George whispered anxiously. "I'm sure it's Orion. Oh, my friend, don't be a part of this for I can't allow a conspirator, or even a sympathizer to continue as a member of the Emperor's personal guard." As Orion reached the stable door, George whispered his plea, "Look away from those who engage in forbidden secret counsels. They take counsel among themselves for iniquity, hostility, and disobedience. Secret counsels are only inspired by the evil one, that he may cause grief to believers. Let the believers put their trust in God."[11] He watched with relief as Orion confirmed the stables were empty and continued with his usual rounds.

*****

Galerius reviewed his plan, checking the things he could control and the things he couldn't. "George showed tolerance for all religions as commander in the northeast," he told the senator. "When challenged regarding religious freedom, he won't back down. Because the Emperor is already planning some action against the Christians, I'm going to use religious freedom as the wedge to separate George from the Emperor.

My cunning plan is falling into place."

"If you can get the Emperor sufficiently enflamed against the Christians to issue a brutal persecution order, George may oppose it," the senator agreed.

"But, if I can get Diocletian to charge George with execution of any persecution orders...Yes, that would surely drive a wedge between them," Galerius spoke excitedly. "I just need to make sure the net for the Christians is cast wide enough to catch sympathizers such as George too. I'll draw George in, keeping him close enough to break him down."[12]

*****

Retiring alone to his quarters, George felt heavy with the weight of evil preparing its assault. Humbly he knelt and raised his voice, "O Lord, I will praise Thee forever. My soul will rejoice in Thee, my God, and the Rock of my salvation. I will walk in Thy paths and be strict in Thy plain roads! O Lord, I have trusted in thee, and I will trust in thee forever. I will not put my trust in the arm of flesh. I will lift up my voice unto Thee. I will cry unto Thee, my God, the Rock of my righteousness. Behold, my voice shall forever ascend up unto Thee, my Rock and mine everlasting God. Amen."[13]

*****

Galerius was not accustomed to making house calls, but he was anxious about his plan and wanted a second opinion that he respected. The deep-voiced counselor stepped outside, closing the door behind him. Together they walked to the seclusion of a nearby olive grove. Quickly Galerius shared his plan. "I'm going to burn the cathedral, inciting the Christians to riot, with the resulting chaos falling right into Diocletian's lap."

His companion hesitated, looking for the right words. "History tells of a fire in Rome that was blamed on the Christians, resulting in a severe backlash of anti-Christian persecution. A well-placed fire may indeed be the spark needed to move the Emperor and the citizens generally to support severe persecutions, for uncontrolled fire is a universal foe. But what if the Christians don't riot? Anyone starting the cathedral fire will have put the entire capital in peril, thus becoming an enemy to all. It seems more likely that burning the cathedral may make many, the Emperor included, sympathetic toward the Christians, believing they are the victims of others' intolerance, unless we prove the Christians started their own fire. The challenge, as I see it, is laying the blame for the fire on the Christians. I don't think anyone will believe they burned their own cathedral."

"You don't think people will declare this as the just retribution of the gods?" Galerius asked.

"They might," the deep voice replied, "but it may not be the sure thing you're looking for."

"Do you have a better idea?" Galerius grunted.

Speaking submissively, the deep voice responded, "The fire is a great idea, but I think there may be a better target for the fire that's much more likely to enrage the Emperor against the Christians. It's a target the people could believe the Christians might burn, providing us with a rich opportunity to fill our pockets from the treasuries of the church."

****

CHAPTER THIRTY-EIGHT
Evil Hearts Aflame – Demand for Persecution

Nicodemia, Eastern Roman Capital
February 303 AD

*"...wicked men...only plot against their own souls,
and they perceive it not."*[1]
Qur'an 6:123

****

Marcus woke with a start. Galerius Caesar had roused him late in the second watch of the night. "Marcus, is it? I have need of two things. First, I have an urgent message for the legion commander in Antioch. I need you to deliver it with an unbroken seal."

"But my lord, I'm a servant in the palace. I cannot go without leave of the Emperor," Marcus replied.

Galerius looked at him sharply and said, "The second thing I need is a new centurion in our Syrian legion. Here are the orders naming you to that position, but you must depart immediately. I'll inform the Emperor of this action in the morning."

Marcus hesitated for only a moment. He was sure he could recognize a golden opportunity when it hit him like this. "I'm your man!" he declared. He accepted the two documents, quickly packed a few personal items, and left the palace, heading for the stables.

*****

Just inside the stables a man was waiting. "Galerius told me the messages you carry are highly confidential," he said. "No one must know that you've taken them. Therefore, we must work in darkness. Take the horse from the second stall and saddle her up. I'll gather all the supplies and money you'll need for your journey."

"Yes, sir," Marcus replied. He led the horse from the stall and prepared to saddle it.

Approaching from behind, the man whispered, "Here's all you'll need for your journey." In the darkness he calmly thrust a long dagger forcefully into Marcus' back, piercing his heart. "A man who would defy his Emperor can't be trusted by the next one, unless it is himself," he said as he withdrew the dagger from the lifeless man.

*****

Galerius quickly gathered the clothing and bedding that had been left in the servant's quarters and put them against the wall that backed to Diocletian's quarters. He touched the pile with his small torch and silently the flames began their rapid ascent and spread. He felt the heat expanding as he thought, *Some would think me reckless, setting the fire myself when it would have been much safer to get an expendable conspirator to take the big risk of getting caught in the palace. But I'm no such coward. I want to keep this matter simple. I want the job done right. If the Emperor dies in the fire, that will serve my purposes just as well. No guts, no glory!* Satisfied with his work, he hurried down the corridor, away from the imperial residence.

*****

Orion was irritated. It was the middle of the night and he was making his usual rounds through the palace. Something just wasn't right, but he couldn't quite put his finger on the problem. He thought about waking George, but for what? Walking with determination he left the hallway by the pagan sanctuary, heading for the servants' quarters and the imperial residence. As he approached, he caught a whiff of smoke and saw what he thought might be the flicker of fire light down the corridor. Running quickly he found Marcus' room fully engulfed in flames. "FIRE!!! FIRE!!! FIRE!!!" he shouted repeatedly as he ran on to the Emperor's quarters.

Diocletian and Alexandria were both awake and on the move when Orion arrived. The fire had already spread through the rafters to the area above their quarters. Though they were able to escape the flames, there was only time for them to save a few personal items. They were a safe distance down the corridor when George arrived with the rest of the palace guard and went to work fighting the fire.

"Don't leave," George advised Diocletian. "This is likely a set up for assassination. If the fire doesn't kill you, other conspirators may try to while your imperial guards are distracted in the chaos."

Diocletian knew George was right, but the fighter in him desperately wanted to go out now, face the traitors and destroy them. He took a deep breath and said, "It's best if I stay close, but by the gods we must catch these actors and kill them all."

A Martyr's Faith

*****

When he was sure the fire was out, George reported to the Emperor. "The imperial residence and servants' quarters are completely destroyed. The great hall and prison are damaged, but they can be cleaned and repaired without much disruption. The tribunes' quarters, pagan sanctuary, archives, imperial council chambers and balcony over the public square suffered no serious damage. I've directed several tribunes to vacate their quarters and temporarily relocate closer to the council chambers and the prison. This gives place for the imperial family and servants in an area still occupied by me and some of the other tribunes."

*****

It was nearly midday and the Emperor was almost settled into his new quarters when the Empress entered quietly to check on him. "I must have answers, and then I'll have heads!" he declared, clearly outraged by the attack on the palace and on him personally.

Trying to calm the rage in her husband, Alexandria said, "You should be still and think. No lives were lost, my love, only things, and things can be replaced," she reminded him.

"Though they didn't kill us, our enemies will grow bolder if they aren't exposed and punished mortally for their treason," Diocletian replied sternly.

"Well, you'll think more clearly to unravel this mystery if you lay aside your rage," she urged again, still hoping to dampen his anger. "Besides, the palace decor was intolerable. This is the perfect opportunity to redecorate our personal quarters to my satisfaction. After all, it's only tax money," she jabbed lightly.

"Would you thus mark as providential the symbolically violent destruction of the old to make way for the new?" Diocletian asked soberly, finally making his point with Alexandria.

*****

The Emperor stood gazing out from the balcony overlooking the public square, still angry over the attack. Galerius stood next to him in the late afternoon sun as they surveyed the damage to the palace. Lest the Emperor should miss it, Galerius spoke brazenly, "Just look at the ashes of the burned out palace! It's quite a contrast with the shining Christian cathedral there. Perhaps the Roman gods have allowed this tragedy because the Christians were allowed to build such a magnificent sanctuary to the glory of their God and to the shame of all others."

"The Roman gods? Seriously?" the Diocletian chided. This was no explanation to him, but it led him to wonder what would happen if that rumor became a common suspicion among the people. "Are you accusing the Christians of starting the palace fire?" he asked directly.

"My lord, by their own admission, their God is a jealous God who hates all other gods," Galerius said. "The Christians are the one group that always places their God before the Emperor. Surely not all Christians are violent, but there are growing rumors of a band of Christian saboteurs."

"I've not heard a word of any alleged Christian saboteurs from George," Diocletian replied.

"The rumors have come from several sources. I expect George would have heard them too. Perhaps his loyalties need further proving," Galerius suggested.

"Don't be ridiculous!" the Emperor boomed, staring Galerius down.

Galerius was pleased that he'd struck a nerve. Backing slightly he continued, "Surely George has heard these rumors too. I just don't understand why he would've said nothing."

Feeling slightly unsettled, Diocletian made no reply.

Galerius continued, "My lord, a few of the rumors are very specific, suggesting the Christians have conspired with someone in the palace to start the fire. To assist you, I've commissioned an investigation into this matter. We shall report to you immediately with any developments or leads. We invite you to assist us in any way you can to identify and catch the perpetrators. We'll find out who did this! Punishment will be swift and severe, I assure you!"

"I want their heads!" the Emperor seethed to the delight of his Caesar.

*****

Night had fallen and the Emperor was exhausted. When George appeared at his door, Diocletian asked anxiously, "What news do you have?"

"The imperial guard has investigated the rumors you spoke of," George replied. "We were unable to identify any credible source connecting the palace fire to the Christians. There were indeed many sources of these rumors, but none had any firsthand knowledge implicating the Christians and none of the rumor sources had their origins prior to the fire. The Christian clergy have denied any involvement and have denied any knowledge of anyone who might be involved. We were able to determine the origin of the fire. It started in

A Martyr's Faith

the quarters of your servant, Marcus. Clothing and bedding were at the base of the fire's origin, next to the wall. We've been unable to locate Marcus anywhere in the palace. No human remains were found in any of the burned areas. Unless you know where we can locate him, it seems he has gone."

"I don't know where Marcus could've gone," Diocletian replied as he thought on George's report and on the rumors Galerius had shared. George hadn't given him much. Galerius may have been right about a conspirator among the palace servants. "This situation is unacceptable," the Emperor stated. "We must identify the guilty parties and punish them. We'll revisit this matter in the morning."

*****

It was late in the morning and the imperial council chambers were full. "The members are buzzing like flies over the palace fire, hoping for a report on the investigation," George said to Constantine. "All in the capital with even the poorest excuse to attend court have come to survey the fire damage for themselves. I've assigned Orion to attend the Emperor, freeing me to examine the crowd more closely."

Constantine stayed close to George, sharing his thoughts and observations quietly.

Solemnly, the Emperor called the council to order and informed them, "To this point, there has been no official claim of responsibility, although there have been a number of unsubstantiated rumors regarding Christian saboteurs. Officials have also reported many signs of agitation among the people in various parts of the capital, but thus far, all potential riots have been suppressed by the imperial guard and elements of my army."

When the Emperor had concluded his report, Galerius stood to offer his measured evaluation of the rumors. "Surely with so many sources implicating the Christians, there must be some truth to it. After all, where there's smoke, there's fire!" With a wink and a nod he signaled his allies on the council for support. This brought a flood of additional charges against the Christians from all sides, along with an emphatic clamor for swift action against them.

"I've heard a lot of rumors, but thus far I've seen no actual evidence against the Christians," Diocletian replied. "I see no reason to incite civil unrest, especially in the absence of any solid evidence," the Emperor concluded, defying the mob as he thought, *What dangerously broad cover such chaos provides for all manner of atrocities and treachery.*

Reacting to Diocletian's comments, the council became ever more raucous until Galerius raised his hands for silence. After the council had quieted, Galerius proposed to the council, "Great leaders of the people, let us not descend into anarchy, but let us be tempered in our response to these Christian atrocities. While many are calling for retaliation and persecution, I call for consultation with the divine. Some weeks ago our wise Emperor made inquiry to the oracle of Apollo at Didyma for guidance regarding the Christian question. With counsel from the oracle, I'm certain we'll know what we must do." Again the council erupted, the clamor manifestly in support of this proposal.

Cautiously Constantine whispered to George, "Are we to expect that the oracle of Apollo will exonerate the Christians?"

"No," George replied quietly. "I'm sure this is all a trap for Diocletian. It has yet to be fully sprung, but the Emperor and his supporters on the council are all standing in the snare. Galerius wants to incite civil unrest to distract everyone from his real treachery. If the Christians take the brunt of the violence, he'll not be disappointed."

Shaking his head in disgust, Constantine offered his hushed response. "Who does more wrong than he who invents a lie against God or rejects the truth when it reaches him? Hell awaits such as these who reject faith and conspire against God."[2]

Diocletian pondered on the scene. *The council is extremely animated which is ironic considering that so few of them actually believe in any of the gods. In either case, going with this proposal should still buy me some time for more investigation and greater consideration of the issues.* Abruptly, he stood and raised his right hand for order and quiet. "Well spoken, noble Caesar," he said to Galerius. Then, turning more fully to the council he continued, "We will bring the matter of the palace fire to light and punish the guilty. If the oracle of Apollo can assist, I welcome it."

As a moderate rumble of approval flowed through the assembly, a messenger suddenly appeared at the door. Seeing this, Galerius addressed Diocletian. "Most noble Emperor, I sent a man to check on the oracle's messenger and he has just arrived. May we hear his report?" he asked.

When a second messenger wearing the symbols of Apollo appeared at the door, Diocletian felt especially wary. Facing the expectant members of the council, he could see no reasonable way to delay the report for a private audience. Therefore, he ordered, "Let him speak!"

Quickly Galerius' messenger spoke from the doorway, "I have located the oracle's messenger and brought him here. He shall speak for the oracle!" This declaration received loud applause.

Slowly the aged messenger of the oracle shuffled half the distance from the door of the chamber to the Emperor's throne. While he walked,

George thought for a moment about the actions of both Galerius and Diocletian. Speaking with a quiet shudder he said, "The kings of the earth stand up and the rulers are gathered together against the Lord and against his Christ. Why do the heathens rage and the people imagine such vain things?"[3]

Taking hold of George's shoulder Constantine replied, "If Diocletian loses the council, he should fear for surely Galerius will grasp for the reins of power. When men grasp for power, the people always suffer. Removing a wicked emperor is a horrible and bloody task."[4]

"I've heard that before, from my father," George replied.

"Then perhaps he was as wise as my mother," Constantine said, still anxious about the message.

As directed by the Emperor, the aged messenger spoke. "The oracle of Apollo desires to serve our great Emperor and this great Republic. Regrettably, the oracle reports that the impious on earth have hindered Apollo's ability to provide counsel on the matter of the Christians."

A hush settled briefly over the council as each man tried to interpret the message of the oracle. Galerius, however, having intercepted the oracle's messenger prior to the meeting, was well aware of the message and the exact wording with which it would be delivered. Wasting no time he stepped forward to frame it to his own purposes. "Most noble Diocletian, we are all aware of the sedition of the Christians in dishonoring the Roman gods and refusing to pay homage to your divinity and right of rule in the empire. Though not all are aware, we've seen this hindrance of the Roman gods before, when the priests at Caesarea were unable to read the sacrificial entrails at the harvest festival because the sacrifices were disrupted by the intolerant Christian zealot, Romanus. Clearly the 'impious' spoken of could only refer to the Christians who are ungodly because they won't respect our sacrifices to the Roman gods, and they refuse to pay homage to your divine nature."

Galerius' allies on the council took the signal, raising their voices against the Christians.

Annoyed by Galerius' voice, Constantine whispered to George, repeating a familiar verse between them. "The harshest sound, without doubt, is the braying of the ass.[5] The words of his mouth are iniquity and deceit. He has left off to be wise and to do good."[6]

George remembered their past exchanges and, turning to Constantine, responded with another verse. "Yet shall we be moderate in our pace and lower our voices, for the truth will bear its own emphasis mildly. Wicked men only plot against their own souls, though they don't recognize it.[7] But the judgments of God will overtake the wicked, and it is by the wicked that the wicked are punished, for it is the wicked that stir up the hearts of men unto bloodshed."[8]

After several minutes of angry clamoring, Galerius called the council back to order and addressed himself to the Emperor on their behalf. "We are also certain of Christian treachery in the matter of the palace fire. Their proud new cathedral stands in stark contrast nearby." Raising his voice dramatically he continued, "My Lord, in light of the oracle's message against the ungodly, the council demands that you immediately issue edicts condemning the Christians for the palace fire and for their seditions. We demand that you order the arrest of their soldiers and clergy, requiring that they renounce their faith and pay homage to the Roman gods and to you or face execution. Further, we demand the destruction of the Christian cathedral, confiscation of their property, and burning of their records for their seditious acts."

The council waited momentarily for any final demands on their behalf. Quickly, Galerius turned to the council and, raising his hands, challenged, "Do we not demand these things?" The council's acclamation in support of the demands quickly grew vicious and chaotic.

Hearing this, Constantine turned to George and said, "The wicked are estranged from humanity. From the womb they go astray, as soon as they are delivered, speaking lies. Their poison is like the poison of a serpent."[9]

"Still favoring the Psalms?" George whispered.

"Oh, was that scripture too?" Constantine asked with sober concern. "I thought it was just another plain truth from my saintly mother's lips."

George replied, "Lo, the wicked bend their bows, they make ready their arrows upon the string, that they may secretly shoot at the upright in heart.[10] Who can be more wicked than he who invents lies against God?"[11]

Diocletian was more than irritated by Galerius' demands. However, he could see the darkness in the faces of the imperial council and knew he had lost them, for now. *Immediate confrontation is an option,* he thought, *but perhaps not the best course, for they are likely ready to deal with that. Now that the battle for control has come to me, I'll bide my time and look for opportunities to reclaim the council's loyalty from Galerius. If I can't muster the strength for this fight, I'll have to abdicate or be removed from the throne by violence.*

Galerius' impatience is a flaw I should have recognized much earlier. I feel both disdain and admiration for the crafty conspiracy gathering around me. I selected Galerius as Caesar precisely because I needed an ambitious and brutal bludgeon that could bear the rigors of travel to put down rebellions in the frontier regions. I needed someone to whom I could confidently delegate a share of the battle load. Now I must bridle

Galerius if possible, or perhaps assassinate him. But first, I must lead the council in the direction they are already going and get George to keep them in check. "I'll prepare my orders and present them for the council's approval tomorrow," he stated with a heavy sigh. Rising, he departed the chamber, ending the debate for the moment.

*****

George returned to his private quarters, distressed by the uncertainty of the Emperor's response. *I've been counting on Diocletian to impose moderation on the ruling council and now that's in doubt. Of course, the Emperor could still issue orders furthering the investigation into the palace fire and placing token restraints on some of the leading Christians, but I have a bad feeling about how this will play out.*

He looked out his window at the Christian cathedral. Anguishing over what was coming but not knowing how to stop it, he thought, *Secret conspiracies seeking power place men in bondage, depriving them of their freedom and agency. Such conspiracies are wicked above all in the sight of God. Our Father does not work in secret conspiracies. He has forbidden that men should shed each other's blood. The sword of justice of the Eternal God shall fall upon any nation that shall uphold such conspiracies and works of darkness, to their overthrow and entire destruction. Those who build them up seek to overthrow the freedom of all lands, nations, countries and peoples to their utter destruction. Such conspiracies are authored by the devil, the dragon who is the father of all lies who has caused men to commit murder from the beginning. He is the beast who has hardened the hearts of men that they have murdered the prophets, and stoned them, and cast them out from the beginning. This nation must repent, that they may come to the Fountain of all righteousness and be saved.*[12]

George pondered on the actions of Galerius and the council, fully recognizing that their demands, if granted, would entangle him too because of his position. Feeling the attack against him personally, he prayed in anguish, "Holy Father, let them be ashamed and confounded that seek to destroy my soul. Turn back them that desire my hurt. Let confusion and shame be their reward.[13] For my enemies speak against me. They that lay wait for my soul take counsel together saying, 'God has forsaken him; persecute and take him, for there is none to deliver him.' Let my adversaries be confounded and consumed. Let them that seek to injure me be covered with reproach and dishonor. My tongue shall talk of Thy righteousness all the day long, for they that sought my destruction are confounded and brought to shame."[14]

Countering the weight of evil he felt, the whisperings of the Spirit filled his mind with light and understanding: *The whole world groans in darkness, under the bondage of sin, because they come not unto Me. For whoso receives not My voice is not of Me. By this you may know the righteous from the wicked, and that the whole world groans under sin and darkness even now. The minds of this people, in times past, have been darkened because of unbelief, and because they have treated lightly sacred things bringing them under condemnation.*[15] *For all men shall live by every word that proceeds forth from the mouth of God. For the word of the Lord is truth, and whatsoever is truth is light, and whatsoever is light is Spirit, even the Spirit of Jesus Christ. And the Spirit gives light to every man that comes into the world, and enlightens every man that hearkens to the voice of the Spirit. And every one that hearkens to the voice of the Spirit comes unto God, even the Father. And the Father teaches men of the covenant which He has renewed and confirmed upon men through faith on the blood of His Son, Jesus Christ.*[16]

George felt an unusual mix of emotions, elated by the peace and joy of the Spirit, but weighed down by the pervasive evil dominating the imperial council and other leaders. Grateful that he answered only to Diocletian, George wondered how things might change if the Emperor were to grant the council's demands, or lose power. With a shudder he whispered to himself, "Gather not my soul with sinners, nor my life with bloody men, in whose hands is mischief, and their right hands are full of bribes. But as for me, I will walk in mine integrity. Lord Jesus, redeem me and be merciful unto me."[17]

****

CHAPTER THIRTY-NINE
Persecution Order

Nicodemia, Eastern Roman Capital
24 February, 303 AD

"Woe unto them that decree unrighteous decrees, and that write grievousness which they have prescribed..."[1]
Isaiah 10:1

****

George appeared at the door to the Emperor's private chambers as the messenger had instructed. "Good, you're here," Diocletian said anxiously. "It's time to present my edicts to the council. There are very few among them that I trust. I don't want this to get out of hand."

"Are you expecting trouble?" George asked. "I was told specifically to bring Ascalon."

"I'm always expecting trouble now," the Emperor replied grimly. "I want you to shadow me closely no matter where I go."

"Why? What have you ordered on the Christian matter?" George probed.

"Would it matter?" the Emperor questioned. "There's no way to please everyone, and anything short of a Christian blood bath may prompt the conspirators to immediate violence."

"I'll stay with you and protect you with my sword and my life," George promised, knowing the Emperor just wanted reassurance. The answer to his question would be clear soon enough.

"I'm grateful," Diocletian sighed as he buckled on his own sword and picked up his documents and seal. "Now let's go swing the axe with our might and see where the chips fall," he said, heading for the council chamber with George keeping pace at his side.

*****

The Emperor strode confidently into the room, though he felt inside like a man overboard in shark infested waters. With determination he took his place on the throne. Standing a step behind and to the right, George scanned the group and noted that his friend Constantine was in attendance. However, Galerius, the perennial irritant, was curiously absent. The assembly seemed very agitated, as if they anticipated disappointment in response to their demands.

The Emperor raised his hand and a hush came over the crowd. After turning his head aside briefly to clear his throat, Diocletian began to read the edicts he had prepared. "First, I order the destruction of the Christian cathedral in Nicodemia. Further, I command the seizure of the church treasury and records for the Republic. All church scriptures are ordered to be burned."

"Next, I command the immediate arrest of all Christian clergy and Christian officers in military or governmental posts in Nicodemia. These are commanded to publicly renounce Christianity, make sacrifices to the Roman gods, and pay homage to the Emperor as a god. Those who refuse will be tried on charges of sedition and treason, and face punishment up to execution."

George was stunned by the orders. If the imperial council chose to riot and attack the Emperor at that moment, he was uncertain which side he would take. However, the council responded in support of Diocletian's edicts. George's mind worked over the orders just presented and their significance. *This aggressive persecution against the Christians shows that Diocletian has chosen to submit fully to the will of the council and to accept its demands.*

"Where's Galerius?" George blurted out.

"Get the full guard and we'll go see," Diocletian replied. "Our work here is done. We're going to the cathedral."

As they hurried on their way, Diocletian confided, "As a gesture of goodwill, I previewed the Christian persecution orders with Galerius last night. He requested and received copies of the orders, stamped with my seal, to take with him on a raid of the cathedral early this morning."

*****

As dawn was about to break, Galerius and his personal security guards took the persecution orders in hand and approached the newly built Christian Cathedral in Nicodemia. They were accompanied by the local prefect of Nicodemia, a few select military leaders, a centurion with his hundred men, and several accountants and records clerks. Galerius had carefully shielded both George and Constantine from the flow of information regarding the planned raid.

"Break the lock and force open the doors!" Galerius commanded, and thus the destruction began. The scene was one of chaos and panic for the keepers and occupants of the sacred house of God. Images and furniture were smashed and the treasury was robbed, its contents to be divided between Galerius and the Emperor, with small tributes distributed among the looting soldiers.

"My lord, we've been unable to locate the church's scriptures and records," a soldier reported. "We've seized this man who says his name is Timothy. He admits he is a caretaker of the church and keeper of the Holy Scriptures, but he won't give them up."

In humility young Timothy stood bound before them, keeping his eyes down. Slapping him viciously, Galerius grabbed his shirt, and pulled him close. "Tell me where the records are hidden and deliver them up to be burned if you want to live," he snarled.

"Had I children, I would sooner deliver them up to be sacrificed, than part with the sacred Word of God," Timothy answered.

"Insolent idiot!" Galerius raged. "The books shall at least be useless to you, for you shall not see to read them. Put this man's eyes out!" he commanded, incensed at Timothy's defiance.

Timothy's patience under the torture was so great that Galerius grew even angrier. "Hang him up by the feet, with a weight tied about his neck, and a gag in his mouth!" he ordered in an attempt to break the keeper's will.

Seeing this, Timothy's wife Maura tenderly urged him, "Please tell them where the records are hidden and spare yourself, for my sake."

When his gag was removed, Timothy responded soberly, "Maura, do not sell yourself for a mistaken love of this mortal life. I will be faithful until death. I plead with you, be faithful too."

In responsive fury, Galerius drew his sword and stabbed Timothy in the heart.

Through her anguish and fear, Maura was inspired by her husband's courage, honor, and fidelity. Summoning her own faith, she pled, "I beg you, let me share the fate of my husband and pass on with him to glory."

"Torture this creature for the location of the records!" Galerius ordered.

After several minutes of useless torture, Galerius angrily executed the woman.[2]

*****

Still numb over the orders that had been issued, George led Diocletian and his guard to the Christian cathedral. Soberly, the Emperor explained, "For some time now Galerius has been warning of a possible informant within the council who has been alerting the Christians to our monitoring and enforcement actions. In order to retain the element of surprise, we agreed to conduct a raid on the Christian cathedral, concurrent with my announcement of the edicts in the imperial chambers this morning. Now we shall see the results of his work."

The commotion around the cathedral was similar to the looting raids George had seen early in his military career. "Be vigilant as we approach the church," he warned the tribunes. "The chaos of the raid offers ample cover for an assassination attempt on the Emperor."

"I want to inspect what has been confiscated!" Diocletian demanded as they met Galerius. "Have we discovered any documents that prove conclusively whether the Christians were responsible for the palace fire?"

Galerius hadn't counted on Diocletian's personal attendance at the raid, but he was prepared. At his direction, one of his record keepers responded, "Here are the documents and records we recovered. They clearly implicate the complicity of the Christian clergy in the palace fire."

"Raze the church!" the Emperor commanded. "Let no stone be left upon another! Burn all that will burn, including the bodies of the caretaker and his wife."

*****

As the Emperor and his guards returned to the palace, George felt growing pain and despair at witnessing the destruction of the cathedral, the sacred scriptures, and the caretaker's family. Fear had been evident in the eyes of the other church leaders as they were arrested, beaten, and carted away. A rush from his memory brought a Psalm of anguish and pleading which filled his mind. *My soul is among lions: and I lie even among them that are set on fire, even the sons of men, whose teeth are spears and arrows, and their tongue a sharp sword. Be Thou exalted, O God, above the heavens; let Thy glory be above all the earth...Awake up, my glory....*[3]

I'm certain the documents implicating the Christians in the palace fire are a deception at the hands of Galerius, he thought. *But I would need undeniable evidence to raise any charges against him. The possibility of getting what I need, making a persuasive case to the Emperor, and getting an agreement from the imperial council to change course appears less than hopeless.* "How could the situation possibly get any worse?" he asked himself.

*****

At Diocletian's command, all of the tribunes remained near his throne in the council chambers. He was still certain of a conspiracy within the council, but he was uncertain how the Christians would react to the persecution edicts and to the immediate destruction of their beloved cathedral. Hearing rumors of the raid, the council had reconvened for an authoritative report on the event. As the Emperor looked at each member of the council, seeking clues as to their true allegiance, the door to the council chamber was abruptly pushed open and in marched a very sweaty but euphoric Galerius, who promptly spilled a chest with the contents of the church's treasury on the chamber floor. It was as if he expected a hero's acclamation for his day's work.

For a moment, Diocletian saw flashes of Christian sympathy confessed on the faces of several council members, but they were fleeting. At the moment he had no plans to initiate any confrontations. *I'll just ride the surge of emotion for now and try to change its course later, when it has mostly played itself out*, he thought. *I'll strike back when I have a better feel for who are my allies and who are my enemies.*

But Galerius had plans for this moment. Playing off his dramatic entrance, he addressed himself to the Emperor, though he spoke for the benefit of the assembly. "Most noble Emperor Diocletian, I return to report on the execution of your order for the destruction of the cathedral. As you've seen, documents discovered in the raid clearly evidence a Christian conspiracy to set the palace on fire in an attempt to assassinate you. As you have commanded, we've confiscated their treasury, destroyed their cathedral, burned their religious records, and arrested their clergy.

"There is still the matter of cleansing the capital, arresting all Christian civil authorities and military officers, and gaining their submission in renouncing their faith in Christ and making sacrifices to the Roman gods and to the Emperor lest they be executed. I urge you to pick a trusted man and charge him to strictly enforce these orders." Galerius was uncertain what Diocletian would do in this moment, but he could only imagine two likely options for the Emperor, and either one would play to his advantage.

"Well spoken," Diocletian replied, suspecting Galerius was simply angling for the transfer of more authority to himself, to make it easier for him to bend the wills of those who might still be supporting their Emperor. Knowing this must not happen, and feeling that hesitation before the entire council was not an option, he turned to his most faithful and trusted tribune. Extending the orders for persecution, Diocletian loudly proclaimed, "George, I solemnly charge you to immediately execute these edicts against the Christians throughout Nicodemia!"

Stupor gave way to a flood of the Spirit as George turned to face the

Emperor. Bridling his anger he scanned the imperial council and spoke boldly the words of Isaiah, "Woe unto them that decree unrighteous decrees and that write grievousness which they have prescribed...."[4]

"What's that? What's the problem, George?" the Emperor asked in surprise and confusion.

Recognizing that his refusal to fulfill these commands would be grounds for his own execution, George proceeded. "These decrees are unlawful. They are a cruel injustice, and I can't enforce them. I won't enforce them. If I must act on them, I shall first arrest myself, rendering me unavailable for further duty."

Rarely in his life had Diocletian been caught off guard, but his instincts did not abandon him. *Play for time!* "Will you be pleading the cause of the Christians before your Emperor then?" he asked George in a playful manner. "This may be somewhat entertaining considering the current mood in this chamber, but I'll hear you out, if you don't make me too cross," he laughed. This prompted a muffle of sympathetic laughter, but no one took George for a jester.

"I beg you to stop for a moment and consider these matters all again," George pleaded. "Could it be that the Roman laws of tolerance toward all religions are extended only to its subjects on condition that they worship gods in whom they have no faith? The Christians, who have been loyal to their God, have also been loyal to this Republic and to you, great Emperor, yet the leaders of this nation seek to heap one abuse after another upon them, and only because the Christian God is not a puppet or idol of men. This nation is full of men who simply fear that which they can't control. The Christians were not responsible for the palace fire and this Republic had no cause to destroy their cathedral. You can't strengthen the weak by weakening the strong.[5] You can't strengthen the Republic by weakening those who are strongest in obedience to its laws, for every house divided against itself shall fall.[6]

"Christian doctrine requires the faithful to be subject to and sustain civil authorities in obeying moral laws. Jesus commanded His disciples: 'Render therefore unto Caesar the things which are Caesar's; and unto God the things which are God's.'[7] The Apostle Paul also taught Christians: 'Render therefore to all their dues: tribute to whom tribute is due; custom to whom custom; fear to whom fear; honor to whom honor.'"[8]

Constantine watched in amazement as George forcefully declared the truth of Christianity. Quietly he pled under his breath, "Throw now thy rod; and behold it swallows up straight away all the falsehoods which they fake."[9]

George continued boldly and deliberately, "Christians accept the admonition of Paul to be true, honest, just, pure, and virtuous in doing good to all men.[10] Under Roman law, Christians seek tolerance for their religious beliefs and claim the privilege of worshipping God according to the dictates of their consciences. Notwithstanding their faith and desire to share the gospel of Jesus Christ with all men, true Christians have tolerance for all men in worshipping how, where, or what they may."[11]

The Emperor listened intently as George made his plea for the cause of the Christians, and for himself. He was still shocked and surprised that George, whom he'd trusted completely and loved like his own son, had taken this defiant position publicly before the imperial council. Diocletian couldn't recall his commands now without appearing to bow to George. He wasn't sure he would even want to recall them if he could. But as he listened, he weighed the effect of George's words on the members of the imperial council. They weren't persuaded by his defense of Christianity, or even by his claimed defense of Roman law, but they feared him physically and his influence as a leader. The council's fear of George was just one more reason Diocletian desperately wanted to preserve him as an ally. *I must get George to submit to my commands, for the good of the empire*, he thought.

As George concluded, Diocletian raised his hand to quiet the council chamber. He looked carefully at George and made his personal plea. "George, you are a tribune of the Roman Empire, sworn to protect your Emperor with your life and to advance your Emperor's will. It is my will, for the good of the empire, that every Christian lay aside his traditions and submit to my commands, for as you've stated, every kingdom divided against itself shall fall.[12] You can do a service of immeasurable benefit to your country and your people by leading this nation in submission to these decrees. I command you now to recall your words, honoring your allegiance to me, and to fulfill all my commands regarding the implementation of these orders against Christianity. As your Emperor, I command your submission."

George felt his heart breaking at the betrayal of a man he had trusted. "I'll submit to your will in all that is right," he replied, "but this is not right! If only you hadn't seated yourself among those who are swayed by ignorance and impatience![13] I pray that we might find common ground, but that can only be in the realm where my faith in Jesus Christ is acknowledged and respected, if not believed. I'll never make sacrifices to the imagined gods of Rome, nor pay homage to a mortal Emperor as a God. I will only worship the one true and living God and His Son, Jesus Christ. My faith is beyond mere tradition, for I know whereof I speak. Though it costs me my life, I will never execute these orders against the Christians, for I am a Christian!"

The imperial council exploded with rancor. "Away with this man who reviles and defies our Emperor and our law! He is a Christian and a traitor! Condemn him to death!"

George turned from the Emperor to the council and took a step toward them, Ascalon still in his hand. As a group the council drew back in fear. Stopping, George spoke, "Do you stand to judge me? Be still and know the things of God.[14] For as surely as you live, God lives! I don't fear your persecution, for all who live after His righteousness shall suffer persecution.[15] Men of true character and faith must all endure these crosses, despising the shame of the world.[16] Yet you are full of unbelief, lifted up in the pride of your hearts, taking glory in your riches and the vain things of the world, worshipping the work of your own hands, denying the true and living God. You refuse to look forward for a remission of your sins, and you lack everlasting faith in that which is to come. Though the Lord wade through much affliction and sorrow with you, no joy shall come because of your unbelief.[17] Oh, that I could persuade all men not to rebel against God, to provoke Him to anger, but that all men would believe in Christ, view His death, suffer His cross, and bear the shame of the world, for the glory of eternity."[18]

After silencing the council, George turned back to Diocletian and pleaded, "I stand at the Emperor's judgment seat, where I ought to be judged lawfully, and where I pray to be judged righteously. Unless there is justice in the persecution of Christians for their faith, I've done no wrong, as all well know. If I'm an offender or have committed anything worthy of death, I will not refuse to die.[19] But the day of the Lord shall be great and terrible unto the wicked, for they shall perish because they cast out the prophets and the saints, and stone them and slay them. Wherefore, the cry of the blood of the saints shall ascend up unto God from the ground against them, and the day of the Lord shall burn up the proud and the wicked as stubble, according to His word."[20]

Again the council chambers erupted in rancor. The Emperor stood up, amazed and bewildered. He hadn't seen this coming. No man had dared speak to him in this tone for more than ten years. George's challenge to his orders could not be ignored. Grief flooded over Diocletian as he thought, *Not you, George. Had I known, perhaps I could have saved you from this chaos. But now, I fear both you and I will be swallowed up by it.*

****

CHAPTER FORTY
Prisoner for Christ

Nicodemia, Eastern Roman Capital
24 February, 303 AD

"But I say unto you, Love your enemies, bless them that curse you, do good to them that hate you, and pray for them which despitefully use you, and persecute you, that ye may be the children of your Father which is in heaven."[1]
Matthew 5:44-45

****

Diocletian needed to put an end to the overflowing passions in the chamber and to regroup with his few remaining allies. "Silence!" he commanded. "George will be held over for trial on charges of insubordination and sedition." Turning to George he said, "Surrender your weapon to me." Tension was evident among all the imperial guards as George slowly rotated Ascalon in his hands and extended the hilt to the Emperor. Taking the sword, Diocletian said, "Orion, bind George and deliver him to the palace prison."

Orion was inspired by George's character and bearing. He didn't want to oppose him in anything. Yet at the command, he moved into position behind his friend, approaching hesitantly. Orion was a mountain of a man and the only tribune who appeared physically capable of overpowering George. But they had done enough earnest sparring for him to know he wasn't taking George unless George was willing to be taken, with or without Ascalon.

George had heard the Emperor's order and he sensed the tension in the tribune. He knew his conflict was with the Emperor and the imperial council, not with his friend. Slowly he turned and looked Orion in the eye and said, "Fear not; do your duty and no harm will come to you."

These words from another man might have been a subtle deception to catch Orion off guard, but coming from George, they were sure and true.

Carefully, Orion tied George's hands behind him. As he guided George down the corridor toward the palace prison, behind them they heard an eruption of excited voices in the council chamber as many began to clamor, demanding George's immediate execution for his defiance. Soberly, Orion leaned in and whispered, "You should submit to the will of the Emperor lest you bear his threatened justice for your refusal to renounce your faith. This cannot end well."

"Since the Theban legion was put to the sword by Maximian for their refusal to deny their faith in Christ, I've often considered how I would respond to such an unjust command," George replied calmly. "Yet, who could be more unjust than me, were I to conceal the testimony I have from God?[2] Submission to the Emperor's unjust commands would leave me more unjust than him, for he's ignorant of much of the things of God, but I know whereof I speak. I'll bear the justice and the injustice of all men that I may secure to myself the mercy of my God. If it be His will, I shall not withhold from Him my life in His cause. The Lord giveth, and the Lord taketh away. Praised be the name of the Lord."[3]

George was too far away to hear when the Emperor finally rose up and declared with finality, "This man is a Roman citizen. He will be accorded his rights under the law. He'll be given a proper trial, as is his right. This Republic will not descend again into mob rule while I stand at the head. I command all men here to uphold the law in this matter, or you shall be subjected to the law for your refusals to submit!"

The force of Diocletian's words brought soberness back to the council. Seeing this, Diocletian left the chamber, headed for his private quarters to consider this unsettling turn of events. His thoughts were a clutter. *This situation is spiraling out of control. If I can just get George back on my side, we can fix this. I must use every means possible to get him to submit publicly to my edicts. He's popular throughout the capital and much of the eastern empire. With him as an example, renouncing his Christian faith, making the required sacrifices to the Roman gods, and paying homage to me as a deity, we can fix this mess.*

"Bring Orion to me," he called to the tribune outside his door.

*****

George sat quietly in his cell, pondering all that had happened and considering his predicament. He thought of Orion's advice and the prospect of escaping death by simply renouncing his faith in Christ, making a token sacrifice to the Roman gods, and carrying out the Emperor's orders. He knew he couldn't do that, nor would he consider it any further. The thought of death hung heavy over him. As he pondered his future, his heart was filled with the emotion of the Psalm: *My God, my God, why hast thou forsaken me? Why art Thou so far from helping me, and from the words of my anguish? O my God, I cry in the daytime but Thou hearest not; and in the night I am not silent. But Thou art holy, O Thou that lives to the praises of Israel. Our fathers trusted in Thee;*

they trusted and Thou didst deliver them. They cried unto Thee and were delivered: they trusted in Thee, and were not confounded.[4]

George remembered his own experiences in life and spoke quietly to himself. "My God has not forsaken me, but He has been my support. He has led me through my afflictions in this life and has preserved me from hell. He has filled me with His love and confounded my enemies. He has heard my cries by day and given me knowledge by dreams and visions in the night.[5] Holy Father, have mercy upon me and send Thy Holy Spirit to comfort me. Fill me with Thy Spirit and with forgiveness, understanding, and peace. Help me to remember Thy hand strengthening me in all things that I may not doubt in my time of need, nor give place within me to the enemy of my soul. As I have seen so great things, why should my heart weep and my soul linger in the valley of sorrow? Why should I yield to sin? Why should I give way to temptations that the evil one have place in my heart to destroy my peace and afflict my soul?[6]

"Lord, wilt Thou redeem my soul? Wilt Thou deliver me out of the hands of my enemies? Wilt Thou make me that I may shake at the appearance of sin? May the gates of hell be shut continually before me, because my heart is broken and my spirit is contrite! Lord, wilt Thou not shut the gates of Thy righteousness before me! Wilt Thou encircle me around in the robe of Thy righteousness! Lord, wilt Thou make a way for my escape before my enemies?[7]

"Awake, my soul! No longer droop in sin. Rejoice, my heart, and give place no more for the enemy of my soul. Do not anger again because of my enemies. Do not slacken my strength because of my afflictions. Rejoice, my heart, and cry unto the Lord. Lord, I will praise Thee forever. My soul will rejoice in Thee, my God and the Rock of my salvation.[8]

"Lord, I have trusted in Thee, and I will trust in Thee forever. I will not put my trust in the arm of flesh. Cursed is he that puts his trust in man or in the arm of flesh. I know that God will give liberally to him that asks. Yes, my God will give me, if I ask not amiss. Therefore I will lift up my voice unto Thee. I will cry unto Thee, my God, the Rock of my righteousness. My voice shall forever ascend up unto Thee, my Rock and my everlasting God. Amen."[9]

George hadn't thought it would come to this, but when he'd been given the command to enforce the persecution orders against the Christians, he knew immediately how he must respond, and what it might cost him. He thought of home and all that gave meaning to his life. He yearned for the company of a faithful companion but knew that any such visitor would come under immediate suspicion and would likely share his fate. He pondered upon the promise of the Lord: *I will not leave you comfortless; but the Comforter, which is the Holy Ghost, whom the Father will send in My name, He shall teach you all things, and bring all things to your remembrance, whatsoever I have said unto you.*[10]

Still praying silently for peace of mind and calm in his heart, George began to feel the promised comfort of the Spirit. Reverently he gave voice to his deepest emotions. "I felt as though the Lord had forsaken me and altogether forgotten me. But He has shown that He has not forgotten me. Were it possible that a woman could forget her sucking child, that she should not have compassion on the son of her womb, yet the Lord would not forget His children. For He has graven us upon the palms of His hands, and redeemed us with His own blood. He will yet lift up His hand to the nations and set His standard to all people and save all His children.[11] For they shall not be ashamed that wait upon the Lord.[12] Lord, I will keep my trust in Thee."

Soon the Spirit filled his mind with the words of the Savior: *Come unto Me, all ye that labor and are heavy laden, and I will give you rest. Take My yoke upon you, and learn of Me; for I am meek and lowly in heart: and ye shall find rest unto your souls. For My yoke is easy, and My burden is light.*[13] *Blessed are they which are persecuted for righteousness' sake, for theirs is the kingdom of heaven.*[14]

George knew no matter how hard it might be to stand by his knowledge of the truth and his faith in God, if he renounced his faith, it would be infinitely more difficult to face an offended God who had blessed him so richly, and would yet bless him with eternal glory. The comfort and peace he felt gave him confidence before the Lord. He prayed, "O Lord, deliver my soul from the wicked men of the world which have their portion in this life and merit no reward in the day of judgment.[15] By Thy words I have been kept from the paths of the destroyer. Secure me in Thy path that my feet may not slip.[16] Keep me as the apple of Thine eye."[17]

*****

George had been alone in his cell for several hours before Orion returned. The key rattled in the lock and the hinges strained, protesting loudly as he entered. Confiding in the prisoner, Orion spoke quietly. "You've had time to think. Now listen. The Emperor is determined to save you but you must help. He's promised to release you from prison and restore you to your position as tribune and captain of his guard if you will publicly renounce your faith in Jesus Christ, make the required sacrifices to the Roman gods, and carry out the persecution orders."

George thought carefully about how he could explain his position to Orion, and to the Emperor for that matter. Calmly he spoke, "The God of heaven forbids that I cover His truth with falsehood or conceal His truth when I know what it is.[18] The Emperor proposes that I forfeit the eternal salvation offered by God, that I might be saved in the flesh by a man. I will not do that. I cannot put off the truth of God. My faith in God and in all truth abides. I will not abandon my inheritance of faith and my hope of a glorious resurrection. I will never renounce my faith in Jesus Christ, nor will I recall my words, for they are true. I've been given into the Emperor's hands as a witness of these truths that he may know of their surety. If God requires it, I will suffer even unto death, but I will not recall my words. They shall stand as a testimony against the evil of these persecution orders and the men who execute them. And if I am slain, my innocent blood will cry from the ground as a testimony against the wicked at the last day."[19]

"I'll tell the Emperor you've...refused his proposal," Orion sighed with resignation. "I'm sure that won't be as convincing as hearing your words directly and feeling your conviction."

"Have no fear, Brother. Do your best to give the Emperor my response in full detail," George encouraged. "I'm confident I'll get another chance to deliver my witness to him personally."

"Very good," Orion replied as he left George's cell, taking care to make sure the cell door was securely locked behind him.

*****

Alone again, George thought more deeply about the likely impact if he didn't submit to the Emperor. He would be marked for death, but if the Lord chose to spare him, no man could take his life away. Otherwise, he would die a martyr's death and the persecution of the Christians would be intensified. The vision in his mind broke his heart as he thought of the innocent people being abused for their faith. Again, the words of Jesus Christ came to his mind: *Blessed are ye, when men shall hate you, and when they shall separate you from their company, and shall reproach you, and cast out your name as evil, for the Son of Man's sake. Rejoice ye in that day, and leap for joy: for, behold, your reward is great in heaven.*[20] These words were spoken to all men. George knew it was not his place to deny anyone the privilege of being tried and proven in the furnace of adversity, that thereby they might gain the heavenly gift from God.

Kneeling alone in faith and with further resignation to the will of God, he prayed, "Thy word is a lamp unto my feet and a light unto my path. I've sworn, and I will perform it, that I will keep Thy righteous judgments. I'm gravely afflicted. Quicken me, O Lord, according to Thy word.[21] I will speak of Thy testimonies also before kings and will not be ashamed.[22] Lord, strengthen me and my brethren, that we may be strong in Thee and in the power of Thy might. Put upon us the whole armor of God that we may be able to stand against the wiles of the adversary. For we wrestle not against flesh and blood, but against principalities, against powers, against the rulers of the darkness of this world, and against spiritual wickedness in high places. Wherefore put upon us Thy whole armor that we may be able to withstand in the evil day, praying always and watching with all supplication for all the saints."[23]

As George waited in the silence, his mind was filled again with the words of the Savior: *But I say unto you, Love your enemies, bless them that curse you, do good to them that hate you, and pray for them which despitefully use you, and persecute you, that ye may be the children of your Father which is in heaven.*[24]

George was uncertain about whether Diocletian was his enemy or just a man who was caught up in a snare of the adversary because he knew not God. Feeling no need to judge the Emperor, George prayed for him too.

*****

"George refused your proposal," Orion reported blankly. "He said he will never deny his God."

"Even though it's what I expected, it still upsets me," the Emperor replied. "I don't want to lose George. He's the son of my old friend and he's been my most trusted tribune. There are few others in the palace that I count as allies against the conspiracy, but I still feel confidence in my Empress and in my imperial priest. Send another tribune to bring them to me. You stay close."

*****

"How may we serve you, my lord?" the priest asked politely.

"I'm frustrated with George," Diocletian growled. "I've loved him like a son. Now he's given the conspirators a wedge with his defiance of my commands regarding the Christian persecution orders. He's standing on his infernal principles. He's bound himself for his own destruction and unless we're careful, he'll take us down with him. I'm determined not to let that happen. He won't remain a witness for Christ or become

His martyr."

"My lord, what can we do to secure our course?" Alexandria asked earnestly.

"We must persuade George to make a public submission to my authority. We must convince him to renounce his Christian faith and pay token homage to the Roman gods and to me," Diocletian replied. "If we work this right, we should be able to save the empire from civil war and save George as well. But we must have his cooperation and his public submission. We can't be sure how long the council will wait before they risk more disruptive action. As far as they're concerned, George has already marked himself for death by his public defiance of me and his witness to the divinity of Jesus Christ. If I withdraw my edicts now, the council will accuse me of submitting to George and the Christians and they'll destroy us.

"When I stand by my edicts, the council believes George will refuse to submit to my will and I'll be forced to execute him. If I'm forced to execute George without his submission, his witness against this empire will be sealed with his blood, magnifying the power of his testimony in the eyes of all the people, him having voluntarily given up his life rather than renounce his faith in Jesus Christ. Not only will George die, but the Christian zealots will be emboldened and the council and people will be turned against me. Either way, one of their two most feared enemies will be destroyed and the power of the other will have been greatly diminished.

"The one thing the conspirators have disregarded is the prospect of George submitting to my commands. If we can convince George to renounce his faith publicly, the Christian masses should follow like sheep and submit themselves to my commands, muting most of the chaos in the council and stabilizing our cause." Diocletian drew a deep breath and continued. "I charge you two with securing George's submission to my will, as soon as possible."

"What leverage do we have in persuading him to submit to you?" Athanasius asked. "Does he have wealth or a family he'll want to protect?"

"His parents are dead and his brother inherited all the property," Diocletian replied. "Besides, he doesn't respond cooperatively to the stick. He would much rather fight than give in to force. I think the carrot will be a better approach, though I have my doubts about even that. George is more motivated by his own sense of right than any man I've ever known."

"I expect sooner or later he'll want to save his own life," the Empress suggested. "He's a proud man, so he may demand at least some amount of torture before he concedes. His submission will likely come at a high price. Perhaps if he were offered some land in the province where he grew up, slaves to work the land for him, livestock, and money to assure his success, he might see the sense in giving us what we must have."

"Do it!" Diocletian declared without hesitation.

"By the gods!" the priest replied impulsively. "I might consider defying the Emperor myself, if only temporarily, in order to get all that." The priest waited, intending to give the Emperor time to reconsider the precedent he would be setting with such an agreement.

Diocletian turned to Athanasius and, after a moment of thought, spoke with increasing urgency, "Tomorrow I'll publish new edicts against the Christians. Based on the documents Galerius provided that link them to the palace fire, I've expanded my orders for destruction of Christian churches and records beyond Nicodemia, all throughout the empire. I doubt these edicts will be sufficient to counter the impact George has had on the council. We must get him to see that his defiance won't change the course of events in the way he hopes. I need your help to quickly gain his submission. Do whatever's necessary to gain his cooperation. Do it now!"

"We'll see to George," the priest replied reassuringly. "Few men have the virtue to withstand the highest bidder."[25]

"George may be the one who does," the distressed Emperor replied.

"We'll meet with George and let you know when we have his agreement to submit," the Empress said confidently as the priest nodded beside her.

Diocletian's face remained shrouded in shadows of doubt. He eyed the Empress and priest warily. "You don't know George like I do. I know this because you're both still smiling, seemingly confident about this battle of wills."

****

CHAPTER FORTY-ONE
Every Man Has His Price

The Palace at Nicodemia
March-April, 303 AD

"Ye are bought with a price; be not ye the servants of men."[1]
1 Corinthians 7:23

****

"Prisoner! Back away from the door!" the tribune commanded. Obediently, George withdrew a few paces. The door opened and a guard entered the chamber. As the tribune closed and locked the door behind him, the guard put shackles on George's hands and feet, suggesting he would either be having an important visitor or he would be taken out for a bit of exercise. With the shackles securely in place, the cell door opened again and the tribune barked, "Bring him out!"

*****

The corridors leading to the pagan sanctuary in the palace were familiar. George felt the evil of the place receding as he approached. He was surprised as he stood in shackles facing the Empress and the imperial priest.

"Why have you brought me here?" George asked blutly.

"Because the stench in the prison makes it impossible to think clearly or hold a civil discussion!" the Empress exclaimed.

"Will we be thinking clearly and holding a civil discussion then?" George mused, annoying the Empress. "I've heard the slander of many, driven by fear on every side, while they take counsel together against me, plotting to take away my life.[2] Are you also with them?"

"We're seeking a solution to save your life," the priest responded. "We're sorry about the shackles, but others in the palace fear you. The shackles seem to put them at ease when you're not locked in a cell."

"You are not new to the political intrigues of the capital," the Empress declared. "The Emperor needs to show strength before the council to maintain order in the empire. He values you as a faithful tribune and an effective leader. He still feels gratitude for the loyalty of your father, and he's grown fond of you. But you've backed him into a corner with your public defiance of his orders. He can back no further. The remedy must be a public display of your submission."

"So you're not expecting me to pay homage to the Roman gods of wood and stone here and now, are you?" George probed.

"No. Your voluntary submission will need to be a public example for the people. But without your cooperation, Diocletian will have to secure your submission by force. He has charged us with your interrogation. He has instructed us to get your agreement on submission, renouncing your faith in Christ, and paying homage to the Roman gods and the Emperor."

"You have my sympathies, for that will never happen," George responded calmly.

"Now let's not be too hasty. You haven't even heard our proposal," the priest replied.

"Oh, I've heard enough to know your terms won't be acceptable to me or to my God."

"Well, just let me get it all on the table. We propose that, in exchange for your public renunciation of your Christian faith and your public display of homage to the Roman gods and the Emperor, Diocletian will dismiss the charges against you and spare your life. He'll also affirm your Roman citizenship. You'll be granted land in your home province of Palestine and money to stock it with cattle. You'll be given sufficient slaves to work your land. If you wish to retain your post as tribune here in the capital, you would be required to lead the enforcement of the persecution orders. That's our offer," Athanasius concluded.

George thought briefly on the wisdom of Solomon: *My son, if sinners entice thee, consent thou not.*[3] After a moment he asked wryly, "Is that your best offer? Have you nothing more to add?"

The priest smiled. "Ah…you can see how desperate Diocletian is to save the empire, so now the negotiations begin in earnest. You name your price and we'll discuss your proposal with him."

"You misunderstand the intent of my questions," George responded. "I want to avoid wasting time in these discussions. I want to draw out your best offer so that, when I reject it, our civil discussion will be concluded."

"Come now, George. Every man has his price," the priest chided. "We know yours will be high, but until you tell us what it is, we won't know if we can find a solution to our problem."

"And what is your price?" George responded abruptly. "Would you bargain your soul and become a servant of hell, tempting me to deny the true and living God?[4] You offer me a bribe for treason against God. This casts you among the wicked who, knowingly or not, only wrong themselves. How shall you stand before the power of God except you repent and turn from your evil ways? Don't you know you are in the hands of God and He has all power? At His great command the earth shall be rolled together as a scroll. Therefore, repent and humble yourselves before Him lest He comes out in judgment against you and none can deliver you."[5] After a brief sigh George asked, "Can the Emperor deliver resurrection from the dead and eternal glory in holiness and righteousness? That is my price!"

After a few moments of uncomfortable silence George calmly continued. "You blind arrogant fools. How long do you suppose the Lord God will suffer you to go on in your ways of sin? You ought to howl and mourn because of the great destruction which awaits you except you shall repent.[6] Your idols are wood and stone, silver and gold, yet all are just the work of men's hands. They have mouths, but can't speak; eyes but can't see; ears but can't hear; neither is there any breath of life in them. Their makers are like them, devoid of life; as is everyone that trusts in them.[7] No one can deliver me if I disobey God, nor can I find refuge except in Him.[8]

"Since you seem uncertain as to what the Emperor's final proposal will be, I'll give you my final proposal. I propose that the Emperor lead this Republic in repentance, turning to the one true and living God and obeying Him. God has promised that those who learn the doctrine of Christ and obey His truths will prosper in the land. Humble submission to God will bring about a mighty change of heart, such that this people will have no more disposition to do evil, and I shall be set free."[9]

"Come now, persisting in this Christian faith has become futile!" the priest replied, his irritation evident. "Christianity will be crushed by the Emperor! With you as a Christian martyr, the flames of persecution will only burn with greater fury. If Galerius succeeds in taking power, there will be no end to the brutal persecution and Christian bloodshed while he reigns."

Boldly George replied, "My life and my service to the Republic witness that I don't fear the shedding of blood. But I do fear for those who shed the blood of the innocent. There are many who seek deep to hide their counsels from the Lord, and their works against the righteous are in darkness. But the blood of the saints shall cry from the ground as a witness against them,[10] and the Lord and Shepherd of all shall sustain His flock and preserve them, that they may prosper in the eternities through the blood of the everlasting covenant.[11] No unhallowed hand can stop His work from progressing.[12] Soon we shall all be laid to rest with our fathers. Our choices now will determine whether we will hang our heads in shame in their presence or whether we'll be bound to them and our Lord as our blood cries out against the unrighteous who pervert the right ways of God. Shall any of us trade our divine birthright of eternal glory for a mess of pottage in a moment of weakness?[13] I won't, for I am a true disciple of Christ."

"George, you must see what you've done," the Empress pleaded, attempting to persuade the prisoner. "Some on the council have been plotting to create a crisis that will bring down Diocletian and elevate Galerius. We don't have clear proof of the conspiracy, but everything points to this conclusion. Just as you can't prove the cathedral documents relating to the palace fire were a fabrication, but it's clear who stands to gain.

"The fire was intended to be the crisis issue, but now you've given the conspirators a bigger issue with your public defiance of the Emperor's commands. The entire capital, from noble citizens to lowly slaves, is buzzing over your defiant stand and speculating as to whether you will ultimately submit to the Emperor's will by choice, or by death.

"If you do submit willingly to the Emperor's commands, many of your Christian brothers are expected to follow your example and do likewise. Those who don't submit will suffer, while those who renounce their faith in Christ will be saved. If you don't submit, many who follow your lead will be lost. George, you can't win in this battle of the wills. If you persist, you face certain death, and your death will be of no benefit to those you love."

George stared into the anguished face of the young Empress. Calmly he replied, "You know nothing of who shall be saved and who shall be lost. You have no faith in the true and living God, and you have no knowledge of His plan of redemption and happiness for His children and the glories of eternity. You say that if I submit to the living God, many of my Christian brethren are expected to do likewise. Thereby they shall gain eternal life. I cannot lead these faithful souls astray.

"Again I ask, why have you brought me here? Perhaps that I may tell you of your iniquities? For you desire to get gain and to be praised of men. You've set your hearts on gold and silver and the riches and vain things of the world, for which you persecute the righteous and do all manner of iniquity.[14] If you were righteous and willing to receive the truth and give heed to it and walk uprightly before God, then you wouldn't revile against the truth I speak.[15] But the pride which you've allowed to enter into your hearts is a curse to you."[16]

Feeling the sting of his accusation and sensing she was in over her head in matters of true faith, the Empress tried another approach. "It makes no difference what you truly believe, as long as you make a public renunciation of Christianity and a proper show of submission to the

Emperor and the Roman gods. Once that's done, you can still have the land, the money, and the slaves, and you can be free of the capital and its political intrigues. Believe what you will, but save yourself and your people from persecution and death. Save Diocletian from this conspiracy."

George felt the earnest conviction of the Empress that, unless she could get him to submit, the Emperor's power and position were in peril, turning her world upside down. Calmly he replied, "I'm sorry for your distress, yet I feel even more sorrow for your lack of understanding of who will be saved and who will be lost. I can't just pick and choose what I believe. I've seen the hand of God so clearly in my life that what I once believed, I now know to be true. I can't deny it without offending a just and merciful God who has enlightened me. I can't be unfaithful to Him simply to please a mere mortal, not even an Emperor. I know there is a God who is the Father of us all, and Jesus Christ is His Holy Son. They live. I'm not ashamed of the gospel of Christ. It is the power of God unto salvation to everyone that believes in Him."[17]

"Why do you persist in this doctrine of Christ?"[18] the priest asked in frustration. "You rely on the merits of a man who was put to death by the Romans. Surely you should seek mercy from the victor and not from the vanquished. The things you call prophecies are simply the foolish traditions of your ancestors. Your hope in a remission of sins is the effect of a deranged and a frenzied mind which leads you to believe in things which are not true. Why subject yourself to such foolish and vain hopes?[19] In this life, men fare according to their cunning and might. It has always been so and will continue to be so well beyond the span of our lives. Death is the end for each man,[20] and unless you agree to submit to the Emperor, your death will be coming very soon, my friend."

George felt an overwhelming peace inside as he responded. "Why do I persist in the doctrine of Christ? Because it is the way of happiness. The prophecies of the holy prophets reveal God's great plan of redemption and happiness for all His children. You see this world from your own experience and you believe every man has his price for submission. I see this world through the knowledge of a loving Father in heaven. I know every man has his price for redemption, and that price has already been paid through the atoning blood of Jesus Christ. I do seek mercy from the Victor of all, not from the vanquished who stand before me.

"Most members of the ruling class don't truly believe in any gods. I give you my word that if you will stop serving these pretend gods made by men's hands and serve the Lord, He will remember His covenants with our fathers and He will bless you.[21] If you continue in His word, you shall know His truth, and that truth will set you free."[22]

"Your truth will not set you free!" the Empress spouted abruptly.

"Oh, but He already has," George replied mildly.

Opening the door to the hallway the Empress called out, "Guards, take this prisoner back to his cell. Now!"

*****

After George was gone, the priest turned to the Empress and with a weak smile said, "That didn't quite go the way we'd planned, did it?"

"No, it didn't," she huffed. "I find his pride and arrogance incredible! But he's very definite in his rejection of lands, money, and slaves in exchange for his submission. Yet I still believe he'll eventually want to save his own life and the lives of his friends. We just need to find a way to get him to open up and consider the immediate consequences of his actions and how things could change for the better if he would just make a token submission to the Emperor."

"I've got an idea about how we can test his resolve to sacrifice his own life, if required, for his cause," the priest offered.

"Enlighten me," the Empress responded with interest.

"Everyone knows about the fire in the palace two weeks ago," Athanasius began.

"Many suspect the Christians, but the documents discovered at the destruction of the cathedral seem a little too convenient," Alexandria responded.

"That's not the issue," the priest replied. "Do you know how the prisoners reacted to the palace fire? They were so desperate to avoid burning that several nearly killed themselves in frantic efforts to break out of their cells. Since then, George has publicly defied the Emperor and he's been cast into prison. If another fire arose in the prison area, it might prompt George to seriously consider his mortality sooner, rather than later. It's fairly risky. It must be carefully coordinated and doused, and nobody but us must ever learn who started it."

"Ooh, I like it!" the Empress praised, studying the priest carefully. "It's cunning and sinister, yet harmless. Let's do it!" she encouraged with an approving nod.

"I won't proceed without Diocletian's full knowledge and approval," Athanasius stressed.

"We'll discuss it with him together," Alexandria assured.

The priest paused, thinking carefully on George's words. "You know, George isn't the blind sheep I've imagined most Christians to be," he said. "He's a thinker. He studies, analyzes, plans and designs. If his plans have any flaws, he modifies them until they work. He has obviously thought very deeply about his religious convictions. Currently, he doesn't see any flaws in the plan of his God. Unless we can show him a flaw in the doctrine, he's not likely to consider our plan. If we're going to find any flaws in God's plan, we'll need to know that plan better than George does. If we're going to out-think him, we'll need to know everything he's thinking."

"And just how do you propose we accomplish that?" the Empress asked.

"I propose that we make an immediate and thorough study of Christianity to accomplish our task," the priest urged.

"Who would be willing to teach us, considering the edicts against Christianity?" the Empress mused.

"We can look to many sources to inform us, but as you suspect, most are unlikely to cooperate because of the Emperor's persecution orders," the priest observed. "If we only had access to someone who knows everything that George knows, and is unafraid of being thrown in prison for advocating the Christian faith."

"Are you proposing that we have George teach us?" the Empress stammered in near disbelief.

"Right now, he may be the best one to teach us, if we can persuade him to do it," the priest replied.

After brief consideration the Empress responded, "Your suggestion has merit. Let's share both ideas with Diocletian, letting him know that we may need a few weeks to accomplish our task. I expect he will cooperate, but his patience may end without warning, depending on the actions of the council. Oh, there is one more thing. From now on, when we entertain our guest, he must be bathed and have fresh clothes. His prison rags carry an air of defiance which sets us apart, creating a barrier to unity in these negotiations."

"Agreed!" the priest replied. "You have a noble motive for your small kindness. As for me, I just want to avoid the gag reflex to the foul prison smells, which linger even after he's gone."

*****

George awoke and sat up, alone in his darkened cell. A flicker of light through the door's small window played on thick smoke in the upper half of his room. *Fire!* He heard a panicked commotion in the corridor outside his cell. Other prisoners were screaming for freedom to escape the flames. Confidently he commanded the guards outside his door, "Go get the water pots from the council chambers and bring them here." Acting on his orders, they quickly doused the flames. Calmly, George lay back down.

*****

"Tribune!" the Empress called out. "Bring George to the priest's sanctuary in an hour. First, make him bathe and get him clean clothes. I won't bear the stench of the prison any longer. Follow these orders each time we call for him in the future."

"And the chains?" Orion asked.

"They stay on," the Empress responded. "I'm not sure they're necessary, but many fear him."

"As you command, my lady," Orion answered, a bit curious as to these sanctuary meetings.

*****

As commanded, the guards presented George at the pagan sanctuary. "Thank you for the bath and clean clothes," he said. "Has the Emperor accepted my proposal so quickly?"

****

CHAPTER FORTY-TWO
God and His Witnesses

The Palace at Nicodemia
March-April, 303 AD

"Wherefore, behold, I send unto you prophets, and wise men,..."[1]
Matthew 23:34

****

"Actually," Athanasius said, "we haven't presented your proposal to the Emperor yet. His offer of money, land, and slaves in exchange for your renunciation of Christianity is still on the table."

"Well, Diocletian's offer has no place at my table," George said quietly. "My table is the table of the living God. I feast upon His promises of immortal glory. I'll not part with eternal life for the paltry trinkets of men. Come, join me at the table of the living God."

"Please, George, hear us out," the Empress pleaded gently. "The fire last night has us greatly disturbed. We're concerned for our safety and yours. It's rumored the Christians are to blame for this fire in retaliation for the loss of their cathedral. There's more talk of a conspiracy that won't rest until they've destroyed the palace, the Emperor, and us too. We must quickly reach an agreement on your submission and get you out of here."

"We must agree to disagree!" George said forcefully. "I won't submit to the Emperor's edicts. I won't renounce my faith in Christ, nor worship the Roman gods or Diocletian."

"In considering your position and the immense gulf separating you from the Emperor," the priest began, "it's clear that we simply aren't looking at this problem the same way. We may not even be looking at the same problem. We're not at the same table, as you say. I think if we could see the problem from your perspective, we would have a better chance of bridging the gap and finding common ground between you and the Emperor. George, we want you to help us by teaching us about Christianity so we can better understand your position."

"Well, you've seized the element of surprise," George confessed, though he doubted the sincerity of their search for Christ. Still, he had invited them to the table of the Lord, and he'd never refused to teach anyone about God.

The priest continued, "We suspect most of the information we have about Christianity is based upon vicious rumors that probably won't be very productive for discussion. Therefore, we would like you to teach us the Christian doctrines, in a logical succession, as we suspect a man like you might have them organized in his own mind."

As George silently pleaded for direction, he felt the quiet whisperings of the Spirit guiding him: *Ye shall not cast them out, but ye shall minister unto them, for ye know not but what they will turn unto Me and repent, and come unto Me with full purpose of heart, and I shall heal them, and ye shall be the means of bringing salvation unto them.*[2]

"If you're sincere in your search for truth, having real intent to obey what you learn, the Holy Spirit will enlighten you by degrees till you understand the doctrines,"[3] George said. "But I warn you, if you seek the truth of God with no intent to learn and do His will, the knowledge you obtain will be a curse to you instead of a blessing, for those that contend against the word of God and deny the truths He has revealed, shall receive no greater light.[4] Do you really want to learn the truth of God?" he probed.

Alexandria responded, "Who can know how a heart will change when it learns truth? We don't know what will come of our study of Christianity, but if, as you say, it's the truth about God, we certainly want to know it. Please help us learn."

George paused a moment in thought. Though fettered in shackles, he felt the flooding warmth and peace of the Spirit confirming again that he should teach them without fear or doubt. "As you wish," he said. "I'll teach you the doctrine of Christ, and I'll do my best to answer all your questions according to the Spirit of the Lord, for I shall say nothing which is contrary to the Spirit.[5] But you won't understand or feel the mighty change of heart until you humble yourselves and exercise faith in the redemption of the true and living God who created you."[6]

"Will you be trying to convert us then?" the priest asked.

"I can't convert you," George replied simply. "You must judge for yourselves the truth of what I teach. If you do so by the light of Christ, you will see clearly to judge all things rightly, knowing good from evil. If you search diligently, laying hold on every good thing and not condemning that which you know to be true, God will lead you into all truth. If you have the courage to embrace all truth no matter where you find it, you will certainly gain the glory and become children of Christ.[7] If you open your hearts to the Holy Spirit and exercise faith in Christ, you'll learn His doctrine and become converted, and that will change everything."

"We'll risk it," the Empress nodded. "Please, proceed."

George hesitated, casting a glance toward heaven and thinking, *O God, I pray that I may open my mouth boldly, to make known the mysteries of Thy gospel. I am Thy ambassador, in bonds that therein I may speak boldly, as I ought to speak.*[8] *Bless and sustain me, I pray.*

Annoyed by the silence, the priest posed his first question. "You say there is one true and living God. What is He like?"

"Yes, there is one true and living God who is the Father of us all.[9] He knows all the thoughts and intents of our hearts, for by His hand were we created, in His image, from the beginning.[10] He loves each of us unconditionally and seeks to bless us in every way possible, on conditions of repentance and righteousness.[11] He blesses those who will have Him to be their God, who seek Him with real intent to obey. To those who love Him and keep His commandments, He offers covenants of honor, power, authority, and eternal life through faith in Jesus Christ."[12]

"And who is this Jesus Christ in whom you say we must have faith?" the priest inquired, asserting himself as the lead in this religious discussion.

"Jesus Christ is the Only Begotten Son of God in the flesh," George replied.

"Is the Son of God the very Eternal Father?" Athanasius asked.

"Yes, the Son of God is the very Eternal Father of heaven and earth, the Creator of all things therein. He is the beginning and the end, the first and the last, the author and finisher of our salvation.[13] He created the earth for the habitation of man, and it is His footstool. He created His children that they should possess the earth in righteousness. He raises up righteous nations and guides them into precious lands. The wicked He brings down, and curses the land unto them for their sakes.[14]

"Because men sin, falling short of the perfection and glory of God, our Heavenly Father sent His Son, Jesus,[15] to offer Himself as the perfect sacrifice to atone for the sins of all men, being lifted up by corrupt men that He might lift all men from corruption and lead us back to the Father.[16] Jesus said, 'And this is life eternal, that they might know Thee the only true God, and Jesus Christ, whom Thou hast sent.'[17]

"Christ alone is our Savior and Redeemer. He came into the world to redeem His people. He took upon Him the transgressions of those who believe on His name, and salvation comes to none else.[18] He is the Law and the Light. Repent and believe in Him and endure to the end and you shall have eternal life."[19]

"And how do the Roman gods fit into the Christian religion?" the Empress asked.

"The Roman gods are no gods at all," George responded. "They are mere graven images of metal, stone, and wood made by the hands of men. They do no miracles. They are myths without witnesses, conjured up to play on the fears and superstitions of an ignorant people to the end that their priests and their craftsmen might get rich upon the meager wealth of the poor and the unlearned, and that rulers and leaders might more easily manipulate the masses."

"You spoke of witnesses," the priest said. "I'm interested in those who testify that they have seen God. What witnesses do you have of your one true and living God that we may question them in order to establish the truth of His existence and the measure of His doctrine?"

"The earth and all things upon the face of it, and its motion, and also all the planets which move in their established order stand as witnesses that there is a Supreme Creator,"[20] George replied. "God's creation of man is the crowning masterpiece attesting to His existence. We are His children. He has designed this experience in mortality to prepare each of us for the richest blessings He can bestow upon us throughout the eternities. Knowing there is a God who loves His children is the beginning of faith.[21]

"Because of His love for us, God has promised He will do nothing concerning His children except He will reveal His secrets to His servants the prophets.[22] To His prophets, God may reveal Himself directly, or send heavenly messengers to declare His word. To others, He sends His prophets and apostles as witnesses to reveal His will, and wise men and women to testify of His truths.[23]

"God has revealed Himself to men on earth since the beginning. He revealed Himself to Adam, the first man of all. He revealed Himself to Noah and to Abraham, Isaac, and Jacob and their posterity. He revealed Himself to Moses, a Levite, and to Joshua, an Ephraimite. There have been many prophets among the children of Israel who have seen God, face to face, and borne His image in their countenances.[24] Now, after the many witnesses that have been sent, God sent His Only Begotten Son, Jesus Christ, to testify of the Father, to redeem all who will believe on Him, and to lead us back to our heavenly home.[25]

"Beyond all of these witnesses, God has promised all His children that they may know His truths for themselves, by receiving the witnessing power of His Holy Spirit. Jesus said, 'If any man will do His will, he shall know of the doctrine, whether it be of God, or whether I speak of Myself.'[26] It is by the Spirit that all things are made known to the prophets, which shall come upon the children of men according to the flesh.[27] It is by receiving this same Spirit that the truth of all things can be discerned by all of God's children."

"What is the nature of this Holy Spirit you say will testify of all

A Martyr's Faith

truth?" the priest asked.

George tried to explain without creating confusion. "The Father, Son, and Holy Spirit are one God. They are united in all things, just as Christ prayed for his disciples to be united.[28] The Lord promised his disciples that the Father would send them the Holy Spirit, or the Holy Ghost. He said, 'The Comforter, which is the Holy Ghost, whom the Father will send in My name, He shall teach you all things, and bring all things to your remembrance, whatsoever I have said unto you.'[29] The Holy Ghost testifies of all truth to those who receive Him.[30] When we are filled with the Holy Ghost, the true word of God will begin to swell within us, enlarging our souls and enlightening our understandings, becoming a fruit most delicious to us.[31] The mighty change of heart we feel through the Holy Spirit is likened unto a baptism by fire."[32]

"And what miracles have been wrought by your God, that we may have signs confirming His power and the truth of your words?" the Empress asked.

"God, even the God of Abraham, and the God of Isaac, and the God of Jacob, is a God of miracles. He created the heavens and the earth and all things. He created Adam, the first man, and by Adam came the fall of man. Because of the fall, God sent His Son, Jesus Christ, to redeem all men who believe in Him.[33] These things are miracles, and God is a God of miracles and an Unchangeable Being. If the miracles of God are hidden from among the children of men it is because they dwindle in unbelief and depart from the right way, not knowing the God in whom they should trust.[34]

"Many are the miracles recorded in the writings of the holy prophets. One of the best known miracles was when God's prophet, Moses, parted the Red Sea so the children of Israel might escape the Egyptian armies on dry ground.[35] There are many witnesses and records of the mighty miracles done by Jesus and His apostles.[36] Finally, Christ performed the greatest miracle of all when He bled and died to atone for our sins. He was buried and rose again on the third day, resurrected in glory, and was seen of many.[37] These records stand as tangible witnesses against all who reject the true and living God.

"We have labored diligently to preserve them, hoping that our children and our beloved brethren will receive them with thankful hearts and study God's words, that they may learn with joy and not with sorrow or contempt concerning their first parents and the covenants of God to all His children. May all our posterity know that we knew of Jesus Christ and had a hope of His glory, as did all the holy prophets which were before us. They believed in Christ and testified of Him. They worshipped the Father in His name. We also worship the Father in

Christ's name."[38]

"Where are the records of these witnesses and miracles, that we may examine them?" the Empress demanded impatiently.

Amazed by the irony of the situation, George answered, "Why Empress, you should have many copies of these records in the imperial archives, unless you've burned them all. The records you seek are the Christian scriptures which the Emperor ordered to be confiscated and destroyed. You would do well to preserve these sacred documents and study them."

"And what if we've destroyed them all?" the Empress asked, embarrassed by the situation.

"Notwithstanding the many witnesses that have been sent, more witnesses with the spirit of prophecy will be sent to testify of Christ.[39] God will reveal Himself to all nations, that all His children may know to Whom they may look for a remission of their sins and for redemption."[40]

"What does this God of yours promise in return for our worship of Him?" the priest asked.

With confidence George replied, "There are few things I want more than for you to understand the promised blessings of the Lord. Knowing God gives meaning to all the adversities of this mortal life. It provides a direct line of communication with the ultimate Power in the universe, reassuring us that we are never alone. We are constantly looked after by our loving Father. God has promised to bless us if we heed the servants of the Lord.[41] Recognizing God's authorized servants and honoring their counsel enhances our connection with God. This allows the faithful to wade through afflictions being filled with the Spirit and guides us in establishing and building proper relationships with God and all mankind, filling our souls with joy and consolation. I know that if we will exercise faith in Christ, He will reveal Himself to us, by degrees, just as the sun rises, until our whole souls are filled with light and understanding. If we continue in the faith, eventually the burden of guilt will be lifted, the Holy Ghost will become our constant companion, and we will be prepared to return to the presence of the Father, as His sons and daughters, heirs to every blessing He has to give."[42] George paused, feeling the flood of the Spirit bringing peace and confirming the truths to which he had just testified.

"Though I'm far from embracing these doctrines of Christ, I'm at least beginning to see why they are so attractive to the masses. Who wouldn't want to believe that he or she was a favored heir, sired by God?" Alexandria offered as the priest nodded slowly in agreement.

George continued, "Have you felt the power of righteousness and truth in your own lives? Do you feel the pleasure of God when you are

A Martyr's Faith

good to others, showing compassion and mercy?"

"We feel the pleasure of the gods when we do right. But all men feel these things, whether they are Christian or not," the Empress challenged.

"That's true," George admitted. "Because these are true principles of God, every man who obeys them will feel His blessings. Happiness is a process of coming to know the full nature of God, that we might please Him and receive the blessings He desires to give us. Because His blessings are conditioned upon our obedience to His laws and commandments, we must be reconciled to Him through Christ, His Only Begotten Son. Thus, having faith, we may obtain a good hope of the resurrection and of glory in the eternal world to come. These things are manifested unto us plainly by the Spirit for the salvation of our souls. And we are not the only witnesses of these things, for God also revealed them to all the holy prophets of old who testified of Him and the promised Messiah, our Savior, Jesus Christ.[43]

"I challenge you to build your lives around what you know to be true, letting go of that which is proven wrong by the truths you know, and by those you will soon come to know."

"I believe in truth," the Empress assured. "But I don't believe everything I hear just because it sounds good. I want to review the records of these witnesses so I can weigh their testimony. I'm looking for truth that can be verified."

"All things testify that these things are true," George replied. "Now, I urge you to seek this Jesus of whom the prophets and apostles have written, that the grace of God the Father and also the Lord Jesus Christ, and the Holy Ghost, may be and abide in you forever.[44] You have all things as a testimony to you that these things are true, if you will just consider the evidence of God and His witnesses."[45]

"We'll consider the evidence," the priest said. "We hope you'll give more consideration to the Emperor's offer, which still stands. Guards, take this man back to the dungeon."

*****

After George had gone, the priest spoke to the Empress. "My Lady, despite the order for the destruction of all Christian scriptures, I know the keeper of the archives maintains copies of these records for purposes just such as ours. I'll retrieve them for our review, if you wish."

"Yes," the Empress replied. "We'll need to do that if we're to have any chance of quickly exposing the flaws in the Christian doctrines and turning George to our purposes. I will admit this much though, George is very persuasive about his convictions of his own faith."

"George's challenge to sincerity reminded me of a similar charge my grandmother made when I was a boy," Athanasius mused. "I was raised by her, and she was a follower of Christ. Her words still kindle in me a sense that if we're not genuinely seeking the truth of God, we won't understand George's faith in Christ as he does, and we won't succeed in fulfilling Diocletian's commands."

*****

Alone in his quarters, Athanasius muttered to himself, "I would've been offended by George's attack on the Roman gods if I didn't know his bold assertions were true. I seem to recall grandma telling me of Christ's death, and of all the witnesses to His resurrection, including the apostles and over 500 men.[46] I can't remember why I abandoned Christianity, other than its disfavor among the elite and powerful. But I know exactly why I became the imperial priest. I wanted wealth and power but I had no stomach for the sword. Though I have no faith in the pagan gods, this was the path best suited to my ambitions. Perhaps now I might really learn something of religious conviction."

*****

Diocletian was pleased to find his young Empress in her private quarters, intently studying some documents. "How did it go with George today?" he asked casually.

"Not well," Alexandria replied. "He didn't have any concern about the fire, and he didn't show any willingness to compromise. He did agree to teach us the Christian doctrines as he understands them, so there's still hope of exposing a flaw in his beliefs that could open the door to his submission. That's why I'm studying all these records as quickly as possible."

"I'm not surprised," Diocletian responded. "Oh, I had a visit from Galerius today. It was tough to keep a straight face when he started passionately accusing the Christians of starting this second palace fire as further sabotage in retaliation for the loss of their cathedral. He claimed he was certain it was them. I almost expected him to produce new evidence to support his claim, but he stopped short of that. I'm certain of his treachery, but without proof that his anti-Christian evidence is false, I won't be able to pacify the council's demands for Christian persecution or their demands for George's trial and execution. Anyway, I'll see to Galerius. You and Athanasius keep working on George. We must stick with our plan."

CHAPTER FORTY-THREE
Dispensations, Apostasy and Restoration

The Palace at Nicodemia
March-April, 303 AD

*"Let no man deceive you by any means: for that day shall not come,
except there come a falling away first,
and that man of sin be revealed, the son of perdition."*[1]
2 Thessalonians 2:3

****

It was several days before the guards took George back to the pagan sanctuary in the palace. His audience had not changed, and his shackles were still in place. "Have you given any further consideration to the Emperor's proposal?" the priest asked. "Land in your native province of Palestine, cattle, slaves, and money, all for your submission to the Emperor's will. It's all still on the table, but we can't guarantee it will remain there long."

"The Emperor's proposal is on the wrong table," George replied patiently. "It can never be put on the right table. Have you presented my proposal to the Emperor yet?"

"No, we haven't," the Empress confessed. "It will be best to complete our study of the Christian doctrines first and explore all possible paths to reconciliation before we unveil your ultimatum."

"Have you started examining the records of the witnesses for God and Christ?" George probed.

"We've begun our review, but we have much left to do," Alexandria replied. "Other than evidence of God and Christ, what else should we look for in our study of these records?"

George smiled lightly. "The records will reveal a repeating pattern of communion between God and His children. When God's children obey His voice, He sends His authorized witnesses, heavenly messengers and prophets, to teach the people and put them under covenant that they may qualify for all His blessings.[2] God pours out His Spirit to the obedient, confirming their faith. This pattern of revelation is known as a 'dispensation' of the gospel of Jesus Christ.

"When God's covenant people abandon the truths they've been given, reviling against His laws and ordinances, embracing darkness and violence, He withdraws His witnesses, His doctrine and covenants, and His Spirit, cutting His children off from His presence so they won't be held accountable for sinning against the greater light.[3] This part of the repeating pattern is 'apostasy.'

"When God's children have been sufficiently humbled through adversity that they're ready to repent and obey His laws again, He sends new witnesses with His priesthood authority. His witnesses teach His doctrine, and administer His covenants and ordinances to His righteous children, that they may again learn of Him and His laws, and receive all the blessings He has prepared for them. This part of the pattern is called 'restoration' and is often evident at the beginning of each successive dispensation of the gospel."

"What if the people won't repent?" the Empress asked.

"If the people continue in sin, God will send more witnesses to warn them again of the judgments to come except they repent. If they don't repent, but become fully ripe in iniquity, God may permit their utter destruction."

"What are some examples of these dispensations of the gospel?" Athanasius asked.

"The first dispensation of the gospel was revealed to our first father, Adam," George replied. "Adam was a righteous man. He had some righteous posterity down to Noah. But in the days of Noah, the people on the earth were so wicked and full of violence that God chose to withdraw His covenants and authority from them. After the people rejected many warning witnesses, God chose to cleanse the earth with a flood, or baptism by water. God revealed to Noah how he and his family could survive the flood. Through strict obedience to God's counsel, Noah and his family were saved. God renewed His covenants with Noah and his sons.[4] Many generations later, the posterity of Noah conspired against God at the tower of Babel. In response, God withdrew his priesthood authority and covenants from most of His children and confounded the language of the people, scattering them abroad into many nations.[5]

"God began a new dispensation of the gospel by restoring His covenants through Abraham and his posterity, including the children of Israel.[6] Abraham was promised that through his posterity all the nations of the earth would be blessed.[7] Eventually the house of Israel went to Egypt seeking refuge from a great famine.[8] In Egypt, God's people forsook their covenants and broke His laws. Again, God withdrew His servants, authority, and covenants.

"After several generations, the Lord revealed Himself to the prophet Moses, ushering in another dispensation of the gospel. Moses was sent as God's witness to restore His laws and covenants to His people. He was also called to restore the children of Israel to their God.[9] Moses showed clear signs of authority from God, smiting Egypt with plagues and parting the Red Sea.[10] Later he introduced seventy Elders of Israel into the presence of their God.[11] He also appeared before the camp of Israel transfigured by the glory of God which reflected from his face.[12]

"At God's direction, the people were organized with God as their King and Moses as His prophet. Leadership of the people was established with a Prince from each of the twelve Tribes[13] and seventy Elders of Israel[14] to be the administrators of God's law and His covenants. They were witnesses to teach the people about their relationship to God. God commanded Moses and the Israelites to build a tabernacle, or portable temple, as the center of their religious worship where He could reveal Himself and His mysteries to His people.[15] The most accurate record we have about God's dealings with His people from the beginning to the days of Moses we have through records Moses kept of God's revelations to him. Moses testified that God spoke to him face to face, as a man speaks to his friend.[16] Moses received and taught God's law, pointing the Israelites to Christ and His atoning sacrifice.[17]

"In subsequent generations the Israelites repeatedly forsook God's laws and broke their covenants. As a result, they were driven and scattered as a people and their temple was destroyed. But always a remnant of the house of Israel has gathered, seeking to reestablish a connection with God and His covenants. For the Lord of hosts has promised them, 'Even from the days of your fathers you are gone away from Mine ordinances, and have not kept them. Return unto Me, and I will return unto you.'[18]

"Each time God's people have returned to Him, the Lord has sent forth authorized servants to teach and testify regarding His laws and commandments and concerning the redemption and resurrection which the Lord has prepared for His people. These witnesses for Christ prophesied and testified boldly of his sufferings and death.[19]

"Finally, after an extended period of apostasy, with little record of prophets in Israel for nearly 600 years, God sent His Son, Jesus Christ, the Holy Messiah, to restore His people to their God and to restore God's covenants to His people, preparing a way for all men to return to God. Under the direction of His Father, Jesus established His church and kingdom with Himself as the Prophet, as had been prophesied by Moses.[20] He called and ordained twelve apostles[21] and seventy others, whom He sent out two by two,[22] to be witnesses of God and to administer His covenants and ordinances, blessing others in His name. Jesus claimed the temple in His Father's name and cleansed it, restoring its holiness for God and His people."[23]

"It's been nearly 300 years since Jesus was crucified and we hear nothing of prophets or apostles living in our day," Athanasius said, testing a theory that was developing in his mind. "So have angels ceased to appear to men on earth? Has God withheld the power of the Holy Ghost from men until He comes again?"[24]

"No," George replied. "God will not withhold the power of the Holy Ghost so long as there is even one man on earth to be saved. But it is by faith that angels appear and minister unto men.[25] God sent His Son to bless all men by turning each of us away from our iniquities. Unless men exercise faith in Christ, they cannot receive His covenants and eternal blessings."

"Will God yet initiate other dispensations of this gospel you preach?" the priest probed further.

George thought for a moment before responding. "The records state that in the end of the world the Father shall again send Christ, Whom the heavens have received until the time of the restitution of all things, which God has spoken by the mouths of all His holy prophets since the world began.[26] The holy records declare that in the last days, before Christ comes again to reign in glory, another angel will fly in the midst of heaven, having the everlasting gospel, to preach unto them that dwell on the earth, to every nation, kindred, tongue and people saying, 'Fear God, and give glory to Him; for the hour of His judgment is come: and worship Him that made heaven and earth....'[27]

"The voice of the Lord, by the mouths of angels, will declare unto all nations that the day of salvation draws near. God will sound these glad tidings of great joy among all His people scattered abroad upon the face of all the earth in plain terms that we cannot err. His word is given to all the children of men that the hearts of all men might be prepared to receive Him at the time of His coming in glory.[28] Moreover, God will gather in the dispersed of His people and will restore unto them His everlasting covenants in the sanctuary of His tabernacle.[29]

"But in the last days, many shall murmur at the servants of the Lord because they shall receive more of God's word. For God's law of witnesses requires the testimony of more than one nation witnessing unto all that He is God, and that He remembers one nation like unto another. Wherefore, He speaks the same words unto one nation like unto another. And when the two nations shall run together the testimony of the two nations shall run together also.[30]

"God does this as a witness to many that He is the same yesterday, today, and forever and that He speaks forth His words according to His own pleasure. Because He has spoken one word we need not suppose He

A Martyr's Faith

cannot speak another, for His work is not yet finished, neither will it be until the end of man, neither from that time henceforth and forever. Wherefore, we need not suppose that the records we have contain all of God's words, nor should we suppose that He has not caused more to be written.[31]

"So you see, you may lead a nation to sin, and God will withdraw for a time, but He is always feeling after the welfare of His children. Even if all the records of God were destroyed by men, God would send more witnesses to His children when they are prepared to return and repent and keep His commandments and covenants. When His children are ready to embrace righteousness, God will restore all that has been lost, and more."

"The scope of the Christian doctrine is beyond what I had imagined," the Empress remarked. "It's much more complex and challenging. It's obvious that we have much to study in these records as we test the truth of what you teach. However, you must consider your own life, which is in great peril. Also, there are the lives of the many faithful Christians who are sure to suffer, not for their apostasy, but for their faith. Your public submission to the Emperor will spare much suffering for many, without the necessity of them changing their true beliefs. Why don't you accept the Emperor's proposal for land, cattle, slaves, and money and by your example save the Christians from a more severe persecution?"

"Jesus willingly suffered death to fulfill God's plan of salvation for all His children. Shall we not be willing to follow His example and suffer unto death in this cause?" George asked.

"Are you really that sure of your cause?" Athanasius asked. "Because suffering unto death is exactly the consequence we fear and the one we hope to avoid for you and us."

"I'm certain of my God and His cause," George said. "I've studied the records of His witnesses. These messengers of the Lord don't teach with the enticing words of men, but with the word of God and with the power of His Spirit. Eye has not seen, nor ear heard, neither have entered into the hearts of men, the blessings which God has prepared for them that love Him. But God has revealed them unto us by His Spirit: for the Spirit searches all things, even the deep things of God. No man knows the things of God but by the Spirit of God. I've felt the Spirit of God, and by that Spirit I know many of the things that are freely given to us of God. But the natural man will not receive the things of the Spirit of God, for they are foolishness to him, neither can he know them because they are spiritually discerned."[32]

"I don't understand this spiritual discernment you speak of," Alexandria confessed.

Speaking gently George replied, "If you don't understand the words which I've spoken, it's because you fail to ask the Lord in faith, wherefore, you are not brought into the light but must perish in the darkness. But if you will enter in by the way and receive the Holy Ghost, it will show you all things what you should do.[33] If you really want to know the truth of the doctrine of Christ, you'll prove the will of the Father through obedience. God has promised that if you do this He will reveal the truthfulness of His doctrine to you.[34] By this you can be reconciled to God and become void of offense toward all men,[35] fully prepared to give and receive mercy at the judgment bar of Christ. The truth of all things will be confirmed to you by the Holy Spirit's still small voice of thunder."

"What is this way by which we should enter, that we might receive God's Holy Spirit?" the priest asked tentatively.

"Jesus Christ is the Way,"[36] George replied. "He set the example for all by submitting His will to the will of the Father and by being baptized to fulfill all righteousness.[37] Humble yourselves and repent, with fasting and prayer and turn away from all evil.[38] Turn to the ways of the Lord. Be baptized as a token of your covenant to take upon you His name in faith. Keep all His statutes and commandments that by faith the breach between you and God may be healed. If you can be healed by merely looking to Christ in faith, should you not look quickly? Or will you harden your hearts in unbelief, embracing doubt and fear till you perish?"[39]

"You challenge us to a covenant that requires faith in Christ as the way to learn all truth, yet we can't have faith unless we believe, and we can't believe until we know what is true," the Empress said, her frustration surfacing.

"There's no escape from the trap you describe except for those who humble themselves and first desire to believe," George admitted. "Eventually, every son and daughter of God will be confronted with all truth. Then every knee shall bow and every tongue confess that Jesus is the Christ.[40] Humility will come to all, yet blessed are they who humble themselves without being compelled to be humble, who believe in the word of God and are baptized without stubbornness of heart, without being compelled to know before they will believe.[41] To them that believe in faith, the Lord God will confirm that belief and faith in truth until it becomes a sure knowledge. Wake to the dispensation of Jesus Christ. Don't sleep through His restoration. There is too much at stake to give only half-hearted effort to your search for truth. We must all work with heart, might, mind, and strength, stepping past our weaknesses to serve the Lord.[42] Awake to God and join the battle against evil now."

George paused to give his investigators time to ponder his words.

With conviction he continued, "I've wrestled with the Lord many times in mighty prayer for a remission of my sins.[43] I will not now relinquish that which is most precious to me for mere physical relief by renouncing my faith. I've fasted and prayed many days that I might know these things of myself. And now I do know of myself that they are true, for God has made them manifest to me by His Holy Spirit, and this is the spirit of revelation and the spirit of prophecy which is in me.[44]

"I know God lives and that He loves us. There is no other name given under heaven, save it be Jesus Christ, whereby man can be saved. Wherefore, these things shall go forth from generation to generation as long as the earth shall stand, and they shall go according to the will and pleasure of God. The nations who possess them shall be judged of them according to the words which are written. The faithful labor diligently to preserve these records, that we might persuade our children, and also our brethren, to believe in Christ and to be reconciled to God, for we know it is by His grace that we are saved after all we can do. And now the right way is to believe in Christ and deny Him not. Christ is the Holy One of Israel, wherefore all must bow down before Him and worship Him with all our might, mind, and strength. If we do this we shall in nowise be cast out.[45]

"Awake your hearts from your deep sleep. Awake unto God, come out of the darkness, and be illuminated by the light of His everlasting word. Be delivered out of captivity and bondage by the mercy and power of God and His word."[46]

"Why don't we call the guard back?" the Empress suggested. "I'm feeling a bit of indigestion just now. We can pick this up again soon."

"Very good, my Lady," Athanasius responded, suspicious of her indigestion.

*****

As the door closed behind the departing prisoner and the tribune, the Empress could no longer contain her agitation. "George is making me crazy," she huffed. "His convictions defy rebuttal, but I don't share them."

"It's not reasonable to me that there should be a Christ, He being the Son of God, the Father of heaven and earth," the priest offered. "I believe this is an evil doctrine promoted by the Christians to deceive us into believing in some supposed great and marvelous thing, that they may gain our submission, for we cannot witness with our own eyes that these things are true."[47]

"We must continue our search of the Christian records if we're to have any hope of confounding George with his own doctrine," the Empress added, feeling the rising magnitude of the challenge.

****

CHAPTER FORTY-FOUR
The Plan of Redemption

The Palace at Nicodemia
March-April, 303 AD

"...therefore only unto him that has faith unto repentance is brought about the great and eternal plan of redemption."[1]
Alma 34:16

****

The Empress and the priest both looked tired as George entered their chamber. "My lady, the prisoner is here, as you commanded," the tribune reported. With the approval of the Empress, the guards withdrew from the room, locking the door behind them.

"George, it would be a great relief to us if you would accept the Emperor's offer of land in Palestine or wherever you like, plus slaves to make your land productive, cattle, and enough money to assure your success, in exchange for your submission," the Empress spoke hopefully.

With a smile George thought, *It might be a great relief to me if I could teach you in my cell where it's easier to feel the Spirit of God flowing freely.*

"Believe what you like," the Empress continued, "but make a way for Diocletian to avoid the shame of your defiance and the pain of losing you."

"Woe unto them which justify the wicked for reward, and take away the righteousness of the righteous from him,"[2] George responded. Looking casually down at his hands and feet he continued, "I'm surprised that you don't take me at my word when I tell you truthfully that these shackles are not necessary. Yet you beg me to lie to all the world and to God, for which you promise to set me free. Roman doctrine is surely confusion. I can't be a part of the Emperor's lie against the God of all truth and against Jesus Christ, for Their doctrine is the doctrine of holiness, truth, freedom, and liberty."

"You say the Christian doctrine is holiness, truth, freedom, and liberty, but I say it is set to bind men down to prophecies which are not true,"[3] the priest challenged.

"Is this what you've learned from your review of the witnesses' records?" George questioned.

"We're still working on that," Alexandria replied. "You've spoken of the nature of God and His purported witnesses. And the records support the pattern of dispensations, apostasy, and restoration which you described. But our review is incomplete. Though we're beginning to understand the doctrine, don't mistake that for a belief that your story is true."

"It's not 'my story,'" George replied. "It's God's truth. Will you reject the words of Christ and the testimony of the prophets who have all witnessed of Christ? After you've been nourished by the good word of God, will you bring forth evil fruit, that you must be hewn down and cast into the fire? Will you deny the power of God and quench the Holy Spirit which confirms the testimony of Christ? For these records truly testify of Christ, the Holy One of Israel, and none of the prophets have written or prophesied except they have testified of Him."[4]

"And how shall I ask your God for a witness of His truths?" Alexandria asked.

"Simple," George replied. "Start by understanding that God is your Father and that He loves you. Then, exercise some faith in Christ's redeeming love for you and in His willingness to endure suffering and death that you might be blessed. From there, follow the promptings of the Holy Spirit, for the Spirit teaches all men to pray.[5]

"If you will exercise even a little faith and do the will of the Lord, your faith will grow and eventually it will become knowledge. When that happens, you will never deny the only true and living God.[6] Then you'll know that I can never deny God the Father or His Holy Son. I beg you to ask God in humble prayer for your own witness of His truths."

"Seeing that we are yet unbelievers, perhaps you would teach us to pray," Athanasius invited.

"Jesus Christ is our perfect example and the only way we can return to the presence of our Father,"[7] George responded. "He taught us to pray[8] to the Father in His name.[9] By doing so, we show that we've taken upon ourselves the name of Christ and that we are His servants. We cannot pray to our Father and yet refuse to be Christ's servants, except we take His name in vain. God will answer our faithful prayers through the Holy Spirit who will enlighten us and bring peace to our minds and hearts as we seek and do the will of the Lord in obedience to the truths He has revealed to us.[10] Further, He will bless us as we plead for that which we need. Oh, that all men might be faithful and heed the counsel to pray to the Lord, that He will not hide His face far from us nor put us away in anger. Pray that the God of our salvation will be our help, never leaving or forsaking us. Wait upon the Lord and be of good courage for He shall strengthen our hearts. Pray and then wait in patience upon the

Lord.[11] The Father will honor all true servants of Christ."[12]

"Why do you persist in teaching this doctrine of Christ?" the priest challenged again.

"Because you asked me to, and that you and all men might know concerning the covenants of the Lord with His people," George replied. "He has spoken by the mouths of His holy prophets, even from the beginning down from generation to generation. He will continue to speak to His children until His people shall all be gathered in with joy and rejoicing to their promised inheritance in His kingdom."[13]

"Are all the Christians familiar with these mysteries?" the priest asked, perplexed by the doctrine.

"None but the truly penitent know these things," George answered. "He that repents, exercises faith, brings forth good works, and prays continually without ceasing, unto such shall the mysteries of God be revealed by the power of His Spirit."[14]

"If you be such a penitent man, reveal to us the secret of God's plan for men," the priest urged.

"Whether I'm sufficiently penitent or not, only God knows," George replied. "But you wrongly imply that penitent men can pick and choose which of God's secrets to reveal. That's not how it works. God alone determines what He will reveal and to whom it will be revealed. Heavenly Father rarely satisfies our curiosities to no purpose but our own condemnation. Instead, He answers our pleas by giving us only what we need to know and what we are ready to obey. Fortunately, God's plan for men on earth has been revealed and recorded many times in the sacred records. There was a creation for us. There was a fall from glory for our experience and learning. There will be redemption through the atonement of Christ for all who love and serve God. Yet it is written: *The hour of temptation shall come upon all the world, to try them that dwell upon the earth.*[15] The short answer is that life is a test."

"I knew it!" the Empress blurted out. Slightly embarrassed she continued, "I mean...all the gods put forth some test of fidelity before they bestow their gifts."

"What test has the Christian God devised for us?" Athanasius asked.

"It is a test of our love for Him and His righteous laws," George answered. "It is not a test of His love for us, which has its evidence in all things. God's plan for us was laid from before the foundations of the earth.[16] Before this life we lived as spirit offspring with our Heavenly Father.[17] Jesus Christ also lived with God in the beginning, before this world was, and the glory of the Father was reflected in Him.[18] We felt God's unconditional love and support. He wanted all His children to grow in obedience, righteousness, and glory. He knew we needed to learn to love righteousness and choose obedience, progressing beyond mere submission to Him. Therefore, He prepared tests outside His immediate presence for our learning and happiness."

"But what are these tests?" the priest persisted.

"There are two major tests for all men," George began. "The first is whether we will choose righteousness over wickedness. The second is whether we will choose to make and keep the covenants God offers us or whether we will pridefully ignore the will of God. Those who submit their wills to the will of God qualify to abide in His glory forever."

"How is this test of righteousness administered?" Alexandria asked with interest.

"Life is full of adversity that God, in His infinite wisdom, has allowed us to experience for our benefit and blessing," George explained. "As part of this brush with adversity, God gave us agency, which is the right to choose between good and evil, yet we are bound by the consequences of our choices. As He did with Adam and Eve, God has given us physical bodies to house our spirits.[19] Thus, we are subjected to the temptations of the flesh, to see if we will choose righteousness when we are shielded from the overwhelming influence of our Heavenly Father. Coupled with life itself, our ability to make choices and learn from the consequences of our own actions is one of the greatest gifts God has given us.

"Agency requires that we be enticed by both good and evil, the Spirit of God and the temptations of the adversary, that we might choose for ourselves. Without choices, righteousness could not be brought to pass, neither wickedness, neither holiness nor misery, neither good nor bad.[20] In order for our tests in life to be fair and just, we must be subjected to the influences of both good and evil in reasonably balanced measures, being overwhelmed by neither so we remain accountable for our own choices. Now, it is given to us to follow the whisperings of the Holy Spirit to righteousness, or to submit ourselves to the rancor and bondage of Satan, the evil one who was cast out of heaven."[21]

"And these tests of mortality began with Adam and Eve?" the priest asked.

"Yes," George replied. "In the beginning, in the garden of Eden, God commanded our first parents not to partake of the fruit of the tree of knowledge of good and evil, but He gave them agency to choose. He explained the consequences of disobedience would be spiritual death, being cut off from the presence of the Lord, and physical death, eventually having their spirits separated from their physical bodies.[22] Adam and Eve were tempted of the evil one and they chose to subject themselves to the pains of adversity for the blessing of knowing good from evil.

"If Adam and Eve had not transgressed they would not have fallen, and they wouldn't have had children, for they were innocent. They would have had no joy, for they knew no misery, doing no good, for they knew no sin.[23] By their fall, they were cast out of God's presence and death was introduced into the world. Sin became a barrier to man's return to the presence of the Father in His holy kingdom.[24] But all things have been done in the wisdom of Him who knows all. Adam fell that men might be, and men are that they might have joy, being filled with the Spirit of God.[25] Now we must endure our own tests of righteousness."

"And what of those who have already departed from the ways of God? Is there a way back?" Athanasius probed further.

"Most definitely! Repentance!" George exclaimed. "God gave man this life as a probationary state that we might repent and turn unto Him while in the flesh. He commanded us that we must repent to escape our fallen state which has come about by sin."[26]

"How does this repentance work?" Alexandria asked, working the doctrine over in her mind.

"Repentance requires faith in Christ and His power to save. Then, we must carefully examine our own conduct for anything offensive to God. Conscience and the light of Christ will reveal where we've sinned, inspiring a godly sorrow within us. Recognition of sin is followed by confession to God and to any we have wronged. True repentance is coupled with our best efforts to put things right and make restitution for our wrongs. If we plead sincerely, our merciful God will renew His covenant of obedience and redemption with us. As we exercise faith in Christ, abandon our sins, and obey His word, God will forgive us."

"How is faith in Christ shown forth?" Alexandria asked.

"Having faith in Christ means truly believing in Him and His covenants," George replied. "But, faith is also a principle of action. Where there is true faith there will be changes that bring us more in line with the will of God. Repentance and baptism are the beginning of such works. Because of the coming judgment and God's unalterable decrees, He has commanded us to repent and be baptized in His name, that we may be sanctified by the reception of the Holy Ghost, that we may stand spotless before Him at the last day. If we choose righteousness without being forced, exercising faith in Christ and repenting, receiving and keeping all the covenants He offers us, we will be filled with the Holy Spirit which brings that joy which surpasses all things.[27] Then may the glory of the Lord be reflected in our countenances.[28] Now we know what we must do, for the works which we have seen Christ do, that shall we also do."[29]

"Must we all die as Christ died, as martyrs for our faith?" the priest scoffed.

"Christ chose righteousness and He made and kept all the covenants given to Him by the Father. We must do the same," George responded. "Christ came into the world to do the will of His Father. The Father sent Him that Jesus might offer Himself as an infinite sacrifice for all men, that after He had been lifted up on the cross He might draw all men unto Him, having purchased them with His holy blood. Then shall all men be brought before the bar of Christ the Son, God the Father, and the Holy Spirit, which is one Eternal God, to be judged according to their works, whether they be good or evil.[30] Those who have repented and been baptized in Christ's name, enduring in faith to the end, He will hold guiltless before the Father at that day when He shall stand to judge the world. Those who don't endure to the end in faith will be hewn down and cast into the fire from whence they can no more return because of the justice of the Father. For no unclean thing can enter into His kingdom."[31]

"Righteousness, obedience, and only the hope of a merciful judgment?" the Empress pressed.

"God's mercy is sure if we love and obey Him," George said. "Because of our agency, we are free according to the flesh to choose liberty and eternal life, through Jesus Christ, the great Mediator of all men, or to choose captivity and death, according to the captivity and power of the devil who seeks that all men might be cast out of God's presence forever, becoming miserable like unto himself. In the fullness of times, in the day of judgment, Christ will come again to redeem from the fall all men who will repent and believe on His name. They who are redeemed from the fall return to God, becoming free forever, knowing good and evil, to act for themselves in obedience to the commandments God has given them.[32] This is His word which He has given to the children of men. And He cannot lie, but fulfills all His words which He has given."[33]

"Does this day of judgment come when we die?" the Empress asked with mild concern as the priest nodded his curiosity.

"Death is only a temporary separation of the spirit from the body," George replied. "The spirits of all men, as soon as they are departed from this mortal body, are taken home to that God who gave them life where they receive a partial judgment. The spirits of the righteous are received into a state of happiness and peace called paradise, where they rest from all pain and sorrow.[34] There they await the resurrection and the great day of final judgment. The disobedient abide in a hellish prison of misery, captives of Satan, the master they have chosen and followed.

These languish in torment and fear, awaiting the resurrection and their terrible day of judgment."[35]

"What exactly is this resurrection?" Athanasius asked.

"Resurrection is the reuniting of the spirit with the body in a perfected and incorruptible form," George explained. "Three days after His crucifixion, Christ was resurrected with a body of flesh and bones and appeared to His disciples. He challenged them saying, 'Behold My hands and My feet, that it is I Myself: handle Me, and see; for a spirit has not flesh and bones as you see Me have.'[36] All men will be resurrected in like manner, with perfected physical bodies to house their spirits, in the great and terrible day of the Lord. Resurrection is a free gift of God that comes to all, both old and young, bond and free, male and female, wicked and righteous. Every body shall be restored as it has been in this life to its perfect frame, this mortal body being raised to immortality, never more to be subjected to corruption, and not one hair of the head shall be lost.[37] This free gift of immortal life offsets the curse of physical death brought on by the fall of Adam and Eve. It is written: *For as in Adam all die, even so in Christ shall all be made alive.*"[38]

"Are you saying that all men everywhere, both good and evil, will eventually be raised from the dead to immortality by a loving God who is the Father of us all?" the Empress asked, beginning to feel the power of this doctrine, in spite of herself.

"That's true," George confirmed.

"With such a guarantee, what motivation would anyone have to obey your God?" Athanasius exclaimed. "What reward beyond immortality awaits the repentant and obedient in this day of judgment?"

"Beyond immortality, they have hope through the atonement of Christ and the power of His redemption to be freed from all bondage and raised up unto life eternal, because of their faith in Christ according to the promise,"[39] George responded. "Those found worthy will be heirs of eternal life in the presence and glory of the Father. Those who overcome all things and return to God's kingdom shall shine forth, reflecting the glory of the Father, being joint-heirs with Christ of all the Father has, whose glory defies all description."[40] Knowing he could never fully describe the glories of God, he added, "The Apostle Paul taught, 'Eye hath not seen, nor ear heard, neither have entered into the heart of man, the things which God hath prepared for them that love Him.'"[41]

"So, those who have chosen righteousness, who have made and kept the covenants of the Lord, will be restored to righteousness, cleansed and sanctified through the redeeming power and the atoning blood of the Son of God?" Alexandria summarized.

"Exactly!" George replied. "Justified by the Holy Spirit, the righteous shall return to the kingdom of the Father, according to the mercy of the Son."

"And the wicked?" the Empress questioned.

George shook his head mildly. "Those who have chosen wickedness can't be restored to that which is righteous, but will be cast out of the Father's presence, according to His justice. Wherefore, the wicked remain as though there had been no redemption made, except that the bands of death are loosed and the spirit and body are reunited again in their perfect form, and they are brought to stand before God to be judged of their works, having a bright recollection of all their guilt.[42] Though these be raised from the dead to immortality, they will suffer the second death, even a spiritual death, being cast out of God's presence and eternally cut off from things pertaining to righteousness and the kingdom of God."[43]

"Why do Christians bind themselves down under such foolish and vain hopes in Christ? What can we possibly know of things to come?"[44] the priest challenged uncertainly.

I've heard many questions such as this before, George thought. *One thing I've learned is that there is no sure correlation between how ridiculous the questions are and how close the investigator is to embracing truth and rejecting self-deceit.* With a respectful soberness devoid of sarcasm he answered, "We know that our flesh must waste away and die. By diligently searching the records of God's witnesses, we can know that we will be raised up after death and again in our bodies we shall see God. We can also know that Christ came in the flesh to His people at Jerusalem and, according to the will of His Father, He suffered Himself to be subjected to evil men and was crucified for all men. We can know that by His atoning sacrifice, Christ has redeemed all men. We are now subject to His judgment."[45]

Anxious about the judgment, Athanasius shot out a string of questions. "If we are to be judged by a perfect Christ, on what basis do we have any hope for salvation? What is the cause of our being loosed from the bands of death and hell? On what conditions are men saved?"[46]

"Men are saved on conditions of faith in Christ, true repentance from sin, and obedience to God's commandments. A mighty change is wrought in the hearts of the sincere, that we may humble ourselves and keep our faith in the true and living God, remaining obedient and faithful until the end. Therefore, through the power of Christ's atonement and resurrection, the bands of death are broken and the chains of hell which encircle us about are loosed, that we may sing the song of redeeming love and be saved. Truly we must be born of God. So now I ask you, have you spiritually been born of God? Have you received His image in your countenances? Have you experienced this mighty change?"[47]

George paused, not really expecting a response, but rather waiting for his questions to fully sink in to their minds and hearts. As neither the priest nor the Empress spoke, he continued. "Personal revelation of these truths from the Lord is a sacred process. It's built upon a foundation of faith that we are truly God's children and that He loves us and is seeking to lift us to glory and bless us in every way possible, consistent with His eternal laws.[48] Beyond the words of the prophets, each of God's children must seek and obtain a personal witness through the Holy Spirit of each of His principles, truths, and covenants. God works patiently with His children, for precept must be upon precept, line upon line, here a little and there a little.[49]

"This is God's plan of agency and redemption, giving us the blessing of learning good from evil by our own experience and mercifully preparing a way that we might be cleansed of our sins. Thus we become clean again through the holy blood of the Lamb of God, freely offered as an infinite payment to redeem our souls on conditions of faith in Christ and repentance from sin. This stands in stark opposition to that cunning plan of the evil one who seeks to subject us and bind us down to endless destruction. God's plan, laid before the foundation of the world, is one of deliverance from death. Before we believed in Christ, He first believed in us, that we would choose righteousness and repent, and He opposed our accuser before God. Now, in the wisdom of a loving Heavenly Father, our righteousness is to be tried, tested, and proven by the adversity of the accuser, the great dragon, that serpent called the Devil, and Satan, who was cast out of heaven down to the earth, and his angels were cast out with him."[50]

Feeling a flood of warmth, Alexandria said, "This revelation of all truth which comes through the Holy Spirit, does it only come after we believe that God lives and that He loves us?"

"The Spirit of Christ is given to all men," George explained. "The way is plain, that all may know with a perfect knowledge to judge good from evil. For that which invites, entices, and persuades to do good and to believe in Christ is of God.[51] In this manner, all who seek righteousness are enlightened, precept upon precept, whether they know God as their Father or are ignorant of Him, all can progress in obedience to His laws. Believing in God and in His love for us opens the floodgates of personal revelation, wherefore, the record of heaven abides in us through the Comforter, bestowing upon all those who receive it the peaceable things of immortal glory, the truth of all things, quickening and making alive those who have been sanctified and made holy, bestowing all knowledge and all power according to wisdom, mercy, truth, justice, and judgment. This is God's plan of happiness for all men, through the blood of the Only Begotten of the Father, even Jesus Christ."[52]

George sensed the priest and Empress had enough to ponder as they continued their review of the records. Feeling the need to emphasize one final point he said, "Before you renew your hopeless bribes and banish me back to my cell to rot, think again on God's gift of agency to His children. Many of life's tests are simple because we generally get rewarded by others for doing good and we generally get punished by others for doing evil. However, some of the most important tests of agency come when we are promised a reward for doing evil, or when we are guaranteed a punishment for choosing righteousness.[53] I will not betray my God when such a critical test is so clearly before me.

"Now I invite you to look to the great Mediator. Have faith in Him and repent. Obey His great commandments. Receive His covenants and be faithful to His words. Choose eternal life according to the will of His Holy Spirit. I plead with you, do not choose eternal death, according to the will of the flesh and the evil therein, which gives the spirit of the devil power to captivate, to bring you down to hell that he may reign over you in his own kingdom.[54] Believe and repent of your sins and be baptized in the name of Jesus Christ, the Son of God, and you shall receive the Holy Ghost, that you may have all things made manifest to you."[55]

*****

Alexandria was quietly studying the Christian records in her private quarters when Diocletian entered. "Are we making any progress in closing the gap with George?" he asked, coming right to the point but not expecting to be pleased with the response.

"Not unless you've come around to his way of thinking," Alexandria replied softly. "I have reviewed the Christian records and listened to George witness his convictions. I'm astonished at the clarity and simplicity of his declaration of God's love for all and His plan of redemption. I don't see any way to turn him."

"What have you found in their records?" Diocletian asked.

Alexandria took a deep breath and began, "True followers of Christ are not usurpers. They truly aren't seeking power, except the right to worship their God according to their religious doctrine. Their God is one of agency and accountability. He invites all men to freely obey His laws. His foundation is one of freedom and righteousness. Bondage and compulsion are the plan of the adversary, for God will force no man to heaven.

"When the Israelites departed from Egypt, they were led by the prophet Moses, and God was their King. They had many generations of freedom and prosperity under the direction of God's prophets until they got jealous of the worldly glory and pomp of the surrounding nations. Their envy drove them to negotiate with God for a lesser blessing, so He gave them men for kings, Saul, David, Solomon and their posterity, who subjected them to the political bondage they had chosen.

"God withdrew by degrees, allowing His people to suffer the natural consequences of their choices, reaping for a time the glory of the world, but in the end, cutting them off from His presence. After many generations, their God sent His Son to restore His children to the true gospel plan of agency and redemption. Though they will never stop preaching and inviting others to come to Christ, true followers of Christ would never force their religion or their God upon anyone. We can be sure that those advancing such schemes of manipulation and bondage for political power are not true Christians at all, no matter what they call themselves or from whom they may claim authority."

****

CHAPTER FORTY-FIVE
The Atonement of Christ

The Palace at Nicodemia
March-April, 303 AD

"For God so loved the world, that He gave His Only Begotten Son, that whosoever believeth in Him should not perish, but have everlasting life."[1]
John 3:16

****

"I may have the key to gaining George's submission," the priest announced with a smile when the Empress entered the pagan sanctuary.

"And what might that be?" Alexandria asked curiously.

"Justice!" the priest declared. "I've been studying the Christian records, but I've also been thinking about all the other gods. Only the Christian God claims to be a perfectly omnipotent champion of absolute justice. The other gods are governed by whims and limited in their power. As such, they are not required to reconcile themselves with injustice. But with all the injustice that is obvious in our world, with endless war, poverty, disease, abuse, power mongers, and conspiracy, how could there possibly be one true God who is all powerful and at the same time is perfectly just with all men?"

"I see your point," the Empress replied. "We'll see what George has to say about that."

"Who cares what George has to say?" Athanasius blurted. "I'm telling you it's an irreconcilable proposition that defies the truth of the Christian God."

"Just keep in mind that we are not about truth. We are about submission," the Empress replied patiently. "Therefore, we care about what George says. If he won't admit a flaw in the doctrine, it won't matter if you are right."

"And I see your point," the priest responded soberly.

*****

"Would you please slip your hands and feet into the shackles?" Orion asked. George noted the new iron rings were significantly oversized and already locked. He gave a quizzical look to the tribune. "They're just for show," Orion assured.

"A brisk bath and a fresh set of clothes have me feeling good," George responded. "I'm not going to let these new chains spoil that. Still, something inside me reviles against bondage, whether malicious or 'just for show.'"

*****

"Your countenance appears much improved," the Empress observed as George appeared in the priest's sanctuary. "We're hoping your disposition is much improved too."

"My disposition is that of a true follower of Christ, bound for my faith," George replied calmly.

"The Emperor's offer is still available, in exchange for your public submission, but time may be running out on us," Alexandria added. "Diocletian has been patient, but we can't be certain when the imperial council will force his hand. George, you know Diocletian will not recall his orders against the Christians nor his demand for worship of the Roman gods and homage to himself. He doesn't want you destroyed, but he's made it clear that it would be better for one man to die than for an entire nation to descend into chaos, anarchy, and destruction."

"It's also better that one man should perish than that a nation should dwindle and perish in unbelief,"[2] George countered, straining for optimism. "Jesus freely gave His life for His people. Shall I not follow His example in all things, though it cost me my life?"

"But you'll die a horrible death," Alexandria cried, barely containing a sudden flood of emotion.

George smiled lightly. "All men must die, but how a man chooses to live, that is the true measure of his character and worth."

"But why must all men die?" Alexandria pleaded in anguish.

George paused for the Empress to regain her composure. With more doctrine to teach, he needed the Spirit to prevail over her anguish. "Through death we are able to lay aside the corruption of mortality. Through the resurrection of our Savior and Redeemer, and His infinite atoning sacrifice, Jesus Christ is able to raise us up in incorruption.[3] On conditions of repentance we can be perfected in Him."

"You say that Christ is our Savior and Redeemer. What is this redemption and why is it necessary?" the priest asked.

George prayed silently as he gathered his thoughts. "With the loving sacrifice of His own precious blood, Christ has paid the price for our sins which we could not satisfy ourselves. He has reclaimed us from death and hell, becoming our Savior. Further, He has covenanted that if we will have faith in Him, repent of all our sins, and keep His commandments, He will exercise His power to heal the breach between us and our Heavenly Father. Thus may we return to the presence of the Father, being redeemed from the demands of justice." As George looked into the still expectant faces of Alexandria and Athanasius, he could see they were looking for something more than the simple explanation he'd given.

"You speak of the demands of justice," the priest noted confidently. "If God is the author of justice, and also an all-powerful being, then how does this atonement work? Will God save His people in their sins?"[4]

"He will not save His people in their sins," George replied. "It's impossible for Him to deny His word. He has said that no unclean thing can inherit the kingdom of heaven. Thus, men cannot be saved in their sins.[5] Therefore none may enter into His rest except those who have washed their garments in the blood of the Lamb of God through faith, repentance of all their sins, and obedience unto the end. Now this is the commandment which He has given: 'Repent, all ye ends of the earth, and come unto Me and be baptized in My name, that ye may be sanctified by the reception of the Holy Ghost, that ye may stand spotless before Me at the last day.'"[6]

"But if we are literally God's children, would He not bear with all things to have us back in His presence?" the Empress challenged.

"Not so," George responded, "for His law must be upheld. He will bear all manner of mistakes, sins, and even the temporary rebellion of His children, if they will repent. But the unrepentant sinner is a measure of filth that He cannot bear, for cleanliness is next to godliness, and all things before Him shall be done in cleanliness."[7]

Seeing doubt in the eyes of the Empress, George turned his head to the left and pressed his face down onto the shoulder of his fresh tunic. Drawing in a slow deep breath he lifted his head again and smiled. "Is it really so hard to believe that the King of kings, the Creator of heaven and earth, would reserve to Himself a sanctuary where none but the clean and properly adorned may approach Him?"

Orion chuckled lightly in the unseen corridor as Alexandria blushed faintly.

"If He is God, why can't He save whom He will and destroy whom He will?" the priest asked.

"Let me try to explain it another way," George replied. "Our Heavenly Father is a God of love. However, He is also a God of truth and justice. He has established laws that govern His kingdom. His law of justice requires that sin must be punished and that no unclean thing can inhabit His kingdom. God cannot violate His own laws or He would cease to be a God of truth and justice. Indeed, He would cease to be God.[8]

"When we came to earth and began to exercise our God-given agency, our Father knew we would be tempted to violate His laws and we would make mistakes as we learned to know good from evil by our own experiences. God knew we would sin, thereby becoming unclean. If it hadn't been for His plan of agency and redemption, there could've been no resurrection of the dead and no redemption in God's kingdom.[9] Men would have been cut off by God's law and become miserable forever because of sin.[10]

"But there is a way prepared for all men from the foundation of the world if they will repent and come unto Christ. For those that diligently seek God shall find Him, and His mysteries shall be unfolded unto them by the power of the Holy Ghost in all ages.[11] Thus, God sent His Son that redemption might come in and through the Holy Messiah, who offered Himself a sinless sacrifice for sin, to answer the ends of the law for all who have broken hearts and contrite spirits. Unto none else can the ends of the law be answered. No flesh can dwell in the presence of God except through the merits, mercy, and grace of the Holy Messiah, who laid down His life according to the flesh and took it up again by the power of the Spirit, that He might bring to pass the resurrection of the dead, being the First to rise. And all men shall stand in the presence of God to be judged of Him according to the truth and holiness which are in Him. And the ends of the law which the Holy One has given inflict punishment upon the wicked, in opposition to the happiness and joy of God promised to all those who exercise faith and obey Him."[12]

"How has this Holy Messiah laid down His life as a sacrifice for sin?" Alexandria asked.

"Well," George began, "Jesus was born of an immortal Father and a mortal mother. From His Father, Jesus had life within Himself and was not subject to death. Yet from His mother, Jesus inherited the ability to die, voluntarily, by simply waiting to exercise His power over death until after He had experienced it, descending below all things that He might rise above all things and lead the captives back to their heavenly home.

"Christ came into the world to suffer the will of His Father. It was the will of His Father that He should die that He might claim the souls of men. Though sinless, He suffered and died to atone for our sins, breaking the bands of death that the grave should have no victory and redeeming us on conditions of faith and repentance, that we might have a hope of glory in the eternities."[13]

"If the whole plan of redemption hinges on Christ simply dying for us, then what does it really matter what we do in this life?" Athanasius asked.

"It hinges on our choices too," George replied. "God's great plan of agency, mercy, and redemption was presented before the foundation of the world. Christ covenanted with the Father and us to set an example for us in all things and to offer Himself as a willing sacrifice, to prepare a way for us, that all who would repent and have faith in Him might be redeemed, holy and without blame, back into the presence and glory of the Father.[14]

"In opposition to the great plan of redemption, Satan came before God. Seeking the honor and power of the Father for himself, he accused us, his brethren, of being unworthy of the test of adversity, and of being weak and lacking the intelligence and faithfulness required to succeed.[15] He tried to intimidate us into surrendering our agency to him, that he might rule over us. He claimed that he would protect us from ourselves and that we would have no responsibility for our own actions, for he would force us to do right and thereby raise us to glory as his subjects.[16]

"Christ pled with us to retain our precious agency, given to us by the Father, and trust in Him to make the required sacrifice, condescending to suffer the will of the Father in the flesh.[17] Christ covenanted to walk the path of adversity we all must take, that we might have confidence in His words, 'Come, follow Me,' leading us to return with Him to our Father's kingdom as glorified sons and daughters of Almighty God.[18]

"Because of His love for His children, the Father invited us to experience adversity and promised to provide a Savior for us. He commanded us to choose righteousness, receive His covenants, and return to Him. Honoring the agency He had given, He let us choose. Satan and his followers rejected God's plan. For their rebellion, they were cast out of God's kingdom.[19] They were sent to earth, being allowed to tempt men in this life until the final judgment. Their evil work continued with our first parents in the Garden of Eden and persists to this day."

"So now we're back to Adam and Eve and their fall from grace?" Alexandria asked. "Are you thinking we'll believe it's true, if you can just tell us the tale three times over?"

"It's a matter of vision and perspective, not a question of truth," George replied. "All I have told you is true, but hearing the principles taught by many witnesses or in different ways, as in the records, gives better understanding, just as viewing the horizon with two eyes gives more clear perspective than viewing it with only one." George smiled as the Empress turned to look out the window, intermittently covering one eye with a hand. After a moment, the priest did the same.

"I see," Alexandria admitted.

"Then I'll continue," George replied. "By the fall of Adam and through our own sins we've become corrupt, unclean and unfit for God's holy kingdom. Thus we've been cut off from the presence of the Lord, suffering spiritual death, and being condemned to physical death.[20] But Christ has atoned for the sins of all who have fallen by the transgression of Adam."

"I'm still stuck on the witnesses," the priest said, shifting uncomfortably. "It makes no sense that such a being as Christ, the Son of God, the Father of heaven and earth, should have come in relative obscurity. If He truly is a God of goodness and power, would He not reveal Himself to all men, that we might witness these great and marvelous things with our own eyes?"[21]

"Your question implies that you haven't finished reviewing the records," George replied. "They teach clearly that in the end of the world God will truly reveal Himself in glory to all men. At that day every knee shall bow and every tongue confess that He is righteousness and life.[22] All men shall come to Him and witness His overwhelming truth, justice, mercy, majesty, and power for themselves.[23] Then shall those who have been offended at God and His plan of agency and redemption be ashamed, while those who have looked to Christ in faith shall be justified, raised to life and glory as His sons and daughters. Before God reveals Himself in His might, we must all face the trials of our faith until we've chosen that which we love, which God will restore to us through the power of the resurrection and the redemption which is in Jesus Christ."

"You say that God is our loving Heavenly Father and that He seeks to bless us in every way possible, and that He is an omnipotent God of justice, mercy, and truth," the priest stated.

"He is," George replied. "God does all in His power to endow us with His glory."

"Yet our world is constantly filled with war, poverty, disease, abuse, and conspiracy," the priest observed. "Such things suggest there either is no God, or that God is not all powerful, or that God is not just. Otherwise, how can these be if there is one true God who is all powerful and at the same time is perfectly just with all men?" he challenged.

"It may be easier to understand if we review the justice of God," George replied. "His justice is not temporary, it is eternal. If you look for it in this life only, you will not find it, for by it we would all be condemned for our sins. Therefore, justice has been temporarily suspended, that we might have time to repent. But the demands of justice will eventually be answered in the day of judgment. So let's consider how justice works in God's plan of agency and redemption.

"God created this earth for the habitation and testing of His children, that He might bless us. It would be unjust of Him to subject us to this mortal suffering against our wills, but He can allow us to voluntarily choose the test of adversity that we might know good from evil. Therefore, justice demands agency, opposition, choices, and consequences for those being tested.

"God created physical bodies for Adam and Eve that were pure and not subject to death. As a just God, our Father would not inflict adversity upon our first parents, who had kept His laws. Instead, He gave them commandments, explaining the consequences of disobedience, and He let them choose. Adam and Eve used their agency to partake of the forbidden fruit and begin the mortal test of adversity. As consequences, justice required them to be subjected to the penalties of spiritual and physical death, according to the word of God."

"Now we bear the burdens of their choices," the priest observed. "Where's the justice in that?"

"As the family of Adam has entered the world, we have borne the curse of being subject to physical death through no fault of our own," George agreed. "Though we did not transgress the law, we are made to suffer the consequence, which is unjust. So what does justice demand?"

"Justice demands that immortal life be restored to us freely," Athanasius replied.

"That's right," George said. "However, during our test in mortality, we all sin against God's laws, staining ourselves and falling short of His glory. God has declared that no unclean thing can enter His kingdom, therefore we are unfit to return. Now what does justice demand?"

"Justice demands that we be cast off from God's presence forever," the priest responded.

"Yes, it does," George affirmed. "However, in His wisdom, God sent His Son, Jesus Christ, as a perfect sacrifice to suffer unjustly for all, that He might be entitled to claim and redeem all that are His, according to the demands of justice. He suffered infinitely for the sins of all men, in Gethsemane and on the cross at Golgotha, giving His life as a ransom for His people. Because of His perfect obedience to the will of His Father, justice entitles Jesus to immortality and glory in His Father's kingdom. Jesus claimed these blessings through His resurrection and His ascension back to His Father."

"But having been rewarded for His obedience, justice now demands that He be compensated for the injustice of His suffering," the priest concluded.

"Very good," George replied. "Through His sacrifice, Christ brought

A Martyr's Faith

about the resurrection of all men, answering the demands of justice. For as in Adam all unjustly die physically, even so in Christ shall all be justly made alive, resurrected to immortality.[24]

"Overcoming the effects of our own sins is a different challenge. Part of Christ's compensation for His suffering is His right to raise all that are His to eternal glory. He extends His mercy to all who repent and exercise faith in Him, answering the demands of justice with His suffering."

"But His suffering was infinite. Can't He extend infinite mercy to all men?" Alexandria inquired.

"The mercy Christ offers is infinite," George explained. "However, what men will receive is limited by our agency. Justice only allows Christ to claim as His own those who have exercised their agency to become His disciples and serve Him. Justice will not allow Christ to claim those who have chosen other masters for themselves. Because our test is one of agency and consequences, justice remains a barrier to those who are not the Lord's because they have not served Him. For how knows a man the Master whom he has not served, who is far from the thoughts and intents of his heart?[25]

"Therefore, redemption in our Father's kingdom is conditioned upon repentance, turning to the Lord and serving Him by covenant. Unto such, the blessings of mercy cannot be denied. Justice sustains Christ's claim to all who are His people, allowing Him to cleanse them with His own blood, bringing them back to the Father, justified and sanctified, pure and holy. This is the balance between justice and mercy. This is why God commands all men everywhere to repent and come unto Him to be justified, sanctified, and glorified."

"Did this Savior of yours give His life to save even a pagan priest such as me?" Athanasius asked with a marked change toward humility.

"Christ came into the world to save all men if they will hearken to His voice," George replied. "He suffered the pains of every man, woman, and child who belong to the family of Adam. He suffered this that the resurrection might pass upon all men, that all might stand before Him at the great judgment day. Now He commands all men that they must exercise faith in the Holy One of Israel and repent and be baptized in His name or they cannot be saved in the kingdom of God. And if they will not believe and repent, being baptized in His name and enduring to the end, they must be damned, for the Lord God has spoken it. But woe unto him that has the law given, that has all the commandments of God and transgresses them, wasting the days of his probation, for awful is his state!"[26]

"And what of those who don't have all the commandments of God?"

Alexandria asked. "Is there no mercy for them?"

"Although the Lord has given His law to us in plainness, that we cannot err, there are many who have been kept in ignorance of God's laws," George admitted. "Many have never attained the age of accountability and therefore are not subject to the laws of performance. And where there is no law given there is no punishment. Where there is no punishment there is no condemnation. Where there is no condemnation the mercies of the Holy One of Israel have claim upon them, because of the atonement.[27] These stand innocent before the judgment seat of God. They are delivered by the power of the Lamb of God, for His atonement satisfies the demands of justice on all those who have no law given to them. They are delivered from death and hell, and the dragon and his endless torment. They are restored to that God who gave them breath, which is the Holy One of Israel."[28]

The group fell silent, each thinking about the doctrine of Christ that had been discussed. After a few moments, Athanasius took a deep breath, let out a mild sigh, and then began his summary. "Just so we're clear, you say we all lived with God before we were born on earth. Our mortal life is a test to see if we'll choose righteousness of our own free will. We all must die, but we'll all be resurrected to immortality. Those who've chosen righteousness in this life, repenting of their sins, having faith in Christ, and being obedient to His commandments will be washed clean and pure through the holy atoning blood of Jesus Christ and will be able to return, as joint-heirs with Christ, to glory in the kingdom and presence of the Father. Those who reject Christ will be cast off by a loving God who is bound by His own law of justice. Do I have all that right?"

"I think you're finally beginning to see the essentials of God's plan. Good for you, Athanasius!" George smiled. "If you keep your focus on Jesus Christ and His central role in God's plan for our redemption, you will do well."

"Justice demands it," the priest replied with a wink to the Empress.

"I understand how it might be possible for one to look down upon the conduct of evil men with their idols of wood, metal, and stone and doubt the existence of any God," George admitted. "But I cannot conceive how a man could look upon all of creation and doubt the existence of the one true and living God.[29] I don't understand everything about the plan of agency and redemption, or about the atonement of Christ, but I know we have a Heavenly Father who loves us all. He is all-powerful, a God of justice, mercy, and truth. His Son is our Savior and Redeemer. Christ's sacrifice was perfect, without blemish, infinite and eternal, withholding nothing that all the demands of justice might be met and mercy dispensed on conditions of repentance. These terms are imposed by the justice of Almighty God. Christ suffered the will of the Father in all things, voluntarily submitting and enduring the suffering which was required of Him, which suffering caused Him to tremble with pain, and to bleed at every pore, and to suffer in both body and spirit.[30]

"The records declare that we must suffer with Christ if we are to be redeemed and glorified with Him.[31] Our sacrifice is born of faith, repentance, coming unto Christ with broken hearts and contrite spirits, withholding nothing, and giving away all our sins to know Him and be saved.[32] He is omnipotent. In mortality, He showed His power to heal and His power over death. He will redeem and glorify all who serve Him.

"You plead with me to suffer the will of the Emperor, that I might not suffer pain and physical death in this life. But I choose to suffer the will of God, that I might not suffer spiritual death for all eternity.

"God counsels in wisdom, justice, truth, and mercy over all His works. Seek His counsel. Be reconciled to Him through the atonement of Christ, His Only Begotten Son, that you may obtain a glorious resurrection, having true faith.[33] Though you may not yet know these things, I've known many of these truths from my youth. If you seek God's will with real intent to obey the truths you learn, the Holy Spirit will confirm these truths to you."

*****

"You seem a bit agitated," the Empress said to the priest after George had gone.

"Perhaps I am," Athanasius responded. "Though I haven't finished my review of the Christian records, I'm perplexed by this doctrine of Christ. When considered fully, it is becoming more and more intellectually persuasive."

"I feel the power of this doctrine too," Alexandria acknowledged. "Why would any man not want to believe that a loving God is his Father? But, I don't know these things are true. They could just be the foolish traditions of a deluded people. George did have an answer for injustice though."

"George seems to have an answer for everything," Athanasius admitted begrudgingly.

"Is he right or is he wrong?" the Empress asked.

"The truth doesn't matter," the priest reminded her. "I fear his growing confidence. Getting his submission now appears more impossible than ever."

"Failure is not an option!" the Empress declared. "We must complete our review of the records and find a fatal flaw in the doctrine that will enable us to gain his submission."

****

CHAPTER FORTY-SIX
Priesthood Keys and Covenants

The Palace at Nicodemia
March-April, 303 AD

"...thou art Peter...And I will give unto thee the keys of the kingdom of heaven: and whatsoever thou shalt bind on earth shall be bound in heaven..."[1]
Matthew 16:18-19

****

As Orion guided him from the bath area to the pagan sanctuary in the palace, George sighed, "If the only benefit from this teaching is the chance to get clean before each meeting, it's worth it."

When they arrived, Alexandria and Athanasius were waiting expectantly in the sanctuary. "We haven't finished our review of the records yet," the priest offered quickly.

"But we're very troubled by the mood of the imperial council," the Empress added. "We need your submission soon if there's to be any hope of sparing your life. The land, money, cattle, and slaves are still yours if that will help, but you must publicly renounce your Christian faith and make a token sacrifice to the Roman gods if you are to live. Your actual beliefs won't matter. Surely the God in whom you trust can see beyond a man's actions to the intents of his heart."

"You almost sound as if you're anxious for my welfare," George quipped. "However, though your tone is soothing, your plea is still unacceptable. God can surely see the desires of my heart, but those desires bind me to honor Him. It's courage, not compromise that brings the smile of God's approval."[2] Boldly George continued, "I worship Jesus, for He is the Christ, my Savior, the Son of the living God. Surely I'm blessed, for God has revealed this truth to me by His Holy Spirit.[3] Of the many witnesses of God and Christ, none compares to the witness of the Holy Spirit. Spirit speaks to spirit in purity and clarity, freeing me from the crafty perversions of men which lead to everlasting destruction."

"Well, we don't know what you claim to know," the priest replied.

"Have you inquired of the Lord?" George asked. "God has promised that if we will not harden our hearts and ask in faith, believing that we shall receive, with diligence in keeping His commandments, the truth of all things shall be made known unto us."[4]

"I don't see how I can ask in faith for anything from a Being in whom I don't believe," Alexandria responded.

"Give place for a desire to believe," George counseled. "Otherwise, for the hardness of your hearts, except you repent the Lord will take away His word and His Spirit from you. He will no longer suffer you, but will turn the hearts of men against you."[5]

Frustrated with George's predictable challenge to prayer, Athanasius issued his own challenge. "We ask for evidence of your God, His laws, and that Jesus who has been crucified is His Son. All we see are whims and dreams, pretended visions and mysteries of this unknown Being. It appears these Christian doctrines are taught to bind simple people down under foolish ordinances and performances crafted by ancient priests to usurp power and authority over the people, to keep them in ignorance and submission, that they dare not think for themselves nor make use of the wealth which is their own, lest they should offend their priest. Your ancient prophecies haven't freed the Christians but have made them slaves to standards that deny them the common pleasures of life. Your Christian traditions lead men away into foolishness, that your priests may glut themselves upon the labors of men, denying them the enjoyment of their rights and privileges.[6] Else, what sign will you show us that there is a God?"

A bit surprised by the aggressive confrontation, George responded, "You know that our priests don't glut themselves upon the labors of the people. They labor for their own support. Most of the church's work is done by the ministration of the members. What profit is it to labor in the church if we receive no wages, except to declare the truth that we may have rejoicing in the joy of our brethren? Do you believe that Christians deceive the people and that this is the cause of the great joy in their hearts?"[7]

"The deceit of leaders is most effective when the masses are celebrating," Athanasius replied.

"I grieve at the perversion and pride of you who persist in leading the people to worship dumb idols of wood and stone, boasting in your gold and silver and costly apparel,"[8] George said. "Why do you speak against the Lord and His witnesses, the holy prophets? Why do you pervert the ways of the Lord, denying the Christ, disrupting the rejoicings of a faithful people?[9] Will you tempt God, demanding more signs when you have the testimonies and records of all the holy prophets laid before you? All things in heaven and on the face of the earth witness that there is a Supreme Creator. You have signs enough before you. I grieve for the

A Martyr's Faith

hardness of your hearts, still resisting the spirit of truth that your souls may be destroyed."[10]

Uncomfortable with the ripening tension, the Empress tried to turn the discussion. "Surely our souls are as precious as others in the sight of God. Therefore, show us in wisdom how to understand the signs that are already evident of God's work and His love."[11]

Somewhat relieved George explained, "In order to understand the doctrine of Christ you must understand that God loves all His children and that He seeks to guide them to the enduring blessings of eternity. He has revealed His laws that we might know concerning the covenants He has made with all His children.[12] Thus all may rejoice and lift up their heads forever because of the blessings which the Lord God shall bestow upon His faithful children.

"All people may exercise faith and seek blessings directly from the hand of the Lord. Where faith is lacking, the desire to believe is a key to the revelation you seek. God will answer those who seek the truth, with real intent to obey Him. However, those who seek to be bound to the Lord must seek out His servants who have been authorized to administer His ordinances and covenants. Jesus told His apostle, Peter, 'I will give unto thee the keys of the kingdom of heaven: and whatsoever thou shalt bind on earth shall be bound in heaven....'[13] This shows that the priesthood authority Jesus gave to Peter had power to validate covenants and ordinances between men and God that would endure and be binding beyond the grave."

"Are you authorized to administer the covenants of God?" the Empress inquired.

"I am a disciple of Jesus Christ, the Son of God," George replied respectfully. "I'm not authorized to command in His name or to administer His covenants and ordinances to His children. But unless the Spirit restrains me, having irrevocably taken upon me His name and knowing His doctrines of salvation, I will teach His words among all people, that they might seek Him and find everlasting life.[14] As with all of God's children who have faith in Christ, I'm obliged to do good and to echo the words of the prophets, testifying of that which I know to be true according to His Spirit."

"How may we know if a man is authorized to administer God's covenants?" Alexandria asked.

"The records speak of various authorized priesthood offices such as apostles, prophets, evangelists, pastors,[15] high priests,[16] elders,[17] priests,[18] teachers,[19] deacons, and bishops[20] who are given of God for the perfecting of the saints, for the work of the ministry, and to edify the church.[21] However, the records declare that no man takes the honor of

God's priesthood to himself. This honor is vested only in those who are called of God, as was Aaron.[22] Now, Aaron's call came from God through the prophet Moses, who also administered to and ordained Aaron to officiate in the priesthood.[23] Later, the prophet Isaiah declared that the Lord's witnesses and servants are chosen by Him.[24] Jesus chose twelve of His disciples and named them apostles.[25] These men He ordained that they should be with Him and that He might send them forth to preach.[26] To all His authorized servants Jesus declared, 'Ye have not chosen Me, but I have chosen you and ordained you…I command you that ye love one another.'"[27]

"So the sign of an authorized servant of God is that he loves others?" Athanasius asked with a strained chuckle.

"Love is not the sign of God's authority, although pure love certainly meets with His approval," George responded patiently. "However, the lack of charitable love is a strong indicator that a man has no authority from God. All men may serve God by choosing righteousness and loving and serving others. However, none may administer the covenants and ordinances of the Lord except they be called of God and properly ordained. An authorized servant of God receives his calling from God, by the spirit of prophecy, through those who are already in authority to preach the Gospel and administer in the ordinances thereof. Ordination to the priesthood is performed by those in authority by the laying of hands upon the head of the man to be ordained.[28]

"At God's command, the word of Christ is declared unto His chosen servants that they may bear witness of Him.[29] The Lord God ordained priests after His holy order, which was after the order of His Son, to teach the people His plan of redemption that all might know to look for salvation in and through the atonement of Christ, that they might also enter into His rest.[30] Thus, God has prepared the way that the residue of men may have faith in Christ, that the Holy Ghost may have place in their hearts.

"True servants of the Lord teach God's plan of redemption and happiness, always pointing others to Christ, inviting all to come unto Christ and be perfected in Him through obedience to the laws and ordinances of His gospel.[31] The records you study will establish that all the holy prophets who have prophesied ever since the world began have spoken more or less concerning these things, teaching plainly that God Himself should come down among the children of men and take upon Him the form of man, going forth in mighty power upon the face of the earth, bringing to pass the resurrection of the dead and the redemption of His people."[32]

Raising his eyebrows slightly, Athanasius asked, "How is this mighty power manifested in true servants of the Lord?"

"True bearers of God's priesthood have power to administer His ordinances," George explained. "Through the prayer of faith they may anoint the sick with oil, and in the name of the Lord, exercise the power to heal.[33] By faith they may move mountains, if such work is expedient to the Lord.[34] When threatened by a storm at sea, the Lord rebuked the wind and the waves and they obeyed Him.[35] The elements will obey God's servants, if they act in faith according to His will. At the bidding of the Lord, Peter walked on water. But when he took his eyes off the Savior and gave place for fear, his power ceased.[36]

"Among the greatest powers God has given some of His servants is the authority to call men to repentance, to work righteousness upon the earth that He may fulfill the covenants and promises which He has made unto the children of men, having prepared a way for us that we may return to Him by taking upon us the name of Christ, becoming His sons and daughters and joint-heirs with Him to all the blessings the Father has to bestow upon His righteous posterity.[37] The records say we must take upon us Christ's name, for by His name shall we be called in the day of judgment. Those who take upon them His name and endure to the end shall be saved at the last day."[38]

"How are these covenants and promises of God received by men?" the Empress asked.

"We prepare to receive the covenants of the Lord by choosing righteousness, exercising faith in Christ, repenting, and obeying the ordinances proscribed by God," George replied. "Jesus said, 'Except a man be born of water and of the Spirit, he cannot enter into the kingdom of God.'[39] Thus, baptism is the ordinance through which we covenant to serve God and Christ. It is the gateway into God's kingdom and the means by which we are taught to look to the Son of God for a remission of our sins, this ordinance being a type of His death, burial, and resurrection.[40] Through baptism, the worldly man is buried with Christ. Men and women then arise from the water as spiritual beings with Christ, having faith in the great plan of the Eternal God, according to His promises and covenants with His children.[41]

"God has promised to send His Spirit to guide us in keeping our baptismal covenants, and to comfort us in adversity. Therefore, baptism by water is to be coupled with the baptism of fire and the Holy Ghost by the laying on of hands.[42] In return for our baptismal covenant, one who possesses the proper priesthood of God can lay hands upon our heads and invoke the baptism of fire and of the Holy Spirit, which will abide with us so long as we remain worthy. Through righteousness we can have the influence of the Spirit in our lives constantly. It is this Holy Spirit of truth which will guide us into all truth."[43]

"And if we don't remain worthy?" Athanasius asked.

"If we sin and offend the Spirit, He will not abide in us," George responded. "However, we may regain the companionship of the Spirit through sincere repentance and a return to our God."

"So, we receive these covenants and ordinances and then look to the Son of God for a remission of sins. Is that the end of it?" Alexandria asked.

"To retain a remission of our sins and keep our covenants in force, we must continually repent and forsake our sins, humbling ourselves before God, standing steadfast in the faith of Christ's atoning sacrifice,[44] with obedience to all the laws of God and to the promptings of His Holy Spirit," George replied.

"As you review the Christian records you'll see that John the Baptist was also a witness to the principles of faith in the Lord, repentance of sins, baptisms by water, and baptism by fire and the Holy Ghost.[45] The apostle Peter was yet another witness. He said, 'Repent and be baptized…in the name of Jesus Christ…and you shall receive the gift of the Holy Ghost.'[46]

"What are all the ordinances and covenants required by God, beyond just baptism and receiving the Holy Ghost?" Alexandria asked.

"Baptism is the gateway, and the companionship of the Holy Ghost is necessary to endure the presence of the Lord in His glory. The records speak of ordination to the various offices of the priesthood, marriage, and the sacred ordinances of the temple. Eventually, all who would be heirs of God's kingdom must receive all the covenants and ordinances the Lord offers them in order to obtain all the blessings that are available through obedience to Him."

"How is the temple different from a church or cathedral?" Athanasius asked.

"Churches and cathedrals are open to all men who desire to worship and draw nearer to God, learning of Him through communion with others of faith. The temple is a place designated by God, where heaven touches earth. It is the house of God. But it's more than just a house dedicated to the Lord. It's where the Lord may reveal Himself and the fullness of His covenants and ordinances to those who are faithful in keeping His commandments. The apostle Paul referenced the temple when he taught of having an high priest over the house of God, inviting us to draw near to God with a true heart in full assurance of faith in Jesus Christ, having our hearts purified from an evil conscience, and our bodies washed with pure water. He testified that we should hold fast to our faith, without wavering, for He that promised us eternal glory is faithful to His word.[47]

Teaching further regarding God's covenants Paul wrote: *This is the covenant that I will make with them after those days, saith the Lord, I will put my laws into their hearts, and in their minds will I write them; and their sins and iniquities will I remember no more.*[48]

"Earlier, Malachi prophesied of this when he wrote: *Behold, I will send my messenger, and he shall prepare the way before Me. And the Lord, whom ye seek, shall suddenly come to His temple, even the Messenger of the covenant, whom ye delight in. Behold, He shall come, saith the Lord of hosts. But who may abide the day of His coming? And who shall stand when He appears? For He is like a refiner's fire, and like fuller's soap.*"[49]

"Who then shall stand when He appears?" the Empress urged.

"The records pose similar questions elsewhere, and provide an answer," George replied. "Who shall ascend into the hill of the Lord? Or who shall stand in His holy place? He that has clean hands and a pure heart, who has not lifted up his soul unto vanity, nor sworn deceitfully.[50] Righteousness, humility, and real intent to keep our covenants with God are essential. God's kingdom is reserved for those who make and keep His covenants. These are they who shall stand with Him when He appears."

"What about those who are inclined to righteousness but die without having their covenants in place?" Alexandria asked.

"I don't know all things," George admitted, "but I do know that God has made provisions for all righteousness. Any who have repented, believed, and worked righteousness in this life, may hope to be among those who are offered and receive God's covenants.[51] The prophet Isaiah speaks of them that dwell in the land of the shadow of death, stating that upon them hath the Light shined.[52] The great apostle Peter also spoke of this when he promised, 'For Christ also hath once suffered for sins, the Just for the unjust, that He might bring us to God, being put to death in the flesh, but quickened by the Spirit: by which also He went and preached unto the spirits in prison.'[53] There would've been no purpose in God preaching the gospel to the spirits in prison if there were no provisions for their covenants. In refuting those who disbelieved in the resurrection, the apostle Paul wrote: *Else what shall they do which are baptized for the dead, if the dead rise not at all? Why are they then baptized for the dead?*"[54]

"So you baptize dead people?" Athanasius challenged, testing for a breach in the doctrine.

"The early disciples didn't baptize the dead. They were baptized as proxies 'for the dead,'" George explained. "Paul used this ordinance as evidence of the reality of the resurrection."

"Are there any other covenants of God that we need to review?" Athanasius pondered aloud.

"There are many covenants of the Lord noted by His witnesses in the holy records. Some covenants are specific to certain individuals, such as the wise and understanding heart He gave Solomon.[55] Others receive covenants that extend to their posterity, such as father Abraham who was promised that through his posterity all the kindreds of the earth would be blessed.[56] The Lord swore in truth unto King David, 'Of the fruit of thy body will I set upon thy throne. If thy children will keep My covenant and My testimony that I shall teach them, their children shall also sit upon thy throne for evermore.'[57]

"Some covenants are extended to all who will receive them, such as the remission of sins on conditions of repentance. And even as this covenant to take upon us the name of Christ establishes us as the people of God,[58] so we become partakers of the covenant of the gathering, which He promised saying, 'Hear the word of the Lord, O ye nations, and declare it in the isles afar off, and say, He that scattered Israel will gather him, and keep him, as a shepherd doth his flock.[59] He shall call to the heavens from above, and to the earth…Gather my saints together unto Me; those that have made a covenant with Me by sacrifice.'"[60]

"What profit is it for those who have kept the ordinances and covenants of your God, walking mournfully before Him?" the priest challenged anxiously. "Aren't the Christians in bondage to us who they castigate as proud and wicked? Surely it is vain to serve your God."[61]

"The profit is God's eternal reward," George replied. "If you can't see beyond this mortal life you can never know the mysteries and glories of God. His blessings are intended for all men, even the proud and the wicked, if they will repent and in humility turn again to Him. God has plainly promised all His children, 'Return unto Me, and I will return unto you.'"[62]

"What shall we do that we may be approved of the God you preach?" Alexandria inquired. "On what conditions are we saved from death and hell?"

"Believe in the words of the holy prophets who speak the words of God,"[63] George replied simply. "Now is the time to repent, for the day of salvation is near. Cast your sins away. Repent and humble yourselves before God, and call on His holy name, watching and praying continually. Bring forth fruit meet for repentance, even a broken heart and a contrite spirit. Take upon you the name of Jesus Christ through baptism and receive the Holy Ghost, having faith on the Lord, having a hope that you shall receive eternal life, having the love of God always in your hearts that you may be lifted up at the last day to enter into the rest of the Lord."[64]

"I think we've had our fill of doctrine for today," Athanasius sighed. "We'll keep trudging through the records and get back to you when we've made more progress."

Hearing more than a hint of sarcasm in the priest's voice, George responded humbly, "I beg you not to strain against the scriptures to your own destruction."[65]

"Enough already," Athanasius spoke with tired determination. "Tribune! Return George to his cell now."

Feeling a burning within, as if this was a critical moment of choice he shouldn't let pass, George ventured boldly further. "You wonder at the doctrines of Christ, but I sense you fail to ask God in faith for the reward of all them that diligently seek Him. If you would hearken to the Spirit, which teaches all men to pray, you would know that you must pray. It is the evil spirit which discourages men from prayer. But we must pray always to the Father, in the name of Christ, that the Father may send His Spirit to guide us into all truth and holiness.[66] When you rend the veil of unbelief which keeps you in your awful state of distress and hardness of heart and blindness of mind, then shall you see great and marvelous things which have been hid up from the foundation of the world. When you call upon the Father in the name of Christ with a broken heart and a contrite spirit, then shall the Father show unto you that He remembers all the covenants which He has made unto His people.[67]

"The law of the Lord is perfect, converting the soul. The testimony of the Lord is sure, making wise the simple. The statutes of the Lord are right, rejoicing the heart. The commandments of the Lord are pure, enlightening the eyes. The fear of the Lord is clean, enduring forever. The judgments of the Lord are true and righteous altogether.[68] All the paths of the Lord are mercy and truth unto such as keep His covenants and His testimonies."[69]

Orion had quietly entered the pagan sanctuary, awaiting further instructions. He'd been ordered to take the prisoner back to his cell, but he stood listening to George's powerful testimony, unwilling to disrupt the spirit he was feeling.

The priest and Empress had listened too, momentarily paralyzed, feeling something they were yet unwilling to acknowledge. At the same time, both were fearful of rejecting the hope that was clearly evident in the countenance of their friend. Wishing to be alone with his thoughts, Athanasius finally spoke. "Tribune, return this man to his cell."

"Yes, my lord," Orion replied.

*****

"I'm not sure we're making any progress in our quest," the priest said. "I've never met a man so skilled at teaching the Christian doctrine as George is. It's easy to believe he's known many of these principles from his youth. But often, when we pose a question or challenge, he pauses momentarily, as if he'd never considered the matter, then he responds with all the wisdom of heaven, guiding us to two or three witnesses of each principle."

"Yes, and when he's done, he marvels at what he's taught us as if it was the first time he heard it himself," Alexandria agreed. "George's conviction seems to be increasing with each visit. Though my review of the Christian records is nearly complete, I haven't found any flaw that will be persuasive with George. We must push on quickly though, lest time and hope depart."

*****

Diocletian was surprised when he entered Alexandria's quarters. She was reviewing some documents with frustrated intensity. After studying her for a moment he said, "I'm not sure I like your brooding, but at least it gives us one more thing in common. What's the matter?"

With an exasperated sigh Alexandria set aside her notes and the Christian records and looked directly at Diocletian. "It's George. This charge of gaining his submission has me unsettled. If you had initially required my life as a penalty for failure, I should have ventured gladly. Now it's clear that such a bargain would have been folly. I see the confidence with which he holds to his covenants with God and with men. I doubt we can turn him with either bribes or logical persuasion. He has his own answers for everything. And they're not just theories in his mind. He knows them to be true and we can't seem to prove otherwise."

"You're a very intelligent woman," Diocletian responded as he glanced casually at Alexandria's notes. "I'm confident you'll uncover some fallacy in the Christian doctrine and draw George to it," he said, though his true feelings were just the opposite.

Alexandria pondered for a moment, lost in a distant stare. "I can't say I know the truth of what he says, but he certainly has opened my eyes to the conflict of interest borne by the professional clergy. I think George has particularly unsettled our esteemed priest, but we remain determined to carry on. Sometimes I feel the weight of this conflict is so great that we shall either prevail soon or be crushed in the effort and die."

Diocletian brooded for a moment before he responded. "If we fail to gain George's submission, we may literally get caught up in a groundswell of chaos that could cost us our lives." Then, with a wry smile he added, "I'm beginning to think that we finally share a common view of the problem presented by our hero, George."

****

CHAPTER FORTY-SEVEN
A House Upon a Rock

The Palace at Nicodemia
March-April, 303 AD

"Therefore whosoever heareth these sayings of Mine, and doeth them, I will liken him unto a wise man, which built his house upon a Rock..."[1]
Matthew 7:24

****

George stood quietly in the pagan sanctuary, despising his bonds but appreciating the fresh clothing he had received after washing.

"The imperial council's rancor over your defiance grows daily," the Empress began. "Their clamor for your trial and execution is deafening and their rage against Diocletian is growing. We must present a solution to silence the mob. Is there any compromise that would have you submit to the Emperor?"

"I will not compromise and betray my God, nor will I recall my words condemning those who execute the edicts for persecution against the Christians," George replied soberly, wondering when this charade of the priest and the Empress would end.

"Would you consider simply paying homage to the Emperor, while avoiding any open Christian worship?" Alexandria queried. "If you would just bow down to Diocletian, publicly, with a great show of respect, honor, and submission, we may be able to satisfy enough of the council to quiet the critics, perhaps defusing the issue of your defiance. Then we could move you from Nicodemia to Palestine, making provisions for all your needs. Before you answer, let me be clear, we have no authority from the Emperor for this proposal. We're simply exploring possible options for resolution."

"Let me confirm the specific terms of your unauthorized proposal," George replied soberly, amazed at their level of desperation. "You suggest that I wouldn't have to actually worship the Emperor, so long as I make everyone believe that I'm worshipping him."

"Well...uh...," the Empress fumbled for a response.

"And," George continued, "you suggest that I can continue to worship the living God, so long as nobody believes that I worship Him."

"Surely true faith is a matter of the mind and heart and not a product of prideful public display," the priest intervened. "Will your God not know your mind and your heart?"

"My God knows my mind and my heart," George assured. "He is my Master. He commands that I take upon me the name of Jesus Christ. In obedience to Him, I cannot refuse to be known by the name of Christ or pretend to worship the name of any other. No man can serve two masters.[2] The life and provisions you propose for me are but further bribery offered for treason against God, by which you only wrong yourselves.[3] I seek no treasures of this world but treasures in heaven, which you should also seek. If your hearts are pure and your eyes are aligned with the glory of God, your whole bodies shall be full of light. But if your eyes are set to evil, the light of your whole body shall be overwhelming darkness."[4]

"The darkened eyes of many on the imperial council witness to their evil intent, confirming the truth of your words, at least on this point," Alexandria responded with distressed intensity. "Won't you work with us to find a solution that will set back their conspiracy?"

"My solution is to trust in the living God," George declared. "I won't compromise in this matter, for I know the will of God on it. Whatever price my faith may require will be answered with courage, not compromise."

"Would you make the token sacrifices in exchange for half the kingdom and the Princess Sabra?" Athanasius goaded sarcastically.

George studied his captors' faces carefully. Seeing distress but no malice, he turned toward the priest. "I would lose my entire eternal kingdom were I to offend God in this way." He continued observing the priest and the Empress, wondering if they planned any manipulating surprises he might not be prepared to endure.

"So, no compromise," Alexandria restated softly.

"No surprise there," Athanasius observed under his breath. Then speaking to all, he asked, "Shall we get back to our study of the Christian doctrines?"

The Empress nodded. Turning back to George she said, "We've nearly completed our review of the Christian records. Are there other Christian doctrines we should note in our studies?"

"Yes," George responded simply. "The doctrine of God is the doctrine of the family."

"What do you mean by that?" Alexandria probed. "How is the family the doctrine of God?"

George thought a moment before explaining. "We are all children of our Heavenly Father, who created our spirits before the world was. God also created physical bodies for Adam and Eve, as temples for their spirits. From Adam and Eve have come all the families of the earth.

"God gave us families to help us learn our true relationship to Him. Not all families are perfect, just as not all people are perfect. But it's in the family where we have the best opportunities to learn to love unconditionally through selfless service to those who we count as our own flesh. Christ set the example, giving His life for all of us. He promised us, 'He that loseth his life for My sake shall find it.'[5] He also said, 'This is My commandment, that ye love one another, as I have loved you. Greater love hath no man than this, that a man lay down his life for his friends.'[6] To follow the Savior's example we must learn to give our lives for others."

"How can we give our lives for others? Must we die for them?" Alexandria asked with concern.

"Mostly, we must live for them, based on covenants of mutual support," George explained. "We owe a debt to our earthly parents for the lives they've given us. This debt is surpassed by the covenant we make with our chosen spouse, to give our whole lives for each other.[7] Marriage and family are ordained of God to help us learn about proper relationships with all men in the eternities. We build on the foundation of our marriage relationships by learning to give our lives in unity for the benefit of our children and then for all men. Just as we seek to bless our own children, our Heavenly Father seeks to bless us. Jesus once told His disciples, 'If ye then, being evil, know how to give good gifts unto your children, how much more shall your Father which is in heaven give good things to them that ask Him?'[8]

"God has warned that those who violate familial covenants, who abuse spouse or offspring, or who fail to fulfill family responsibilities will one day stand accountable before Him. Further, He has warned that the disintegration of the family will bring upon individuals and nations the calamities foretold by His prophets.[9] God's grief knows no bounds when we reject His blessings, choosing for ourselves to embrace darkness rather than His marvelous Light. But as we obey the truths we know, the Spirit bears witness to our spirits that we are God's children and therefore, we are His heirs and joint-heirs with Christ to all that the Father has to give if we suffer with Christ, that we may also be glorified together.[10]

"The Almighty speaks frequently of the family of Abraham and the house, or family, of Israel. The sacred records use the house of Israel as a type or symbol for the family of God. The scattering of the house of Israel from the promised land and their being gathered home in the last days mirror the experience of all of God's children. We've been scattered from our heavenly home to be tested in the wilderness of adversity and affliction. Yet all who will heed God's call shall be gathered back to our Heavenly Father's kingdom in the great day of the Lord as we discussed in God's transcendent plan of agency, redemption and happiness."

"So we're all God's children, and therefore we're all brothers and sisters. Romans, Egyptians, Persians, Visigoths, and Sarmatians; from the beggar to the Emperor, all are equal in our relationships to God?" Athanasius challenged with a slight laugh.

"Exactly! God is our loving Father in heaven and every one of us is beloved of Him," George replied. "However, the key is more than just knowing we're all His children. Jesus commanded that we must also learn to love each other as He loves us."[11]

"And it's God's plan that we should all be gathered back to our heavenly home?" the priest questioned.

"Yes," George confirmed. "God's love has no conditions, but His blessings are conditioned on our obedience to His laws. In families we can learn the principles of God's love, that we may begin to love as He loves and to obey His laws as He obeys them, thereby becoming holy even as He is Holy, as He has commanded us to be,[12] for He is our Father and Holy is His name.[13] Jesus commanded us to be perfect, even as our Father which is in heaven is perfect.[14] Fulfilling this commandment would only be possible if we truly had a pathway to complete perfection, through repentance and the atoning sacrifice of our Lord and Savior, back to the kingdom of our Father."

"You mentioned suffering with Christ. How must we suffer with Him?" Alexandria asked earnestly.

"Our suffering began when we left the glory of the Father's presence to have a mortal experience with adversity. We put aside the glory we had with the Father that we might come to earth, to receive physical bodies and learn from our own experiences to know good from evil. If we could remember the glory we had with God, this test of adversity wouldn't be hard and we would firmly submit our wills to God, to ensure our return to glory. But the test is one for each man's heart and must be balanced in the justice of God. We suffer further with Christ when we take upon us His name, and obey His will. This brings upon us the mockery of the world but allows us to be filled with the joy of the Holy Spirit in this life and to be clothed with glory in the life to come. The sufferings of this present time cannot compare with the glory which God shall reveal in us if we are faithful."[15]

"You said that 'house' often symbolizes 'family' in the sacred records?" Alexandria mused.

"Absolutely!" George responded enthusiastically. "Jesus taught His disciples, 'In my Father's house are many mansions. I go to prepare a place for you.'[16] The Lord was teaching that in His Father's family there are many great and noble families. Jesus came to earth to prepare the path back to the family of our Heavenly Father, but we are meant to return as families. Jesus also taught, 'Whosoever heareth these sayings of mine and doeth them, I will liken him unto a wise man who built his house upon a Rock: and the rains descended, and the floods came, and the wind blew and beat upon that house; and it did not fall, for it was founded upon a Rock.'[17] The 'house' the wise man built was his family."

"Then what is the 'Rock' upon which we are to build our families?" Athanasius asked.

"The apostle Paul told the Corinthians very clearly, the Rock is Christ," George replied.[18] "Truly it is upon the Rock of our Redeemer, who is Jesus Christ, the Son of God, that we must build our foundation, that when the devil shall send forth his mighty winds, when all his hail and mighty storm shall beat upon us, it shall have no power over us to drag us down to the gulf of misery and endless woe because of the Rock upon which we are built, which is a sure foundation, a foundation whereon if men build they cannot fall.[19] Now I ask you, will you build your houses upon the Rock of salvation?" George paused a moment for Alexandria and Athanasius to consider his question, but neither offered a verbal response.

"Early on in the sacred records it is made clear: 'except the Lord build the house, they labor in vain that build it,'[20] George explained. "In other words, except a family is bound together by receiving and honoring the covenants of the Lord, the family will not endure in eternity. The apostle Paul taught the Hebrews that though many of their ancestors had wrought righteousness and obtained a good report through faith, they received not the promise. But God is faithful, making these covenants available to all the families of the earth who will receive them, in some manner whereby without us they should not be made perfect.[21] Through the prophet Malachi, God promised that those who fear and honor the Lord shall be His, saying, 'In that day…I will spare them as a man spareth his own son that serveth him…[22] Behold, I will send you Elijah the prophet before the coming of the great and dreadful day of the Lord: and He shall turn the heart of the fathers to the children, and the heart of the children to the fathers, lest I come and smite the earth with a curse.'[23]

"We must prepare ourselves as families, turning our hearts to both ancestors and posterity. We must be bound together by His priesthood authority and keys which Elijah held anciently. In the last days, before the day of judgment, Elijah will be sent back to earth to restore these keys and authority, that we might prepare as families to receive our God. If we are one in Christ, we will be one together forever with the righteous of our families."

"Based on what you have taught us," the Empress deduced excitedly, "the house of God should be the place where we receive the covenants that bind us together as eternal families within the family of God."

George smiled. "The truth has distilled upon your soul as the dews from heaven.[24] The house of God is the family of God. The mansions within God's house are the noble and great families who are bound together by His covenants in that holy place where heaven touches earth. If our families are faithful, God will share all things with us in the eternities, and thus, as part of the family of God, we become joint-heirs with Christ to all that the Father has to give."

"What evidence do the records show of these familial covenants you describe?" the priest asked.

George thought carefully for a moment. "In the Garden of Eden, another place where heaven touched earth, God joined our first parents, Adam and Eve, as husband and wife before they fell from glory and before death had entered into the world.[25] Therefore, if they hadn't partaken of the forbidden fruit they wouldn't have been separated by death and they would have retained the eternal marriage God had administered. As a result of the fall, the blessings of immortality and eternal marriage were lost. Adam and Eve became subject to death, to the separation of the body from the spirit, and to the separation of the husband from the wife at death.[26]

"However, through His infinite and eternal atoning sacrifice, Christ overcame all the negative effects of the fall. The resurrection, or restoration of the body and the spirit, reunited in a perfect and incorruptible form, is a free gift for all of God's children. Other blessings are available to all but may be restored only on conditions of repentance and obedience to God's laws. Christ established a path for all of God's children back to the presence of the Father, promising a restoration of all the blessings that were lost with the fall, including the restoration of faithful husbands and wives to an eternal bond of marriage which no man may put asunder.[27] Peter also wrote of the husband and wife, *as being heirs together of the grace of life.*[28]

"The apostle Paul compared the relationship between husband and wife to the relationship between Christ and the church, for whom He gave His life and who will certainly be bound to Him beyond the grave and for eternity.[29] Paul also wrote, *Neither is the man without the woman, neither the woman without the man, in the Lord.*"[30]

After considering for a moment, Alexandria asked, "Beyond this ordinance of binding in marriage for eternity, what evidence do the records provide that the family structure beyond this life includes relationships between parents and children?"

George had a ready answer for this question too. "The apostle John taught that there is no greater joy than to hear that our children walk in truth.[31] The records teach that children are a heritage of the Lord. The fruit of the womb is His reward. As arrows are in the hand of a mighty man, so are children. Happy is the man that has his quiver full of them.[32] What is a heritage from God if it does not remain with you according to the covenant?

"The records show that God appeared unto Isaac and renewed with him the covenant He had made with Abraham, that in his seed all the nations of the earth should be blessed.[33] This references generations before and after, all bound together by a covenant of the Lord. Righteous posterity is unquestionably a blessing, and God has promised that no blessings will be withheld from the faithfully obedient. What value is such a promise if, after this life, there is no continued association with your righteous posterity, nor with the righteous of all nations who have been blessed by your righteousness to become a part of God's family in the eternities?

"In His ministry, Jesus shared the parable of the beggar, Lazarus, and a rich man. Using simple truths to emphasize eternal principles, the Lord taught that after this life, the righteous posterity of Abraham will be gathered to his bosom in glory. In like manner, when we die, the righteous will be gathered as families with their righteous ancestors. In the parable, after the rich man died, he still had concern for the eternal welfare of his father and brethren. He asked father Abraham to send Lazarus as a heavenly messenger from the dead to warn his brethren. Abraham said that if his brethren would not hear Moses and the prophets, they would also reject other messengers, even those sent from the dead."[34]

Thinking there might be a hitch in this doctrine, the priest asked, "What is the state of little children who die before they are old enough to make these familial covenants with God?"

"All little children without God's law remain pure and innocent before the Lord," George responded confidently. "In their innocence, little children have no need to be baptized for the remission of sins. However, those of faith may bring their children before the Lord to have their names included in the records of the church and to receive blessings by the authority of God's priesthood. Jesus set the example when He said, 'Suffer the little children to come unto Me and forbid them not, for of such is the kingdom of God. Verily I say unto you, whosoever shall not receive the kingdom of God as a little child, he shall not enter therein.'[35] Thereafter, Jesus took the little children up into His arms, put His hands upon them, and blessed them. Yet even without such formalized blessings, these little children remain holy and acceptable to the Lord, covered by His great atoning sacrifice."

"So, the doctrine of God is the doctrine of His family and all the families of man," Alexandria summarized.

"That's right," George confirmed. "This is the great plan of happiness God has established for His children, conditioned upon obedience to His laws and ordinances. That's why God invites us again and again to come unto His Son, for Christ has graven us in the palms of His hands through His atoning sacrifice.[36] After His resurrection, Christ appeared to the apostle John saying, 'Fear not, I am the First and the Last. I am He that lives and was dead, and behold, I am alive for evermore and have the keys of death and hell, Amen.'[37] He is the Faithful Witness of the Father, the Only Begotten Son of God in the flesh, and the First Begotten of the dead in the resurrection. He loves us and will wash our sins from us with His own blood. He will make us kings and priests unto God and His Father. To Christ be glory and dominion forever and ever."[38]

"You say all these things are manifest in the records?" Alexandria asked.

"Yes," George replied. "The prophets have labored diligently to write the things of God. The faithful preserve these records that they might persuade all men to believe in Christ and to be reconciled to God, for we know it is by His grace that we are saved, after all we can do. We are made alive in Christ because of our faith. We talk of Christ, we rejoice in Christ, we preach of Christ, we witness of Christ, and we record our testimonies that our children may know to what source they may look for a remission of their sins. We pray they will look forward unto that life which is in Christ."[39] Tears came to George's eyes as he testified again of our loving Heavenly Father and His Son, Jesus Christ. He paused, knowing Alexandria and Athanasius were feeling the truth of his words. Silently he prayed they would open their hearts to the joy of God's Spirit.

After a few moments George continued. "The blessings of the Lord are still available to you, but you must stir yourselves more diligently for the welfare and freedoms of this people. You have neglected them such that the blood of thousands shall come upon your heads for vengeance except you repent. For known unto God are all their cries and their sufferings. If you have supposed that you could stand as idle witnesses to their persecution and that the God of heaven would sustain you, you have supposed in vain. Many innocent people have fallen by the sword of this government and it is partially to your condemnation."[40]

"If there is a living God of love, why would He allow His faithful children to be so brutally abused and slain?" the priest asked.

"God suffers the righteous to be slain that His judgments may come in justice upon the wicked," George declared. "Fear not for the slain of the righteous, for they enter into the rest of the Lord their God. Rather, fear greatly that the judgments of God will come upon this nation because of the great neglect of the leaders, modeling immorality and usurping the rights and freedoms of the innocent among this people."[41]

Hearing these sober accusations, the Empress and the priest both felt an unmistakable conviction of conscience. Finally, Alexandria gathered herself and spoke. "What must one do to have this redemption of which you've spoken? How can one be born of God, having this wicked spirit rooted out of one's breast?"[42]

George responded firmly, "If you would receive God's Spirit and be filled with this promised joy, you must repent of all your sins and iniquities and believe in Jesus Christ, that He is the Son of God, that He was slain for the sins of the world, and by the power of the Father He has risen again, whereby He has gained the victory over the grave, and in Him the sting of death is swallowed up. He brings to pass the resurrection of the dead and the redemption of the world, whereby he that is found guiltless may dwell in the presence of God in His kingdom. Therefore, repent and be baptized in the name of Jesus and lay hold upon the gospel of Christ. And if you believe in Christ and are baptized, first with water, then with fire and the Holy Ghost, following the example of our Savior as He has commanded us, you shall join the people of the covenant and it shall be well with you in the day of judgment."[43]

"This redemption you speak of seems impossible," Alexandria replied. "How can justice remain except the wicked be condemned?" she asked somberly.

"Look to Christ," George urged. "Though His people disobey and kindle His anger against them, yet His arms are stretched out still to receive them who will turn again to Him, that He may heal them. His ensign is lifted to all nations, calling all His people home.[44] Those that believe in Him and are baptized are His people.[45] If you do this, according to your faith, a mighty change of heart will be wrought within you if you humble yourselves and put your faith in the true and living God. If you are thus spiritually born of God, receiving His image in your countenance and remaining faithful until the end, you shall be saved in His kingdom at the last day. Look forward with an eye of faith to the redemption of God when this mortal body shall be raised in immortality and incorruption.[46] The eternal purposes of the Lord shall roll on until all His promises shall be fulfilled."[47]

*****

The tribune had taken George back to his cell and the pagan sanctuary was quiet. The priest and the Empress had remained to review their notes and to consider any options that might bring them success in their quest. With a strained smile Athanasius declared, "At last we've exposed an undeniable flaw in the doctrine."

"And what's that?" Alexandria asked in surprise.

"It's the mother-in-law doctrine," the priest replied coyly. "If the doctrine of God is the doctrine of the family, then men and women will be bound to their families for eternity. A married couple will then be bound to both their families for eternity, meaning that each one will be bound to his or her mother-in-law for eternity. Who would believe that to be the capstone of glory?"

Alexandria rolled her eyes as she replied, "Only those truly seeking perfection. Besides, we don't know if George even has a mother-in-law. All we know is that his brother is a farmer in Palestine and that he visits each winter."

After studying his notes more seriously, Athanasius glanced at the Empress who sat motionless, her head bowed, her eyes closed. "Are you thinking, sleeping, or praying?" the priest joked.

In response, Alexandria slowly lifted her right hand just high enough to signal the priest to stop his interruption. After a few more moments she lifted her head, opened her eyes, and looked silently at the priest.

"You're starting to scare me," he said. "For a while there at the end I was starting to feel like you were buying the doctrines George was peddling so well."

"Should I not desire eternal joy and love?" Alexandria questioned. "Should I not believe in a God who is centered in righteous family relationships that endure forever? Is it wrong for me to embrace the concept of an afterlife in which all the injustices of this world are made right?"

Athanasius furrowed his brow with grave concern. "I admire your courage in admitting your true feelings," he acknowledged. "If I've felt some of these same sentiments, I'm yet too proud or too cowardly to confess them."

After another quiet moment had passed, the Empress realized the priest was still studying her expressions intently. "Oh, don't worry!" she blurted out. "I'm just trying to see this from George's perspective. It doesn't mean I believe it. Although," she continued hesitantly, "I'm now quite certain that George believes so deeply in the doctrines he teaches that he'll never submit to Diocletian's edicts."

****

CHAPTER FORTY-EIGHT
Obedience and Repentance

The Palace at Nicodemia
March-April, 303 AD

"Behold, to obey is better than to sacrifice..."[1]
1 Samuel 15:22

****

"You seem agitated," the Empress observed. "Do we need to reschedule our time with George?"

"No," the priest replied. "I'll gather my wits for our meeting," he promised just as George was escorted into the pagan sanctuary, still in chains.

"Are you feeling okay?" George asked as he observed the priest's sullen countenance.

Frustrated, Athanasius erupted, "George, you claim faith in the only true and living God! You implicitly condemn all other religions. You label as false the beliefs of all men who don't share your faith. Therefore, you must think ill of me and my work among the people of this Republic. Your doctrine that all men are equal is rebutted by sound evidence on every side. All can clearly see that very few men are capable of leading other men. Conversely, we see so many people around us who clearly lack the capacity to do anything but follow. At least your God named them aptly when He called His people 'sheep.' Now, seeing that simple-minded sheep need a shepherd, why should your God condemn those who accept payment for their preaching, who array themselves in fine apparel that they might appeal more broadly to the ignorant who stand in such desperate need of their guidance? And surely a benevolent Father-God of love would decree that all His children should be saved at the last day, leaving no man to fear nor tremble at His presence. Truly all men should lift up their heads and rejoice, for if God has created all men, surely He will redeem all men and raise them to eternal life."[2]

By the shocked look on Alexandria's face, George could tell the priest's outburst was spontaneous and not a concerted effort. "Whoa. Whoa there," he said, straining to defuse the flood of emotion and set the stage for additional teaching. "Did I miss the first part of our meeting? I haven't heard anything about land in Palestine, cattle, slaves, money, the good of this nation, or even some tarts to sweeten the previously rejected offers for my submission. Is the Emperor's bribe for treason against God off the table now, or has Diocletian finally accepted my proposal?"

After a few moments the Empress broke the foreboding silence. "This is a pleasant surprise, Athanasius. All this time we thought George wasn't even listening to our offers for submission," she teased. Turning to George she asked, "So, what room is there for compromise now?"

"None at all," George replied. "I was just so surprised by Athanasius' initial challenge that I wanted us to start over on a more familiar path, though I do want to clarify a few points that he raised. First, it's not my place to judge any other man in his standing before God; to do so would be contrary to true faith in Christ. However, when the Spirit whispers to me that a man is evil, I listen. I have no such feeling about either of you. Next, when I teach that all men are equal before God, that is to say that they are all answerable directly to Him for their choices based on the light, truth, and knowledge He has given each one. Generally, I don't know which of God's truths have been revealed to any other man, so I can't possibly know the standard by which each man will be judged by a merciful and loving God.

"Christians believe that some men are given more talents and abilities than others, according to their capacity. Yet all are accountable to God for that which they've received, be it talents or truth.[3] When I teach doctrines I know to be true, I don't presume that you believe them or that God will hold you accountable for them the same as if He had revealed them to you through His Holy Spirit. However, I promise that if you will ask God in faith, with real intent to obey whatever He reveals, the Holy Spirit will reveal to you the truth of all that I have taught.[4]

"In my experience with men, one truth I've learned is that I have more in common with men of other faiths who honestly live their religion, abiding by the truths they know, than I do with men of my own faith who don't live their religion. My hope is that each man will obey the truths he knows and that each man will diligently seek further light and knowledge and then abide by the truths he receives. I know this path will lead all men to Christ and the Father."

"Very well," the priest acknowledged, imagining to himself that he had achieved at least a minor submission getting George to back away from the condemnation of all non-Christians. "What new doctrines shall we explore today?"

"Obedience to God's laws and commandments," George answered.

"Please continue," Alexandria urged gently.

"God's laws were irrevocably decreed in heaven before this world was created. When we obtain any blessing from God it is through obedience to the law upon which that blessing is predicated.[5] All who will have a blessing at the hand of God shall abide the law and conditions which were appointed for that blessing, which were instituted from before the foundation of the world."[6]

"In the Roman Empire there is little difference between the Emperor's commandments and the law, for his word is law," the Empress observed. "What then is the difference between God's laws and His commandments?"

Bypassing the obvious contrast between mortal man and Deity, George explained, "God's word is law, but God's laws of which I speak are more about defining how things operate, whereas God's commandments are more about defining what He requires of us. Obedience to God is the first law of heaven, which means it is a condition associated with every commandment that God has given. As you study the Christian records you will find that Jesus Christ repeatedly testified that He came not to do His own will but in obedience to the will of His Father who sent Him.[7] The records also teach plainly that obedience to God's laws has greater value than sacrifice alone.[8] Christ testified further, 'If any man will do His will, he shall know of the doctrine, whether it be of God.'[9]

"God's laws are principles of righteousness, designed to free us from sin and endow us with spiritual power. Because of God's love for us and His endless desire to bless us, He sends His servants to teach us His laws and commandments as we are prepared to receive them, that we may obey them and thereby gain the promised blessings. Thus, He invites us to act in all holiness, binding ourselves to Him.[10] Because He is a God of truth, the Lord is bound to bless us when we obey Him."[11]

"Would you give us an example of one of God's commandments and the promised blessings associated with obedience to that commandment?" Alexandria requested.

"One of the greatest tests of true faith is a man's purse," George explained. "Through the prophet Malachi the Lord commanded, 'Bring your tithes into the storehouse, and prove Me now herewith, saith the Lord of hosts, if I will not open you the windows of heaven, and pour you out a blessing, that there shall not be room enough to receive it.' As a further blessing for obediently paying an honest tithe, the Lord promised, 'and I will rebuke the devourer for your sakes, and he shall not destroy the fruits of your ground…And all nations shall call you blessed, for you shall be a delightsome land, saith the Lord of hosts.'"[12]

"Are you saying that faithful followers of Christ voluntarily pay a full tithe of their wealth to His authorized servants?" the priest asked in amazement.

"I'm saying that God promises great blessings for obedience to His commandments. We qualify for God's continuous blessings in this life and in eternity when we receive His covenants and act in righteousness and obedience to His laws and commandments. There are two great commandments which, if kept faithfully, will qualify us for all of God's blessings."

"But I was sure there were at least ten commandments in the Christian theology, and even hundreds subscribed to by some sects among the Jews," Athanasius offered tentatively.

"The ten commandments you speak of are fully encompassed in the two great commandments of which I speak. The first great commandment is to love God with all our hearts. The second great commandment is to love others as we love ourselves. The law of love is the foundation for all the doctrine of Christ.[13] If you review the ten commandments revealed by God through Moses, you'll see the first four focus on man's relationship to God. The last six of those ten commandments address our relationships with each other."[14]

After a quick review of the records, the priest responded simply, "I see you are right."

Encouraged, George explained further, "Civil laws and governments are ordained of God for the benefit of man. They are given to help us manage our relationships with others in righteousness. However, many of man's laws are designed to restrict and restrain us, serving as the basis for punishments when they are violated. Yet if there are two or more people who don't love others as themselves, who are selfish and conceited, it is impossible to make enough laws to govern their relationships with each other. In the alternative, it's an eternal principle that if there are two people who truly love each other and put the other's interest ahead of their own, no other laws or commandments are needed to govern their behavior together."

"So the more laws required by a society, the less likely that group is to meet with the approval of the true and living God?" Alexandria asked curiously.

"That's not an absolute, but excessive laws and an overabundance of lawyers are frequently strong indicators that the will of God has been abandoned or is being supplanted by the philosophies of men. You both have servants. You know the attitude that makes them valuable and trustworthy. Those who must be commanded in all things are slothful and unwise servants. The Lord would have us be anxiously engaged in good causes and do many good things of our own free will, bringing to pass much righteousness. The power to choose has been given to us by our Father in heaven. Those who use it wisely shall in no way lose their rewards.[15]

"God has commanded us to make ourselves clean before Him and cease all evil. He commands us to do good, seek judgment, relieve the oppressed, and tend to widows and orphans. By these actions and our covenants with Him, He has promised to make our scarlet sins as white as snow. Further, He's promised that if we are willing and obedient, we shall eat the good of the land. But if we refuse and rebel, we shall be devoured with the sword, for He has spoken it.[16]

"The tests of mortal life are simple to understand but most complex to master. Each man must choose between righteousness and iniquity. Those who choose righteousness must also choose whether to put the will of God ahead of their own designs. Will it be my way or God's way? Even the Son of God groaned in agony under the weight of what was required of Him, yet He set the perfect example of submission when He said, 'Father, if it be possible, let this cup pass from Me: nevertheless not as I will, but as Thou wilt.'[17]

"The delicate balance between good and evil is maintained for this life only. Evil has no power over righteousness in the eternities. God's power will be shared with those who do His will in this life, receiving and keeping all the laws, commandments, covenants, and ordinances He offers His children. If we prove trustworthy, then God will share all things with us in the eternities and thus we become joint-heirs with Christ in all that the Father has, having glory added upon us forever."[18]

George paused a moment for consideration, and then concluded, "You see, we aren't obedient because we are blind. We're obedient because we can see."[19]

Intrigued by the claim that men might see all truth, Alexandria posed a question that had been growing in her mind. "Does God favor or oppose the Emperor?"

George was a little surprised, but he sensed she was sincere. "God favors the righteous in all cases," he replied. "Is our Emperor righteous and in favor with God? Answer yourselves, for God is no respecter of persons, only righteousness, honor, and truth."[20]

"If the Emperor holds no privilege with God by virtue of his position, then how does he qualify for God's blessings?" the Empress probed further.

"If he acts in righteousness," George explained, "the Emperor is entitled to the inspiration of heaven in the management of all the affairs of the Republic, for that is his stewardship. To act in righteousness the Emperor must keep all of God's commandments and call upon Him in faith. Jesus said, 'If ye love Me, keep My commandments.'[21] This statement of the Lord establishes an eternal correlation between the first law of obedience and the great law of love. These define the path for the favor of the living God."

"What about God's commandment to everyone to repent? Why is it that men must repent?" the Empress asked.

"Must we go on and on about repentance?" Athanasius whined, cringing and hanging his head.

"If you were holy I would speak to you of holiness," George replied. "But as none of us are holy, wisdom urges that we speak of the consequences of sin and of repentance, God's narrow but sure path to redemption."[22]

Turning more fully to the Empress, George continued, "The first law of heaven is obedience. Knowing of our imperfections, God knew we would sin and fall short of His glory. When we sin, we turn away from the Lord and His ways, banishing the Holy Ghost from us through our unrighteousness. If we desire the return of God's Spirit, we must seek Him through repentance, with broken hearts and contrite spirits. When we repent, we must deny ourselves of all sin and turn again to the Lord and His ways that we might become worthy and qualify for His blessings. When we've humbled ourselves as little children before the Lord, God will send His Spirit again to comfort us and to illuminate our lives. When we're filled with the Holy Ghost, we're prepared to enter into the presence of our God. In this state of preparation we must endure to the end by accepting and keeping all the covenants offered to us by the Lord. Thus we become partakers of the heavenly gift.

"Wherefore, all men everywhere must repent or they cannot inherit the kingdom of God, for no unclean thing can dwell there in His presence, for He is a Man of Holiness.[23] God's call to repentance is His sign to us that, though we are not yet perfect, He hasn't given up on us. He desires that we voluntarily deny ourselves of all ungodliness, that we may become perfected in Him.[24] God's commandments to us are filled with hope and love, not laced with wrath and condemnation."

"If this hope and love is to prevail, then why must you condemn this nation for iniquity?" Alexandria begged earnestly, causing Athanasius to lift his head with admiring interest.

"It's not this nation, but the iniquity that I condemn," George rebutted. "I raise a warning voice of hope and an invitation to return to righteousness. The lust for power and the secret works of darkness by evil men threaten the righteous. Through immorality many men have broken the hearts of their tender wives and lost the confidence of their children. The sobbing cries of innocent hearts ascend up to God against the wicked, and He commands repentance, lest the tender hearts of His children wax cold, pierced with deep wounds.[25] Rather than condemn others, I invite faith in Christ and repentance, that this Republic and its people might be blessed. It is the unrepentant that condemn themselves and their nation to the wages of sin, which is death and the wrath of Almighty God. But the gift of God for the repentant is eternal life through Jesus Christ our Lord."[26]

"So it's not you, but this nation that condemns itself before God?" the priest chided smugly.

"Unless they repent," George affirmed. "Christ bears record of the Father, and the Father bears record of Christ.[27] The Holy Spirit bears record of the Father and Jesus Christ.[28] Jesus Christ testifies that the Father commands all men everywhere to repent and believe on His Son. And whoso believes in Christ and is baptized, the same shall be saved. They are they who shall inherit the kingdom of God, while he that rejects Christ and is not baptized shall be damned.[29] Choose to repent. Work righteousness that the Lord may grant mercy to you."[30]

"But what chance would a couple of hellions like us have in pleading for mercy before such a holy God as you profess?" the priest challenged somewhat sarcastically.

Sincerely George replied, "The Lord has promised that in the last days He will make a new covenant with His people, taking those who will have Him to be their God and writing His law in their hearts. In that day they shall all know their God and He will forgive their iniquities and remember their sins no more."[31]

"How is it possible that any might approach and know such a holy Being as you describe?" Alexandria inquired.

"Where there is a prayerful heart, a hungering after righteousness, a forsaking of sins, and obedience to the commandments of God, the Lord will be merciful, pouring out more and more light and knowledge until there is finally power to pierce the heavenly veil. Every person of such righteousness has the priceless promise that one day he or she shall see the Lord's face and know that He is.[32] And again, the Lord has promised that those who have repented of their sins will be forgiven and He will remember their sins no more."[33]

"How can a God who is all-powerful and all-knowing ever forget our sins which burn so deeply within our own minds that we can never forget them?" Athanasius challenged, believing he may have found the elusive breach in the Christian doctrine. "If God knows our thoughts, He must continually know our sins."

"You misunderstand the promise," George replied. "God will not forget our sins, neither can He, for He knows all things from the beginning. Jesus taught, 'If thy right eye offend thee, pluck it out and cast it from thee...and if thy right hand offend thee, cut it off, and cast it from thee, for it is profitable for thee that one of thy members should perish, and not that thy whole body should be cast into hell.'[34] Using the physical to emphasize the spiritual, Christ was pleading with all men to 'dismember' from themselves all that is offensive in the sight of God.

"Jesus Christ has promised that He will help us separate our sins from our characters, or 'dismember' them from us, and He will not 'remember' or reattach them to us ever again. He will be our Advocate before the Father, dispensing mercy to those who have repented of their sins. He will rebuke the accusers and boldly testify that, notwithstanding the sins of our past, we have become new creatures in Him, and we are no longer who we were when we committed our sins. Christ will witness that we have covenanted with Him and kept our covenants, that thereby He might redeem us by the power of His infinite atoning sacrifice and claim us as His own. Thus, He will lead us forward and upward to eternal perfection back in the presence of our Heavenly Father."

"So just repent and obey and it will all work out well in the end?" Athanasius sighed.

"Yes," George confirmed. "But true obedience requires that we come unto Christ and receive all the covenants and ordinances He offers us in order to obtain all the blessings He desires to bestow upon us. Many of the covenants and blessings of the Lord are contained within the Christian records you possess. I won't pretend to know them all, nor do I claim that I've made a proper application of God's word in all that I've taught you, but you have my word that I've done my best to teach you the true doctrines of Christ. If there are any discrepancies between my words and the holy records, I defer to the holy records in every particular, for I still have much to learn of the Lord and His ways."

"What is it about this doctrine of Christ that's so compelling to the masses?" Alexandria asked.

George looked intently at the Empress and then at the priest. "The doctrine of Christ is the pleasing word of God which heals wounded souls.[35] It is the gospel of love and miracles. Unlike the parting of the Red Sea, most miracles are unseen, wrought in the quiet chambers of men's hearts. Many miss the miracles because of the hardness of their hearts towards God. That happiness which is prepared for the saints shall be hidden forever from those who are puffed up because of their wealth, learning, and wisdom.[36] They resist the truth and thus they cannot be healed. Seeing, they see not. Hearing, they hear not."

"These doctrines you teach, are they common among all the Christians throughout the empire?" Athanasius asked with interest.

"Not all the followers of Christ are clear on many of these doctrines,"

George admitted. "But even if some of the local clergy and church members are unclear or misguided, the apostles and prophets were clear on them. In fact, many of the sacred records written by the apostles and prophets were letters of correction, given in opposition to false doctrines and evil practices which had arisen locally among God's people.

"The apostle Paul warned church leaders that after he departed from them, grievous wolves would enter in among them, not sparing the flock, and that from among their own group men would arise speaking perverse things to draw away disciples after them.[37] He further warned the members not to be deceived, for the great day of the Lord would not come, except there be a falling away first, and that man of sin be revealed.[38] Paul warned Timothy to turn away from those who have a form of godliness but deny the power thereof.[39] He warned Titus against those who profess to know God but through their actions deny Him, being disobedient and reprobate in good works.[40]

"What warnings and corrections did other apostles give the Christians regarding their leaders?" Alexandria asked.

"Peter taught that prophecy did not come by the will of man in times past, but holy men of God spoke as they were moved by the Holy Ghost. He warned there would be false prophets among the people. He would've had no need to distinguish false prophets from true prophets if no true prophets were to come in the future.[41] We've already discussed how the Lord restores truth when His children are ready to obey.

"The apostle John recorded praise from the Lord for the saints who exposed liars, testing those who claimed they were apostles but were not.[42] This suggests that tests will always be needed to determine who are the true servants of the Lord, as not all prophets and apostles are false. Again, we've already discussed how we can discern authorized servants of the Lord.

"Consider your own study of the witnesses and records and the many questions with which you still struggle. Where would you be in your understanding of the gospel if you remained ignorant, either through illiteracy, lack of access to the sacred records, or through a lack of diligence in studying the truth you have at hand. Let's not judge too harshly those who are uncertain about the points of Christ's doctrine, but let us diligently seek the truth, for God has turned judgment away from us because of His Son. Look to Christ and begin to believe, that you may be healed. For Christ has surely come to redeem His people, suffering death that He might atone for the sins of all who will believe on Him, that He might bring to pass the resurrection, that all men might stand before Him to be judged of their works."[43]

"George," the priest laughed softly, "you've trod us in the winepress to the last drop. Again we offer the land, the cattle, the slaves, and the money, and to enhance our final offer we'll throw in a basket of tarts to sweeten the deal if you'll just submit to the Emperor's commands and pay public homage to him and the Roman gods."

"Do you mock me and the living God?" George challenged. "By now I'm certain you've both felt the Spirit of God as we've discussed the doctrines of Christianity, and yet you go on seeking my treason against Him."

"We make no mockery of you, nor of any gods," Alexandria protested. "Your words are soothing, but we don't know that they are all true. We tolerate your views as they don't offend. However, if we were convinced of the truthfulness of all your doctrine, we would be your advocates. As we are not yet convinced, we earnestly plead again that you seek a path of reconciliation with the Emperor. This reconciliation is expedient. The path to the goal is much less important than achieving the ultimate goal."

"Tolerance is good," George replied. "But, apathy cloaked in tolerance is damnation, a barrier to glorification and progress in the eternities. God has declared there is only one true path to reconciliation with the Father and that is through faith in Jesus Christ and sincere repentance. Having wrestled with the Lord in mighty prayer many times for a remission of my sins, I will not now relinquish that which is most precious to me for mere physical relief by renouncing my faith in the God I know.[44] I shall not abandon the true and living God for the favors of any man. As for you two, know that if you reject these sacred truths, the power of the redemption and the resurrection, which is in Christ, will bring you to stand with awful guilt and shame before the throne of God and Him who has purchased you with His holy blood. And if you have rejected the heavenly gifts of God, according to the power of justice which cannot be denied, you must be consigned to endless torment in the lake of fire and brimstone.[45]

"Now, after you have been nourished by the good word of God all the day long, will you bring forth evil fruit, that you must be hewn down and cast into the fire? Will you reject these words? Will you reject the witnesses of the prophets, and will you reject all the words which have been spoken concerning Christ, after so many have spoken concerning Him? Will you deny the good word of Christ and the power of God and the gift of the Holy Ghost, quenching the Holy Spirit and making a mock of the great plan of redemption which has been prepared for you?[46]

"I challenge you to build your lives around that which you know to be true. Be quick to let go of that which is contradicted by known truth. If you follow the example set by our Savior, with full purpose of heart, acting no hypocrisy and no deception before God but with real intent to obey Him, repenting of your sins, witnessing unto the Father by baptism that you've taken upon you the name of Christ, following your Lord and Savior down into the water according to His word, then shall you receive the baptism of fire, and of the Holy Ghost. Then shall you speak with the tongue of angels and shout praises to the Holy One of Israel. Wherefore, do the things which your Lord and your Redeemer has done and endure to the end in faith and be saved."[47]

"Tribune!" Alexandria called out. "Come and take this prisoner back to his cell."

"Yes, my lady," Orion answered.

*****

After the tribune had escorted George away, Alexandria lingered in the pagan sanctuary. Cautiously she broke the silence. "Is George right or is he wrong in all his religious doctrine?"

"What difference does it make?" the priest responded, raising his eyebrows. "Even if he's wrong, he still won't submit to the Emperor or renounce his faith in Christ."

"But if he's right," Alexandria spoke intently, "then surely all the judgments he has testified against us will come upon us, for we know he's testified correctly concerning the iniquities of this people, which are many. He knows all that shall befall us as he knows of our iniquities. If he didn't have the spirit of prophecy, he couldn't have testified concerning all these things."[48]

Athanasius thought for a moment, sensing the personal concern the Empress had for her own soul. "Calm your fears," he soothed. "If George is right, there's still time to seek the mercy of the Lord. There's still time to repent," he added smugly.

"But could the Lord truly be merciful to such as us?" Alexandria questioned in anguish.

Sensing her distress, Athanasius discarded his smug demeanor. "George has testified that the Lord is merciful to all who will, in the sincerity of their hearts, call upon His holy name. The gates of heaven are open to all who believe on Jesus Christ. Those who will may lay hold upon the word of God which leads past the snares and wiles of the devil and leads the man of Christ in a strait and narrow course across that everlasting gulf of misery prepared for the wicked, landing their immortal souls at the right hand of God in the kingdom of heaven, to sit down with all our holy fathers, to go no more out.[49] If George is right about the other doctrine, then he must be right about this also."

Even as he spoke, they both felt something reassuring them that these words were true, yet neither one was prepared to admit it. Still, feeling a change, they began to search the scriptures more diligently.[50]

****

CHAPTER FORTY-NINE
The Eve of Trial

The Palace at Nicodemia
April, 303 AD

"Whether ye hide what is in your hearts or reveal it, God knows it all."[1]
Qur'an 3:29

****

"The Emperor will never recall the Christian persecution orders," Orion whispered quietly as they walked toward the prison area. "They are his word to the imperial council, and he's coupled them again and again with reassurances that you'll either submit to his commands, in which case they have much to gain, or you'll be executed for your defiance, establishing a deterrent for all who might venture to follow your example. You've been his most trusted friend and support. He loves you like a favored son, but even so he won't recall his words."

"I know," George responded with a wistful sigh. "He invites me to yield to him, and with him submit to the secret works of corrupt leaders, partaking of their spoils, promising that by thus aligning ourselves, we will not be destroyed.[2] His promises will never be sufficient to justify treason against God. He only wrongs himself with such oaths. He knows I will never yield."

"I don't understand why the Empress and the imperial priest want to know so much about Christianity since the Emperor has outlawed it and they're seeking to destroy it," Orion said, keeping his voice low.

"They're trying to undermine my faith in God, hoping I will then submit to the Emperor," George answered. "But they are at a disadvantage. They don't know the doctrine of Christ as I do. Because of the anti-Christian laws they can't get anyone else to teach them."

"Why are you teaching them if they only want to tear down your beliefs and use them against you?" the tribune asked.

"I'm not exactly sure how to answer that except to say that I've never refused to teach anyone about the true doctrine of Christ, and the Spirit bids me to teach them," George replied.

Orion chewed on his own thoughts until they reached the cell door. He followed George inside and removed the shackles. "It's all true, isn't it?" he asked intently as he unfastened the locks.

"Yes, it's all true," George confirmed. "There is no greater truth in this world than the love of God for His family."[3]

"How can I know the truth of what you've taught?" Orion questioned. "I have your witness, and I truly respect that, but I have no records to study which would enlighten me."

"Simply seek the will of God and do it. His Spirit will confirm truth to you," George explained. "As you obey every truth you know, God will give you more and more truth, by degrees, until your understanding is clear and sure. Then shall you rejoice, for you shall know it is a blessing from the hand of God, and the scales of darkness shall fall from your eyes.[4] But remember that the Lord will try His servants with adversity, and you receive no witness until after the trial of your faith.[5] If you persist in faith, obeying every truth you know, you will qualify for all the blessings of eternity and none will be denied. Never let what you don't know cause you to doubt what you do know. Doubt your doubts before you ever doubt your faith in Christ."[6]

"What is the trial of faith that comes before the witness you mentioned?" Orion asked.

"That depends upon the witness you seek," George replied. "But generally, there are two major decisions that will determine your course in this life and throughout eternity. The first decision or test is whether you will choose righteousness or unrighteousness as your way of life. Will you love and embrace good, or evil? In order for this test to be fair, the invitations to good and evil must be fairly balanced. However, the balance between good and evil is maintained for this life only. Evil has no power over righteousness in the eternities.

"The second major decision or test for the righteous is whether they will do things their own way or whether they will seek the word and will of God and obey Him. Will pride constrain you to declare, 'My way!' Or will humility enable you to embrace God's way? In the eternities God's power is shared with those who prove in this life that they can be trusted to always do His will. Jesus set the perfect example when He was faced with great personal suffering. He said, 'Father, if it be possible, let this cup pass from Me: nevertheless not as I will, but as Thou wilt.'"[7]

"But why would the Father will the suffering of His own sinless Son?" Orion asked.

Though he knew the answer, George had pondered this question many times himself, seeking greater understanding. "In order to bring about the great plan of mercy and redemption, the Father commanded His Beloved Son to submit to the abuses of evil men who trampled the very God of Israel under their feet, setting Him at naught, and rejecting the voice of His counsels. The world, because of iniquity, has judged Him to be a thing of naught. They scourged Him, and He suffered it. They smote Him, and He suffered it. They spat upon Him, and He suffered it. He suffered all these abuses and more because of His love for His Father and His loving kindness and long-suffering towards the children of men. The Mighty God of Abraham, Isaac, and Jacob, even yielded Himself as a Man into the hands of wicked men and was lifted up, crucified, and buried in a sepulcher.[8] But now, He is risen from the dead, with healing in His wings,[9] giving life to all who will look to Him in faith.

"Now it is given to each man to choose whether he will bear the cross of the Lord. All the righteous believing saints must take upon them the name of Christ, bearing His cross and despising the shame of the world.[10] Knowing these things, we are free to choose the way of life, which is righteousness and obedience to God, or to choose rebellion and death.[11] Oh, that I could persuade all men not to rebel against God, to provoke Him to anger, but that they would believe in Christ and view His death, suffer His cross, and bear the shame of the world.[12] For Christ truly has overcome the fall through His great and last sacrifice, by which mercy may satisfy the demands of justice in answering for the transgressions of God's children."[13]

"Choose righteousness, obey God, have faith in Christ…" Orion spoke the words and knew they were true. Yet his heart was filled with anguish for George over what was coming. With sadness and desperate confusion he looked at his friend and asked, "What can I do for you?"

Quickly George replied, "Trust in God with all your heart, never favoring your own wisdom over strict obedience to His word. In all things acknowledge the Lord and He shall direct your paths.[14] Seek not to counsel the Lord but to take counsel from Him, for He counsels in wisdom and justice and in great mercy over all His works. Wherefore, be reconciled to the Father through the atonement of Christ, His Only Begotten Son, that you may obtain a resurrection and be presented as the first-fruits of Christ unto God and be glorified in Him."[15]

*****

Soon after Orion had left, George heard the key rattling in the lock of his cell door. A moment later, Constantine stepped in, closing the door quickly but quietly behind him. "How are you, Brother?" he asked.

"Just the same as you will be if they find out you're here," George cautioned. "Have you no fear of being cast with the Christians? No fear of retribution?"

Constantine smiled. "They keep me here in the east as leverage against my father and his army in the west. Though it's restraining to me, it's been something of a blessing in disguise. It comes with certain privileges, for they dare not lose their leverage. They rightly fear to poke the bear, lest in the eyes of the people he gains just cause for retribution against them. Besides, Diocletian and Maximian are both too old to match my father in battle, and Galerius isn't wise enough to match him."

"I see your point. How did you get past Orion?" George asked.

"I asked for the keys and he gave them to me," Constantine whispered.

"Brother, I know your counsel is safe, but I fear for Orion," George said. "He's too trusting of others. We must make him understand that those who betray the righteous servants of God are often their closest confidants, who through transgression offend the Spirit of God and are left with no influence in their lives but that of the devil, who bids them to sin and murder."

"He's sick about you," Constantine responded. "He doesn't know what to do to help. I think he's hoping I'll ask for his help in starting an uprising to free you from prison. There's a popular sentiment that way among the people too. I've considered it, but I keep having a stupor of thought every time I try to devise a plan with any chance of success."

The words of his friend sounded good, but escape from the palace just didn't feel right. "Have no fear, Brother," George reassured. "I feel I'm where the Lord wants me to be and I should stay until His purposes are all fulfilled. Let us trust in the Lord who rules all things to bring me safely home. I'm confident my situation is really a blessing in disguise too."

"If that's true, Brother, your blessing has a really good disguise. Prison, trial, torture, execution…surely a most convincing disguise," Constantine replied in a vain attempt to keep things light. "If your work is here, I shall honor that."

"So, my bonds in Christ are manifest in the palace and to all in the empire?" George asked.

"Yes," Constantine answered. "And I hear that many of our brethren in the Lord are waxing confident by your bonds and are much bolder to speak the word in faith, hearing that the gospel is yet being preached even in the palace.[16] Do you have any message for the Christians?" Constantine asked.

"I dare not send any letters. They would only make it easier for the conspirators to identify targets for their persecutions," George observed cautiously. "Tell the saints I salute them.[17] Tell them to humble themselves in adversity and seek the will of the Lord, counseling with

A Martyr's Faith

God in all their doings.[18] Exhort them to pray unto Him with exceeding faith and He will console them in their afflictions. Christ will plead their cause, and God will send down justice upon those who seek their destruction.[19] Urge them to call upon the Lord, denying themselves of all ungodliness.[20] Tell the saints to be calm and secure in the hope of a glorious resurrection and redemption, which comes only in and through Christ the Lord, who is the very Eternal Father.[21] And may the grace of Jesus Christ be with them all."[22]

"Whoa, George!" Constantine interjected. "If I can't write it down, you'll have to keep the message short and simple. Remember, at least one of us here is still just a mere mortal."

George blinked his eyes and looked at his friend's smiling face. Relaxing his shoulders some, he smiled weakly. "Come now, Brother, you know all this too, don't you?"

"I know Christ set the example when He gave his life for all of us and that we must learn to live our lives, and sometimes give our lives, for others," Constantine replied. "But I don't know the details of the doctrine as you do, and I think I just believe most of what you seem to know."

"Clearly you understand the essential doctrines, and I think you actually know more than you think you know," George assured. "I suspect you still have access to the imperial archives so you can review copies of the sacred records. I find it easy to remember and to teach the simple doctrine that it is upon the Rock of our Redeemer, who is Christ, the Son of God, that we must build our foundations, that when the devil shall send forth his mighty winds and his shafts in the whirlwind, and when all his hail and his mighty storm shall beat upon us, it shall have no power over us to drag us down to the gulf of misery and endless wo, because of the Rock upon which we are built, which is a sure foundation, a foundation whereon if men build, they cannot fall."[23]

"'The Rock' it is!" Constantine agreed. "If you need anything, send for me without fear. Take care." He gave his friend a quick brotherly hug and headed out the door. The key rattled slightly engaging the lock and then his footsteps faded down the corridor.

*****

The Emperor found Alexandria in her quarters. The Empress was shrouded in distress, which seemed to be her persistent companion of late. "Still brooding, eh? Did your beauty fail to beguile him?" Diocletian jabbed in sarcastic frustration.

"Not all men are so shallow as to entertain such lusts, much less give in to them," Alexandria responded, disheartened by Diocletian's inference of her vanity. "George is a man true to his convictions, who properly disciplines his passions. He is truly a follower of Christ and His doctrine. He is the perfect ally of the righteous. If you want his submission, perhaps you should pray to his God and plead for His mercy in helping you to accomplish your purposes."

Diocletian mused on the thought. *Pray to George's God for help in getting George to deny Him.* Alexandria was not making any sense at all. But he wasn't surprised by the situation. He hadn't really overestimated the persuasive abilities of his Empress nor had he underestimated George. As he pondered a bit longer he realized things had turned out just as he had always expected they would. His frustration was with the situation, not with Alexandria or Athanasius. "So we're not making any progress in gaining George's submission," he said.

"No," the Empress scowled. "There's been no compromise in George's convictions to his God or his principles. According to your instructions we've made many offers of land, money, and slaves if George will renounce his faith in Christ and pay the required homage to the Roman gods and to you as a divine Emperor. But George has always refused." Alexandria scanned her notes on the doctrines George had taught. "I keep looking for a wedge to split any of the Christian doctrines George has presented, but every time I try my mind goes into a stupor, and I just can't compose any solid arguments against what he has taught."[24] She kept to herself how simply the principles and doctrines flowed together whenever she looked for truth in them.

Diocletian reached out for her notes, which she handed to him. Looking at the headings of each successive page he read, "God and His Witnesses. Dispensations, Apostasy, and Restoration. God's Plan of Agency, Redemption, and Happiness. The Atonement of Jesus Christ. Priesthood Keys and Covenants. Eternal Marriage and Families. Obedience and Repentance." At the bottom of the final page he read the underlined words, "The Family of God."

"Would you like me to explain any of them?" Alexandria offered with some resignation.

"Would it make any difference?" Diocletian responded. "I need George's submission regardless of whether I understand these doctrines or not, whether they are true or not."

Alexandria was a little surprised at her own emotional response. She said nothing, but felt her heart screaming: *Of course it would make a difference! It would make all the difference in the world, in time and in eternity, if these doctrines are true!*

Diocletian continued, "Assuming we fail to gain George's submission, his death may be our only path to survive the coming chaos." With a sober grimace the Emperor shook his bowed head and whispered, "Damn you, George…you and your uncompromising pride!"

*****

Finally alone, George tried to prepare emotionally and spiritually for his coming trial and likely punishment. He thought, *No doubt the intent of the trial and torture will be to set a very intimidating public example of me for my refusal to submit to the will of the Emperor and comply with his orders. I expect I'll be found guilty and an order for my execution will be issued. All this will be inflicted because of my faith in Christ. It's no worse than Jesus, who was accused of blasphemy by the Jews. Their leaders knew who Christ was and condemned Him for it. Before the Romans they accused Him of sedition. Pilate and the Romans didn't know who Christ was, but even though they found no fault in Him they condemned Him to appease wicked men. Sometimes the prophets and apostles were saved for other work, and other times their lives were given as enduring witnesses of God's truth. What kind of witness will I be? Will God choose to spare me? My soul is filled with sorrow because of the wickedness of the evil men seeking to destroy me and to destroy the family of God.*[25]

Weighed down with depression, he prayed to the Lord, "Holy Father, I thank Thee for the faith and prayers of the saints for me. I plead with Thee to inspire Thy saints to join in fasting and mighty prayer in behalf of the welfare of those who are yet strangers to Thy ways."[26]

As he prayed, George's mind was filled with enlightenment. *The faithful will receive a heavenly habitation, even a holy city which I have prepared for them, and I will not be ashamed to be called their God.*[27] *My people shall not be ashamed, for My people are they who wait for Me, who still wait for the return of the Messiah.*[28] *They who abide in Me shall have confidence in My presence and not be ashamed before Me at My coming.*[29]

George's mind returned to the doctrines he had taught Alexandria and Athanasius about the family of God. *I'm certain that if we are one in Christ we will be one together forever with the righteous of our families as a part of the family of God. Paul promised the Hebrews that God would provide a path to all His blessings for the righteous of all generations of men, noting the binding link required for perfection.*[30]

George prayed fervently, "Father, extend Thy mercies to Alexandria and Athanasius as they study Thy word, for I love them and their righteous desires, which struggle against evil."

George waited for inspiration and his mind was filled with the words of Jesus: *Blessed are they who hunger and thirst after righteousness, for they shall be filled with the Holy Ghost.*[31] *Blessed are they who shall believe in your words and humble themselves unto baptism, for they shall be visited with fire and with the Holy Ghost and receive a remission of their sins.*[32]

George prayed for his family and then for his own blessing, that fear might be removed from him. As he waited, he thought on the promise of the Lord: *Be strong and of a good courage; be not afraid, neither be thou dismayed. The Lord thy God is with thee whithersoever thou goest.*[33]

As he began to take comfort in these spiritual promptings, he thought, *God knows what is in the heavens and what is in the earth, for He has power over all things. Surely He knows what is within my heart, whether I hide what is there or reveal it. But mine is a day of testimony, not a day of silence. On the day when every soul will be confronted with all the good it has done and all the evil it has done, may there be a great distance between me and all evil.*[34] On this thought, George pled further, "God, I remember and serve Thee. Remember Thou me with kindness and mercy.[35] Lord, cleanse my hands, purify my heart, purge me of vanity and lies, that I may ascend to the mountain of Thy house and stand with Thee in Thy holy place."[36]

Focusing on the Lord's holy place, George's mind was filled with the words of the apostle John: *I saw under the altar the souls of them that were slain for the word of God and for the testimony which they held. And white robes were given unto every one of them, and it was said unto them that they should rest yet for a little season until their fellow servants also and their brethren, that should be killed as they were, should be fulfilled.*[37]

Sensing that the blessing he sought would be his if he remained faithful, George thought, *Awake, my soul! No longer droop in sin. Rejoice, O my heart, and give place no more for the enemy of my soul.*[38] And he was filled with the joy of the Spirit.

Quietly he lingered in the joy of the Spirit, pondering the Lord's promises to His faithful children. After several minutes, feeling spiritually filled, he posed one more tentative question. "Lord, is there more?"

Quickly into his mind came the responsive promise: *The dragon shalt thou trample under thy feet.*[39]

How shall this be done, Lord? George pondered.

The words of Jesus came into his mind: *Greater love hath no man than this, that he lay down his life for his friends.*[40] *He that loseth his life for My sake shall find it.*[41]

George had taught this doctrine of love and the doctrine of witnesses. He knew the principles of testimony and the words of Paul written to the Hebrews: *For where a testament is, there must also of necessity be the death of the testator. For a testament is of force after men are dead: otherwise it is of no strength at all while the testator liveth.*[42] By this George understood that the force of a man's word of truth was magnified by his death, amplified by his endurance to the end of mortality, and given a sure foundation that could never be renounced in mortality by him. If God were to come out in judgment against the Roman Republic based on his testimony, that testimony would need to be in full force first. *What shall I do?* George thought.

Into his mind came the question, *Who shall declare My generation?*[43]

Inspired by the Spirit which filled him, George responded with faith and determination, "I shall declare Thy generation!"

****

CHAPTER FIFTY
Trial and Testimony of Hope in Christ

The Palace at Nicodemia
April, 303 AD

"If any of you lack wisdom, let him ask of God..."[1]
James 1:5

****

"Bring in the prisoner!" At Diocletian's command, the tribunes brought George into the council chamber. He was shackled hand and foot and attended by four guards, one on either side and two behind holding restraining chains. Still, he walked with purpose and determination.

Stepping forward, Galerius made an overly dramatic bow and began, "Great and beloved Emperor, the defiant man before you has been charged with insubordination and sedition. He has spoken evil against this nation and the leaders of this people, including you, most noble Diocletian. He has threatened our destruction unless we repent of our supposed iniquities and embrace his religion. We know we are a great people, favored of the gods, devoid of iniquity that we should be judged or condemned of this man. He has lied and we are guiltless. We are strong, and we shall continue to prosper in the land. Therefore, we deliver this liar to you that you may condemn him and destroy him."[2]

"Who charges this man with crimes against the Republic?" Diocletian asked solemnly.

Galerius was disappointed that his informal proposal of summary condemnation had been ignored, but he was prepared for a formal trial, so he continued. "Divine Emperor, your imperial council brings charges of insubordination and sedition against George, son of Gerontius, citizen of Rome, tribune of the Roman army and member of your imperial guard."

"Do you speak for the council, Galerius?" the Emperor inquired.

"On this matter, yes, I speak for the council," Galerius responded.

"Please read the charges as they've been submitted for the record," Diocletian directed.

Galerius proceeded in an unnaturally slow and artificially deepened voice, "George, son of Gerontius, citizen of Rome, you are charged with insubordination for your refusal to comply with lawful military orders in the arrest of Christian subversives and the confiscation and destruction of Christian property. You are also charged with sedition for your conspiracy and treason against the Emperor and the empire. You are accused of conspiring with the Christian enemies of the empire to avoid submission to the Emperor's edicts by giving them advanced notice of planned enforcement raids. You're also charged with lying to the imperial council and personally refusing the Emperor's orders to make sacrifices to the Roman gods and to pay homage to the Emperor's divinity. These are the charges."

Diocletian turned from Galerius to George and, bearing his most stoic expression, asked simply, "George, citizen of Rome, how do you answer these charges of insubordination and sedition?"

George knew he had the right as a Roman citizen to answer and dispute the charges. He also knew that he wouldn't be allowed endless rambling so he must speak boldly. He thought, *How misguided these charges are, much like when the leaders of the Jews accused Jesus of blasphemy in their own council and then accused Him of sedition before Pilate and the Romans.*

"As to the charge of sedition," he began, "I declare that I have ever been and will always be completely faithful to the Roman Republic, to the Emperor who by right leads her, and to the cause of Rome which is the liberty and prosperity of all men. I have never sought for power. I've spent all my energy and influence in advancing the cause of peace through the strength of this Republic. I do not fear the power or authority of this tribunal, but it is God I fear, and it is according to His commandments that I have taken up my sword to defend the cause of our great Republic.

"In my defense I would speak of the Christians and the doctrines of Christ, which have been condemned by this nation, and I would speak of the true enemies of Rome and their conspiracy."

At this the council erupted, shouting George down with enraged demands for immediate judgment and execution. However, the Emperor was interested in what George might reveal regarding the conspiracy against him and how the council members would react to George's accusations. Thus he was determined to give his prisoner broad latitude in his remarks. "There will be due respect given to the rights of this citizen of Rome in this chamber!" Diocletian commanded in a warning tone. "The prisoner may continue with his pleadings."

"Thank you, my lord," George sighed. "I plead the cause of the Christians, who have been condemned without trial. We have been branded subversives solely for our faith in and worship of a God who wasn't created by men. God holds our primary allegiance, but we have also been loyal to this nation and to you, most noble Diocletian. Christian doctrine requires the faithful to be subject to and sustain civil authorities in obeying moral laws. The words of Christ are given to all men, and He teaches all men that they should do good.[3] Jesus commanded His disciples, 'Render therefore unto Caesar the things which are Caesar's; and unto God the things which are God's.'[4] Christ's apostles taught, 'Render therefore to all their dues: tribute to whom tribute is due; custom to whom custom; fear to whom fear; honor to whom honor.'"[5]

Abruptly Galerius challenged, "If the Christian doctrine enjoins obedience and submission to the Emperor, why do you persist in defying his commands?"

"Except they blind themselves, all can clearly see the edicts for Christian persecution are not moral, just, or right," George responded. "They defy the Roman laws of religious tolerance extended to all. We seek tolerance for our religious beliefs, that we might worship God according to our faith. Though we desire to share the good news of Christ with all men, we respect the rights of others to worship freely as they choose. It is our faith that all men who seek truth, with real intent to obey it, will receive greater light from God according to their obedience until they are completely united in truth.

"As followers of Jesus Christ, we know life is a test for each of us to prove whether we will choose righteousness and receive the covenants of the Lord or whether we will reject God's covenants and choose iniquity in violation of His commandments. Because God is our Father, He loves us and wants us to succeed in this life, learning to love righteousness and returning to our heavenly home pure and holy, without blemish.

"Our Father knew that in this test of adversity we would make mistakes and sin, becoming unworthy to return to His holy kingdom. Therefore, He prepared a plan of redemption for all who would believe in His Son and repent. God's witnesses, all the holy prophets and apostles, have testified of Christ's central role in our mortal journey on earth. Though sinless, Jesus gave Himself as a voluntarily sacrifice, suffering all things that He might redeem us from sin and death, having paid the price for those who believe on Him. Faith in Jesus Christ, repentance from sin, and receiving the covenants of the Lord from His authorized servants, including baptism by water and the baptism by fire and by the Holy Ghost, are essential to our return to the kingdom of God.

"We must experience a mighty change of heart, becoming sufficiently humble to embrace all truth wherever it is found, if we are to see as God sees, with an eye single to His glory. We are all His sons and daughters.

Therefore we are all brothers and sisters, from the least of us to the greatest. Families are ordained of God and they help us understand our true relationship to Him. The house of God is where we receive covenants that bind us together with our families eternally into the family of God. Through our faith in Christ and our obedience to God's commandments, we can partake of all the blessings of heaven."

"My lord, have we not heard enough of these foolish traditions?" Galerius interjected, prompting a supportive clamor from the council.

"I will hear and consider what this citizen has to say in his own defense!" the Emperor declared.

George felt the illuminating power of the Holy Spirit prompting him further. "The Spirit of God carries truth to the hearts of all men who will receive it. But many harden their hearts against His Holy Spirit, that He has no place in them. Wherefore, they cast many things away which are of great worth, esteeming them as naught.[6] I urge you to partake of the goodness of God and respect the words of the Jews, and also the words of Christ, and of all His holy prophets and apostles, lest your end shall be terrible, for my words shall condemn you at the last day."[7]

"Great Emperor," Galerius spouted, "how long must we suffer the judgment and condemnation of this traitor?"

"Patience!" Diocletian responded. "I will hear this man's words, though they may be his last."

Anxiously, George continued. "No man shall be able to deny Christ on the day of judgment.[8] For this life is the time for men to prepare to meet God. As you have had so many witnesses, I plead with you again, do not procrastinate the day of your repentance until the end. For after this day of life, light, and preparation comes the night of darkness wherein reconciliation with God cannot be made. For that same spirit which possesses your body at the time you go out of this life will have power to possess your body in the eternal world. If you have procrastinated the day of your repentance even until death, you will become subjected to the spirit of the devil, and he will seal you his and exercise all power over you, which is the final state of the wicked.[9]

"I plead with you to ask God, the Eternal Father, in the name of Christ, for the truth of these matters. God has promised those who ask with a sincere heart, with real intent to obey revealed truth, having faith in Christ, that His truth will be revealed to them by the power of His Holy Spirit. And by the power of His Holy Spirit all men may know the truth of all things.[10] For the Holy Spirit persuades men to do good. It speaks of Jesus, and persuades men to believe in Him, and to endure to the end, which is life eternal.[11] Jesus Christ is the Light and the Life of the world; a Light that is endless, that can never be darkened, and a Life which is endless, that there can be no more death.[12]

"The time shall come when all shall see the salvation of the Lord, and all men shall know that redemption comes only through Christ the Lord, who is the very Eternal Father."[13] Even this mortal shall put on immortality, and this corruption shall put on incorruption, and all shall be brought to stand before the bar of God, to be judged of Him according to their works whether they be good or whether they be evil. If their works are good, they will be resurrected to endless life and happiness, and if they are evil, they will be resurrected to endless damnation, being delivered up to the devil who has subjected them.[14] Every nation, kindred, tongue, and people shall see eye to eye and shall confess before God that His judgments are just.[15]

"Now look to Christ and live, for if He hadn't come into the world there could've been no redemption. If Christ hadn't risen from the dead and broken the bands of death there could've been no resurrection. But there is a resurrection and there is a redemption, therefore the grave has no victory and the sting of death is swallowed up in Christ.[16]

"As a witness for our loving Heavenly Father and His Son, Jesus Christ, I exhort all men to come unto Him and lay hold upon every good thing. Set aside your worship of lifeless idols that have no power to bless or heal you. Come unto Christ, be perfected in Him, and deny yourselves of all ungodliness. If you deny yourselves of all ungodliness and love God with all your heart, might, mind, and strength then is His grace sufficient for you, that by His grace you may be perfect in Him. If by the grace of God you are perfected in Christ and deny not His power, then will you be sanctified in Christ by the grace of God through the shedding of Christ's blood, which is in the covenant of the Father unto the remission of your sins that you become holy, without spot.[17] He has promised that all who will repent and come unto Him will be the covenant people of the Lord."[18]

"My lord!" Galerius interrupted, looking first to the Emperor and then to the council. "How long must we endure this man's babble? His message is clear. He admits his guilt and then challenges us to join his cause. He commands us to prepare for the judgments of his God and repent or be damned!"

"You've completely missed my message," George responded. "I plead with all to repent and be blessed. This has always been the word of the Lord and His plan to bless all His children on earth who will receive Him. For your iniquities have you sold yourselves into bondage, and for your transgressions shall you be put away.[19] But the hand of the Lord is stretched out still to redeem you and deliver you from an awful hell.[20] Repent and turn to the ways of the Lord. Keep all His statutes and commandments, as given through all His holy prophets, and become partakers of the heavenly gift and receive of His blessings. It's a message of glory, peace, and reconciliation for the obedient."

"Have we not heard enough?" Galerius sighed dramatically.

"My lord, I haven't finished my answer to the charges," George appealed again to Diocletian.

"The accused will continue and answer the charges!" the Emperor ordered.

"Thank you, my lord," George replied. "As to the charge of insubordination, I have refused orders to arrest Christians for their faith, to confiscate their wealth, to destroy their property and records, and to otherwise unjustly abuse them. However, I dispute the legality of those orders attacking religious beliefs. Roman law has historically been very tolerant of every citizen's religious beliefs. There has never been a nation on earth that has sanctioned more imagined gods than this Republic has. Our laws have been justly swift to punish criminal actions infringing upon the rights of others, but the right of free thought and worship we have held dear.

"I have refused and I will always refuse to worship any gods in whom I lack faith. Great Diocletian, I faithfully honor you as our Emperor, but I'm constrained, according to the covenants I've made to keep the commandments of the true and living God, to only worship Him and His Son, Jesus Christ. I would that all men should hold fast to the word of God.[21] These orders requiring Christians to worship anyone other than the true and living God are simply an attack on the rights of all men to believe and worship freely."

"Thank you for your bold and candid admissions to the charges!" Galerius sneered emphatically.

"Diocletian, I beg you, stop for a moment and consider all these matters again," George pleaded. "All the Christians records confiscated at the destruction of the cathedral were written in either Hebrew, or more predominantly, Greek. These are the languages of the people and of the church. However, the supposed evidence, the documents implicating the Christians regarding the first palace fire, were written in Latin, the language of government officers. The Christians were not responsible for the palace fires. The leaders of this nation seek to heap one abuse after another upon the Christians, and only because the Christian God isn't a puppet or idol of men. This nation is full of men who simply fear anything they can't control.

"The time is now at hand that except we repent and withdraw from our persecution of the innocent Christians, except we rouse ourselves in defense of religious freedom for all in this Republic and for our posterity, the sword of justice hangs over us, and it shall fall upon us and visit us with war and desolation to our own destruction. I don't seek power or the honors of the world. I seek for the glory of God and the freedom and prosperity of all people."[22]

As George concluded, Galerius stepped brashly toward Diocletian with his reply, "Great Emperor, have we not been rebuked beyond reason by this man?" Turning back to face the imperial council and making a grand gesture to the whole assembly, Galerius asked pointedly, "What further need have we of any witnesses? For this man has confessed to the acts with which he has been accused. Now he asserts as his defense that his acts weren't wrong, but that our law and our divine Emperor are wrong. He declares his God, seeking to set at defiance all other gods and the divinity of our holy Emperor.

"He claims this Empire is under condemnation for some supposed iniquity and that all who oppose him are possessed of devils. We know all is well in the Roman Empire, aside from these vexing Christians. The empire prospers and all is well. We know there is no hell as George has described. There's no devil that possesses us. There is no such creature!"[23] Seething with contempt, Galerius turned back to the Emperor. "This council demands prompt condemnation and execution of this man for his insubordination and sedition!" Taking his signal, the imperial council unleashed an angry, chaotic clamor demanding George's immediate execution.

Raising his hand to calm the unruly chamber, Diocletian turned back to George and quietly asked, "Have you anything further to say in your own defense?"

George considered for a moment. Although he disagreed with the legality of the Emperor's edicts, he had defied them and he was certain to be punished for his actions unless the Emperor's edicts were withdrawn. He held no hope that the Emperor would take back his commands, but he still saw one more way that he might help the Emperor and the Republic. "Galerius claims that I've spoken against Roman law, but I've spoken in favor of the law, to the condemnation of him and this council. By their evil designs they are laying the foundation for the destruction of this nation and for you as its head.[24] All here today know this Republic is not well. The men of deceit in this council, who seek a scapegoat for their own betrayal, have fixed their eyes upon the Christians. But the Christians aren't seeking power. They are only seeking the freedom to worship Almighty God."

Deliberately, George looked directly at Galerius and continued. "Why do you build up your secret conspiracies to get gain, causing widows and orphans to mourn before the Lord as the blood of their fathers and their

A Martyr's Faith

husbands cries unto Him from the ground for vengeance upon your heads? The sword of God's vengeance hangs over you, and the time shall come that He will avenge the blood of the saints upon you, for He will not suffer their cries any longer."[25]

Turning back to the Emperor, George pled, "Great Emperor Diocletian, those who seek power have betrayed you and this Republic. They're a wicked and perverse generation of serpents and vipers, laying traps and snares to catch the holy ones of God, perverting the way of righteousness and peace.[26] Surely, they shall not escape the damnation of hell.[27] This great Republic will never be destroyed from the outside. If we falter and lose our freedoms and our place at the head of all nations, it will be because we destroyed ourselves through treachery from within![28] If this nation chooses iniquity and remains in transgression, it will quickly ripen for destruction."[29]

George scanned the sea of angry faces in the council and continued, "Any nation that shall uphold such murderous secret combinations to get power and gain until they have spread over the nation, shall be destroyed. The Lord will not suffer that the blood of His saints, which shall be shed by them, shall always cry unto Him from the ground for vengeance upon them and yet He avenges them not.[30] If you persecute and destroy the righteous from among you, then will the Lord come out in His fierce anger against you, and you shall be smitten by famine and by the sword. This shall be your end, except you repent.[31] You who have led this treachery against God and this nation shall be cut off from the presence of the Lord, being left desolate, both root and branch,[32] and your heritage is become a waste place for the dragons of the wilderness."[33]

When George had said these words, a spirit of conviction fell over all the assembly. Those who were receptive to the Spirit of God were convinced of the treachery from within the council. The conspirators became pale and trembled in fear, sensing they were completely exposed. Galerius was gripped with fear at the convincing power of God. He was also convinced that God had given George knowledge of the thoughts and intents of his heart. He trembled with fear but remained silent, waiting for the Emperor's reaction.[34]

Caught in the conflict of his own misguided sense of honor and legacy, Diocletian sensed neither the truth nor how to defeat the conspiracy under foot. He desperately wanted more time to consider George's words.

George broke the lingering silence with a final plea. "Most great and noble Emperor Diocletian, I beg you to withdraw your edicts of condemnation and persecution against the Christians, and pardon my faults."

Despite his love for George as a trusted friend and faithful servant, there was no doubt he had defied the imperial edicts, and Diocletian would not recall his words. Sensing the moment required decisive action, the Emperor turned to his prisoner and, with his eyes passive and stoic, issued his pronouncement. "George, son of Gerontius, citizen and soldier of the Roman Empire, you are convicted of both insubordination and sedition. The penalty for these crimes is torture and execution, to which you are hereby condemned by my order unless you will recall the words which you have spoken against this empire, renounce your faith in Jesus Christ, and pay homage to the Roman gods and to your Emperor."

Calmly George replied, "I will not recall the words which I have spoken concerning Christ, for they are true, and that you may know of their surety, I've been given into your hands as a sure witness. Though I suffer death, I will not recall my words. They shall stand as a testimony against you. If you shed my innocent blood, this shall also stand as a testimony against you at the last day."

Diocletian couldn't deny the power of George's testimony. As he considered releasing him for fear that the judgments of God would come down upon him, the council raised their voices against George, accusing him of having reviled the Emperor. Fearing the loss of the council, Diocletian allowed his anger to be stirred against George. Therefore, he commanded, "Guards, take him to the prison chamber and await my orders!"[35]

Quietly George sighed, "If it be God's will that I die, I shall go to rest in the paradise of God until my spirit and my body shall again reunite and I am brought forth triumphant to meet you before the pleasing bar of Jesus Christ, the Eternal Judge of both the quick and the dead."[36]

****

CHAPTER FIFTY-ONE
Conversion of Others

Nicodemia, Eastern Roman Capital
April, 303 AD

"O God...if there is a God, and if Thou art God, wilt Thou make Thyself known unto me, and I will give away all my sins to know Thee...."[1]
Alma 22:18

****

Alone in the solitary confines of his darkened cell, George thought upon the events of the day. *Is there anything more to say? Still I mourn the wickedness, ignorance, unbelief, and stubbornness of the leaders. They refuse to search or understand great knowledge when it is given to them in plainness, as plain as words can be.*[2]

*****

Constantine retired to his quarters where he met with his mother, Helena. Carefully he recounted the events of the day, reporting in detail on the trial and George's defense of Christianity. "Some within the council chambers believed George's words, knowing in their hearts that idol worship and persecution of the Christians are wrong. Many know of the treachery and conspiracy that are pervasive within the ruling class. They know of the iniquities which George witnessed against them.[3]

"I felt the Spirit of God testify to the truthfulness of George's testimony," Constantine acknowledged humbly. "I've known George for more than ten years now. Of all the men I've ever met on the battlefield or otherwise, George is one of the very few I feel a desire to follow, wherever he might lead," he noted with admiration.

"I feel the Spirit in your witness of George's testimony," Helena replied. "This is of God."

"I pray the council members have departed in search of refuge and solitude, that they might try the word of God and ask Him in faith, that thereby they might obtain knowledge of the truth and wisdom about what they must do to repent, that they might please the one true and living God,"[4] Constantine responded earnestly.

After his mother left, Constantine pondered on what he must do next.

I feel a desire to intervene with my sword on George's behalf, but I feel no inspiration as to how I might do that. I know that becoming like Christ will be a lifetime pursuit, but if the Spirit is ever going to provide me with clear direction, I hope it will be now. Nothing? With no idea on how to help George, I'll continue to wait upon the Lord for guidance.

*****

The Empress entered her chambers seeking solitude. Diocletian had not yet returned, so she spent the time pondering on all that had taken place. *I confess that for the past few weeks, every time George has testified of God's love for His children and of His commandments as guides to His blessings, I have felt something good inside. Perhaps it's just a yearning to believe. But deep down I feel certain it is the Spirit of God witnessing the truth of George's testimony to me.* Carefully she reviewed her notes and thought back over all George had taught her about God and the atoning and redeeming power of Jesus Christ.

As she retired for the night, she began to feel the burden of George being unjustly condemned and she wondered what she should do. As her anxiety increased, she carefully opened her covers and knelt down beside her bed. She was not used to praying vocally, so she whispered quietly, "Dear Father, where is Thy peace? Where is Thy balm for my soul? I need Thy wisdom to calm my troubled heart. When I shall be called to account before Thee, how shall I stand? My soul thirsts for Thy presence. My tears shall burst forth as a fountain day and night, as Thine adversaries continually challenge me saying, 'Where is thy true and living God?'[5] O Jesus, thou Son of God, have mercy on me, who am in the gall of bitterness, and am encircled about by the everlasting chains of death."[6]

Quietly, she waited. Like the growing illumination of the rising sun, the Empress felt the clear impression: *Believe these things which have been spoken of Me, and I will visit you with the manifestations of My Spirit. Through My Spirit you shall know that these things are true, for they persuade men to do good. You shall know and bear record of Me.*[7] With this came the desired relief from her anguish and the harrowing memory of her many sins. The Spirit filled her with marvelous light and her whole soul was filled with joy as exquisite as had been her pain![8]

Finally feeling the Spirit of peace, the Empress laid down to rest. She was still unsure of what the Lord would have her do, but she was certain He was there, His gentle love for her being tender, merciful, and sweet above all things.

A Martyr's Faith

*****

Athanasius had come from the council chambers and entered his quarters. He was astonished by the false witnesses of the imperial council. They knew the truth of George's testimony against them, unlike the blinded masses of people who had been deceived. Anguish mounted as he considered the impact of his own lying words in the deceptions. He was overwhelmed by the power of George's witness.

His thoughts were interrupted by a heavy knocking at his door. Desiring solitude, he opened the door reluctantly. "My lord," the guard began, "some members of the council are here to see you. They want to discuss the doctrines George declared in his defense of Christianity. Will you see them now?"

"I'm engaged presently. Tell them I'll attend to them this evening," Athanasius answered.

"Very good," the guard replied and then took his leave.

Perhaps there were some on the council who wanted to know the truth and make changes in their lives. The priest shook his head in disgust and muttered his own scathing self-criticism, "You hypocrite! First cast the board out of your own eye. Then shall you see clearly to cast the sliver out of your brother's eye."[9] Yes, he knew the Christian scriptures, but he'd never previously experienced the "mighty change of heart."

In solitude he felt the growing weight of his offenses toward God, and the fear of the Lord came upon him. *My soul is harrowed up under a consciousness of my own guilt, and I feel the encircling pains of hell.*[10] *Now I clearly understand that the devil has deceived me into believing there is no God, and that I would benefit by appealing to the carnal minds of men, which I've done very effectively, bringing a great curse upon them and me.*[11] *My mind is sore with my iniquities. I feel a sickness of burning fever coming upon me.*[12]

Athanasius examined the trappings of his craft that adorned the sanctuary. In callous torment he lashed out against the idols of wood and stone, beating them with his staff and tilting them off their pedestals. These, he knew, were without any power of retribution, much less the power to heal or change the hearts of men. In the midst of his fit of anguish, he left the sanctuary for his private quarters. Immediately upon leaving the area of pagan worship, a realization washed over him like a reviving spring rain. *I felt the Spirit of God witness to me the truth of George's testimony. I wouldn't have received that witness if there was no possible redemption for me.*

Viewing himself in his own carnal state, even less than the dust of the earth, he cried aloud saying, "O God, have mercy and apply the atoning blood of Christ that I may receive a forgiveness of my sins and that my heart may be purified, for I believe even as George has testified, in Jesus Christ, the Son of God, who created the heavens and the earth, and all things. I believe Christ came down among the children of men to offer Himself a sinless sacrifice to atone for the sins of all men who have faith in Him and keep His commandments." When he had finished calling upon God and witnessing his faith in Christ, the Spirit of the Lord came upon him, and he was filled with joy, feeling a remission of his sins, and having peace of conscience because of his faith in Jesus Christ.[13]

Athanasius rejoiced to himself, "Truly God is good to those who serve Him, even to such as are of a clean heart. But as for me, my feet were almost gone astray. My steps had well nigh slipped off His path forever. For when I saw the prosperity of the foolishly wicked, I was envious of them. Therefore pride surrounded me as a chain, and violence covered me as a garment. I was corrupt and spoke loftily and wickedly concerning oppression. I set my mouth against the heavens, speaking evil throughout the earth. I was among the ungodly who prospered in the world, increasing in riches. But now I've cleansed my heart of vanity and washed my hands in innocence. I was so foolish and ignorant, as a beast before God. Now the Lord shall guide me with His counsel and afterwards receive me into His glory. It is good for me to draw near to God. I've put my trust in the Lord God, that I may declare all His works."[14]

Carefully he drew the sacred records from his table. Opening them, he read this passage: *But when the Comforter is come, whom I will send unto you from the Father, even the Spirit of truth, which proceedeth from the Father, He shall testify of Me: and ye also shall bear witness...*[15] Athanasius knew all would be different going forward in his life, for now he truly had a great fear to do evil in the sight of the Lord because of his sore repentance for his many sins.[16] As he moved back into the pagan sanctuary to clean up the refuse of his fit, he continued pondering on what the Lord would have him do, but without any clear direction from the Spirit.

*****

With the Emperor's condemnation and sentencing, Galerius felt he'd finally overcome a major obstacle in his quest for George's blood. He left the council chambers and went to the public square to verify that all the preparations were in order for the coming spectacle.

"The trial was a success," the senator praised. "Fate was with us. Diocletian's pride in his word and his legacy kept him on the path to

A Martyr's Faith

destruction. For his defiance, George will soon be dead."

"I'm determined that George will still make a public submission, renouncing his Christianity and pleading for a quick and merciful death," Galerius replied. "But mercy is the furthest thing from my mind. I hate him!" As he said the words, that cold sick feeling of fear he had felt during the trial returned and was magnified.

"If you go about your work patiently, you will accomplish your purposes," the senator replied.

Galerius knew patience wasn't his strongest quality, but he was determined to control himself in the execution of this foe. Having assured himself that the stage would be ready for his spectacle of torture and submission, he left the square. Next, he stopped at the blacksmith's shop, taking time to personally sharpen both edges of his sword. He was excited for the prospects of the coming day. Tormentors would do much of the torture, but he would do the public interrogation of the prisoner, and he personally would act as executioner, bringing down the sword of his own justice upon George, spilling his blood. He wouldn't allow George to die with either the courage or the dignity that might inspire the masses to more bold defiance of their rulers.

*****

The Emperor sat alone in a private chamber room. Subconsciously he polished the signet ring on his left hand with his right thumb. He wanted to think about what George had said, but regaining the support of the imperial council had won his attention. "The divide in the council is getting wider and my allies are in the minority," he mumbled to himself. "Though they aren't Christian, they believe in George's ability to manage the capital and the economy to the benefit of everyone. I'm sure they're concerned for their own futures under the anticipated brutality of Galerius. That's likely why so many of them privately encouraged me to find a way to reconcile with George. Either way, I can't recall my words to save George without losing the council.

"The conspiracy has already gotten me, for I can't do as I please. I can't retain my credibility and authority, restore George to honor, and avoid making any martyrs for a religious cause that's unsettling me. George urges me to trust in God, but I can't control the growing Christian ranks." Diocletian paused in his mumbling. Finally he shouted, "Without control, it all goes wrong!"

****

CHAPTER FIFTY-TWO
Sabra Visits

Nicodemia, Eastern Roman Capital
22 April, 303 AD

"Behold, God is my salvation; I will trust and not be afraid;..."[1]
2 Nephi 22:2; Isaiah 12:2

****

George sat motionless, his back against the cold stone wall of his prison cell. An anguished yearning to commune with God welled up in his soul. Quietly he recited a Psalm, "Then will I go unto the altar of God, unto God my exceeding joy. Upon the harp will I praise Thee, O God my God. Why art thou cast down, O my soul, and why art thou disquieted within me? Hope in God, for I shall yet praise Him, who is the health of my countenance, and my God."[2]

He also thought through the Song of Moses, but he'd never quite gotten a tune for it:

Great and marvelous are Thy works, Lord God Almighty;
Just and true are Thy ways, Thou King of saints.
Who shall not fear Thee, O Lord, and glorify Thy name?
For Thou only art holy.

For all nations shall come and worship before Thee;
For Thy judgments are made manifest.
Who shall not fear Thee, O Lord, and glorify Thy name?
For Thou only art holy.[3]

After a few moments of quiet reflection, George bowed his head in prayer.

*****

"I can't sleep," Diocletian growled in frustration.

"What's vexing you?" Alexandria asked patiently.

"Thoughts of a humble old man from long ago," he replied. "He warned me, 'The way you gain power will likely be the way you are doomed to maintain it.' I took the empire with my sword. Although my actual throne is luxury without blemish, I feel ill at ease in it. It's as if every conquering stroke of my sword has hacked at the perfectly smooth surface until the seat, back, and arm rests have become a cactus of endless splinters, each one pricking my bare flesh. My jeweled crown matches my throne in opulence, yet it pierces like a crown of thorns upon my head. Now I've turned my conquering sword against George whom I love, to retain the throne and crown I despise. I must be mad."

"What are you going to do?" Alexandria inquired.

"I honestly don't know," the Emperor replied. "I've thought about slaughtering my opponents on the council, but I've worked too hard to establish a legacy of prosperity, benevolence, and peaceful transitions of power to have it all come crashing down in a flood of blood with an uncertain outcome. Besides, I don't know if the people are with the council or the Christians. I've seriously considered the prospect of abdicating my throne if I can't regain control of the council. But I put aside that thought because of my concerns over Galerius."

"I doubt he'll champion your legacy when he succeeds you," Alexandria observed.

"I'm going to the throne to see if there is any way to scrape away the splinters and smooth it out," Diocletian said soberly as he picked up his sword and joined the tribune at the door.

*****

The Emperor sat upon his throne, brooding. The only other person in the room was the tribune who stood beside him with his eyes fixed on the doorway, expressionless. "I feel sick inside," Diocletian confided. "With all my power, I can't see any way to keep George alive and reclaim the loyalty of the council." The tribune remained silent, as if he had heard nothing, which was a relief to the Emperor. Shifting uncomfortably Diocletian thought, *How truly irritating this throne is. Others may lust after it, but any who ascend to it will soon become aware of its curse.*

*****

The mysterious young woman appeared unexpectedly, disrupting the quiet of the night in the palace. "My name is Sabra," she told the tribune. "I beg leave to see the condemned man before his execution that I might try to save his life."

Orion was George's friend, as were many in the palace. But friend or not, he couldn't see any way George's life could be saved. Still, something about this woman's countenance gripped at his core. Though he was concerned that an unsolicited interruption might bring retribution from the Emperor, for it was well past the time for receiving such petitions, he was willing to take a chance. *The Emperor might be intrigued by this woman's choice of names, though I doubt it's her real one*, he thought. Hesitating only a moment, he ordered her, "Follow me!"

*****

"My lord, I beg pardon for the interruption, but a woman named Sabra is here seeking leave to see George. Will you hear her request or shall I send her away?" Orion asked.

Diocletian turned abruptly at the inquiry. "Did you say her name is Sabra?" he asked, fighting through the fog of depression that had long been his unwelcome companion.

"Yes, my lord, Sabra," Orion affirmed.

Curiosity soon got the better of Diocletian. "Check her for weapons, then show her in and stay with us," he instructed.

Sabra entered quietly and waited for the Emperor to address her. She wore a hooded cloak which hid much of her face. "Come close before me and remove your hood so I may see you more clearly," Diocletian directed. Silently, Sabra did as she was commanded.

The Emperor carefully evaluated the woman standing before him. She was young and attractive, with a soft face and intense deep brown eyes. She wasn't dressed in the prevailing styles of the capital. Yet, although her clothes were very modest, they were neat and clean. She was still and patient, apparently having been taught much more than most about proper respect and decorum. Mostly, she was a mystery. "You are permitted to speak," he directed.

"Most noble Emperor, I am Sabra, a free born citizen of the Republic from the province of Palestine. I seek permission to speak with the prisoner, George, before his execution."

"Why would you speak with my condemned prisoner?" Diocletian inquired.

"George once saved my life," Sabra replied. "I would like to return the favor."

"Really? How did George save your life?" the Emperor challenged.

"He helped me return to my mother," she replied.

"And how might you return the favor, my dear?" Diocletian probed.

"I will question his faith and his refusal to renounce Christianity,"

Sabra responded.

"Are you the Sabra from the legends?" Diocletian asked curiously.

"Please, my Lord, could anybody truly be the Sabra of the legends?" she responded.

"How strange that you should answer me in precisely the same manner as George did when I challenged him. Still, it was an amusing thought, but I see your point."

After a quiet moment, the woman renewed her plea. "My lord, I beg leave to speak with your prisoner. Will you graciously grant my petition?"

Diocletian was surprised at Sabra's respectful assertiveness but he wasn't put off by it. "If you hope to save George's life by challenging his faith, you must not know him very well," he mused. "Perhaps you suspect that I'm willing to try almost anything to save him. Very well, you may visit him in his cell and question his faith. Afterwards, you will return directly to me to report. Tribune, take this woman to see George. Bring her back to me when she's done."

"Yes, my lord. As you command," Orion replied.

*****

Orion led the way into the prison past several other guards to George's cell. Banging on the door he called out, "Prisoner, back away where I can see you." After looking through the small window to confirm that George had moved to the far side of the cell, he unlocked the door. Opening it only slightly, he let Sabra slip in before he closed it again.

As Orion locked the door, the Emperor appeared behind him in the corridor. Putting a finger to his lips, Diocletian signaled for the tribune to be silent. With a whisper he commanded Orion, "Wait at the main entrance to the prison." When Orion hesitated a moment, the Emperor brushed him back with his hand, sending him on his way. Keeping close to the wall so he couldn't be seen, Diocletian eased himself down beside the cell door to sit and listen.

Sabra's eyes hadn't fully adjusted to the darkness in the cell, so she was uncertain of the expression on George's face. George, however, could clearly see the expression on her face. He simply didn't believe she was really there.

"How did you get in here?" he whispered anxiously.

"Through the door," Sabra replied innocently.

"It's dangerous for anyone to come see me, but especially for you," George whispered.

"Too late. I'm here already," Sabra replied. Seeing her answers were not amusing George, she continued quietly, "If you must know, I told the Emperor if he would let me in, I would question your faith to see if you will comply with his orders, that your life might be spared."

"The Emperor and many on the imperial council are still desperate to claim my reputation as their prize," George muttered. "They've already proposed every bribe they can imagine."

"Do you need any money? I brought some," Sabra offered.

"Still doing well with your copy work, eh?" George asked.

"Well enough to take care of the children in case anything unfortunate should happen to their father, or farmer Gregor," Sabra explained in a hushed voice. "I've been saving carefully."

"Well, I doubt you have enough to square things for me with the Emperor and the council," George said as he shook his head in disbelief. "I still can't believe you're here. It's like I'm seeing a spirit or an angel."

"Behold, it is I myself: handle me and see…," Sabra teased.

George stepped closer and, wrapping his arms around his beloved Sabra, finished the verse, "…for a spirit hath not flesh and bones as I see you have.[4] Therefore, you must be an angel."

"I'm your guardian angel, and don't you forget it," Sabra whispered emphatically.

"I won't forget. And no, I don't need any money," he assured her. Then quietly he whispered into her ear, "I only need to know that your love is stronger than death, as is mine for you."

"Only a love stronger than death would have me follow you here," she replied almost inaudibly.

"How did you know to come?" George whispered anxiously.

"Constantine wrote to Gregor after you were imprisoned," Sabra replied. "I've been here for several weeks seeking reports on your status. When I heard about the trial, I knew it was time."

"I love you with my whole soul, but you are in great danger here," George spoke quietly. "If our relationship is revealed, some would be willing to torture and even kill you to try and manipulate me. We must be careful, and you must leave quickly."

As Sabra held tightly to George, she considered that the guard may have been ordered to listen to them. Raising her voice casually, she fulfilled her word to the Emperor. "Why do you testify against this people whom you say God will visit with terrible punishments and destruction except they repent? What purpose will be served by your death for your refusal to comply with the Emperor's orders to renounce your faith and pay homage to him and the Roman gods?"

For the benefit of any unseen witnesses, George responded with firm resolution, "My purpose is to discharge my duty to God, that all men may repent and honor the one true and living God, who is full of mercy, grace and truth.[5] The prophet Daniel was once threatened with death if he prayed to God. Daniel remained faithful and was blessed of the Lord. I know wherein my salvation is made perfect, and I will not cease to take counsel and sustenance from my God. While my breath is in me I will not remove my integrity from me.[6] Truly, my prayer and my service of sacrifice, my life and my death, are all for God.[7] I'll give my life freely knowing that, as I pass through the veil of death, I shall be wrapped in His arms and taken to His throne of mercy where I shall await a glorious resurrection, receiving an immortal body, being raised in incorruption, a reflection of God's glory, love, and peace. God knows his purposes. His Spirit bids me be true in my witness of Him. Perhaps the Lord will stay the executioner's hand, as He did with Abraham and Isaac. But if He requires that I suffer His will in the flesh, for His glory, it doesn't matter, if at the last day I'm saved in His kingdom."[8]

Sabra knew these words of truth were coming, yet they hit with great force, and tears rolled down her cheeks despite her determination to bear up in support of George's faithful obedience to God. George pulled her close again and whispered, "Your secret yearnings and tearful pleadings will touch the hearts of the Father and the Son.[9] If the Lord takes me from you, He is bound by covenant to answer your needs and the needs of our children, in the absence of my sustaining support."

Sabra adjusted to wipe away a tear and George reached carefully down to help her, wiping away a few more tears. Regaining her composure, she smiled weakly at him. He knew she was strong, perhaps stronger than him, but that didn't relieve the pain or anguish of this adversity. Only God could take away the pain, in His own time and in His own way.

"I sorrow for Diocletian," George said.

"How can you sorrow for the man who has ordered your death because you worship your God?" Sabra asked with a tinge of sincere bitterness.

"It's all a matter of perspective," George replied. "We can complain because rose bushes have thorns, or rejoice because thorn bushes have roses.[10] I believe Diocletian is trying to do right by his people, but he is simply not acquainted with Almighty God, and therein is the thorn. He issued persecution edicts against the Christians. Now he can't go back on them or he'll suffer open revolt by the council. Besides, he that loves not his brother abides in death, rather than simply passing through it."[11]

"And who is your brother?"[12] Sabra challenged.

"That fact is established by who I know my Father to be, and who I know His children are. I know God is my Heavenly Father. He loves me and all men and women on earth, as they are all His children. I know in this life families are ordained of God. For the righteous, bound by God's covenants, family relationships endure beyond the grave. I love my God and my family with all that I am. I rejoice in the hope of a glorious resurrection, united with all those I love. Shall we not move forward in so great a cause as that of our God, moving courageously on to victory, bringing Him an offering in righteousness?"[13] George asked.

"We shall submit ourselves to the will of God in all things, as did our Brother, the Lord Jesus Christ," Sabra affirmed beyond mere patient devotion. "As much as we shall put our trust in God, even so much shall we be delivered out of our trials, our troubles, and our afflictions and we shall be lifted up at the last day."[14]

George was hesitant to speak of his concerns, but the strength he felt from Sabra whenever he had confided in her had always been a blessing to him. "If I must go down to my grave soon, I know my spirit will go to the place of my rest, which is with my Redeemer, for I know in Him I shall have rest," he reassured. "I rejoice in the day when my mortal shall put on immortality, and I shall stand before Him. Then shall I see His face with pleasure, and He will say to me, 'Come unto Me, ye blessed. There is a place prepared for you in the mansions of My Father.'"[15]

Sabra felt the truth of George's premonition. Lovingly, she echoed the consoling words of the Savior, "Be not afraid. Only believe.[16] Be of good courage, and He shall strengthen your heart; you and all that hope in the Lord.[17] Through God we shall do valiantly, for it is He that shall tread down our enemies."[18]

"Sabra, before you leave I pray that you will give me your word," George pled anxiously.

"The fervent prayer of a righteous man avails much," Sabra replied emotionally.[19] "Ask what you will, for I freely give you everything. Shall I die for you?"

George pulled Sabra close again and whispered very quietly, "If it is the Lord's will that I give my life tomorrow as a witness for Him, I pray you will guard our little kingdom well. For I have no greater joy than to hear that my children walk in light and truth.[20] Give me your word that you will fill our children with light and truth and teach them to forgive all men?"

"Yes, of course," Sabra replied. "You have my word, as God is my witness."

Still whispering, George added, "Live in joy, not in fear. Follow the promptings of the Spirit and you'll be safe, whatever the future holds.

You'll be shown what to do.[21] Together we will rejoice when you pass through the veil to join me. Be faithful my love. I would ask you to pray for me, but what I really want is to hear you sing. Please sing for me, the song you sing to our children when you put them to bed."

Sabra hugged George tightly and said, "The song of the righteous is a prayer unto God.[22] I love that song too." With an emotionally strained swallow, Sabra relaxed her embrace a little, leaned her head gently on George's chest, and reverently began to sing:

I feel my Savior's love
In all the world around me.
His Spirit warms my soul
Through ev'rything I see.
He knows I will follow Him,
Give all my life to Him.
I feel my Savior's love,
The love He freely gives me.

George responded in a similarly subdued tone:

I feel my Savior's love
And know that He will bless me.
I offer Him my heart;
My Shepherd He will be.
He knows I will follow Him,
Give all my life to Him.
I feel my Savior's love,
The love He freely gives me.

Sabra followed with another verse as she hugged George closely and the tears flowed freely down their cheeks:

I feel my Savior's love;
Its gentleness enfolds me,
And when I kneel to pray,
My heart is filled with peace.
He knows I will follow Him,
Give all my life to Him.
I feel my Savior's love,
The love He freely gives me.[23]

George finished the song as his hand gently wiped more tears from

Sabra's face:

I will not fear the end.
My Savior will receive me.
He'll wash away my sin,
With joy He'll set me free.
I'll know I have followed Him,
Giv'n all my life to Him.
I'll feel my Savior's love,
The love He freely gives me.

"In heaven," George promised quietly, "God will wipe away all our tears and heal our broken hearts.[24] The way of Life is Righteousness."[25]

*****

Outside the cell door other tears were flowing. Battle and politics had left Diocletian calloused in body and spirit. He was more than a little surprised at the flood of emotion that overcame him now. He couldn't remember any other time when his heart had broken and tears had flowed. *Perhaps I really am getting soft in my old age*, he thought. As his emotions had gotten the better of him, he rose and left before he was exposed by his deepening involuntary gasps for breaths.

He stopped in the corridor a short distance from the main gate to compose himself. *George, you've been like a son to me, the best I've ever had. I can't see any way to save you*, he thought. *If only I hadn't signed those cursed edicts.*

Slowly he proceeded to the gate. "Go and get the woman from George's cell," he instructed the waiting tribune.

"Shall I bring her to your chamber to report on her visit?" Orion asked.

"No. Escort her wherever she desires, within the city, and leave her in peace. Then return to me and report."

"As you command, my lord," Orion replied.

*****

"Prisoner, back away from the door and your visitor," Orion ordered.

At the tribune's command, Sabra prepared to leave. "What shall I do now?" she asked George, earnestly seeking comfort in his direction.

"Let the Holy Spirit guide you home," was his heartfelt reply as he hugged her one last time.

A Martyr's Faith

*****

"Are you coming to bed?" Alexandria urged.

"No," Diocletian replied. "I'm waiting on one more report. I can't sleep anyway. I wish tomorrow would never come. George won't renounce his faith before the tribunal in the morning, or ever. I don't know God, but I know George is certain of all to which he has testified. I cringe at the torture that will be inflicted. I almost wish George's God would stop the executioner's blade and spare him the torture and death that are coming, thus sparing me my own pain and loss. But a God of peace and love will not answer the prayer of a man with hands such as mine that are stained with blood. Without God in the world there is only bitterness."[26]

"Isn't this worse that recalling your words against George and the Christians?" Alexandria asked.

"I will never recall my words!" Diocletian thundered. "If I did, the only possible result of George's defiant stand against my orders would be confusion for my empire."

****

CHAPTER FIFTY-THREE
Preparing to Meet God

Nicodemia, Eastern Roman Capital
22 April, 303 AD

"Therefore thus will I do unto thee...and because I will do this unto thee, prepare to meet thy God..."[1]
Amos 4:12

****

With Sabra's departure, George was alone with his thoughts. *Beloved Sabra, may you pass safely home. I haven't eaten since early today. My afternoon ration remains untouched in the corner. More than food, I need communion with God which is facilitated by fasting and prayer. I doubt I will sleep tonight and if I don't, fatigue might make it harder to sustain the courage and strength needed to endure the coming tortures.* As he pondered further he knew, *The strength I need now will not come from either bread or sleep.*

George knelt lightly on the cool stone floor and bowed his head. His mind was racing. *All rests in the hands of God. He alone has power to accomplish all things for the benefit and blessing of His children. But I have never before felt this helpless in all that is important to me.* Quietly he began his earnest prayer. "O Lord, forgive my unworthiness, and remember me in Thy endless mercy.[2] I trust in Thy infinite mercy, yet I'm uncertain of the timing of its application. Still I know Thou wilt be merciful at the final judgment, where it will be most essential and beneficial."

Pondering further, he recalled the words of the apostle Paul, warning: *All that will live godly lives in Christ Jesus shall suffer persecution.*[3] He continued his prayer, "Though I embrace the honor of being counted worthy to suffer shame for Christ's name, that won't make the suffering any less painful."[4]

Several psalms ran through his mind which captured some of his feelings:

Hear me, O Lord, for Thy loving kindness is good. Turn unto me according to the multitude of Thy tender mercies. Hide not Thy face from Thy servant, for I am in trouble. Hear me speedily. Draw nigh unto my soul, and redeem it. Deliver me because of mine enemies.[5]

O God, Thou art my God, early will I seek Thee. My soul thirsts for Thee. My flesh longs for Thee in a dry and thirsty land, where no water is. I yearn to see Thy power and Thy glory, so as I have seen Thee in the sanctuary. Because Thy loving kindness is better than life, my lips shall praise Thee. Thus I will bless Thee while I live. I will lift up my hands in Thy name.[6]

As with a sword in my bones my enemies reproach me; while they say daily unto me, Where is thy God?[7] *They that hate me without a cause are more than the hairs of my head. They that would destroy me, being mine enemies wrongfully, are mighty. O God, Thou knowest my foolishness, and my sins are not hidden from Thee. Let not them that wait upon Thee, O Lord God of hosts, be ashamed for my sake. Let not those that seek Thee be confounded for my sake, O God of Israel.*[8]

They that sit in the gate speak against me, and I was the song of the drunkards. But as for me, my prayer is unto Thee, O Lord, in an acceptable time. O God, in the multitude of Thy mercy hear me, in the truth of Thy salvation. Deliver me out of the mire, and let me not sink. Let me be delivered from them that hate me, and out of the deep waters. Let not the waterflood overflow me, neither let the deep swallow me up, and let not the pit shut her mouth upon me.[9]

Why art thou cast down, O my soul, and why art thou disquieted within me? Hope thou in God, for I shall yet praise Him, who is the health of my countenance, and my God.[10] *Truly my soul waits upon God. He only is my Rock and my salvation. He is my defense. I shall not be moved. He is my salvation and my glory. He is the Rock of my strength. My refuge is in God.*[11]

Restraining his anxiety, George earnestly resumed his vocal prayer. "Dear God in heaven, I beg Thee to hear my plea and grant me Thy mercy. Thou knowest all the thoughts and intents of my heart, and Thou canst purify me with Thy Holy Spirit and Thy love, that I may be fit to enter into Thy presence and dwell with Thee in holiness. I beg Thee to forgive all Thou seest amiss in me. Enlighten my understanding that I may know Thy will, and I shall be obedient to Thee in all things. I beg of Thee, grant me the courage and strength to endure all the adversity that shall be thrust upon me for Thy name's sake."

As George pondered how God might answer him, the thought flowed through his mind: *They will break my body, but I need not fear, for God shall heal me, if I abide in Him.* Tears rolled down his cheeks as his mind was filled with greater understanding of the coming suffering. He thought of the Savior's admonition: *And whosoever doth not bear his cross, and come after Me, cannot be My disciple.*[12]

My suffering will be unbearable, George thought, *but it will be of benefit to those who witness my faith and testimony. The Spirit whispers that the greater the injustice of my suffering in Christ's name, the more compelling and motivating my witness will be to those whose hearts are softened. Many will begin to exercise hope in Christ, making their own changes to follow His example and to obey God's commandments.*

Although Jesus Christ is the Light of the world, He taught that the faithful are also lights unto the world. He commanded His disciples to let their lights of righteousness shine, reflecting His glory to all men that others might also glorify our Father which is in heaven.[13] *As I see Thy hand revealed ever more clearly in what is to come, my faith in Thee swells, instilling confidence regarding the salvation of my soul, which brings unspeakable peace.*

As George's thought turned back to Sabra and their children, his anguish returned. *My beloved family will be without their father, but they will be sustained just as I have been by our Heavenly Father.* With immense confidence in his approach to his loving God, George continued his prayer, pleading desperately for the welfare of his wife and their children. Again the Holy Spirit spoke peace to his mind and heart.[14]

Reassured, George turned his pleas to the welfare of all those who would soon suffer for their faith in Jesus Christ. "Dear God, please deliver thy righteous children from the hands of wickedness and from the calamity before us, for their souls are precious before Thee. Remember them who have been driven from their inheritance for Thy name's sake. Break off the yoke of affliction that has been put upon them. Remember all Thy faithful servants. Sanctify and adorn us that our garments may be pure, that we may be clothed upon with robes of righteousness, with palms in our hands and crowns of glory upon our heads, that we may reap eternal joy for all our sufferings.[15] Above all, Thy will be done, O Lord, and not mine."

Again, the Spirit spoke peace to George's mind and heart, inspiring him with the words of the apostle Paul who recounted: *others had trial of cruel mockings and scourgings, yea, moreover of bonds and imprisonment. They were stoned, they were sawn asunder, were tempted, were slain with the sword, not accepting deliverance, that they might obtain a better resurrection.*[16]

With increasing fervor George pled for those like Diocletian, who were wrongly persecuting the faithful. "Have mercy, O Lord, upon the wicked who persecute Thy saints, that they may repent of their sins if repentance is to be found,[17] for many of them also know not what they do.[18] May the prejudices of the Emperor give way before the truth, that Thy people may obtain favor in the sight of all, that all the ends of the earth may know that Thou hast spoken and that Thy Son has come and

A Martyr's Faith

fulfilled Thy will in all things.[19] I've forgiven every man his trespasses against me, and now I pray for Thy mercy to cover them too." He felt the Spirit whispering reassurance to him that even such as these could partake of the Lord's mercy, but only on conditions of faith in Christ, sincere repentance, and obedience to God's commandments, these requirements being the same for all of God's children.

"May Thy church be adorned as a bride for that day when Thou shalt unveil the heavens, and Thy glory shall fill the earth."[20] As he concluded his prayer, George thought how much he desired the sustaining support of his father Gerontius, prior to the coming torture. He was confident the Lord could send his father, because of the experiences he'd previously had with him. However, no manifestation came to him, but yet again the calm assurance of the Spirit spoke peace to his mind and heart.[21]

Outside there was a gentle rumble of distant thunder, like the whispered voice of Almighty God. George couldn't hear words in the thunder, but as the gentle patter of rain began, overwhelming peace filled his soul.

****

CHAPTER FIFTY-FOUR
Sabra Prepares

Nicodemia, Eastern Roman Capital
22 April, 303 AD

*"...and He doth suffer that they may do this thing...
according to the hardness of their hearts,
that the judgments which He shall exercise
upon them may be just..."*[1]
Alma 14:11

****

Orion escorted Sabra to her lodgings for the night. His body filled the frame of the doorway as he peered inside to make sure she was safe. His concern for her safety went beyond this evening. There had been a slight pause in enforcement of the Christian persecution orders so the Emperor and the council could attend to George's trial and execution. Like many others, Orion sensed that this was only a temporary calm before the raging storm to come.

Feeling the danger, he spoke with quiet intensity to Sabra. "You should not attend George's torture and execution tomorrow. It won't be safe for anyone and especially not you. The entire nation knows of George's unyielding principles. There's no chance he'll renounce his faith and live. Therefore, there's no point in witnessing the exhibition, as there's no doubt of the outcome. There is great danger of rioting between the army and the Christians. Much blood may be spilled, including yours if you are there. The safest course to avoid violence is to leave Nicodemia early, before the torture starts, and definitely before the execution is complete."

"What will they do to George?" Sabra asked as she weighed his counsel.

"They'll break him, one way or another," Orion replied. "I've never seen a torture victim remain unbroken. If they break a man's spirit first, they'll still beat him and mark him, but they may let him live. If the man's will is strong, like George's, and they can't break his spirit, they'll break his body to attack his spirit."

"But how will they torture him?" Sabra pressed.

"I'd rather not go into the details. I don't like to think about it, much

A Martyr's Faith

less talk of it." In frustration Orion declared, "I just can't believe the Emperor has condemned George as an enemy!"

"Well, if you won't explain it to me, then I'll have to go see it for myself," Sabra suggested.

"No, Ma'am. You mustn't do that." Orion hesitated, considering the matter, and then continued. "Listen...I'll sketch it out for you so you won't have to go see...but I warned you. First, you need to understand this is a propaganda event, not the carriage of justice. It's a test of wills and a show of power. It's not about torture or execution. Intimidation and submission are the objectives. George may not submit, but in the end he'll be subjected to the Emperor's will when he's executed.

"Prisoners are handled carefully to inflict the greatest amount of pain while generating the least amount of mob sympathy. The Emperor wants to get a plea of submission while the people are still uncertain why the prisoner is submitting. This leads the crowd to believe that the prisoner's resolve is weak because his cause is not just.

"Often, the tormentors will inflict hidden injuries before the prisoner is presented to the crowd. Breaking ribs is a common tactic that's hard for the crowd to notice, but extremely painful. With some prisoners they might break the wrists or the ankles, without breaking the skin. They avoid damaging the head or jaw so that when the prisoner breaks...and he will break...the crowd will clearly hear his cries for mercy.

"The next phase is usually a thorough scourging. A common myth among the crowd is that if a man's cause is just, a severe whipping can and should be endured courageously. But many men have died from being scourged. The man wielding the scourge will know whether the prisoner is to live or to die at his hand, and he can make either one happen. If the prisoner is bleeding too much, the guards may sear his wounds with red hot irons to stop the bleeding and prolong the torture. With George, the goal is submission, so the torture will be carefully controlled to encourage his plea for mercy."

"What follows the scourging?" Sabra asked.

"That often depends on the mood of the crowd. If there's little or no sympathy for the prisoner, such as in the case of a known murderer, the brutality of torture may be unbounded. If a prisoner has simply defied the Emperor's will, as the crowd begins to sympathize with the prisoner, the process can move quickly to execution. With any prolonged attempt to gain the prisoner's submission, the Emperor risks riot, chaos, and a blood bath among his subjects. I have no doubt he is taking such a risk with George.

"Another common torture is dragging the scourged prisoner behind a horse through the square. Several factors show the intent of this torture.

The longer the distance and the faster the speed, the more likely the prisoner is to die from the dragging. Being pulled by your feet is more dangerous to the head. Being pulled by the hands often dislocates the shoulders or shatters the elbows. When submission is desired, it may be a slower, shorter pull. In most cases the prisoner is stripped of clothing. Can you see it in your mind, or shall I go on?" Orion asked.

"Please continue," Sabra replied soberly. "I need to be prepared for whatever happens."

"Why? You're not going to witness this torture, are you?" Orion challenged.

"I hope I don't have to, but I must follow the Spirit wherever He may lead. He may bid me to go and offer George my support," Sabra responded simply.

Orion shook his head in protest. "Your support isn't likely to help George. It's likely to distract him, making it harder for him to endure the torture. It's also likely to get you killed. I beg you not to make matters worse for yourself and others by going to the execution tomorrow."

"If God bids me to go, I'll go, and it will be the best thing I can do for myself and all others," Sabra stated with firm resolve.

With increasing concern Orion continued. "Well, if the prisoner survives the dragging, other tortures will follow. Forcing the prisoner's feet into molten lead may be done. This is extremely painful and would require amputation of both lower legs for the prisoner to have any chance to live. However, if this is done, the prisoner is surely marked for death.

"They may also use a wheel of swords if the prisoner refuses to submit. In that case, the guards take the wheel of a cart and replace the spokes with sharpened sword blades. The prisoner then has his arms and legs pulled through the wheel, between the sword blade spokes. Hands and feet are tied together on the other side. The wheel is then rotated in either direction, causing the sword blades to lacerate the limbs and slice the muscles down to the bone. Often the wheel rotations dislocate joints and break limbs. This torture is a signal that the goal of submission has been abandoned, and death is near. Few men survive.

"Of course you're familiar with crucifixion. It's not common when the goal is submission, but sometimes it's done anyway. It frequently follows a thorough scourging. Also, one concern with Christians is that they'll be viewed as more valiant martyrs for Christ if they're put to death in the same way Jesus was.

"At any time, the Emperor can order an immediate beheading of the prisoner. This is usually considered a token of mercy but often it's because he's become impatient. It's also a common choice of condemned Roman citizens who are sometimes given the privilege of choosing their own manner of death." Orion paused again, thinking. Finally he said, "Mum, I beg you not to attend the torture and execution. I really can't help you any more with this."

Sabra was silent for a long moment, trying to absorb what she could without breaking down. "Thank you for being honest with me," she said quietly. Silently, she turned and disappeared through the doorway into her lodgings.

Alone in her room, Sabra dropped to her knees beside the bed. She pulled her bag from under the bed and reached inside. Moving a few personal items she saw the dagger she had brought for protection. It was useless against the tide of anguish that was flooding over her. Quickly, she moved the dagger aside and removed the scriptures that had been carefully packed at the bottom. She opened the pages in an anxious search for guidance and answers. Silently she read the words of James: *If any of you lack wisdom, let him ask of God, that giveth to all men liberally, and upbraideth not; and it shall be given him. But let him ask in faith, nothing wavering.*[2]

Sabra felt that God might require the sacrifice of all things by her cherished husband, but the burden upon her was growing by the moment. Her flood of emotions broke forth in gasping sobs as she felt the weight of the loss that would surely come. She wondered, *What consolation might the Lord, in His mercy, provide? What might I venture to ask of the Lord that would not be amiss and can be paired with real faith?* She prayed, "Holy Father, I give thanks unto Thee, for Thou hast made us to be partakers of the inheritance of the saints in light.[3] Hear my plea and bestow Thy mercies liberally. Do not leave me comfortless. Send Thy Comforter, that He may abide with me forever."[4]

****

CHAPTER FIFTY-FIVE
Truth Stands

Nicodemia, Eastern Roman Capital
23 April, 303 AD

"I love them that love Me; and those that seek Me early shall find Me."[1]
Proverbs 8:17

****

George spent a sleepless night seeking communion with God to bear him up through the coming trials. He thought and felt the earnest pleadings of David's psalms: *Show me Thy ways, O Lord. Teach me Thy paths. Lead me in Thy truth, and teach me, for Thou art the God of my salvation. On Thee do I wait all the day. Remember, O Lord, Thy tender mercies and Thy loving kindnesses, for they have been ever of old. Remember not the sins of my youth, nor my transgressions. According to Thy tender mercies remember Thou me, O Lord.*[2] *For I have trusted in Thee, O Lord. Thou art my God. My times are in Thy hand. Deliver me from the hand of mine enemies, and from them that persecute me. Make Thy face to shine upon Thy servant. Save me for Thy mercies' sake. Let me not be ashamed, O Lord, for I have called upon Thee. Let the wicked be ashamed, and let them be silent in the grave."*[3]

As George pondered on the anticipated events of the day, his mind was filled with a clear impression that he was not alone. It was as if he could hear the words of his unseen Companion: *The night is far spent, the day is at hand: let Us therefore cast off the works of darkness, and let Us put on the armor of light.*[4]

With the dawn, George asked the prison guard to have the tribune bring paper and ink so he could record his testimony and will. The tribune was well known to George, but not a partisan as to the Christian persecutions. He knew events in the square wouldn't begin until about the third hour so he took the time to write as George requested.

George's personal effects remained undisturbed in the tribunes' quarters. He thought of Sabra but decided he couldn't direct anything to her without risking the safety of his family. He also considered all his faithful and trusted companions in the northeast and concluded that the peace and prosperity he had helped established among the people, with righteous leaders, was the best and only thing he could give them at this time. Nor could he attempt to convey anything to the church without putting the saints in peril. "The money I have in my quarters is to be distributed for the benefit of the poor in Nicodemia," he directed.

When he thought about his most prized possession, his copy of the scriptures written in Sabra's hand, he desperately wanted to preserve them but knew he couldn't will them specifically to anyone, as his will was sure to be reviewed by someone in authority at some time either before or after his death. Remembering that this treasure was in his saddlebags, he thought of his horses and felt a strong impression. "I leave my horses to Constantine, with the desire that they be granted the honor of continued service to the Republic. With this bequest I include my saddle, saddlebags, and their contents." George hoped no one would dare to inspect the saddlebags' contents before transferring them to such a highly honored military officer.

"Finally, I ask that my body be returned to Palestine for burial beside my parents. I ask that my battle sword, Ascalon, and my signet ring be sent along with my body." The tribune accepted George's instructions for his personal effects and made the arrangements. However, he made no such promise as to his body and burial. Those requests would require the Emperor's approval.

*****

Shortly, the tribune returned to escort the prisoner to the priest's sanctuary. Sober about his future, George imagined that a final desperate proposal would be made for his submission. By now he was sure they knew their efforts would be futile.

As they entered the sanctuary, George saw Athanasius and Alexandria, as he'd expected. What he hadn't expected was the personal appearance of the Emperor. Diocletian looked old and tired, but he was determined. "George, my allies report there is no progress with you on submission to my edicts. They say you're certain of your one true and living God. Will you preach this doctrine of Christ to me also?"

"My lord, I will preach Christ to all men if you desire it," George replied.

"Then tell me of this God that I may take the measure of Him with whom I compete for your loyalty and faithfulness!" Diocletian commanded.

"How can one measure the infinite?" George asked, feeling the Spirit guiding him. "The one true and living God is the Father of us all, infinite and eternal. He loves us and will do all things necessary for our blessing. He sent His Only Begotten Son, Jesus Christ, to come down among the children of men and dwell in the flesh. After working many mighty miracles among the children of men, Christ suffered Himself to be abused, mocked, scourged, cast out, and spit upon, being disowned by His own people, yet He reviled not. He subjected His flesh to the will of His Father in all things, even until He was led as a Lamb to the slaughter, being crucified for the sins of the world, becoming subject even unto death, the will of the Son being swallowed up in the will of the Father.[5] All this was done that Christ might redeem His people.

"Because He was perfectly obedient to His Father, death could not hold Him. He reclaimed His body through the justice of the Father, gaining the victory and breaking the bands of death, thus claiming the power of the resurrection. He ascended into heaven, having His bowels filled with mercy, being filled with compassion towards the children of men. Now He stands between justice and all men, having taken upon Himself their iniquities and their transgressions, having redeemed them and satisfied the demands of justice, receiving the power to make intercession and grant mercy to all the children of men who will exercise faith in Him unto repentance.[6]

"Who shall declare His generation, and who shall be the children of His redemption? Those that have received the words of all the holy prophets and, believing in Him, have looked forward to that day of redemption with faith and hope for a remission of their sins. These are His children and heirs of the kingdom of God. These are they whose sins He has borne, for whom He has died, to redeem them from their transgressions. Seeing that He has purchased them with His own blood, are they not His children? Now the time shall come that the salvation of the Lord shall be declared to every nation, kindred, tongue, and people. The watchmen of the Lord shall lift up their voices and sing, for they shall see eye to eye when the Lord shall bring again Zion. The Lord will make bare His holy arm in the eyes of all the nations, and all the ends of the earth shall see the salvation of our God."[7]

Diocletian looked into the prisoner's eyes and spoke in a low but firm voice, "George, the games are over. We must resolve this impasse now or you will be executed. I cannot recall my edicts. We can still save you and get you away from here if you'll submit to my decrees and make a token public offering of homage to the Roman gods and to me as the divine authority on earth. In addition to saving you, we'll give you land in Palestine, along with the cattle, slaves, and money necessary for you to prosper. You can find peace, and perhaps raise a family. Take this offer. Help save us all," the Emperor pled, exhausted by the conflict within himself.

"Nothing has changed," George replied calmly, still bound in chains.

"I cannot recall my words, for they are true.[8] I cannot make sport of the God of heaven, for the word of His truth is inviolable. I know my God can deliver me from death, but if He doesn't, I will be faithful and never serve your gods or worship you.[9] Till I die I will retain my integrity."[10]

"What benefit can there possibly be in you being executed for your principles?" the Emperor challenged, chiding George for his stubbornness.

George responded calmly, "If my faithfulness to God has no influence on anyone but me that will be sufficient. I will not relinquish my claim to be, 'Always faithful!'"

"Don't be naïve and act the fool! It's unbecoming of you," Diocletian growled, his mood darkening measurably. "And don't force me to have you put to death for your arrogance."

"Shall I be put to death for my arrogance, or for yours?" George asked.

"Enough!" the Emperor boomed. Silently he struggled with the anger, frustration, and anguish within himself. He knew there would be no compromise between them, and his hands would be stained with George's blood. He knew Galerius and the imperial council would also be stained with blood, but this was no consolation.

"You believe you have no choice but to execute me, and so you shall," George replied softly. "But I warn you not to disregard the true and living God simply because He requires that my testimony be sealed with my blood. For the Lord suffers the righteous to be slain by the wicked according to the hardness of their hearts, that the judgments which He shall exercise upon the wicked in His wrath may be just. Therefore, you need not suppose that the righteous are lost because they are slain. They enter into the rest of the Lord their God.[11] Yet shall the blood of the innocent stand as a witness against the wicked and cry mightily against them at the last day.[12]

"The gates of history turn on small hinges, and so do people's lives.[13] I speak openly of what I know to be true. Long have I believed and hoped in a God of righteousness and love. At length, I've passed beyond faith to a sure knowledge that such a God lives and that Jesus Christ is His divine Son. Divine authority on earth flows from Christ. The signs of God will come, such that none can deny them. It will do no good for a soul to believe in them then, if it did not believe them before or work righteousness through its faith.[14]

"I cannot separate truth from truth. My faith in God and the truth will abide. I choose not to leave my eternal inheritance of faith, hope, and glory. I shall never regard you as more than the clear signs of God that I've received, or as more than Him Who created us. So decree what you will. Your words and your power touch only the life of this world.[15] There's only one solution to our impasse and that is for you to move toward God, for He is unchanging, having established Himself in righteousness forever. I will not recall my words, for to do so would be to offend the one true and living God, to whom I look for salvation in the eternities."

Diocletian was agitated but had been unable to interrupt. When George had concluded, he raised his voice in response. "George! You must set aside all this talk of God and truth and just look at this matter realistically. I don't care what you really believe, or even what's true for that matter. What I care about is sparing your life and averting civil chaos. I have no hope of doing both if you persist in your refusal to submit. Your continued defiance will surely result in the deaths of many innocent people before peace and order are restored. You can't want that on your conscience. Do the right thing now. Save your people and the empire as well."

George felt indignation well up inside him as he replied with a subtle voice of thunder, "You weary the Lord with your words when you say everyone who does evil is good in the sight of the gods.[16] I will do the right thing, by God. If you will repent and turn to Him, He'll save you, the people, and the Republic. But being part of a wicked and perverse generation, you harden your hearts and stiffen your necks against the word of the Lord. How long do you suppose the Lord will suffer you? How long will you suffer yourselves to be led by foolish and blind guides? How long will you choose darkness rather than light?"[17]

Diocletian hadn't been rebuked like this in almost twenty years. It irritated him more than a little. He was calloused to taking a man's life, but he believed he was able to assert his will and save a man's life at his pleasure. George had shattered that image with his rolling thunder. Still, Diocletian tried to regain his stoic façade.

After a short pause, George pled more gently, "Beloved Emperor Diocletian, again I beg your tolerance and ask that you withdraw your edicts of condemnation and persecution against the Christians and that you pardon my faults."

Feeling the futility of his efforts at gaining George's submission, the Emperor emphatically declared, "I can't take back what I've decreed! I can't submit to you and maintain order in the empire! George, you leave me no choice but to proceed with your scheduled torture and execution! And now you've made me angry!" he shouted as he turned and stormed out of the pagan sanctuary.

It had been a long time since they had seen Diocletian passionate with anger. Alexandria and Athanasius looked at each other with questioning

A Martyr's Faith

eyes as if to say, *What now?* They had been unable to identify any objective flaw in the Christian doctrine, and all their bribes offered for George's submission had been soundly rejected. The Empress turned to George and probed, "Have you no fear of death then?"

"At this point, I would still prefer life," he responded. "However, the terms must be acceptable to God, in either case. Death is not as strong a motivator for me as the choice of how I live the next few hours of my life. I know my choices will have an impact on the lives of others, and I dare say, many who witness my submission to God may be influenced for good. So, shall we agree to disagree?" George proposed.

"I believe we are more in agreement than what you may think," Alexandria responded. "Still, that doesn't bring us any closer to reconciliation with Diocletian."

"If I could see any way to end this madness and restore unity with the Emperor, I would take us down that path," Athanasius offered sincerely.

"I have a better idea," George said quietly, drawing their gazes. "Let's agree to reconcile ourselves with all truth. Diocletian's iniquity is born of his love of the glory and the vain things of this world. He knows he transgresses the laws of God and tramples them under his feet. If the rulers of this people don't repent of their sins and iniquities, the judgments of the Almighty against them will no longer be stayed.[18] They must awake from the deep sleep of hell and shake off the awful chains of iniquity with which they are bound, which bind the children of men, that they are carried away captive to the eternal gulf of misery and woe. If all men will hearken unto the words of the Lord and His holy prophets, they shall not perish, but be blessed. But if they reject the words of the Lord and the witnesses of His servants, their blessings shall be taken away and given to those who will obey Him.[19]

"The voice of the Lord is unto all men, and there is none to escape. There is no eye that shall not see, neither ear that shall not hear, neither heart that shall not be penetrated. And the rebellious shall be pierced with much sorrow, for their iniquities shall be spoken upon the housetops, and their secret acts shall be revealed. Wherefore the voice of the Lord is unto the ends of the earth, that all who will hear may hear. Prepare for that which is to come, for the Lord is nigh, and the arm of the Lord shall be revealed. The day will come that they who will not hear the voice of the Lord, neither the voice of his servants, neither give heed to the words of the prophets and apostles, shall be cut off from among His people."[20]

George paused for a moment, considering that this might be his final witness and testimony to these two souls that he had grown to love. Earnestly he continued, "We cannot hide our crimes from God. Except we repent, they will stand as a testimony against us at the last day. Therefore, let us repent and forsake our sins and go no more after the lusts of our eyes. Cross ourselves in all these things, for except we do this, we can in nowise inherit the kingdom of God. Remember, and take it upon you to cross yourselves in all these things.[21] Prove God's word by doing His will and you shall know that the doctrine is of God.[22] I've come to know all these things for myself, and that is why I will never deny the only true and living God."

"George, we know you are convinced of the doctrine of Christ," Alexandria spoke mildly. "We can see it in your countenance and bearing. Your convictions do you great credit and honor, yet they will cost you your life. We do not yet possess the faith you have, and therefore we fear to walk the path you have chosen."

George heard her words, but more importantly, he felt the Spirit whispering of changes that were real, though not yet complete. "I would to God that I could persuade you and all men to trust fully in God and not provoke Him to anger, but that all would believe in Christ, view His death, suffer His cross, and bear the shame of the world."[23] Patiently he asked, "Are you yet ashamed to take upon you the name of Christ? Do you still think the miserable praise of the world is of greater value than an endless happiness of eternal glory?"

"What do you know of the true desires of my heart?" Alexandria whispered.

George studied her countenance for answers. "I know you have taken notice of the needs of others. You begin to give heed to the hungry, the needy, the naked, the sick, and the afflicted, to the satisfaction of your own soul.[24] You yearn to do good, and I glory in your desires." George paused for rebuttal, but there was none. With slight relief he continued, "Whether you hide what is in your heart or reveal it, God knows it all. He knows what's in the heavens and what's in the earth. He has power over all things. God invites all to remember Him, for He is full of kindness to those that serve Him.[25] This is why I'm not ashamed of the gospel of Christ. It is the power of God unto salvation to everyone that believes."[26]

"But it's a salvation that only comes after indescribable suffering," Alexandria anguished.

"If it is the will of God that we also suffer, it is better to suffer at the hands of this world for doing good than to suffer at the hand of God for doing evil,"[27] George replied hopefully.

****

CHAPTER FIFTY-SIX
Torture and Dragging

Nicodemia, Eastern Roman Capital
23 April, 303 AD

"...it is by faith that angels appear and minister unto men;..."[1]
Moroni 7:37

****

As the third hour came, the spring morning remained cloudy and threatening. Many leaders were already in place to watch the ordeal from the palace balcony above the square. Alexandria, Athanasius, and Constantine, along with many from the imperial council were in position to witness it. The Emperor would be one of the last to arrive, with his full complement of tribunes.

"The gathering crowd is already large, perhaps 10,000 or more," Athanasius observed.

"Everyone knows of George," Alexandria responded. "His legend preceded him and he has done little to tarnish it since he arrived in Nicodemia. He has searched out the poor and oppressed, working with them to generate sources of honest income. His work has significantly reduced crime and abuse among the people. Not everyone knows him personally, but most know somebody who knows him. Nearly all believe him to be a good and true friend of the people and of the Republic. They don't understand why Diocletian has commanded that George be publicly tortured and executed over a question of religion."

"And there's the catch," Athanasius whispered. "Diocletian has convinced himself that the injustices he inflicts upon George are necessary to keep his other subjects submissive to his commands. This is where he risks civil unrest, for the mob will only bear so much injustice before it reacts in violent ways with unpredictable results. This crowd knows of the edicts against the Christians and they know George has openly defied the Emperor, refusing to implement them. They expect this defiance will come to an end this day, one way or another. Most don't believe in any of the gods or their religious tales, but they revel in the celebrations. They're here out of curiosity for the spectacle. Few understand why George would be willing to die for his faith. This causes the people to have questions brewing in their minds. George knows

Saint George and The Dragon

these questions will be answered in error if he recants his testimony of Jesus Christ as the Son of the living God. But if he endures to the end, many may be convinced of the Christian God."

*****

  The guards who came for George were not the regular tribunes. They were a group of blood lusting curs handpicked by Galerius for this task. Before they presented him to the public, they began their brutal torture according to the commands they'd been given. George had been taken to the stocks in the dungeon. With his legs confined, the guards forced him to lay back while they placed a heavy stone on his chest, keeping it balanced there against his movements. With the weight on his chest, each breath he let out was almost impossible to recover. George had to keep his lungs inflated or the weight of the stone would have crushed his ribs.
  With the stone still on his chest, the guards strapped wooden blocks, like shoes, to his feet. However, the blocks were filled with nails pounded through and protruding inward toward the soles of his feet. Next, they gave his head and face a rough shave, a standard for prisoners. Then they cut away the Roman legion emblem tattoo from his right shoulder, searing the wound with a heated knife blade. George knew if he cried out in anguish, he would likely succumb under the weight of the stone, so he bore this abuse in silence to the surprise and begrudging admiration of his tormentors. With no apparent progress in breaking the prisoner into submission, and with a schedule to keep, the brutes removed the stone and simply broke several of George's ribs with wooden clubs.
  As they forced him to stand, he realized there were barely enough nail points to carry his weight, if he remained balanced. As his balance shifted, the nail points worked their way into the soles of his feet. George could barely breathe after the clubbing his ribs had taken, and it was difficult for him to stand upright and still. At least the pain in his ribs distracted him from the pain on his right shoulder. He watched his tormentors carefully, but didn't recoil from them. He couldn't stop them from doing what they would do, but he could be ready and control his reactions as much as possible, showing his own courage and strength.

*****

  Sabra's hooded figure moved quietly through the somber crowd. She could see George, who stood in chains, stripped of his shirt, having an odd pair of shoes strapped tightly onto his feet. His shoulder was mangled and bloody. He looked physically weak, which she had never seen before. She thought, *I doubt he'll see me in the sea of faces open to his view. I'm not as tall as most men, which is just as well, as it seems best not to attract any attention to myself in this place. I've followed the promptings of the Spirit thus far. I've pled to the Lord for additional guidance. I'll wait upon the Lord before I go further.*

*****

The crowd was full of Christians and non-Christians alike but few were trying to promote their beliefs or to attract the attention of anyone. Most were intently watching the raised platform where a man they knew as very handsome and strong stood, stripped half naked, shackled and wary, having obviously been given a beating.

The crowd hushed as the Emperor appeared on his balcony overlooking the public square, flanked by his Empress, his imperial priest, many of the council, and a few other leaders. Raising his voice he ordered, "Galerius, Caesar of the eastern empire and general of the Roman legions, present the condemned prisoner to the people and proceed with the punishment, as I have commanded."

Galerius stepped forward on the platform near George, who stood with hands chained to separate wooden restraining posts. Pointing at the condemned man, Galerius boomed out to the crowd, "George, son of Gerontius, citizen of Rome, you have disgraced yourself and shamed this people. You've been tried and convicted on charges of insubordination and sedition. On this 'Good Friday' of the Christians, you've been sentenced to torture and death for your refusal to obey our divine Emperor by renouncing Christianity, paying homage to the Roman gods, and worshipping the Emperor. You see the crowd. Will you persist in leading them down a pointless path of pain and torment, or will you renounce your faith in Christ as the Son of God?" Galerius framed his question as simply as he could to be sure George would remain defiant.

George tried to draw breath so he could respond with boldness. He nearly fainted with the pain, but fainting could not be the end of this day of testimony. In a voice just loud enough for Galerius to hear George charged, "Bask in your brief bit of power! For truly, you are making straightway for hell!"[2]

Before Galerius could think to respond, George took a painfully deep breath and loudly proclaimed for all to hear, "I worship Jesus Christ, the Son of the living God. I invite all men to exercise faith in Christ and do His will. Thus shall you surely come to know the divinity of Christ and of His power to redeem and glorify all who believe on Him.[3] I will never recall my words, and I will never deny Almighty God, nor His Holy Son."

Seeking to antagonize George further, Galerius loudly challenged, "If your God has such power, call upon Him to deliver you from torture and death.[4] But there is no God of the Christians. Else show us a sign that we may be convinced there is a God. Show us He has power and then we will believe.[5] Otherwise, plead for mercy and a swift execution."

George responded to Galerius, loud enough for all to hear. "You've had signs enough. You have the testimonies of the holy prophets. The sacred records are laid before you. Even the earth and all things upon the face of it, and its motion, and also all the planets which move in their regular form stand as witnesses that there is a Supreme Creator.[6] Will you tempt the anger of a just God further by denying the signs which you have, and yet demanding more?" After a brief pause, George whispered to Galerius. "All can see that you are possessed with a lying spirit, having put off the Spirit of God that it has no place in you, but the devil has power over you, leading you by the nose to persecute the children of God."[7]

Galerius was more than a little annoyed with George, who always had more to say than just 'yes' or 'no.' *I'm not going to let that ruin my victory today,* he thought. *I'll make the torture as painful as possible, careful to avoid inflicting any mortal wounds, prolonging your ordeal to emphasize my own power and, if possible, to extract a plea for a merciful death from a broken man. The Emperor wants you to renounce your faith, but I just want you to die, slowly and painfully.* "Scourge him! Forty lashes!" Galerius commanded the tormentor.

The whip cracked as it tore at George's skin. The tormentor was skilled. He opened narrow bands of flesh from the base of the prisoner's neck all the way down to his calves. George's back was angry with pain, but he solidly stood his ground. When the scourging had ended, there was a scuffling of feet behind him and suddenly he felt the tinge of red hot iron searing several spots where the bleeding was excessive. This raised an involuntary cry of agony and George felt his legs nearly fail him.

Galerius smiled cruelly as he taunted, "Recall your words now and plead for mercy!"

George gasped in pain but rising with courage he declared, "I will not recall my words, for they are true! I will suffer even until death and yet I won't recall my words, and they shall stand as a testimony against you in the day of God's judgment."[8]

"Oh, you most certainly will suffer, even until death!" Galerius mocked.

A slight breeze arose from the northeast and the clouds became noticeably more ominous. The crowd was beginning to get anxious over the torture. Questions kept growing in their minds. *Is there truly a living God? Can such a God be known, as this man has testified? If the Roman gods truly exist, why don't they inflict their own punishments on George? Will George's God save him somehow? Will there really be a day of God's judgment?* Although the answers were still unclear to the people, sympathy was growing for this tortured man, and for his faith.

"Drag this traitor through the square for all to see!" Galerius commanded next. According to prior instructions, several guards took hold of George's shackles and pulled him off the raised platform. After tying him by his wrists behind a large horse, a guard led the horse around the square at a moderate trot. The crowd parted in front of the horse as it went.

To keep from being dragged, George had to run behind the horse. This drove the nails within his shoes deep into the soles of his feet, which soon lost their function. Falling forward, he rolled onto his back, his arms and hands stretched overhead toward the trotting horse. The torn flesh of his back dragged across the stones leaving a trail of blood wherever he was pulled. He feared to roll over as that would expose his face and elbows to the cobblestones. Suddenly, he felt the horse lunge ahead, bouncing him up awkwardly. When he came down, the back of his head struck on the stone and all went black.

*****

Relieved of pain, George felt himself passing calmly from darkness into light. But this wasn't the dark light of day. As he moved forward, this shockingly bright light was driving the darkness away. His shackles were gone and he was dressed in a white robe. He saw his father, Gerontius, dressed in white and transfigured in glorious light, coming towards him.

Father called gently, "George, you are blessed for bearing persecution in the Lord's name and for His sake. Great shall be your reward, for so persecuted they many righteous men before you."[9]

"Father, oh my father, is it done?" George pled earnestly.

"My son, your mission is not yet complete. You must return and finish the work of the Lord, testifying boldly of Father, Son, and Holy Ghost. I'll be here waiting for you when you come again. Don't fear my son, for the Lord redeems the souls of those who serve Him. None of them that trust in Him shall be left desolate."[10]

In humility George responded, "Be it unto me according to thy word."[11]

Tears filled his eyes as Gerontius commanded, "Awake thou that sleepest! Arise from the dead and Christ shall give thee light!"[12]

****

CHAPTER FIFTY-SEVEN
The Quicklime Casket

Nicodemia, Eastern Roman Capital
23 April, 303 AD

"Therefore shall all hands be faint, and every man's heart shall melt..."[1]
Isaiah 13:7

****

The wind picked up a little and the clouds grew darker as the lifeless body was drawn to the platform at the front of the square. The crowd was uncertain, but few had enthusiasm for this killing. The guards untied George's body from the horse. After checking and finding no pulse, they carried him back onto the platform. Galerius looked at his men and asked, "Is he dead?" As their heads began to nod affirmatively, George's body stirred. *Never mind their incompetence*, Galerius thought with a cruel smile, *I'm not done with George.*

"Sear his bleeding wounds!" Galerius shouted.

The burning pain of the hot irons nearly caused another loss of consciousness. A bucket of water and some smelling salts were administered to rouse George's senses more fully. Along with consciousness came the return of unbearable pain. George felt certain his left hip had been dislocated or broken by the pull. The pain there was sharp and grinding and he could not bear weight on it. Into his mind came the Psalm: *O Lord, Thou hast brought up my soul from the grave: Thou hast kept me alive, that I should not go down to the pit.*[2] Knowing the Lord had further work for him to do, George didn't question his situation, but he did wonder again why so many blessings that come to us in life are disguised so thoroughly as curses.

"George! Confess that your God cannot save you," Galerius demanded. "Beg for mercy and perhaps our holy Emperor will grant you a quick death."

George could barely breathe through the pain, but he knew he must now testify again. With intense but reverent conviction he spoke, "I worship God, our Father, and His Son, Jesus Christ, the Lord of Life. There is none but Him to whom we may look for redemption, through His atoning blood and the sanctification of the Holy Spirit. Cursed with the sword be those workers of darkness who conspire for power except they repent."[3]

Galerius felt anger every time George warned of conspirators. Each time the warning was raised, his allies on the imperial council became paralyzed, fearing they would be exposed. It was time to silence George forever. "Throw the prisoner in quicklime!" Galerius ordered.

Up on the balcony, the Emperor sat seething and sullen, his mood seeming to darken with the sky. *I'm helpless to stop this madness,* he thought. *If I intervene, I risk losing the imperial council or the crowd. I can't bear to watch, but I dare not leave.*

Constantine also watched from the palace balcony, a silent witness to the torture of his friend. *I have the courage to act and intervene,* his mind raced. *I must stop this injustice, but the Spirit constrains me to be still.*[4] *Did Peter have similar feelings as he watched the torture and execution of the Lord, uncertain of how the terrible scene served God's purposes, but constrained by the Spirit? My anguish is full of guilt, frustration, confusion, and helplessness.* Still, he kept his vigil, waiting with restrained impatience.

A gasp arose from the crowd as the guards brought out a coffin sized wooden box filled with limey alkaline powder. Picking George up by each limb, they raised him over the open box and dropped him in, being careful not to get any of the powder on themselves. George's reaction was immediate as the chemicals began to burn in the lacerated flesh of his body. He didn't have much strength left, but he was able to throw his right leg over the side of the box, tipping it on its side, allowing him to roll out before he succumbed to the burning pain.

*****

For a second time George found himself relieved from his suffering, moving from darkness into a shock of bright light. Again he had no wounds and his garments were white and luminescent. He saw his shining father coming towards him, with tears rolling down his glowing face.

"Father, is it done? May I stay with you and rest now?" George begged.

"Not yet, George. It's not done yet. The Lord yet has work for you to do. My son, have faith in the Lord and His ways, for He will bring about all His purposes in fulfilling the covenants and promises He has made unto the children of men. Do not fear to serve God further, my son. I'll come again to meet you when you return. Now awake, and endure in faith to the end."

****

CHAPTER FIFTY-EIGHT
The Wheel of Swords

Nicodemia, Eastern Roman Capital
23 April, 303 AD

*"Who shall separate us from the love of Christ?
Shall tribulation, or distress, or persecution,
or famine, or nakedness, or peril, or sword?"*[1]
Romans 8:35

****

Galerius stared at George's lifeless body as the quicklime continued to react with his flesh. There was no respiration in his chest. Impatient, Galerius again ordered his men to check George's body for signs of life. The crowd waited in hushed anticipation as the guards approached cautiously, trying to avoid the caustic powder on their victim for fear of burning themselves. As one guard reached out slowly to assess the prisoner, George turned his head and reached up with his right arm, as if pleading for help. The startled guards recoiled with fear and surprise showing in their eyes.

Speaking deeply to the hushed crowd, George testified boldly declaring, "God lives! Jesus Christ is His divine Son!"

Galerius felt his rage increase with each word from George's mouth. The crowd was manifestly against the quicklime torture. They were uncertain of the justice of any of this abuse. Among them a growing chant for mercy had begun. With a fierce passion Galerius spewed the order to his men, "Rack the prisoner on the wheel of swords!"

Afraid of touching the quicklime on George's body, the guards doused his forearms and lower legs with water in a vain attempt to make those areas safe to touch. Still wary, they wrapped their hands in rags and then pulled George to the wheel of swords. They threaded his arms and legs through the sword blade spokes, tying his hands and feet together so they couldn't be withdrawn. Angry, Galerius commanded, "Deny your God and beg for a merciful death!"

"I will never deny my God! I look only to Him for mercy!" George replied solidly. Then, directing himself to the crowd he implored, "We must all turn from our wicked ways. Repent of your evil doings, of your lies and deceits, your whoredoms and your idolatries. Set aside your murders, your priestcraft, your envy, and strife. Deny yourselves all wickedness and abominations. Come unto Christ and be baptized in His name that you may receive a remission of your sins and be filled with the Holy Ghost, that you may be numbered among His people and be lifted up at the last day."[2]

"Mercy! Mercy!" The rising chant of the crowd intensified, becoming almost aggressive.

Galerius was insensitive to the crowd. He'd never been one to rule with compassion or by gentle persuasion. He counted those among Diocletian's occasional weaknesses. Fear and intimidation were the tools he embraced, ever seeking to strike greater terror into the hearts of his enemies and allies alike. His heart was hardened, delighting continually in the shedding of blood.[3] *The more brutal, the better*, he thought. Firmly he gripped the wheel of swords and abruptly rotated it hard to the right. The blades immediately inflicted lengthy lacerations to each arm and leg, slicing the flesh deep to the bone. An involuntary gasp escaped George's lips and his body went limp. Galerius turned the wheel back to the left causing more deep lacerations, but there was no more resistance or reaction from the body. Though the wounds were deep, there was no gushing of blood. Galerius was sure George's heart had failed and was no longer beating. Brashly he cut the bindings and ordered his men, "Remove his body from the wheel!" Still careful of the quicklime, they laid him on a beam, tying him across the chest and feet. Raising the head of the beam, they showed the crowd that the Emperor's will had clearly been done.

Covered by her cloak and hood, Sabra stood still in the crowd, drawing no attention. Her heart had risen to her throat, choking her breath as tears rolled down her cheeks. She now sought mercy herself as she whispered, "Lord, how long wilt Thou look on? Rescue my darling from these lions, and our souls from their destructions."[4]

*****

For the third time George felt himself emerge from darkness, moving toward bright light. His body and garments were white and glowing brighter than before. His glorious father came towards him. "Father, is it done? Please say I may stay with you now," George pleaded.

"Not yet, my son," Gerontius replied earnestly. "Now we know the Lord, and now is our salvation nearer than when we only believed. We have put on the armor of light. Let us endure till all the works of darkness be cast off us forever. Your mission is nearly complete, but now it is high time for you to awaken out of your sleep.[5] You must go back once more, but fear not. The next time you come through the veil from mortality to eternity, your mission will be complete and you will be received by the Lord. He will wipe away your tears and fill your heart with His joy and peace. His priests will be clothed with righteousness, and His saints will shout for joy.[6] I'll be here awaiting your return. All glory be to God the Father and His Son Jesus Christ. Now awake my son, and be faithful to the end. I love you."

Encouraged by his father's promise that he was near the end of his ordeal, George spoke, "I love you too, Father. Not my will, but the will of God be done."[7]

The veil began to part again and George felt himself returning to the pain of his mortal body. Before the veil closed, he glanced back toward heaven and pled humbly, "O God, forsake me not until I have shown Thy strength unto this generation and Thy power to everyone that is come to witness. Thou, which hast shown me great and sore troubles, shall quicken me again, and shall bring me up again from the depths of the earth."[8] And then the veil was drawn.

****

CHAPTER FIFTY-NINE
Testimony and Execution

Nicodemia, Eastern Roman Capital
23 April, 303 AD

*"Nor can a soul die except by God's leave,
the term being fixed as by writing."*[1]
Qur'an 3:145

****

Suddenly, George stirred visibly. The crowd was astonished. Constantine looked down from the palace balcony and whispered under his breath, "Thou art poured out like water, and all thy bones are out of joint. Thy heart is like wax melted in the midst of thy bowels. Thy strength is dried up, yet thou endurest in faith.[2] Nor can a soul die except by God's leave, the term of life being fixed as by writing.[3] It's as if the Lord God poured His Spirit into thy soul."[4]

Galerius was mortified. He didn't believe in George's God, but he began to fear he might be mistaken in his unbelief, yet he could not change his course. Hoping there would be no response, he challenged George. "Will you now renounce your God and plead for mercy?" As Galerius looked on for any answer, he saw a visible transformation occurring. He could tell by the united gasps from the crowd that they were seeing it too.

George's entire countenance began to radiate with intensifying light as he was filled with the Spirit of the Lord. His face shone like that of an angel, a visible witness to all that God was with him.[5] As he began to speak, the guards stood forth and attempted to lay their hands on him, but he withstood them, crying with a voice of thunder for all to hear, saying, "Touch me not, for the living God will not suffer that I shall be destroyed at this time, but He shall smite you if you lay your hands upon me before my witness of Him is complete."[6]

When George had spoken these words, no man dared lay hands upon him, for the flame of the Spirit was upon him, and his face shone with exceeding luster, even as Moses' did while on Sinai. Looking from Galerius to those on the palace balcony, George spoke with authority saying, "You see that you have no power to slay me, therefore I finish my testimony. I see that my words cut you to your hearts because I tell you the truth concerning your iniquities, and my words fill you with wonder and amazement, and with anger."[7]

George now fixed his gaze upon Diocletian and spoke, "Beloved Emperor, God knows how often you have transgressed His commandments and His laws, going on in the persuasions of men. You should never have feared man more than God. Although men set at naught the counsels of God and despise His words, yet you should have embraced Him and been faithful, and He would have extended His arm and supported you against all the fiery darts of your adversaries. He would have been with you in every time of trouble.[8] Yet now, you have no promise.

"You leaders of this nation, I speak to those who do not believe in Jesus Christ. There surely will be a great day in which you shall be brought to stand before the Lamb of God, and you shall behold the holiness of His Being while you are racked with a consciousness of your own guilt, that you have ever abused His laws and His children. When you shall be brought to see your nakedness before God, and also the glory of God and the holiness of Jesus Christ, it will kindle a flame of unquenchable fire upon you. Lest this be your end, turn unto the Lord and cry mightily unto the Father in the name of Jesus that you may become spotless, having been cleansed of all your sins by the blood of the Lamb at that great and last day.[9] For the day of the Lord is near upon all the heathen, and as thou hast done, it shall be done unto thee. Thy reward shall return upon thine own heads.[10]

"Without sincere repentance, you will be encircled about by the bands of death and the chains of hell, consigned to an everlasting destruction, you workers of iniquity, professing righteousness but rejecting the call of the Fountain of Righteousness. In His own name does He call you, which is the name of Jesus Christ. If you do not hearken to His call, taking upon you His name, then you are not His and you cannot be saved, for the devil is your shepherd.[11]

"Now I say to all that are desirous to follow the voice of the Good Shepherd, come out from among the wicked. Separate yourselves. Deny yourselves of all ungodliness. Touch not the unclean things of the unbelievers and you shall receive an inheritance at the right hand of God.[12]

"Think on these things, for the Spirit of God bears record of the truth which I speak concerning the day of judgment which is to come. Do you imagine that in the day of judgment you can lie to the Lord, when you are brought before the tribunal of God, your souls filled with guilt and remorse, having a perfect knowledge of all your wickedness, remembering you have ever set at defiance the commandments of God?

Can you look up to God at that day with a pure heart and clean hands, having His image engraven upon your countenances? Can you hope for salvation when you have yielded yourselves to become subjects to the devil?[13]

"You will know at that day that you cannot be saved, for no man can be saved except his garments are washed white, purified and cleansed from all stain through the blood of Him who came to redeem His people from their sins. How shall you stand before the bar of God, having your garments stained with all manner of filthiness and the blood of innocent men? These things will testify against you, that you are murderers and guilty of all manner of wickedness. How can you have place in the kingdom of God and sit down with all those whose garments are pure and white?[14]

"Who can stand against and despise the works of the Lord? Who can deny His sayings? Who will despise the children of Christ? All you who are despisers of the works of the Lord, you shall wonder and perish. O then despise not and wonder not, but hearken unto the words of the Lord and ask the Father in the name of Jesus for what things you shall stand in need. Doubt not but believe, and come unto the Lord with all your hearts, working out your own salvation with fear and trembling in humility before Him. Be wise in the days of your probation. Do all things in worthiness, and in the name of Jesus Christ, the Son of the living God. If you do this and endure to the end, you will in no wise be cast out.[15]

"Now, seeing you know these things and cannot deny them except you shall lie, therefore in this you have sinned, for you have rejected all these things, notwithstanding so many evidences which you have received of God and His creations. You have received all things, both things in heaven and all things which are in the earth, as a witness that they are true. But you have rejected the truth and reviled against your holy God, heaping up for yourselves wrath against the day of judgment instead of laying up for yourselves treasures in heaven where nothing doth corrupt, and where no unclean thing can come. Behold now the day of judgment is even at your doors. Prepare yourselves and enter in unto the judgment-seat of God.[16] He shall search your hearts and administer justice according to your rebellions and mercy according to your faith in Christ and your sincere repentance."

Turning his head to gaze upon the people who were gathered in the square, George continued, "Repent my beloved people, for the kingdom of heaven is soon at hand. The Son of God will come again in His glory, might, majesty, power, and dominion. We shall see the glory of the King of all the earth, and also the King of heaven shall very soon shine forth

A Martyr's Faith

among all the children of men.[17] Wherefore, choose you this day whom you will serve,[18] whether the true and living God of heaven or the lifeless dross of metal, wood, and stone. For you are all free to choose for yourselves the way of eternal life or the way of everlasting death. Wherefore, reconcile yourselves to the will of God and not to the will of the devil and the flesh. And after you are reconciled unto God, remember that it is only in and through the grace of Jesus Christ that you are saved.[19]

"I soon go down to my grave, yet I know that my spirit will go to the place of rest, which is with my Redeemer; for I know that in Him I shall have rest with my Father and my God, in whose mighty legion I shall not now be ashamed, neither shall my face wax pale at His presence.[20] My Lord and Savior Jesus Christ has willingly given His life for me. I now willingly give my life to Him. I rejoice in the day when my mortal shall put on immortality and I shall stand before Him; then shall I see His face with pleasure."[21]

With his final words, George's entire body collapsed in physical exhaustion, and the glorious light of his countenance began to fade. Sensing the departure of the miraculous power that had sustained him, Galerius muttered to himself in frustration and rage, "I knew we should have broken his jaw before the scourging."

Diocletian was unnerved by George's resuscitation and transfiguration, his testimony of the true and living God, and his warning of the judgments to come. *These public tortures are a huge risk if the prisoner doesn't break,* he thought. *The people are superstitious. They greatly revere the final words of any man facing death. All have heard George reaffirm his testimony of God and Christ three times already, each instance in the face of a most painful death. And now George has testified again with miraculous power!*

The righteous among the crowd began to sense the whisperings of the Spirit in a still small voice that pierced them that heard it to the very center, such that every part of their frames began to quake. The Spirit pierced them to the very soul, causing their hearts to burn within them.[22] The crowd began to shout of miracles and worship for the true and living God proclaimed by George.

I must stop this now!, the Emperor thought. *I'm sick of the torture and sick of Galerius' insufferable rage. But I shall not risk anarchy by taking back any of my words!* "Enough!" Diocletian shouted down. "Take the prisoner outside the walls of the city immediately and behead him! Galerius, see to it now and then clear the square!"

Unwilling to bear the scene any further, Diocletian left the balcony and entered the palace, followed closely by Alexandria and Athanasius.

His chest swelled with anguish as he considered the torture inflicted upon his friend at his command. *I will not witness the beheading,* he thought. *I have no desire to personally see George suffer further and die. I fear I've made a grave error in believing it was necessary for him to die to prevent chaos in the empire, but there is no turning back now. My course is set.* The storm gathering outside suddenly pounded with thunder. Instinctively he thought, *The God of nature suffers for this injustice to His son, George.*[23]

*****

Constantine continued his vigil from the imperial balcony. He saw that George's face retained a mild glow, but he was broken, torn, bloody, and raw. The thunder rolled again as a gentle rain began to wash George's body. Silently, Constantine pled with God for relief from his anguish over George's torture and coming execution. Into his mind came the clear impression: *Be still, and know that I am God. I will be exalted among the heathen. I will be exalted in the earth.*[24]

*****

At the Emperor's order, Galerius and his men had placed George onto a cart. He was still tied to the beam against which he had been laid. Extra soldiers were called in to open a path for the small band to pass through the agitated crowd to the city gates. As the beam was laid outside the city wall, George opened his eyes to heaven and raised his voice in one final plea, "Merciful Father, receive my spirit unto Thee.[25] Thou hast redeemed me, O Lord God of truth."[26]

After George had said these words, he was completely overcome with exhaustion by his ordeal. Still, he whispered, "O Lord, my God!"[27] as he watched the sword swing down upon his throat. In that instant he knew, his mortal mission for God was complete. He suffered death by beheading because he would not deny the true and living God or His Son, Jesus Christ, or the workings of the Holy Spirit, having sealed the truth of his words in blood by his death.[28]

****

CHAPTER SIXTY
Behold the Glory of the Lord

The Throne of God

"O then, my beloved brethren, come unto the Lord, the Holy One. Remember that His paths are righteous...and the Keeper of the gate is the Holy One of Israel: and He employeth no servant there... He cannot be deceived, for the Lord God is His name."[1]
2 Nephi 9:41

****

At the moment of execution, George's spirit passed through the veil between mortality and the spirit world for the final time. Rather than encountering a shock of bright light, he moved from the darkness into a thunder of overwhelmingly brilliant light, much more intense than his three prior experiences during his torturous ordeal. Within the intense light, George detected Beings of glory, but it was difficult for him to observe much detail because of Their immense brilliance.

"Awake, thou that sleepest, and arise...and Christ shall give thee light!"[2] the Lord declared. "Awake, awake! Put on thy strength. Art thou not he that hath wounded the dragon?[3] Awake, and put on thy beautiful garments of glory and light.[4] Learn of Me, and listen to My words; walk in the meekness of My Spirit, and you shall have peace in Me. I am Jesus Christ; I came by the will of the Father, and I do His will.[5] Fear not. Believest thou the words which I shall speak?"[6]

George answered, "Yea, Lord. I know that Thou speakest the truth, for Thou art a God of truth, and canst not lie.[7] Make Thy face to shine upon Thy servant, and teach me Thy statutes."[8] Suddenly, the Lord revealed Himself and that which had been too bright to discern became perceptible, and George began to reflect more fully the glory of the Lord in his own countenance.

And the Lord spoke again, "Because thou knowest these things, ye are redeemed from the fall; therefore ye are brought back into My presence; therefore I show Myself unto you. Behold, I am He who was prepared from the foundation of the world to redeem My people. Behold, I am Jesus Christ. I am the Father and the Son. In Me shall all mankind have life, and that eternally, even they who shall believe on My name; and they shall become My sons and My daughters.[9] Come unto

Me ye blessed, for behold, your works have been the works of righteousness upon the face of the earth."[10]

Although no others were currently conversing with Jesus, George could see many beings, clothed in brilliant white garments like his own, standing nearby at the altar of the Lord. Perceiving George's thoughts, the Lord explained, "These are the souls of them that were slain for the word of God, and for the testimony which they held. These shall rest yet for a little season, until their fellow servants also and their brethren, that shall be killed as they were, shall be fulfilled."[11]

"Lord, how these have suffered!" George exclaimed in anguish.

"I suffer the righteous to be slain by the wicked, who do these things according to the hardness of their hearts, that the justice and judgments which I shall exercise in My wrath upon the wicked may be just,"[12] the Lord replied. "Therefore, no man need suppose that the righteous are lost because they are slain. Behold, they have died in My cause; therefore they have entered into My rest, and they are happy.[13] These shall be Mine, in that day when I make up My jewels; and I will spare them, as a man spares his own son that serves him.[14] And there is no other way or means whereby man can be saved, only in and through Christ, for I am the Life and Light of the world, the Word of truth and righteousness.[15]

"These are they whom I shall bring with Me, when I shall come in the clouds of heaven to reign on the earth over My people.[16] These are they who are just men made perfect in Me, the mediator of the new covenant, having wrought out a perfect atonement through the shedding of My own blood.[17] These are washed and cleansed from all their sins, receiving the Holy Spirit, and they shall have part in the first resurrection, coming forth in the resurrection of the just.[18] Their names are written in heaven, where God and Christ are the judge of all,[19] that they who fear Me and think upon My name should be remembered in My house,[20] having been sealed by the Holy Spirit of Promise, which the Father sheds forth upon all those who are just and true.[21]

"These righteous heirs of celestial glory come unto Mount Zion, unto the city of the living God, the heavenly place, the holiest of all.[22] These are priests and kings of the Most High, who have received of His fullness, and of His glory, being ordained after the order of His Only Begotten Son, into whose hands the Father hath given all things.[23] Wherefore, as it is written, they are even the sons of God. Wherefore, all things are theirs, whether life or death, or things present, or things to come, all are theirs and they are Christ's, and Christ is God's, before Whose throne all things bow in humble reverence, and give Him glory forever and ever."[24]

George felt tears flow as he asked, "How long, O Lord, holy and true, dost Thou not judge and avenge our blood on them that dwell on the earth?"[25]

"That My covenants may be fulfilled which I have made unto the children of men, that I will do unto them while they are in the flesh, I must needs destroy the secret works of darkness, and of murders, and of abominations. Wherefore, he that fights against Zion, both Jew and Gentile, both bond and free, both male and female, shall perish, for they are they who are the whore of all the earth, for they who are not for Me are against Me.[26]

"And when the second trump shall sound then shall they that never knew Me come forth and shall stand before Me.[27] The blood of the innocent shall stand as a witness against the wicked and cry mightily against them at the last day.[28] Then shall all return, and discern between the righteous and the wicked, between him that serves God and him that serves Him not.[29] Then shall they know that I am the Lord their God, that I am their Redeemer; but they would not be redeemed. And then will I confess unto them that I never knew them; and they shall depart into that everlasting fire prepared for the devil and his angels, for he that will not hear My voice, the same I will not receive at the last day, and he shall not be numbered among My people."[30]

As the Lord spoke, He carefully wiped away George's tears and put His arms around him. "Blessed art thou, Georgios, My servant and My son, because of thy exceeding faith in My words.[31] Thy weeping may endure for a night, but joy comes in the morning.[32] They that sow in tears shall reap in joy.[33] It is I that have taken upon Me the sins of the world, for it is I that have created all men. It is I that grant unto those that endure to the end a place at My right hand. For behold, in My name are they called, and if they know Me they shall come forth, and shall have a place eternally at My right hand.[34] Sit thou at My right hand, until I make thine enemies thy footstool."[35]

"And what of my family?" George asked, still anxious for Sabra and their children.

And the Lord answered, "Blessed are you because of your faith in My work. I will bless you and your family, yea, your little ones; and the day cometh that they will believe and know the truth and be one with you in My house. Wherefore, your family shall live. Behold, verily I say unto you, I will prepare a place for them.[36]

"And blessed are they that will believe in the words of thy testimony, and exercise faith in Me unto repentance, who are willing to bear My name, and suffer for My name's sake, for in My name shall they be called, in this life and in eternity, and they are Mine.[37] For behold, this is

My work and My glory—to bring to pass the immortality and eternal life of man."[38]

When George had heard these words, he was comforted, and said, "O Lord, Thy righteous will be done, for I know that Thou workest unto the children of men according to their faith.[39] Wherefore, bless this people with faith that they might have grace and charity."[40]

With gentleness the Lord replied, "If they have not charity it mattereth not unto thee. Thou hast been faithful, wherefore thy garments are made clean.[41] I will make thee ruler over many things.[42] Come unto Me, ye blessed, there is a place prepared for you in the mansions of My Father."[43]

****

CHAPTER SIXTY-ONE
Habeas Corpus
Sabra Seeks George's Body for Burial

Nicodemia, Eastern Roman Capital
23 April, 303 AD

"Sir, if thou have borne Him hence, tell me where thou hast laid Him, and I will take Him away."[1]
John 20:15

****

The multitude had witnessed all that George had spoken in the course of his torture and execution. Their astonishment gave way for a beginning of faith, and the power of God had come upon them. Their hearts had swollen within them for the cruelty and injustice which George had endured and they were overcome, unable to move.[2] A deep clap of rolling thunder sounded, as if it were the voice of the Lord.[3] Tears from heaven followed the thunder, along with a flood of emotions. As if to honor the Lord's martyr, the rain beat down persistently, washing the spilt blood from the square and prompting the crowd to disperse. Still filled with the Spirit of truth they returned to their homes, witnessing to their families and friends all that they had seen and heard and felt.[4]

Yet a solitary woman in a hooded cape remained, motionless and reverent in the public square as the blood of her righteous man seeped down between the cobblestones and into the earth, away from her view. With bowed head and anguished tears, Sabra spoke to her Father. "Dear God, Thou who knowest the pain and anguish at the suffering and death of Thine own Son, hear my cry. All this is come upon us, yet have we not forgotten Thee, neither have we dealt falsely in thy covenant. Our hearts are not turned back, neither have our steps declined from Thy way, though Thou hast sore broken us in the place of dragons and covered us with the shadow of death. For Thy sake are we killed all the day long. Redeem us for Thy mercies' sake."[5]

She continued to stand, waiting upon the Lord, silently watching the blood fade away. Into her mind came a clear impression: *For by water ye keep the commandment; by the Spirit ye are justified and by the blood ye are sanctified.*[6] *Be still, and know that I am God. I will be exalted among the heathen. I will be exalted in the earth.*[7]

Sabra needed direction now, more than ever before in her life. She remained resolute, waiting patiently upon the Lord until His guidance for her path was clear. "Take me home," she heard George say softly. She turned to look for him, but he was not there. Still, she heard his voice again, "Fear not to take me home."

Sabra knew the only path to recovering George's body for burial back home was through the Emperor. She had feared further contact with him because of George's warnings, and because she had not fulfilled his command to return and report after her visit to the prison. Still, the voice had bid her not to fear. Again she looked to heaven and spoke with her Father. "Hear, O Lord, when I cry with my voice. Have mercy also upon me, and answer me.[8] Have mercy upon me, O Lord, for I am in trouble. My eye is consumed with grief and my soul is in anguish. But I will be glad and rejoice in Thy mercy, for Thou hast considered my trouble. Thou hast known my soul in adversities.[9] Look upon my affliction and my pain. Forgive all my sins. Consider my enemies, for they are many. O keep my soul, and deliver me. Let me not be ashamed, for I put my trust in Thee. Let integrity and uprightness preserve me, for I wait on Thee."[10]

*****

Fearing the Emperor's dark mood, the tribune approached cautiously. "My Lord, the woman Sabra has come to plead for George's body. Shall I bring her to you?"

Diocletian felt some connection and sympathy for this woman who had tried to save George's life. There were few he wanted to see at this time, but this woman he would hear. "Yes, bring her in that I may consider her plea."

Sabra approached reverently. With eyes down to the floor she waited for the Emperor to speak.

Curiously, Diocletian observed the shadows in the room appearing to flee as she entered, which only added to the mystery surrounding her presence. "You are permitted to speak. What matter do you bring before your Emperor?" he asked.

Sabra began, "Lord, forgive me for not returning to report to you after my visit with George last night. As you know I was unable to change the path he had chosen. Afterwards, the tribune told me you had commanded him to take me to my lodgings instead of returning me to you."

"Have no fear," the Emperor replied. "He was obedient to my

A Martyr's Faith

command. Coming here today you have also fulfilled my command to return and report. Do you have other business for me?"

"Yes, my Lord," Sabra responded quietly. "I've come to plead for George's body so he may be buried with his father and mother in Palestine. My Lord, if you've carried him away, tell me where you've laid him, and I'll take him away."[11]

Diocletian considered her request. He could not give George an honorable burial without losing the influence he had just gained over the council. He chafed at the leash they held on him but he chose a compromise he was willing to risk. "George's head will remain in the capital. You may take his body with you tomorrow morning if you will leave immediately and conceal your business from all until you reach Palestine. I'll provide George's body, prepared and sealed in a coffin, and I'll give you documents and an escort to assure your safe passage."

"Thank you, my Lord," Sabra replied. Knowing that she should take what was offered and leave, she hesitated before making her next request. "I know that no honors of the empire will be accorded for the burial, but I humbly ask that the coffin be draped with the family's banner that has been made for it." Sabra handed Diocletian the white banner with the red cross on it.

"I'll consider your request for the banner, but I make no promises," the Emperor responded. "If it's on the coffin in the morning, it will stay on the coffin. Otherwise, you'll know your request has been denied." Diocletian was concerned about how the council members would react to the banner, but out of love and respect for both George and his father, Diocletian determined to show them this private honor.

As the grieving woman left his presence, Diocletian felt the light go with her. Once again he was shrouded in shadows, alone with the weight of the evil he had done, his throne and crown were more painful than ever. Darkness closed in on his soul. The testimony of his friend George was already dimming to barely a whisper in his mind.

*****

The Empress had been alone in her bed chamber for over an hour. Her heart had broken as she watched the torture preceding George's execution. *One thing I know more than anything else is that George knew the truths whereof he spoke and testified,* she thought. *I'm certain he knew this God of love, into whose gentle arms he has surely been received.*

She had pondered on all George had taught her, principle by principle. "It's all true!" she exclaimed. Her heart burned within her at the sure realization. "God is my loving Father, and His Son, Jesus Christ, is my Redeemer, who offered Himself as an atoning sacrifice to prepare a way for me to return, pure and holy, back to my Father." Kneeling, she prayed, "Great and marvelous are Thy works, O Lord God Almighty! Thy throne is high in the heavens, and Thy power, goodness, and mercy are over all the inhabitants of the earth. Because Thou art merciful, Thou wilt not suffer those who come unto Thee that they shall perish![12] I take upon me the name of Christ, confessing my many sins, rejoicing in the love I feel for Thee and for Thy plan of redemption and happiness. In the hope of a glorious resurrection I promise to obey every word that cometh of Thee. I beg of Thee, guide me to a true administrator of Thy covenants, that I may be baptized for a remission of my sins and as a token of my covenant to take upon me the name of Christ forever."

*****

Athanasius stood alone in his chamber, staring at himself in the mirror. Carefully he removed the vestments of his priestly office. He was unsettled by what he had just witnessed. In his mind he knew, *George's execution was wrong but I was powerless to intervene. Yet the manner in which George endured the tortures and held power over death until his testimony was complete was astonishing. The influence of this event has permeated the hearts and minds of the people. Although I can't say for sure when I began to believe, my knowledge of the truth of George's testimony has been reconfirmed.* Looking blankly in the mirror he spoke to God, "What is man that Thou art mindful of him?[13] Truly we are Thy sons and daughters."[14]

He felt confused, unable to reconcile his knowledge of God with his occupation in life. They were completely inconsistent. He thought, *How much more cursed will I be, knowing the truth about God and persisting in my priestcraft?* He had been wrong before when he only had cause to believe but had acted without sure knowledge.[15] *Now my course must change despite the consequences,* he thought. Calmly, he began to evaluate his options. *I can't truly rest until I have abandoned this charade of false priesthood, standing up for truth. But wait! Perhaps, if I wait for the right moment, I can make my exit from the imperial stage without attracting too much attention.* Cautiously he began to formulate his plans for the necessary changes.

*****

Orion was grateful Galerius had used his own men for the torture and execution. Grateful was an understatement. Though he was a battle-hardened veteran, Orion still had his integrity. He knew the condemnation, torture, and execution of George, his friend and hero, were not right. He wanted nothing to do with it but he'd been obliged to stand as a witness with the Emperor's guard on the balcony. As with all the other witnesses, he'd seen the revivals and transfiguration of the Lord's martyr. He had a deep conviction that George knew whereof he spoke.

In the transition between duties in the palace and the prison, he made time to test the words of his friend. Alone, he knelt down before the Lord. Prostrating himself on the ground, he cried mightily saying, "O God, will Thou make Thyself known unto me, and I will give away all my sins to know Thee and to partake of Thy blessings, that I might be raised from the dead and be saved at the last day in Thy kingdom."[16]

The response was immediate and complete as Orion was filled with joy and peace. This was coupled with the strong impression that he needed to separate from the capital and the Emperor's service as soon as possible. The capital wouldn't be a kind place for Christian converts who meant to change their lives completely to comply with their new faith. Suddenly, an idea came. He would go to the Emperor and request dismissal, offering to take as his final assignment the escort of George's coffin back to Palestine. Though he was uncertain how his proposal would be received, he felt it was the right action to take, and he was determined to do it.

*****

As Sabra walked towards her quarters for the evening, she felt grief begin to release from her soul. George was gone, and no power would bring him back to this mortal life. Her only path was forward, until that day when she would pass through the veil of death and, having kept the faith herself, be reunited with him. Her thoughts were interrupted by the playful imaginations of a darling young girl, maybe five or six years old. She sat at the side of the road in her own little world of pretended distress. Joyfully the girl quietly pled, "George. Oh, George! Please save me. Don't let the dragon destroy me!"

As these words ran through Sabra's mind, they became her own and the floodgate of emotion burst open. Tears flowed as she sat down on a crate and began to tremble. Immediately the child stopped her play and approached. Taking Sabra's hand, she declared with conviction, "If you need help, George will be there for you."

"Out of the mouths of babes hast Thou ordained strength that Thou mightest still the enemy and the avenger,"[17] Sabra responded, prompting a confused look from the young girl. Sabra added, "Yes, my dear. I know George will be there for me, along with the legions of heaven."

"Yes, mum," the child confirmed with a knowing smile.

Off in the distance Sabra thought she heard the faint melody, "I feel my Savior's love…"[18] She did feel her Savior's love, and His tender mercies. Gradually, her pain was overcome by the joy of God's plan of happiness for all His children. In this, and in thoughts of her own children, she found the courage and determination to press on.

****

CHAPTER SIXTY-TWO
The Mantle Passes

Nicodemia, Eastern Roman Capital
24 April, 303 AD

*"He took up also the mantle of Elijah that fell from him…
And when the sons of the prophets…saw him, they said,
The spirit of Elijah doth rest upon Elisha."*[1]
2 Kings 2:13, 15

****

Constantine left the palace very early and went to the stables to rub down his horses and to think. *I feel torn by George's torture and execution. I know he spoke the truth about God and Christ and the judgments to come. I feel sick at my failure to intervene and save my friend. Is this feeling cowardice?* Weighed down by his weaknesses, he set aside the horse's brush and looked to heaven. Bowing his head he pled, "Father, forgive me for failing both Thee and Thy son, George." Peace came immediately into his mind and heart. *I don't know what to do, but I know that God loves me and will still be with me.*

As he resumed grooming his horses he continued to ponder, thinking of the dream Joseph had received telling him that Herod would seek the baby Jesus' life, and warning him that he needed to take Mary and Jesus and depart from the land.[2] In that moment Constantine knew he needed to separate himself from Galerius, Diocletian, and Maximian, as each would seek to kill him. His mind and heart were turned to his father, Constantius. "I will reunite with my father in Britannia at the earliest opportunity." Recalling George's testimonies he felt delight and the flooding inspiration of the Spirit igniting an earnest desire to study the statutes and precepts of the Lord and meditate upon them, knowing they would liberate him.[3]

After Constantine finished grooming his horses, he was drawn to George's two horses. They were magnificent animals. As he began to brush the white one, Orion entered the stables and quietly approached the coffin-laden cart. The tribune was relieved to see the white banner with the red cross draped over the coffin, hanging down to the bed of the cart on all sides. Moving easily he lifted a corner of the banner and slid Ascalon under it, next to the coffin where it wouldn't be noticed or disturbed. In his pocket he held George's signet ring for Sabra.

Noting Constantine's presence, Orion reviewed some documents and approached. Swallowing hard he began, "I have a personal note to you from George. Also, he requested that his chargers be given to you upon his death. The Emperor has ordered that one be used to pull the cart and coffin. You shall receive the other one. The choice is yours. Take your pick and I'll hitch the other to the cart. Then I'll need you to sign the acknowledgment and receipt for me."

Reverently Constantine opened the note which read: *C- Beloved Brother, do not run faster or labor more than you have strength, but be diligent unto the end. Pray always, that you may come off conqueror, that you may conquer Satan, and that you may escape the hands of the servants of Satan that do uphold his work.*[4] The note and gifts were signs to him that George knew he would be martyred. They confirmed that their brotherhood was unbroken, bringing him additional peace.

He looked carefully at the two horses. He remembered them from when he and George had served together in the Danube River region. He had envied George his horses then, but he never would have traded his friend for these animals. He had trouble deciding which horse he liked best, but he had no trouble deciding which would be most appropriate to carry George home. "Hitch the white one to the cart. His name is Caleb. I'll keep the black one for myself."

"As you will, my lord," Orion responded.

When Constantine had signed the required documents, Orion pointed out, "The property conveyed includes the tack and saddlebags, along with George's riding cloak."[5]

"Thank you," Constantine said as Orion closed his pouch of paperwork. Constantine set Caleb's tack and saddlebags aside. Together he and Orion led the white charger and hitched him up to the cart bearing George's coffin.

After Orion had gone, Constantine returned to George's saddlebags and examined their contents. Inside was a large collection of papers bound in leather. To his surprise, he discovered that the leather bound papers were beautiful well-worn copies of many of the writings of the ancient prophets and more recent apostles. Carefully he opened the text and his eyes fell upon this verse: *The Lord is my light and my salvation. Whom shall I fear? The Lord is the strength of my life. Of whom shall I be afraid?*[6] Turning a few pages further he read: *Rest in the Lord, and wait patiently for Him: fret not thyself because of him who prospers in his way, because of the man who brings wicked devices to pass. Cease from anger, and forsake wrath. Fret not thyself in any wise to do evil, for evil doers shall be cut off. But those that wait upon the Lord, they*

A Martyr's Faith

shall inherit the earth.[7] Turning a few more pages he read: *But the path of the just is as a shining light, that shineth more and more unto the perfect day.*[8]

What about Diocletian's order to destroy all Christian scriptures? I would die first! he thought as he examined the treasure. *This I will entrust to my mother's care.* Carefully he returned the text to the saddlebag. Looking to heaven he spoke reverently, "My Light, my Salvation and my Strength, guide my steps I pray, and I will walk in Thy paths all the days of my life."

Quickly he saddled his new black horse. Feeling greatly relieved, he wrapped himself in George's cloak and mounted the powerful charger. "Hiyah, Joshua!" he called as he guided the horse away, seeking a quiet place to think about George's witness of the living God. As he rode, he quoted, "O give thanks unto the God of gods: for His mercy endureth for ever."[9]

*****

Few on the imperial council had slept well the night following George's execution. As the day dawned, to their relief, the world had not yet come to an end. With few duties to attend to in the early hours, several gathered at the palace stables to see the coffin taken to the pauper's field. To their great distress, they found the coffin on a cart, secured for transport, a white banner with a red cross draped on it and an honor guard beside. "What's the meaning of the honor guard, and this banner covering the coffin?" one senator demanded as the Emperor approached.

"I placed the banner there," Diocletian responded boldly. "It has no significance of imperial or military honor. However, it will be a symbol to all Christians suggesting that their courage and faith in their God will lead them to purification, represented by the white banner, through bloodshed and death, represented by the red cross. The guard will disperse any crowds from gathering round the cart."

There were no further questions as the slight hooded woman led the horse and cart carefully out of the stable. Orion, the solitary tribune in battle uniform and armed with sword and shield, accompanied the cart on its journey.

*****

Sabra was familiar with the horse hitched to the cart. It was George's white charger Caleb, who favored peace. As she led the horse and cart down the cobblestone road to the main gate of the city, a growing crowd gathered around them. Seeing the coffin draped with the white banner and red cross, they felt compelled to mourn the martyr. None blocked her path, but many fell in behind the cart after it had passed. Sabra sensed this gathering crowd might bring unwanted attention endangering her journey home. Worse yet, there was always a chance that the Emperor would change his mind and order that George's body remain in the capital.

As the somber procession reached the city gate, Sabra stopped the cart and climbed upon it. Overlooking the crowd she slowly pulled back her hood so all could see her face. Tears stained her cheeks but no words were spoken as she searched the crowd with her eyes. Their faces all seemed to ask, *What do we do now?* Sabra searched their souls with a piercing glance. Reverently she clasped her hands together just below her chin in prayer. Looking to heaven, and bowing her head again, she modeled the counsel, *Look to God.* After another searching scan through the silent crowd she again lifted her eyes toward heaven and then bowed her head. Quietly she climbed down off the cart. With the palm of her right hand she signaled the crowd to stop. Gently she pulled the hood back over her head and led the horse out through the gate. Only Orion followed.

****

CHAPTER SIXTY-THREE
Other Martyrs

Nicodemia, Eastern Roman Capital
27 April, 303 AD

*"Yea, and all that will live godly in Christ Jesus
shall suffer persecution."*[1]
2 Timothy 3:12

****

Four days after George's execution, Alexandria entered the council chambers. She heard many voices of alarm at the increasing boldness of defiant Christians. Some of the concern appeared genuine, but she suspected many of the complaints were reports manipulated by Galerius to support his call for the empire to respond with even more widespread brutal repression.

The Emperor sat quietly as Galerius spewed forth his claims in the name of the council. "With each incident of violence, the Christians become more resolute in the worship of their God, causing great concern, especially among those of us who personally witnessed the crowd's reaction to George's execution. We must immediately crush this defiance by those who seek to unite against the empire. We must purge our nation of this Christian scourge. We've prepared an order for your seal requiring all Christians to worship Roman gods. Any who refuse to comply will face the threat of execution."

The Emperor felt his own fury rising as he scanned the raucous assembly. He desperately wished that just this once his sovereignty would merit the obedience of all to one simple command; that everybody just "SHUT UP!" Diocletian was exhausted by the rancor. However, he still couldn't see a more likely path to stability for the empire than these persecutions.

Alexandria felt a swelling grief in her heart for the monstrous injustices that were being perpetrated in the name of the Republic. Prompted by the Spirit and unable to contain the testimony she had received, she approached the Emperor with her passionate plea. "Most noble Diocletian, how long will you suffer these fools to drag you down to hell?"[2] She scanned the angry faces in the room. "We are cursed for our rebellion and we stand guilty before God. George, whom we have slain, is truly innocent. Because of the hardness of our hearts, God shall surely exercise His just judgments against us in His wrath, and the blood of this man shall stand as a mighty witness against us at the last day.[3] There will never be enough Christian blood to satisfy this godless council, as there is no peace for the wicked. They're a pack of ravenous fools who despise wisdom and instruction.[4] Cast them aside and do right by your people and by God.

"I prayed to God to know the truth of what George taught and the Holy Spirit confirmed it to me. That confirmation was reinforced with each lash of the whip on the martyr's back. Witnessing George's three miraculous recoveries from death further magnified the faith and knowledge I have. Surely you witnessed how George was sustained in the torture, and how his life couldn't be taken from him until his testimony was complete. Pray to God to know the truth of his witness. The Holy Spirit will reveal to you that Jesus Christ is the divine Son of God. Let us stop this fight against the true and living God, lest we all be cast down to hell forever."

Diocletian raised his eyebrows, staring in disbelief, caught off guard, too surprised to speak.

"I have repented of my sins that I might be redeemed of Christ, and I have been filled with the joy of the Holy Spirit," Alexandria continued. "Now I know that all mankind, men and women, all nations, kindreds, tongues, and people must repent and be born again, even born of God, changed from their carnal and fallen state to a state of righteousness, being redeemed of God, becoming His sons and His daughters. Thus, they become new creatures. Unless they do this, they cannot inherit the kingdom of God, but they must be cast off.[5]

"These things I know, for I was on the path to be cast off. But now I know that at the great day of the Lord, every knee shall bow and every tongue confess before Him. Even at the last day, when all men shall stand to be judged of Him, then shall they confess that He is God. Then shall they who have lived without God in the world confess that His judgments of everlasting punishment are just upon them, and they shall quake and tremble and shrink beneath the glance of His all-searching eye. I seek to repair the injuries I've done to all men through my rebellion against God, confessing my sins and testifying of all that has been revealed to me through His Holy Spirit."[6]

Recovering from their shock and utter disbelief at what they'd heard, the council erupted with angry voices. "She is possessed by demons![7] Condemn her to death!" they clamored.

Diocletian scanned the council, measuring the intensity of their reactions. Stoically he turned back to face his Empress. Raising his hand for silence he asked, "Alexandria, the serene, have you been beguiled by the beauty and majesty of our hero George, or have you been snared by this madness of Christianity?"

Alexandria responded quietly, her eyes locked on the Emperor's stare, "I have been snared from the jaws of hell by the arms of our loving Father in heaven. His arms are stretched out still to save all who will believe in His Son, Jesus Christ."

Suddenly Athanasius, who had never before broken protocol by speaking without invitation from the Emperor, spoke out to the assembly. "Why do you stand in amazement at the witness of the Empress? I too have weighed George's testimony and the cause of the Christians. I was raised by my Christian grandmother. Even so, I never had known much of the ways of the Lord and His mysteries and marvelous power. But I'm mistaken, for I've seen much of His mysteries and His marvelous power in the preservation of this people and this nation. Yet I hardened my heart, for I was called many times, but I would not hear. Therefore, I knew concerning these things, yet I would not know, and thus I went on rebelling against God in the wickedness of my heart.[8] I am guilty, and George truly is spotless before God.[9] But the Spirit of God has filled me with understanding, confirming the truths of the Christian doctrines. The Spirit of God will manifest these truths to you too, if you will ask God with a sincere heart, with real intent to obey all revealed truth, having faith in Christ.[10] We must stop these Christian persecutions."

After Athanasius had testified of Christ, the council was even more stunned and amazed. Now there were three witnesses who had testified of their wickedness in fighting against God and rejecting His word and the prophecies of that which is to come.[11] But the lust for blood had already rooted itself deep within their souls and their anger soon broke through again.

As chaos engulfed the imperial council chamber, Diocletian considered this surprising turn of events. George was a solitary public witness against him, the council, the Roman gods and the empire. He'd been given a public forum in which to plead his case, which he'd done manfully and miraculously, sealing his testimony of Christ with his blood to the condemnation of his persecutors. Now the abuse and injustice heaped upon the Christians was leading many of the non-Christians to sympathize with the humble followers of Christ. Few, if any, of the other abused Christians had been given a public forum to speak against the iniquities of the empire and the worship of the Roman gods. Diocletian was determined there wouldn't be any other public witnesses against them.

The Emperor stared with regret at the unsigned order in his left hand, as he raised his right hand for quiet. With determination he declared, "Empress Alexandria, and Athanasius, imperial priest, I find you both guilty of treason and sedition. I hereby strip you of your titles and honors, and order your immediate executions."

"Beloved Diocletian," Alexandria pled passionately, "I am willing to die for the truth, but I beg of you, permit me to be baptized Christian before I'm executed."

"You have pled your cause before me, and I have pronounced my judgment," Diocletian replied, maintaining his stoic expression as he looked carefully into the face of the former Empress. "If it's a covenant with your God you seek, plead your cause to Him, for you shall meet Him soon, if He exists." With a sigh of angry resignation, but without objection, Diocletian signed and sealed the new persecution order and the hastily written orders of execution for the Empress and priest. "Galerius, see to the immediate execution of Alexandria and Athanasius," he commanded. Turning away, he walked briskly from the council chamber to his private quarters, flanked by his personal guards.

*****

Galerius was struck with surprise at this amazing turn of events. He realized that quick action would best serve his purposes, solidifying the operation of his plans. "Tribunes, restrain the traitors!" he ordered. The tribunes promptly obeyed, binding the arms of Alexandria and Athanasius behind them. With a menacing sneer, Galerius approached his prisoners. "How shall I look when I am damned?"[12] he gnashed sarcastically as he gave each prisoner a vicious slap across the face, knocking them off balance. As they righted themselves and braced for more abuse, he spat in the face of each one. "Take them to the dungeon!" he ordered. Turning to the council he proclaimed, "The die is cast. Use your influence immediately to destroy the Christians, starting in Nicodemia and spreading throughout the empire. You may keep whatever treasure you confiscate. No questions will be asked. I'll fulfill the Emperor's commands regarding these prisoners and then join with you soon."

*****

In the dungeon chamber, Alexandria and Athanasius were forced to kneel before Galerius. "What a delight it will be for George to be so quickly reunited with his most celebrated converts," he crowed. "Ladies first then, shall we?" Most unceremoniously he brought his sword down twice, beheading them. His only real regret was there hadn't been any order for torture. No matter, his presence was needed elsewhere.

*****

As the spirits of Alexandria and Athanasius passed through the veil of death, they moved from darkness into the same thunder of overwhelmingly brilliant light to which George had advanced upon his final death. The Light was astonishing, the Beings of glory, easily detectible, but with details barely discernible due to the brightness of the light emanating from Them.
"Fear not!" the Voice spoke. "Because of thy faith in Christ, thy sins are forgiven thee, and thou shalt be blessed."[13]
A flood of joy and glory filled each of them. As they knelt instinctively to worship their God, the glory emanating from their own countenances and clothing intensified, reflecting the glory of the Lord which now covered them.

*****

Diocletian entered his private chambers. "I'm not to be disturbed until I call for you!" he ordered his tribunes. Alone, he dropped beside his bed, feeling broken inside. He thought more carefully on the testimonies and executions of George, Alexandria, and Athanasius. These had been his most faithful supporters against the conspiracy, and he'd had them all killed. Raising his eyes to heaven in realization and fear, he whispered in agony, "Gods of heaven, have I not gained anything in this life that I may retain with love? Oh, all is lost."

****

CHAPTER SIXTY-FOUR
Rest in Peace

Lydda, Palestine
30 April, 303 AD

"I am to be gathered with my people: bury me with my fathers...."[1]
Genesis 49:29

****

When they finally arrived back in Lydda, Sabra was exhausted physically and emotionally. "Gregor and I will take care of the cart so you can focus on your family," Orion offered.

"Thank you," she replied gratefully, leaving quickly to find her mother and children.

As they surveyed the cart and its contents, Orion raised the corner of the family banner which was still draped over George's coffin. "George instructed that this be returned to you," he said, pointing to Ascalon.

Immediately Gregor's eyes flooded with tears. "I want George, not the sword," he whispered.

"It is a sword of righteousness," Orion responded. "It remains an honored symbol of many principles that George held dear."

Gregor nodded numbly as he carefully removed the heirloom from the cart. "To honor George, I'll clean and sharpen it and return it to its place in the family library," he said.

*****

After the young ones were asleep, Sabra embraced her aged mother. "Though I'm heart-broken, the tender hours spent with my family have reinforced that there is still much in life for me to love," she told Callidora. "I marvel at the strength I feel as you hold me. You understand my pain like no other mortal."

*****

At the interment service the next day, Sabra explained the symbols of the banner to Gregor and her children. "The cross is a symbol of Christianity. It is a symbol of Christ's atoning sacrifice. Red is for courage, the courage to sacrifice one's own blood, if required, in the cause of Christ. White is for purity. The white field of the banner signifies how we can be washed pure in the atoning blood of Christ and be made holy and sanctified by the Spirit of God.

"Many people may speak evil of your father for his refusal to submit to the Emperor," Sabra explained to her children. "But those who worship the one true and living God will always honor him for his courage, integrity, and his refusal to deny his faith in Jesus Christ, our Savior and Redeemer."[2]

Gregor spoke next, offering a few words of comfort to the family. "United as family we bear this grief, mourning greatly for the departure of our husband, father, and brother. These are days of solemn sorrow and a time for much fasting and prayer.[3] Truly we mourn the death of our kin, yet we rejoice in the hope and even know, according to the promises of the Lord, that George will be raised up to dwell at the right hand of God, in a state of never ending happiness. But the battle is not yet over, so still we hear the call of the Lord to diligence in laboring in His vineyard, that we may behold the miracles of joy because of the light of Christ unto life."[4]

Gregor, Sabra, and Callidora watched with tears as George's coffin was lowered into the grave. Each family member took a turn to add a handful of dirt to bury the coffin. Gregor offered a prayer to dedicate the grave as the final resting place for George's body until his resurrection clothed with righteousness, glory, and light reflecting the image of God. When he had concluded, he heard in the distance the unmistakable call of a rooster, *Urha-urha-urrr!* A flood of emotion overwhelmed him as he responded through tears, "I hear you brother, and I'll answer the call. Urha-urha-urrr!"

Gregor's reply was quickly echoed by a chorus of three small voices answering, "Urha-urha-urrr!"

Sabra felt a gentle tug on her dress. "Mama, what will we do without Papa?" her daughter asked.

A calm assurance came over Sabra as she replied, "The Lord has called your father home. Now, He is bound by covenant to answer our needs in the absence of your father's sustaining support. God knows how our hearts ache without your father here. He will take care of us. Seek God's blessings with joy, not fear. If we follow the promptings of the Spirit, we'll be safe, whatever the future holds. We'll be shown what to do.[5] The Lord is good to all, and His tender mercies are over all His works and all His saints shall bless Him."[6]

Sabra looked carefully into the faces of her children and kindly shared more of her own faith, to prepare them. "Come and hear the pleasing word of God, which heals the wounded soul.[7] You little ones that are pure in heart, look to God with firmness of mind, and pray unto Him with exceeding faith, and He will console you in your afflictions. He will plead your cause with our Heavenly Father. Lift up your heads and receive the pleasing word of God, for death is not the end, but only the beginning. Let your minds feast upon His love, forever.[8] It is true that because of our faith in Christ we shall be hated of men. But, if we stay true, trusting in God and enduring to the end in faith, we shall be saved,[9] and God will not be ashamed to be called our God.[10] As heirs to God's kingdom, surely we shall see your father again in the flesh."[11]

****

CHAPTER SIXTY-FIVE
The Dragon Wounded

Paradise of God

"Awake, awake! Put on Thy strength...Art Thou not He that hath wounded the dragon?"[1]
Isaiah 51:9

****

Gerontius and Polychronia stood in awe at the glory of the Lord reflected in their son as he stood with them and shared a few details of his redemption. George was wearing a linen robe of pure snowy white, with a golden belt just below the chest.[2] His whole being was as brilliant and radiant as the sun, as if he stood in the midst of a flaming fire.[3] His face shone like lightning.[4] His voice had taken on the quality of mighty rushing winds.[5] "Father and Mother," he said, "being with you only adds to the joy of being redeemed in the presence of the Lord, which surpasses all understanding.

"After my death, the Lord bade me awake and arise from my sleep and put on the beautiful garments of glory. I beheld the heavens open, and I was clothed upon with glory,[6] and I was prepared that the covenants of the Eternal Father which He had made might be fulfilled for me. Christ bade me come unto Him and be perfected in Him.[7] He then spoke of my mortal mission and made it known that I had done well with the work He had given me. The Lord explained that because I had overcome the adversity of the flesh and endured in faith to the end, I would abide with all those who have not defiled their garments, being clothed as He is clothed in white raiment of glory.[8]

"My name was written in His Book of Life, and He confessed my name before the Father and before His angels.[9] Thus am I preserved from the second death, never again to be cut off from the presence of the Father.[10] And the voice of God declared, and I saw that I was created in His own image and in the image of His Only Begotten, Who is full of grace and truth.[11] All things are present before Him, for He knows them all, for all is as one day with God, and time only is measured unto men.[12] And wisdom remains in God, and for His own purposes has He created all things and required this work at my hands.[13]

"And the Lord said unto me, 'Look, and I will show unto thee the world for the space of many generations.'[14] At His command, I looked and beheld the earth and the inhabitants thereof, and there was not a soul which I did not behold, discerning all by the Spirit of God.[15] And I beheld my people at war, and a curse was upon all those who fought against God's purposes. In the midst of the war I beheld a man, and the Spirit of God wrought upon the man, that he went forth conquering, bringing peace to my people and sanctuary to the people of the Lord.[16] From that time, the fear of the Lord was upon the surrounding nations, so great was the grace of the Lord which was upon His people. And the Lord blessed the land, and they were blessed upon the mountains and upon the high places and did flourish.[17]

"From that time forth there came generation upon generation, and the power of Satan was again upon all the face of the earth, and there were wars and bloodshed among all men. And Satan veiled the whole face of the earth with darkness, and he looked up and laughed, and his angels rejoiced. And God looked upon the residue of the people and He wept.[18] And I asked the Lord, 'How is it that Thou canst weep, seeing Thou art holy, and from all eternity to all eternity? Thou art just and kind forever and mercy shall go before Thy face and have no end. Therefore, how is it Thou canst weep?'[19]

"And the Holy One said, 'Behold, these thy brethren are the workmanship of Mine own hands, and I gave unto them their agency. I commanded them to love one another, and that they should choose Me, their Father, but they are without affection, and they hate their own blood.[20] Satan shall be their father, and misery shall be their doom. The whole heavens shall weep over them, and why shouldn't the heavens weep, seeing these shall suffer?[21] My Beloved, which I have chosen, hath suffered for their sins, inasmuch as they will repent in the day that My Chosen shall return unto Me, and until that day these shall be in torment. Wherefore, for this shall the heavens weep.[22] But My blood hath been shed, that all they that mourn may be sanctified and have eternal life.'[23]

"And I asked God, 'Wilt Thou not come again upon the earth? Thou hast made me, and given unto me a right to Thy throne, and not of myself, but through Thine own grace, wherefore, I ask Thee if Thou wilt not come again on the earth.'[24]

"And the Lord said, 'As I live, even so will I come in the last days, in the days of wickedness and vengeance, to fulfill the oath which I have made concerning My people. But before that day the heavens shall be darkened, and a veil of darkness shall cover the earth. The heavens shall shake, and also the earth, and great tribulations shall be among the children of men, but My people will I preserve. And righteousness will I send down out of heaven, and truth will I send forth out of the earth, to bear witness of Mine Only Begotten, His resurrection from the dead, and also the resurrection of all men. Righteousness and truth will I cause to sweep the earth as with a flood, to gather My people from the four quarters of the earth.'[25]

"The Lord explained that the time shall come when the knowledge of a Savior shall spread throughout every nation, kindred, tongue, and people, and when that time comes, none shall be found blameless before God, except it be little children, only through repentance and faith on the name of the Lord God Omnipotent.[26]

"Further, the Lord revealed that many would be converted through the testimony and sacrifice He had required at my hands. He showed me that soon the Republic will be given into the hands of a faithful follower of God, and that an innumerable host of His children will receive the gospel of Jesus Christ, through all generations unto the end of the earth. He declared, 'From the rising of the sun even unto the going down of the same, the Lord's name shall be great among the Gentiles…for His name shall be great among the heathen, saith the Lord of hosts.'[27] This is why my testimony and death were so valuable to the righteousness of His children.

"He also renewed His promise that because of my faithfulness and obedience, none of my blessings would be lost in the eternities, neither for me, nor for our family. Because of my faithfulness in mortality, I shall be made ruler over many things, through all eternity. Thus have I entered into the joy of the Lord.[28]

"And the Lord showed unto me the day of the righteous and the hour of their redemption, and I received a fullness of joy.[29] Then the Redeemer fed me with manna and gave me a white stone with a new name written upon it that is sacred to those who receive it.[30] He declared that He had placed His new name upon me and that I should be a pillar in the temple of God.[31] According to His word, even as the Lord has overcome and has been set down with the Father in His throne, because I have overcome through Christ and kept His commandments, the Lord has granted that I be set down with Him in His throne.[32] There I shall be given power over many kingdoms, that I might join with Him in ruling over them according to the word of God. They shall be in my hands as the vessels of clay in the hands of a potter, and I shall govern them by faith, with equity and justice, even as I received of our Father."[33]

As George concluded his report to his parents, Polly spoke. "The Spirit of the Lord has enlightened us in many details, bestowing greater knowledge and understanding than mere words alone can provide. We are warmed by our love for each other, and we feel the growing joy of unity in our eternal family. Our presence together has a magnifying effect on the glory that each of us radiate."

Gerontius beamed with appreciation for his son and all he had endured to fulfill the will of the Lord. Reverently he spoke, "George, no matter how many times I heard it, I always enjoyed hearing the story of your rescue of the Princess Sabra, even when the retelling became sheer fantasy. In light of the blessings that will come to the Christians, in part through your example of obedience and faith, and by your witness and martyrdom, let me tell the story as I now see it."

"That would be wonderful, Father," George agreed with restrained embarrassment.

Humbly, Gerontius began:

And there appeared a great wonder in heaven, a woman clothed with the sun, and the moon under her feet, and upon her head a crown of twelve stars. And she being with child cried, travailing in birth, and pained to be delivered.[34]

And there appeared another wonder in heaven. Behold a great red dragon, having seven heads and ten horns, and seven crowns upon his heads. And there was war in heaven. Michael and his angels fought against the dragon. And the dragon fought, and his angels, and prevailed not, neither was their place found any more in heaven. And the great dragon was cast out, that old serpent, called the Devil, and Satan, which deceiveth the whole world, he was cast out into the earth, and his angels were cast out with him, and his tail drew the third part of the stars of heaven, and did cast them to the earth.[35]

Woe to the inhabitants of the earth and of the sea! For the devil is come down unto you, having great wrath, because he knoweth that he hath but a short time.[36]

And when the dragon saw that he was cast unto the earth, he stood before the woman which was ready to be delivered, for to devour her Child as soon as it was born.[37] *And she brought forth a Man Child, who was to rule all nations with a rod of iron. And her Child was caught up unto God, and to His throne.*[38]

And the dragon was wroth and persecuted the woman which brought forth the Man Child, and went to make war with the remnant of her seed, which keep the commandments of God, and have the testimony of Jesus Christ.[39] *And the dragon made war with the saints and prevailed against them, until the Ancient of days came.*[40] *And the saints cried: O Lord God Almighty, ...Thy power, and goodness, and mercy are over all the inhabitants of the earth, and because Thou art merciful, Thou wilt not suffer those who come unto Thee that they shall perish!*[41]

And I heard a loud voice saying in heaven, Now is salvation, and strength, and the kingdom of our God, and the power of his Christ.[42] *And He was clothed in a vesture dipped in blood, and His name is called The Word of God. And the armies which were in heaven followed Him upon white horses, clothed in fine linen, white and clean. And out of His mouth went a sharp sword, that with it He should smite the nations, and He shall rule them with a rod of iron, and He treads the winepress of the fierceness and wrath of Almighty God. And He has on His vesture and on His thigh a name written, KING OF KINGS, AND LORD OF LORDS.*[43]

And He called to all His servants: Awake, awake, put on strength, take hold of the arm of the Lord, ye that have wounded the Dragon.[44] *And the Ancient of days came, and judgment was given to the saints of the Most High. And the time came that the saints possessed the kingdom.*[45] *And the kingdom and dominion, and the greatness of the kingdom under the whole heaven, was given to the people of the saints of the Most High, whose kingdom is an everlasting kingdom, and all dominions shall serve and obey Him.*[46]

And they overcame the dragon by the blood of the Lamb, and by the word of their testimony, and they loved not their lives unto the death.[47] *And He laid hold on the dragon, that old serpent, which is the Devil, and Satan, and bound him…and cast him into the bottomless pit, and shut him up, and set a seal upon him, that he should deceive the nations no more till the thousand years should be fulfilled.*[48]

Therefore rejoice, ye heavens, and ye that dwell in them, for the accuser of our brethren is cast down, which accused them before our God day and night.[49] *Let us be glad and rejoice, and give honor to Him: for the marriage of the Lamb is come, and His wife hath made herself ready. And to her was granted that she should be arrayed in fine linen, clean and white; for fine linen is the righteousness of saints.*[50]

And I saw thrones, and they sat upon them. And I saw the souls of them that were beheaded for the witness of Jesus, and for the word of God, and which had not worshipped the beast, neither his image, neither had received his mark upon their foreheads, or in their hands; and they lived and reigned with Christ a thousand years…This is the first resurrection. Blessed and holy is he that has part in the first resurrection. On such the second death hath no power, but they shall be priests of God and of Christ, and shall reign with Him a thousand years.[51]

And I heard a great voice out of heaven saying, Behold, the tabernacle of God is with men, and He will dwell with them, and they shall be His people, and God Himself shall be with them, and be their

God. And God shall wipe away all tears from their eyes. And there shall be no more death, neither sorrow nor crying, neither shall there be any more pain, for the former things are passed away. And He that sat upon the throne said, Behold, I make all things new. And I will give unto him that is athirst of the fountain of the water of life freely. He that overcometh shall inherit all things, and I will be his God, and he shall be My son.[52]

Great and marvelous are Thy works, Lord God Almighty. Just and true are Thy ways, Thou King of saints.[53]

As Gerontius finished his recital of this revelation, Polly casually noted, "I didn't hear the mention of George's name once in your story."

Tenderly, George put his arm around his mother and said, "That's because the Lord has always held His own sword in this battle against sin, just as He did with Gideon. I saw myself among God's faithful servants, and I saw Sabra and our family among the saints of His church. I may have wounded the dragon with my sacrifice, but only through the Lord can he truly be overcome."

Father embraced George, and quietly shared the words of Jesus: "'Greater love hath no man than this, that he lay down his life for his friends.'[54] We have come to the Lord and He has claimed us as His own, that we may not perish, but be glorified in Him for all eternity."

****

EPILOGUE
The Ripple Effect

The Roman Empire
303 AD and Beyond

"For your obedience is come abroad unto all men...but yet I would have you wise unto that which is good, and simple concerning evil. And the God of peace shall bruise Satan under your feet shortly."[1]
Romans 16:19-20

****

The Christian persecution launched by Emperor Diocletian[2] was the last and most severe in the history of the Roman Empire. Christians were forbidden to worship in groups, many were deprived of official ranks, and their churches and scriptures were destroyed. Christian clergy and military officers were thrown into prison, to be released only after making the required sacrifices to the Roman gods, or to be executed.[3] Thousands of true Christians suffered martyrdom, being executed for their refusal to deny their faith.

George's faith and courage in the face of torture and execution inspired many to believe in the God of Abraham and to endure their persecutions with patience, determination, and faith in Christ. The testimonies and martyrdoms of the Empress and the imperial priest stand as powerful evidence of the reality and depth of their conversions, and of the marvelous spirit with which they received George's testimony of Christ.

Many Roman subjects believed in religious tolerance and chafed at the abuse of the Christians. Spurred by these injustices, interest in the faith was magnified. The hope and love embodied in the doctrines of Christ brought about the conversion of many more people than the number of those who were put to death for their faith. Thus, the ranks of Christians rapidly increased.

Unfortunately, some opponents of the Republic professed Christian faith merely as a cloak for their efforts to undermine the government and incite chaos. From the time of George's execution, violence in the capital increased to the point that Galerius[4] departed for Rome, declaring Nicodemia unsafe. Diocletian followed Galerius to Rome soon thereafter.[5]

As the persecution and conflict intensified, much ground was hallowed by the shedding of innocent blood. Those who remained became ever more determined that these martyrs would not die in vain. Still, the faithful believers in Christ, who were the saints of God, suffered great persecutions, wading through much affliction. Many passed through these trials, rejoicing that they were also counted worthy to suffer the shame of the world for Christ's name.[6]

*****

Another prominent martyr during this period was Florian.[7] He was born around 250 AD. He joined the Roman army where he rose to become a commander in Noricum province. He organized and trained elite groups of soldiers whose primary duty was to control fires. He greatly advanced the science of fire fighting and also used fire as a strategic weapon in battle.

During the Christian persecutions, Florian was reported for not enforcing the edicts in his province. The Emperor sent an officer who ordered Florian to make sacrifices to the Roman gods. When he refused, he was condemned to death. At his execution on 4 May 304, Florian challenged the Roman soldiers saying, "If you wish to know that I am not afraid of your torture, light the fire, and in the name of the Lord I will climb onto it." Unsettled by his reputed mastery of fire, the soldiers chose instead to tie a millstone around his neck and drown him in the Enns River. He was beatified as a saint and is recognized as the patron saint of firefighters. The most common modern symbol for fire and rescue units is the "Florian Cross."

*****

By the summer of 304, Diocletian and Galerius had made their way back to Nicodemia, where the Christian persecutions continued. They spent the fighting season that year on the northeast frontier, with Constantine[8] still tethered on a very short leash.

In late 304, Diocletian fell gravely ill. At a public appearance in March 305, he was so emaciated that he was barely recognizable.[9] On 1 May 305, under pressure from Galerius and the imperial council, Diocletian abdicated the throne, elevating Galerius to senior Augustus. With his new power, Galerius aggressively intensified the persecution of the saints.

On the same day a parallel ceremony was held in the western empire in which Maximian[10] abdicated his throne, elevating Constantius[11] to

Augustus in the west. The two most obvious candidates for appointment as Caesars were Constantine, son of Constantius, and Maxentius,[12] son of Maximian. However, fearful of his rivals, Galerius chose his own men over these best qualified candidates. He named his own nephew, Maximinus Daia,[13] as his Caesar in the east. Denying Constantius the right of naming his own junior emperor, Galerius named Severus[14] as Caesar in the West. He also retained Constantine in the east as leverage against Constantius.

Continually fearful of Constantine's proven military skill and rapidly growing popularity, Galerius sent him to the eastern battle front many times with inadequate armies, commanding him to personally lead the charges on these suicide missions. Although Constantine won victory after victory against all odds, he understood clearly that he had to leave the east as soon as possible or Galerius would ultimately succeed in having him killed.

One night at a palace celebration, he approached Galerius publicly and made an impassioned plea, asking permission to join his father in the west, to help in putting down the rebellions in Britannia. Galerius had been drinking heavily and he gave in to the sentiment of the assembly, granting Constantine permission to go to his father's aid. He had assumed that Constantine wouldn't leave until the next morning, giving him time to privately rescind his publicly magnanimous approval.

However, rather than retiring for the night, Constantine immediately slipped out to the stables. Grabbing the barest of essentials and the best available horse, he began his westward ride by moonlight. He rode three consecutive horses nearly to death along the post line before daybreak, putting enough distance between himself and the palace so that Galerius couldn't reach him with orders to return. Days later he arrived in Britannia and joined his father.

Constantius and Constantine were a formidable team in battle, having great success in Britannia in 305 and the first half of 306. It didn't take long for the men under Constantine's command to gain a deep trusting admiration for his courage, fighting skills, and genius in battle strategy.

In the summer of 306, Constantius fell gravely ill. Feeling the end was near he counseled his legion commanders and made them swear an oath to proclaim Constantine as Augustus after his death. He died in July 306. Faithful to their oaths and genuinely inspired by Constantine, the commanders proclaimed him Augustus in his father's stead on 25 July 306, defying Galerius.

This created a huge problem for Galerius. He didn't want to grant any power to Constantine. But with the army in the west declaring loyalty to Constantine, and many in the eastern army also inclined towards him, Galerius needed a way to honor Constantine but still restrict his power. His solution was to elevate Severus to Augustus in the west, granting Constantine a promotion to junior emperor as Caesar in the west, but not to Augustus.

Constantine accepted this compromise without great objection, retaining the largest and most battle-seasoned army in the empire. He chose to actively consolidate other elements of his power base rather than immediately engaging in open conflict with the other tetrarchs. However, he did put an immediate end to the persecutions of Christians in his quarter of the empire, and offered full restitution of what had been taken from them.[15]

With the largest loyal army in the west under Constantine's control, the western Augustus, Severus, located in Milan in northern Italy, appeared suspiciously weak. Therefore, Maximian's son, Maxentius, gathered an army and declared himself Augustus of Rome and southern Italy.

Severus took a large army and marched against Maxentius in 307. As they arrived at Rome, they found Maximian allied with his son. Seeing their old commander with his son, many of Severus' men abandoned him to join the army of Maxentius. A short time later, Severus and the remainder of his army surrendered to Maxentius on condition that their lives be spared.

Near this time, Constantine married Fausta, the daughter of Maximian and the sister of Maxentius. Seeing no point in appealing to Constantine and his army for help, Galerius took his army to the aid of Severus later that year. However, when Galerius arrived in Rome he too learned that many in his army preferred Maxentius to him as their emperor. Although Galerius didn't surrender, these defections forced him to withdraw and resulted in the execution of Severus as a conspirator in his uprising.

In 308, with the empire still on the brink of chaos, Diocletian briefly returned from retirement to the political scene at the Conference of Carnuntum to aid Galerius in an attempt to avert full scale civil war. Unable to command the respect required to succeed, Diocletian immediately withdrew back into retirement where he remained until he died sometime between 311 and 316.

At Carnuntum, Galerius appointed Licinius as the new Augustus in the west and charged him with regaining his domain from Maxentius. Sensing an opportunity, the ever ambitious Maximian tried to regain the position of Augustus in the west by deposing his own son. This time the army sided with the younger, more energetic Maxentius, causing Maximian to flee to his son-in-law, Constantine, for security.

In 309, Maximian tried to persuade his daughter to murder her husband so he could take Constantine's throne. Fausta revealed the plot to Constantine who then allowed Maximian to choose his own manner of execution. After nearly twenty years as an Augustus, Maximian was hanged, a penalty insufficient to answer for his slaughter of the Theban Legion. Relations between Constantine and Maxentius deteriorated rapidly after Maximian's death.

Within a few years of his ascension to the throne, Galerius realized that his strongest base of economic support and the most secure regions of the empire were the provinces where Christianity was on the rise. He could see that the faithful Christians were prospering in the face of constant adversity, while those around them struggled. He knew the Christians were very tolerant and peace-loving, with no manifest ambition as a group to seize political power except to secure religious freedom and tolerance. Still, he continued his Christian persecutions.

By 311, Galerius had become somewhat obese and had been stricken with a genital disease. As the disease progressed, he was beset by severe ulcerous lesions which generated extensive amounts of putrid discharge so sickening and foul that even his doctors would rather be put to death than to approach him, having to confess that they could not help him.

By April, Galerius was fully incapacitated by his disease. Given his plight, he considered that this curse might be God's retribution for his persecution of the Christians. He acknowledged that all his efforts to suppress Christianity had come to naught. In a move calculated to shore up waning popular support, he issued an edict officially ending persecution of Christians, but not restoring their property. In his order he commanded the Christians to pray to God for his benefit. Death came for him within a month of his edict.

When Galerius died, his nephew, Maximinus Daia, ascended to Augustus in the east. Maximinus Daia then entered into a power sharing agreement with Licinius, who still needed an army to help him recover his own throne from Maxentius in Rome.

In the summer of 311, Maxentius mobilized against Constantine in the west, possibly hoping to defeat him before being attacked by Licinius and his forces. Very late in the year, Constantine formed an alliance with Licinius against Maxentius. In response, Maxentius then entered a secret alliance with Maximinus Daia against both Licinius and Constantine.

Having survived 311, Constantine determined to take the battle to Maxentius in Rome in 312. On his campaign southward, he ordered his army not to loot the towns or abuse the people who they defeated in battle. Soon the other towns began surrendering without resistance, with the assurance that they would be treated fairly.

Outside Rome, Constantine had a vision in the night in which a heavenly messenger told him to go forth with the Chi-Rho sign of the cross on his arms, which he did.

Maxentius consulted a soothsayer who assured him that on the sixth anniversary of his ascension to the throne in Rome, he would again ascend to the throne. Therefore, on 28 October 312 AD, the sixth anniversary of his conquest of Rome, he agreed to leave the protection of the city's walls and meet Constantine in open battle. On that date, Constantine's forces defeated Maxentius and his army, gaining complete control of the western empire. In his retreat, Maxentius fell from his horse into the Tiber River and drowned. Thus, his spirit ascended to God's throne for preliminary judgment.

Constantine was received most honorably in Rome, which celebrated for seven days. His image was set up in the marketplace, holding in his right hand the sign of the Chi-Rho cross, with this inscription: *With this wholesome sign, the true token of fortitude, I have rescued and delivered our city from the yoke of the tyrant.*[16]

With Constantine in full control of the western empire and possessing the largest loyal army, it became obvious to Licinius that his path to power was through Maximinus Daia. The latter was much like Galerius had been in his management of people, but he was far inferior in his military bearing and understanding of battle strategy. Licinius quickly began organizing loyal forces in the east to challenge Maximinus Daia, and he strengthened his alliance with Constantine.

Though they remained the law, orders for persecution of Christians had generally not been enforced in the west after the abdication of Diocletian and Maximian. In February 313, Constantine met with Licinius in Milan where they developed the "Edict of Milan." The edict granted Christians the privilege to openly practice their faith without oppression, removing penalties for professing Christianity and effectively legalizing the religion. The edict protected not only Christians but all other religions from persecution, allowing anyone to worship whichever gods they chose. The edict included several provisions for the previously persecuted Christians, including the return of all Church property which had previously been confiscated.

The "Edict of Milan" created an open rupture between Licinius and Maximinus Daia, who was an avowed pagan and persecutor of Christians. As a result, the two leaders met in battle on 30 April 313. Licinius defeated his opponent, gaining sole control of the eastern empire. Maximinus Daia fled to Tarsus where he died the following August.

A Martyr's Faith

However, the empire simply wasn't big enough for both Constantine and Licinius. After more than ten years of recurring wars and uneasy truces, Constantine finally defeated Licinius and unified the Republic under his command in 324. Constantine publicly proclaimed his Christianity and provided state protection for Christian worship, saving many Christians temporally from Satan's destructive power. He also renewed and extended religious tolerance to many other faiths. He organized the council of Nicea in 325 to formalize the laws of religious tolerance for all faiths and to encourage uniformity of doctrine among the Christians.

With control of the entire empire, Constantine designated his mother, Helena,[17] as Augusta Imperatrix or Empress, and gave her full access to the imperial treasury with a charge to locate and preserve Christian relics and sacred sites. She is reported to have located and preserved the cross and nails used for the crucifixion of Jesus and the robe of Jesus for which the Roman soldiers cast lots.[18] She commissioned the construction of many Christian churches in Jerusalem and the Holy land, including the Church of the Nativity in Bethlehem, the Church of Eleona on the Mount of Olives (the traditional site of Christ's ascension),[19] the Church of the Holy Sepulcher, the Church of the Burning Bush in the Egyptian Sinai, and many others. Worthy of special note is a cathedral she had constructed in Lydda, Palestine, dedicated to the memory of a noble follower of God. She is known as the patron saint of archaeologists.

Also noteworthy is Bishop Nicholas of Myra,[20] who was born in 270 AD, making him five years older than George. Like George, his parents were Greek Christians. Tales of his youth include travel to Egypt and a pilgrimage to the Holy Land. Soon after his return he became Bishop of Myra. Much of his ministry took place not far from Nicodemia, overlapping the period of the Diocletian persecution and George's trial, torture, and execution. Around that time he was cast into prison for his faith. He may have spent as much as twenty years in prison, reportedly being released after Constantine's ascension to the throne. He was on a list of attendees at the Council of Nicaea in 325. However, legends suggest that he was temporarily banished and imprisoned during the council for his aggressive opposition to what he considered heresy. He died in December 343. He is considered a saint by many faithful Christians, being revered as the patron saint of, among others, repentant thieves. His legendary reputation of secret gift-giving gave rise to the traditional notion of Saint Nicholas, Sinterklaas, or Santa Claus.

Constantine appears to have been a witness to George's trial, torture, and execution.[21] Perhaps like Peter who watched in anguish but did not intervene as the Savior was abused, tried, scourged, and crucified,

Constantine may have watched in anguish as George suffered torture and death for the glory of God. Though he may not have been prompted by the Spirit to intervene in George's suffering, he was prompted later to significant action in securing freedom of conscience and worship for all throughout the Roman Empire. With his support, knowledge of Jesus Christ spread rapidly among vast numbers of God's children within his domain. In his Book of Martyrs, Foxe proclaims, "Constantine so established the peace of the Church that for the space of a thousand years we read of no set persecution against the Christians, unto the time of John Wickliffe."[22] Constantine died in Nicodemia (Izmet, Turkey), on 22 May 337.

****
****

AUTHOR'S WITNESS

No man can be reconciled with the history of humanity if he looks for justice in mortality alone. Embracing the eternal perspective is the foundation for understanding, reconciliation, and peace.

Though the world is full of injustice, this life remains a test of adversity given to us by our loving Heavenly Father for our learning and benefit. Success in the great tests of adversity is manifest when we work righteousness though we are assured of the world's punishments for our actions, and when we reject sin despite the promises of worldly rewards for evil works.

God will set all things right in the eternities, blessing all who obey Him, and punishing those who persist in rebellion against Him. The Lord has promised, "Mine indignation is soon to be poured out without measure upon all nations; and this will I do when the cup of their iniquity is full…And all they who have mourned shall be comforted. And all they who have given their lives for My name shall be crowned. Therefore, let your hearts be comforted concerning Zion; for all flesh is in Mine hands; be still and know that I am God. Zion shall not be moved out of her place, notwithstanding her children are scattered. They that remain, and are pure in heart, shall return, and come to their inheritances, they and their children, with songs of everlasting joy, to build up the waste places of Zion—And all these things that the prophets might be fulfilled."[1]

Accepting God's plan allows us to more easily access the sublime redemptive and healing power of Jesus Christ which is the fruit of His atoning sacrifice and His pure love for us.

It has been said the gospel is so simple that a child could not err therein, and yet it is so profound that it can never be fully comprehended in mortality. Still, God intends for all His children to live by His word, studying and pondering how each passage, principle, and truth might help us to understand our own experiences in life. Each principle of righteousness and holiness is not so much a mystery as it is a puzzle. We are invited to work at them and solve them as we each gather experiences from day to day. With a bit of thoughtful effort we can organize our experiences, like pieces in a puzzle, in a way that refines our growing understanding of the true principles of God's laws and His kingdom. The mysteries of God are not secret, but they are sacred. They are available to all who will honor them.

True principles of righteousness are eternal and unchanging. Each person's puzzle in life contains all God's principles of righteousness and holiness. Each of us has the opportunity of learning the very same laws and truths, completing the very same puzzle picture, even if the puzzle pieces in our own lives have shapes and sizes that differ from those in the puzzled lives of others. When each person's unique life puzzle is properly assembled, the completed picture is the same for everyone. It is a glorious and loving Savior who smiles with outstretched hands, inviting us to come to Him, promising He will lead us back to the glory of our Heavenly Father.

The Holy Scriptures contain the fullness of the gospel and God's plan for His children. When the Lord tells us to live by every word that proceeds from the mouth of God, we should understand that as an invitation to study a completed puzzle (the fullness of the gospel as contained in the scriptures) which will strengthen our ability to recognize the eternal principles intended in the adversity we encounter, as we piece together our own lives. The more familiar we are with the completed picture of the puzzle revealed in the scriptures, the easier it is for us to see the hand of God in the patterns of anguish and joy we experience.

The commandments of God given in holy writ are similar to edge pieces on a puzzle. They are easy to find, relatively easy to order and attach, and they provide a solid framework from which to begin making sense of the rest of life's chaos. However, there is so much more color, meaning, and glory within the completed picture than is evident in the borders alone. God gives us piece by piece, that our light and understanding may increase, and shine brighter and brighter unto the perfect day.[2]

The Book of Mormon prophet Nephi wrote about his own application of this process thus: *"...but that I might more fully persuade [my people] to believe in the Lord their Redeemer I did read unto them that which was written by the prophet Isaiah; for I did liken all scriptures unto us, that it might be for our profit and learning*[3] *...For I will liken his words unto my people*[4]*....Behold, my soul delighteth in the things of the Lord; and my heart pondereth continually upon the things which I have seen and heard."*[5]

I testify that those who study and live by the word of God will see the hand of God in their own lives, if not in all things.

We can all help others as we witness of truths we know, like showing them a small section of our partially completed puzzle. However, no matter what we show others, they eventually must find and reattach, or "remember" their own puzzle pieces, and have their work sealed by the witness of the Holy Spirit. Our puzzles become easier as we learn to embrace all truth, wherever we find it, for the gospel of Jesus Christ encompasses all truth.

The passages and references incorporated in this book represent some of the truths I have come to know for myself. They are a connected part of the puzzle I am working on to make sense of my own life and experiences.

What could be worse than having a tough experience in life? Having a tough experience and not learning from it. It's a great blessing when we come to understand our experiences and when we can see the hand of God in all things.

The Psalmist wrote: *The counsel of the Lord standeth for ever, the thoughts of His heart to all generations. Blessed is the nation whose God is the Lord; and the people whom He hath chosen for His own inheritance. The Lord looketh from heaven; He beholdeth all the sons of men. From the place of His habitation He looketh upon all the inhabitants of the earth. He fashioneth their hearts alike; He considereth all their works.*[6]

It is my intent to honor God's word in all things as I apply it and what little I understand of His mysteries to my life and my work. The truths in this work are God's. The errors are mine.

—Brent Colton

****
****

Discussion Questions
SAINT GEORGE and THE DRAGON:
A Martyr's Faith

Choose those questions most relevant to your group.

1. Athanasius says, "Every man has his price." Can integrity be bought? Does every man have a price? Who will be affected by George's choices? Do your choices affect others? What hard choices have you faced?

2. The empress states, "It makes no difference what you truly believe, as long as you make a public renunciation of Christianity and a proper show of submission to the Emperor and the Roman gods. Once that's done, you can still have the land, the money, and the slaves, and you can be free of the capital and its politics. Believe what you will, but save yourself and your people from persecution and death." Is there ever justification for denying your beliefs? Have you ever been in a situation where you needed to lie to protect yourself or others?

3. George says we should seek for all truth, wherever it is found. Should we accept all truth regardless of the source? How does the source impact our ability to embrace truth?

4. As a young man, George memorizes scripture passages to fill his mind. What thoughts do you cultivate in your mind? Does it matter how we occupy our minds during our free time? (What are the long term consequences of how we use our time?)

5. Gregor and George urge their mother to stay home from delivering bread and clothes to the poor. She answers, "Thank you boys, but I need to do it. The greater the distance between the giver and the receiver, the more the receiver develops a sense of entitlement, which undermines the motivation to self-reliance intended by the giver.[1] Let us never distance ourselves from the Ultimate Giver, nor take Him for granted or fail to do our part."[2] Do you agree with her? How does distance affect the giver and the receiver? How did Christ dispense the gifts that He had for others?

6. When George conquers a town, he trains the population to defend themselves and arms them with weapons. How does this affect those captured? Is an armed population a safer population?

7. Are there any justifications for war? If so, what are they?

8. Is it true that life's biggest tests are when you are assured of rewards for doing evil and punishments for doing good? Why or why not? Have you ever encountered a situation where you were punished for doing what was right?

9. The emperor issues edicts to worship him and the Roman gods. Can belief be legislated, or is freedom of thought inherent in people?

10. Why may George have waited before declaring he was a Christian? How can we promote religious tolerance when we don't agree with other's beliefs?

11. How does "fake news" affect George's situation? Does "fake news" occur today? If so, what impact does it have?

12. Should George have shared the gospel with the priest and the empress when he didn't believe they were sincere in their desires to learn about God? How do we sometimes judge others unnecessarily?

13. How should prisoners of war be treated? What are the pros and cons of each side of this issue?

14. Why did the author leave out details of George's marriage and family life on his journeys home during the off season? Should he have included these? Would they add to or detract from the story?

15. What are the risks related to Sabra's visit to George in prison? Was this wise?

16. Why didn't the emperor go against the council? What "mobs of opinion" challenge us today?

17. Does God sometimes tell us not to intervene when we see injustice? If so, how does He do it and why? (Peter, Constantine, others)

18. How does God prepare us to accomplish difficult tasks in our lives? (Present vs. future) How was George prepared?

19. You can give your life for someone by dying for them, or you can give your life for someone by living for them. Which is harder? How do those options compare?

20. George dies for what he believes. Did George's life make a difference? What, if anything, did George's death accomplish? What things are worthy of your sacrifice? What things are worth the ultimate sacrifice?

CHAPTER NOTES

Old and New Testament references are from the *King James Version of the Bible* unless identified as "JST" for Joseph Smith Translation.

References for 1 Nephi, 2 Nephi, Jacob, Enos, Jarom, Omni, Words of Mormon, Mosiah, Alma, Helaman, 3 Nephi, 4 Nephi, Mormon, Ether, and Moroni are found in *The Book of Mormon: Another Testament of Jesus Christ.*

"D&C" references are found in *The Doctrine and Covenants of The Church of Jesus Christ of Latter-Day Saints.*

References for Moses, Abraham, Joseph Smith History, and Articles of Faith are found in *The Pearl of Great Price.*

"Qur'an" references are found in *The Holy Qur'an*, text and translation by 'Abdullah Yusuf 'Ali.

****

Introduction

1. Deuteronomy 8:3

Chapter 1

1. Psalm 68:5
2. Alma 37:35
3. 2 Nephi 32:8-9; D&C 10:5

Chapter 2

1. Matthew 24:35
2. Genesis 25:29-34
3. Lincoln, Abraham; 16th U.S. President, 1861-1865

Chapter 3

1. 1 Samuel 2:30
2. Matthew 16:19
3. John 14:15

Chapter 4

1. Judges 7:20
2. 1 Corinthians 13:11
3. Judges 7:1-22
4. Judges 7:20

Chapter 5

1. 1 Peter 1:16
2. Moroni 7:45-47
3. Psalm 37:28-29
4. Matthew 4:4; Deuteronomy 8:3
5. 1 Corinthians 1:2
6. 1 Corinthians 13:1-8
7. 1 Peter 1:14-16; Revelation 13:10
8. 1 Nephi 11:17
9. Hebrews 11:1
10. Galatians 5:6
11. Hebrews 11:6
12. Alma 32:21-43
13. Matthew 5:48; 3 Nephi 12:48
14. Matthew 26:39
15. Moroni 7:47
16. Mosiah 4:30

Chapter 6

1. Matthew 22:21
2. Lincoln, Abraham; 16th U.S. President, 1861-1865
3. Matthew 22:21
4. Mosiah 29:21-23
5. Matthew 6:33
6. Packer, Boyd K. (2000, May) The Cloven Tongues of Fire, *Ensign*, 7.
7. Jacob 2:18-19
8. Proverbs 29:2

Chapter 7

1. Mark 8:35
2. 2 Timothy 3:12
3. Hebrews 10:23
4. 2 Nephi 26:3-4
5. Alma 31:26, 30-31
6. Foxe, John; 1516-1587; *Foxe's Book of Martyrs*, Chapter II, The Ninth Persecution.
7. 2 Timothy 3:12
8. 2 Thessalonians 1:4-5
9. Alma 60:13; Alma 14:11
10. Psalm 35:13
11. Helaman 3:35
12. Hebrews 9:16-17
13. Psalm 116:15-16, 8-9, 7

Chapter 8

1. 2 Nephi 9:29
2. Matthew 5:25
3. Lincoln, Abraham; 16th U.S. President, 1861-1865
4. 1 Timothy 4:14

Chapter 9

1. 1 Samuel 17:46
2. Lincoln, Abraham; 16th U.S. President, 1861-1865
3. 1 Samuel 17:33-51

Chapter 10

1. Genesis 48:19
2. Exodus 20:17
3. 1 Samuel 16:7
4. Genesis 48:13-20

5. Mosiah 2:17
6. John 13:34-35
7. Lincoln, Abraham; 16th U.S. President, 1861-1865

Chapter 11

1. Malachi 3:1
2. Exodus 33:7-10
3. Psalm 48:1-2, 9-11, 14
4. Matthew 23:37-38
5. Luke 22:39, 41
6. Mark 14:33-34
7. Luke 22:41-44
8. Matthew 26:42
9. Luke 22:44
10. John 17:1, 5
11. Matthew 4:4
12. Durrant, Devin G. (2015, November) My Heart Pondereth Them Continually, *Ensign*, 112.
13. Matthew 27:33, 35, 37
14. Matthew 27:46
15. Luke 23:45
16. John 19:30
17. Luke 23:46
18. Mark 15:39
19. Isaiah 63:3-4
20. Matthew 27:59-60
21. Matthew 27:59-66
22. Matthew 28:1
23. Matthew 28:2-6
24. Matthew 28:6
25. JST Luke 2:46-47
26. Psalm 26:8
27. Zechariah 13:6
28. Psalm 24:3-5
29. Psalm 27:4, 8

Chapter 12

1. Alma 37:37
2. Matthew 26:52
3. Revelation 13:10
4. Romans 8:16-18
5. Deuteronomy 8:3; Matthew 4:4
6. Psalm 112:1
7. Mormon 9:28; Moroni 4:3; Moroni 10:30
8. Alma 45:8 (2-8)
9. Luke 12:48
10. JSH 1:33

11. Proverbs 1:8
12. Jacob 4:10
13. Proverbs 3:11-12
14. Alma 37:37; Proverbs 3:6
15. Psalm 119:26-27
16. Revelation 2:10
17. Mormon 9:27
18. Psalm 91:11-13
19. Proverbs 2:1-2; D&C 6:12; Matthew 7:6

Chapter 13

1. 1 Samuel 2:26
2. Packer, Boyd K. (2000, May) The Cloven Tongues of Fire, *Ensign*, 7.
3. Packer, Boyd K. (2014, May) The Witness, *Ensign*, 94.
4. Moroni 7:41
5. 2 Corinthians 6:18
6. Alma 56:47-48
7. D&C 88:6
8. James 1:27
9. 1 Corinthians 13:1-3
10. Moroni 7:47
11. Mosiah 2:17-18
12. Matthew 25:40
13. Acts 9:32-35
14. Acts 9:36-42

Chapter 14

1. Luke 12:48
2. Matthew 20:15
3. Johnson, Benjamin F.; 1818-1905

Chapter 15

1. Proverbs 24:29
2. Luke 2:52
3. Lincoln, Abraham; 16th U.S. President, 1861-1865
4. Matthew 26:11
5. Joshua 14:2-3 (12:1 to 17:8)
6. Matthew 7:12
7. Proverbs 24:29
8. Romans 12:15, 21
9. Anderson, Wilford W. (as quoted by Renlund, Dale G.) (2016, May) That I Might Draw All Men Unto Me, *Ensign*, 39.
10. Renlund, Dale G. (2016, May) That I Might Draw All Men Unto Me, *Ensign*, 39.

Chapter 16

1. Romans 5:2, 5
2. Acts 9:32-42
3. John 3:2
4. Lincoln, Abraham; 16th U.S. President, 1861-1865
5. Proverbs 1:8
6. Alma 56:47-48
7. Daniel 2:31-46
8. 3 John 1:4
9. Qur'an 7:55
10. Qur'an 6:106
11. Washington, George; 1st U.S. President, 1789-1797
12. D&C 135:4
13. John 14:23, 26
14. D&C 8:2
15. Alma 17:11
16. MacArthur, Douglas; U.S. Military General, WWII, 1941-1945
17. D&C 10:5

Chapter 17

1. Luke 2:49
2. 3 Nephi 22:14
3. Enos 1:3
4. Alma 5:14
5. Zechariah 1:16-17; 2:1-5, 10-12; 8:3-9
6. Psalm 38:21-22
7. Joshua 4:1-9, 19-24
8. D&C 82:10
9. John 14:15-16
10. Luke 15:11-32
11. 2 Nephi 32:3
12. 2 Nephi 4:15-17

Chapter 18

1. Ephesians 6:13
2. Daniel 2:40
3. Ephesians 6:10-18
4. 1 Nephi 19:23
5. Qur'an 7:26
6. Genesis 3:17
7. Matthew 4:4

A Martyr's Faith

8. Hebrews 12:5-10
9. 1 Nephi 3:7
10. Deuteronomy 8:3
11. 1 Corinthians 13:1-8
12. 1 Peter 1:14-16; Revelation 13:10
13. Jacob 4:10
14. Proverbs 3:11-12
15. Psalm 119:26-27
16. D&C 6:12
17. Revelation 2:10

Chapter 19

1. Joshua 4:21
2. Psalm 111:10
3. Matthew 17:19-21; Alma 17:2-3
4. Qur'an 6:14
5. Jackson, Thomas Jonathan "Stonewall"; Confederate General, U.S. Civil War, 1861-1865
6. Qur'an 3:154
7. Alma 60:13
8. 1 Nephi 11:17
9. Matthew 11:28-30
10. Joshua 3, 4:1-9, 19-24
11. 1 Nephi 2:7
12. Alma 48:10
13. Alma 48:11
14. Alma 48:12-16

Chapter 20

1. Proverbs 2:8
2. Psalm 77:18
3. Psalm 106:1
4. Alma 43:9
5. Alma 60:29, 24, 27
6. James 1:20
7. 3 Nephi 11:29
8. Lincoln, Abraham; 16th U.S. President, 1861-1865
9. Romans 8:31
10. Proverbs 2:5-9
11. Romans 14:8
12. Hebrews 13:6
13. Psalm 25:2
14. Alma 48:12, 7-10, 15-16, 20
15. Qur'an 59:13-14

16. Carlyle, Thomas; *Lecture on Martin Luther*, The Deseret News Press, 1926, 20.
17. Mosiah 4:9-12
18. Alma 3:26-27
19. Alma 60:14, 16
20. Alma 28:12, 14
21. Alma 57:19-21
22. 1 Samuel 3:19
23. Genesis 39:2-4
24. Qur'an 2:256
25. Ether 4:11

Chapter 21

1. Job 33:15-16
2. Moroni 7:29-30
3. Proverbs 1:10, 13-16, 18-19
4. JSH 1:33
5. 1 John 2:28
6. D&C 6:12
7. https://en.wikipedia.org/wiki/Saint_Florian
8. Howe, Julia Ward; *Battle Hymn of the Republic*; 1861
9. Romans 8:31
10. D&C 123:17
11. Hebrews 13:6
12. Qur'an 29:69
13. Mosiah 29:20
14. JSH 1:24-25
15. Qur'an 6:157
16. Psalm 31:1
17. Alma 2:30
18. Alma 58:10
19. Alma 58:11

Chapter 22

1. Proverbs 16:19
2. Mosiah 20:11
3. Alma 43:54
4. Alma 44:3, 1
5. Proverbs 3:13, 17-18
6. Alma 58:40
7. Alma 57:35-36
8. Psalm 119:162
9. Proverbs 16:18-19

Chapter 23

1. James 1:27
2. James 1:27
3. Moroni 7:45-47
4. Alma 53:5
5. Mosiah 20:12
6. D&C 24:1-2
7. Lincoln, Abraham; 16th U.S. President, 1861-1865; *Gettysburg Address*, 4 July 1863
8. Ibid.
9. Ibid.
10. Ibid.
11. Ibid.
12. Exodus 20:17
13. Genesis 4:8-9; Moses 5:31-33
14. 1 Corinthians 15:34
15. D&C 88:86
16. Mosiah 21:17
17. Mosiah 21:17-18
18. Mormon 9:19
19. Mormon 9:20

Chapter 24

1. Romans 12:18
2. 1 Nephi 7:11-12
3. Qur'an 41:34
4. Qur'an 8:70
5. D&C 88:86
6. Mark 5:36
7. Qur'an 9:71
8. Chase, Salmon P.; U.S. Treasury Secretary, 1861-1864; U.S. Supreme Court Chief Justice, 1864-1873.
9. Alma 41:14
10. Lincoln, Abraham; 16th U.S. President, 1861-1865
11. Alma 1:13
12. Alma 3:19
13. Helaman 12:21
14. Alma 24:13
15. Isaiah 14:18-20
16. Alma 30:7-11
17. Joshua 24:15
18. Qur'an 6:108
19. Alma 1:21-22, 25
20. Mosiah 27:2-5
21. Psalm 37:3

Chapter 25

1. Isaiah 54:10
2. Mosiah 18:9
3. Alma 50:39
4. Alma 50:39
5. Lincoln, Abraham; 16th U.S. President, 1861-1865
6. Revelation 13:10
7. D&C 130:20
8. Isaiah 28:10; Ephesians 4:13
9. Qur'an 106:1-4
10. Alma 60:28-29, 34, 36
11. Alma 53:17-19
12. Alma 33:1, 3-5, 7, 10-11, 13
13. Moroni 8:25-26
14. Proverbs 3:9-10
15. Alma 1:27
16. Alma 1:29-30
17. Mosiah 24:14-16
18. Mosiah 25:24
19. Qur'an 60:12
20. Jonah 3:5-8
21. Alma 12:33-34
22. Mosiah 5:6-7
23. Qur'an 60:10, 12
24. Hebrews 5:4; John 15:16
25. https://en.wikipedia.org/wiki/Saint_Nicholas
26. Mosiah 5:15
27. Helaman 3:27

Chapter 26

1. Alma 37:6
2. Tolstoy, Leo; 1795-1881; *War and Peace*.
3. McKay, David O. (1967, June) Consciousness of God—Supreme Goal of Life, *Improvement Era*, 80.
4. 2 Nephi 33:3
5. Mark 5:36
6. Alma 37:6-7
7. Joshua 6
8. Alma 62:9
9. Alma 57:35-36
10. Qur'an 3:17
11. Lincoln, Abraham; 16th U.S. President, 1861-1865
12. Mosiah 2:18
13. Nehemiah 4:16-23; 6:1-3

14. Qur'an 2:261
15. Alma 46:13, 16, 18
16. Alma 58:11-12
17. Alma 61:15

Chapter 27

1. Matthew 5:39
2. 2 Chronicles 26:14
3. Joshua 10:7
4. Alma 20:17-18
5. James 1:20
6. Lincoln, Abraham; 16th U.S. President, 1861-1865
7. Young, Brigham (as cited by Hanks, Marion D.) (1974, January) Forgiveness: The Ultimate Form of Love, *Ensign*, 21.
8. Romans 12:19-21
9. Proverbs 1:5
10. Hebrews 11:34
11. Ether 12:27
12. Alma 55:19
13. Alma 48:11-13
14. Alma 48:7-8
15. Alma 48:10
16. Alma 48:15-16
17. Alma 48:17-18
18. Pope Gelasius I; Beatification of St. George; 494 AD
19. Matthew 6:4
20. D&C 31:9, 7
21. Alma 44:11

Chapter 28

1. Proverbs 3:5
2. Psalm 120:7
3. Mormon 4:5
4. 1 Corinthians 3:19
5. Alma 56:47-48
6. Matthew 25:21
7. Genesis 3:19
8. Amos 5:12, 14; 1 Samuel 12:3
9. Proverbs 1:10-16, 18-19
10. Mosiah 7:33
11. Mosiah 2:17-19
12. Psalm 24:8
13. Jacob 4:10
14. Alma 37:37

15. Alma 32:16
16. Proverbs 3:5-7, 4
17. Alma 5:28-29
18. 3 Nephi 11:29-30
19. 1 John 3:14
20. Luke 10:29

Chapter 29

1. Alma 62:5
2. Lincoln, Abraham; 16th U.S. President, 1861-1865
3. Mosiah 29:10-11, 14, 32, 34, 36
4. Washington, George; 1st U.S. President, 1789-1797
5. Holland, Jeffrey R. (2014, May) The Cost—and Blessings—of Discipleship, *Ensign*, 6.
6. 3 Nephi 27:14
7. Alma 24:14
8. Alma 22:6
9. Moroni 7:3-4, 19-22
10. Proverbs 1:7
11. 3 Nephi 29:5-6
12. Alma 32:41-43
13. Alma 41:14-15
14. Omni 1:26
15. Mosiah 29:37-40
16. Alma 31:5
17. Moroni 7:41
18. Psalm 33:18-19, 21-22
19. Mormon 4:18
20. Mosiah 5:2-4
21. Alma 22:18
22. Alma 27:30
23. Psalm 60:12

Chapter 30

1. Qur'an 4:75
2. 1 Timothy 3:5
3. Exodus 18:13-26
4. Psalm 18:43-44, 46
5. Qur'an 5:82
6. Lincoln, Abraham; 16th U.S. President, 1861-1865
7. Washington, George; 1st U.S. President, 1789-1797
8. Qur'an 8:61
9. Wallace, William Ross; *What Rules the World?*; 1865
10. Mosiah 29:40

11. Alma 22:7-8
12. Isaiah 40:28-31
13. Alma 7:9-13
14. Alma 7:14
15. Alma 32:28
16. Alma 33:23
17. D&C 84:44-45
18. D&C 84:46-48
19. Alma 5:33-35
20. Alma 7:14-16
21. Alma 5:57-58
22. Mosiah 21:32
23. Psalm 74:13
24. Alma 43:46-47
25. Alma 43:9
26. Alma 46:12
27. Alma 46:22
28. Alma 46:23-24
29. 4 Nephi 1:2-3

Chapter 31

1. Genesis 39:3
2. Alma 48:12
3. 2 Nephi 1:1, 4-5
4. 2 Nephi 1:7
5. 2 Nephi 1:21-23, 19
6. Psalm 118:24
7. Psalm 107:21-22
8. Alma 34:38
9. James 2:18
10. Lincoln, Abraham; 16th U.S. President, 1861-1865
11. Ether 4:11
12. Alma 61:15, 21
13. 2 Timothy 3:12
14. Psalm 62:8
15. 2 Nephi 31:7, 10
16. Psalm 117:1-2
17. Mosiah 5:1-2
18. Alma 17:4
19. Alma 61:9
20. Psalm 72:4-5, 7, 9, 12-14
21. Alma 26:1, 26
22. Alma 26:12-13
23. Alma 26:6
24. Alma 26:29, 4, 15, 13
25. Alma 26:11, 13, 7
26. Alma 26:37
27. 2 Nephi 4:17
28. 2 Nephi 4:19-20
29. Psalm 35:27-28
30. Psalm 116:17

Chapter 32

1. Ecclesiastes 3:1, 7
2. Romans 16:22
3. Qur'an 2:86
4. Lincoln, Abraham; 16th U.S. President, 1861-1865
5. Psalm 40:4

Chapter 33

1. Judges 7:2
2. Proverbs 6:16-19
3. Proverbs 1:10-16
4. 3 Nephi 11:29-30
5. 1 Samuel 12:3; Amos 5:12; Exodus 23:8; Deuteronomy 16:19
6. Exodus 20:14; Acts 15:20
7. Genesis 3:19
8. Qur'an 6:141
9. Alma 60:14
10. Qur'an 7:180
11. D&C 6:12
12. Qur'an 6:70
13. 1 Nephi 16:2
14. Mormon 3:12
15. Psalm 133:1

Chapter 34

1. Psalm 75:6-7
2. Eban, Abba; Speech in London, 16 December 1970.
3. Sun-tzu; Chinese General & Military Strategist (~400 BC)
4. Proverbs 28:1
5. Leviticus 26:15, 19-20
6. 2 Nephi 4:20-28
7. Psalm 37:23-24
8. Psalm 75:6-7
9. Psalm 91:11-13
10. D&C 49:27-28
11. 2 Nephi 4:30
12. Alma 7:22-25, 27

Chapter 35

1. Psalm 91:13

A Martyr's Faith

2. *Troparion of St. George, Tone 4:* http://www.antiochian.org/saint_george
3. Philippians 4:8; Articles of Faith 1:13
4. Alma 18:17

Chapter 36

1. Exodus 13:21
2. Genesis 39:21-23
3. Alma 18:10

Chapter 37

1. Psalm 2:2
2. Mormon 9:4
3. Alma 46:4-5
4. Ether 8:15, 14
5. Helaman 16:22
6. John 11:47-48
7. 3 Nephi 11:29
8. 2 Nephi 26:22-23
9. Mark 4:22
10. Matthew 23:27
11. Qur'an 58:8, 10
12. Sun-tzu; Chinese General & Military Strategist (~400 BC)
13. 2 Nephi 4:30, 32, 34-35

Chapter 38

1. Qur'an 6:123
2. Qur'an 29:68
3. Acts 4:25-26
4. Mosiah 29:21
5. Qur'an 31:19
6. Psalm 36:3
7. Qur'an 6:123
8. Mormon 4:5
9. Psalm 58:3-4
10. Psalm 11:2
11. Qur'an 6:93
12. Ether 8:18-19, 22-26
13. Psalm 70:2-3
14. Psalm 71:10-11, 13, 24
15. D&C 84:49-55
16. D&C 84:44-48
17. Psalm 26:9-11

Chapter 39

1. Isaiah 10:1
2. Foxe, John; *Foxe's Book of Martyrs*, Chapter II, The Tenth Persecution; adaptation of similar story.
3. Psalm 57:4-5, 8
4. Isaiah 10:1
5. Lincoln, Abraham; 16th U.S. President, 1861-1865
6. Matthew 12:25
7. Matthew 22:17-21
8. Romans 13:7
9. Qur'an 7:117
10. Philippians 4:8; Articles of Faith 1:13
11. Articles of Faith 1:11
12. Matthew 12:25
13. Qur'an 6:35
14. D&C 101:16
15. 2 Timothy 3:12
16. 2 Nephi 9:18
17. Alma 7:6, 5
18. Jacob 1:8
19. Acts 25:10-11
20. 2 Nephi 26:3-4

Chapter 40

1. Matthew 5:44-45
2. Qur'an 2:140
3. Job 1:21
4. Psalm 22:1-5
5. 2 Nephi 4:20-23
6. 2 Nephi 4:26-27
7. 2 Nephi 4:31-33
8. 2 Nephi 4:28-30
9. 2 Nephi 4:34-35
10. John 14:18, 26
11. 1 Nephi 21:14-16; Isaiah 49:14-16
12. 1 Nephi 21:22-23; Isaiah 49:22-23
13. Matthew 11:28-30
14. Matthew 5:10-12
15. Psalm 17:13-14
16. Psalm 17:4-5
17. Psalm 17:8
18. Qur'an 2:42
19. Mosiah 17:9-10
20. Luke 6:22-23
21. Psalm 119:105-107
22. Psalm 119:46
23. Ephesians 6:10-13, 18
24. Matthew 5:44-45; 3 Nephi 12:44-45
25. Washington, George; 1st U.S. President, 1789-1797

Chapter 41

1. 1 Corinthians 7:23
2. Psalm 31:13
3. Proverbs 1:10
4. Matthew 16:23
5. Mormon 5:22-24
6. Helaman 9:21-22
7. Psalm 115:4-8; 135:15-18
8. Qur'an 72:22
9. Mosiah 5:2
10. 2 Nephi 28:9-10
11. Hebrews 13:20
12. Smith, Joseph (2002, July) The Wentworth Letter, *Ensign*, 31.
13. Genesis 25:29-34
14. Helaman 7:13, 21
15. 1 Nephi 16:3
16. Helaman 7:26
17. Romans 1:16
18. Alma 30:13
19. Alma 30:14, 16, 13
20. Alma 30:17-18
21. Deuteronomy 4:28-31
22. John 8:31-32

Chapter 42

1. Matthew 23:34
2. Jeremiah 3:22; 3 Nephi 18:32
3. Moroni 10:4; Isaiah 28:10
4. Ether 4:8
5. Alma 11:22
6. Alma 5:13-15
7. Moroni 7:18-19
8. Ephesians 6:19-20
9. Alma 11:26-27
10. Alma 18:32, 34
11. D&C 138:19
12. 1 Nephi 17:40; Genesis 28:13-15; John 3:14-15; John 3:36
13. Alma 11:38-39
14. 1 Nephi 17:36-38; Genesis 3:17
15. John 5:37
16. 3 Nephi 27:14; John 12:32
17. John 17:3
18. Alma 11:40
19. 3 Nephi 15:9; John 12:34-36
20. Alma 30:44
21. 1 Nephi 11:17
22. Amos 3:7
23. Matthew 23:34
24. Exodus 33:11; 34:29; Matthew 17:2-3
25. John 3:16
26. John 7:17
27. 1 Nephi 22:2
28. John 17:20-23
29. John 14:26
30. Moroni 10:5
31. Alma 32:28
32. Matthew 3:11
33. Mormon 9:11-12
34. Mormon 9:19-20
35. Exodus 14:15-31
36. Mormon 9:18
37. Matthew 26-28; Mark 14-16; Luke 22-24; John 18-21; 3 Nephi 11-26
38. Jacob 4:3-5
39. Revelation 19:10
40. Mark 13:10
41. 3 Nephi 12:1
42. Romans 8:16-18
43. Jacob 4:11-13
44. Ether 12:41
45. Alma 30:41
46. 1 Corinthians 15:3-8

Chapter 43

1. 2 Thessalonians 2:3
2. Acts 7:52-53
3. Matthew 13:12
4. Genesis 9:8-17
5. Genesis 11:1-9
6. Genesis 17:1-7
7. Genesis 22:18
8. Genesis 46-50
9. Exodus 3
10. Exodus 4-14
11. Exodus 24:1, 9-11
12. Exodus 34:29-35
13. Numbers 7:1-3
14. Exodus 24:1, 9; Numbers 11:16
15. Exodus 25-27
16. Exodus 33:11
17. Deuteronomy 18:15-19
18. Malachi 3:7
19. 3 Nephi 6:20
20. Acts 3:19-26
21. Luke 6:13
22. Luke 10:1, 17-19
23. John 2:13-16
24. Moroni 7:36
25. Moroni 7:36-37
26. Acts 3:26, 20-21
27. Revelation 14:6-7
28. Alma 13:21-24
29. Ezekiel 37:21-27
30. 2 Nephi 29:8
31. 2 Nephi 29:9-10
32. 1 Corinthians 2:4-5, 9-12, 14
33. 2 Nephi 32:4-5
34. John 7:17

35. D&C 135:4
36. John 14:6
37. Matthew 3:13-17
38. Jonah 3:5-8
39. Alma 33:21
40. Philippians 2:10-11
41. Alma 32:16
42. Uchtdorf, Dieter F. (2014, May) Are You Sleeping Through the Restoration?, *Ensign,* 58.
43. Enos 1:2
44. Alma 5:46-47
45. 2 Nephi 25:20-23, 29
46. Alma 5:7, 4-5
47. Helaman 16:18, 20

Chapter 44

1. Alma 34:16
2. Isaiah 5:22-23
3. Alma 30:24
4. Jacob 6:7-8; 7:11
5. 2 Nephi 32:8
6. Alma 32:33-34
7. John 14:6, 11-12
8. Matthew 6:6-13
9. John 16:23
10. D&C 8:2
11. Psalm 27:9, 14
12. John 16:23-27
13. 2 Nephi 9:1-3
14. Alma 26:21-22
15. Revelation 3:10
16. Hebrews 1:1-2, 8-10; Abraham 1:2-3
17. Hebrews 12:9; Acts 17:28-29; Job 38:4-7
18. John 1:1-3; 17:5
19. 1 Corinthians 6:19
20. 2 Nephi 2:11, 14-16
21. Revelation 12:7-10
22. Genesis 2:16-17
23. 2 Nephi 2:22-23
24. Alma 12:22-24
25. 2 Nephi 2:24-25
26. 2 Nephi 2:21
27. Romans 15:13
28. 3 Nephi 19:25; 2 Corinthians 3:7
29. 3 Nephi 27:20-21; John 14:12
30. 3 Nephi 27:13-15; Alma 11:43-45
31. 3 Nephi 27:16-17, 19
32. 2 Nephi 2:27, 26
33. 3 Nephi 27:18
34. Alma 40:11-12
35. Alma 40:13-14; 1 Peter 3:18-20
36. Luke 24:39
37. Alma 11:43-45

38. 1 Corinthians 15:22
39. Moroni 7:41
40. Alma 40:25; 1 John 3:2; Romans 8:17
41. 1 Corinthians 2:9
42. Alma 11:41
43. Helaman 14:18
44. Alma 30:13
45. 2 Nephi 9:4-5
46. Alma 5:10
47. Alma 5:9, 13-14
48. 1 Nephi 11:17
49. Isaiah 28:10
50. Revelation 12:7-10
51. Moroni 7:16
52. Moses 6:61-62
53. 1 Peter 2:20
54. 2 Nephi 2:28-29
55. Moses 8:24

Chapter 45

1. John 3:16
2. 1 Nephi 4:13
3. 2 Nephi 9:6-7
4. Alma 11:34
5. Alma 11:34, 37
6. 3 Nephi 27:19-20
7. D&C 42:41
8. Alma 42:13
9. Alma 12:31-32, 25
10. 2 Nephi 2:5
11. 1 Nephi 10:18-19
12. 2 Nephi 2:6-8, 10
13. Alma 22:14
14. Ephesians 1:3-4; Moses 4:2
15. Revelation 12:10
16. Moses 4:1, 3-4
17. John 1:14; 3 Nephi 11:11
18. Luke 18:22
19. Revelation 12:7-9
20. 2 Nephi 9:6
21. Helaman 16:18
22. Romans 14:11; Mosiah 27:31
23. D&C 109:77
24. 1 Corinthians 15:22
25. Mosiah 5:13
26. 2 Nephi 9:21-24, 27
27. 2 Nephi 9:25
28. 2 Nephi 9:26
29. Lincoln, Abraham; 16th U.S. President, 1861-1865
30. Luke 22:44; 3 Nephi 11:11; Mosiah 3:7; 15:5; D&C 19:16-18; 45:4
31. Romans 8:17; 2 Timothy 2:12; 1 Peter 2:20; Jacob 1:8
32. Alma 22:17-18

Chapter 46

1. Matthew 16:18-19
2. Monson, Thomas S. (2004, May) The Call for Courage, *Ensign*, 54.
3. Matthew 16:15-17
4. 1 Nephi 15:8, 11; James 1:5-6
5. Helaman 13:8
6. Alma 30:23-24, 28, 27
7. Alma 30:32-35
8. Alma 31:1, 24-25, 28
9. Alma 30:22
10. Alma 30:44, 46
11. Alma 31:35
12. 2 Nephi 9:1
13. Matthew 16:19
14. 3 Nephi 5:13
15. Ephesians 4:11
16. Hebrews 10:21
17. James 5:14
18. Luke 1:8
19. Ephesians 4:11
20. 1 Timothy 3:1-10
21. Ephesians 4:12
22. Hebrews 5:4
23. Exodus 28:1, 41; Leviticus 8:12
24. Isaiah 43:10
25. Luke 6:13
26. Mark 3:14-15
27. John 15:16-17
28. Articles of Faith 1:5
29. Moroni 7:31
30. Alma 13:1-2, 5-6
31. Moroni 10:32; Articles of Faith 1:3
32. Mosiah 13:33-35
33. James 5:14-15
34. Matthew 17:20
35. Mark 4:36-41
36. Matthew 14:25-33
37. Romans 8:17
38. 3 Nephi 27:5-6
39. John 3:5
40. Alma 13:16
41. Colossians 2:12
42. Acts 8:18; Acts 19:6
43. John 16:13
44. Mosiah 4:10-11
45. Mark 1:3-8; Matthew 3:1-3, 8, 11
46. Acts 2:38
47. Hebrews 10:21-23
48. Hebrews 10:16-17
49. Malachi 3:1-2
50. Psalm 24:3-4
51. Qur'an 28:67
52. Isaiah 9:2
53. 1 Peter 3:18-19
54. 1 Corinthians 15:29
55. 1 Kings 3:5-12
56. Genesis 12:1-3; Acts 3:25; Abraham 2:9-11
57. Psalm 132:11-12
58. Galatians 3:29
59. Jeremiah 31:10
60. Psalm 50:4-5
61. Malachi 3:14-15
62. Malachi 3:7
63. Alma 5:10-11
64. Alma 13:21, 27-28, 13, 28-29
65. Alma 13:20
66. 2 Nephi 32:8-9; Hebrews 11:6; John 14:26
67. Ether 4:15
68. Psalm 19:7-9
69. Psalm 25:10

Chapter 47

1. Matthew 7:24
2. Matthew 6:24
3. 3 Nephi 3:7, 11
4. Matthew 6:19-23
5. Matthew 10:39
6. John 15:12-13
7. Genesis 2:24
8. Matthew 7:11
9. Hinckley, Gordon B., et al. (1995, November) The Family: A Proclamation to the World, *Ensign*, 102.
10. Romans 8:16-17
11. John 15:11-12
12. 1 Peter 1:14-16
13. Luke 1:49
14. Matthew 5:48
15. Romans 8:18
16. John 14:2
17. Matthew 7:24-27
18. 1 Corinthians 10:4
19. Helaman 5:12
20. Psalm 127:1
21. Hebrews 11:32-40
22. Malachi 3:16-17
23. Malachi 4:5-6
24. D&C 121:45
25. Genesis 2:18, 21-25
26. Genesis 2:16-17; 3:2-6, 22-24
27. Matthew 19:4-6; Mark 10:6-9
28. 1 Peter 3:7
29. Ephesians 5:25-32
30. 1 Corinthians 11:11
31. 3 John 1:4

A Martyr's Faith

32. Psalm 127:3-5
33. Genesis 26:1-5
34. Luke 16:19-31
35. Mark 10:14-16
36. Isaiah 49:16
37. Revelation 1:17-18
38. Revelation 1:5-6
39. 2 Nephi 25:23, 25-27
40. Alma 60:10-12
41. Alma 60:13-14
42. Alma 22:15; Acts 2:37
43. Mormon 7:5-10; Acts 2:38
44. Isaiah 5:25-26
45. Mosiah 26:21-22
46. Alma 5:12-15
47. Mormon 8:22

Chapter 48

1. 1 Samuel 15:22
2. Alma 1:3-4
3. Matthew 25:14-30; Luke 12:47-48
4. Moroni 10:4-5
5. D&C 130:20-21
6. D&C 132:5
7. John 6:38
8. 1 Samuel 15:22
9. John 7:17
10. D&C 43:9
11. D&C 82:10
12. Malachi 3:10-12
13. Matthew 22:35-40
14. Exodus 20:1-17
15. D&C 58:26-28
16. Isaiah 1:16-20
17. Matthew 26:39
18. Romans 8:16-18; Abraham 3:26
19. Packer, Boyd K. (1983, May) Agency and Control, *Ensign*, 66.
20. 2 Chronicles 19:7
21. John 14:15
22. 2 Nephi 9:48
23. Moses 6:57
24. Moroni 10:32
25. Jacob 2:35
26. Romans 6:23
27. Matthew 15:15-17; Mark 9:7; John 6:38-40
28. John 15:26
29. 3 Nephi 11:32-34
30. Alma 13:10
31. Jeremiah 31:31-34
32. Kimball, Spencer W. (1980, March) Give the Lord Your Loyalty, *Ensign*, 6.
33. D&C 58:42
34. Matthew 5:29-30

35. Jacob 2:8
36. 2 Nephi 9:42-43
37. Acts 20:28-30
38. 2 Thessalonians 2:3
39. 2 Timothy 3:5
40. Titus 1:16
41. 2 Peter 1:21-2:1
42. Revelation 2:2
43. Alma 33:11, 22
44. Enos 1:2
45. Jacob 6:9-10
46. Jacob 6:7-8
47. 2 Nephi 31:13, 17, 15
48. Helaman 8:8-9
49. Helaman 3:27-30
50. Alma 14:1

Chapter 49

1. Qur'an 3:29
2. 3 Nephi 3:7
3. John 3:16; Moses 1:39
4. 2 Nephi 30:6
5. Ether 12:6
6. Uchtdorf, Dieter F. (2013, November) Come, Join With Us, *Ensign*, 21.
7. Matthew 26:39
8. 1 Nephi 19:7, 9-10
9. 2 Nephi 25:13; Malachi 4:2
10. 2 Nephi 9:18
11. 2 Nephi 2:27
12. Jacob 1:8
13. Alma 34:10-16
14. Proverbs 3:5-6
15. Jacob 4:10-11
16. Philippians 1:13-14
17. Philippians 4:21-22
18. Alma 37:37
19. Jacob 3:1
20. Moroni 10:32
21. Mosiah 16:15
22. Philippians 4:23
23. Helaman 5:12
24. D&C 9:8-9
25. Helaman 7:9
26. Alma 6:6
27. Hebrews 11:16
28. 2 Nephi 6:13
29. 1 John 2:28
30. Hebrews 11:32-40
31. 3 Nephi 12:6; Matthew 5:6
32. 3 Nephi 12:2
33. Joshua 1:9
34. Qur'an 3:29-30
35. Qur'an 3:30
36. Psalm 24:3-4

515

37. Revelation 6:9, 11
38. 2 Nephi 4:28
39. Psalms 91:13
40. John 15:13
41. Matthew 10:39
42. Hebrews 9:16-17
43. Mosiah 15:10; Acts 8:33

Chapter 50

1. James 1:5
2. Mosiah 12:9, 12-16
3. 2 Nephi 33:10
4. Matthew 22:17-21
5. Romans 13:7
6. 2 Nephi 33:1-2
7. 2 Nephi 33:14
8. Mormon 9:3
9. Alma 34:32-35
10. Moroni 10:4-5
11. 2 Nephi 33:4
12. Mosiah 16:9
13. Mosiah 16:15
14. Mosiah 16:10-11
15. Mosiah 16:1
16. Mosiah 16:6-8
17. Moroni 10:30, 32-33
18. 2 Nephi 30:2
19. Isaiah 50:1
20. Isaiah 10:4
21. Alma 60:34
22. Alma 60:29, 36
23. 2 Nephi 28:21-22
24. Alma 10:26-27
25. Mormon 8:40-41
26. Alma 10:17-18
27. Matthew 23:33
28. Lincoln, Abraham; 16th U.S. President, 1861-1865
29. Alma 10:19
30. Ether 8:22
31. Alma 10:23
32. Malachi 4:1
33. Malachi 1:3
34. Alma 12:7
35. Mosiah 17:11-12
36. Moroni 10:34

Chapter 51

1. Alma 22:18
2. 2 Nephi 32:7
3. Mosiah 17:2
4. James 1:5-6
5. Psalm 42:2-3
6. Alma 36:18
7. Ether 4:11
8. Alma 36:19-20
9. Matthew 7:5
10. Alma 14:6
11. Alma 30:53
12. Alma 15:5
13. Mosiah 4:2-3
14. Psalm 73:1-3, 6, 8-9, 12-13, 22, 24, 28
15. John 15:26-27
16. Alma 27:23

Chapter 52

1. 2 Nephi 22:2; Isaiah 12:2
2. Psalm 43:4-5
3. Revelation 15:3-4
4. Luke 24:39
5. Qur'an 7:164
6. Job 27:5
7. Qur'an 6:162
8. Ether 15:34
9. Packer, Boyd K. (2014, May) The Witness, *Ensign*, 94.
10. Lincoln, Abraham; 16th U.S. President, 1861-1865
11. 1 John 3:14
12. Luke 10:29
13. D&C 128:22
14. Alma 38:5
15. Enos 1:27
16. Mark 5:36
17. Psalm 31:24
18. Psalm 60:12
19. James 5:16
20. 3 John 1:4
21. Packer, Boyd K. (2000, May) The Cloven Tongues of Fire, *Ensign*, 7.
22. D&C 25:12
23. "I Feel My Savior's Love" *Words Verses 1-3:* Ralph Rodgers, Jr.; K. Newell Dayley; and Laurie Huffman (Ref. John 15:10-12) *Music:* K. Newell Dayley © 1979 K. Newell Dayley; Used with permission. Jackman Music Corporation is the publisher of commercial arrangements of this song.
24. Revelation 7:17; 21:3-4
25. Proverbs 12:28
26. Alma 41:11

Chapter 53

1. Amos 4:12
2. Alma 38:14
3. 2 Timothy 3:12
4. Acts 5:41
5. Psalm 69:16-18
6. Psalm 63:1-4
7. Psalm 42:10
8. Psalm 69:4-6
9. Psalm 69:12-15
10. Psalm 42:11
11. Psalm 62:1, 6-7
12. Luke 14:27
13. Matthew 5:14-16
14. D&C 8:2
15. D&C 109:46, 43, 47, 72, 76
16. Hebrews 11:36-37, 35
17. D&C 109:50
18. Luke 23:34
19. D&C 109:56-57
20. D&C 109:73-74
21. D&C 8:2

Chapter 54

1. Alma 14:11
2. James 1:5-6
3. Colossians 1:12
4. John 14:18, 16

Chapter 55

1. Proverbs 8:17
2. Psalm 25:4-7
3. Psalm 31:14-17
4. Romans 13:12
5. Mosiah 15:1-2, 5-7
6. Mosiah 15:8-9
7. Mosiah 15:10-12, 28-29, 31
8. Mosiah 17:9
9. Daniel 3:17-18
10. Job 27:5
11. Alma 60:13
12. Alma 14:11
13. Monson, Thomas S. (2004, November) Choose You This Day, *Ensign*, 67.
14. Qur'an 6:158
15. Qur'an 20:72
16. Malachi 2:17
17. Helaman 13:29
18. Alma 60:32-33
19. 2 Nephi 1:13, 23, 28-29
20. D&C 1:2-3, 11-12, 14
21. Alma 39:8-9
22. John 7:17
23. Jacob 1:8
24. Jacob 2:19
25. Qur'an 3:29-30
26. Romans 1:16
27. 1 Peter 3:17

Chapter 56

1. Moroni 7:37
2. Qur'an 14:30
3. John 7:17
4. Alma 14:24
5. Alma 30:43
6. Alma 30:44
7. Alma 30:42
8. Mosiah 17:9-10
9. 3 Nephi 12:10-12; Matthew 5:10-12
10. Psalm 34:22
11. Luke 1:38
12. Ephesians 5:14

Chapter 57

1. Isaiah 13:7
2. Psalm 30:3
3. Alma 37:31
4. Alma 14:11

Chapter 58

1. Romans 8:35
2. 3 Nephi 30:2
3. Mormon 4:11
4. Psalm 35:17
5. Romans 13:11-12
6. Psalm 132:9
7. Luke 22:42
8. Psalm 71:18, 20

Chapter 59

1. Qur'an 3:145
2. Psalm 22:14-15
3. Qur'an 3:145
4. Jacob 7:8
5. Exodus 34:29-35
6. Mosiah 13:2-3
7. Mosiah 13:5-8

8. D&C 3:6-8
9. Mormon 9:1-2, 5-6
10. Obadiah 1:15
11. Alma 5:7, 37-39
12. Alma 5:57-58
13. Alma 5:17-20
14. Alma 5:21-24
15. Mormon 9:26-29
16. Helaman 8:24-25, 27
17. Alma 5:50
18. Joshua 24:15
19. 2 Nephi 10:23-24
20. 2 Nephi 27:33
21. Enos 1:27
22. 3 Nephi 11:3
23. 1 Nephi 19:12
24. Psalm 46:10
25. Acts 7:59
26. Psalm 31:5
27. D&C 135:1
28. Mosiah 17:20

Chapter 60

1. 2 Nephi 9:41
2. Ephesians 5:14
3. Isaiah 51:9
4. Isaiah 52:1
5. D&C 19:23-24
6. Ether 3:11
7. Ether 3:12
8. Psalm 119:135
9. Ether 3:13-14
10. Alma 5:16
11. Revelation 6:9, 11; Qur'an 3:169; 3:140
12. Alma 14:11
13. Alma 60:13; 56:11
14. Malachi 3:17
15. Alma 38:9
16. D&C 76:63
17. D&C 76:69
18. D&C 76:52, 64-65
19. D&C 76:68
20. Malachi 3:16
21. D&C 76:53
22. D&C 76:66
23. D&C 76:56-57, 55
24. D&C 76:58-59, 93
25. Revelation 6:10
26. 2 Nephi 10:15-16
27. Mosiah 26:25
28. Alma 14:11
29. Malachi 3:18
30. Mosiah 26:26-28, 32
31. Mosiah 26:15
32. Psalm 30:5
33. Psalm 126:5
34. Mosiah 26:23-24
35. Psalm 110:1
36. D&C 31:1-2, 5-6
37. Mosiah 26:16-18, 20
38. Moses 1:39
39. Ether 12:29
40. Ether 12:36
41. Ether 12:37
42. Matthew 25:21
43. Enos 1:27

Chapter 61

1. John 20:15
2. Alma 24:24
3. Psalm 29:3
4. Acts 22:15
5. Psalm 44:17-19, 22, 26
6. Moses 6:60
7. Psalm 46:10
8. Psalm 27:7
9. Psalm 31:9, 7
10. Psalm 25:18-21
11. John 20:15
12. 1 Nephi 1:14
13. Psalm 8:4
14. Hosea 1:10; 2 Corinthians 6:18
15. Alma 32:19
16. Alma 22:18
17. Psalm 8:2
18. "I Feel My Savior's Love"
    Words: Ralph Rodgers, Jr.; K. Newell Dayley; and Laurie Huffman
    (Ref. John 15:10-12)
    Music: K. Newell Dayley
    © 1979 K. Newell Dayley; Used with permission. Jackman Music Corporation is the publisher of commercial arrangements of this song.

Chapter 62

1. 2 Kings 2:13, 15
2. Matthew 2:13-15
3. Psalm 119:23-24, 15, 45
4. D&C 10:4-5
5. 2 Kings 2:13-15

6. Psalm 27:1
7. Psalm 37:7-9
8. Proverbs 4:18
9. Psalm 136:2

Chapter 63

1. 2 Timothy 3:12
2. Alma 30:60
3. Alma 14:7, 11
4. Proverbs 1:7
5. Mosiah 27:24-27
6. Mosiah 27:31, 35
7. Alma 14:7
8. Alma 10:5-6
9. Alma 14:7
10. Moroni 10:4
11. Alma 10:12
12. Alma 14:21
13. Enos 1:5, 8

Chapter 64

1. Genesis 49:29
2. Joseph Smith History 1:33
3. Alma 28:5-6
4. Alma 28:12, 14
5. Packer, Boyd K. (2000, May) The Cloven Tongues of Fire, *Ensign*, 7.
6. Psalm 145:9-10
7. Jacob 2:8
8. Jacob 3:1-2
9. Matthew 10:22
10. Hebrews 11:16
11. Job 19:26

Chapter 65

1. Isaiah 51:9
2. Revelation 15:6
3. Revelation 1:14-16; Acts 7:30
4. Matthew 28:3; Helaman 5:36
5. Acts 2:2
6. Moses 7:3
7. Moroni 10:31-32
8. Revelation 3:4
9. Revelation 3:5
10. Revelation 2:11
11. Genesis 1:26-27
12. Moses 1:6; Alma 40:8
13. Moses 1:31

14. Moses 7:4
15. Moses 1:27-28
16. 1 Nephi 13:12
17. Moses 7:17
18. Moses 7:16, 24-26, 28
19. Moses 7:29-31
20. Moses 7:32-33
21. Moses 7:37
22. Moses 7:39-40
23. Moses 7:45
24. Moses 7:59
25. Moses 7:60-62
26. Mosiah 3:20-21
27. Malachi 1:11
28. Matthew 25:21
29. Moses 7:67
30. Revelation 2:17
31. Revelation 3:12
32. Revelation 3:21
33. JST Revelation 2:26-27
34. Revelation 12:1-2
35. Revelation 12:3, 7-9, 4
36. Revelation 12:12
37. Revelation 12:13, 4
38. Revelation 12:5
39. Revelation 12:17, 13, 17
40. Daniel 7:21-22
41. 1 Nephi 1:14
42. Revelation 12:10
43. Revelation 19:13-16
44. Isaiah 51:9
45. Daniel 7:22
46. Daniel 7:27
47. Revelation 12:11
48. Revelation 20:2-3
49. Revelation 12:12, 10
50. Revelation 19:7-8
51. Revelation 20:4-6
52. Revelation 21:3-7
53. Revelation 15:3
54. John 15:13

Epilogue

1. Romans 16:19-20
2. https://en.wikipedia.org/wiki/Diocletian; https://en.wikipedia.org/wiki/Diocletianic_Persecution

3. https://en.wikipedia.org/wiki/Diocletianic_Persecution; embedded footnote 1.
4. https://en.wikipedia.org/wiki/Galerius
5. https://en.wikipedia.org/wiki/Diocletian; embedded footnotes 177-178.
6. Acts 5:41
7. https://en.wikipedia.org/wiki/Saint_Florian; embedded footnotes 3-5.
8. https://en.wikipedia.org/wiki/Constantine_the_Great
9. https://en.wikipedia.org/wiki/Diocletian; embedded footnote 192.
10. https://en.wikipedia.org/wiki/Maximian
11. https://en.wikipedia.org/wiki/Constantius_Chlorus
12. https://en.wikipedia.org/wiki/Maxentius
13. https://en.wikipedia.org/wiki/Maximinus_II
14. https://en.wikipedia.org/wiki/Valerius_Severus
15. https://en.wikipedia.org/wiki/Diocletianic_Persecution; embedded footnote 173.
16. Foxe's Book of Martyrs, Chapter II, The Tenth Persecution
17. https://en.wikipedia.org/wiki/Helena_(empress)
18. John 19:23-24
19. Acts 1:9-11
20. https://en.wikipedia.org/wiki/Saint_Nicholas
21. https://en.wikipedia.org/wiki/Constantine_the_Great; embedded footnotes 52-56.
22. Foxe's Book of Martyrs, Chapter II, The Tenth Persecution

Author's Witness

1. D&C 101:11, 14-19
2. Isaiah 28:10; Proverbs 4:18; D&C 50:24
3. 1 Nephi 19:23
4. 2 Nephi 11:2
5. 2 Nephi 4:16
6. Psalm 33:11-15

Discussion Questions

1. Anderson, Wilford W. (as quoted by Renlund, Dale G.) (2016, May) That I Might Draw All Men Unto Me, *Ensign*, 39.
2. Renlund, Dale G. (2016, May) That I Might Draw All Men Unto Me, *Ensign*, 39.